Pasquale Villari

The Two First Centuries of Florentine History

Outlook

Pasquale Villari

The Two First Centuries of Florentine History

1. Auflage | ISBN: 978-3-73262-438-6

Erscheinungsort: Frankfurt am Main, Deutschland

Erscheinungsjahr: 2018

Outlook Verlag GmbH, Frankfurt.

Pasquale Villari

The Two First Centuries of Florentine History

Outlook

The Two First Centuries
of
Florentine History

THE MERCATO VECCHIO BEFORE ITS DEMOLITION.

The Two First Centuries of
Florentine History

THE REPUBLIC AND PARTIES
AT THE TIME OF DANTE

BY

PROFESSOR PASQUALE VILLARI

TRANSLATED BY

LINDA VILLARI

FOURTH IMPRESSION

ILLUSTRATED

London

T. FISHER UNWIN

1 ADELPHI TERRACE

1908

AUTHOR'S PREFACE TO THE ENGLISH VERSION.

BEFORE deciding to issue this translation I had first to reflect whether my Florentine studies could be of any use to the English public. Since Roscoe's day English literature has been enriched by works of much importance on different phases of the political, literary, and artistic history of Florence. Both Napier and Trollope have bequeathed very complete narratives of Florentine events, and translations of notable foreign works have also been produced. But nearly all these works appeared before any scientific research as to the origin of the City and Commonwealth had begun, or, at least, before it had reached the results I have briefly expounded, and which deserve notice, not only on the score of intrinsic worth, but also because they throw new light on the subsequent history of Florence.

To attempt any new delineation of the special vicissitudes of the Florentine Republic, already so exhaustively and lucidly treated by other historians, would have been outside my purpose. As stated in the preface to the Italian edition, my sole aim was to investigate in what manner the Republic was formed, the nature of its constitution, the why and wherefore of its continual transmutations, the first causes and genuine motives of the factions by which the city was torn, and likewise to ascertain how it came about that—despite all this turbulence and strife—commerce and industry, the fine arts and letters should have been able to achieve such marvellous results. Now, so far as I know, English literature contains nothing on this particular theme, although one that can scarcely fail to be of some use and interest even to readers familiar with greater works and more extended and detailed accounts of Florentine history.

These researches are not pursued beyond the times of Dante and Henry VII., inasmuch as that term actually marks the close of the period during which the Republic took shape and built up its constitution. This was followed by a new phase of equally high importance but very different character, during which the Republic entered, instead, on a course of decomposition. In fact, we have only to draw a comparison between the "Divine Comedy" and the "Decameron," to instantly perceive how deep was the change a few years had wrought in the spirit of Florence and of all Italy. These two works were almost contemporaneous, yet when reading them they seem to us the product of two entirely different ages. Whether in politics, religion, morals, or letters, the character of these two periods is seen to be essentially diverse. The Middle Ages, with all their rough primitive originality, have come to an end;

3

classic learning and the Renaissance have begun. Touching this second period, there is no scarcity of information, documents, or chroniclers, as in the case of the first. The historian is confronted by totally novel problems to which numerous modern writers have given their attention, and which have also been investigated in previous works of my own.

Even this second period would certainly afford matter for another work on the gradual course of political and moral dissolution, during which art and literature blossomed to new splendour. Such investigations, however, would transport me beyond the limits I have set to this book. Under what conditions and amid what difficulties these researches were begun and carried forward has been already plainly told in my preface to the Italian edition. It only remains for me to crave the indulgence of English readers.

PASQUALE VILLARI.

AUTHOR'S PREFACE.

A WORD of explanation is due to my readers touching the genesis of the present work.

In 1866 I began a course of lectures at our Istituto Superiore on the History of Florence, chiefly for the purpose of examining the political constitution of the Republic, and investigating the various transformations it had undergone during the long series of internal revolutions by which the city was harassed. In this way I hoped to ascertain the veritable causes of those revolutions, to discover some leading thread through the mazes of Florentine history, which even when treated by great writers has often been found exceedingly involved and obscure, and likewise to determine the most logical mode of arranging it in periods. Even a partial solution of these problems would have been of some use. I continued the lectures for a considerable time, but suspended them on reaching the period of Giano della Bella's "Decrees of Justice" (*Ordinamenti di Giustizia*), 1293. Some of these discourses were published in the Milan *Politecnico*, others in the *Nuova Antologia* at Florence. It was then my intention to collect them in a volume; but after some hesitation I renounced the idea. It seemed indispensable to at least add some outline of the course of events subsequent to the fall of Giano della Bella and the exile of Dante, in order to conclude the first and most important period of the political history of Florence. Besides, I saw that the necessity of continuing these lectures on fixed days had not always allowed sufficient time for overcoming obstacles encountered by the way. Accordingly, more than a superficial revisal was required; gaps had to be filled in, certain pages re- written. Hence fresh researches were demanded, for which other labours granted no leisure at the moment.

Meanwhile new documents, new dissertations, and monographs on Florentine history were continually appearing, besides notable works on a larger scale such as those of Capponi, Del Lungo, Hartwig, Perrens, &c. All this increased the difficulty of revising and correcting lectures, now lapsing inevitably more and more out of date. On the other hand I sometimes found previous deductions confirmed by recently discovered documents, and that certain general ideas I had enounced were accepted and followed by writers of note. This naturally inclined me to be less severe in judging my work, and more disposed to listen to the tried friends who were urging its republication.

Being thus encouraged to resume my forsaken studies, I lectured in 1888 on the times of Henry VII. of Germany and the exile of Dante. Later on, in 1890, recognising that my previous work on the origins of the city and its commonwealth had become altogether inadequate since the appearance of so much new material, I returned to the subject in a fresh course of lectures, which likewise saw the light in the *Nuova Antologia*. Then, I finally began to put the scattered papers together to revise and correct them.

Hence it will be plainly seen that this book is composed of various separate parts which, although informed, one and all, by the same leading idea and treating of the same argument, were produced at distant intervals during a quarter of a century, in which the study of Florentine history had made rapid advance through the labours of numerous and competent writers. Therefore, in spite of devoting my best efforts to pruning, revising, and arranging my lectures, they are still old essays more or less disjointed, and containing many unavoidable repetitions. Greater organic unity could only have been attained by re-writing the whole and composing a new book; whereas my intention was merely to republish a series of scattered compositions, under the fitting title of "Researches."

What finally decided me to reprint them was, that, as I venture to think, their dominant and fundamental notes still ring true, even after the numerous works produced by other hands. Indeed, unless I be mistaken, those works frequently support my observations, and confirm the ideas expressed throughout on the general character and progressive development of Florentine history. Whether I be right or wrong in this belief the reader must decide. At any rate I venture to hope that, in judging this book, he will kindly make allowance for the time and manner in which it came into existence.

CONTENTS.

ILLUSTRATIONS.

VARIOUS REMAINS DISCOVERED IN THE MERCATO VECCHIO OF FLORENCE.

(Now in the Etruscan Museum.)

[*To face page 1*

INTRODUCTION.[1]

I.

THE history of Italian freedom, from the Middle Ages to the new series of foreign invasions, dating from the descent of Charles VIII. in 1494, mainly consists of the history of our communes. But this history is as yet unwritten, and, worse still, can never be written until the material required for the task shall have been brought to light, sifted, and illustrated. What were the most ancient political statutes, what those of the guilds of art and commerce, what the penal and civil laws, the individual conditions, revenue, expenditure, trade, and industry of those republics? To all these questions we can give but imperfect replies at the best, and some are left altogether unsolved. Yet until all are decided the civil history of our communes remains involved in obscurity.

Through Machiavelli and Giannone Italy gave the world the first essays in constitutional history, and by Muratori's gigantic labours inaugurated the great school of learning that is the only settled basis of modern and, more especially, of constitutional history. But we soon allowed the sceptre we had won to be snatched from our grasp. It is true that we have never experienced any dearth of great scholars or historians, but the complete national history of a people is a task exceeding the powers of one or of several individuals. Such history must be produced, as it were, by the nation itself. Only the combined efforts of many scholars and of many generations can succeed in co- ordinating and investigating the vast mass of material that has to be ransacked in order to trace through the vicissitudes of numerous municipalities, all differing from, and at war with one another, the history of the Italian people. It has been long the custom with us for every one to work independently: hence we lack the spirit of agreement and co-operation required to enable individual efforts to carry forward the work of the whole country at the same pace. Certainly, however, I must not forget to note the example of our various national historical societies, subsidised by the Government, and composed of most learned and deserving men. But these associations and commissions have as yet no general nor united plan of work; and, in fact, some of their members are apt to devote their energies to labours which, however important, are disconnected from the main object. Thus there will be much delay before our learned men complete the investigation of any one period of our history. Yet the rules which should be followed are not far to seek, since Italians were the first to discover them, and we still bear them in mind. Nor has the issue of highly important collections of documents been relegated exclusively to our societies and commissions. None can have forgotten the untiring labours of the worthy Vieusseux and his friends in their management of the "Archivio Storico Italiano"! To show what excellent results may be achieved by the publication of a single series of State papers, it is sufficient to mention the Despatches (*Relazioni*) of Venetian Ambassadors, given to the world by Alberi, and whereby not only Italian but European history has been so greatly profited. What progress might not be made would all Italian scholars consent to devote their labours to a common end! We have seen how much Professor Pertz was enabled to achieve at Berlin, with a subsidy from the Confederation, and aided by all the scholars of Germany. Truly, his "Monumenta" form an enduring memorial of the national history of the Fatherland, and has become the nucleus of a new school of scholars and historians.

Now that Italy is united, and her many states fused into one, she should know the history of her communes, and trace out the history of her people. It should also be kept in view that the Commune was the institution by whose means modern society was evolved from the Middle Ages. Rising in the midst of a throng of slaves, vassals, barons, marquises, dukes, the Commune gave birth to the *third estate* and the people which, after first destroying feudalism in Italy, subsequently by the French Revolution, destroyed it throughout Europe. Even Augustin Thierry notes that "thus was formed the immense congregation of free men who in 1789 undertook for all France that which had been achieved by their forefathers in mediæval municipalities."[2] Accordingly, since Italy was the centre and seat of municipal liberty, the purpose of the present work is not only to investigate our civil history, but to demonstrate how much we contributed to the discovery of the principles of modern society and civilisation. All careful students of the history of Roman law in the Middle Ages will have occasion to remark that our commentators while reviewing ancient jurisprudence, unconsciously modified it in adapting it to their own times. Francesco Forti has declared that no student of our statutes can fail to perceive that many of the regulations found in the Napoleon Code, and supposed to be created by the French Revolution, already formed part of the old Italian law. I have come to the conclusion that in every branch of Italian civil life our history will be able to prove that the same remark holds good, inasmuch as our civil institutions contained the primary germs of modern freedom. But no one has yet dared to attempt this task, and, as I said before, no single strength could suffice for it. We have now to deal with a far humbler theme. By tracing in bold outline the history of a single commune, we desire to show what fresh researches remain to be made, and how many problems to be solved.

The vicissitudes of the Florentine Republic can only be paralleled with those of the most flourishing periods of Athenian freedom. Throughout modern history we might seek in vain the example of another city simultaneously so turbulent and prosperous, where, despite so much internecine carnage, fine arts, letters, commerce, and industry, all flourished equally. The historian almost doubts his own veracity when bound to recount how a handful of men settled on a small spot of earth, extended their trade to the East and the West; establishing banks throughout Europe; and accumulated such vast wealth, that private fortunes sometimes sufficed to support tottering thrones. He has also to relate how these rich merchants founded modern poetry with their Dante, painting with their Giotto; how with the aid of their Arnolfo and Brunellesco, and of their Michelangelo, who was poet, painter, sculptor, and architect in one, they raised the stupendous buildings which the world will lastingly admire. The first and subtlest of European diplomatists were Florentines; political science and civil history were born in Florence with Machiavelli. Towards the end of the Middle Ages this narrow township seems a small point of fire shedding light over the whole world.

It might well be thought that all difficulties regarding the history of this commune must have been already overcome, seeing that the finest Italian writers, the greatest modern historians, have for so long made it the theme of extended labours. In fact, what other city can boast annals penned by such men as Villani, Compagni, Machiavelli, Guicciardini, Nardi, Varchi? And, in addition to histories and chronicles, we find an endless string of Diaries, *Prioristi* (Notebooks), Reminiscences, before coming down to modern writers. Among the Florentines it was a very common practice to keep a daily register of events, and in this wise their splendid store of historic literature was continually enlarged. But, nevertheless, no history bristles with so many difficulties as that of Florence, nor offers so many apparently insurmountable contradictions. Events pass before our eyes, well described, vividly coloured; they flit past in a rapid and uninterrupted whirl, never resting, subject to no law, and seemingly obedient to chance alone. Personal hatred, jealousy, and private revenge produce political revolutions, drenching the city with the blood of its children. These revolutions endure for months, perhaps even for years, and end with arbitrary decrees, which are violated or undone the moment they have received magisterial sanction. Thus we are often moved to inquire, How can this be the work of far-seeing diplomats, of great politicians? Either lofty commendations for political good sense and acuteness were falsely lavished on men incapable of giving their country sound laws and stable institutions, and who in the gravest affairs of State were solely influenced by personal loves and hates; or else for centuries past we have accorded unmerited praise to the historians who have described impossible events to us in the most vivid colours. In fact, how could it possibly be that so much good sense should breed so much disorder? How, too, in the midst of this disorder, with the vessel of the State at the mercy of every wind that blew, could art, science, and literature give forth so glorious a harvest?

Undoubtedly history, as we interpret it to-day, was unknown to the ancients. We seek the causes of events, whereas they merely described them. We wish to know the laws, manners, ideas, and prejudices of mankind, whereas our forefathers were exclusively concerned with human passions and actions. In the fifteenth century political science was chiefly a study of human nature, while at this day it is mainly a study of institutions. Modern history aims at the examination of mankind and society in every form, and from every point of view. That is why we have had to so often re-fashion the work that, nevertheless, had been splendidly performed by writers of old.

Leaving aside all compilers of those fables and legends on the origin of Florence found repeated in even later works, Florentine historians may be divided into two great schools. First come the authors of Chronicles or Diaries, who flourished chiefly in the fourteenth century, although they continued long after that period. These writers record day by day the events they have witnessed and in which they have often taken part; stirred by the very passions they describe, they sometimes rise to eloquence, and the heat of their own words leaves them no time to dwell on abstract ideas. They presuppose in their readers their own detailed knowledge of the political institutions among which their lives were spent, but which are unknown to us, and the object of our keenest desire. Frequently, however, some fourteenth- century chronicler, such as Giovanni Villani, with his incomparable gift of observation, supplies such minute descriptions of events, reports so many details, that, almost unawares, we find ourselves carried back to his day. Sometimes, when descending to particulars, he apologises for detaining the reader on topics of small moment, little foreseeing what value we later generations would attach to all those details of the trade, instruction, revenue, and expenditure of the Republic, or how we should long for more facts of the same kind. But as soon as these writers touch upon times and events outside their own experience, they have either to copy verbatim from other chroniclers, or their narratives remain cold, colourless, and devoid of merit or authority. We pass at once from the most lively and graphic descriptions to the strangest fables, the greatest incoherence, since these men are incapable of using any discernment even in copying literally from others. Proofs of this are seen in their puerile accounts of the foundation of Florence. Historical criticism was as yet unborn.

The scholarship of the fifteenth century gave rise to the study and imitation of Sallust and Livy; and Italian writers were no longer content to register facts from day to day, unconnectedly and without order. Many wrote in Latin, others in Italian; but all sought to compose historical narratives in a more artistic, or at all events, more artificial way. They launched into exordiums and general considerations; gave lengthy descriptions, eked out by many flights of fancy, of wars they had never witnessed, and of which they knew little or nothing; they attributed imaginary speeches to their personages, and sometimes fashioned their narratives in the shape of dialogues, to increase the distance between themselves and their fourteenth-century predecessors.[3]

It was a period of rhetorical essays and servile imitations of the classics, during which Italian history and literature declined, although preparing for revival in the coming age. In fact, we find the art of history notably advanced in the sixteenth century. Machiavelli, who may be styled the most illustrious founder of that art, begins with a word of blame to preceding historians exactly because "they had said little or nothing of civil discords, or of existing internal enmities and their effects, and described other matters with a brevity that could be neither useful nor pleasing to the reader." Indirectly, these words serve as a faithful portrait of the book that has proved the most lasting monument to his own fame. He inquires into the causes of events, the origin of all the parties and revolutions of the Republic; thus creating a new method and opening a new road. He reduces the whole history of the Commonwealth into an admirable unity; he rejects with profound contempt the fabulous tales bequeathed by the chronicler regarding the foundation of Florence, and throws an eagle glance on party manœuvres from their origin down to his own day. He was the first to undertake these researches, and, notwithstanding all newer investigations, his fundamental idea maintains its value.

But Machiavelli gave little heed to institutions, scarcely any at all to laws and customs. Furthermore, he was so entirely guided by his instinct of divination as to care little for the historic exactitude of particular facts. To ascertain the infinite number of inaccuracies and blunders contained in his book, and which would be unpardonable in a modern writer, his narrative must be compared with the contemporary accounts of the old chroniclers, some of which were known to him. Not only are there frequent errors of date, but also of the names and number of magistrates and of the framework of institutions. It would seem that while divining the spirit of events, he simultaneously remoulded them according to his own fancy. Sometimes we find him appropriating entire pages from Cavalcanti's history, even transcribing the fictitious speeches attributed by that chronicler to historic characters, and by a few touches of his own pouring new life into the dull narrative without troubling to undertake any fresh research. Thus, his book, although a valuable guide, is also an unsafe one. He cannot always abstain from transplanting a true fact to the place best suited to his own theories, thus filling up inconvenient gaps without many scruples of conscience. His aim, so he tells us, was to investigate the causes of parties and revolutions. What is now designated as local colour—*i.e.*, the historic colour of facts—is entirely absent from his narrative, and particularly from that of the earlier days of the Republic. Men adhere to different factions, sometimes commit evil, sometimes generous deeds, but are apparently always the same in his eyes. To what extent the clear appreciation of events is hampered by this theory may easily be imagined. Then, too, as Machiavelli draws nearer to his own times, he sees the constitution of the Republic changing and decaying, freedom disappearing, and a thousand personal passions arising to hasten the overthrow of enfeebled institutions. A knowledge of minute particulars would be doubly desirable at this period to make us understand the social revolution in question; but Machiavelli, though always a fifteenth-century Florentine, never lost sight of the example of Titus Livy and other Roman writers, and consequently, like all the scholars of his age, was inspired with a lofty contempt for any small details apt to endanger the epic unity of historic narrative. Then, later on, in approaching the distinct domination of the Medici, under whose rule he was living, he turns aside with ill-concealed disgust from the internal vicissitudes of the Republic and gives his whole attention to external events. He then discourses of warfare and of the Italian policy that was the passion of his life. In the midst of court intrigues and the contested predominance of this or that party, we find him chiefly concerned in ascertaining how a new prince might best reunite the scattered members of his torn and oppressed motherland; and note that this noble design frequently makes him forget the history of Florence.

In reading old chronicles of contemporary events, we see before our eyes the living, speaking figures of Giano della Bella, Farinata degli Uberti, Corso Donati, and Michele di Lando. Their feelings, loves, and hates are known and almost familiar to us; but we are plunged in a restless, unrestrained tumult of passions, without knowing whence blows the blast driving men and things onward in a whirl of confusion, without one moment's truce. No sooner do we pass beyond the visual horizon of the writer, than all images become confused, and our sight is no less obscured than his own. Even at moments of most eloquent description we hear of institutions and magistrates conveying no meaning to our ears, and often see these change, disappear, and return without grasping the why and wherefore. But when, on the other hand, by the study and imitation of ancient authors, the art of embracing a vaster circle of facts springs into being, and the causes and relations of those facts are investigated in order to weld them into visible unity, historic criticism is still lacking to verify events, to examine and define laws and institutions, to colour and almost revive the past in all its varied and changeful aspects. The genius of the historian emits, as it were, flashes of light; but these, while illuminating some occasional point, only leave a confused and uncertain view of past ages in our mind. We require to know men and institutions, parties and laws, as they really were; nor is this enough: we must also comprehend how all these elements were fused into unity, and how laws and institutions were begotten by those men in those times.

This was the task modern writers should have performed, but many reasons have prevented its completion. First of all, the progress achieved by art and literature while liberty was perishing in Florence, and their great influence on all modern culture, fixed the principal attention of writers on this section of Florentine history as being one of very general importance, and more easily intelligible to all. Accordingly, the greater number of modern, and especially of foreign students neither examined nor understood the precise period in which all the noblest qualities of the Florentine nature had been formed, and during which were evolved and trained the intellectual powers afterwards expressed in art and letters to the admiration of the whole world. Many foreigners seemed to believe that art and letters had not only flourished when manners were most corrupt, but were almost the result of and identified with the corruption that led to their decline. For the fine arts, being the offspring of liberty and morality, could not long survive their parent forces.

It should be also observed that no great modern writer has yet produced any work specially devoted to the political and constitutional history of Florence.[4] It must be confessed that more than by any modern pen was achieved to this effect by the elder and younger Ammirato, who, although writers of the seventeenth century, already began to ransack State papers, and composed a work that was new and remarkable at that period. But they neither proposed to write a history of the Florentine constitution, nor possessed sufficient critical equipment for the purpose, had they sought to fulfil it. They often overload new and valuable information regarding events, and even institutions, with a mass of useless detail, destructive to the general unity of their narrative.

It is scarcely requisite to add that modern writers, only treating of Florence in general histories of Italy, were necessarily compelled to pass briefly over secondary parts of their work. They often relied too blindly on old authors of acknowledged repute and influence, without using enough discrimination in sifting material of undeniable value from other parts composed of second-hand narratives and repetitions of fabulous tales. We have only to compare Villani with Malespini to see that one of the two undoubtedly copied many chapters from the other.[5] Nor is this a solitary example. As we have before remarked, Machiavelli borrowed whole chapters from Cavalcanti;[6] Guicciardini often translated from Galeazzo Capra, better known under the name of Capella;[7] Nardi reproduced Buonaccorsi verbatim. Therefore, without critical examination of these writers, and careful decision as to their relative value and the confidence to be accorded to different parts of their works, it is uncommonly easy to be misled. For this, and many other reasons, modern historians of Italy encounter numerous pitfalls when treating of Florentine matters. Now and then we see them halting, in common with chroniclers of the widest renown, to define the precise functions of the Captain of the people, or Podestà, or Council of the Commune, and afterwards finding it extremely difficult to make their definitions agree with actual facts whenever those titles recur in their pages. Such mistakes nearly always proceed from a double source. The definitions supplied by old writers regarding magistrates and their functions were extremely slight, when they alluded to their own times, and often inexact where other periods were in question. Also, modern writers generally demand a precise and fixed definition of institutions which were subject to change from the day of their birth, and unalterable only in name. The name not only remains intact after the institution has become entirely different from what it was at first, but often long outlives the institution itself. It is curious to see what ingenious theories are then started to give substance and reality to names now become ghosts of a vanished past. The only way to thread this labyrinth is by endeavouring to reconstruct the series of radical changes every one of those institutions underwent, and without once losing sight of the mutual relations preserved between them during the continual vicissitudes to which they are subject. Only by seeking the law that regulates and dominates these changes is it possible to discern the general idea of the Republic and determine the value of its institutions.

But what can be done while we lack so many of the elements most needed for the completion of this task? The learned have yet to arrange, examine, and illustrate the endless series of provisions, statutes, *consulte*, *pratiche*, ambassadorial reports, and, in short, of all the State papers of the Republic, many of which are still unsought and undiscovered. Nevertheless, we believe that, without attempting for the present any complete history of Florence, some rather useful work may be performed. We may certainly follow the guidance of old chroniclers and historians regarding events of which they had ocular testimony, trying, when needed, to temper their party spirit by confronting them with writers of an opposite faction. Vast numbers of documents have been published in driblets, and many learned dissertations, although the series is still incomplete; besides, one may easily resort to the Florence archives in order to vanquish difficulties and bridge the principal gaps. And after undertaking researches of this kind, it seems easy to us to clearly prove how the whole history of Florence may be illumined by a new light, and its apparent disorder made to disappear. In fact, as soon as one begins to carefully examine the veritable first causes underlying the apparent, and often, fallacious causes of political revolutions in Florence, these revolutions will be found to follow one another in a marvellously logical sequence. Then in the wildest chaos we seem rapidly able to discern a mathematical succession and connection of causes and effects. Personal hatreds and jealousies are not causes, but only opportunities serving to accelerate the fast and feverish sequence of reforms by which the Florentine Commune, after trying by turns every political constitution possible at the time, gradually attained to the highest liberty compatible with the Middle Ages. It is this noble aim, this largeness of freedom, that rouses all the intellectual and moral force contained in the Republic, evolves its admirable political acumen, and allows letters and art and science to put forth such splendid flowers in the midst of apparent disorder. But when strictly personal passions and hatreds prevail, then real chaos begins, the constitution becomes corrupt, and the downfall of freedom is at hand.

The sole aim of the present work is to offer a brief sketch of the history of Florence during the foundation of its liberties. So great is the importance of the theme that the historian Thiers has given long attention to it, and we know that an illustrious Italian has already made it the object of many years of strenuous research.[8]

II.

The history of every Italian republic may be divided into two chief periods: the origin of the commune, the development of its constitution and its liberties. In the first period, during which an old state of society is decaying and a new one arising, it is hard to distinguish the history of any one commune from that of the rest, inasmuch as it treats of Goths, Longobards, Greeks, and Franks, who dominate the greater part of Italy in turn, reducing the country, almost throughout its extent, to identical conditions. The position of conquerors and of conquered is everywhere the same, only altered by change of rulers. Amid the obscurity of the times and scarcity of information, there seems scarcely any difference between one Italian city and another. But differences are more clearly defined, and become increasingly prominent after the first arisal of freedom. Most obscure, though not of earliest date, was perhaps the origin of Florence, which tarried long before beginning to rise to importance. Our present purpose being merely to throw light on the history of the Florentine Constitution, we need not devote many words to the first period mentioned above—namely, of the origin of Italian communes in general. At one time this question was the theme of a learned, lengthy, and most lively dispute, chiefly carried on by Italian and German writers. But the scientific severity of researches, in which Italian scholars won much honour, was often impaired by patriotism and national prejudice. It being recognised that the origin of the Commune was likewise the origin of modern liberty and society, the problem was tacitly transformed into another question—*i.e.*, whether Italians or Germans were the first founders of these liberties, this society? It is easy to understand how political feelings were then imported into the controversy, and effectually removed it from the ground of tranquil debate.

Towards the end of the last century the question was often discussed in Italy by learned men of different views, such as Giannone, Maffei, Sigonio, Pagnoncelli, &c. Muratori, though lacking any prearranged system, threw powerful flashes of light on the subject, and raised it to higher regions by force of his stupendous learning. But the dispute did not become heated until Savigny took up the theme in his renowned "History of Roman Law in the Middle Ages." In endeavouring to prove the uninterrupted continuity of the said jurisprudence, he was obliged—inasmuch as all historical events are more or less connected together—to maintain that the Italians, when subject to barbarian and even to Longobard rule, lost neither all their personal liberty nor their ancient rights, and that the Roman Commune was never completely destroyed. Accordingly, the revival of our republics and of Roman law was no more than a renewal of old institutions and laws which had never entirely disappeared. Germany was quick to see to what conclusions the ideas of our great historian tended, and thereupon Eichorn, Leo, Bethmann, Karl Hegel, and others, rose up in arms against the theory of the Italian Commune being of Roman birth. They maintained, on the contrary, that the barbarians, and more especially the Longobards, whose domination was harsher and more prolonged than the rest, had stripped us of all liberty, destroyed every vestige of Roman institutions, and that, consequently, the new communes and their statutes were of new creation, and originally derived from Germanic tribes alone.

To all appearance these views should have stirred Italian patriotism to furious opposition, and made Savigny's ideas universally popular among us. Yet this was not the case. We supplied many learned adherents to either side.

At that time our national feeling had just awakened; we already desired—nay, claimed—a united Italy, no matter at what cost, and detested everything that seemed opposed to our unity. Well, the Longobards had been on the point of mastering the whole of Italy, and the Papacy alone had been able to arrest their conquests by securing the aid of the Franks. But for this, even the Italy of the ninth or tenth century might have become as united a country as France. Already the school of thinkers had been revived among us that, even in Machiavelli's day, had regarded the Pope as the fatal cause of Italy's divisions. Therefore, naturally enough, while confuting Savigny's views, our nineteenth-century Ghibellines exalted the Longobards, ventured to praise their goodness and humanity, and hurled invectives against the Papacy for having prevented their general and permanent conquest of Italy. But, on the other hand, there was also a political school that looked to the Pope as the future saviour of Italy, and this school, prevailing later on during the revolution of 1848, adopted the opposite theory, and possessed two most illustrious representatives in Manzoni and Carlo Troya. At any rate, they had little difficulty in proving that barbarians had been invariably barbaric, killing, destroying, and trampling down all things, and that the Papacy, by summoning the Franks, no matter for what end, had certainly rendered some help to the harshly oppressed masses. The Franks, in fact, gave some relief to the Latin population, sanctioned the use of Roman law and granted new powers to Popes and bishops, who undoubtedly contributed to the revival of the communes. Thus, although for opposite ends, identical opinions were maintained on both sides of the Alps. Throughout this controversy learning was always subordinated to political aims, although the disputants may not have been always aware of it; and historic truth and serenity consequently suffered unavoidable hurt. Balbo, Capponi, and Capei, after throwing their weight on this side or that, ended by holding very temperate views, and their teachings cast much light on the point at issue.

The main difficulty proceeds from the fact that few persons are willing to believe that in the Middle Ages, as well as throughout modern history, we can always trace the continuous reciprocal action of the Latin and German races, and that it is impossible to award the merit of any of the chief political, social, or literary revolutions exclusively to either. On the contrary, wherever the absolute predominance of one of the two races seems most undoubted, we have to tread with most caution, and seek to discover what share of the work was due to the other. Likewise, in order to justly weigh and determine their reciprocal rights in history, impartial narrative would have a better chance of success than any system based on political ideas. Assuredly, when facts are once thoroughly verified, no system is needed, since general ideas result naturally from facts. Were it allowable to introduce here a comparison with far younger times, we might remark that when French literature invaded Germany in the eighteenth century it obtained general imitation there, and unexpectedly led to the revival of national German literature. In order to glorify the national tone of this literature, would it be necessary to maintain that the great previous diffusion of French writings was only imagined by historians? Later, the French flag was flaunted in nearly every city of Germany, and the people humiliated and crushed. From that moment we see the national German spirit springing to vigorous life. Must we say that this revival was due to the French? Is it not better to describe events as they occurred, rejecting all foregone conclusions? I am quite aware of the abyss between these recent events and those of old days; but, nevertheless, I consider that Balbo was right in remarking that the fact of the origin of the communes being disputed at such length and with so much heat and learning by the two rival schools, proved that the truth was not confined exclusively to either. Accordingly, we will rapidly sum up the conclusions we deem the most reasonable.

Every one knows that, after the earlier barbarian descents, by which the Empire was devastated, and Rome itself frequently ravaged, Italy endured five real and thorough invasions. Odoacer, with his mercenary horde, composed of men of different tribes, but generally designated as Heruli, was the leader who dealt the mortal blow in 476, and becoming master of Italy for more than ten years, scarcely attempted to govern it, and only seized a third of the soil. But a new host poured in from the banks of the Danube, commonly styled Goths, and subdivided into Visigoths and Ostrogoths. The former division, commanded by Alaric, had already besieged and sacked Rome; the latter, led by Theodoric, appeared in 489, and speedily subjected all Italy. Theodoric's reign was highly praised. The chiefs of these early barbarian tribes had often served for many years in Roman legions, and had sometimes been educated in Rome. Accordingly they felt a genuine admiration for the majesty of the very empire that the heat of victory now urged them to destroy. Theodoric organised the government; and, according to the barbarian custom, seized a third of the land for his men; but he left the Romans their laws and their magistrates. In every province a count was at the head of the government, and held jurisdiction over the Ostrogoths. The Romans were ruled according to their own laws, and these laws administered by a mixed tribunal of both races. But Theodoric's government became gradually harsher and more intolerable to the Romans, so that, after his death, they revolted against his successors, and invoked the aid of the Greeks of the Eastern Empire. But revolt brought them nothing save increased suffering, inasmuch as the Goths began to murder the Romans in self-defence, deprived them of what liberty and institutions they had been allowed to retain, and organised a military and absolute government. This was the government Belisarius and Narses found established on coming from Constantinople to deliver and reconquer Italy; this was the government they copied with their dukes, or *duces*. The Ostrogoths had ruled Italy for fifty-nine years (493–552), and the Greeks held it for sixteen more (552–568). Theirs also was a purely martial government, under the General-in-chief Narses, but with dukes, tribunes, and inferior judges nominated by the Empire. As usual, the newcomers appropriated a share of the soil, and probably this share now went to the State. Their tyranny was different from that of the barbarians, but it was the tyranny of corrupt rulers, and therefore more cruel. The Greeks had expelled the Goths, and next came the Longobards to drive out the Greeks. They gradually extended their conquests, and in fifteen years became masters of three-fourths of Italy, leaving only a few strips of land, mainly near the sea, to the Greeks whom they never succeeded in expelling altogether. The Longobards struck deep roots in Italian soil, and dwelt on it for more than two hundred years (568–773), ruling in a very harsh and tyrannous fashion. They took a third of the land, reduced the Italians almost to slavery, and respected neither Roman laws nor Roman institutions. Beneath their sway the ancient civilisation seemed annihilated, and the germs of a newer one were prepared, although its first budding forth is still involved in much obscurity. Every controversy as to the origin of our communes started from inquiries into the condition of the Italians under the Longobard rule. If ancient tradition were at any time really broken off and replaced by a totally new one, it must have occurred under that rule. Or, if it only underwent a great change before assuming new life and vigour at a later time, the process must have dated from the same period.

Nevertheless, wherever the Byzantine domination had obtained, a feebler and more vacillating government weighed less cruelly on the people; therefore, as early as the seventh and eighth centuries, certain cities were seen to develop new life. The Commune speedily took shape, even in Rome, where the power of the Papacy, hostile to the Longobards, had greatly increased. On first coming among us, these barbarians of the Arian creed respected neither the Catholic bishops, the minor clergy, nor anything sacred or profane, and later on menaced the Eternal City itself. Accordingly, as a means of defence against the threatening enemy at his gates, the Pontiff summoned the Franks to save the Church and country from oppression. They came in obedience to this call, led first by Pepin and then by Charlemagne, who, driving out the Longobards, and fortifying the Papacy by grants of land, enabled the Pope to inaugurate his temporal dominion. In reward for this Charlemagne was crowned emperor; and thus the ancient Empire of the West was re-established by the new Empire of the Franks, to which the Holy Roman-Germanic Empire afterwards succeeded.

Thereupon the dissolution of barbarian institutions, already begun in Italy, proceeded at a more rapid pace. There was a ferment in Italian public life, heralding the approach of a new era. Institutions, usages, laws, traditions of all kinds—Longobard, Greek, Frankish, ecclesiastical, Roman—were found side by side and jumbled together. Next ensued a prolonged term of violence and turmoil, during which the name of Italy was scarcely heard. All old and new institutions seem at war, all struggling in vain for supremacy, when suddenly the Commune arises to solve the problem, and the era of freedom begins. But what gave birth to the Commune? This is the question by which we are always confronted.

It would be outside our present purpose to follow the learned scholars who have sought to deduce ingenious and complicated theories from some doubtful phrase in an old codex, or the vague words of some chronicler. It is certain that the Roman Empire was an aggregation of municipalities exercising self-government. The city was the primitive atom, the germ-cell, as it may be called, of the great Roman society that began to disperse when the capital lost the power of attraction required to bind together so great a number of cities separated by vast tracts of country either totally deserted, or only inhabited by the slaves cultivating the soil. The barbarians, on the other hand, knew nothing of citizen life, and the *Gau* or *Comitatus* (whence the term *contado* is derived), only comprising embryo towns, or rather villages, which were sometimes burnt when the tribes moved on elsewhere, resembled the primitive nucleus of Teutonic society. In the *comitatus* the count ruled and administered justice with his magistrates; the chiefs of the soldiery were his subordinates, and became barons later on. Several countships joined together formed the dukedoms or marquisates into which Italy was then divided, and the whole of the invading nation was commanded by a king elected by the people.

When, therefore, the Germanic tribes held sway over the Latin, the *Gau* held sway over the cities which indeed formed its constituents. And the counts, as military chieftains, ruled the conquered land, of which the victors appropriated one-third. The Goths pursued the same plan; so too the Greeks, who replaced all counts by their own *duces*; and so also the Longobards. Only the latter's rule was far more tyrannous, especially at first, and their history is very obscure. They began by slaughtering the richest and most powerful Romans; they seized one-third of the revenues, it would seem, instead of the lands, thus leaving the oppressed masses without any free property, and consequently in a worse condition than before. The Goths had permitted the Romans to live in their own way, but the Longobards respected no laws, rights, nor institutions of the vanquished race. On this head Manzoni remarks[9] that no mention is found of any Italian personage, whether actual or imaginary, in connection with any royal office or public act of the time. Nevertheless, from absolute tyranny, and even downright subjection, to the total destroyal of every Roman law, right, and institution, there is a long step. In order to attribute to the Longobards—numbering, it is said, some 130,000 souls in all—the total extinction of Roman life in every direction, we must credit them with an administrative power, far too well ordered and disciplined, too steadfast and permanent, to be any way compatible with their condition. How could a tribe incapable of comprehending Roman life persecute it to extinction on all sides? Granting even, although this is another disputed point, that the Romans were deprived of all independent property; granting that Roman law was neither legally recognised nor respected by the Longobards, it by no means follows that every vestige of Roman law and civilisation was therefore destroyed at the time. Far more just and credible seems the opinion of other writers who have maintained that when the Longobards descended into Italy they thought chiefly of their own needs, made no legal provision for the Italians, and were satisfied with keeping them in subjection.[10] Thus, in all private concerns, and in matters beyond the grasp of the barbarian administration, the conquered people could continue to live according to the Roman law and in pursuance of ancient customs. In fact, Romans and Longobards lived on Italian soil as two separate nations; the fusion of victors and vanquished, so easy elsewhere, is seen to have been difficult in Italy, even after the lapse of two centuries. So great is the tenacity and persistence of the Latin race among us, that it is easier to reduce the conquered to slavery, or extirpate them altogether, than to deprive them of their individuality. In fact, whenever, by the force of things, and by long intercourse, conquerors and conquered come into closer contact, the barbarians are unavoidably driven to make large concessions to the Latin civilisation, which even when apparently extinguished is always found to have life. How explain otherwise the gradual yielding of Longobard law to the pressure of Roman law; how explain the new species of code that gradually took shape, and was styled by Capponi *an almost Roman edifice built upon Germanic foundations*?

As the Longobards became more firmly established in Italy, they began to inhabit the cities which they had been unable to entirely destroy; they also began to covet real property, and accordingly, during the reign of their king Autari, instead of a third of the revenues, seized an even larger proportion of the land. This measure aggravated the condition of the vanquished on the one hand, but greatly improved it on the other, by leaving them in possession of some independent property.[11] And although, as Manzoni observed, we find no royal officials, great or small, of Roman blood, it is no less certain that the Longobards, having need of mariners, builders, and artisans, were obliged to make use of Romans and their superior skill in those capacities. It was in this way that the ancient *scholae*, or associations of craftsmen, continued to survive throughout the Middle Ages, as we know to have been the case with the *magistri comacini*, or Guild of Como Masons, to whose skill the conquering race had frequent recourse. In however rough and disorderly a fashion these associations contrived to withstand the barbarian impact, they were certainly an element of the old civilisation, and kept the thread of it unbroken. Other remains and traditions of that same civilisation also clung about them; and when every other form of government or protecting force was lacking to the inhabitants of cities, these associations guarded the public welfare to some extent. Do we not find that an ancient municipality, when first left to its own resources, sometimes closed the city gates against the barbarians, and defended itself, almost after the manner of an independent state? Was it not sometimes successful in repulsing the foe? Even when conquered, trampled, and crushed, can we suppose it to have been destroyed everywhere alike, or so thoroughly cancelled from the memory of the Latins, that, on seeing it reappear, we must attribute its resurrection to Germanic tribes, to whom all idea of a city was unknown until they had invaded our soil? Did not the resuscitation of the Greek cities of Southern Italy begin as far back as the seventh and eighth centuries— namely, in the time of the Longobards—and assuredly without the help of Germanic traditions? Did not the Roman Commune arise at the same period? And if the ancient municipalities, fallen beneath the Longobard yoke, and therefore more cruelly oppressed, delayed almost four centuries longer, did they not also follow the example of their fellow-cities at last? What is the meaning of the widely spread tradition, that only in that paragon of independent, free republics, Byzantine Amalfi, were preserved the Roman Pandects, which were then captured by Pisa, and cherished as her most valued treasure? Does not the whole subsequent history of the Commune consist of the continual struggle of the re-born Latin race against the descendants of Teuton hordes? If Latin civilisation had been utterly destroyed, how came it that the dead could rise again to combat the living? Therefore, it seems clear to us that, although the Longobards accorded no legal rights to the conquered people, they could not practically deprive them of all; they either tolerated or were unaware of many things, and the tradition, usage, and persistence of the race kept alive some remnants of Latin civilisation. Thus alone can it be explained how, after enduring a harsh and long-continued tyranny that apparently destroyed everything, no sooner were a few links snapped off the strong, barbaric chain, by which the Italian population was so straitly bound, than Latin institutions sprang to new life, and regained all the ground they had lost.

Barbarian society, both in form and tendency, was essentially different from the Latin. Its predominant characteristic was the so-called Germanic individualism, as opposed to the Latin sociability. We note a prevalent tendency to divide into distinct and separate groups. As a body, it no sooner lost the force of cohesion and union induced by the progress and rush of conquest, than it immediately began to be scattered and disintegrated. Owing to their nomadic and savage life, as well as to the blood in their veins, the barbarians seemed to have inherited an exaggerated personality and independence, making it difficult for them to submit for long to a common authority. Thus, when peace was established, germs of enfeebling discord soon appeared among them. In fact, when the Longobards had completed the conquest of nearly the whole of Italy, they divided the land into thirty-six Duchies, governed by independent dukes enjoying absolute rule in their respective territories. Under the dukes were sometimes counts, residing in cities of secondary importance, and at the head of the *comitati*; while still smaller cities were often ruled by a *sculdascius*, or bailiff. Both dukes and bailies administered justice according to the Longobard code, together with the assistant judges, who, under the Franks, developed into *scabini*, or sheriffs. Little by little military leaders gained possession of the strongholds, and subsequently became almost independent chiefs. Then, too, the royal officials, styled *gasindi*, likewise exercised great power. And even as the dukes finally asserted their independence from the king, so counts and *sculdasci* sought emancipation from the ducal sway, although without immediate success. In the first century, after the conquest, there was no law, no recognised protection for the vanquished, nor was the authority of the bishops and clergy in any way respected. The history of the Longobard rule shows it to have been so tremendously oppressive as to apparently crush the very life of the people, so that even at the most favourable moments no serious revolts were attempted. Even the example of the free cities in the South failed to excite them.

Nevertheless, as we have already noted, the Church, having gained meanwhile a great increase of power, refused to tolerate the pride and arrogance of barbarians who showed her so little respect. Hence the Pope resolved to expel these strangers by the help of others, and called the Franks into Italy. Charlemagne, the founder of the new Empire, could not regard the Latins, to whom the growing civilisation of his states was so much indebted, with the inextinguishable barbarian contempt felt by the Longobards. He sought to extend his conquests and his power. He wished to assist the Pope, in order to be consecrated by him and obtain his moral support. Therefore he came to Italy, and the already disintegrated Longobards could ill withstand the firm unity of the Franks, strengthened as it was by the prestige of his own victories. In vain the Longobards had already chosen and sworn fealty to another monarch; in vain they prepared for defence. After two hundred and five years of assured and almost unchecked domination, their kingdom was overthrown for ever. In 774 Charlemagne became master of Italy, and in the year 800 was crowned emperor by the Pope in Rome. Thus the Western Empire became reconstituted and consecrated in a new shape, entirely separate and independent from the Empire of the East. The Franks deprived the Longobards of all their dominions, excepting the Duchy of Benevento in Southern Italy. The power of the Pope was greatly increased by his assumption of the right of anointing the emperor, who rewarded him with rich donations and promised additions of territory. Rome, however, was ruled as a free municipality; and Venice, after the manner of the Greek cities in the South, had already asserted her freedom. Such was the state of Italy after the last barbarian invasion—that, namely, of the Franks.

As usual, the new masters appropriated one-third of the land; but the condition of the natives was now decidedly changed for the better. Roman law was recognised as the code of the vanquished, and this is an evident sign that it was never entirely obsolete during the two centuries of Longobard rule. Charlemagne greatly improved the condition of the Latins, and sometimes promoted them to *honours*, *i.e.*, to offices of royal appointment. But the special characteristic of his reign in Italy was the new hierarchy he established there. He destroyed the power of the dukes, whose attitude was too threatening to the unity of the Empire, and raised instead the position of the counts. Even in the Marches, or border-provinces, he retained no dukes, but replaced them by marquises (Mark-grafen, Praefecti limitum). In this manner the ancient unity of the *comitatus*, or *Gau*, became likewise the basis of the new barbarian society. Nor did Charlemagne stop at this point, but began to distribute offices, lands, and possessions in *beneficio*—i.e., in fief—and therefore on condition of obligatory military service. This proved the beginning of a social revolution, possibly originated at an earlier date, but now carried to completion under the name of feudalism. Not the emperor only, but kings, counts, and marquises also granted lands, revenues, and offices in fief, in order to obtain a sufficient supply of vassals. Thus an infinite number of new potentates was created: *vassalli, valvassori,* and *valvassini,* the latter being lowest in degree. Gradually the whole society of the Middle Ages took a feudal shape; the recipient of a grant of land was bound to yield military service, at the head of the peasants employed on his ground. Similar privileges, similar obligations, accompanied every donation of land or bestowal of office; for even official posts were generally supplemented by a concession of land or of revenue. Thus the Germanic tendency to division and subdivision in small groups was satisfied, while, at the same time, the Empire, the cities, and even the Church itself, assumed a feudal form. The bishops in their turn soon began to possess benefices, and gradually rose to increased power, until we find them in the position of so many counts and barons. Both in their own persons, and those of their subordinates, they enjoy immunity from ordinary laws and tribunals—an inestimable advantage, serving to enhance their independence and unite large clusters of population beneath their sheltering sway. Feudalism, accordingly, is a new order, a new and thoroughly Germanic aristocracy, yet at the same time it is the root of a veritable revolution in barbaric society, the which revolution will continue to grow and extend through many vicissitudes. Step by step the Crown will begin to exempt the benefices or fiefs of the vassals from subjection to the count, and will then declare them hereditary by means of a series of laws, all designed for the purpose of irritating the lesser potentates against their superiors, and of giving increased strength to the royal authority; but which served, on the contrary, to open a way of redemption to the downtrodden people. All this, however, was still unforeseen in the days of Charlemagne. He organised the feudal system, and kept his realm united and flourishing, although soon after his death (814) the Empire was split into several kingdoms.

The rule of the Franks in Italy lasted to the death of Charles the Fat, in 888. And throughout this rule of 115 years, the revolution to which we have alluded was steadily making way. On all sides the number of benefices or fiefs continually grew, and year by year exemptions increased at an equal rate. These were conceded more easily to prelates than to others, since when laymen received benefices they were entitled to leave them to their heirs, and thus became inconveniently powerful. This state of things proved very favourable to cities in which bishops held residence. At first the count was sole ruler of the city, save the portion appertaining to the Crown, and called *gastaldiale,* as being under the command of a *gastaldo,* or steward; then, as the power of the bishop increased, another portion was exempted from the count's jurisdiction, as being *vescovile, i.e.*, the property of the bishop. Step by step this portion was enlarged until it included nearly the whole of the town: many cities, in fact, were ruled solely by the bishop. Thus the fibres of barbarian society were weakened, and we might almost say unknit, by a method that would have served to keep it in subjection to the supreme authority of the monarch, but for the fact that the people, deemed to be dead, was not only breathing, but on the point of asserting its strength against nobles, kings and emperors, prelates, and Popes.

Two revolts in the cause of liberty successively took place, and both began under the Carlovingians, and continued during the reigns of their successors. The first enervated and enfeebled the barbarian society to which the soil of Italy was so ill suited; the second prepared the way for the rise of communes. With the death of Charles the Fat the rule of the Franks lapsed, and barbarian invasions likewise ceased. The Germanic tribes had settled down on Italian soil and were becoming civilised. Nevertheless, Italy had still to pass through a string of revolutions and years of ill fortune. At the dissolution of the Empire of the Franks, certain counts and marquises, especially the latter, who, by the union of several counties, had gained the power of dukes, were found asserting extravagant pretensions, even endeavouring to form independent states, and often with success. To this day, in fact, there are reigning families descended from Frankish marquises and counts. To compass their destruction benefices and immunities had been granted in vain: their power was not to be so easily extinguished. For, even in Italy, where, owing to the different character of the country, the ancient civilisation had tenaciously lingered on, and now began to awake to new life, and where, too, the Papacy and the Greeks of Byzantium had impeded the absolute triumph of Germanic institutions, feudal counts and marquises now arose to contest the crown. Next followed long years of renewed devastation and conflict, ending by the crown being retained in the grasp of German emperors and kings. The first wars and quarrels were carried on by Berengarius of Friuli and Guido of Spoleto, with other Italian and foreign nobles, a German king, two Burgundian monarchs, and finally by King Otho of Germany, who remained victor. It was during these seventy odd years of continued strife that Italian kings first reigned in Italy, though with an always uncertain and disputed rule. Then came a forty years' peace (961–1002), during which Otho I., II., III. reigned in turn, and another Italian marquis, Hardouin of Ivrea, disputed the crown of Italy with the German kings. But in 1014 Hardouin was vanquished by Henry of Germany, surnamed the *Saint*, to whom succeeded Conradin of the Franconian or Salic dynasty.

These two German sovereigns completed the feudal revolution, already mentioned by us, the which, begun by the Carlovingians, and continued by the Othos, had failed nevertheless to assure the supremacy of kings and emperors over Italy. But, at all events, seeing that the Othos had purposely exempted numerous lesser vassals from rendering allegiance to the counts and barons, and had accorded many cities to prelates; also seeing that the renascence of communes was considerably promoted by all the aforesaid exemptions, some writers conceived the idea that this renascence was chiefly owed to the initiative of the Othos. But these emperors had a very different aim in view, and had failed to achieve it. They sought to undermine the strength of all possible assailants of the Crown, when threatened by revolts such as that of the Marquis of Ivrea. For this reason Henry the Saint continued to favour the greater feudatories at the expense of "holders of honours"—that is to say, of counts and marquises—and in fact almost annihilated the latter class. Conradin the Salic carried out the scheme more completely, by favouring even the minor feudatories and making benefices hereditary. From that moment the victory of the German sovereigns over the feudal lords was assured; for vassals once rendered masters of their fiefs owed obedience to the Crown alone, and thus the pride of the great nobles was permanently abased. Not so the new popular pride, which had grown to be a power unawares.

Accordingly, we find a multitude of facts showing that the condition of the Roman race was continually improving; that feudal society, by the action of its own sovereigns, was daily losing substance and strength; that as the Latin civilisation revived by the natural force of events, it changed, assimilated, and absorbed the principles of Germanic society. Even before the two races came into conflict, the traditions of the conquered had frequently combated and overcome those of victors. The latter, indeed, had already accepted the Roman law to some extent, when the once subject race pleaded the sanction of their municipal statutes.

Italians were in a state of ferment and of radical transformation when the first signs of a revival of the communes appeared. Neither the barbarian rule nor the Empire had ever really mastered the social order of the peninsula; and exactly when feudalism was first founded and seemed likely to spread everywhere and assure the quiet supremacy of the emperors over Italy, fresh causes of peril and strife suddenly sprang into existence. Papacy and clergy attained to loftier and more menacing power; the immunities lavished on prelates, from dread of the laity, rendered them temporal potentates dependent on the emperors, while as spiritual dignitaries they owed obedience to the Pope: thus practically enjoying a double investiture. This led to much disorder and scandalous corruption in the Church, since prelates were converted into feudal lords, holding sway over cities, making war on other territories, keeping open court, and indulging in every worldly pleasure. The Popes wished to re-establish discipline, to maintain absolute rule over the bishops, and nominate them unhindered; but this was opposed by the emperor, since the temporal authority of the prelates made them logically subject to his rule as well. Thus began the famous war of investitures between the Papacy and the Empire, the issue of which was so long undecided. Meanwhile neither the Church, the Empire, nor the feudal system could obtain complete mastery over the social movement, and the confusion was increased by their continual disputes. This state of things weakened even the authority of the prelates; and then the communes, having necessarily learnt the art of self-government during the period when dioceses were left vacant, having noted the prosperity of the Southern republics, and found their strength increased by the extension of commerce and the feudal disorganisation, finally saw that the moment to achieve freedom had arrived. Even in cities ruled by lay nobles, things followed the same course, since to side either with the Empire or the Church always served to excite much enmity against those in power, and procured many allies for the weaker party.

Accordingly the eleventh century witnessed the arisal of communes throughout Italy, and the joy of independence once realised, it was impossible to return to a state of vassalage, whether under bishops, counts, or the Empire itself. At first these communes were hemmed in on all sides by a vast number of dukes, counts, and barons of various degrees of strength, inasmuch as the feudal order was still very powerful and still supreme in all country districts. Of German descent and trained to arms, these nobles fought in their own interest, although nominally for the Empire and its rights, against the new communal order that suddenly faced them with such menacing strength. They swooped down from their strongholds to bar the trade of the towns; they levied tolls, threatened violence, and tried to treat free men as their vassals. Thereupon the indignant citizens were stirred to vengeance from time to time, and often ended by razing great fortresses to the ground. On the other hand, the nobles still remaining in the cities became wearied of living among men who no longer respected the distinctions of class or race, and often departed to rejoin their friends. They frequently emigrated in such numbers that the citizens suffered injury by it, and issued decrees forbidding their exodus. The Pope gave encouragement to the communes, because the reduction of his prelates' temporal power did not displease him, and the abasement of the Empire was indispensable to his aims. Thus the struggle of the working classes against feudalism finally began, and with it the real history of our communes.

But it should not be thought that the Commune arose to champion the rights of man or in the name of national independence. Nothing of the kind. The Empire was still held to be the sole and universal fount of right. Almost to the close of the fifteenth century, in fact, all cities, whether Guelph or Ghibelline, foes or friends of the Empire, continued to indite their State papers in its name.[12] The revived republics always acknowledged its supremacy, and their own dependence, almost, one might say, as though in claiming a new and more general exemption, they only sought to be, as it were, their own dukes or counts. They combated the nobles and combated the Empire; but victory once assured, they recognised the authority of the emperor, and prayed him to sanction the privileges they had won. Nor was the destruction of the Empire at any time desired by the Popes; its protection was often indispensable to them, and they too recognised it as the legitimate heir of ancient Rome, and consequently as the only source of political and civil rights. Their purpose was to subject the temporal to the spiritual power. Therefore, during the rise of the Commune, theocracy and feudalism, Papacy and Empire, still subsisted together and always in conflict. The Commune had to struggle long against obstacles of all kinds; but it was destined to triumph, and to create the third estate and people by whom alone modern society could be evolved from the chaos of the Middle Ages. This constitutes the chief historical importance of the Italian Commune.

CHAPTER I.

THE ORIGIN OF FLORENCE.

I.

THE origin of Florence is wrapped in great obscurity, and little light is to be derived from chroniclers, who either avoided the subject altogether or clouded it over with legends. Much has been written of late touching these chroniclers and on the value and varying credibility of their accounts. But in endeavouring to ascertain everything, and push research too subtly, long and learned disputes have sometimes arisen on particulars which can never, perhaps, be verified and are scarcely worth knowing, while more significant and easily investigated points have been left untouched. By this method some risk is incurred of building up from those writers a species of occult science for the sole benefit of the initiated, whereas all that is absolutely known of the origin of Florence may be expressed in a few words.

The Florentine Commune being of tardier birth than many others, its historians and chroniclers were likewise of later date, since no commune possesses a written history until conscious of its own personality. Thus, it was only in the twelfth century that yearly records were first started, registering some of the more important events of Florence, giving dates, and names of places and persons, while, at the same time, lists were made of the Consuls, the first magistrates of the Commune, and afterwards supplemented with the names of the Podestà, who succeeded to the Consuls. These magistrates being changed yearly, and even more frequently, this catalogue served as a chronological guide, and was soon converted into a register of contemporaneous events in the town.

THE ARNO RIVER-GOD.

(Bas-relief now in the Etruscan Museum, Florence.)

[To face page 39

A very early fragment of these annals is preserved in the Vatican, and is written on the back of a sheet forming part of a codex[13] of Longobard laws. It contains eighteen records, running from 1110 to 1173, in different handwritings, all, however, of the twelfth century, with some blunders and no chronological arrangement. Nevertheless these records are of much importance, being the earliest we possess. A similar and longer series of records of much later date, running from 1107 to 1247, is to be found in a thirteenth-century MS.[14] in the National Library at Florence.

Both collections have been recently republished and illustrated by Dr. Hartwig, under the title of "Annales florentini," i. and "Annales florentini," ii.[15] The Codex containing the second series also comprises the oldest list extant of Consuls and Podestà, from 1196 to 1267, and has been rendered more complete by the results of fresh research.[16]

Other and similar records must have been certainly made, first in Latin, then in Italian, and, in passing from this family to that, from hand to hand, enlarged, revised, and altered according to the taste, or even the fancy, of their transcribers. But, from the remains of those records and all matter copied from them by the chroniclers, it may be inferred with almost absolute certainty that they told little or nothing of the origin of the Commune. We are therefore inclined to believe that this was neither the outcome of virulent conflict nor of downright revolution, for either would have been undoubtedly registered in the annals, but that it gradually evolved and developed amid struggles of secondary importance.

If in these days we desire to ascertain the origin of the Florentine Commune, it is only natural that older generations should have felt even a keener interest in the theme. They, however, lacked the art and critical method enabling us to track and often lay bare the darkest and most remote periods of history by means of public documents, although many now perished must have been at their disposal. But our forefathers were readier to draw on their own imagination, and thus a legend regarding the origin of the city was created, and soon became widely diffused.

The primary germ from which this legend was developed and expanded must date from the twelfth century, seeing that it was known and recorded by the chronicler Sanzanome, who wrote during the first years of the thirteenth century. It cannot be much older than this, seeing that the events and dates to which it alludes, in however vague and shadowy a fashion, carry it down beyond the eleventh century. Several inedited copies of this legend are still to be found in Florentine libraries,[17] and it has been published in three different compilations. The most ancient of these, in Latin, is contained in a codex dating from the end of the thirteenth or beginning of the fourteenth century.[18] The second, in Italian, is in a Lucchese MS.,[19] compiled between 1290 and 1342; at one point it gives a record of 1264,[20] and was probably written at that time. The third and later version, known as the "Libro fiesolano", is comprised in an Italian codex dated 1382, in the Marucellian Library at Florence, was discovered by Signor Gargani and published by him in 1854.[21] Dr. Hartwig discovered the second, which is identical, save in language, with the first, and published all three under the title of "Chronica de Origine Civitatis,"[22] found in the Lucca MS.; although in other MSS. it is styled "Memoria del Nascimento di Firenze."

Such was the material at the service of the old chroniclers, and all they had to rely upon regarding the origin of Florence. The earliest chronicler of whom any remains are extant is the judge and notary Sanzanome, who, as already noted by us, wrote his "Gesta Florentinorum" at the beginning of the thirteenth century. We find him mentioned more than once in Florentine documents from 1188–1245.[23] Although we cannot be certain that this name always referred to the same individual, it is certain that the same chronicler records his presence in the war of Semifonte in the year 1202, and in that of Montalto in 1207. Besides, his work is found in a Florentine codex of the thirteenth century, and if not in his own hand, in the character of about the same period.[24] This first attempt at Florentine history, written in Latin by a judge and notary, supposed by Milanesi and Hartwig to have been a native of a neighbouring town, but resident in Florence, has a stamp of its own, very different from that of all subsequent Florentine chronicles. Sanzanome says nothing as to the origin of the Commune and its internal constitution. After a vague and hasty allusion to the old legend,[25] he starts with the war and destruction of Fiesole in 1125, "cum eius occasione Florentia sumpsisset originem." Thus, from the beginning, he shows us the Commune already established, with its consuls and captains, and proceeds to recount its conflicts with neighbouring powers in a stilted, rhetorical fashion, with uncertain and often erroneous dates, and with speeches in strained imitation of ancient Roman historians. Consequently some writers refused to assign any historic value to his work. But, on the other hand, critics of greater weight and impartiality, such as Hartwig, Hegel, and Paoli, have recognised that the work of this notary, who was almost a precursor of the fifteenth-century humanists, is a literary phenomenon, and that the fact of its isolation makes it the more remarkable as a proof of ancient Florentine culture, and also because we find beneath its rhetorical flourishes much useful information on the early history of Florence.

Hence all the other chroniclers had to face one and the same problem: how to write a history, or even a bare chronicle of the earliest beginnings of Florence, from the scant and fragmentary accounts at their disposal? The notary Sanzanome shirked the difficulty by saying nothing of the foundation of the town, and then expanding his narrative with rhetorical flights, fictitious speeches, and descriptions of battles, in which his own fancy and imitation of the classics played the main part. But this method was neither congenial nor possible to the simpler folk of a later day, who sought to write as they spoke, and whose culture was slighter, or at all events very different from the notary's. These chroniclers, therefore, had no basis to build upon save one legend and a few scraps of information that could not possibly satisfy their patriotic pride.

Fortunately for their purpose, just at this time—namely, towards the middle of the thirteenth century—an event of great literary importance occurred, serving to put the Florentine chroniclers on a new track. A Dominican monk, one Martin of Troppau, in Bohemia, surnamed therefore *Oppaviensis*, vulgarly known as Martin Polono, chaplain, apostolic penitentiary, and afterwards archbishop, wrote an historical work which, although of no remarkable merit, had an extraordinary and rapid success. It was a species of manual of universal history, chronologically arranged under the names of the various emperors and Popes, down to the year 1268. Its author afterwards carried it down to a few years later, with an introduction treating of the times anterior to the Roman Empire.[26] This book was mechanically arranged, and stuffed with anecdotes, blunders, and fables; but was the work of an eminent prelate, inspired with the Guelphic spirit. The author's method of arranging the events of the Middle Ages under the headings of Popes and Emperors served as a leading thread through the vast labyrinth. It is certain that his book was rapidly diffused throughout Europe, especially in Italy, and above all in Florence. As Prof. Scheffer Boichorst remarks: "Its first translator was a Florentine, and another Florentine, Brunetto Latini, the first to make use of it." In fact, the Florence libraries have numerous copies of it in Latin MSS. of the fourteenth century, while others of the same period comprise an Italian translation that, according to the results of learned research,[27] must have been produced in Florence towards 1279.[28] This fact alone is a most luminous proof of the rapid popularity and diffusion of the work. As it was a common practice with the scribes of that period to insert alterations of their own in the works they copied out, it may have easily occurred to some transcriber of this translation to enrich it here and there with the more important of the few facts then known of the early history of their city. But as Martin Polono's work was only brought down to the end of the thirteenth century, and items of Florentine history had increased in number and extent, so it came about that all these additions forsook universal history and were solely devoted to that of Florence. In this way the former merely served, as it were, as an introduction to the latter; a result highly gratifying to municipal self-complacency.

One of the first works introducing Martin Polono's book, translated, shortened, re-written, and with several interpolated Florentine items, is that entitled "Le Vite dei Pontefici et Imperatori Romani," once attributed to Petrarch, and existing in several Florentine fourteenth-century codices. In this work, however, Florentine history is still given very secondary importance, and indeed when at last, after various sequels and alterations, it finally appeared in print in 1478, Polono's primitive method was still maintained by giving summaries here and there of the lives of the other emperors and Popes. But other versions soon appeared in which Florentine history filled a larger space.[29] In a fourteenth-century MS. of the Naples National Library, first examined by Pertz, we find Martin Polono's share of the work considerably curtailed, and the history of Florence not only much extended, but likewise carried down to 1309.[30] Here one begins to see that the writer was chiefly interested in Florentine events. Professor Hartwig was so struck by this fact as to be at the pains to extract everything relating to Florence from the MS., and print it apart, as one of the authorities probably recurred to by Villani.[31] In a chronicle attributed to Brunetto Latini the same purpose is still more clearly indicated. Some of the Florentine news contained in it were long and frequently extracted, printed, and employed; notably the list of Consuls and Podestà used by Ammirato, and a narrative of the Buondelmonti tragedy (1215), differing considerably from Villani's version of the tale. It was speedily decided that the author must have written in 1293, since he records an event of that year, and says that he witnessed it with his own eyes.[32] Later, this Chronicle was attributed to Brunetto Latini, although the narrative is carried down to a date when Dante's master must have certainly ceased to exist.[33] During his learned researches in Florence Dr. Hartwig discovered a MS. that, in all probability, is the original autograph of the Chronicle.[34] Although mutilated—starting only from 1181—this Codex is doubly precious, as it clearly shows the method on which this and many similar works were compiled. There is a middle column containing the usual mangled version of Martin Polono[35]; and here on the margins, between the rubrics and sometimes even the lines, are added notices of general history, drawn from other sources, and special records of Florentine events.

The history is thus brought down to 1249, where a gap occurs extending to 1285, from which year the author continues his narrative to 1303.[36] But in this second part the character of the work is entirely changed. Having no longer Martin Polono as a guide, he now forsakes that prelate's method. The affairs of the Empire and the Church are reduced to still smaller proportions, more space is given to those of Florence, and instead of being scattered haphazard over the narrative, they are now united and carried steadily on. Thus we see a real chronicle of Florence gradually developing before us and acquiring a special value of its own. Its discoverer, Dr. Hartwig, at first considered it an autograph, but finally conceived doubts on that score. The great disorder of the manuscript; its mutilated commencement; the gap between thirty-six years in the middle; the absence of certain records, comprised in certain excerpts from it, quoted by old writers; the discovery that many of these writers quoted from another MS. of the Chronicle belonging to the Gaddi Library; all this justified his statement that the problem could not be finally solved without the aid of the Gaddi Codex, which he had not yet been able to discover.

On the other hand, Professor Santini maintained, in a prize essay, that the Gaddi Codex could only be a copy of that found by Hartwig, and that the latter must be the mutilated original manuscript. After a short time the question was ultimately decided by another student of our Istituto Superiore, Signor Alvisi, who, having unearthed the Gaddi Codex in the Laurentian Library, found it to be a fifteenth-century copy.[37] Here the various fragments —arranged in separate columns in the original MS.—are joined with the remainder of the text, though often in an arbitrary fashion. Here, too, there is the gap between 1249–85, but the Chronicle, instead of starting from 1181, begins, like Martin Polono's first compilation, with Jesus Christ—*primo e sommo Pontefice*—and the Emperor Octavian. Thus, it may now be affirmed, that the Codex in the Florence National Library is a genuine and, as it were, photographic representation of the method employed for the earliest compilations of Florentine historiography. It allows us to see the author at work, as it were, before our eyes.

Another, but far less perfect, specimen of this kind of production is afforded by the Lucca MS., to which previous allusion has been made. The author carefully tells us that it was composed between the years 1290 and 1342. He transcribes the whole legend of the origin of Florence, and then gives his Italian *pasticcio* of Martin Polono, beginning from the Emperor Octavian. But he intersperses it with "many things relating to the affairs of Tuscany, and especially of Florence ... the greater part being found in divers books on Tuscany, of which some contain more, some less" (*qual na più, qual na meno*). Having reached the year 1309 in this fashion, he continues his narrative by borrowing from Villani, several books of whose history had already appeared in 1341, and with this assistance carries his work down to 1342. He continues by reproducing a Latin description of Florence written in 1339, and then gives the Latin introduction that Martin Polono had added to his history. The compiler of this Lucca Codex avows that his method is neither logical nor chronological; but craves the reader's indulgence, saying that in this work he had first put together all the Italian and then all the Latin portions, with the intention of arranging them better afterwards, by fusing them together and writing the whole in Latin. This intention he seems to have found no time to fulfil. From this Codex also, all the portions relating to Florence were subsequently extracted and printed.[38] As may be seen, the compiler's method is always the same, although in this case heavier and more mechanical than usual, for lack of any inherent connection between the different parts. The only novelty consists in transcribing the entire legend to make it serve as an introduction to Florentine history; an example that, as will be seen, was afterwards followed by others.

But however flattering to Florentine self-love this system of fusing the history of the Commune with that of the universe might be, it was clearly apparent that the former remained crushed, as it were, by the contact. Hence even the fourteenth century witnessed attempts to expound it apart. Paolo Pieri begins his Chronicle from 1080, the year from which the other writers also date their earliest historical account of Florence, and continues it, with slight allusions to the Popes and slighter to the emperors, down to 1305, including the scanty Florentine records "gleaned from many chronicles and books, with certain novel matters seen by me, Paolino di Piero, and written *ad memoriam*." On the other hand, Simone della Tosa, who died in 1380, begins his "Annals" with a list of Consuls and Podestà (1196–1278), and then passes to the death of Countess Matilda (1115) and on to 1346, supplementing towards the close his meagre account of Florentine affairs with details about his own family. But simple summaries such as these, consisting only of a few pages, were more inadequate than ever to satisfy the needs of a city that now, in the fourteenth century, had already won a foremost place in Italy, was proudly asserting equality with Rome, and aspired to have a history similar to that of the ancient metropolis of the world.

Such was the ambitious problem that Giovanni Villani as shown by his own words, proposed to solve. In the year 1300, he says, "being in Rome for the Jubilee, admiring the grand memories of that city, reading the glorious deeds narrated by Virgil, Sallust, Lucan, Titus Livy, Paul Orosio, and other masters of history, who recounted, not the events of Rome alone, but likewise strange events of the universal world: I borrowed their style and form."[39] Reflecting that "our old Florentines had left few and confused records of past deeds in our city of Florence,[40] and that our city, the child and creature of Rome, was on the upward path, and about to achieve great things, whereas Rome was on the decline," I resolved "to bring into this volume and new chronicle all the events and beginnings of the city of Florence, ... and give henceforth *in full* the deeds of the Florentines, and *briefly* the notable affairs of the rest of the universe."[41] Thus, according to Villani, the course to be pursued was to connect the history of Florence with that of the world, as others had done before him, but in such wise that Florence should not be the loser, but rather play the chief part. Hence his work is no longer a mechanical mosaic; he arranges his history, dividing it in books and chapters, after the manner of the ancients. We do not know all the authorities from whom his work was derived, for this question has not yet been completely investigated.

But we know that they were many in number. For general history, Martin Polono was still the main source; but Villani also drew from the "Gesta Imperatorum et Pontificum" of Thomas Tuscus,[42] the "Vita di San Giovanni Gualberto," the "Cronache di San Dionigi" (an Italian translation of which was printed—1476—before the original text), and the "Libro del Conquisto d'Oltremare," which was a history of the Crusades, translated from the French into almost every other language during the Middle Ages.[43]

That Villani is a very valuable authority in Florentine history dating from the end of the thirteenth century, is a fact well known to all, and need not be discussed here. As to the origin of the city, he has little that is genuinely historical to tell us. His accounts begin, as usual, from 1080, are more or less identical with those disseminated by other writers, not unfrequently charged with the same blunders, and often in the same words. This singular resemblance between many of the Florentine chroniclers when treating of early times, and remarked upon later, was easily explained so long as it was taken for granted that some chroniclers had copied from others. But when it could be proved, as was often the case, that the same resemblance existed even between totally independent writers, the problem was not so readily solved. For this reason, Prof. Scheffer-Boichorst, in noting the fact, after impartial and keen investigation, suggested the theory that all the different chroniclers had drawn from some common source, of which nothing was now known. Seeing that Tolomeo of Lucca, whose Annals were already concluded before Villani began to colour his design, often quotes from "Gesta" and "Acta Florentinorum," "Gesta" and "Acta Lucensium," the German critic assigned the name of "Gesta Florentinum" to what, in his opinion, must have been the original source used by all the chroniclers of Florence down to the beginning of the fourteenth century. This hypothesis became generally accepted as the most probable explanation of a fact that was otherwise inexplicable. But when attempts were made to precisely define the nature and limits of the "Gesta"—to define, not only its language, but in which year it was begun, in which ended, together with the style and exact character both of the work and its author—the question then stood on very disputable ground. Accordingly, I will leave discussions of this kind on one side, as beyond the sphere of a general outline. Besides, I must agree with Prof. C. Paoli[44] in considering that the "Gesta" cannot have been a strictly individual work, but rather a collection of Florentine news, originally of very meagre proportions, but gradually enriched by fresh annalistic matter and new additions, as it passed from hand to hand. Some compilation of this kind, but of greater weight and repute (now unluckily perished), must have fallen into the hands of various chroniclers, who made use of it in turn, unconscious that it had served others before them. And these chroniclers were again copied by several of a later period.

Villani begins with the Tower of Babel and the confusion of tongues and then passes on to the legendary origin of Florence, dividing it in chapters and expounding it as though it were genuine history, but inserting various alterations, to which we shall refer later on. He then proceeds with a general history of the Middle Ages, and from the year 1080 engrafts on this stock all the accounts of Florence he had been able to collect, and even colours these by a variety of other legends much diffused among the people at the time, and often, also, by the addition of fantastic considerations of his own. What amount of accurate knowledge can be derived from all this? Substantially we find a single legend, and a small number of historical facts of undoubted value, though not free from errors, floating, as elsewhere, in an ocean of events quite unconnected with Florence, intermixed with scraps of misty traditions or legends, arbitrarily interpreted and explained. Therefore, the first question to be decided is that of the origin and value of the legend itself. Can any historical information be derived from it, either directly or indirectly? The second question is: Can it be ascertained with any certainty what original nucleus of authentic information the "Gesta Florentinorum" must have contained? The latter at least presents no serious difficulty, seeing that when we compare the various chroniclers, particularly those who worked independently, and extract what Florentine material they used in common and often gave in the same words, the main point is won. But, after all this, and after trying to extract some substance (scant enough, as will be seen) from the legend, very little genuine information is gained. It is therefore an absolute necessity to seek the aid of all public and private documents contained in our Archives, and of all learned modern investigations regarding mediæval history in general, and that of Florence in particular. Florentine historical research, first inaugurated by Ammirato, was diligently pursued in the eighteenth century by Borghini, Lami, and numerous other scholars, down to the present day. Nevertheless, the definite results of these prolonged inquiries, this vast display of learning, were still very few. For instance, we find that even the illustrious Gino Capponi, after a short introduction to his History of Florence, is compelled, like the ancients, to leap to the death of Countess Matilda, and makes his first mention, so to say, of the Commune after it had already existed for some time. Then the history of almost two centuries, to the year 1215, or thereabouts, is summed up in twelve pages, and only from the thirteenth forward are events related really in full.

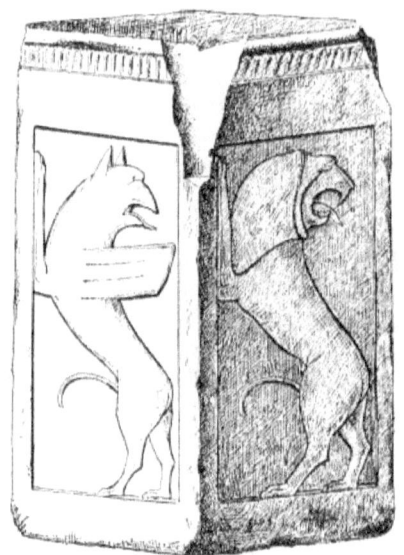

ETRUSCAN TOMBSTONES, FROM THE MERCATO VECCHIO, FLORENCE.

But in these days the study of mediæval documents has made extraordinary progress, above all in Germany, and accordingly the Florentine question has been again reopened. Dr. O. Hartwig was the first to apply his learning to the task, employing the scientific method. He not only examined all that was published on the subject, but made fresh researches in Italian libraries and archives, further aided by precious notes of documents newly discovered in Tuscany by D. Wüstenfeld. Thus, in the work from which we have frequently quoted, he was enabled to give a collection of valuable documents and of learned dissertations which have been already turned to account, will serve as a basis for future researches, and would be still better known and appreciated were they penned in a more popular style. Much has been found, very much read by Prof. Perrens, who has devoted his life to Florentine history, and already published eight volumes of his work. His first volume, of five hundred pages, only extends to the middle of the thirteenth century, and therefore treats of the origin of the city learnedly and at length. All Italians owe him gratitude for this; but it must be confessed that his untiring zeal, vast learning, and prodigious reading have not always resulted in a due amount of historical accuracy, and sureness of method. Treating of a period in which all has to be built up on a very scanty number of known facts, unless these facts are thoroughly ascertained disastrous consequences are apt to ensue. For example, in investigating the first origin of the Consuls, he still relies on the document of Pogna, dated March 4, 1101, in which they are named, and without remarking that Capponi, from whom, nevertheless, he continually quotes, had proved that, although long thought correct, this date was erroneous, and should be altered to March 4, 1181, Florentine style, the which signifies 1182 in the modern style. Thus Prof. Perrens introduces Consuls long before they were born.[45] Elsewhere he plunges into the very intricate dispute as to the jurisdiction exercised over their own territory by the Florentines of the twelfth century. He repeats with the old chroniclers that in 1186 Frederic I. deprived them of all jurisdiction beyond the city walls, but that they re-acquired it in 1188. He adds that on the Emperor Frederic's decease in 1190, his successor, Henry VI. "comme don de joyeux evènement, multiplie les privilèges." He fails to reflect that the patent quoted in support of the latter assertion bears the date of 1187, and that he gives the date in a note of his own.[46] How is the reader to disentangle this skein? As another example, we may add that the author gives as an historical fact the legendary tale of the origin of the Colombina festival held on Holy Saturday. The Florentines are sent to the Crusades by their archbishop, Ranieri, in 1099: that is several centuries before Florence possessed an archbishop. Pazzino de Pazzi, in reward for his feats of valour at the taking of Jerusalem, receives the *mural crown* from Godfrey de Bouillon, together with the right to change his arms and adopt the crosses and dolphins, the which change was only effected by the Pazzi several centuries later.[47] Pazzino returns to Florence in triumph, mounted on a car, of which the description is given; and at a time when the Commune was not yet established,[48] is received in the style of a Roman conqueror by the people, the clergy, and the magistrates. He has brought three stones from the Holy Sepulchre, and these are the flints from which the sparks are still struck to fire the Car of the Dove. All this is derived from Gamurrini's "Storia genealogica," an utterly valueless work.[49] Readers may consider it strangely invidious on my part to be at the pains to refer to certain blunders contained in a work of which I am the first to recognise the merits, and by which I have often profited. But it seemed necessary to explain why, in spite of having praised, I should so seldom quote it. The work undeniably comprises abundant historic material, is written with vivacity and clearness, contains many keen observations, and does honour to an author to whom Italians are bound to be grateful. But although for all these reasons it is a book deserving attention, no possible use can be made of it, without continually verifying the authorities cited in it.

Here a word must be said touching another and far less imposing work, to which we have been able to refer with far greater security. Already, in certain short papers appearing in the "Archivio Storico Italiano," Prof. Santini had proved his power of keen research on the early history of Florence, and has now had the happy idea of collecting all the documents on the subject, both published and unpublished, existing in the Florentine Archives. After copying and verifying them from the originals, he is now bringing them out in a bulky volume. It would be well if he or other writers could complete the same task in all cities, or at least in those of Tuscany, which had so many ties in common. Meanwhile, his book will form a new and solid foundation for Florentine historic research. We are doubly grateful for his kindness in allowing us to examine his press proofs. Thus we have been enabled to profit by his forthcoming book in advance of its publication, and shall have frequent occasion to quote from it. Other works, unmentioned in the text, will be recorded in the notes for our readers' benefit.

SITE OF A ROMAN VILLA DISCOVERED NEAR S. ANDREA, FLORENCE.

II.

Turning away for the moment from codices and chroniclers, we now come to the legend presenting the first problem that has to be solved, or at any rate discussed. Undoubtedly this legend was very widely circulated among the people. Even the "Divina Commedia" (Par. xv. 125) tells us how the

Florentine dame at her spinning wheel—

"Favoleggiava con la sua famiglia
De' Troiani di Fiesole e di Roma."

Nevertheless, it appears to have had a literary rather than a purely popular origin. In fact, it is only a strange medley of classical and mediæval traditions, chiefly taken from books, and more or less arbitrarily altered, regarding the siege of Troy, the flight of Æneas, and the origin of Rome; and as municipal pride sought to connect the latter with that of Florence, all the scanty and vague notices, or rather traditions, existing on the subject had been carefully scraped together. The legend begins with Adam, but quickly leaving him aside, strides on to the foundation of Fiesole by Atlas and his spouse, aided by the counsels of Apollonius the astrologer. Fiesole was the first city built; it was erected on the healthiest spot in Europe, and hence its name—*Fie sola*. The children of Atlas spread over the land and populated it. The eldest son was called Italo, and gave Italy its name; the third was Sicano, who conquered and named Sicily. The second son, Dardano, wandered farther a-field, and founded the city of Troy.[50] The legend next passes rapidly to the Trojan war, the flight of Æneas, and the foundation of Rome, of which city Florence is the favourite offspring. It then goes on to speak at much greater length, of Catiline, regarding whom so many particulars are given, that he must have been the subject of a separate legend which either, when united with the rest, at a later date, formed the so-called "Chronica de origine Civitatis," or was, more probably, anterior to this, and only amalgamated with it in subsequent compilations.

After conspiring against Rome Catiline came to Fiesole, whither the Romans pursued and attacked him, under their consuls Metellus and Fiorinus. The latter falling in battle, their army was totally defeated on the banks of the Arno. But Julius Cæsar came to avenge them, besieged and destroyed Fiesole; and then, on the same spot where Fiorinus had fallen, a new city was built, and called Fiorenza to commemorate his name. Catiline fled to the Pistorian Appennines, but was pursued there and routed. So great was the number of the killed, that a pestilence broke out, and from this Pistoia derived its name.[51]

PAVEMENT OF ROMAN HOUSE UNDER THE MERCATO VECCHIO, FLORENCE.

MOSAIC PAVEMENT OF ROMAN BATHS, FLORENCE.

[To face page 59

In the legend the nomenclature of Tuscan cities is always explained on the same principles, Pisa, for instance, being derived from *pesare* (to weigh). For the Romans received their tributes there, and these were so numerous that they had to be weighed in two different places. This is why they spoke of the city in the plural, *Pisae Pisarum*. Lucca comes from *lucere* (to shine), because it was the first city converted to the light of Christianity. When the Franks[52] marched against the Longobards in the South they halted at a place in central Italy, and left all their aged people behind them. Thus the city built on that site received the name, likewise in the plural, of *Senae Senarum*. Florence, however, according to the legend, derived its name from Fiorinus, although later writers declared it to be taken from the word *Fluentia*, because it stood by the river Arno; others, again, from the numerous flowers springing from its soil. It was built in the likeness of Rome, with a capitol, forum, theatre, and baths, and was consequently called Little Rome. Its friends are always the friends of Rome; the foes of the one are foes of the other.

After five hundred years, so runs the legend, *Totila flagellum Dei* came and destroyed Florence, and immediately rebuilt the rival city of Fiesole. This clearly alludes to Attila, since he bore the title of *flagellum Dei*, and in the Middle Ages was the real type of the devastator and destroyer of cities. As he never came to Florence he was converted into Totila, who had been there, although never designated by the same appellation. This exchange of names was aided by their resemblance, nor is it the sole example the Middle Ages afford of the confusion of Attila with Totila. In the "Divina Commedia" ("Inferno," xiii. 148–9) we find Dante attributing the destruction of Florence to Attila, when he says:

"Quei cittadin che poi la rifondarno
Sovra il cener che d'Attila rimase."

And hereby he doubly deserts the legend; for, according to that, Florence was rebuilt by the Romans and then, naturally, on the pattern of Christian Rome, with churches dedicated to St. Peter, St. John, St. Laurence, &c., as in the Eternal City.

Thereupon more than 500 years[53] elapsed in peace; but then Florence, finally resolving to be revenged on its perpetual rival, suddenly attacked and destroyed Fiesole. At this point we may remark that, if Florence had been first founded in Cæsar's time, and adorned with Roman monuments at a later date; if, after 500 years,[54] it was destroyed by Totila, and then itself overthrew Fiesole after another interval of 500 years, the chronology of the legend clearly brings us to the eleventh century at least. If we also add that the assault and partial destruction of Fiesole really occurred in 1125, it follows that, as we have noted, the legend cannot have been framed before the twelfth century.

Here, then, it should end and give place to history. In fact, Sanzanome, the earliest of the chroniclers, begins his work with the destruction of Fiesole. But the "Libro fiesolano" sometimes introduces capricious turns in the framework of the legend, and at this point makes an addition worthy of note as an evidence of the mode in which these fantastic stories were built up. The added portion refers to the Uberti, powerful citizens always opposed to popular government in Florence. According to tradition, they came originally from Germany with the Othos. Evidently, however, this theory was repugnant to the author of the "Libro fiesolano," possibly an adherent of the Uberti, and he therefore remarks, with some heat, that, on the contrary, the Uberti were descended from Catiline, "most noble king of Rome," with Trojan blood running in his veins. Catiline's son Uberto Cesare had a Fiesolan wife, who bore him sixteen children; and he was afterwards sent by Augustus to reconquer Saxony, which had risen in rebellion. While in that country Uberto Catilina married a German lady of high position, and from this union sprang "the lineage of the good Ceto [Otho] of Sansognia." Thus it is false that the Uberti were "born of the Emperor of Germany, the truth being that the emperor was born of their race."[55] This addition, posterior to the rest of the legend, shows that the author desired to exalt the Uberti; but, remembering their constant hostility to the Florentine government, declared them descended from Catiline and his Fiesolan bride. Also, being unable to deny outright their Ghibelline proclivities and Germanic origin, yet unwilling to acknowledge their descent from the Othos, he converts them into the latter's progenitors. Thus the legend is brought into harmony with its compiler's views, or rather, with his intent of magnifying his friends.

Inquiry into the sources of this legend would only lead us astray, without throwing any new light on the origin of Florence, since the fable has no real historical value. We need only say that, besides Darses' "De excidio Troiae," the commentary to Virgil of Servius; Orosio's History, Paolo Diacono's Roman History, and the "Storia Miscella," &c., must have been consulted for its compilation.[56] Leaving the question aside, we may rather note that, although Villani and Malespini both give the legend as a preface to their histories, they not only refer to two separate compilations, but use them in a totally different way.[57] This is another proof that even if Malespini's chronicle were copied from Villani, it is not always an exact reproduction. He refers to the "Libro fiesolano,"[58] but enlarges it with two entire chapters of his own, containing a complete story, probably derived from some episode of the Catiline legend. And although teeming with the strangest anachronisms, it is better written and far livelier than the rest.

In this tale we find Fiorino converted into a Roman king, married to the most beautiful woman ever seen, appropriately named Belisca. After the defeat and death of her husband, Queen Belisca remained the captive of a wicked knight named Pravus, but Catiline causes him to be put to death, and carries off Belisca, of whom he is desperately enamoured. The queen, however, is in despair concerning the fate of her lovely daughter Teverina, imprisoned in the house of one Centurione, and adored by him. In kissing Teverina's beautiful hair this man had exclaimed: "It is these that enchain me, for lovelier locks have I never seen." On the day of Pentecost the mother attended mass in the Fiesole church, and with bitter tears bemoaned the loss of her child. Her prayer was heard by a serving-maid, who knew where Teverina was hidden, and revealed it to the weeping mother. On receiving the news, Catiline instantly attacked Centurione's palace, and, after a fierce struggle, succeeded in capturing him. The prisoner owed his life to Belisca's intercession; for, having regained her child, she desired to save him, dressed his wounds, and urged him to fly from Catiline's wrath. Centurione consented to escape, and having mounted his horse, implored permission to bid a last farewell to Teverina. But when she appeared, he caught her in his arms, and galloped away, followed by his men. The mother fainted from grief, and Catiline, "with all his barons," a thousand horse and two thousand foot, pursued the traitor to the castle of Naldo, ten miles off, and proceeded to attack him there. But at that moment news came that the Romans were marching on Fiesole, so he was obliged to hasten back there before the siege should begin. Thus ends the singular episode annexed to the legend, when, having lost its primitive character, it became a fairy tale while pretending to be history.

Villani, on the other hand, follows a more ancient compilation, and rejects the Belisca story. He, too, is acquainted with the "Libro fiesolano," makes some use of it, but considers it unauthentic exactly at the point where we find Malespini adhering to it. In fact, when recording the pretended descent of the Uberti from Catiline, Villani adds: "We find no proof of these matters in any authentic history."[59] Also, in trying, as far as possible, to give the legend a more genuine and historical appearance, he often inserts alterations drawn from the sources on which the legend itself was based, sometimes quoting Roman poets and historians such as Ovid, Lucan, Titus Livy, and, above all, Sallust, to whom he refers when adding certain historical particulars to the Catiline legends. A permanently instructive psychological fact is afforded us by the men of this period, and most of all by Villani. How was it that a contemporary of Dante— a man practised in affairs, cultivated, intellectual, and acutely observant— could mingle so much and such puerile credulity with great intelligence, culture, and common sense?

In short, what substantial information can be gleaned from the "Chronica de origine civitatis"? Besides the ambitious aim, common to nearly all the cities of Italy, of trying to trace their origin back to the Romans and Trojans, the "Chronica" wishes to impress upon us that the Etruscan Fiesole was the constant rival of Roman Florence, which could not prosper until the former was destroyed. Therefore, Catiline, the enemy of Rome, is the defender of Fiesole, Cæsar, Augustus, the emperors, are the founders, champions, and restorers of Florence, which is always described as being in the likeness of Rome and styled little Rome, Augusta, Cesarea, &c. Totila or Attila—that is, barbarians who overthrew the Empire—are likewise destroyers of Florence. Another legend of later date attributes the rebuilding of the city to Charlemagne, the restorer of the Empire. So at least the tale runs in Villani and Malespini; but there is no trace of it either in the "De Origine," or the "Libro fiesolano," both impregnated with Roman traditions only, and the legends of chivalry being as yet unknown to Florence. In fact, Villani remarks, when repeating the tale: "We find (it) in the 'Chronicles of France.'"[60]

We may accept as a certainty that the first origin of Florence was owed to Etruscan Fiesole, and that this was known even in the days of Dante is proved by his lines to the Florentines ("Inferno," xv. 61–3):

"Ma quell' ingrato popolo maligno,
   Che discese da Fiesole ab antico,
  E tiene ancor del monte e del macigno."

And Niccolò Machiavelli, leaving all legends aside (as Aretino had done before him), justly declared that the traders of Fiesole had begun from very remote times to form a commercial settlement on the Arno, at the pointwhere the Mugnone runs into the river. So gradually a cluster of cabins arose, grew into houses, and finally became a rival city. But the city was entirely constructed by the Romans, though at what precise period is still unascertained. It is scarcely probable that the event can have occurred earlier than two centuries before Christ. Perhaps the city began to rise when, to protect Tuscany against Ligurian invaders, the Romans made a network of roads through the valley of the Arno; that is, when (according to Livy) C. Flaminius *viam a Bononia perduxit Arretium*, the which road crossed the Ponte Vecchio. Strabo says nothing of Florence; Tacitus and Pliny are the first to mention it. But in the second century of the Vulgar Era Florius already styles it *Municipium splendidissimum*, and records it among the cities which suffered most in the days of Sulla.[61] Recent excavations made in digging new sewers under Florence have furnished proofs that in Sulla's time the city must have already possessed buildings of no small importance, including an amphitheatre.[62] The restoration of Florence, after the serious injuries inflicted on it in Sulla's day, is generally attributed to Augustus, who is supposed to have made it the seat of one of the twenty-eight colonies founded by him, whence the name *Julia, Augusta, Florentia*. The "Liber Coloniarum" (p. 213, 6) numbers Florence among the colonies formed by the *Triumviri* (45 B.C.), and it certainly must have been a colony in 15 B.C., when the city sent a deputation to Tiberius asking him to forbid the junction of the river Chiana with the Arno, on account of the damage this would cause (Tacitus, "Ann.," i.

79). But the weighty authority of Mommsen supports the view that, in spite of the testimony given by Florius, the colony of Florence was founded instead by Sulla.[63] The same date may be assigned to the construction of the oldest circuit of walls, existing during a great part of the Middle Ages, and some remains of which have been discovered in our own day.

PISCINA FRIGIDARIA.

Discovered near the Campidoglio, Florence.

[*To face page 66*

Florence would seem to have been built in the form of the ancient Roman *Castrum*, a quadrangle traversed by two wide and perfectly straight streets, crossing it in the centre at right angles and dividing it into quarters. The Campidoglio stood in the middle on the site afterwards occupied by the Church of Santa Maria in Campidoglio, and the Forum was near at hand, on the site of the now demolished Mercato Vecchio. There was also the amphitheatre, known in the Middle Ages as the *Parlascio*, of which some traces exist near Borgo de' Greci; a theatre (in Via de' Gondi.); a temple of Isis (on the site of San Firenze); and baths in the street still known as Via delle Terme.[64] Accordingly, it is not surprising that the city, which was then very small and limited to this side of the Arno, should have been called Little Rome, and sought to base its origin on Roman traditions. The whole spirit of its monuments spoke of Rome, and the same spirit was echoed by the minds and imaginations of those who invented the legend. Even now, after so many centuries, so many changes, we still find remains of Roman buildings, and of so-called Byzantine architecture, but no single trace of the real Gothic or Longobard style.

Florence gradually extended as time went on, and *borghi* were built outside the walls, the largest of these suburban quarters being the *Borgo*, connected with the city proper by the Ponte Vecchio. In the second half of the eleventh century, and in the year 1078, if Villani's statement be correct (iv. 8), new walls were built to replace the palisades surrounding the *Borghi*. Villani may be accepted as an authority, now that he is known to have superintended the construction of the third and last circuit of walls begun in 1299 (viii. 2 and 31), and now almost entirely destroyed save for a fragment here and there.

For a long time after the epoch of the barbarian invasions the history of Florence is involved in great obscurity, and what little information we have on the subject is either entirely legendary or jumbled with legends.

In 405 Radagasius led a horde of Goths, mixed with other tribes, into Tuscany and lay siege to Florence. But the walls held out until the Roman general Stilicho came to the rescue, defeated the assailants, and put their leader to death. The resistance of Florence was greatly magnified, and Stilicho's victory attributed to a miracle. Tradition added that the battle having been fought on the 8th of October, the Feast of Santa Reparata, the Florentines inaugurated their Pallio races on that day, and founded the Church of Santa Reparata; but both these events were of later occurrence. The tradition merely serves to show how long Florence preserved the memory of its narrow escape from destruction.

Regarding the next century there is an absolute blank; but then comes the legend that even Villani accepts, relating how Totila, *flagellum Dei*, destroyed Florence and re-built Fiesole.[65] To this the chronicler appends a second tale to the effect that after the city had remained thus devastated and ruined for 350 years, Charlemagne summoned the Romans to join him in rebuilding the city in the likeness of Rome, and that it thus arose anew, adorned with churches dedicated, like those of Rome, to San Pietro, San Lorenzo, Santa Maria Maggiore, &c., and was also granted a territory extending three miles beyond the walls.[66] Here one sees that although the chronicler had already recorded, on the authority of the "De Origine," that Florence was rebuilt immediately after its pretended destruction by Totila, he thought that date premature, seeing that Florence really remained for long after in a very desolate and obscure condition, and therefore, to save trouble, he also jots down the posterior legend attributing instead the reconstruction of the city to Charlemagne, the saviour of the Empire.

What germs of truth can be gleaned from all this? Totila really entered Tuscany in 542, and sent part of his host to besiege Florence. Justin, the commander of the Imperial garrison there, then sought aid from Ravenna; and when the relieving force approached the city, Totila raised the siege and withdrew towards Sienna. Pursued by the Imperial troops, he succeeded in routing them, but instead of returning against Florence, directed his march towards Southern Italy. So at least runs the account given by Procopius, and also followed by modern writers.[67] The Goths, it is true, made another descent later, easily mastered Tuscany and Florence, and committed much cruelty there, though without destroying the city. These are the facts; all the rest was a legendary excrescence signifying that the Florentines endured a long period of obscurity and oppression, and only began to emerge from it in the time of the Franks.

In fact, the Longobard occupation of Tuscany took place towards 570, and we have two centuries of utter darkness. We find mention of one *Gudibrandus, Dux civitatis Florentinorum*, appointed by the conquerors; but nothing else is known to us. Amid the many calamities wrought by invasion, war, and harsh tyranny, not only was the trade, to which Florence owed its existence, entirely ruined, but many families escaped from the plains to safe places among the hills, and a good number accordingly took refuge in Fiesole, which city profited as usual by the ill fortune of Florence. And this to so great an extent, that during the latter half of the eighth century we find documents alluding to Florence as though it had become a suburb of Fiesole.[68] But soon, beneath Charlemagne's rule, times of greater order and tranquillity were inaugurated. Men began once more to forsake the hills for the valley; Florence began to prosper at Fiesole's expense. And as the Franks replaced the Longobard dukes by counts, so Florence too had its count, exercising jurisdiction throughout the territories of the bishopric that had been carved out of the old Roman division. This was the so-called *contado fiorentino*, stretching on the one side to a place called I Confini, near Prato, and thence towards Poggio a Caiano, sweeping round by the Empoli district, and conterminous with the borders of Lucca, Volterra, and the *contado* of Fiesole.[69]

Charlemagne halted in Florence, and celebrated Christmas there in 786;

he likewise defended the property of the Florentine Church against Longobard aggressions. This gave rise to the legend that the rebuilding of the city was his work. Regardless of anachronisms, Villani not only adds that many imaginary privileges were conceded by him, but attributes to this period the birth of the Commune which only took place several centuries later. "Charles," he tells us, "created many knights, and granted privileges to the city by rendering free and independent the Commune, its inhabitants, and the *contado*, with all dwellers therein, for three miles round, inclusive of resident strangers from other parts. For this reason many men returned to the said city, and framed its government after the Roman mode, namely, with two consuls and a council of one hundred senators."[70] But this addition is made by the chronicler, and in a more arbitrary way than the legend itself.

Nor was this all. Not Charlemagne only, but likewise Otho I., the regenerator of the German Empire, must be necessarily the patron of Florence, "because," continues the chronicler, "it had always appertained to the Romans and been faithful to the Empire."[71] In the year 955 the emperor halted in Florence on the way to Rome for his coronation, and on this occasion the chronicler makes him grant the city a territory of six miles in extent, that is, one as big again, but no less imaginary, than that bestowed by Charlemagne. Villani goes on to relate how Otho established peace in Italy, overthrew tyrants, and left many of his barons settled in Lombardy and Tuscany, the Counts Guidi and Uberti among the rest. He fails to reflect that some of these Tuscan families were of much earlier origin, and that even in his own day the leading nobles of the *contado* bore the name of Cattani Lombardi, in remembrance of their Longobard descent. Also, he again forgets that Florence was not then a free city to whom the emperor could concede a portion of territory, which, as we have seen, already belonged to his own jurisdiction, and, towards Fiesole at least, could not possibly be of six miles in extent.[72]

Another fabulous narrative, also given by Villani, is that of the destruction of Fiesole in 1010. On the day of St. Romolo's feast the Florentines, bent on revenge, are supposed to have entered the rival city with arms concealed under their clothes, and suddenly drawing their weapons and summoning comrades hidden in ambush, to have rushed through the streets, seizing everything and destroying all houses and buildings excepting the bishop's palace, the cathedral, two or three churches, and the fortress, which refused to surrender. After this, safety was promised to all disposed to migrate into Florence, and many profited by the offer. Thus the two peoples were made one, and even their flags united. That of the Florentines bore the white lily on a red field, that of Fiesole a demi lune azur on a white field; and thus was formed the red and white banner of the Commune.[73]

According to Villani this union of two separate peoples proved the chief cause of the continual wars by which Florence was harassed, together with the fact of the city being built "under the sway and influence of the planet Mars, the which always leads to war and discord." Then again, as though forgetting he had already made the same statement regarding the times of Charlemagne, he repeats the almost equal anachronism that the Florentines "then made common laws and statutes, and lived under the rule of two consuls and a council of senators, consisting of a hundred men, the best of the city, according to the custom introduced in Florence by the Romans."[74] It is plain that he does not know how the Commune arose, but feels persuaded its origin was derived from Rome, and therefore records the fact as having occurred at the moment suiting him best, or seeming least improbable. But it is hard to see why he assigned the war and destruction of Fiesole to the year 1010 when aware that those events occurred, on the contrary, in 1125, as he afterwards relates in due place. The most probable explanation is, that finding the legend gave an account of the war and overthrow of Fiesole *more than five hundred years* after the destruction of Florence by Totila, whose invasion occurred *five hundred years* after the city was founded, the chronicler described the destruction twice over, namely, in 1010 and 1125; thus following first the legendary account, which had retraced its steps in a very vague fashion, and next the historical account, commonly known in his day. As for the causes of civil war being derived from the forced junction of two hostile nationalities, it may be observed that the diversity between the Germanic strain in the nobility and the Latin blood of the people, really constituted a strong element of discord, and this may have been felt, if not understood, by the chronicler.

It is certain that from the Frankish times downward the prosperity of Florence slowly but surely increased. Nevertheless it is true that, as Villani says, its whole territory bristled with the castles of feudal barons of Germanic descent, all hostile to Florence, and many of whom, safely ensconced on the neighbouring hill of Fiesole, were always ready to swoop down on Florentine soil.

In spite of this the geographical position of the city, on the road to Rome, proved increasingly advantageous to its commerce. As early as 825 the *Costitutiones olonenses* of the Emperor Lothair proposed Florence, with seven other Italian cities, as the seat of a public school, thus attesting its importance even at that date. Besides, the German emperors nearly always halted there on their way to coronation in Rome. More often, and for longer periods, the Popes made sojourn there, whenever—a by no means uncommon occurrence—popular disturbances expelled them from Rome. Victor II. died in Florence in 1057, and had held a council there two years before; in 1058 Stephen IX. drew his last breath there; three years later Nicholas II. and his cardinals stayed in the town pending the election of Alexander II. Full of Roman traditions and monuments, in continual relation with the Eternal City, Florence was subject to its influence from the earliest times, and showed the Guelph and religious tendencies afterwards increasingly prominent in the course of her history. Towards the close of the tenth century many new churches arose within and without the city walls. At the beginning of the eleventh century the construction of an edifice such as San Miniato al Monte, in addition to the other churches built about the same period, affords indubitable proof of awakening prosperity and religious zeal. In fact, Florence now became one of the chief centres of the movement in favour of monastic reform that, after its first manifestation at Cluny, spread so widely on all sides. St. Giovanni Gualberto, of Florentine birth, who died in 1073, inaugurated the reformed Benedictine order known by the name of Vallombrosa, in which place he founded his celebrated cloister, and subjected many of the monasteries near Florence to the same rule.

ATTACK ON THE MONKS OF S. SALVI.

(Bas-relief by Benedetto da Rovezzano in the National Museum, Florence.)

[*To face page 74*

Before long this religious and monastic zeal burnt so fiercely in Florence, that when its bishop, Pietro da Pavia, was accused of simony, all the people rose against him. The friars declared that he owed his high office to the favour of the emperor, and of Duke Goffredo and Beatrice his wife, and that he had bought their protection at a very heavy price. The multitude sided with the friars, and the quarrel was carried on for five years (1063–68), and with so much heat as to lead to bloodshed. The bishop, enraged by these accusations, and emboldened by the duke's favour, caused an armed attack to be made on the monastery of San Salvi near Florence. The first promoter of the religious movement, St. Giovanni Gualberto, was, fortunately for him, elsewhere at the time; but his altars were pillaged and several of his monks injured. This incident naturally added fuel to the fire, and St. Giovanni Gualberto, who had already inflamed men's minds by preaching in the city streets, now cast aside all reserve, and openly declared that no priests consecrated by a simoniacal bishop were real members of the clergy. The popular excitement rose to so high a pitch, that it is asserted that about a thousand persons preferred to die unassoiled, rather than receive the sacrament from priests ordained by a bishop guilty of simony.[75] Strange though it seem, this was by no means incredible in times of earnest religious faith!

Pope Alexander II. vainly endeavoured to pacify the people; vainly sent the pious, learned, and eloquent St. Pier Damiano to achieve that end. The holy man came with the words of peace, afterwards repeated in his letters addressed to *Dilectis in Christo civibus florentinis*. He censured simony, but likewise blamed too easy credence of the charge. It were better, he said, for the Florentines to send representatives to the Synod in Rome, whose authority would decide the quarrel; meanwhile they must remain quiet, without yielding to the blind and heinous illusion that had left so many to die without the "sacraments" to their souls' peril. Woe to those who seek to be juster than the just, wiser than the wise. Through too great zeal, they end by joining the foes of the Church. Croaking even as frogs (*velut ranae in paludibus*), they throw everything into confusion, and may be likened to the plague of locusts in Egypt, since they bring equal destruction on the Church.[76]

This movement much resembled that carried on about the same time by the Patarini in Milan against the simony of the archbishop. There too, as in Florence, St. Pier Damiano played the part of peacemaker, and there also many preferred to die unassoiled, rather than take the sacrament from simoniacal priests.[77] But, despite the resemblance of the two insurrections, they led to different final results, owing to the different conditions of the two cities, and the very diverse attitude respectively assumed towards them by the Court of Rome. At any rate, the exhortations of St. Pier Damiano had no effect in Florence. The Vallombrosa monks sent representatives to Rome, but only to declare before the Council, then in session, their readiness to decide the question by appeal to the judgment of God. Not only was their proposal rejected by Pope and Council, but they were also severely censured for suggesting it, although the Archdeacon Hildebrand, there present, who had already risen to great authority in the Church, tried to defend them, as he had previously defended the Patarini of Milan. The Council ordered the monks to withdraw to their monasteries, and abide in them quietly, without daring again to inflame minds already unduly excited. St. Giovanni Gualberto would have obeyed willingly now; but it was too late: he could no longer quell the storm he had raised. For when the populace heard of what the monks had proposed in Rome, they insisted on the ordeal by fire. The champion chosen for the purpose, already prepared and impatient to stand the test, was a certain Brother Pietro, of Vallombrosa, afterwards known by the name of Pietro Igneo, who, according to some writers, had been cowherd to the monastery, although others assert him to have belonged to the noble family of the Counts Aldobrandeschi of Sovana. Guglielmo, surnamed Bulguro, of the Counts of Borgonuovo, offered the monks a free arena for the ordeal, close to the Abbey of San Salvatore, in his patronage, at Settimo, five miles from Florence.[78] The bishop, however, not only rejected the challenge with indignation, but obtained a decree to the effect that whoever, whether of the Church or the laity, should refuse to obey his authority, the same would be seized, bound, and *not led, but dragged* before the chief of the city.[79] Likewise the goods of all persons having fled in alarm were to be confiscated by the *Potestà*, that is, by Duke Goffredo, who favoured the bishop. Meanwhile, certain rebellious ecclesiastics who had sought refuge in an oratory,[80] were driven from it by force. Naturally, these measures only increased the heat of the popular fury. Pietro Igneo declared his readiness to pass through the fire, and, if need be, alone. On February 13, 1068, an enormous crowd of men, women (some about to be mothers), old people, and children, set forth to Settimo, chanting prayers and psalms by the way. There, by the Badia, two piles of wood were fired, and, as related by one who claims to have witnessed the sight, the friar passed through the roaring flames miraculously unhurt. This aroused an indescribable enthusiasm; the sky echoed with cries of joy, and Pietro Igneo, though unscathed by the fire, was nearly crushed to death by the throng pressing round him to kiss the hem of his robe. With great difficulty, and only by main force, some ecclesiastics succeeded in rescuing him.[81] The news flew to Rome with lightning speed, and then, when all the details reached the Pope's ear, he was compelled to bow to the miracle. The bishop of Florence retired to a monastery; Pietro Igneo was named cardinal, made bishop of Albano, and worshipped as a saint after his death.

MIRACLE OF SAN GIOVANNI GUALBERTO.

(Bas-relief by Benedetto da Rovezzano in the National Museum, Florence.)

[To face page 78

This reminds us of the other ordeal by fire proposed in Florence in 1498, and that led to Savonarola's martyrdom, shortly before the fall of the Republic, of which the birth and death would thus seem to have been preluded by similar events. For, albeit the account of the affair may have been exaggerated by party feeling and superstition, and although the terms of "Preside" and "Podestà" employed in the old narrative only indicate in a general way the ruling powers in Florence at the time, all shows that a new state of society had begun. We find that there was a Duke of Tuscany, a military president, apparently his representative in the city, and, what is more, a people which, though only appearing as a fanatic mob, is plainly conscious at last of its own strength, since it struggles against the bishop, resists both the duke and the Pope, and finally obtains what it desires. In addressing the Pope it assumes the title of *populus florentinus*; and is addressed by St. Pier Damiano as *cives florentini*. It is true, of course, that these were mere forms of speech imitated from the ancients; assuredly the Commune was still unborn, and much time had yet to elapse before its rise; but an entirely new condition of things had begun, in which the elements conducing to its rise were already in course of preparation. Accordingly, we must now retrace our steps, in order to study the question more closely.

CHAPTER II.

THE ORIGIN OF THE FLORENTINE COMMUNE.[82]

I.

WHEN the Longobards became masters of nearly the whole of Italy, and subjected it to their long and cruel sway, they are known to have appointed a duke to every one of the principal cities they occupied. Rome remained free from them, having a Pope; Ravenna also escaped because an Exarch was soon to hold rule there, and almost all the cities by the sea were likewise exempted, inasmuch as the Longobards were ignorant of navigation, and needed assistance for their maritime trade. It was for the same reason that republics such as Venice, Amalfi, Pisa, Naples, and Gaeta, were of earlier origin than the rest. The dukes enjoyed great authority and independence; indeed, some of the duchies, especially on the borders, became so extended as to resemble small kingdoms—*e.g.*, the dukedoms of Friuli, Spoleto, and Benevento. This circumstance greatly contributed to the decomposition of the kingdom and to the fall of the Longobards, whose strength and daring were never conjoined with any real political capacity.

On the arrival of the Franks, counts took the place of dukes, but with less power and smaller territories. Charlemagne, with his genuine talent for statesmanship, refused to maintain lords who, in seeking their own independence, might endanger the existence of his empire. Nevertheless, as it was indispensable to keep his borders more strongly defended, he constituted *marches*, on the pattern of the greater Longobard duchies, and entrusted them to margraves, or marquises (*Mark-grafen*—frontier counts, marquises, or margraves). Thus too the marquisate of Tuscany was formed and the government centred in Lucca; for this city having had a duke of its own ever since the times of the Longobards, was already of considerable importance, while, as we have seen, Florence had fallen so low that the documents of the period merely refer to it as a suburb of Fiesole. Nearly all the margraves acquired great power, and aspired to still higher dignities. From their ranks in fact came men such as Hardouin and Berengarius, who, aspiring to form an Italian kingdom, became formidable opponents of the Empire, often wrought it much harm, and involved it in sanguinary wars.

Hence it is not surprising if, later on, the policy of the German emperors should have constantly aimed at the enfeeblement of the leading Italian counts and margraves, and, by granting exemptions and benefices to prelates or lesser feudatories, and making all benefices conceded to the latter hereditary estates, rendered these independent of all greater and more dangerous potentates. Therefore, particularly in Lombardy, this class rose to importance, and so, too, the political authority of the bishops, who in point of fact held the position of counts. But in Tuscany things took a different turn. Whether feudalism there, having smaller strength and power of expansion, seemed less formidable to the Empire; whether the country, being more distant, proved less easy to govern; or because a strong state in central Italy was felt to be needed to arrest the growing power of the Papacy; whether the latter may have favoured its formation, as a possible check to the Empire; or again, as seems probable, for all these reasons combined, it is certain that the dukes or marquises of Tuscany (either title was borne by them) increased in power and consequence, and afterwards, in their turn, became a danger to the Empire. But in Tuscany the power of bishops and counts suffered more reduction than in Lombardy from the growing strength of the margraves, whose sway was extending on all sides, so that they sometimes appear to be virtual sovereigns of central Italy. The same reasons served to delay the rise of cities, and specially hindered that of Florence.

Already, from the second part of the tenth century, a Marquis Ugo, surnamed the Great, of Salic descent, ruled over Tuscany, the duchy of Spoleto and the *march* of Camerino. He reigned in Lucca almost in the guise of an independent monarch, and enjoyed the favour of the Othos. His successors continued to govern with much the same authority as the dukes of Benevento; and Bonifazio III. extended his State even to Northern Italy, thus giving umbrage to Henry III., whom he often outrivalled in cunning. Bonifazio being voracious for power, and of tyrannical temper, stripped many prelates, counts, and monasteries of their possessions, either to seize them in his own grasp or give them to better trusted vassals. He also tightened his grasp on all cities which, having risen to some importance, coveted increased freedom. This was specially the case with Lucca and Pisa. The former had prospered through being long the chief seat of the duchy, while the latter owed its prosperity to the sea, on which, as Amari happily phrased it, Pisa was already a free city, while still a subject city on land. Florence, however, still existed in humble obscurity, trading in a small way, and girt about on all sides by feudal strongholds.

In 1037 Bonifazio had taken to wife Beatrice of Lorraine, who in 1046 gave birth to a daughter, Matilda, the celebrated countess or *comitissa*, as she is entitled by the chroniclers. After the death of Bonifazio, by assassination, in

1052, Matilda was soon associated with her mother in the government of Tuscany and of the whole duchy, and when left an orphan in 1076, became sole ruler of those extensive dominions. Beatrice had remarried, and as she was very religious, and her second husband, Goffredo of Lorraine, was brother to Pope Stephen IX., this served to increase their common zeal for the papal policy, afterwards so devotedly pursued by Matilda. When this high- minded, energetic woman became sole ruler, she held the reins of government in a firm grasp, and was often seen on battle-fields with a sword at her side. Her political position was one of great peril, for she was driven to take part in the fierce quarrel, recently begun, between the Church and the Empire. At first the great, high-tempered Hildebrand conducted the struggle as the inspiring genius of various Popes; later on, when raised to the pontifical Chair as Gregory VII., he fought in person against Henry IV. of Germany, and found Matilda his strongest and best ally. In this conflict, stirring and dividing all Europe, it was only natural that many opposing passions should be excited in Italy. All cities that, like Pisa and Lucca, considered themselves wronged by Duke Bonifazio, now declared for the Empire, and the Empire sided with them against Matilda. The same course was followed by all dissatisfied feudatories, especially by those whom Bonifazio had stripped of their possessions. More than once, it is true, Countess Matilda seized estates which had been arbitrarily alienated; but she seldom restored them to their original owners, preferring instead to bestow them on churches, convents, and trusty adherents of her own. This added fresh fuel to the flame. Hence an increasingly tangled web of opposing passions, of conflicting interests, from which at last some profit accrued to Florence. The Guelph spirit of the city and its commercial position, on the highway to Rome, had from the outset inclined it to the Church, and now, as a declared ally, was actively favoured by Beatrice and Matilda.

II.

It was long believed that Florence had had Consuls, and consequently an independent government, from the year 1102, since Consuls are mentioned in a treaty of that date, whereby the inhabitants of Pogna swore submission to the city. But it was difficult to reconcile this fact with the clearly proved dependence of Florence on Countess Matilda at the time. It was afterwards ascertained that the document in question bore a wrong date, and that the correct one was 1182, when the submission of Pogna really took place. Accordingly, the independence of the city was transferred to after 1115, the year of the countess's death. But it was still difficult to explain the wars previously carried on by the city on its own account, and other events of a like nature. The fact is that no fixed year can be assigned to the birth of the Florentine Commune, which took shape very slowly, and resulted from the conditions of Florence under the rule of the last dukes or marquises. We have already recorded the popular riots of 1063–68 against the bishop Mezzabarba, when accused of simony, and we have related how they ended with the ordeal of fire, braved by Pietro Igneo in 1068. On this head we have cited the letters of St. Pier Damiano addressed *civibus florentinis*. We also referred to a document[83] in which the *clerus et populus florentinus* made appeal to the Pope, and, in narrating what had occurred, mentioned a *municipale praesidium*, a *praeses* of the city, and a superior *potestas*. This proved, before all, that the civic body of the period was already conscious of its personality, and that there was already an embryo local government within the city walls. Doubtless the supreme *potestas* was the Duke Goffredo, husband to Beatrice; the *praeses*, his representative in Florence. It was before him that, as we have seen, the bishop threatened to drag his adversaries, whose property was to be confiscated should they persist in disobedience. This *preside* commanded the *praesidium*, designated *municipal* even before the municipality had come into being, and at least the name shows that the majority of the *praesidium* must have consisted of citizens. But all this makes it equally plain that, while Florence was still an integral part of the margraviate, Roman forms, traditions, and ideas already prevailed there to the extent of assigning Roman names to institutions of feudal origin. We must pause to consider this fact, since it gave rise to a question, not only of form, but of genuine historical importance.

A ROMAN HYPO-CAUST, PARTLY CONSTRUCTED.

EXTERIOR VIEW OF CALIDARIUM AND FURNACE.

[To face page 85

The employment of Roman terms need cause little surprise when we remember that the study of elementary Roman law, as well as of rhetoric,[84] the *ars dictandi* then formed part of the *Trivium*, and was therefore widely taught in Italy. In the first half of the eleventh century a still more advanced study of law already flourished at the school of Ravenna, and as its influence increased, extended through Romagna into Tuscany. This system of law seemed to spring to life again spontaneously from the midst of Latin populations, with whom it had never entirely died out, and now in its new vigour brought modifications and changes into the different institutions and legislations with which it came in contact.[85] In fact, in the sentences pronounced by Beatrice and Matilda, we find occasional quotations from the *Digesto*, or Code, that, according to the procedure of the time, was carried to the tribunals by those basing their rights on its clauses.[86] The works of St. Pier Damiano afford satisfactory proof that the Florentines pursued the same study, and set great value on Roman law. The saint mentions a juridical dispute of the Florentines, regarding which, towards the middle of the eleventh century, they had asked the opinion of the *sapientes* of Ravenna, who, much to his own disgust, presumed to alter the prescriptions of canonical law on the authority of the *Digesto*. Among those wise men, he adds, the most impetuous and subtle chanced to be a Florentine.[87] Another proof might be deduced from the remark previously made by Ficker,[88] namely, that the courts held in Florence and its territory were seldom attended by the Romagnol assessors, or *causidici*, frequenting other Tuscan tribunals. This would seem to imply that in this respect Florentines had no need to recur to Romagna. Later—that is towards the end of the century—the school of Irnerius (Werner) began to flourish at Bologna, the which school aimed at an exact reproduction of Roman law and promoted its genuine revival. But at the time of which we speak the Ravenna school represented, on the contrary, a continuation of the ancient jurisprudence, partly decayed and partly changed by the diverse elements of civilisation in the midst of which it had survived, and in which it was now producing radical changes.[89] One of these changes— leading to very remarkable consequences of a political as well as a legal kind —took place in the constitution and attributes of the margravial tribunal.

We know that Matilda, after the fashion of her predecessors, administered justice in the name of the Empire, presiding in state over the tribunals. Indeed, this was one of her chief functions. Some sentences given by her have survived, and serve to show us how her tribunal was composed. Certain high feudatories had seats flanking her throne; next came the judges, assessors, pleaders (*causidici*), and witnesses, and lastly, the notary. Prof. Lami has observed that the judges, and more particularly the assessors, were changed as the countess moved from city to city, which would prove that not a few of them were inhabitants of the towns wherein they administered justice.[90] In fact, what names do we find among them in Florence? Those of the Gherardi, Caponsacchi, Uberti, Donati, Ughi, and a few others.[91] These were already the first and most influential citizens, the *boni homines*, the *sapientes*, the men we afterwards find officiating as Consuls. Thus there were certain families who first formed part of the margravial tribunal, and were afterwards at the head of the Commune.

Political changes were facilitated and prepared by a juridical change, followed by the increased action of the revived Roman law. What was the nature of this change? The exact definition of the functions respectively assigned by the Germanic code to the president of the tribunal who gave sentence, or to the judges who led up to the same by administering the law, had been gradually lost sight of. Sometimes the countess pronounced sentence without the aid of judges; but more often they conducted the trial, applied the law, and formulated the verdict, to which the countess merely gave assent. Thus, as Ficker states, her office was reduced to that of a passive president.[92] This is confirmed on seeing that tribunals sometimes sat in her absence, when the trials were entirely managed by the judges. A method of this kind once adopted, Matilda's grave and numerous affairs of State, together with the continual warfare in which she was involved, must have augmented the number of the cases settled by local judges. This must have been a matter of weighty importance at a time when the administration of justice was one of the principal attributes of political sovereignty. Hence these citizen tribunals are a precursory sign of civic independence before the Commune had asserted its real autonomy and individual position. The strange dearth of documents certifying that any tribunal in Florence was presided over by Matilda during the last fifteen years of her life, serves to confirm our remarks. A similar fact is also verified in the Tuscan cities remaining faithful to the Empire; for these too had tribunals in which justice was administered, not by feudal potentates, but by citizens invested by the emperor with judicial authority.[93] These, too, served as a preliminary to communal independence, although hardly forming, as some thought, its actual beginning.

DESCENT TO A ROMAN WELL.

Discovered beneath the Campidoglio, Florence

[To face page 89

It is certain that in this and other ways, during the contest between Henry IV. and Matilda, many Tuscan cities, siding either with the Empire or the Church, and therefore highly favoured by the one or the other, were able to achieve a commencement of freedom. After Henry IV. had defeated Matilda near Mantua in 1081 he granted large privileges to Pisa and Lucca, in return for their proofs of goodwill to his cause. In a letter patent issued at Rome June 23, 1081, he not only guaranteed to Lucca the integrity of its walls, but also authorised it to forbid the construction of any castles in the city or territory within a circuit of six miles, and promised to exempt it from building an Imperial palace. He likewise declared that no Imperial envoy should be sent to give judgment in Lucca, but made a reservation in case of the personal presence there of the emperor, or his son, or his chancellor. In conclusion, he annulled the "evil customs" (*perverse consuetudini*) imposed by Bonifazio III.[94] to the hurt of Lucca, and granted it full permission to trade in the markets of San Donnino and Capannori, from which he expressly excluded the Florentines. This final clause not only proves the hostility of the Empire to Florence, but the importance the latter's trade must have assumed by that time. In the same year Pisa received a patent guaranteeing the maintenance of its ancient rights, and Henry declared that no Imperial envoy belonging to another territory should be sent to plead suits within the walls, or within the boundaries of its *contado*. And, what was still more to the point, he also declared that no marquis should be sent into Tuscany without the consent of twelve *buoni uomini* chosen by the popular assembly, summoned in Pisa by sound of bell.[95] Here, if no Consuls yet appear on the scene, we already find their precursors in these worthies, or *sapientes*, elected of the people, and we have already a popular assembly. Even though the Commune be still unborn, its birth is now, as it were, in sight. Further (provided nothing was interpolated in the document), it is most remarkable to find the appointment of an Imperial margrave subject to the sanction of the people. There is also a hinted desire— unattainable during Matilda's life—to assume the government of the margraviate in person; after her death an attempt to this effect was actually made, but, as we shall see, with very brief and partial success.

III.

Nevertheless the condition of Florence was considerably different from that of Pisa or Lucca. These two cities, as we have seen, had long enjoyed greater prosperity. They had often fought against each other; Pisa, haughty and daring by sea, had begun, even in the middle of the tenth century, a long and arduous war against the Mussulmans[96] of Sicily, Spain, and Africa. Florence, on the other hand, in siding with Matilda, became necessarily the foe of all the great feudal nobles of the *contado*, surrounding the city on all sides, and who, disgusted by their treatment at the hands of the marquises of Tuscany, since the time of Bonifazio III., now, for the most part, adhered to the Empire. Their antagonism towards the Florentines was not only heightened by the fact of these nobles being of Germanic origin, even as feudal institutions were Germanic, whereas the population of Florence, consisting chiefly of artisans, was of Roman origin and full of Roman traditions; but it was likewise increased by the geographical position of the city. Had Florence been situated in a plain like Pisa and Lucca, or like Sienna and Arezzo on a height, the feudal nobility could have promoted their interests better by settling within its walls. But it lay in a valley in the midst of a girdle of hills bristling with feudal turrets, whence the nobles threatened it on all sides, raiding its lands and closing all outlets for its commerce.

These geographical conditions had no slight effect on the future destiny of Florence; and, in fact, largely contributed to form the special character of its history. As a primary result, conflict between the feudal nobles and the city was more inevitable and more sanguinary than elsewhere, while the city being, from the first, of far more democratic temper than the rest, was therefore longer prevented from asserting its independence, since this result could only be achieved when Florence had gained sufficient strength to cope with the numerous enemies girding it about. Until that moment arrived its interests were best forwarded by remaining friendly and submissive to Countess Matilda, the only power able to hold the barons in check, and the loss of whose aid would have left Florence a prey to its foes. This explains not only the city's delay in asserting its independence, but also the total lack of documents concerning the origin of a commune that had already risen to considerable strength, and started wars on its own account before its existence was officially recognised. These wars were still carried on in the name of the Countess, who occasionally visited the camp in person; the city was unmentioned in public documents, because it had as yet no personal existence. Nevertheless, we are forced to recognise the first signs of its communal life in the campaigns undertaken by Florence in defence of its trade against the nobles of the *contado*; the which campaigns were continued on an increasing and more vigorous scale until they ended in the total annihilation of the feudal lords. This was both the starting point and the aim of all Florentine history.

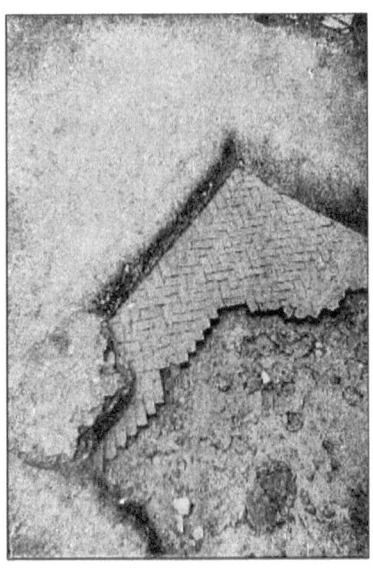

IMPLUVIUM OF ROMAN HOUSE, FLORENCE.

ROMAN CALIDARIUM,FLORENCE.

[To face page 96

From the very beginning, it is true, we find that even Florence possessed some families that may be called noble. Such were the Donati, Caponsacchi,

Uberti, Lamberti, and others whose names were included on the lists of the judges and soon to be found on those of the Consuls. These were the ruling, governing families at the head of the city. But they were neither counts, marquises, nor dukes; they were not as the Counts Cadolingi, Guidi, and Alberti, who dwelt in the outlying territory or *contado*; nor did they belong to those *Cattani Lombardi* so-called at the time, in remembrance of their Germanic descent. Rather than veritable nobles, they were "worthies" (*boni homines*), "great ones" (*grandi*),[97] owning no feudal titles; natives of the city risen to high fortune, or scions of petty feudal lines, who, unable to hold their own against greater neighbours of the country side, had sought safety within the town. They quickly amalgamated with the people, sharing and taking the lead in all the latter's expeditions against the strongholds outside the city. Nor, as will be shown, was it a rare case, later on, to find some of these nobles engaged in trade, or heads of trade guilds, as soon as the latter became more firmly established. And it is by no means an insignificant fact that during disturbances at Pisa, Sienna, and elsewhere, we often see the names of real citizen-nobles, counts, viscounts, and so on, never to be met with in Florence. In documents concerning the Florentines the word *nobiles* seldom occurs, whereas it is often used in speaking of the Pisans, Siennese, &c. The term *milites*, it is true, frequently occurs in Florentine records; but although the *milites* could not be *popolani*, since the lower classes were not then admitted to knighthood, neither could they be feudal nobles in Florence: they were the leading citizens who exercised no trade, the *grandi*, in fact, to whom we have previously alluded. They were members of Matilda's courts, were employed by her in various ways; they commanded the *municipale praesidium*, probably filled the office of *praeses*, and they were leaders of the army. Richer, more cultivated and better fitted than other citizens for politics and warfare by their freedom from daily toil, they were the *boni viri*, the *sapientes*, the *milites* found more or less in all cities, but of a separate stamp in Florence.

Notwithstanding our knowledge of this *preside* and *presidio* and of these Florentine tribunals, very little is known as to the government and administration of the social body already beginning to prosper and to have varied interests of its own. Matilda's sway in Florence must have been of a shadowy kind, when the city was able to start wars on its own account and to its own profit, albeit still undertaken in her name. As its commercial prosperity increased and Matilda became more absorbed in her struggle with the Empire, the city must have been left more to itself. Consequently this is the time when the associations serving to classify and organise the citizens were formed, which we presently find flourishing and strongly established. Thus, being almost without a central government, a local one could assert its existence, and the strength of the Commune be developed long before its independence was proclaimed. The same fact explains why the Commune, its individuality once declared, should have made such rapid progress and leapt to the headship of Tuscany. At any rate, by the second half of the twelfth century we find on the one side the *grandi*, or nobles—if we prefer to give them that name—formed in Societies of Towers (*Società delle torri*), with statutes soon to be made known to us; while, on the other we find trade guilds or associations not only in existence, but sometimes with sufficient political importance to entitle them to the honour of representing the Republic. Can we possibly suppose that such results could be achieved without a long, preliminary course of preparation? Did not the *scholae*, progenitors of the guilds, survive during the Lower Empire and throughout the Middle Ages? do we not find them dividing all society, including both the soldiery and foreigners in Rome and in Ravenna? How could they be destroyed by barbarians ignorant of crafts which were nevertheless indispensable to their own needs?

Florentine commerce and industry undoubtedly increased during the rule of Countess Matilda. This has been proved by the patent of 1081, and the first wars undertaken by the Florentines in the interest of their trade afford sure confirmation of the fact. Were we to exclude trade associations from the conditions of the period, we should have to admit the existence, at that day, of the modern workman, isolated and independent: a decided impossibility in the Middle Ages. Those were times in which every trade was exercised by distinct groups of families, and handed down by them as a tradition from father to son. Frequently, even offices of the State were the monopoly of certain families. It was from a society split into groups and castes that the Commune eventually developed the modern State, but in old times the very idea of the latter was unconceived. It is absurd to suppose—though a few writers accept the notion—that the guilds only began when they had regular statutes. These statutes only formulated what had already existed for some time, and undoubtedly in Florence everything conduces to the belief that the associations of the trades and of the towers, though still embryonic, must have preceded the formation of the Commune evolved in their midst.

IV.

For on all sides, if in diverse modes, we perceive that a long period of incubation was needed to form the Commune, which naturally owed its birth to pre-existing elements. The celebrated agreement or *concordia* made at Pisa by Bishop Daiberto, about 1090, or even, perhaps, a year or so earlier, shows that the nobles were organised and waging fierce war against one another from their towers. The bishop induced them to partly demolish these towers, and solemnly vow never to carry them above the height of thirty-six braccia (about one hundred feet), as previously decreed by the patent of Henry IV. in 1081.[99] And the agreement proceeded to set forth that any man believing his houses to have been unjustly damaged was to bear his complaint *ad commune Colloquium Civitatis*; nor could the dwelling of the offender be demolished without the general consent of the citizens.[100]

MOUTH OF ROMAN FURNACE,

Discovered beneath the Mercato Vecchio.

CALIDARIUM.

Ibid.

[To face page 96

The whole tenor of this document not only proves that the Pisan nobles were already an organised body, but that they also boasted a civic importance never attained by the nobles of Florence.[101] Evidently Pisa had no Consuls as yet, or they would have been certainly mentioned in the document. But all the elements destined to make it a far more aristocratic commune than that of Florence were already existent.[102] We see that there was a *commune consilium* of *sapientes* or *boni homines*, which was a species of senate, and a *commune colloquium*, a general assembly of all the citizens, afterwards developing into a parliament or *arrengo*. Five *sapientes*, whose names are given, sat in council with the bishop.[103] These were the immediate precursors or, as Pawinski rightly calls them, the *vorbilder* of the Consuls, who are actually mentioned shortly after this time, in 1094, in another agreement (*concordia*), also drawn up by Daiberto. He makes an explicit appeal to their authority (*huius civitatis consulibus*) in decreeing that all smiths engaged on work required for the Duomo should be left unmolested.[104] Thus the rise of the Pisan Commune was preceded by a conflict waged by belligerent nobles from their respective towers, and the Consuls of the town were first named as the protectors of the smiths.

The existence of guilds in Venice as far back as the ninth century is certified by the Altino Chronicle, proving that, even then, there were some leading industries exercised by certain families only, and that humbler trades, or *ministeria*, were already constituted, as it were, in associations, the members of which pursued their avocation according to traditional and definite rules. These craft-guilds or *ministeria* implied certain accompanying obligations, since all members of them were bound to yield some gratuitous service to the State. On the other hand, the higher trades, such as mosaic work, architecture, and so on, requiring more culture and talent, were exercised by the leading families, and members of these guilds remained eligible for the political offices of the State.[105] There is a document of the eleventh century showing that the guild of smiths was constituted under the rule of a *gastaldo* (or steward), against whom one of the members appealed for justice to the doge, according to a custom as yet unwritten.[106] All this compels us to believe that the existence of art and trade guilds, and in general of all the associations into which the citizens of the communes were afterwards divided, dates from a very remote period, and that in Florence, as elsewhere, all similar associations were constituted before the Commune had proclaimed its independence. Otherwise it would be impossible to explain the existence of a city that, almost without any visible government, was already prosperous in commerce and able to make war on its own account. For otherwise all the ensuing facts, although beyond the reach of doubt, would remain unexplained.

V.

Therefore, even in the days of Countess Matilda, we find the mass of the citizens divided and arranged in groups. We see on the one side the ancient *scholae* transformed into associations of arts and trades, containing the germ of future greater and lesser guilds; on the other, family associations and clans of the *grandi* or leading citizens, embryos of future societies of the towers. All these associations already formed the practical government of the city, in which the principal offices were filled by *grandi* of Matilda's choice. It is quite probable that the post of *preside* was reserved, in accordance with mediæval usage, to a single family or clan, perhaps to that of the Uberti, who were, as we shall see, among the most powerful in the city, and boasting a Germanic descent. Nevertheless, there was then no hostility, no separation between the great folk or *grandi* and the people, all being united by common bonds and interests. In fact, as we have said, there will be soon documentary evidence that some of the *grandi* engaged in commerce were chiefs of guilds, and already beginning to fight, side by side with the people, against the outlying nobility. It is true that they owned lands and herds, but these were then the main source of that Florentine trade and commerce in defence of which the first wars were undertaken. The castles surrounding the city barred all outlets for commerce; armed men were always swooping down from them to attack and maltreat all pack trains issuing from the city to convey its products and merchandise to neighbouring towns. With continual wars on her hands, the Countess Matilda could seldom afford any help, and consequently the Florentines, although fighting in her name, were practically left to their own resources. It was this alliance of all classes of citizens, united by identity of interests and singleness of purpose against a common foe, that then constituted the strength of that Florentine people whose loyalty, purity, and valour were so fervently praised by Dante and the chroniclers. This was the moment when virtue laid the foundations of the Commune's future freedom and wealth.

Villani is given to exaggerate, but there is a basis of truth in his words when he states in the year 1107 (iv. 25) that "the city being much risen and increased in population, men, and power, the Florentines determined to extend their outlying *contado*, and widen their authority, and that war should be waged against any castle refusing obedience." This year, in fact, they began military operations by attacking the fortress of Monte Orlando, near

Lastra a Signa, also described by the chroniclers as the castle of Gangalandi or Gualandi, a fief of the Counts Cadolingi,[107] then a very powerful family, and soon becoming bitterly hostile to Florence. During the same year they captured and demolished the stronghold of Prato, owned by the Counts Alberti, also very formidable enemies. But as on this occasion the Countess was present in the camp, their success is more easily explained.[108]

In 1110 we hear of another war. "Florentini iuxsta Pesa comites vicerunt," we read in the "Annales," i. which start with this event and date it the 26th of May. The *comites* here mentioned cannot be the Counts Guidi, then on friendly terms with Matilda and Florence, although, when fighting against both at a much later date, they were specially designated as "The Counts." In 1110 Florence attacked and conquered the Cadolingi, also known as the *Cattani Lombardi*, whose lands extended from Pistoia, by the Val di Nievole, towards Lucca, and by the Lower Val d'Arno to the vicinity of Florence. If the city could rout these nobles, it must have acquired great strength, even admitting the probability that on this occasion also it had the aid of Matilda's troops.

In 1113 there were two other military campaigns which, owing to the very different accounts narrated by the chroniclers, have given rise to an infinity of learned disputes. First of all came the assault and destruction of Monte Cascioli, assigned by some to the year 1113, by others to 1114, and postponed by a few to 1119, when it was supposed to have been defended by an Imperial German vicar named Rempoctus or Rabodo, who perished in the fight. Other chroniclers assign the overthrow of the castle to three different years, and Villani puts a climax to the confusion by jumbling together the various assaults described, assigning them all to 1113, and saying that the castle had revolted against Robert the German, vicar of the Empire, holding residence at San Miniato al Tedesco (iv. 29). But in 1113—that is, before the Countess's death—there was no Imperial vicar in Tuscany, and consequently none could be installed at San Miniato, to which the appellation "al Tedesco" was not yet applied. But the confusion can be cleared, the chroniclers made to agree, and the different narratives easily explained, if it is admitted that only the first attack upon Monte Cascioli took place in 1113, when the castle was held by the Cadolingi and could be vigorously defended.[109] As the walls on that occasion were only partially destroyed, it was necessary to renew the assault in 1114, when they were totally demolished. They were afterwards rebuilt by the Cadolingi, and therefore, in 1119, when Florence had achieved independence, two more attempts were made to capture the stronghold; the Imperial envoy was killed while assisting in its defence, and the building was finally demolished and burnt to the ground. But without anticipating events we may conclude that even before Matilda's death the Florentines had succeeded, by their expeditions against Monte Orlando, Prato, Val di Pesa, and Monte Cascioli, in opening the highways of Signa, Prato, and Val d'Elsa to their trade.

Another event, likewise occurring in the years 1113–15, although dated by the chroniclers in 1117, namely, the Pisan expedition to the Balearic Isles, also led to a somewhat complicated dispute. As already related, the Pisans began to make war on the Mussulmans from the middle of the tenth century, and during the latter half of the next century the strife was pursued more hotly than ever. In 1087 Pisa and Genoa combined, displayed a fleet of forty sail in battle array before Mehdia, and in 1113 both cities joined in the more important expedition to the Balearic Isles. They were also accompanied by many counts and marquises from Lombardy and Central Italy, likewise including a few from the Florentine territory. Then, combining with the Counts of Barcelona and Montpellier, the Viscount of Narbonne, and others, they attacked the Balearic Isles, and, in spite of a very obstinate resistance, seized the castle of Majorca, and captured young Burabe, the last scion of the ruling dynasty there. Villani, in alluding to this war of 1113–15, assigns it, like the other chroniclers, to the year 1117, adding that the Pisans fearing, when about to set sail, that the Lucchese might, as once before, take advantage of their absence to attack their city, entrusted the Florentines with its defence. The latter immediately encamped two miles from the walls and forbade their men to enter Pisa, under penalty of death; for, seeing that scarcely any males were left in the city, they feared some attempts might be made on the honour of its women, to the grave discredit of Florentine loyalty. And this decree was rigorously enforced. One soldier who dared to violate the rules of discipline was condemned to death, notwithstanding the prayers of the Pisans, who, as the only chance of saving the man's life, protested that they could not permit a capital sentence to be executed on their territory. Whereupon the Florentines, showing even in this matter their scrupulous regard for others' rights, purchased a scrap of land, and there put the culprit to death.

Meanwhile, the Pisans returning from Majorca, laden with spoil, offered in token of gratitude to their faithful friends the choice of accepting either two bronze doors or two porphyry columns. The Florentines preferred the latter. The columns were consigned to them wrapped in scarlet cloth, in token of their value, and now stand in the chief portal of San Giovanni. However, when the cloth was stripped off, it was seen that some envious person had injured the columns with fire. Evidently part of this account is legendary, and we also discern that something must have been added to it afterwards, when

Pisa and Florence were separated by long and inextinguishable animosity. 110

But the wrong date repeated in Villani and many other chroniclers, regarding a war that lasted several years, and was apparently only recommenced in 1117, does not justify us in denying a fact so constantly affirmed by many writers. [111] The Balearic expedition certainly took place, and there is equal certainty that it was led by the Pisans, with the help of various friends and allies. Their fear lest the city should be attacked by the Lucchese in their absence was justified by the fact that this had really happened in former times. The Pisans were now foes of Lucca and friends of Florence, whose loyalty during that early period was very generally recognised. Why should it be incredible that these friendly Pisans should have entrusted the city to their care, or that they should have proved worthy of the confidence reposed in them? Paolino Pieri not only repeats the story as told by all the other chroniclers, but also adds that the bit of ground upon which the guilty soldier was executed had been purchased with the help of Bello the Syndic, and that even in his own day he saw that it was still left uncultivated in memory of the deed: "it was on the fourth day of July, three hundred and two years more than one thousand, when I saw that ground untouched." At any rate, this is a proof that the tradition of the fact still survived in the fourteenth century, and that every one had the fullest belief in it.

VI.

The death of Countess Matilda, in 1115, was followed by a period of so much disorder as to mark the beginning of a new era for all Central Italy, and more especially for Florence. The countess, as we know, left a will bequeathing all her possessions to the Church; but this donation could only affect her allodial estates, since all those held in fief naturally reverted to the Empire. It was not always easy to precisely distinguish these from those; often, indeed, impossible: hence an endless succession of disputes. And such disputes became increasingly complicated by the pretensions of the Pope and the emperor, each of whom asserted his right to the whole inheritance, the one as Matilda's universal legatee, and the other as the supreme head of the margraviate. Then, too, as we have seen, many considered themselves to have been unjustly deprived of their estates, in favour of others with no rightful claim. All this led to a real politico-social crisis that brought the disorder to a climax. Thereupon the emperor, Henry IV., sent a representative, bearing the title of *Marchio, Iudex, Praeses*, to assume the government of Tuscany in his name. Of course, no one could legally contest his right to do this; but the

Papal opposition, the attitude of the cities now asserting their independence, and the general disorder split the margraviate into fragments. Accordingly the representatives of the Empire could only place themselves at the head of the feudal nobility of the various *contadi* and, by gathering them together, form a Germanic party opposed to the cities. In the documents of the period the members of this party are continually designated by the name of Teutons (*Teutonici*).[112]

Florence, surrounded by the castled nobility occupying her hills, could only decide on one of two courses. Either to yield to those who had always been her mortal enemies, and were now emboldened by Henry's favour, or to combat them openly, and thus declare enmity to the Empire, the which, in the present state of affairs, would amount to a proclamation of independence; and the latter was the course adopted. Florence was now conscious of her own strength, and recognised that safety could only be gained by force. The change was accomplished in a very simple and almost imperceptible way. The same worthies who had administered justice, governed the people, and commanded the garrison in Matilda's name, now that she was dead, and no one in her place, continued to rule in the name of the people, and asked its advice in all grave emergencies. Thus these *grandi* became Consuls of the Commune that may be said to have leapt into existence unperceived. This is why no chroniclers mention its birth, no documents record it, and a plain and self-evident fact is made to appear extremely complicated and obscure. In endeavouring to discover unknown events and lost documents which had never existed, the solution of a very easy problem was hedged round with difficulties, while evident and well-established particulars best fitted to explain it were entirely lost sight of.

Nevertheless, we are not to believe that the event was accomplished without any shock, for the change was of a very remarkable kind. It is true that the actual government remained almost intact; but its basis was altered, since it was now carried on in the name of the people, instead of that of the Countess. This, in itself, signified little, inasmuch as for some time past the city had been practically, if not legally, its own master, and the people beginning to feel and make felt its personality. But the social and political results of the change were neither few nor inconsiderable. Naturally, during Matilda's reign, the governing authorities were men of her choice; and although all official and judicial posts changed hands from time to time, they became increasingly monopolised by a small cluster of families, chief among whom, as we have already said, were most probably the Uberti and their clan. Now, however, that the authorities were to be elected by the people, there was a broader, although still somewhat limited, range of choice. Accordingly, there was more change of office, and men were removed in turn from one to another. This custom already prevailed in other communes, and had been adopted even in Florence both by popular associations and those of the *grandi*. Hence it necessarily prevailed in the formation of the new government.

Nor can we believe that those always to the front in former times could have now withdrawn without resistance, or without attempting to maintain their position by favour of the Empire and the *Teutonici*; nor is it credible that those now entitled to a larger share in the government should have refrained from relying, in their turn, on the strength of the popular favour, backed by the most vital interests of the city. Friction between the leading families seems inevitable to us in this state of things, and Florence must have witnessed some such conflict as at Pisa in Daiberto's day, and in almost all other Italian communes. We learn from Villani (v. 30), from the "Annales," and many other works, that there was a great fire in Florence in 1115, a similar one in 1117, and that "what was left unburned in the first fire was consumed in the second." It was certainly an exaggeration to say that the whole city was destroyed, but the fact of the fire is generally affirmed.[113] We also know that in those times, before gunpowder was invented, fire and arson were the most efficacious weapons in popular riots. Villani says, farther, that "fighting went on among the citizens ... sword in hand, in many parts of Florence." It is true, that, in his opinion, the fight was *for the faith*, seeing that the city being given over to heresy, licence, and the sect of the Epicureans, God therefore chastised it with pestilence and civil war. But, although we find no certain traces in history of any widely diffused heresy in Florence at the time, it is undoubted that from 1068 the earliest gleams of Florentine freedom were mixed and confused, as we have seen, with a religious movement, and it is also certain that the "Annales," i., of the year 1120 record the fact of one named Petrus Mingardole being condemned for heresy to the ordeal by fire,[114] and also add that, between 1138 and 1173, the city was thrice smitten by an interdict, all of which goes to prove a continued religious agitation. Besides, Florence, and particularly her people, remained constantly faithful to the Church party, while the Uberti and their adherents, who sided with the Empire, were opposed to it, and consequently, in those days, may have easily incurred the charge of heresy. Even in Villani's time the general name of *Paterini* was bestowed not only upon all heretics, but on Ghibellines as well.[115] Besides, as he had placed the origin of Florence before Charlemagne's day, and then again immediately after the imaginary destruction of Fiesole in 1010, he naturally refused to recognise that origin for the third time at the moment of the Commune's real birth. Accordingly, slurring over the political movement, that was undoubtedly the main factor in the change, he tried to exaggerate the religious movement that played a very minor part in it.

At any rate, since it appears certain that the Uberti asked the support of the Empire, they must have been now necessarily driven to prove themselves foes of the Church. Therefore, it cannot have been unusual for them to be styled heretics or *Paterini*, especially by so pronounced a Guelph as Villani. We know that the Uberti were already powerful in Matilda's time, from the frequent appearance of their name in contemporary documents. That they also enjoyed a lion's share of the government, and that the revolt was chiefly directed against them, is explicitly proved by the words of a chronicler—so far little read, we might almost say unknown—whose work being derived from different sources than that of Villani, shows some events in a new light. The pseudo Brunetto Latini, in fact, agrees with the other chroniclers in ascribing the first fire to the year 1115, saying that it began at the Santi Apostoli, and spread as far as the bishop's palace, "whereby the greater part of the city was burnt, and many folk perished in the flames." He says nothing concerning heresy, but touching the second fire of 1117, he adds: "In this year a fire broke out in Florence in the houses of the Uberti, who *ruled* the city, whereof little was saved from the burning, and many folk perished by fire and sword."[116] It is evident that there was a real outbreak, almost a revolution waged with fire and sword, against the Uberti, rulers of the city.

Can we be surprised at the hatred roused by the Uberti, or at the civil war of which they were the cause? As we know, they were traditionally supposed to have come with the Othos from Germany; and we have seen how the legend of the *Libro fiesolano*, while refusing credence to this, spoke of them as descended from "the most noble race of Catiline," the enemy of Florence. Even on historical evidence, were they not the forefathers of those Uberti, who afterwards, in 1177, proved the first to attack the Consular government and begin the civil warfare by which the city was so long torn asunder? Were they not the forefathers of the Schiatta Uberti, ringleaders of the band that stabbed Buondelmonti to death, by the statue of Mars on the Ponte Vecchio, in 1215? Were they not the ancestors of the celebrated Farinata, who routed the Guelphs at Montaperti, and attended that Council of Empoli where such fierce measures were proposed against Florence, the perpetual nest of the Guelphs—the same Farinata described by Dante among the heretics in the bog of hell?[117]

VII.

Meanwhile, which party conquered in the struggle following Matilda's death? Facts prove it clearly enough. In the year 1119 the Florentines made that final assault on the castle of Monte Cascioli, to which reference has been already made. This is the moment when the before-mentioned *Rempoctus*,[118] or Rabodo, really comes upon the scene, although Villani (iv. 29) and other chroniclers make him appear in 1113, under the name of Robert the German, Imperial vicar, and suppose him to have fallen in fight that year while defending the castle. We have shown that there could be no Imperial vicar in Tuscany at that date, seeing that none was sent until after Matilda's decease. In fact, no documents mention any vicar before then, and only on September 11, 1116, we find one recorded as "Rabodo ex largitione Imperatoris Marchio Tuscia,"[119] and then in 1119, "Rabodo Dei gratia si quid est,"[120] the identical formula that had been employed in Matilda's patents. In 1120 Rabodo's name disappears, and is replaced by that of the Margrave Corrado. It may therefore be taken for granted that Rabodo really perished in 1119 during the defence of Monte Cascioli against the Florentines, who now succeeded in finally demolishing the stronghold and burning it to the ground.[121] Thus their first achievement, after Matilda's decease, was the destruction of a Cadolingi castle, together with the defeat and death in battle of the first Imperial vicar then established in Tuscany. This is more than enough to show the nature of their attitude with regard to the Empire and the Teutonic party.

Shortly after, an event of even greater significance occurred in the capture and sack of Fiesole during 1125. Sanzanome, whose so-called modern history of Florence starts with this war, describes it at much length, in flights of wordy rhetoric. The gist of it is that the chief cause of the conflict was a commercial dispute. The people of Fiesole would seem to have maltreated and plundered a Florentine trader who was quietly passing through the city with his goods. This incident, added to the remembrance of past rancours and other recent depredations, seems to have stirred the Florentines to war. Instantly, "factum est Consilium per tunc dominantes Consules de processu." One of the leading citizens harangued the people, beginning his speech with these words: "Si de nobili Romanorum prosapia originem duximus ... decet nos patrum adherere vestigiis." Thereupon, "illico a Consulibus exivit edictum." A man of Fiesole, on the other hand, began his address by alluding to the legendary origin of his city: "Viri, frates, qui ab Ytalo sumpsistis originem, a quo tota Ytalia dicitur esse derivata." Although so much learned rhetoric in a writer of the early part of the thirteenth century is another proof of the strong influence of Roman tradition on ancient Florentines, both before and after the rise of their Commune, it cannot conceal the real cause of the war, as proved even by the evidence of Villani, whose chronicle begins to acquire greater historic value at this point. The latter relates that Fiesole had become a veritable nest of *Cattani* and brigands, who infested the Florentine highways and territories.[122] As usual, the feudal barons were swooping down from their strongholds to hinder the trade and traffic of the Commune.

At this moment also there were special causes tending to provoke a war of an unusually sanguinary kind. The counties, or *contadi*, of the two cities, as sometimes occurred elsewhere, had been carved out of the territories of bishoprics, based, in their turn, on ancient Roman partitions of the soil. Accordingly, these counties being not only adjacent, but wedged in and almost tangled one with the other, and their respective bishops having never wielded, as in Lombardy, the authority or power of counts they had ended by forming a single, combined jurisdiction. In fact, many documents refer to the county or jurisdiction of Fiesole and Florence, as though it were one and the same thing. Hence it was only natural that on becoming an independent Commune, after Matilda's death, Florence should seek to dominate over both counties, and equally natural that Fiesole should be violently opposed to the idea, and, notwithstanding the inferior size of the town, should have trusted to the superior strength of its fortified position, and, making alliance with the nobles of the *contado*, should have harboured them in the citadel, and joined them in continual attacks on Florentine traders or in raiding Florentine lands. This was the beginning of the war. Its details are unknown to us, those supplied by Sanzanome being too extravagant for belief,[123] and other chroniclers furnishing none at all. Seeing the strength of Fiesole's position, the campaign could have been neither short nor easy, and undoubtedly ended in cruel slaughter and the almost total destruction of the town. The chroniclers are not the only authorities for this fact. Shortly afterwards, the Abbot Atto of Vallombrosa implored a pardon from Pope Honorius II., *pro Florentinorum excessibus*, urging in their favour that there were many aged persons, women, and children, in Florence, who had assuredly taken no part in the *destruccio fesulana*, and also that many participants in the war now confessed the error of their ways, and sincerely repented all the excesses that "non meditata nequitia commisere."[124] The event was long remembered in Florence, is frequently recorded in documents,[125] and, together with the rout of the Imperial vicar at Monte Cascioli, undoubtedly contributed to establish the independence of the Commune on a firmer basis.

VIII.

It is certain that Florence now had a separate government under Consuls of her own, although there is no documentary proof to this effect earlier than 1138. Sanzanome, however, makes explicit allusion to it at the time of the Fiesole campaign, when, as we have seen, war was declared by the Consuls. But what was the real nature and origin of this new magistracy? Formerly it was opined by many writers that the Consuls were an institution derived in general from the judges of older days. In Lombardy they would have been merely another form of the Frankish *scabini*, and accordingly in Florence it was natural to suppose them to be an altered survival of those judges of the margravial tribunal to whom, for some time before her death, Matilda had accorded the right to give sentence. But this view can be no longer maintained, since it does not comprise the whole truth of the matter. For even when the Consuls are seen in the exercise of their functions, what are they, what do they do, according to chronicles and documents? They conduct wars, conclude treaties in the name of the people, of whom they are the representatives; they govern the city; they administer justice. And at Florence, as elsewhere, the latter is only one of their duties, and only undertaken by them because so closely connected with the exercise of the political power that is, above all, their genuine and principal function. Besides, what was it that really led to the birth of the Florentine Commune? What save the lack of the higher political authority hitherto ruling Tuscany, and the necessity of making war against old and new foes! Accordingly the military and political elements unavoidably prevailed.

We are further confirmed in this idea by examining the constitution of the Consular bench. At first it would seem that all or some of the Consuls presided without distinction, while later, three members were chosen in turn, and entitled *Consules super facto iustitiae*, or even *Consules de iustitia*, to preside for one month; at a still later date two Consuls presided for a term of two months, and finally, after the nature of the primitive government has been changed, we find a single Consul acting as president throughout a whole year.[126]

They might be, but were not necessarily, legal experts, since they only pronounced and confirmed the judgment decided upon without either preparing or formulating it. This duty fell to a real *iudex ordinarius pro Comune*, together with three proveditors or *provisores*, who examined the case and wrote the sentence. The Consuls merely sat as presidents of the tribunal, and when, as sometimes occurred, they failed to appear, the tribunal acted on its own account. Therefore their office was practically the same as that of Countess Matilda herself—*i.e.*, to represent sovereignty without filling the place of judges.[127]

The real nature of the new government will be best understood after investigating the different elements of the civic body from which that government was necessarily evolved. As we are aware, there were two leading classes and interests dividing the city between them—that is, the trade guilds, and the associations of worthies, or of the Towers. In numerical strength the people had greatly the advantage; but the worthies (*grandi*) were far more cultivated, trained to arms and politics, and already somewhat versed in the art of government. Therefore, the Consuls were recruited from this class, and at first always chosen from so small a number of families, that the office appeared to be almost an hereditary one. The misfortune of Florence, as indeed of all the other communes, Venice excepted, was that the *grandi* were never agreed among themselves. Feudal nobility in Italy resembled an exotic plant transferred to uncongenial soil. Elsewhere, being of German origin, it formed part of an entire political system; it was under the orders of the emperor to whom it adhered; it had certain heroic qualities; it created a special form of civilisation, and a literature that flourished in France and Germany, but it never throve in Italy, and in Tuscany least of all. Our feudal lords, being solely dominated by personal interests, leant on the Empire, the better to combat the Pope; on the Pope, to combat the Empire; on the one or the other indiscriminately to combat the cities. Even on Florentine territory the same thing continually occurred. The *grandi* established within the city walls were, it is true, of a very different temper, and much nearer to the people, whose life they shared; but they comprised very discordant elements; for whereas some of these *grandi* had risen from the people, others were descended from feudal houses, with whom they maintained friendly relations and on whose aid they could rely. Thirst for power was a speedy cause of division among them, and the ease with which one party gained favour with the working classes, while the other was backed by the nobles of the *contado*, fostered the growth of civil strife. Then, later on, as more nobles deserted their castles for the city, a regularly aristocratic and Ghibelline party was formed in opposition to the Guelph and popular side. This point, however, was still far removed, for the common necessity of making head against the baronage of the *contado* long prevailed over all other interests, since the very life of the Commune was involved in that struggle.

All that we have so far related serves to show with increasing clearness that two quite distinct classes of citizens already existed in Florence—namely, that of the people or trades (*arti*), and that of the worthies (*grandi*). Had the new government been evolved from the trades alone, it would have assumed a form constituted on the basis of a trade guild. Had it issued from the *grandi* alone, it would have given rise to a regional and local constitution, corresponding with the *sestieri* of the city over which their abodes were scattered. In all Italian communes this double tendency is to be found. In Rome the constitution by districts, or *rioni*, prevailed; while at Florence, after a time, the constitution by guilds obtained in consequence of the enormous prosperity of commerce and industry in that city. Meanwhile, however, the moral predominance of the *grandi* and the pressing exigencies of war favoured a division of the city in *sestieri*, whereby the first assembling and organising of the army was greatly facilitated. It was for this reason that the Consuls were elected by their respective *sestieri*.[128] That the *grandi* were already organised in "Societies of the Towers" there is written evidence to prove. A document of 1165 alludes to these societies as having been in existence for some time,[129] and the parchments of the Florence Archives comprise actual fragments of their statutes dated only a few years later on.[130] The "Tower" was possessed in common by the partners or associates, and no share in it could be bequeathed to any one outside the society, or to any member elected by less than all votes save one. Women were naturally excluded. The expense of maintaining and fortifying the Tower, which always communicated with the houses of neighbouring members, and served for their common defence, was divided among them all. Three or more rectors, also sometimes called Consuls, managed the society, settled disputes, and named their own successors. These rectors and their companions are the men we now find at the head of the government; and there is clear documentary evidence that the Consuls of the Commune were almost invariably chosen from families belonging to the Societies of the Towers. When, too, we observe that some of them were occasionally nominated Consuls of the guilds,[131] as Cavalcanti, for example, and several others, we gain an undoubted proof of the friendly terms preserved, as we have previously noted, between these nobles and the people. The societies were organised somewhat after the fashion of the guilds, by which they may have been originally inspired, and were not on a strictly feudal basis.[132]

Had the more aristocratic Uberti achieved sole predominance in the city, things would have assuredly taken a different turn; but these patricians were compelled, although reluctantly, to yield to the force of events frequently opposed to their views. In fact, they were seldom Consuls before the year 1177, when, after exciting a genuine revolution, they were more frequently named to that post. This confirms the fact of their previous defeat in 1115. The consular government had then fallen into the hands of several noble families on good terms with the people. And it was the popular voice that prevailed in the assemblies where all the chief questions and interests of the State were decided.

The Consuls[133] were elected at the beginning of the year, two for each *sestieri*. At least, this seems to have been the ordinary number, although we cannot be quite certain, since the number was not invariably the same. Two of the twelve, chosen in rotation, acted as heads of the college, and were styled *Consules priores*. For this reason the chroniclers only mentioned two Consuls as a rule, and sometimes one alone. In documents two, three, or even more are mentioned, but always as representing the rest of their colleagues, whose names are often added. Most rarely and only at exceptional moments do we find record of a higher number than twelve.[134] Then perhaps because the retiring Consuls continued in office with the new ones for a few days, or from some other passing cause that is unknown to us. Such variations are not surprising if it is kept in mind that the constitution of Florence, being then in course of formation, must have been liable to uncertainty and change, as will often be seen further on.

IX.

Attention should now be called to the popular element in the constitution. That the guilds were solidly established by the early part of the twelfth century is indubitably proved. Villani says that towards the year 1150 the Consuls of the Merchants, or rather of the "Calimala Guild," were entrusted by the Commune of Florence with the building works of "San Giovanni" (i. 60). Of still greater significance is the fact that on February 3, 1182, the men of Empoli, in making submission to Florence, were bound to make a yearly payment of fifty pounds of "good money" (*buoni denari*) to the Consuls or Rectors of the city, and, failing these officials, to the Consuls of the Merchants,[135] as representing the Commune. Now, if these Consuls had reached so high a degree of importance in 1182, we are entitled to believe that the guild was of no recent origin. And remembering that the guild in question was the Calimala—*i.e.*, that of finishers and dyers of woollen cloths manufactured abroad, and more especially in Flanders, imported by Florence, and thence despatched to foreign markets—we shall understand that Florentine commerce must have already attained a prodigious development, and consequently that many of the guilds must have been already long established. A solitary instance would naturally afford little proof, since it might be open to various interpretations; but others can be adduced to the same effect. In a treaty between Lucca and Florence of July 21, 1184, we find a stipulation according to which the terms might be modified by the Florentine Consuls *comuni populo electi*, and by twenty-five counsellors, provided, as was expressly declared, the Consuls of the merchants were comprised in the number.[136] Likewise, when the men of Trebbio made submission on July 14, 1193, the power of incorporating the agreement in the City Statutes was exclusively reserved to the seven *Rectores qui sunt super Capitibus Artium*.[137]

But a final observation occurs to us at this point, again showing the very uncertain and changeable nature of this consular government. In mentioning the chief authorities of the Commune, almost all documents refer to them as "*Consules seu rectores vel rector*," with the addition, at a later date, of "*Potestas sive dominator*."[138] All these terms had a very general meaning at the period. Nevertheless, there must have been some reason for employing the formula—Consuls or Rectors or *Potestà*—in treaties of peace, or alliance, or state documents of high importance; and probably a special reason, seeing that we often find the formula ending as follows: "*Consules qui pro tempore erint, et si non erint*," the Rectors or the *Potestà* or the Consuls of the guilds were to act in their stead. Why so much vagueness in indicating the chief magistrate of the Republic? Only one explanation is possible. The real practical government of the city was carried on by the various associations; the office of Consul had few attributes and never attained the power and importance due to a central government, as conceived in the modern sense. The same remark may be also applied to the Priors, the Ancients, and other officers of later date; but it is specially true as applied to the consuls, under whom the various civic societies were first united in a single government. Therefore, to meet the eventuality of no Consuls being in office at the moment, it was provided that the Rectors of the Towers or of the guilds should naturally assume the power directly emanating from them. But as no public acts performed in the name of the Rectors are extant, we may conclude that the contingency arranged for seldom arose.

Frequent mention occurs of *counsellors* (*consilarii*), and we note that representatives of the guilds were comprised among them. We know, in fact, that there was a council in Florence, as in other Italian communes, and Villani tells us (iv. 7, and v. 32) that this council was called a senate "according to the custom given by the Romans to the Florentines," and composed of one hundred worthies (*Buoni Uomini*). In documents, however, they are nearly always entitled *consiliarii*, the term "senator"[139] only occurring once; but in those days the term *senato* or *consiglio*, *senatori* or *consiglieri*, were often indiscriminately applied, particularly with regard to the limited or *Special* Council, as it was afterwards called. No documents supply us with the precise number of the councillors; but we believe the one hundred recorded by Villani must be somewhat under the exact figure, since a form of oath sworn by 133 councillors is extant.[140] Perhaps each *sestiere* elected about twenty or twenty-five members, without this being the invariable rule, and thus the Council might be approximately designated as that of the "Hundred." Then, too, there was the parliament, also known as the *Arengo*,[141] which was a general assembly of the people, held on great occasions for the gravest affairs of the State.

X.

Thus the Florentine Commune resembled a confederation of Trade Guilds and Societies of the Towers. Its directing authorities for affairs of war, finance, justice, and other matters of the highest importance, were the Consuls, elected yearly, with a senate or council of about a hundred worthies, likewise elected yearly, and lastly a parliament. The Consuls were almost invariably chosen from members of the Companies of the Towers, and if, for any reason, no election of Consuls took place, the rectors of the Towers or of the guilds were provisionally empowered to act in their stead. But the guilds predominated in the Council, and as a natural consequence the government assumed a popular character from that time, and the whole policy of Florence always tended to promote the trade and commerce of the city.

Nevertheless, to obtain a still clearer idea of a government of this kind, it would be requisite to ascertain exactly who and what were the citizens entitled to a share in it, and this point is still somewhat doubtful. The outlying territory (*contado*) was entirely excluded from citizenship, nor was this privilege granted to all dwellers within the walls, the lower class of artisans and the populace being excluded from it.[142] Hence the government was concentrated in the hands of a few powerful families, the heads of the guilds, and their principal adherents. In fact, even down to the last days of the Republic real citizenship—the possessors of which alone were eligible to political posts— was a privilege conceded to few, and even in 1494 the number of citizens scarcely exceeded three thousand. For this reason, even at the present day, we may find a few humble families asserting their inheritance of old Florentine civic rights, as a rare privilege and almost as a title of nobility. At Venice, even in the eighteenth century, to the last days of the Republic there still existed different grades of citizenship, and the right of government was restricted to a small caste. This is one of the points in our history demanding closer investigation. It is true that the whole people met indistinctly in parliament; but such assemblies were mostly of a purely formal kind. For, seeing that the parliament was convoked either in some square, often of small extent, or inside a church, we are bound to infer that the privilege accorded to all the inhabitants of the city was nominal rather than real.

It were likewise superfluous to add that the exact division of power, as in modern constitutions, was entirely ignored in those days. Affairs were divided according to their importance and the quality of the individuals concerned in them, rather than according to their nature. The Council of the Hundred was not, as might be supposed, at this day, a legislative assembly, nor was the executive power vested in the Consuls. The latter gave judgment, administered affairs, commanded armies, executed the will of the people, and occasionally completed legislative acts even without the aid of the Council. This, however, was always consulted regarding very important reforms, but often voted for or against them without any discussion. On questions of extraordinary moment the parliament gave its *placet* without always understanding the nature of the question. On the other hand, not only affairs of some gravity, and particularly those for which money was needed, were referred to the Council; but this could also be consulted, at the Consul's pleasure, on any question whatever, from the proposed execution of some political offender to granting some citizen permission to transfer his abode from one *sestiere* to another.[143] Although a question of the latter kind seems very insignificant to us nowadays, it was an important one then, since it altered the distribution of the inhabitants in different parts of the city, and consequently the relative strength of these parts and the proportional right of the citizens to fill public offices—a point that was very jealously watched.

BELFRY OF S. ANDREA, MERCATO VECCHIO, FLORENCE.

[To face page 130

Such was the first form of government adopted by the Florentine Commune. But the Commune was not yet consolidated nor sufficiently sure of its strength. The territory beneath its sway was very limited in extent, with ill-defined, disputable and disputed frontiers. Even within these borders the Commune had very little power, inasmuch as the castled nobility not only vaunted their independence of the city, refusing to acknowledge any authority save that of the Empire, to which they were not always submissive, but waged constant war on the Commune, and perpetually incited neighbouring lands to rebellion. Accordingly, the first thing to be done at this juncture was to seize the *contado* by force of arms, reduce it to subjection and govern it, the which, as we shall see, led to many new and serious complications, both within and without the walls. These vicissitudes constitute the real civil history of Florence, which finally starts from this moment.

CHAPTER III.

THE FIRST WARS AND FIRST REFORMS OF THE FLORENTINE COMMUNE.[144]

I.

AFTER Countess Matilda's death the envoys despatched from Germany to reassume the margraviate of Tuscany in the name of the Empire followed one another in rapid succession.[145] But almost all were men of small ability, pursuing a vacillating policy that led to no results. They tried to exercise the power of margraves, but were merely temporary officials of the emperor. Without resources, without knowledge of the country, they relied now on this party, now on that, incapable of distinguishing friends from foes, and never understanding the causes of the wars continually breaking out on every side. This state of things, well adapted to promote communal independence, lasted to 1162, when Frederic Barbarossa began to make the weight of his hand felt by initiating a clearer and more determined policy, although even his talent failed to obtain any notable results.

The Florentines were those best able to profit by the weakness of the Empire. In 1129 they took possession of the Castle of Vignalo in the Val d'Elsa;[146] and in 1135 destroyed the stronghold of Monteboni, belonging to the Buondelmonti, whose name was derived from it, and who were now forced to submit to the Commune, yield it military service, and dwell in the city a certain part of the year.[147] On this head Villani remarks that the Commune now began to extend its borders "by violence rather than by reason, ... subjecting every noble of the *contado*, and demolishing fortresses." This was, in fact, the policy of Florence, and it led to two inevitable results. An increase of territory was the first; the second, that the always-increasing number of nobles brought into the city paved the way for the formation of an aristocratic party opposed to the people, and consequently promoting civil strife and future changes of government.

In June, 1135, the Imperial envoy Engelbert entered Florence, and seemed amicable to the Commune.[148] He speedily moved on to Lucca, where he met with a serious defeat. The succeeding envoy, Errico of Bavaria, came with a considerable force, and appeared ill-disposed towards the Florentines. His stay, however, was short, and his successor, Ulrico d'Attems, showed friendly intentions, and in 1141 even aided the Florentines in a skirmishing expedition against Sienna.[149] But all these envoys came and disappeared like meteors. Florence was now beginning its great war with Count Guido, surnamed the Old, who had become their foe. A contested inheritance served as a pretext for the rupture; but the real cause must have lain in the increased power and menacing attitude of the count. His possessions hemmed in the Republic on all sides, and Sanzanome said of him, "Per se quasi civitas est et provincia."[150] The citizens first seized a castle of his near Ponte a Sieve, and then attacked his stronghold of Monte di Croce. But, aided by neighbouring towns, the count succeeded in defeating the Florentines on June 24, 1146. Nevertheless, they contrived even then to extort advantageous terms, namely: that part of the walls should be dismantled, and that the castle should hoist the banner of Florence.[151] All this was done, and there was truce for a time, while the count seems to have been engaged on distant expeditions. But later, the walls were restored, and thereupon the Florentines,[152] declaring that the agreement had been violated, suddenly stormed the castle in 1153, and rased it to the ground. And thus, wrote Sanzanome, "*Mons Crucis est cruciatus.*" Certainly all this could not lead to peace. Count Guido ceded part of Poggibonsi to the Siennese on condition of their fortifying and defending it against the Florentines, who were preparing to make an assault. By accepting the gift Sienna stood pledged to play an active part in the war, which thus continued to spread.[153]

II.

Just at this time, however, the state of affairs changed, for Tuscany was beginning to feel the influence of Frederic I. (Barbarossa). This emperor, finding that Duke Guelfo was unable to make himself respected, despatched (1162–3) the Archbishop Reinhold of Cologne, a man of energy and brains, with the title of "Italiae archicancellarius et imperatoriae maiestatis legatus," and charged to reorganise the Imperial administration on a new plan. Frederic regarded the dissolution of the margraviate as an accomplished fact, and wished to assume the direct government of its various component parts by means of German counts or Podestà, in the manner already adopted by him in Lombardy. Reinhold set to the task with zeal, establishing German governors and garrisons in the principal castles of the *contado*; and where no castles remained new ones were erected.[154] San Miniato, with its tower on the hill, dominating the suburb of San Genesio below, was the headquarters of this new administration. Here Reinhold established Eberhard von Amern with the title of *"Comes et Federici imperatoris legatus."*[155] Frederic's scheme of policy was clear and precise; but in order to carry it into effect against the will of communes that were already emancipated, and against the interests of many native counts, would have required much time and a great army, both of which were lacking at the moment. Reinhold was soon called elsewhere for other undertakings, and although his successor, the Archbishop Christian of Mayence, was likewise a man of ability, their efforts led to few practical results. Their only success consisted in the amount of money squeezed from the people; for, as a chronicler puts it, "like good fishermen, they drew everything cleverly into their nets." But they established no firm political basis.

It is true that the new German Podestà, or *Teutonici*, as they were called, were seen springing up on all sides. We now find, in fact, continual mention of the *Potestas Florentiae and Florentinorum*, and of the same dignitaries in Sienna, Arezzo, and many other towns. Nevertheless, they exercised little or no power in great cities: these being still governed by Consuls, who disputed the authority of the *Teutonici* of the *contado* outside the walls. This state of things could not be of long continuance. By special permission from the emperor, the Consuls of certain well-affected cities were allowed to exercise jurisdiction, in his name, not only within the walls, but even sometimes over part of the *contado*; always, however, with a reservation in favour of nobles, and often of churches and convents, who were to remain subject to the Imperial authority alone.[156] Everywhere else in Central Italy the Imperial Podestà were to take the entire command, for the emperor admitted no doubt as to the complete and absolute nature of his rights. But the question now hinged on facts rather than on rights, and was only to be solved by a greater force than that possessed by the Empire in Tuscany. Hence, an enormous confusion ensued. All the great cities, and more especially Florence, continued to rule themselves as before; while in the rural territories (*contadi*), Imperial Podestà, Tuscan counts, feudal lords, Consuls great and small, or other officers of the Commune, daily contested one another's authority, and the masses no longer knew whom to obey. Even the cities and nobles siding with the Empire not only failed to carry out Frederic's designs, but actually opposed them; for, in point of fact, this Teutonic over-lordship, wielded by grasping and tyrannous Imperial officials, was equally odious to all.

A sufficiently accurate idea of this state of things may be gleaned from the accounts of contemporary witnesses, who were summoned at various times to furnish authentic details as to the condition of the country. Those sent to report upon the monastery of Rosano describe it as being subject to Count Guido, who was continually driven to defend it "against the warden of Montegrossoli, other Teutons, and the Florentine Consuls," all of whom tried to exercise authority there. They also describe how at Monte di Croce, the Consuls of that place and the *vice comites* all held command simultaneously, and were compelled to defend themselves from the *Teutonici*, and against the encroachments of the Consuls and other officers of the Florentine Commune.[157]

On another occasion an equally chaotic state of things is described in the reports on the castle and valley of Paterno, of which Florentines and Siennese disputed the dominion. One witness tells us that in his day he saw a certain Pipino, *Potestas Florentiae*, holding sway there, and over all the rest of the Florentine *contado*. Another records how he visited the Paterno valley and the whole of the *contado*, together with the consuls of the Commune and a *Teutonico*. Several declare to have gone there now with Pipino, now with other *Teutonici*, and at other times with the Consuls, and that all received obedience and levied taxes in the same way. Then we have the curious deposition of one Giovanni *de Citinaia*, who gives a long account of recent events in the district. He tells us how a big pillar was uprooted by a priest, who, not knowing for what purpose it had been planted, wanted to use it for the church he was building. But it was so heavy that even with a cart and two oxen he failed to remove it. And some peasants who were looking on, cried out to him: "Domini sacerdos, male fecisti, quia est terminus inter Florentinos et Senenses" ("Master priest, thou hast done ill, for this is the boundary stone between Florence and Sienna"). After this, the witness continues, two persons went to the warden of Montegrossoli, and said that if he would help them to rebuild the Castle of Paterno, they would furnish him with proofs of his right over it. The warden cheerfully hastened to Florence to get the permission of the authorities, but quickly returned, saying that the building could not go on, for the Florentines refused consent, because the Archbishop Christian of Mayence was already in Lombardy on the way to Tuscany. Thereupon the Siennese made use of the favourable opportunity to demolish the neglected works, and play the masters themselves. It is certainly impossible to conceive a greater multiplicity and confusion of contrasting rights and authorities.[158]

Hence the only course open to Florence and the Tuscan communes in general was to seize every convenient occasion of asserting their rights either by craft or by violence. The war between Pisa and Lucca had already broken out, and as Count Guido, the foe of the Florentines, had joined with Lucca, they formed an alliance with Pisa. This treaty was very advantageous to their commerce, but it pledged them to an active share in the war.[159] They willingly undertook this, for it was an opportunity of fighting not only the Lucchese, but also the latter's patrons, Count Guido and Christian of Mayence. At first it seemed as though Pisa would be forced to make peace, for on March 23, 1173, Christian declared that city to be under ban of the Empire, thus stripping it of all the privileges it had previously enjoyed. In fact, on the 23rd of May an agreement was concluded (witnessed also by the Florentines) to the effect that Pisa and Lucca should proceed to an exchange of prisoners. The ban was raised on the 28th of the same month, and peace was solemnly proclaimed in Pisa on the 1st of June.

But two months afterwards an unexpected event caused the war to be speedily renewed. The archbishop had invited the Consuls of Pisa and Florence to come to San Genesio on the 4th of August, and on their arrival had them promptly seized and cast into prison. What could have caused an act rendering war unavoidable, after such strenuous efforts to establish peace? Many explanations have been suggested, but one fact alone is well ascertained. Certain men of San Miniato, having been expelled as rebels to the Empire, had sought the Bishop of Florence[160] in his palace, and sworn not only to make common cause with the Pisans and Florentines, but to cede them the territory of San Miniato, should they succeed in retaking it, and even if the fortress remained in the hands of the Germans.[161] This is certainly true, for the document containing the agreement is still extant. It is no regular treaty, being unwitnessed by Consuls, and lacking the proper legal formulas. But the fact of its having been sworn to and signed in the bishop's palace; of some leading citizens, including one of the Uberti,[162] having been parties to it; and of the document being preserved in the Archives,[163] proves that the rulers of the two cities were not unaware of the agreement, but merely preferred to hide, or rather disguise the real importance of it. All this, joined to their reluctance and delay as to the exchange of prisoners, persuaded Christian that they were trying to trick and betray him by a fictitious peace. Accordingly, his patience being exhausted, he was led to commit an imprudent and ill- considered action, that destroyed all hope of the peace he was so anxious to conclude.

In fact, by August the Florentines were already at Castel Fiorentino, and, reinforced by a contingent of 225 horse, accompanied by two Consuls from Pisa, encamped at Pontedera. Christian quickly marched against them, together with Guido and the Lucchese, but the latter were obliged to forsake him, for the Pisans, by advice of the Florentines, had entered the Lucca territory and were laying it waste. Notwithstanding his diminished force he attacked the enemy, and valiantly defended his banner, but was worsted in the fight. How the war went on is unknown to us; but it is certain that Christian soon took his departure, that in 1174 the rebels of San Miniato returned with honour to their native town, and that finally in the following year peace was concluded between the three hostile cities.[164]

Meanwhile the Florentines continued to subject the towns and castles of the territory to their rule.[165] Before this, in 1170, they had wrung hard conditions from the Aretines,[166] who were friendly to Count Guido, and they now marched against Asciano, a walled town near Arezzo, partly under their rule and partly under that of the Siennese, who were now trying to get full possession of it. The latter were routed on July 7, 1174, and leaving a thousand prisoners in the enemy's hands were accordingly obliged to submit to very disadvantageous terms.[167] The negotiations were carried on slowly, but peace was concluded at last in 1176.

The Florentines were acknowledged as the legitimate masters of the whole *contado* of Fiesole and Florence, and obtained part of the Siennese possessions at Poggibonsi, the said Siennese being bound to help them in all wars,[168] save against the emperor or his envoys, and likewise pledged to use every endeavour to conciliate the latter in favour of Florence. Several more of the conditions were particularly harsh.[169] That the Florentines could extort such terms as these after the petty war of Asciano is an undeniable proof of their increased power; but it is equally certain that unless the Siennese were hopelessly ruined, this was only a fictitious peace, concluded after great hesitation, and for the sole purpose of securing the release of the prisoners.

III.

Nevertheless, these triumphs abroad were counteracted by unforeseen events in Florence itself. Owing to the prevalence of the popular party in the consular government, powerful houses in general, and the Uberti faction in particular, were increasingly excluded from public affairs, and naturally showed signs of discontent. At this moment we seldom find any of their names at the head of the Commune.[170] Meanwhile, however, many neighbouring castles and lands having been reduced to submission, the number of nobles of the *contado* dwelling in the city had been greatly augmented. These, being merely counted as *assidui habitatores* or *cives salvatichi*, could have no share in the government, but there was nothing to prevent them from joining the disaffected party and swelling its numbers and strength. And when, in course of time, they became full citizens, their power of action was enlarged. Accordingly, at last, in 1177, the Uberti were encouraged to hazard the revolution that first initiated civil war in Florence.

All the chroniclers speak of this war, and it must have been of considerable importance, seeing that it was pursued for nearly two years with much bloodshed and the destruction by fire of the greater part of the city. Likewise, the river Arno overflowed and broke down the Ponte Vecchio. Villani describes the two fires of 1177, saying that the first extended from the bridge to the Old Market; the second, from San Martino del Vescovo to Santa Maria Ughi and the Cathedral. He also relates the fall of the bridge, adding, as usual, that all this was a righteous chastisement from Heaven on the proud, ungrateful, sinful city. He speaks of the revolution that occurred at the same time as though it had nothing to do with the burning of the town. He goes on to say that the Uberti, who were the "principal and most powerful citizens of Florence, with their followers, both noble and plebeian, began to make war against the Consuls, lords and rulers of the Commune, at a fixed moment and on a fixed plan, from hatred of the Signory, which was not to their liking. And the war was so fierce, that in many parts neighbours fought against neighbours from fortified towers, the which were 100 to 120 *braccia* in height (150 to 180 feet). Likewise certain new towers were erected by the street companies with monies obtained from neighbours, and these were called the Towers of the Companies.

For two years the fighting went on in this fashion, and with much slaughter; and the citizens became so inured to perpetual strife, that they would fight one day and eat and drink together the next, recounting one to another their various deeds and prowess. At last, tired out, they made peace, and the Consuls remained in power; but these things created and gave birth to the accursed factions which soon broke out in Florence."[171]

On the other hand, the pseudo Brunetto Latini dates the first fire extending from the bridge to the Old Market, on August 4, 1177. But he quickly adds that in the same year began the "discord and war, for the space of twenty-seven months, between the Consuls and the Uberti, who refused to obey either the Consuls or the Signory, yet nevertheless formed no government of their own. This strife among the citizens caused great mortality, robbery, and arson. The city was set on fire at five different points; the Sesto d'Oltràrno, and the part between the Churches of San Martino, del Vescovo, and Sta. Maria, were burnt down."[172] According to the same

105

chronicler, the fall of the bridge took place on November 4, 1178, and the civil war only came to an end in 1180, with the triumph of the Uberti, one of whom, Uberto degli Uberti, actually became Consul. "The which afterwards led to the creation of Podestà, who were nobles, powerful, and of foreign birth."[173]

In spite of a few seeming contradictions on the part of both chroniclers, their evidence, joined to that of others, clearly proves that in 1177 a revolution led by the Uberti took place and lasted about two years, accompanied by rapine, murder, and arson. The Uberti did not gain a complete victory, since the consular government survived; but they and their friends were in power more frequently than before, and for this reason the pseudo Brunetto Latini considers them to have conquered. All this gave the government a more patrician tendency. It heralded the change that replaced the Consuls by a Podestà, and cast the first seed of the factions and civil wars destined to involve the city in long-continued strife and bloodshed. Such, in fact, is the gist of the chronicles, and all later documents and events serve to confirm it. Nevertheless, peace was re-established within the walls for the nonce, and the policy of Florence remained unaltered. The partial triumph of the aristocracy had at least one good effect; inasmuch as the nobles, being satisfied for the moment, lent efficacious assistance to the Commune, and enabled all its affairs to be pushed forward more briskly.

In fact, on February 3, 1182, the people of Empoli were reduced to submission, bound over to pay annual tribute and to yield military service at the request of the Florentine Consuls, whether of the Commune or the Guilds, save in the event of a war against the Counts Guidi.[174] The people of Pogna, which was a fief of the Alberti,[175] were the next to make surrender on the 4th of March. And these Pognesi not only pledged themselves to take the field at the command of the Florentine Consuls, but to abstain from constructing new walls or fortresses, either on their own territory or the neighbouring lands of Semifonte. Also, should others attempt to fortify those places, they (the Pognesi) were bound to oppose it and give notice of the fact to the Florentines, who, on their side, promised friendship and protection.[176] In the same year the Castle of Montegrossoli was captured by the Florentines.[177] On July 21, 1184, they made an alliance with the people of Lucca, who promised to send them yearly a contingent of one hundred and fifty horse and five hundred foot, for at least twenty days' service, in all wars waged within Florentine territory.[178]

In October the Florentines attacked the Castle of Mangona in the Mugello, but as this fortress belonged to the Alberti, the latter stirred Pogna to rebellion, and the Florentines quickly marched against that town.[179] Count Alberti seems to have taken part in the fight that ensued at Pogna, for it is known that by November he was in captivity and forced to accept very hard terms for himself, his wife and his children. He had to promise to dismantle his fortress of Pogna the following April, only retaining his own palace and tower; to demolish the tower of Certaldo, and never rebuild that of Semifonte. He was to cede to the Florentines whichever one of the Capraia towers they chose to take; he was to give them one-half of the ransom or tax to be levied on all his possessions in general between the Arno and the Elsa. Finally, as soon as he should be released from prison (*"postquam exiero de prescione"*), he was pledged to compel all his men to swear fealty, and to the payment of four hundred pounds of good Pisan money. His sons were to reside in Florence two months of the year in time of war, one month in time of peace.[180] The subjection and humiliation of this Count Alberto was a very significant fact in itself. And when we reflect that it occurred after Florence had already overthrown the Cadolingi, lowered the power of the Guidi house, and concluded most favourable alliances with Pisa, Sienna, and Lucca, it will be easily seen how quickly the Commune had been able to soar to a position of very great and almost menacing strength.

IV.

All this certainly contributed no little to hasten the coming of the Emperor Frederic I., and, in fact, we find him in Tuscany for the deliberate purpose of reducing the country to subjection in the year 1185. But he came without an army, reliant on the might of the Empire, on his own shrewdness, and his own reputation. He believed in the possibility of achieving his plans by alienating some of the Tuscan cities from Florence, and compelling them to side with the Empire against her. Above all, he counted upon Pistoia, situated between Lucca and Florence, and hostile to both; upon Pisa, whom he hoped, by means of large concessions, to win back to the Imperial cause, to which she had so often adhered before. He became still more hopeful of success when, on reaching San Miniato, in the summer of 1185, many nobles of the *contado* came to do him homage, with loud complaints of the oppressive rule of the free cities. On the 25th of July he emancipated many of these nobles, and some of their fiefs, from the jurisdiction of Lucca.[181] On the 31st of the same month he entered Florence, still surrounded by nobles of the *contado*, who, as Villani says, complained bitterly of the city, "which had seized their castles, and thus grossly insulted the Empire."[182] Hereupon, the chroniclers affirm that Frederic deprived Florence of the right of jurisdiction over her own territory, even just outside the city walls; and even assert that he adopted the same measure with regard to all the Tuscan towns, excepting Pisa and Pistoia.[183] But this point has been seriously disputed, many refusing to admit the possibility of a fact unsupported by any documentary proof. On the other hand, some writers consider it to be proved by a later event, the which is not only related by several chroniclers, but also confirmed by existing documents.

In fact, by a patent dated June 24, 1187, Henry VI., in reward, as he expressed it, for services rendered by the Florentines to his father and himself, granted them judicial rights over the city and the *contado* beyond, to the distance of one mile in the direction of Fiesole, of three towards Settimo and Campi, and of ten in all other directions.[184] Even within these narrow limits, however, the nobles and soldiery were to be independent of the city. In token of gratitude for this liberality on the part of the emperor, the Florentines were bound to present him every year with a piece of good samite, *bonum examitum*.[185] Similar and equally limited concessions were granted to other cities also.[186] Accordingly, some have said, since Henry restored right of jurisdiction to the Florentines, it is clear that his father had deprived them of it. In fact, we know that throughout Tuscany Frederic established Imperial Podestà, who bore the names of their respective cities.[187] Also, reasoning in this style, those writers went so far as to suppose Florence to have been deprived of judicial powers even within the city walls. But, as we have seen, Henry's patent does not speak of restitution—only of the liberality shown in rewarding the services of the Florentines, although it is impossible to understand what those services could have been.[188] On the other hand, it is hard to believe that Florence, who had dared, in weaker times, to use violent measures against the Imperial envoys, murdering Rabodo and putting Christian of Mayence to flight, should now, when so much stronger, and the chief power in Tuscany, unresistingly submit to deprivation of judicial rights throughout her own territory, and even within the city walls. In addition to all this, there seems no doubt that there were Consuls of Florence during the same period, and therefore the theory of there being Imperial Podestà in the city itself naturally falls to the ground. In fact, the Consuls' names are recorded in documents of 1184. It is true that, for the three following years, the pseudo Brunetto Latini is the only authority by whom they are mentioned; but it is difficult to suppose that he invented them all, or that he could have been mistaken three consecutive times. Although during these three years no documents give the names of the Consuls, they afford, indirectly, continual hints of their existence.[189]

Hence it is necessary, in my opinion, to begin by recognising that, according to the ideas and the policy of Frederic I., there was no question as to his right of exercising jurisdiction over Tuscany; and that if the cities had virtually exercised this right without a special grant to that effect, they had violated thereby the rights of the emperor, who was accordingly justified in resuming them. For this end, he had commissioned Reinhold and Christian to establish Podestà everywhere,[190] and to restore affairs to what he deemed their sole legal and normal condition. Only the difficulty here was not in proving his right, according to the Imperial theory, but in being able to enforce it. It was a question of fact, only to be resolved by force. As we have seen, Imperial Podestà were established on all sides; and while even in the *contado* they could only obtain partial and somewhat contested obedience, in the greater cities, and particularly in Florence, they obtained none at all. The *Potestates Florentiae*, or *Florentinorum*, as of Sienna or the Siennese, whose names so often occur, are almost invariably—and in the case of Florence, one may say quite invariably—Imperial Podestà, established in the *contado*, and disputing its jurisdiction with the Consuls. Now, seeing that the commune considered the *contado* to be its own territory, and therefore craved the sole command of it, while from the Imperial point of view city and *contado* were equally subject to the Podestà of the Empire, it naturally followed that these dignitaries were commonly styled Podestà of Florence or of the Florentines; and in the same way, Podestà of Sienna or of the Siennese, of Arezzo or the Aretini, &c. But, as a matter of fact, they not only failed to command obedience within the gates of great cities, but even in the *contado* outside were continually in conflict with the consular authority. We have already seen what a chaos was the result. Nevertheless, it seems natural to believe that the arrival of Frederic I. in Tuscany must have strengthened immensely the power of these Podestà, and that, at least for a time, they must have been enabled to enforce their judicial rights throughout the country, and to the very gates of the town. This made the chroniclers assert that the emperor had stripped Florence of its *contado*. It is certain, however, that on his departure things rapidly lapsed into their previous condition. That is to say, the consuls did their utmost to neutralise the action and authority of the Imperial officials. The rise of the communes had created a new state of things which the Empire was powerless to destroy, even while refusing to acknowledge its legal value. Therefore Henry was finally driven to accord a partial valuation, in the guise of a generous concession, to an actuality that by this means he might at least hope to keep within definite limits.

And in reality his patent of 1187 granted Florence much less than she had possessed for some time before. If, in fact, the territory of the Commune was not to extend more than one mile in the direction of Fiesole, this latter city remained outside the border, although already subjected to Florence by force of arms, together with the whole of its *contado*, which, indeed, as proved by every treaty, had been incorporated in the Florentine territory since 1125. Also, as though this were not enough, Henry declared all nobles within the circumscribed area left to the city, to be exempted from its jurisdiction, even including those who had legally and officially made submission to it. Notwithstanding all this, Florence found it best to accept the Imperial grant. Thus things remained practically as before—that is to say, the Commune could continue to hold the virtual command, and snatch as much more as should be possible. The chronicler Paolino Pieri, in recording this concession, states that the Florentines regained the *contado*—"that is, they took it back," and by this phrase he unconsciously defines the real condition of things. Meanwhile, the Empire yielded the point legally by recognising the judicial rights of the Consuls within the city and over part of the *contado* outside. As to the rest, it was left to be decided, as in the past, by force of arms. All this serves, in our opinion, to make things clear, and likewise to explain the inexactitude and confusion of the chroniclers, who, unable to distinguish between the practical and legal side of the question, continually jumbled both together. Undoubtedly it was hard to disentangle them, seeing that the fact was confronted by two, or rather three, separate rights, each refusing to acknowledge the others—namely, the right of the Empire, that of the Commune, and, lastly, that of the Pope, whose voice was always heard repeating—although always in vain—that the Church was Matilda's sole heir.

V.

Nevertheless, the presence in the *contado* of German Podestà or counts exercised some influence, even if indirectly, on the city itself. Or rather, their presence contributed to modify its constitution by promoting in a certain way the creation of a new civic magistracy, bearing their own title. In fact, the Latin term of *potestas*, *potestà*, or *podestà* was given to every chief authority during the Middle Ages; even in 1068 it was the title attributed to Duke Goffredo of Tuscany. Later, it was bestowed on the German counts governing the *contado* in the name of Frederic I. From them it was afterwards transferred to municipal magistrates. It seems to have been given first to officials despatched by the Commune to the *contado*, when this was already occupied by German counts, in order to imitate and oppose them. At least, there is reason to believe that certain officials with Italian names, and bearing the title of Podestà of Florence—or of Florentine Podestà—before any such post had been created in the city, must have been of this class. Two of these officials, Renuccio da Stagia and Guerrieri, are known to us and mentioned more than once in the Rosano reports.[191] It seems probable enough that Renuccio may have been appointed before the year 1180[192]—that is, when there were assuredly Consuls in Florence.[193] Hence it is to be concluded that he held office in the *contado*. But whether or no this theory be admissible, it should be noted that all Florentine documents of the time, when mentioning the Consuls, always add the words: "sive Rector vel Potestas, vel Dominator." At first it is merely a generic formula, vaguely suggesting the possibility of another magistrature. But little by little the formula assumes a more concrete character; the term *Potestas* becoming of so much more importance, as to often precede that of *Consules*.[194] Then, the new office is on the point of birth; and finally, in 1193, makes its appearance in the person of Gherardo Caponsacchi, a Florentine belonging to a consular family.

Ammirato was mistaken in thinking that there had been a magistrate of this kind in the year 1184, because he found that the treaty of alliance between Florence and Lucca mentioned no individual in particular, but made a general allusion to the office of Podestà.[195] As we have observed, however, too many similar allusions occur in State papers, even when Florence was certainly ruled by Consuls, to allow us to draw the same conclusion. It may be that Florence had a Podestà even earlier than 1193, but until we find some document specifying the name of a person filling that office, we cannot venture to assert it as a fact.

At any rate, the institution of the new magistracy was preceded by an increased influx of nobles within the city walls. This, indeed, was one of the chief causes of the change. Continual proofs to this effect are afforded by contemporary documents, and confirmed by the narratives of the chroniclers. The pseudo Brunetto Latini tells us that in 1192 the Consuls included "Messer Tegrino of the Counts Guidi, 'paladin' in Florence, and Chianni de' Fifanti." Now, to find a count and count palatine or paladine among the Florentine Consuls is an absolutely new thing. The same writer also says that in the same year "a decree was issued in Florence that the Counts Guidi and the Counts Alberti and the Counts da Certaldo, Ubaldini et Figiovanni, Pazzi and Ubertini, the Counts of Panago, and many other nobles, being citizens, were to dwell in the city of Florence during four months of the year." However much or little value this chronicler may have, his statement agrees with the information found in documents, and explains the origin of the new magistrature. Assuredly the nobles cannot have relished being subject to the popular consular government, against which they had struggled since the year 1177, and must have particularly disliked being under the jurisdiction of persons they deemed their inferiors in rank and dignity. Besides, as the elements composing the mass of the citizens became more heterogeneous, thus increasing the danger of civil war, so much the more the possibility of being judged by their political adversaries must have seemed unbearable to them. Hence the need was felt of a new magistrature of a different and, preferably, of an aristocratic character, and an Imperial institution, such as that of the Podestà, was chosen for a model. The holder of this office is no mere judge, as many believed and recorded; he is the positive head and representative of the Commune; he signs treaties, commands the army, and fills the place of the Consuls.

In fact, when on July 14, 1193, the Castle of Trebbio made submission to Florence, the Commune was officially represented by Gherardo Caponsacchi *Potestas Florentie et eius consiliarii*, together with the seven rectors of the headships (*Capitudini*) of the guilds.[196] The councillors, whose names are inserted in the document, are likewise seven, and almost all of consular houses; two, indeed, are nobles—namely, a Count Arrigo (perhaps of Capraia) and a Tegghiaio Bundelmonti. It seems certain that Consuls were again chosen in 1194, since the pseudo Brunetto Latini names two, one of whom was an Uberti. In 1195 a Podestà reappears in the person of *Rainerius de Gaetano, cum suis consiliariis*, among whom a *Consul iustitiae* is included.[197] It may be considered a certainty that these councillors, whose number is continually varying in the documents, were no other than the Consuls, who survived in this transitory form for some time, with the Podestà as their chief. Together with him they represent the Commune, sometimes even without him. But by degrees their importance diminishes, while that of the Podestà is increased. In short, there is a period of transformation during which the new, and as yet, ill-defined form of government alternates with that of the Consuls.

In 1200 the Podestà is no longer a Florentine, but a foreigner, and already represents the government, unaided by councillors, who have disappeared altogether in 1207—namely, when the government has assumed its definite shape. Or, to express it more accurately, their function was continually changed and their number increased, until they were converted into a special council of the whole city, beside the ancient council or senate that was changed into a general council. On arriving at that time we shall find the government represented by the Podestà and two councils, sitting either separately or jointly, and styled in the latter case the general and special council. Thus the consular office may be considered to have been altogether extinguished. In fact, excepting one final attempt in 1211 and 1212, when Consuls were once more elected, we never meet with them again. What we have related will make it easier to understand why the chroniclers attribute the origin of the Podestà to various dates. The pseudo Brunetto Latini makes the office begin in 1200— namely, the year when it was first held by a foreigner, and alien birth considered an indispensable qualification for the post. Therefore, before that time, the chronicler seems to regard the Podestà chiefly as a head Consul. [198] We can also understand why Villani, on the contrary, should have dated the origin of the office from 1207. This, in fact, was the year in which it assumed a really definite shape, since the Podestà was not only a foreigner, but appears unescorted by councillors. Nevertheless, Villani makes a mistake in representing him as a magistrate chosen for the sole purpose of administering justice more impartially, and in adding that "the signory of the Consuls did not cease then, inasmuch as they continued to hold power over all other affairs of the Commune." He makes two blunders here, but the second is little more than a simple anachronism. In fact, although his statement cannot be true as regards 1207, it may have been at least partially true with reference to the preceding years, when the Consuls still survived their own decease, as it were, in the guise of councillors to the Podestà.

VI.

It is certain that there was a recurrence of consular government between 1196 and 1199. [199] But just at that time an event of considerable importance worked a radical change in the general policy of Tuscany, and is accordingly worthy of notice. The Emperor Frederic I. died on September 27, 1197, and his death led first to the abandonment and then to the total ruin of the Imperial system he had so persistently striven to establish throughout central Italy. The people of San Miniato destroyed the fortress held by the Germans, and subsequently the walls of St. Genesio.[200] The Florentines bought back the Castle of Montegrossoli, which had been re-occupied and fortified by nobles, who proved very troublesome.[201] After this Florence set a greater undertaking on foot, by forming a league of the Tuscan cities against the Empire. It was finally arranged at St. Genesio on November 11, 1197, when first the Lucchese, and then the Florentines, Siennese, the people of San Miniato, and the Bishop of Volterra made oath to maintain it, and the solemnity of the occasion was enhanced by the presence of two cardinals of the Church. The main terms of the treaty were, an alliance for the common defence against all opponents of the League, and a pledge that neither peace nor truce should be made "cum aliquo Imperatore vel Rege seu Principe, Duce vel Marchione," without the consent of the Rectors of the said League. It was also agreed to attack all cities, towns, counts, or bishops refusing to join the alliance when requested so to do.[202] What was the pressing danger? Why this alliance against the Empire at the moment when it was no longer a source of alarm? There is one stipulation that best explains the real object in view. It is to the effect that castles, towns, and small domains were only to be admitted to the League as dependents of the legitimate owners of the territory whereon these castles or domains might be situated; but a single exception was made in favour of Poggibonsi,[203] because its dominion was disputed by many claimants. Montepulciano was to be admitted as a dependence of Sienna whenever that city should be able to prove its right of dominion.

It seems clear from all this that the genuine purpose of the League was to take advantage of the emperor's decease in order to secure to the cities the complete possession of their respective territories. To this end it was necessary that Tuscany should be united, and consequently adherence to the League was to be, as far as possible, obligatory. Its subsequent documents leave no doubt as to the true aim in view; indeed, they furnish very ample proof that Florence had promoted the League, in order that all Tuscany might aid her to regain speedy possession of the *contado*. But, although the League was against the Empire, it was by no means intended for the defence of the Pope, since it utterly disregarded his pretensions to Matilda's inheritance. For refusing to recognise any emperor, king, duke, or margrave, without the approval of the Roman Church, a proviso was added showing that should the Pope desire to join the League, he must accept its terms in order to win admittance. Should he request assistance to reconquer his own territories, everything was to be done according to the orders of the Rectors of the League. But should the territory he wished to reconquer be already in the hands of the communes, or of any of the allied cities, the League could afford him no help. It was impossible to speak more clearly. Accordingly, when

Innocent III. became Pope, early in 1198, we soon find him manifesting much disapproval of the conduct of the League, in spite of being adverse to the Empire and favourable to the national Italian spirit.

At Castel Fiorentino, on December 4, 1197, the Rectors of the League were sworn in. First among them were the Bishop of Volterra and the Florentine Consul Acerbo, who was practically the head, although that title was accorded to the bishop by reason of his ecclesiastical rank. For the moment Pisa and Pistoia held back; but these and other Tuscan cities had retained the right of adhering to the League.[204] Arezzo had already joined on the 2nd of December, Count Guido gave his oath on February 5, 1198, and Count Alberto on the seventh of the same month. Nevertheless, in signing the second of these two treaties, the Florentines expressly reserved their right to attach Semifonte, and procure the submission of the Alberti estates of Certaldo and Mangone, even by force if required.[205] Thus many other adhesions were obtained by means of stipulations virtually implying acts of submission to Florence.

This was the moment chosen by the newly elected Pope Innocent, soon after his consecration in the same month of February, to write to the two cardinals who had witnessed the oath to the League, stating that on many points he considered the said treaty "nec utilitatem contineat, nec sapiat honestatem," inasmuch as it neglected the fact of the Duchy of Tuscany appertaining to the Church, "ad ius et dominium Ecclesiae Romanae pertineat." He intended, therefore, to enforce his rights. If the members of the League submitted to him, he would compel the Pisans, under threat of interdict, to likewise join them against the Empire; otherwise he would leave them at liberty to do as they chose.[206] But as no attention was paid to him, he had to make a virtue of necessity and considerably lower his tone.[207] Some slight concessions, though of what nature is unknown, seem, however, to have been made to him, for afterwards, when writing to the Pisans, he appeared to be better satisfied, and urged them to join the League. It is, however, certain that they persisted in their refusal, and although the Pope, grown shrewder by experience, afterwards became a declared and energetic champion of the League against the Empire, this fact only availed to augment his moral and political influence, without winning him a single handsbreadth of territory, or enabling him to enforce any one of his pretended rights over Tuscany. The Florentines, on the contrary, profited more and more by this state of things. On April 10, 1198, Figline entered the League, not only made submission to Florence, but paid a yearly tribute also[208]; and on the 11th of May Certaldo agreed to identical terms.[209] The Republic persevered in the course it had marked out with equal shrewdness and energy. It allowed the nobles to take an increasing part in the government, so as to secure their hearty co-operation in achieving the aim it had in view. The same Count Arrigo da Capraia, who in 1193 was on the council of Podestà Caponsacchi, was actually promoted to the consulship in 1199.[210] Finally, in 1200, a foreigner was elected Podestà,[211] in the person of Paganello Porcari of Lucca, a measure that, as we have already noted, the nobles had long desired to carry out. And as Porcari showed energy and daring in the conduct of the war he was again chosen the following year. Then, in February, 1201, Count Alberto made oath to cede the height of Semifonte, with its fortress and walls, to the Florentines; and to assist them, whenever required, to gain possession of Colle, Certaldo, and the town of Semifonte.[212] The Bishop of Volterra likewise made oath to assist them in these campaigns.[213] All this seemed to come about as an inherent consequence of the terms of the League, and before long the allies, finding themselves reduced to serve the interests of Florence alone, naturally began to show signs of weariness and suspicion. But, heedless of all else, the Commune made ready for the expedition against Semifonte, for which all these treaties had paved the way.

Florence had long contemplated the seizure of that stronghold, for, owing to its strategic advantages and the ease with which the position could be reinforced by friendly neighbours, it had been a thorn in her side. Accordingly the now haughty Republic determined to make an end of it. We have already related how in 1184 Count Alberto had been compelled to accept the same terms exacted from the people of Pogna in 1182—namely, to give his solemn promise to build no defences. Nevertheless, profiting by the arrival of Frederic I. and the difficulties in which Florence was then involved, he had presently erected the Castle of Semifonte on the Petrognano rock, and Florence had never forgiven this offence. He had also assumed the title of *Comes de Summofonte*. Near the castle a town had sprung up, and, as many sought refuge there from neighbouring places conquered and taxed by Florence, its population had rapidly increased. Indeed there was already this rhyme afloat in the *contado*:

"Firenze, fatti in là,
Che Semifonte si fa città."[214]

It was for these reasons that the Republic so persistently tried to secure pledges of help from its neighbours by the numerous treaties to which reference has been made, and likewise by others concluded through the efforts of the energetic Podestà. But Sienna had still to be reckoned with, and Sienna might do good service to the hostile Alberto, who was already prepared for defence. Accordingly the Florentines signed an alliance with that state on March 29, 1201, promising their aid against Montalcino, which showed as threatening a front to Sienna as the Semifonte position towards their own city.[215] Also Colle was made to swear to accord no help to the people of Semifonte.[216] Thereupon the war finally began.

The chronicler Sanzanome, who witnessed it, declares, with his habitual exaggeration, that it lasted five years, but he may have counted in all the preliminary skirmishes.[217] At any rate, it was a hard struggle, for, treaties notwithstanding, Semifonte received help from all its neighbours, whose jealous dread of Florence had considerably increased. Then, too, owing to the strength of its position and the ability of Scoto, its valiant Podestà, the castle opposed so vigorous a resistance to the beleaguring army surrounding it on all sides, that the Florentines, seeing no hope of winning it by force, called treason to their aid. A certain Gonella, with some other fugitives, escaped from an adjoining territory, had taken refuge in the castle, and been entrusted with the defence of the Bagnuolo tower. This man made use of his post to betray the place to the enemy. But at the moment that he and his comrades were in the act of opening the gate, the defenders of Semifonte fell on them with fury and killed them all. Nevertheless, the evil deed had done its work, for Semifonte was speedily forced to surrender. Even if this was not brought about by treason alone, as Villani asserts (v. 30), the betrayal of the tower undoubtedly contributed to that result. In fact, on February 20, 1202, the Consuls, then returned to office in Florence, granted a perpetual exemption from all dues or taxes to the descendants of Gonella and his companions fallen in the cause of the Republic.[218] The same year, on the 3rd of April, the terms of the castle's surrender were subscribed and sworn. The Florentines assured pardon, protection, and the return of all prisoners to the people of Semifonte, but the latter were bound to demolish their fortress and walls; were to desert the hill and settle in the plain; and all save the soldiery and the churches were to pay a yearly tax of twenty-six *denari* on every hearth.[219]

The Pope expostulated strongly with the Florentines for their cruelty towards Semifonte, but after sending him a letter of justification in reply, the Consuls continued to follow their own course, and picked a quarrel with the Siennese.[220] The point of dispute was the Castle of Tornano, in the Paterno valley. Florence wished to get possession of it, and the Siennese declared that it was not theirs to give, seeing that it was the property of independent lords.

Thereupon the Florentines set to work in their usual way, by persuading Montepulciano, a large town belonging to Sienna, to swear submission to them, and also promise an annual tribute.[221] Accordingly, war would have broken out at once, but for the intervention of Ogerio, the Podestà of Poggibonsi. Being accepted as arbiter, he carefully studied the question of border lines, and conscientiously defined them. His verdict was given on June 4, 1203.[222] According to the boundaries traced by Ogerio, Florence retained the whole of the Fiesolan and Florentine *contado*, and the valley of Paterno was comprised in these limits. The Siennese were to do their best to persuade the lords of the castle to cede that as well. Both sides agreed to this arrangement;[223] it was scrupulously respected by the Siennese, and on May 15, 1204, it was sanctioned by Pope Innocent III., at the express desire of the Florentines.[224] Nevertheless, the latter continued their secret practices with Montepulciano, and on the 30th and 31st of May induced that town to renew its oath of offensive and defensive alliance against Sienna.[225] As soon as this became known, there were fresh complaints, fresh protests from the Siennese. They brought the affair before the League, and the Rectors of the same were expressly assembled at San Quirico di Osenna, April 5, 1205, under the presidency of the Bishop of Volterra, the Florentines and Aretines having declined to appear. By the examination of witnesses, it was clearly proved that Montepulciano appertained to the Siennese.[226] We do not know whether the verdict was then pronounced, nor do we know the final result of the quarrel. But it seems clear that from this moment the League was virtually dissolved, and by the act of the Florentines, its original initiators. Their primary object was now achieved in the main, and henceforth they could expect nothing from their allies save impediments to the fulfilment of their ulterior designs. For, more or less, all distrusted their ambition, and were tired of playing the part of passive tools.

But the Florentine Consuls allowed nothing to check their course of action, and quarrelled next with the Counts of Capraia owning a castle of the same name on the right bank of the Arno, near the Pistoian frontier. In conjunction with the Pistoiese, these nobles could easily bar the Arno against the Florentines. Accordingly, before this, in 1203, the latter had deemed it well to erect another castle on the opposite bank at a place called Malborghetto. The very significant name of Montelupo that they gave to the new building was sufficiently expressive of its purpose. In fact, men already repeated the saying, "To destroy this goat, there needs a wolf."[227] This affair also would have provoked strife had not the Florentines, with their

118

accustomed diplomatic subtlety, profited by the friendly offices of the Lucchese to turn it to their own advantage, and avoid coming to blows. In fact, a treaty was arranged in June, 1204, by which Florence was bound to leave the right bank of the river unmolested, and the Counts of Capraia to respect the left bank of the same.[228] And before long the count decided to swear alliance and fealty to the Florentines, together with his dependents, all of whom, excepting the soldiery, became subject to a yearly hearth tax of twenty-six *denari*. He also ceded his castle and other possessions on the left side of the Arno, near Montelupo, being likewise pledged to the defence of this fort.[229]

According to the pseudo Brunetto,[230] and one of the old lists of Consuls, although with no documentary evidence of the fact, Count Rodolfo, son of Count Guido di Capraia, became Podestà of Florence in 1205. Now, if this be true, it must be concluded that his nomination had been also stipulated in the treaty.[231] In the ensuing year the consular government seems to have been resumed, but in 1207 we come at last to the genuine Podestà of foreign birth, in the shape of Gualfredotto Grasselli of Milan, who henceforth represented the Commune without requiring the assistance of his *consiliarii*. Grasselli, too, was re-elected the following year, to enable him to carry on the campaigns the Florentines had planned with so much ardour some time before. An occasion for renewing hostilities was not long delayed. The Montepulciano question had become angrier; and accordingly the Siennese, considering that territory to be theirs by right, resolved to attack it. In the certainty of being reinforced, Montepulciano made a most obstinate defence; and the Florentines, after waiting awhile, also recurred to arms in 1207. In co- operation with Lombard, Romagnol, and Aretine allies, they marched with their *Carroccio* to the assault of the Castle of Montalto della Berardenga, between the rivers Ambra and Ombrone, which the Siennese had guarded on all sides with their Pistoian, Lucchese, and Orvietan friends. These were all routed on the 20th of June, leaving many prisoners in the enemy's hands. According to Paolino Pieri the number taken was 1,254. The castle was destroyed, but the war went on, notwithstanding the Pope's efforts to bring about a peace. The Florentines then made a furious attack on the Castle of Rigomagno, and when the scaling ladders broke down they climbed on one another's shoulders and thus won the walls. The capture of this stronghold made them masters of the Ombrone valley.[232] Thereupon (February, 1208) the Siennese were forced to accept peace on very hard terms. By the treaty concluded between the 13th and 20th of October,[233] they were pledged to yield all their possessions at Poggibonsi, to cede Tornano and its tower, to observe the boundaries adjudged by Ogerio, in every direction, and to leave Montepulciano unmolested. The prisoners on either side were exchanged.

But this war already betokens the advent of a new period in Florentine history. The conquest of the *contado* was no longer in question, for the Republic already possessed it in full. With the growing prosperity born of its numerous victories, the city had now to open roads for its vast commerce. It was not only the vagueness of their respective frontiers and the wish to enlarge them that caused Sienna and Florence to be continually at strife; it was their commercial rivalry in the markets of Italy, and especially as regarded the trade with Rome; this near neighbour having become, through the widespread relations of the Church, the principal centre of financial affairs in the civilised world. For some time past it had been the aim of Florence to obtain a monopoly of these affairs, and this was one reason why she had always adhered to the Guelphs. She had had frequent disputes with Arezzo, Volterra, and above all with Sienna, as being the most powerful city on the road to Rome. So the two rivals were perpetually stirred to fresh and fiercer strife. So, too, before long, the irresistible need of Florence for free communication with the sea became the chief cause of her equally long and sanguinary wars with Pisa, the city barring her way to the coast. But as this conflict had not yet begun, the subject will be resumed in due time. In fact, the peace of Sienna was followed by some years of truce with foreign foes, although there was little peace within the city, where the seeds of civil war were already on the point of bursting forth.

The foreign Podestà, unattended and unchecked by the former councillor-consuls, as they might be called, has now become a settled institution; and, save for their brief re-establishment during 1211 and 1212, the Consuls, as already related, have vanished for ever. This was undeniably a triumph for the patricians, to whom the working people had bent for the nonce, in order to secure their co-operation in the difficult task of reducing the *contado* to submission. The achievement of this conquest gave an extraordinary impulse to trade, and by opening an increasingly wide field for commercial enterprise, induced the desire to develop it still more. Hence, it was not to be expected that a republic whose prosperity and strength were wholly based on its industry and commerce, could or would be satisfied, in the long run, with a government suited to nobles, whose constant tendency was to grow stronger, haughtier, and more overbearing. From this moment, therefore, a struggle between the people and the patricians (*grandi*) was inevitable. The long series of civil wars, lacerating the city and staining its stones with blood, is in fact on the point of beginning.

CHAPTER IV.

STATE OF PARTIES—CONSTITUTION OF THE FIRST POPULAR GOVERNMENT AND OF THE GREATER GUILDS IN FLORENCE.[234]

I.

AFTER the office of Podestà had been permanently established in 1207, its main favourers and promoters, the aristocrats, became more daring, and forming a military organisation, of which the Podestà was the head, took a more active part in all wars abroad. Everything seemed progressing rapidly and well, when the Buondelmonti affair in 1215 caused an outbreak of civil war. Dissension was already lurking among certain of the nobles, and particularly between the Buondelmonti on the one hand, the Uberti and Fifanti on the other, either side numbering many adherents. Accordingly, in the hope of pacifying the dispute, a marriage was arranged between Bundelmonte Buondelmonti and a maiden of the Amidei house. But when all the preliminaries were concluded, the wife of Forese Donati called Buondelmonti to her and said: "Oh! shameful knight, to take to wife a woman of the Uberti and Fifanti. 'Twere better and worthier to choose this bride." So saying, she pointed to her own daughter. Buondelmonti accepted the offer, and, forsaking his betrothed, speedily married the girl. Thereupon the kinsfolk and friends of the deserted maiden assembled in the Amidei palace and vowed to avenge her wrongs. It was then that Mosca Lamberti turned to those charged to execute revenge, saying, "Whoever deals a light blow or wound, may prepare for his own grave." And then, to show that the quarrel was to the death, he added the memorable words: "Once done, 'tis done with" (*"Cosa fatta, capo ha"*). So bloodshed was ordained.

It was the Easter Day of 1215. The handsome young knight Buondelmonti, elegantly attired and with a wreath on his head, mounted his white horse and crossed from Oltrarno by the old bridge. He had reached the statue of Mars, when he was suddenly attacked. Schiatta degli Uberti hurled him to the ground with a blow from his mace, and the other conspirators quickly fell upon him and severed his veins with their knives. Afterwards the corpse was placed on a bier, the bride supporting the head of her murdered husband, and both carried in procession round the city, to move men to fresh deeds of hatred and revenge.[235] And this was the beginning of the series of internecine wars, from which many chroniclers date the origin of the Guelph and Ghibelline factions in Florence. No modern historian, however, will be apt to attribute so vast an importance to a private feud, nor to believe that a breach of promise to an Amidei maiden could be the real primary cause of the party strife that from the year 1177 had already more than once drenched the city in blood. Even Villani, although considering the Buondelmonti affair to be the origin of the Guelphs and Ghibellines, is careful to add: "Nevertheless, long before this, the noble citizens had split into sects and into the said parties, by reason of the quarrels and disputes between the Church and the Empire."[236] The Buondelmonti catastrophe, with all the private enmities it involved, undoubtedly served to inflame the political passions of two already existent parties, which now, in the days of Frederic II., acquired a political importance of a far wider nature by their connection with the general affairs of Italy. It was only then that the parties in Florence assumed the German appellations of Guelphs and Ghibellines. Also, it is worthy of remark that July, 1215, was the date of the second Frederic's state progress to Aix la Chapelle, to be crowned king of Germany, a fact of some significance, as regards the history of parties in Italy. This may easily explain why the chroniclers should have attributed to the Buondelmonti tragedy, occurring in the same year, the origin of the Guelphs and Ghibellines. The names began then it is true, but the parties were of older date.

Villani's Chronicle (v. 39) now gives a list of the principal Guelph and Ghibelline families, showing that the majority of the older houses was almost invariably Ghibellines, whereas the Guelph party included many "of no great antiquity," but "already beginning to be powerful." Later on, when the Ghibellines are destroyed, we shall find the Guelph nobles merged in the party of the well-to-do burghers (*popolo grasso*). At present these patricians, being hostile to the Uberti, begin to make advances to newly enriched families, and even to the people, by siding with the Church. Fortunately Pope Innocent III. started a Crusade at this time, and thus many powerful Florentines went to the East and employed their fighting powers in a better cause. At the siege of Damietta, in fact, they distinguished themselves greatly: Bonaguisa dei Bonaguisi the first to scale the walls, planted the banner of the Republic beside the Christian flag. In Giovanni Villani's time this banner was still preserved and held in the greatest honour.

In 1218 Florence resumed hostilities in the *contado*, and by 1220 had subdued various castles and domains, and exacted oaths of fealty from all defeated foes. But immediately afterwards a far graver war broke out with

Pisa. The jealousy of the two rival republics was always on the increase, and for some time past each had struggled against the other for absolute commercial supremacy in Tuscany. Pisa commanded the sea, Florence the mainland, therefore each city required the other's help. Hence, in spite of repeated agreements and treaties, their mutual jealousy remained undiminished. The Florentines adhered steadfastly to the Church; the Pisans to the Empire. Things had gradually become inflamed to so high a pitch that the smallest trifle was enough to excite war, or rather to provoke the endless series of wars destined to change the character of the Tuscan factions.

In fact, the first pretext for strife, at least as related by Villani (vi. 2), is futile to the point of utter absurdity. Many ambassadors attended the coronation of the Emperor Frederic II. in Rome (1220), and among them, says the chronicler, were those of Pisa and Florence, who had long eyed one another with distrust. It chanced that one of the Florentine ambassadors, while feasting with a cardinal, begged the gift of a certain very beautiful dog, and his host promised to grant it. The next day the cardinal entertained the Pisans, and one of them, happening to make the same request, the animal was promised likewise to him. But the Florentine, being the first to send for the dog, he actually obtained it. This led to quarrels and violence, not only on the part of the ambassadors and their trains, but also between all the Pisans and Florentines in Rome at the time. We can hardly assign any historical value to this tale; but it shows that the amount of ill-feeling between the rival states rendered any trifle a sufficient pretext for bloodshed. The real fact, even according to the testimony of Sanzanome, is that Pisans and Florentines came to blows in Rome. The Pisans were the assailants, but had the worst of the bout. There was great wrath in Pisa at the news of the riot, and as a speedy reprisal all Florentine merchandise in the town was made confiscate. Florence then seems to have done her utmost to avoid open war, but to no purpose. Preparations went on for some time on either side, and then in 1222, when war had burst forth between the Lucchese and Pisans, the Florentines profited by the opportunity to attack the latter near Castel del Bosco, defeated them, and, according to the chroniclers, carried off thirteen hundred prisoners. Other attacks ensued, and various small castles were captured between this time and 1228, when we see the Florentines engaged in more serious strife with the Pistoians, and reducing them to accept their terms. It is in 1228 that we find the first mention of the *Carroccio* on a Florentine battle-field.[237] The Milanese had been the first to use the *Carroccio*, but in course of time, and with slight modifications, the custom had been adopted by the other Italian cities, who, with increasing wars and larger forces, recognised the need of a rallying point in their midst. The *Carroccio* was a chariot drawn by oxen with scarlet trappings and surmounted by two lofty poles bearing the great banner of the Republic, swinging its red and white folds on high. Behind, on a smaller car, came the bell, called the *Martinella*, to ring out military orders. For some time before a war was proclaimed the *Martinella* was attached to the door of Sta Maria in the New Market, and rung there to warn both citizens and enemies to make ready for action. The *Carroccio* was always surrounded by a guard of picked men; its surrender was considered as the final defeat and humiliation of the army.

Another prolonged and sanguinary conflict with Sienna was undertaken and resumed almost yearly from 1227 to 1235. The Siennese suffered severe losses, but were able to seize Montepulciano, demolish its towers and ramparts, and do some damage to Montalcino, which had joined alliance with the Florentines. The latter, however, not only devastated the Siennese *contado* time after time, and captured a large number of prisoners, but also besieged the hostile capital, and although failing to win it, pressed close enough to the walls to hurl donkeys over them with catapults, to prove their contempt for the town. Finally, through the mediation of the Pope, peace was concluded very advantageously for Florence. The Siennese had to forfeit a large sum of money for the rebuilding of the walls and towers of Montepulciano, were sworn to leave that territory for ever unmolested, and likewise compelled to repair the castle of Montalcino, at the pleasure of the Florentines, who still retained their hold on Poggibonsi.

II.

Thus, throughout all these wars, in which the influence of Pope and emperor was felt on this or the other side, we are enabled to trace the gradual formation of parties in Tuscany, and to witness the process by which the political and commercial supremacy of Florence was built up. Her present rivals, Sienna and Pisa, both adhere to the Empire; whereas Florence clings more and more closely to the Church. Pisa shuts her out from the sea: hence the origin of their mutual rivalry and continual strife. How, indeed, could war be avoided, when the commercial power of Florence felt the increasingly imperative need of free access to the coast? Sienna, on the other hand, competed with Florence by trying to get all the affairs of the Roman *curia* into the hands of its own bankers, those affairs being so numerous and lucrative as to enrich all concerned with them. These continual jealousies invariably urged Pisa and Sienna to favour the Empire. Lucca, as the rival of Pisa, inclined towards Florence, and became Guelph. Pistoia, planted between two Guelph cities, and continually menaced by them, naturally adopted the Ghibelline cause. Thus, the division of parties in Tuscany afterwards reacted on the formation of Florentine sects, and as the latter began to assume a more general character, through the growing influence of Frederic II. in Italy, they adopted the German names of Guelphs and Ghibellines. The Florentine Republic, having triumphed over Pisa, Sienna, and Pistoia, was virtually the chief power in Tuscany; but had one danger to face, in the possible augmentation of Frederic's power. Frederic II. was the enemy of the Pope, who had excommunicated him, and of all Guelphs! He had gone away for a time to lead the Crusade in the East; was now in Germany engaged in a struggle with his rebellious son, and all this had greatly advanced the fortunes of Florence. But he was about to return to Italy, and his presence might again embolden the foes of the Republic.

Meanwhile, under the rule of successive Podestà, Florence had prospered in war, and devoted times of peace to internal organisation and embellishment. At the instance of the Podestà Torello da Strada (1233) all the male inhabitants of the *contado* were summoned to inscribe their names and specify their condition, whether freemen, serfs, or dependents, with a view to ascertaining the real state of the population and providing for its better government. In 1237–38 the Podestà Rubaconte da Mandello built a new bridge over the Arno, which was first designated by his own name of Rubaconte, and afterwards as the Ponte alle Grazie, in honour of an adjoining church. It was also by order of the same Podestà that all the streets of Florence were first paved, and other works completed for the improvement of the public health, or the decoration of the city. Thus a magistrate originally appointed—according to the chroniclers—to do the work of an ordinary judge is seen gradually fulfilling the functions of the head of the Republic. And the patricians over whom he presided daily rose to greater power and daring, and particularly when the arrival of Frederic II. began to encourage the Ghibelline party throughout Italy. In fact, when Brescia was besieged by the Ghibellines in 1237, we find many Florentine nobles in their camp. Every day brought fresh proofs that the emperor might count on many friends and much assistance from Florence. Consequently numerous riots took place, for the Guelph nobles offered violent opposition and joined with the people, which was entirely Guelph.[238] In 1240 we find that three citizens were nominated to collect funds in aid of the Imperial army: surely a strange proceeding in a republic[239] where the mass of the population was thoroughly Guelph! But it is not surprising that such events should have inevitably caused a reaction.

Already in 1246 Frederic II. had appointed his natural son, Frederic of Antioch, vicar-general of Tuscany, and also sent other vicars to Florence to fill the office of Podestà. This aroused discontent on the part of the Guelph nobles, who wished their own faction to regain the upper hand in the city.

About this time, 1247, Frederic was in Lombardy,[240] and at almost open war with the Pope, who continued to launch excommunications at him, deprived him of the Imperial title, and stirred enemies from all sides against him. Accordingly, Frederic sent messengers to the Uberti in Florence, advising them that the moment had come for them to assume the government of Florence. Provided they had the courage to fly to arms, his succour would not be long delayed. The Uberti were not deaf to his words. The heads of the chief Ghibelline houses met in council and decided on immediate resort to violence. There was instant division in the city; the Ghibelline aristocracy on one side, the Guelph nobles, with all the people on the other; and the alarm bell was pealed. Fighting went on from street to street, by day and by night, behind barricades, from tower-roofs, and with catapults, rams, and other engines of war. As the popular excitement increased the strife became general. The Ghibellines had the advantage of superior military training; they were confident of receiving reinforcements; and, massed under one leader, took all their orders from the Uberti palaces. The people, on the contrary, fought at random, and were soon surrounded and repulsed. Nevertheless, at one moment their very defeat seemed about to win them the victory. Hard- pressed on all sides, they were gradually driven back towards the chain barricades (*serraglio*) of the Bagnesi and Guidalotti mansions; and being massed about this defence, fought so vigorously as almost to regain their former position. But just then the Imperial contingent appeared on the scene, and all was lost. The vicar-general Frederic, son of the emperor, entered Florence at the head of sixteen hundred German knights, and made furious charges on the people. The latter opposed a sturdy resistance, prolonging the fight for three days, but it was a vain struggle. The Ghibellines were victorious on all sides, and the emperor could have sent fresh reinforcements if required. One of the most valiant of the Guelphs, Rustico Marignolli, who had borne the standard of the people throughout the mêlée, fell wounded to the death by a shot in the face from a crossbow. Thereupon the leaders of the party finally decided to surrender and fly into exile on Candlemas night (February 2, 1249). All those resolved on flight gathered together fully armed, and taking possession of Marignolli's corpse, bore it away in a solemn procession with a crowd of *popolani*, and a great show of weapons and torches, to celebrate the funeral at San Lorenzo by night. The bier was carried on the shoulders of the worthiest cavaliers, and the defeated but not dishonoured banner hung trailing from it to the ground. The whole function resembled a pact of vengeance sworn on the body of the dead warrior rather than a mere burial ceremony.

After this the leading Guelphs fled the city and took refuge in neighbouring castles; the same in fact from which, at the cost of much blood, they had once ousted the feudal lords. These latter, having been compelled to settle in the town, had now won their revenge for past injuries. Thirty-six Guelph houses were pulled down: among them the Tosinghi palace in the New Market, a building measuring one hundred and thirty-five feet in height, and faced with many tiers of marble columns. Party hatred reached such a pitch as to justify the belief expressed by many that the Ghibellines had positively decreed the destruction of San Giovanni, because the Guelphs had used that church as a place of assembly. It was affirmed that the victors had undermined the foundations of the adjoining Guardamorto tower, hoping that this might fall down on the temple and crush it. The failure of the attempt was attributed to the fact that the tower had miraculously fallen in another direction. A more credible account is given by Vasari. He says that the Guardamorto was only demolished in order to widen the Piazza, and that Niccolò Pisano, being charged with the work, cut the tower in two and arranged its fall in a way to avoid any damage to the church or neighbouring houses.

At all events, this proved the beginning of the long list of savage reprisals darkening the history of Florence, when the winning faction not only destroyed the dwellings of the defeated, but banished their foes *en masse*. The Ghibellines were now masters of all, and for their greater security retained the services of Count Giordano Lancia and his eight hundred Germans. It seemed as though the party, being of Teutonic origin, could not yet grasp the reins of government without the support of German soldiery, and could only command the Republic in the emperor's name. This was the final result of admitting the Imperial feudal nobility within the walls of Florence, and allowing them to institute a political and military chief instead of an ordinary judge in the person of the Podestà.

III.

The Ghibelline victory over the Guelphs of Florence in 1249, with all its violence and bloodshed, was by no means an assured triumph. The Ghibellines had destroyed free institutions and exiled a vast number of adversaries; aided by the Imperial vicar, Giordano Lancia and his eight hundred men, they were absolute masters of Florence; nevertheless, the populace, the burghers, and the greater part of the citizens still remained Guelphs. Besides, Pope Innocent IV. roused so many enemies against the emperor in Italy, that the latter's success was destined to a speedy decline. The Florentine exiles were biding their time in neighbouring strongholds, and above all in the Castles of Montevarchi and Capraia in the upper and lower

Val d'Arno. From these points they made frequent skirmishing expeditions, clearly showing that they had by no means lost hope of soon re-entering the city. Accordingly, the conquerors had to be perpetually on the alert against them to provide against some sudden attack restoring them to power.

Therefore Ghibellines and Germans marched against Montevarchi; but almost the whole storming force was killed or captured. This defeat opened the eyes of the Florentine Ghibellines to the danger of their position, and decided them to lay regular siege to the Castle of Capraia, headquarters of the principal Guelphs, chiefs of the party or League, as it was called at the time, directing all the movements of the rest. Although the beleaguering force greatly outnumbered their own, the besieged decided on an obstinate defence, and the Ghibellines were bent on winning the castle either by violence or starvation. But they would have failed to accomplish this but for the arrival of reinforcements from the emperor, who, having been compelled to raise the siege of Parma, had now advanced into Tuscany. But, in spite of these fresh foes, hunger alone drove the Guelphs to surrender. Their leaders were given up to Frederic II., who was then at Fucecchio. He carried them with him to the kingdom of Naples, and, according to the Florentine chroniclers, had them barbarously blinded, beaten to death with clubs, or drowned in the sea, with the exception of one alone, whose life was spared after his eyes had been torn out.

By this time the emperor was irritated and exhausted by the continual wars thrust on him by the Papacy. He had enjoyed no peace since the day (June 24, 1243) when Sinibaldo de Fieschi ascended the Chair of St. Peter as Pope Innocent IV. This pontiff had pronounced his deposition at the Council of Lyons in 1245. He had then secretly excited many conspiracies against him, and attempted more or less to ensure their success. The emperor had been led to suspect his most devoted friend and secretary, Pier delle Vigne, of complicity in one of these plots. Accordingly this faithful servant was thrown into the tower of San Miniato al Tedesco, condemned to lose his eyes, and then transferred to another prison in Pisa, where he dashed out his brains against the wall. Frederic's spirit was alternately cowed and irritated by the hostility he encountered; for, with all his philosophy and unbelief, he greatly dreaded the thunders of the Vatican. He sought reconciliation with the Pope, wished to return to the East to fight the infidels; and Innocent chose that moment to rouse all the Guelph cities against him, thus again forcing him to fly to arms to support the Ghibelline cause and maintain his own sway over Italy.

This he was unable to effect without recurring, as we have seen, to incredible excesses of violence, which naturally increased the number of his enemies on all sides. The Guelphs of Germany had already refused to acknowledge the authority of his son Corrado, whom he had sent as his representative. The army commanded by the emperor in person had been routed at Parma. All the Guelph cities of Romagna, with Bölogna at their head, marched a powerful force against the Ghibellines under King Enzo, another of Frederic's natural sons, and defeated them at the battle of Fossalta on May 26, 1249. Enzo himself was captured and carried in triumph to Bologna, where he remained a prisoner till his death in 1271. But the emperor did not live long enough to feel this last blow. On December 13, 1250, he ceased to breathe in a castle near Lucera in Apulia, and his death completed the downfall of the Ghibelline party in Florence and throughout Italy. For religious hatred was now combined with political enmity against this party. Not only because the Ghibellines combated the Pope, but still more, because the various heresies gradually spreading through Italy found many followers in their ranks, in consequence of frequent marks of tolerance and favour received from the emperor. The heretical poison now slowly infecting the Italian social body was a grave anxiety to the Popes. The Albigenses had first roused attention and found adherents in Provence, where native bards had devoted their talents to attacking the Roman Court. But the religious orders of St. Francis and St. Dominic were bent on crushing the new creed. Innocent III. had founded the Holy Inquisition for the same purpose, and St. Dominic, at the head of mobs thirsting for heretic blood, had ordained the massacre of the Albigenses and ravaged all Provence. Some fugitives, however, had escaped into Italy, to spread the same hatred against Rome, the same poison of heresy. In fact, the *Paterini*, opposed to the Pope, denying the virginity of the Madonna, and having no belief in transubstantiation or other dogmas of the Catholic faith, found followers everywhere and held public gatherings. The Epicurean, Averrhoistic, and other philosophical tenets were rapidly propagated among Italian scholars. For some time, during the most brilliant period of the Imperial Court in Sicily, all this intellectual and religious turmoil seemed to be chiefly centred at Palermo. For there Frederic II. had gathered about him a throng of scholars, troubadours, poets of every kind, Mussulmans, Greek schismatics, Provençal Albigenses, and materialistic philosophers; and although a crusader and persecutor of heretics, took singular delight in this mixed society, in whose midst, and in a storm of sarcasm, doubt, and hatred of priests, Italian poetry first sprang to life, and later on, in the Divine Comedy, gave forth so great a wealth of earnest faith and lofty aspiration. In the meantime, however, heresy and scepticism were current throughout the Peninsula. The *Paterini* quickly obtained many converts among the Ghibellines in Florence, and the Pope established the Inquisition there for the trial and punishment of backsliders. In 1244 Fra Pietro of Verona, moved by religious fury rather than zeal, came to stir the orthodox spirit by his inflammatory sermons; and founded the Society of the Captains of Holy Mary or of Faith, composed of men and women vowed to the extermination of heretics. Public feeling caught fire in 1245, and a real battle between Catholics and heretics raged in the Florence streets. Both at Santa Felicità and in the space by the Croce al Trebbio, where a column still commemorates the ill-fated event, the *Captains of the Faith*, robed in white, bearing the badge of the cross, and commanded by their big, strong, dare- devil chief, Friar Pietro of Verona, routed the *Paterini* and drove them from Florence. In reward for this sanguinary triumph the friar was appointed Inquisitor of Tuscany, and subsequently of Lombardy as well. There in the north, between Milan and Como, he finally met his death at the hands of men wearied of his persecutions. This gained him the title of a martyred saint, and he was known henceforth as St. Peter—Martyr of Verona.[241]

IV.

Meanwhile, in 1250, the year now claiming our attention, Frederic II. passed away, his son Enzo lay captive in Bölogna, Innocent IV. was stirring the Guelphs to action, and Pietro of Verona had become the scourge of all heretics and foes of the Papacy in Tuscany and Lombardy. Accordingly the Ghibelline domination in Florence was approaching its end. In fact, from the moment that the emperor withdrew into Apulia, already stricken with mortal disease, the Guelphs showed so much boldness that the Ghibellines decided on a fresh expedition to oust them from the Castle of Ostina, in the Valdarno, where they had assembled in great force. But while laying siege to the stronghold the Ghibellines were compelled to keep a strong reserve at Figline to protect their rear from the many Guelph partisans lurking at Montevarchi. The latter, however, made a night attack on the force encamped at Figline, and routed it so thoroughly that when the news reached Ostina the Ghibellines raised the siege and marched back to the capital. Thereupon both the people and burghers of Florence, tired of the unbearable load of taxation imposed on them by the continual wars undertaken by the Ghibellines, and worn out by the "grave extortions and acts of violence of these tyrannical masters," felt that the moment for vengeance had come, and rose in open revolt. The rebels were led by the more influential citizens of the so-called middle class, then acting as heads of the people. These men first held their sittings in the Church of San Firenze, then in Santa Croce, and finally, still dreading attack from the Uberti, assembled in smaller numbers and with greater safety in the houses of the Anchioni family. Here, in October, 1250, they proclaimed the nomination of thirty-six "Corporals of the people," six to each *sestiere*, forming the basis of the third Florentine Constitution, known as the First Popular Government (*Primo Popolo*), because its main purpose was to organise and strengthen the people in opposition to the nobles, and by this time the latter being much disheartened, unresistingly submitted to the new government. The first measure adopted was the dismissal of all the magistrates in office, and reforms were then undertaken. The post of Podestà was retained, and henceforth this official became still more exclusively the head of the patricians, being now counterbalanced by the newly instituted Captain of the people, as chief of the *popolani*. But, as in this way the Republic was divided in two parts, a central, presiding body was established consisting of twelve elders (*anziani*) of the people, two for each *sestiere*. These *anziani* had some of the attributes of the Consuls of former days, with this difference, however, that not only were they men of the people, but that the chief government of the city was now entrusted to the Podestà and the Captain. In fact, the new and most important part of the reform was this institution of a Captain as commander of the people, who were now organised on a military footing. The city was divided into twenty armed companies, with twenty gonfalons or banners, under as many gonfalonieri. The *contado*, on the contrary, was organised in ninety-six companies, corresponding with its ninety-six existing parishes (*pivieri*). These town and country companies combined formed a united popular militia, ready for action at any moment, either against foreign foes or to curb patrician tyranny at home. The whole of this armed multitude was under the orders of the Captain, and as he combined the functions of tribune, general, and judge, he afterwards bore the additional titles of *Defender of the Guilds and the People, Captain of all the Guelphs*, &c. Similarly to the Podestà, the Captain held office for one year, and it was indispensable that he should be a Guelph, a noble, and an alien. He came to Florence provided with his own judges, knights, and war-horses, inasmuch as he was leader of the people in war and administrator of justice in times of peace. But, as we have already stated, the Podestà still retained his civil and military importance. In right of his office, he had to give judgment in all civil and criminal cases, those reserved for the Captain's decision being usually acts of violence committed by the *grandi* against the people, questions regarding taxes or valuations, and certain cases of extortion, perjury, and violence, provided these had not been already cited before the Podestà, or unless he should have refused them his attention.[242] Also, in the above-mentioned cases, the Captain was likewise empowered to adjudge capital punishment. The red and white gonfalon or banner of the people was in his charge, and by ringing the bell of the so-called Lion's Tower he summoned the people to assembly. He resided in the Badia, together with the elders, who acted as his counsellors in many respects. Messer Uberto of Lucca was the first Captain of the people. As to the Podestà, although certain writers, misled by the somewhat obscure statements of Villani and Malespini, believed his office to have been at least temporarily abolished, it is certain that he remained at the head of what was specially called the Commune.[243] He, too, had his companies of armed men, and likewise commanded the mounted bands composed almost exclusively of nobles, the bowmen and crossbowmen, bucklermen (*palvesari*), &c., forming conjointly the so-called host, or nucleus of regulars in the mass of the Republican army. The Podestà was often commander-in-chief of the whole army, but his special function was the command of the cavalry and the host (*oste*).[244] And for the further enhancement of his dignity, it was decided to build a great and monumental palace,[245] in which he was to hold residence with his attendant officers and counsellors. But, on the other hand, as nothing was neglected to increase the strength of the people against the patricians, it was decreed that the towers of all powerful houses should be cut down so that none should exceed the height of seventy-five feet (fifty *braccia*), and the superfluous material was used to wall in the city on the south side of the river (*oltr'Arno*).[246]

This third constitution of Florence, known as the *Primo Popolo*, or First Popular Government, was in fact a politico-military constitution, dividing the Republic into two halves, the Commune and the people, and in which the aristocrats and democrats formed, as it were, two opposing camps. The army was marshalled under the banners both of the Commune and the people; all important measures required the sanction both of the Commune and the people. A similar division of authority may seem strange at this day, but it was common enough in the Middle Ages. It was customary to many Tuscan cities, and we find an example of it at Bölogna, where the nobility and people formed, as it were, two distinct republics, having different laws and statutes, and two separate palaces for their respective magistrates. At Milan we find a tripartite republic in the Credenza dei Consoli, the Motta, and the Credenza di Sant Ambrogio, consisting respectively of the greater and middle nobility and the people. This seemed a perfectly natural arrangement, seeing that social conditions are reflected in the institutions to which they give birth; the social body was divided, because it owed its origin to the struggle between the Latin and Teutonic races, between conquerors and conquered. Accordingly, the remote heirs of either race stood arrayed in two opposite camps, armed and prepared for conflict.[247]

PALACE OF THE PODESTÀ, FLORENCE.

[*To face page 192*

In this state of things it is easy to understand why the central government had so little authority in Florence, and why, during the continual clash of opposing interests and jealousies, the power of the Podestà and the Captain should have steadily increased. The former, although his functions were now shared by other magistrates, still remained the chief official representative of the Republic; for he signed treaties of peace, accepted concessions of territory in that capacity, received oaths of submission to Florence from other towns, and, as in times past, still continued to preside over two councils—*i.e.*, the Special and the General, respectively composed of ninety and of three hundred members. The Captain had likewise two councils, the which, according to the usage of the time, consisted of a Special Council, or *credenza*, of eighty members, making, in junction with the Council-General, a total of three hundred. This body included the elders, the heads of guilds, the gonfaloniers of companies, and others, and, unlike the councils of the

135

Podestà, to which nobles were admitted, solely consisted of plebeians. Members of the Special Council frequently sat in the General Assembly, which was therefore usually styled the General and Special Council of the Podestà, or the Captain, as the case might be. The elders had a privy council of their own, composed of thirty-six plebeian worthies; and the parliament must not be forgotten, although at the time of which we are treating it was only summoned on occasions of exceptional importance. But, as will be shown, some time elapsed before these councils were established on a definite basis; none for the moment, save those of the Podestà, which were of older origin, having any settled formation.[248] At any rate, the Republic, as regarded its general outline, was ordered in the following manner: the elders, the council of thirty-six, and the parliament, formed a central government, already much weakened, however, by the constitution and growing strength of the Commune and people, inasmuch as these latter, commanded by the Podestà and Captain, and with their respective greater and lesser councils, formed, as it were, two opposing republics. The Commune undoubtedly enjoyed superior authority and legal importance; but the popular party became daily bolder and more numerous. Before long, in fact, ancient families began to change their names and drop their titles, in order to join the ranks of the people.

The great political writers of Florence differed in opinion with regard to the new constitution. Donato Giannotti censured it, declaring it to be "a cause of sedition, instead of a bond of peace and concord, because the founders of that government directed it entirely against the nobles, its former rulers in the days of Frederic, and who now being in constant fear of attack, were obliged to fly to arms on every occasion."[249] Machiavelli, on the contrary, praised the Constitution, and wound up by saying: "With these military and civil institutions the foundations of Florentine freedom were laid. Nor is it possible to imagine how much authority and strength Florence thereby gained in a short space. For she not only became the head of Tuscany, but was counted among the foremost of Italian cities, and might have risen to any height had she not been afflicted by new and frequent divisions."[250] Machiavelli judged rightly. Both contemporary chroniclers of these events and the impartial voice of history fully confirm the truth of his words.

The city now began to be enriched by new public monuments. The Communal palace, otherwise known as the palace of the Podestà, rose from the ground, and the Santa Trinità bridge was built, chiefly at the expense of a private citizen. The gold florin was now issued, and, being mixed with the best alloy, speedily obtained currency[251] not only in all European markets, but even in the Levant, greatly to the advantage of Florentine commerce, which was daily becoming more widely extended. The nobles were discontented, of course, and hastened to show their ill-feeling, in 1251, by their almost unanimous refusal to join in the war against Pistoia. But when a few of them were sent into banishment the others soon quieted down. The Guelph exiles were recalled, adversaries within the city made peace, and now, that Frederic II. was dead, the aristocracy was kept in check by the strength and self-confidence of the popular party. Shortly afterwards external wars began, and these were carried on with so much success that the following ten years were known as the years of victory.

V.

This First, or Old Popular Government, as it was called, because it was in fact the first time that the people had a political and military organisation of their own, quickly asserted its strength. In order to give the spreading Florentine trade free access to the sea, without yet coming to blows with Pisa, the city concluded an agreement on April 30, 1251, with the Counts Aldobrandeschi, powerful lords of the Maremma, by which Florence was granted right of passage through their territories to Porto Talamone and Port' Ercole and the free use of these harbours for its merchandise.[252] Thereupon the Pisans, being naturally annoyed by this measure, hastened to contract an alliance with Sienna, to which Pistoia also adhered. Thus the three Ghibelline cities were banded together against the Florentine Guelphs. Nor was this the worst. On July 24, 1251, the Ghibellines of Florence joined the League by a secret agreement with Sienna, binding either side to cooperate towards their common aim—*i.e.*, the triumph of their party throughout Tuscany. And as the other Ghibellines of the country-side naturally adhered to the treaty, the whole faction was united to the hurt of the Republic.

Then the Florentines, finding themselves surrounded by so many foes, began their defence by a rapid march on Pistoia, but the Ghibellines of the city refused to take part in a war openly directed against their cause. Accordingly, when the army returned from a successful skirmishing expedition, many leading Ghibellines, including the Uberti and the Lamberti, were driven into banishment. The affair must have been really serious, for the exiles hoisted the banner of the Republic, whereupon the State banner was changed, and instead of bearing the white lily on a red field, henceforth displayed the red lily on a white field; but the flag of the people remained as before, half white and half red. During the summer of this year the Ubaldini, reinforced by a body of exiles, rose to arms in the Mugello, but suffered defeat. The Florentines at last realised the danger of their position. Therefore, with the help of their former friends the Lucchese, they concluded an alliance (August, 1251) with the town of San Miniato al Tedesco—where there was no Imperial vicar for the moment—renewed in September their former treaty with Orvieto, and in November made alliance with Genoa, which was still hostile to Pisa.

Thus the whole of Tuscany was divided between the Guelph and Ghibelline factions. The exiles, together with some German soldiers who had served under Frederic II., occupied the Castle of Montaia, belonging to Count Guido Novello, in the upper Val d'Arno. The Florentines marched to the assault of the stronghold towards the end of the year, but were ignominiously repulsed. On their return to the city, they rang the alarm-bell, collected a large force, again took the field, people and Commune combined, and pursued the war with energy during the month of January, regardless of frost and snow. The general condition of affairs in Tuscany enlarged the proportions of this war; for on the one side Lucchese troops co-operated with the Florentine army, while the exiles on the other received reinforcements from Pisa and Sienna. The First Popular Government now proved its mettle. The adversaries were driven off, the Castle of Mentaia captured and demolished, and its defenders were led captives to Florence in January, 1252.[253]

The Florentines then marched into the Pistoian territory, laid it waste, and halted to attack the Castle of Tizzano on their return. But while thus engaged they heard that the Pisans, having routed the Lucchese, were moving homewards with prisoners and spoil. Accordingly, they raised the siege, hastened in pursuit, and giving battle to the Pisans at Pontedera on July 1, 1252, completely defeated them. Even the Podestà of Pisa was captured, and another curious incident took place. The Lucchese prisoners who were being dragged to Pisa in bonds not only regained their liberty, but were enabled, by the help of the Florentines, to convey to Lucca as captives the same Pisans by whom they had been previously seized.

Meanwhile, profiting by the absence of the Florentine troops, the exiles and Count Guido Novello had taken refuge at Figline and made it the centre of continual skirmishing expeditions. Hence it was indispensable to unearth them all without delay. The town surrendered, but only on condition that the strangers defending its wall should be allowed to go free, and the exiles readmitted. This was granted but then, in violation of the stipulated terms, Figline itself was sacked and burnt (August, 1852).[254]

But, the Siennese having simultaneously profited by the opportunity to lay siege to Montalcino, a border fortress always claimed by the Florentines, the latter hastened to its relief, and after routing its assailants and providing everything for the future defence of the stronghold, marched back to Florence in triumph.

These successes were not unproductive of results. For when the Florentines next attacked Pistoia in 1253, the town surrendered after a brief resistance, and agreed (February 1, 1254) to forsake the Ghibelline League, to grant readmittance to the Guelphs, and to be entirely at the service of Florence.[255] Thereupon the Florentines hastened to defend Montalcino against another attack by the Siennese; and thus the war with the latter, begun at the end of 1253, was vigorously pursued in 1254, to the month of June. Then, having lost many strongholds—some captured by Florentine arms, others gained by purchase from the Counts Guidi—Sienna was forced to end the war and tender submission. On their way back to Florence the victors reduced Poggibonsi, a large and important territory adhering to Sienna and the Ghibellines. They next proceeded to devastate the lands about Volterra, although the city itself seemed impregnable from the strength of its position. But when the Volterrani, counting upon this, ventured to sally forth and give battle, they were defeated and pursued with so much vigour, that the Florentines found themselves inside the city before they had even conceived the possibility of storming its walls. There was such general alarm among the inhabitants that a great throng of old men, women, and children, with the bishop at their head, came as suppliants to make surrender. The Florentines showed much generosity, prohibiting pillage, and merely reforming the government of the city by transferring it to the Guelphs. And now Pisa, being bereft of all allies, finally agreed to surrender, and the terms were subscribed on August 4, 1254. As a result of this treaty the Florentines had right of passage through Pisa, with their merchandise, and exemption from all taxes, dues, or imposts, whether by sea or by land. Moreover, in all contracts made with them, the Pisans were bound to employ Florentine weights and measures, and also, to some extent, Florentine money. They yielded several districts and castles, that of Ripafratta included. And they were compelled to give 150 hostages to secure their observance of these conditions and of the friendship to which they were sworn. Shortly after this event Arezzo likewise made submission (25th of August), and accepted a Podestà from Florence.[256]

These were the "victorious years" of the First Popular Government, whose merits and virtues received such high praise from the chroniclers. Villani tells us, in words afterwards repeated by his plagiarist, Malespini, that it took "much pride in great and lofty undertakings," and that its rulers "were very loyal and devoted to the Commune."[257] And he presently adds: "The citizens of Florence lived soberly, on coarse viands and at little expense; their manners were very good; they had courteous ways; they were plain and frugal; and used rough stuff for their own and their women's dress. And many wore skins uncovered by cloth, and caps on their heads; all were shod with leather; and the Florentine women wore plain hose, and only the greater among them donned very narrow petticoats of coarse scarlet Ipro or Camo cloth, gathered in at the waist by a leather belt in the old style,[258] and a fur- lined mantle with a hood attached to cover the head;[259] and common women wore gowns of coarse green Cambragio stuff, made in the same fashion. And one hundred *lire* was the usual dowry for a bride, two or three hundred *lire* being considered in those times a splendid sum, and even the most beautiful maidens were not given in marriage until they were aged twenty years, or more."[260] Even the evidence of the "Divina Commedia" fully corroborates this account of the goodness and honesty of the Florentines of old, and events continued to prove the truth of the verdict.

Fortune favoured the city not only in war, but also in peace both within and without the walls. In addition to the many great public works we have already mentioned, and which were now completed, other buildings were in course of erection on various sites bought by the *anziani* for the purpose in different parts of the city. These officials, together with the captain of the people, Lambertino di Guido Lambertini, likewise decreed (1252–53) that the register of all the communal deeds should be re-copied and carried on regularly, in order, as they said, that the *jura et rationes Communis* might not be left unknown nor neglected, but open to the public in various places. These papers are the *capitoli* still preserved at the present time, and affording so much useful information on the history of Florence.[261]

Now, however, the state of affairs was about to take a fresh turn. In consequence of Conrad's decease, Manfred, the other son of Frederic II., succeeded to the Neapolitan throne. The new sovereign, being dauntless, ambitious, and full of talent, devoted all his powers to forwarding the interests of the Italian Ghibellines; and the Florentines, with their usual shrewdness, immediately became more cautious in their proceedings. In 1255 they made alliance with Sienna, the following year with Arezzo, severely blamed their captain, Count Guido Guerra, for expelling the Ghibellines from the latter city, and compelled him to recall them. They even treated their own exiles with greater indulgence and liberality, permitting some of them to return from time to time. But on either side these were false demonstrations, leading to no result. All were temporising, waiting to see what fresh turn the general affairs of Italy might take.

Supposing Manfred's fortunes to be really restored, the Florentines would suffer severely, and of this they were perfectly aware. A first warning was received by them in 1256, when the Pisans, oblivious of sworn terms and promises, made an attack upon Ponte a Serchio, a castle held by the Lucchese, the allies of Florence. Accordingly the Florentines hastened to their friends' relief, and routed the assailants, many of whom were drowned in the river in their flight. After this victory the troops marched towards Pisa and coined money in sight of the walls, an act then considered to inflict deep humiliation on the enemy. In addition to this the Pisans were not only forced to renew (September 23, 1256) the ignominious peace concluded in 1254, but also to cede many castles to the Florentines, and some few to the Lucchese. [262] And another clause was added to the terms stipulating that the Castle of Mutrone, a position of great strategical importance both to Lucchese and Florentines, should be given up to the latter, with power to destroy or preserve it, as their magistrates might decide. Accordingly the question was discussed by a council of elders in Florence, and one of the number, Aldobrandino Ottobuoni, who, although poor and plebeian, had much influence as a patriot, asserted the necessity of demolishing the fortress. His proposal was carried, but with the proviso that it should be first submitted to the approval of the parliament. Meanwhile the Pisans, unaware of the result of the discussion and of Ottobuoni's amendment, but knowing that the castle, if held by the Lucchese, would be a serious menace to themselves, sent to offer Ottobuoni four thousand florins—in those days a prodigious sum—if he would address the council in favour of the very plan he had already pleaded with success. But this offer merely opened his eyes to the blunder he had committed, and returning to the council, he induced the elders to reverse their decision. Aldobrandino's reputation was so greatly enhanced by this affair, that on his death it was decreed that a monument should be erected to him in the Duomo of greater height than any other, and at the public expense. [263]

Many men were famed for their virtue in the time of the First Popular Government; but this government only lasted ten years, and a period of new reforms and revolutions, costing much travail to the Republic, is already near at hand.

VI.

The seeds of revolt were already lurking in the Constitution, and, as we have seen, only waiting a convenient opportunity to break forth. Nor was the moment long delayed. The Ghibelline party, after declining in consequence of

Frederic's decease, was now revived in Italy by the strenuous efforts of Manfred in its cause. This monarch's envoys finally came to Florence in 1258, and naturally made their abode with the Uberti, whom they found quite prepared to try the hazard of war. These nobles quickly assembled their adherents, and formed a plot for the overthrow of the popular government. But the times were not yet ripe, because, as Machiavelli has justly remarked, "In those days the Guelphs had much more power than the Ghibellines, partly because the people hated the latter for their arrogant conduct as rulers in Frederic's time; and partly because the side of the Church was in greater favour than that of the emperor, seeing that with the aid of the Church they [the Florentines] hoped to preserve their liberty, and feared to lose it under the emperor."[264] The conspiracy was soon discovered, in fact, and the Uberti were cited to appear before the elders. But, instead of obeying the summons, they barricaded themselves within their own dwellings by the advice of their chief, Farinata. Thereupon the enraged people flew to the assault; the houses of the Uberti were sacked; some of their friends captured, others killed, and no mercy shown even to those merely suspected of complicity. The Abbot of Vallombrosa, one of the Beccaria of Pavia, was beheaded, although his innocence was afterwards acknowledged by many.[265] The whole Uberti family and their principal followers had to seek safety in exile and fly to Sienna, the which city was the declared ally of Manfred, and the headquarters of all Tuscan Ghibellines. The exiles collected there chose Farinata, the most daring and influential member of the band, for their leader. Upon this the Florentines justly complained that the Siennese violated the treaty of 1255 by harbouring the fugitives; but Sienna, having been long the secret ally of the Ghibellines, was deaf to remonstrance.

Hence collision was inevitable, and Florence dealt the first blow by speedily attacking several castles and villages in the Siennese Maremma.[266] Then the *Martinella* was hung in the arch of the Mercato Nuovo, and repeatedly rang the alarm, announcing an expedition of far greater importance. Both sides began to prepare for war, and even summoned their friends to assemble. Florence had sent Brunetto Latini on an embassy to Alfonso of Castile, one of the aspirants to the Imperial crown, inviting him to march into Italy against Manfred. The Siennese, however, had already, and with greater hopes of success, applied for help, through the Florentine exiles, to Manfred in person. This monarch being much occupied with his own kingdom at the time, despatched Giordano d'Anglona, Count of San Severino, with about one hundred German knights, who reached Sienna in December, 1259, bearing the royal banner. At last, in April, 1260, the Florentines set forth with the *carroccio*, people and Commune in full array, with the *Podestà*

Iacopino Rangoni, the elders and leaders of companies at their head, and encamped close to the walls of Sienna, near Porta Camollia. On the 17th of May a battle took place on the site of the monastery of Santa Petronilla. It is related that when Farinata degli Uberti, who, as chief of the exiles, had done much to promote the war, saw how small a contingent Manfred had sent with the standard, he exclaimed: "We will lead it into such straits, that he [the king] will fain be the enemy of the Florentines, and will give us more [knights] than we shall want."[267] It is also told that the German soldiers were purposely intoxicated to make them fight with blind fury.[268] What is certain is that the Siennese citizens marched out under the command of their Podestà, and that the Germans, jointly with the exiles, of whom Farinata was still the chief, were led by Count Guido Novello. The Germans began the engagement with so furious an onslaught that the Florentines, believing a formidable army was on them, scattered in dismay; but then, perceiving the hostile force to be inferior to their own, stood their ground valiantly, and after a sanguinary mêlée repulsed the foe, and capturing Manfred's flag, dragged it in the mud. There was much rejoicing in Florence, although the victory had been dearly bought, and it was seen that a small band of well-trained German cavalry had put to the rout, at least for a moment, a large army of peasants and artisans. The Siennese derived courage from the same fact, particularly now that their chief citizen, Provenzano Salvani, and other ambassadors, were returning from Naples with a stout contingent of eight hundred[269] Germans, also under the command of Count Giordano, now promoted to the post of vicar-royal to Manfred in Tuscany.

Accordingly the war had to be pursued; for with the Siennese already in the field to subdue Staggia and Poggibonsi, and devastate Colle, Montalcino, and Montepulciano, the Florentines were compelled to resume hostilities. Farinata degli Uberti and his fellow-exiles continually cast fresh fuel on the flame by using every device of ingenuity to provoke their foes, and weave treasonable plots within the walls of Florence. In fact, two friars were sent there to inform the elders, with great affectation of secresy, that Sienna was weary of the Ghibellines and of Provenzano Salvani's domination, that accordingly it would be easy to have the gates opened to the Florentine army by means of a bribe of ten thousand florins. The friars, being deceived themselves, as it appears, had no difficulty in duping others. According to Villani's account, on arriving in the city, they asked leave to confer with two elders alone, under pledge of the strictest secresy. Two members were deputed to receive their proposals, who, believing the men to come from the exiles, sons of their own Republic, and forgetting how they had always been dominated by party hatred, accepted the false message in good faith.

Although great mystery was observed in the affair, yet it was necessary to consult the citizens before deciding on war. For that purpose a numerous council of nobles and *popolani* was assembled, and the elders, under more or less plausible pretexts, urged the necessity of quickly resuming the war against Sienna. Nevertheless, there was much disagreement. Although the Florentine laws opposed every possible check to general discussion, and especially when directed against any proposal brought forward by a magistrate,[270] the import of this question was seen to be so grave, that several speakers combated it, pointing out the enormous folly of plunging into war at this moment, when it was known that Sienna had no means of maintaining the Germans for long. The nobles were specially adverse to the proposal, for they had recognised the superiority of the German cavalry, and judged that no army composed of artisans and traders, little practised in war, could possibly make a stand against it, especially now that it was in much greater force. Also, seeing what progress had been already made in the art of war, battles could no more be won by deeds of personal prowess alone. Unluckily the opposition of the nobles inflamed the people in the contrary sense, and set them shouting that they must arm and march forth without delay. Tegghiaio Aldobrandi degli Adimari was one of the first patricians to speak against the proposal and in favour of delay. But an elder named Spedito, and, according to Villani, one of the two sharing the secret, replied to him in insulting terms, winding up with a coarse sneer at Adimari's supposed cowardice.[271] Whereupon Messer Tegghiaio retorted, exclaiming that Spedito would lack the courage to follow far at his heels in battle. After this squabble Cece Gherardini rose up and openly inveighed against the war proposed by the elders. The latter then insisted on his silence, in the name of the law, threatening to make him pay the fine of one hundred *lire* imposed by the statutes on all venturing to speak without the permission of the magistrates; but Gherardini replied that he would pay it and speak. Accordingly they increased the fine to two hundred, then to three hundred *lire*, but only succeeded in silencing him by threats of capital punishment.[272] So the motion for war was finally carried, although even without the secret intrigues retailed and exaggerated by the chroniclers, the heated state of public feeling made hostilities unavoidable.

The Florentine army was still commanded in 1260 by the same Podestà who had led it to battle the previous May. But it was now reinforced by all the Guelphs of Tuscany, from Perugia, Orvieto, Bölogna, and many other cities, so that its total strength amounted to thirty thousand foot and three thousand horse. This large force marched forth in the month of August, with all its chiefs, with the *Carroccio*, and a well-furnished baggage train, crossed the

Siennese border, and reaching Pieve Asciata on September 2nd, halted there to rest. The intrigues carried on by the exiles had produced two results; for on the one hand they had inspired Florence with the vain hope that Sienna could be gained without bloodshed, merely by spending money and making a great show of strength; on the other hand there were traitors in the army itself, actually pledged to secret agreements with the enemy. The first measure adopted was to send messengers to the city haughtily demanding its surrender. But when these envoys entered Sienna they found the whole population burning for war and revenge. They were solemnly received by the Council of Twenty-four, the heads of the State; and these, on hearing their demands, made reply: *"That they should have an answer, by word of mouth, in the field."* Hence the only thing to do was to prepare for a decisive engagement.

On the morning of the 3rd of September a herald went through the streets of Sienna calling on all men to hasten to join his own flag, "in the name of God and the Virgin Mary."[273] Thus a considerable army was collected and marched the same day to encounter the Florentines. The details supplied by the chroniclers are so discrepant that it is difficult to decide as to the exact strength of the force. The Germans, the exiled Ghibellines of Florence, and several contingents from allies swelled the Siennese ranks. Nevertheless the total number was certainly inferior to that of the enemy. According to custom, the Podestà, Francesco Troghisio, held the post of Commander-in-chief. But the actual leaders of the army were Count Giordano and Count D'Arras in command of the German horse and foot; Count Aldobrandino of Santa Fiora, and other valiant captains. The Florentine exiles, including Farinata degli Uberti, who was excited to the highest pitch, were under the command of Count Guido Novello. The army of Florence was also led by its Podestà, Jacopo Rangoni; but its captains were untrained men, who still clung to the hope of winning the victory without striking a blow. They advanced with the *Carroccio* as far as Monselvoli in Val di Biena, and encamped at a short distance from the Arbia stream and the fortress of Montaperti, some four miles from Sienna. On the morning of the 4th of September the Siennese, and more especially the Germans, began the battle by a tremendous onslaught. The Count of Arras kept his men in ambush in order to fall on the enemy's flank at the best moment. Until the hour of vespers, the Florentines made a steadfast resistance, but then began to show signs of failing strength. Thereupon Arras led up his reserve with cries of "St. George," and attacked them so furiously in flank that they were speedily routed. At the same moment Bocca degli Abati, one of the Florentine traitors, severed at a blow the hand of Jacopo dei Pazzi, the standard-bearer of the cavalry. As the flag fell the troop, composed almost entirely of nobles, instantly took to flight, some from panic, others with treasonable intent. But the infantry, consisting

145

of stout *popolani* and faithful allies, stood its ground for a time; then wavered, gave way, and was involved in the general rout. Only the guards of the *Carroccio*, commanded by Giovanni Tornaquinci, a veteran of seventy years, who fought like a lion, maintained their position until the last man fell dead defending the banner. Then, finally, the *Carroccio*, the *Martinella*, and the flag of the Republic were captured by the foe, who bore their spoil to Sienna in triumph and reduced it to atoms.[274] Great slaughter took place, and although many Florentines sought safety in the castle of Montaperti, crying, "Mercy, I surrender!" no mercy was shown them. Finally the Siennese captain, Count Giordano, by the advice of Farinata degli Uberti and with the consent of the gonfaloniers of the people, gave orders that the slaughter should be stopped, and safety granted to all who surrendered.[275] It is difficult to decide how many were killed on that fatal day. Villani, keeping to the minimum, states that all the cavalry escaped by flight, the slaughter being confined to the infantry, of whom 2,500 were killed and 1,500 captured. The Siennese, reducing their own losses to 600 killed and 400 wounded, estimate those of the Florentines at 10,000 killed, 15,000 taken prisoner, 5,000 wounded, and 18,000 horses either killed or strayed. These figures may be exaggerated, but Villani's are certainly below the real number.[276] Nevertheless, the chronicler shows the true state of things when he says in conclusion, "and then the ancient Florentine people was put to rout and annihilated."[277] This, in fact, was the ultimate result of the battle *"that stained the Arbia red"* (*"che fece l'Arbia colorata in rosso"*).

Sienna triumphed with great rejoicing, great festivities; but there was a terrible outcry and lamentation in Florence, where no family had escaped loss. The leading Guelphs knew that their last chance of safety had vanished, and therefore many of their noble families fled into exile together with a considerable number of *popolani*. They escaped from the city on the 13th of September, and although a few of them were scattered among the Tuscan castles, the majority repaired to Lucca, this being still the chief centre of the Guelph faction.

On the 16th of September Count Giordano entered Florence with his German troops, accompanied by the Ghibelline exiles laden with spoil and ready to play the conquerors. One of their first deeds was the destruction of the Ottobuoni monument in the Duomo, forgetful that whether Guelph or Ghibelline that virtuous citizen deserved honour as a patriot. Thus, from the beginning, the Ghibellines did their best to make themselves more detested and unbearable. Poggibonsi, Montalcino, and many of the castles which had cost so much strife, were given up to Sienna. The "ordinances of liberty" were annulled, and Count Giordano nominated Count Guido Novello Podestà of Florence for two years.[278] The latter immediately took possession of the Communal palace, and opened a road thence to the city walls, with the name it still bears of Via Ghibellina. Meanwhile sentences of banishment and persecution of all sorts befel the Guelphs. Their houses and towers were demolished, and their confiscated property devoted to the service of the Ghibelline cause, which was everywhere destined to triumph. Brunetto Latini was also condemned to exile. As we have seen, he had been an ambassador to Alphonso of Castile, and was now in France, where he wrote the "Tesoro" containing an account of his mission.

Count Giordano, being recalled to Naples by Manfred, soon took his departure, leaving Guido Novello to replace him. Thereupon all the Ghibelline chiefs met in council at Empoli to arrange what was to be done. As an instance of the pitch of ferocity to which party hatred against Florence had attained, it was proposed at this meeting to demolish the city walls, pull down all the houses, and reduce this "nest of Guelphs" to a mere suburb, since otherwise they would be sure to revive there once more. But Farinata degli Uberti had the generosity to oppose the suggestion, and in the impulse of his wrath clapped his hand on his sword-hilt, and declared to Count Giordano and the other captains that he had fought to regain his country, not to lose it, and would defend it against all would-be destroyers even more zealously than he had fought against the Guelphs.[279] These words caused the wild proposal to be instantly rejected.

Count Guido appointed several Ghibelline Podestà in Tuscany, while retaining the general government of that province in his own grasp, and likewise ruling Florence as vicar to King Manfred. He basely allowed himself to be the tool of Ghibelline vengeance, although his uncertainty of conduct and weakness of character did little service to the party. Nevertheless, the Guelphs continued to suffer persecution, not only in Florence, where confiscation of their property and destruction of their dwellings and towers were long the order of the day,[280] but also in the neighbouring castles and at Lucca, whence all fugitive Guelphs were expelled. It was on this occasion that Farinata degli Uberti, having seized Cece dei Buondelmonti, hoisted him on his saddle and carried him off, either to save his life, as some have said, or, according to another version, as prisoner of war. But his brother Pietro degli Uberti was so maddened at the sight, that he clubbed the captive to death on Farinata's horse. Such was the ferocity of party hatred at the time. After the defeat of 1260 many Guelphs wandered homeless about the world. Some devoted their swords to the service of their faction in Emilia, and became experts in the newest developments of military science; while others settled in

France as traders, thus giving a fresh and much increased impulse to Florentine commerce.

VII.

From the close of 1260, the year of the battle of Montaperti, down to 1266, when the rule of Count Guido and King Manfred came to an end, the history of Florence records no remarkable event. The city's freedom is crushed, its wars reduced to petty and inglorious party strife, and its new institutions, if worthy to be so called, have no effect on the historical development of the Florentine constitution. In trying to discover the logical connection between the various forms assumed by it in the history of the Republic, no attention need be given to the checks suffered by freedom nor to the intervals wherein tyranny breaks the regular course of events and institutions, seeing that these resume their normal march as soon as liberty is restored to life.

The Podestà ruling in Manfred's name retained the two councils, *i.e.*, the general council of three hundred, and the special of ninety members, in both of which the nobles and the Ghibellines naturally prevailed. But we hear nothing more of the Captain of the people and his councils, nor of the elders and their assembly. But we find in their place a body of twenty-four citizens, four to each *sestiere*, privileged to sit in council with the Podestà.[281] Of the ancient Constitution a few fragments alone remain, and even these are ancient only in name. As a matter of fact the Ghibellines had succeeded, with Manfred's assistance, in establishing an aristocratic despotism, as strangely different from the constitution preceding it as from that destined to replace it, these being in perfect harmony and connection one with the other.

Meanwhile the war against the Guelphs was carried on, not only by razing their houses and confiscating their goods, but by the imposition of repeated fines weighing heavily on the lower classes who were now deprived of all share in the government. But in 1264 Farinata degli Uberti died, in 1265 Dante Alighieri was born, and Italy began to be stirred by novel events soon to be echoed even in Florence.

For some time past, in truth, Italian politics had showed signs of approaching to a radical change. Frederic II., although often cruelly despotic, had gathered about him, nevertheless, all the most cultured men of the country and was highly popular among them. His successor, Manfred, was an adventurous and unfortunate prince, whose loftiness of spirit deservedly gained him numerous admirers. It is true that the Papacy had combated both in their quality of Ghibellines; but the policy of Rome was gradually becoming no less hostile to communal freedom than to the Ghibelline cause, inasmuch as the Papal ambition daily increased and sought to strengthen the temporal power at the expense of the communes. Florence still remained Guelph; but with changed times the character and value, if not the names of parties were beginning to suffer alteration throughout Italy. Hence men often changed sides with small hesitation, nor was it always easy to say whether those who deserted their own party had changed, or whether the alteration of the party itself had caused it to be forsaken. Also the general confusion was greatly increased now that the Popes, with their usual anxiety and dread of losing their supremacy in Italy, resolved on calling fresh strangers to their aid and thus drew fresh miseries on the land.

Alarmed by the great power and reputation gained by the Swabian line, they sought defence in the course of policy so well described by Machiavelli when he remarks that the Popes, "sometimes for the love of religion, at others to forward their own ambitions, never ceased to call fresh humours into Italy and stir fresh wars. And no sooner had they raised a prince to power than they repented and sought to compass his ruin, nor would they consent that any province their own weakness prevented them from seizing should be possessed by another."[282] Thus, after many persistent intrigues, they finally decided the Angevins to undertake an expedition against Manfred, and for the conquest of the Neapolitan kingdom.

With the aid and benediction of Pope Clement IV., Charles of Anjou brought an army composed not only of his own subjects, but of many Italians, among whom the exiled Florentine Guelphs were some of the most distinguished for bravery.[283] He advanced to the Neapolitan frontier, and near Benevento, on February 26, 1266, gave battle to the foe. King Manfred fought valiantly, and when forsaken and betrayed by his soldiery, died the death of a hero on the field. For three days, vain search was made for his corpse among the slain, then it was found, and carried off on the back of an ass. The French monarch refused Manfred burial in consecrated ground, because the Pope had declared him excommunicate. Accordingly he was laid in a ditch by the bridge of Benevento, where the French soldiers, casting each a stone on the corpse, raised a pile that proved a fitting monument to the courage and ill fortune of a warrior slain sword in hand. But Pope Clement grudged him even this humble grave, and at his command the Archbishop of Cosenza persuaded the Angevin monarch to have the corpse exhumed, and thrown beyond the frontier of the Neapolitan kingdom, on the banks of the river Verde.[284] All these events completed the overthrow of the Ghibelline party in Italy. The

Imperial throne stood vacant, the Suabians were crushed, and another foreign dynasty succeeded them in Naples, summoned thither by the Pope. If Frederic's decease had caused the decline of the Ghibellines in Florence, it is easy to imagine what was to befal them now that their evil sway had accumulated such increased detestation of their rule, and that the death of Manfred not only deprived them of a friendly sovereign, but extinguished in Italy the domination of an Imperial and royal line that had been their strongest support.

In fact, when the result of the campaign was announced in Florence, the whole population was moved and stirred to fresh courage against the nobles still holding rule over them. And when it was known that the majority of the Florentine Guelphs, who had done such brave service in the ranks of King Charles, were returning to Florence under his flag, the populace seemed so ready to revolt that Count Guido and his followers were stricken with fear. Therefore, as Machiavelli says, "the Ghibellines judged it well to conciliate by some acts of beneficence the people they had hitherto overwhelmed with injuries; but although these remedies would have succeeded had they been applied before the emergency arose, now, on the contrary, being used too late, not only failed of effect, but hastened the party's ruin."[285] In fact, when Count Guido and the Ghibelline leaders sought to pacify the people by certain liberal concessions they knew not where to begin. The old laws had been annulled, and these men had so completely alienated the people by their arbitrary government and exactions, that no concession could now be made without yielding on all points. On the other hand, the people, being excluded from all share in the management of the State, had turned to trade and commerce, employing therein all the power and energy they were forbidden to bring to bear upon politics. Accordingly all branches of trade were marvellously developed and organised more firmly than before in the shape of politico-industrial associations, entitled Greater and Lesser Guilds (*Arti maggiori ed Arti minori*), the which, dating from the earliest years of the Middle Ages, had gradually become significant political forces, and exercised very great civic influence. Thus many new powerful families had arisen, constituting a new aristocracy, as it were, of wealthy traders, or, according to the designation already bestowed on them, of *popolani grassi* (stout burghers) now the virtual masters of the Florentine citizens.[286] Gradually, therefore, the Ghibellines in power were reduced to an isolated caste, and only enabled to maintain their position by Manfred's friendly support and the help of his German contingent. Being accordingly in the attitude of invaders encamped on alien soil, their moral and political ascendency, their civil authority daily declined; while the burghers under their rule had won by means of trade and commerce a separate world for themselves and constituted a separate body, independent to some extent of the governing authorities. It was both difficult and dangerous to seek the help of the leading burghers, for these, being chiefs of the Guelph population, would undoubtedly insist on giving the latter a share in the government, the which would lead to the speedy downfall of the nobles and Ghibellines. Neither was it easy for the nobles to initiate partial reforms, since they neither knew what concessions to make, nor how to grant any at a moment when the people were conscious of sufficient strength to dominate the city. It was accordingly decided to summon from Bologna two knights of a new order known as the *Frati Gaudenti*, whose mission it was to succour widows and orphans and reconcile hostile parties. Also, as a visible sign of impartiality, one of the chosen knights was to be a Guelph, the other a Ghibelline. All this was arranged with the consent and almost at the instance of Pope Clement IV., who, being of Provençal birth and a strenuous supporter of Charles of Anjou, continually addressed imperious missives to the Florentines,[287] as though the Imperial throne being vacant, its authority had devolved upon himself, and the victory gained by King Charles had made him master of Florence.

But, according to Villani's account, the short-lived order of Frati Gaudenti consisted of men chiefly devoted to their own pleasures, and little fitted for the serious task of acting as Podestà of Florence, and promoting novel reforms there. This was so evident that the two knights speedily saw the necessity of consulting and coming to an understanding with the guilds. Therefore, on reaching the city, they made their abode in the palace of the Commune, and convoked a council of thirty-six Guelph and Ghibelline merchants. The members soon began to hold daily discussions in their meeting-place, the court of the Calimala, or Clothdressers' Guild. The business of dressing foreign woollen stuffs had made great progress in Florence, and the guild was more powerful than any of the others. The council soon agreed that the first measure proposed should be the conversion of the seven greater guilds into an industrial and political body, with special banners, weapons, and chiefs of its own. So they began to organise all the details, assigning a gonfalon to each guild, and arranging them as follows: Judges and Notaries; Calimala, or Dressers of Foreign Cloth; Woollen Trade; Money- changers; Physicians and Druggists; Silk Trade, and Fur Trade. The Ghibellines, however, foresaw that this course would inevitably lead to the reconstruction of the *Primo Popolo* under another name. Accordingly the Uberti, Lamberti, Fifanti, and Scolari decidedly opposed these innovations, and impressed Count Guido with the necessity of putting a stop to them at once if he wished to keep the government in his grasp. This being precisely what the count most desired, he instantly sent to demand aid from Ghibelline cities. Arezzo, Sienna, Pisa, Pistoia, Colle, and San Gimignano contributed some cavalry, which, with his German guard, raised his forces to fifteen hundred. But, although these troops were under Count Guido's command, they were also at his expense; his Germans were already clamouring for their pay, and all his money was spent. Accordingly, while still negotiating terms of agreement with the people, he decided to levy an additional income tax of ten per cent. in Florence. But the citizens were already so heavily burdened that this new impost was more than small fortunes could support. The people were already weary of misgovernment, and much irritated by the count's action in stripping the Communal palace of its armoury to enrich his own castle at Poppi; also being encouraged by commercial success and increasingly hostile to the Ghibellines, they now made vigorous protest, and clearly showed their readiness to fly to arms. Then the Council of Thirty-six tried to pacify the citizens, and acting as mediators, proposed to undertake the collection of the new tax, levying it in such wise as to make it fall chiefly on the rich and powerful.

Just then, however, the nobles, emboldened by the arrival of reinforcements, thought the moment had arrived for a decisive blow, and rose to arms in the city. The Lamberti took the initiative by rushing to the Piazza, sword in hand, shouting, "Out with these thieves, the Thirty-six; let us cut them to pieces!" At this outcry all shops were closed; the Thirty-six broke up their council, and the people rising in revolt took their orders from them and from the consuls of the guilds, with Giovanni Soldanieri as their leader-in- chief. The latter was a patrician, urged by personal ambition to join the riot at the head of the people. Concentrating in Piazza St. Trinità, they were soon attacked by Count Guido and his cavalry, who thought to make short work of them. But, on the contrary, the crowd threw up barricades and made a stubborn resistance, while such a storm of stones and darts rained down from windows and roofs that the Germans began to lose heart, and the count, stricken with dismay, ordered his standards to withdraw, retreated to Piazza St. Giovanni, and then hurrying to the two *Gaudenti* in the Communal palace, demanded the keys of the town in order to effect his escape. Neither his friends' supplications nor the wrath of his followers could persuade him that the danger was not serious, and that he might safely remain in the town. He was so bewildered by fear that, having obtained the keys, he insisted on being escorted by three of the Thirty-six, lest he should be shot from some window by the way. So, on St. Martin's Day, November 11, 1266, he left Florence by the so-called Gate of the Oxen, and fled with his followers to Prato.

The following day, being cured of his panic, he perceived his mistake, and by the advice of the Florentine Ghibellines in his company tried, as Machiavelli puts it, "to recapture by force the city he had forsaken from cowardice." 288 He came with his men in order of battle as far as the Gate by the Carraia Bridge, on the site of the present Borgo Ognissanti; but the people who could have scarcely succeeded in expelling him before, save for his own exaggerated fears, had no difficulty in repulsing him now. When the count demanded admission with a mixture of threats and entreaties, the only reply was a shower of arrows from the walls. He was therefore compelled to retreat, and his men were so enraged and humiliated that on the way back they tried to capture a neighbouring castle in order to prove their strength. But even this small attempt failed, and they reached Prato more humbled than ever, and with much dissension in their ranks. The count, convinced of the hopelessness of recovering the state, sought refuge in the Casentino, and the Florentine Ghibellines dispersed to various fortresses and mansions about the *contado*.

VIII.

The Guelphs were now masters of Florence. They set to work at the changes required for the reorganisation of the popular government, and were favoured with much imperious advice from the Pope. However, they only gave heed to his epistles in sufficient measure to avoid exciting his wrath. Their first act was the dismissal of the two *Gaudenti* friars, whose incapacity had been well proved; their next to request Orvieto to furnish them with a Captain of the people, a Podestà, and a body of knights to guard the safety of the Commune. Accordingly one hundred knights arrived, with Messer Ormanno Monaldeschi as Podestà, and a Messer Bernardini as Captain. For the sake of peace they allowed the Ghibellines to return to Florence, and arranged various reconciliations and marriages between them and the Guelphs, hoping thus to promote unity among the people and mitigate party hatred. But, in the still heated state of the public mind, these measures only excited fresh rancour.

At this juncture Florence seemed to have lost all her former self-reliance, so that, in the midst of the grave complications of Italian politics, even the Guelphs felt the need of foreign support. It was a fatal habit, first owed to the Ghibellines, who, in token of respect toward the Empire, had requested the presence of an Imperial vicar in Florence. So, now that the people had won the victory because the Angevins had succeeded the Suabian line on the Neapolitan throne, recurrence to the same perilous measure seemed almost unavoidable. The Pope, with an assumption of Imperial prerogative, had nominated Charles of Anjou, first as peacemaker, and then as actual vicar-imperial, in Tuscany, for a term of ten years. The Florentines considering it a duty to conform with this new state of things, and even to accept it with a good grace, accordingly offered Charles the lordship of their city for six years, a term afterwards extended to ten. But either because the conditions attached to the offer were distasteful to the French monarch, or because he wished it to be pressed more energetically, he certainly showed much hesitation in deciding to accept it. Shortly afterwards he despatched to Florence Philip de Monfort, who made his entry with eight hundred knights on Easter Day, 1267, the anniversary, as it was remarked at the time, of Buondelmonti's assassination. The king subsequently sent Guy de Monfort as his vicar;[289] and at last came in person to lead the war against the Ghibellines in Tuscany.

The Ghibellines being now expelled, and the supremacy of Charles accepted as an accomplished fact, the necessity remained of establishing the government of Florence on a definite basis, and endeavouring to secure its freedom amid new and hazardous complications. To this end the fourth constitution of the Republic was evolved. The state of Florentine society had undergone considerable change, and this implied a corresponding change in the character of the new constitution. The Ghibelline or patrician party was now reduced to a small number of nobles, soldiers by profession, and eager to exercise tyranny. But, as we have seen, almost a new aristocracy had come to the front, composed of nobles, who, renouncing their titles and altering their names, had joined the popular side, and likewise of well-to-do burghers (*popolo grasso*), who, having leapt to fortune as traders, had now entered a new sphere of civil life, and dominated the city.[290] Another point to be noted is that both burghers and populace were rapidly losing their aptitude for arms, and this not merely because in all wars of the period the superiority of trained soldiers was a recognised fact, and popular armies seen to be of small use, but also because commerce had become too important for busy traders, engaged in their shops or travelling about the world, to be able, as in past times, to spend two or three months of the year in the field. Commerce was now the chief occupation and almost the very life of the Florentines, so that they really deserved to be called a people of bankers and merchants.

In addition to all this there was now a foreign power upheld by foreign soldiery in Florence. Whether in person or by means of other officials of his own nomination, Charles of Anjou filled the post of Podestà of the city, and even the Captain of the people was often a man of his choice. Therefore, with their usual sagacity, the Florentines re-established the twelve elders, two for each *sestiere*, under the name of the Twelve Worthies, as advisers to the Podestà. Also, in place of the Thirty-six, they constituted a council of one hundred worthies of the people, "without whose sanction no important measure nor any expenditure was to be undertaken." With this council and with the parliament, which legally, at all events, never ceased to exist in Florence, we see the reconstitution of a central and popular government, limiting the authority of the Angevin Podestà.

It was, indeed, almost a revival of the old consular government by which the Podestà and Captain, now to be made subordinate to it, had been originally raised to power. Nor did matters stop at this point. The two councils, special and general, of the Podestà and Captain were likewise repristinated. With this difference, however, that whereas by the constitution of 1250 the Captain of the people had been second in command, and then almost abolished under the Ghibelline sway, now at this date he not only resumed his functions, but was given precedence over the Podestà.

In fact, any Bill proposed by the Twelve to the Hundred and approved by the latter, was passed on to the Captain's two councils, in the first place to his special council of the *capitudini*—also known as the *credenza*—consisting, as formerly, of eighty members. Approved by this assembly, the Bill was then proposed to the council-general and special and of the *capitudini*, comprising three hundred members. As a rule, all the three councils put it to the vote the same day. Then, on the following day, the Bill was presented to both the councils of the Podestà, first to the special council of ninety, next to the general council of three hundred, sometimes increased to 390 by deliberating jointly with the special assembly. We know very little regarding the mode of election to these councils, but they usually lasted six months. Nevertheless, as they were very large and, on the other hand, the number of the citizens was small, we opine that all eligible persons—*abili a sedere*, namely, fully qualified citizens—must have been chosen in turn. It should also be added that projected motions were neither all nor invariably submitted to every one of these different councils. Both by law and usage the magistrates were often privileged to recur to certain councils only, even as they were allowed the right of assembling a preliminary and more restricted council of *richiesti* (or invited persons), composed solely of officials or citizens whose experience might be useful in drawing up the required schemes. At other times even a few outsiders were invited to the councils. Thus, for instance, when affairs of war were under discussion the presence was requested of those charged to superintend them. The statutes were neither very precise nor very stringent on this point. Special efforts, however, seem to have been used to put checks on free discussion, possibly to prevent the multitude of councils from causing undue delay. The right of proposing any measure or decree was strictly reserved to magistrates, by whom some notary or other qualified person was commissioned to support it in their name. Save in very grave cases, the councillors only said a few words before voting. The opposition was never more than a small minority, partly because every project brought before the councils had been already sifted several times. Later on, while still allowing men to vote against the magisterial proposals, no one was permitted to speak save in their favour. Hence, in spite of possessing so many public assemblies, Italy produced no real political oratory, and in fact our literature is very poor in this branch of eloquence. And another point should also be noted here. The Council of One Hundred was entirely plebeian, so too those of the Captain; on the other hand, nobles, as well as plebeians, sat in the Podestà's councils. The *capitudini*, or guild-masters, were always admitted, as we have shown, to the Captain's councils, and very frequently also to those of the Podestà. All this plainly proves that the democratic party and the greater guilds constituting its main nucleus were decidedly predominant.[291] Thus, although King Charles obtained the lordship of Florence, his power was fettered by so many restrictions that all administrative authority remained vested in the people, and particularly in the well-to-do burgher class (*popolograsso*).

The new laws examined by us contain very few allusions to Guelphs and Ghibellines, many to nobles and people (*grandi* and *popolani*); for party conflict was beginning to wear its real name, and plainly signified the struggle between the aristocracy and democracy. Nevertheless, the Ghibelline faction still survived and constituted in fact the aristocratic party. For this reason the people desired its total destruction, and another clause of the new constitution aimed at the same result. A list was drawn up of all who had suffered persecution from the Ghibellines between 1260 and 1266, together with an inventory of their confiscated property. The number of victims was found to be very great, and their losses to amount to the then enormous sum of 132,160,8,4 *lire*.[292] It was accordingly resolved to treat the Ghibellines in the same way, and during the years 1268 and 1269 about three thousand were condemned, including contumacious rebels, and as many sentences of confiscation pronounced, which remained enforced for a long period.[293] At first, all confiscated property was collected to form a so-called "*monte*," or fund; then afterwards it became the custom to divide this into three parts: one to the Commune; one to individual Guelphs as indemnity for past losses; and the other third to the party, in order to strengthen it at the Ghibellines' expense. In course of time, however, almost all confiscated estates were granted to the party alone, and their administration entrusted to six governors, chosen for the purpose, three of whom were nobles and three men of the people. These officials were originally styled consuls of the knights, then captains of the Guelph party, in deference to the ill-omened counsels of Pope Clement IV. and Charles of Anjou. As every important magistracy of the time was associated with two councils, so the Captains of the party also possessed a special or privy council of fourteen, and a council-general of sixty members.[294] The Captains kept office for two months, and held their sittings in the Church of Sta. Maria sopra Porta. Later on they had a palace of their own, and were entrusted with the superintendence of public works, of the officials of the Towers, and other functions of a similar kind. But their chief duty was always to promote the cause and persecute Ghibellines. They performed their task with so much zeal, pursuing their adversaries so fiercely, that at last the ruling spirit among the Captains of the party was the virtual ruler of Florence. By excluding all opponents from public posts, sentencing them to exile, and confiscating their goods, these functionaries rose to increasing power, and injured the Republic they served.

Taking a general view of the new constitution, with all its intricate multiplicity of councils and magistracies, our first impression is that all was confusion and arbitrary rule. But on looking more closely into the purpose for which it had been formed, we are obliged to admit that this government was singularly well adapted for success. Civil war is not yet stamped out: on the contrary, must undoubtedly continue for a long time; democracy is pressing on towards the fulness of its triumph and the complete destruction of the aristocracy. Nor will democracy be satisfied with ousting the nobles from the government of the republics, but will seek to deprive them of life itself, and this is only to be accomplished by much bloodshed and many revolutions.

In the new political organisation, the central power, soon to be changed every two months, occupies a very feeble position compared with the high importance, permanence, and strength now assigned to the Podestà and the Captain. These officers are at the head of the Commune and the people; each of them presides over two councils: they are, as it were, the chiefs of two armed and hostile republics. But in that of the people, hitherto the weaker, no patrician is admitted; while in that of the Commune, the people has assumed a very important position relatively to that of the nobles, and therefore has legally obtained the casting vote in all decisions, notwithstanding the supremacy virtually exercised by Charles of Anjou in moments of the gravest emergency. It is easy to foresee the bitterness of strife to be engendered by this state of things. If we likewise remember that this Republic, as though foredoomed to civil war, included so important a magistracy as the Captains of the party, apparently created for the sole purpose of perpetuating discord, as an engine of war, serving to keep all these heterogeneous forces in continual agitation and promote ceaseless bloodshed and destruction, we can understand the course of coming events in Florence. We must be prepared for continual struggles, restless changes of institutions and laws, prepared to behold webs carefully woven one month pulled to pieces before the next moon begins to wane. Nevertheless, the whole machinery of the government was singularly fitted to compass the end that the Republic from the first had constantly in view.

IX.

Much more, however, remains to be said in order to give our readers a lucid and adequate idea of the Constitution and society of Florence in the latter half of the thirteenth century. So far we have dwelt too slightly on the most important detail of the new reforms—*i.e.*, the organisation of the guilds. The measures suggested for this purpose by the Thirty-six from their first meetings in the Calimala Court, and against which the nobles had most strongly protested, were speedily approved by the people, and from that moment became the chief basis of the Florentine statutes. Associations of arts and trades had existed throughout Italy from a very early date, and had soon attained greater development in Florence than in other communes. For, as we have had occasion to note, the whole life of the people was concentrated in these associations when the Ghibelline tyranny, upheld by Manfred, excluded the lower classes from participation in the government of the city. Therefore all that was done now was to embody naturally evolved results in a more regular and legal shape. Only the greater guilds, seven in number, had risen to any really great political importance in 1260; the others had to wait much longer before being reorganised on the same footing. What was the position attained by the seven greater guilds at the moment we are now studying? By devoting our attention to the guild that was first and foremost in the race it will serve as a model, and enlighten us as to the others.

At the period of which we treat the fine arts flourished in Italy side by side with trade, and this was not only advantageous to the national culture, but already enabled our manufactures to dictate the laws of taste to all Europe. In those times Florence, Milan,[295] and Venice set the fashions, as Paris sets them now. The fine Italian taste helped to create the *Calimala*[296] trade, and secured its rapid prosperity. This trade was the art of dressing foreign cloths—from Flanders, France, and England—and dyeing them with colours known to Florence alone. Then, in their finished state, these stuffs were sent to all the European markets stamped with the mark of the Calimala Guild. This mark was highly prized as a proof of good quality, as showing that the exact length of the pieces had been scrupulously verified in Florence, and as a guarantee against any falsification of material. It is therefore easy to see why the Calimala merchants had trading relations with all Europe, and interests extending to every place where civilisation and luxury were known.

Hence the necessity, even in early times, of choosing directors of the guild, framing statutes, and appointing consuls abroad as well as at home, to protect its undertakings. Now, however, with the newly inaugurated reforms, the Calimala, together with the other greater guilds, was constituted on the

lines of a miniature republic.²⁹⁷

Every six months, *i.e.*, in June and December, the heads of warehouses and shops held a meeting, and this *Union*—exercising much the same function in the guild as that of the parliament in the Republic—chose the electors to be charged with the nomination of the magistrates. First came four consuls, who administered justice according to the statutes, acted as representatives of the guild, and ruled it with the assistance of two councils, one being a special council with a minimum of twelve members, and the other a general assembly often varying in number and sometimes limited to eighteen. With the consent of these councils the consuls were even empowered to alter the statutes. They carried the banner of the guild, and in emergencies the citizens assembled at arms under their command. Then there was the *camarlingo*, or chamberlain, holding office for one year, who administered the revenue and expenditure of the association. And even as the Republic had a foreign magistrate in the person of the Podestà, so the guild had one also in the person of its notary, likewise appointed for one year. He was chosen by the council-general, had to speak in both councils as the representative of the consuls; was often employed on missions for the guild, and was specially charged to enforce scrupulous observation of the statutes, with the power of inflicting severe punishment on all violators of the same, were they even the consuls themselves. All these officials were sworn adherents of the Guelph party. The notary's stipend was fixed from year to year. The consuls were bound to accept office if elected, and could not be re- elected under an interval of one year; their salary was first fixed at ten *lire*, and the product of certain fines; but was afterwards reduced to several pounds of pepper and saffron, and a few wooden baskets and spoons. The *camarlingo*, or *camerario*, was remunerated even more slightly, and much in the same way. Three accountants were chosen every year to investigate the actions of the outgoing consuls, *camarlingo*, and other magistrates. Twelve statutory merchants were similarly elected, with authority to revise and improve the statutes of the guild; but all reforms suggested by them had to be approved first by both councils, and then by the Captain of the people. The consuls who, under the title of *capitudini*, took part in the councils of the Captain and Podestà, were pledged to protect the interests of the guild and advocate laws in its favour. But what were these statutes for the good of the trade of which so many magistrates enforced the observance? They prescribed fixed rules and regulations for the exercise of the business. Very severe punishments were enacted when the merchandise was of bad quality, defective, or counterfeit. Every piece of cloth was bound to be labelled, and any stain or rent unrecorded by this label entailed punishment on the merchant concerned. Above all, there was great strictness as to exactness of

measure. The officers of the guild frequently inspected the cloth, and made a bi-monthly examination of the measures used in all the shops. Models of the prescribed measures were exhibited to the public in certain parts of the city. Nor was this all. The consuls sent delegates to every counting-house to verify the merchants' books and accounts, and punished every deviation from established rules. Every guild had a tribunal composed either solely of its own members, or jointly with those of another, for the settlement of all disputes connected with the trade, and enforced severe penalties on all who referred such disputes to ordinary courts. It may be asked how the consuls were enabled to give effect to their verdicts? The punishments were generally fines, and persons refusing to pay them, after receiving several admonitions and increased fines if still recalcitrant, were excluded from the guild and practically ruined. From that moment their merchandise, being unstamped, was no longer guaranteed by the guild; they also lost many other notable advantages, and were finally unable to continue their business in Florence, and not often elsewhere. In fact, as we have seen, the consuls chosen in Florence guarded the interests of the guild even outside the State by deputing vice-consuls for that purpose to other parts of Italy and Europe, and increasing their number in proportion with the increase of their commercial relations. The two more important consuls abroad were those in France. All these delegates were charged with even the choice of the inns to be frequented by the members of the guild. Whenever, according to the usage of the day, any state exercised reprisals on the members' goods, the consuls were bound to assist and defend them. Thus, wherever he might be, a member of the guild was sure of protection from every sort of injury or loss. The guild was a jealous custodian of its members' rights, and, in order to defend them in foreign countries or to obtain justice for injuries received, often despatched ambassadors to the governments concerned.[298] This was an invaluable help at a time when no international law existed for the protection of foreigners, and reprisals were continually used. Accordingly merchants found it better to submit to any penalty rather than be dismissed from the guild; no worse threat was needed to enforce obedience to the statutes. The six other greater guilds were all governed on the same principle as the *Calimala*. Their united body of consuls formed the *capitudini*, and these were afterwards headed by a proconsul, a magistrate held in the highest esteem.

Putting aside the immense commercial and industrial advantages that this organisation of the guilds afforded to the Republic during the thirteenth century, we shall see that they were equally useful from the political point of view. All these merchants, constituting a large majority of the citizens, were continually engaged in directing great undertakings, settling commercial disputes, discussing statutes and laws; they maintained relations with all parts of the known world, and travelled to all parts on special missions in defence of their common interests. We see that they all took a continuous and eager share in political life, inasmuch as every guild was an independent, self-ruling institution, with separate magistrates, laws, statutes, and councils, and that it became a centre of industrial, intellectual, and political activity. Thanks to this freedom of circulation, the pulse of the Florentine people was quickened to redoubled strength, and every faculty of the human mind, all moral and political energy of which man is capable, suddenly rose to a prodigious height in Florence. Choosing any one of these merchants almost at random, one might be sure to find him capable of governing the Republic; a man to be trusted with the most delicate of diplomatic missions, and honourably acquit himself of it; one able to command a respectful hearing from Pope, king, or emperor, without allowing himself to be duped, yet without failing to conform to the requirements of court ceremonial. Thus the Florentines rose to great fame throughout Europe for their shrewdness and subtlety, and as in the midst of all this extraordinary commercial and political activity Italian art and literature also developed, the small mercantile Republic soon shed its lustre over the whole world.

The greater guilds also achieved another good result in Florence. At a time when the State organisation divided the city in two halves, as it were; at a time when the strife of factions was about to be fiercely renewed, when party leaders excited men's passions by nourishing the flame of discord, and the continual change of the supreme Council of Twelve transferred the direction of the government to citizens of all tempers, and all devoted to their respective parties, then the decentralisation of the government in a large number of small associations was indeed an inestimable benefit. If nobles or people rebelled against their rulers in order to change the Twelve, or the Podestà, the Captain, or even the statutes, the suspension of public business that inevitably ensued produced much less real than apparent confusion. Being split up into so many small associations, the Republic could exist without a government even for several months; since the armed, disciplined, and strongly constituted guilds, were now even better prepared than in past times to seize the reins, and prevent the troubles which would have certainly befallen the city had it been left without guidance. Thus the constitution of the guilds, as established in 1266, likewise serves to explain how it was that poetry, painting, sculpture, and architecture were enabled to flourish among a people of traders; even as it explains why so much progress was possible amid such, apparently, enormous confusion, and how democracy succeeded in destroying every relic of feudalism in Florence, and in achieving absolute equality together with the highest degree of freedom known to the Middle Ages. The Florentine Commune was the centre of so much culture because it was also the seat of the largest freedom compatible with the times. Of this culture the best and loveliest fruits are owed to the democracy; for we find in Arnolfo's towers and churches, in the paintings of Cimabue and Giotto, as also in Dante's verse, the special stamp and characteristic of the Florentine people. During the Middle Ages in Provence, France, Germany, and England, many nobles rose to literary fame, and indeed nearly all the poets of those lands were of patrician birth. But Florentine art and letters, constituting the most fertile seeds of art and letters in Italy, were essentially republican; many writers, and most of the artists, of Florence were the offspring of traders or labouring men.

CHAPTER V.

FLORENCE THE DOMINANT POWER IN TUSCANY.[299]

I.

AFTER the death of Frederic II., the Imperial throne long remained vacant. For twenty-three years no king of the Romans was definitively proclaimed in Germany, and sixty-two years elapsed before any prince came to Rome to assume the crown of the Empire. Therefore during this interval the Ghibelline party was left to its own resources, and its leaders tried to maintain their feudal rights by employing their forces and prestige against all communes and small potentates enjoying no chance of gaining the Imperial protection. Hence petty tyrants began to arise on all sides, Ghibelline lords for the most part, who, notwithstanding the many defeats endured by the aristocracy in Italy, derived new and unexpected advantages from the changed conditions of the times. Another factor of this result was the new mode of warfare. Men-at-arms were now the chief strength of an army, and these mounted soldiers, cased as well as their horses, in heavy armour and armed with long spears, were able to overcome infantry before the latter's halberds could come into play. But a lengthy training was required for cavalry service, and it was increasingly difficult for artisans or merchants to pursue the military career to any effect, whereas war was becoming the chief occupation of the nobles. In fact, many of the leading patricians were acquiring a reputation in the new mode of war, gaining followers, and by taking the command of small companies gradually rising to power, and aspiring to become tyrants. For this and other reasons, to be made clearer farther on, nearly all the Lombard cities, and some of those in Central Italy, were now losing their independence.

PALAZZO VECCHIO, FLORENCE.

[To face page 241

The same ambitions doubtless existed among the Guelphs, but the feudal aristocracy had far less influence in their party, the majority of which consisted of merchants and wealthy men of the people. Besides, the Pope was a near neighbour during the interregnum of the Empire, the Guelph cities were at the same time under the dangerous protection of an ambitious pontiff, and that of the equally ambitious Charles I. of Anjou, peacemaker and vicar- imperial of Tuscany. Charles nominated the Podestà of every Guelph Tuscan city, and whenever he failed to appear in person, sent a representative, called by the chroniclers a royal *maliscalco*, with an escort of some hundred horse and foot. Pisa, Arezzo, and all other Ghibelline cities refusing to acknowledge his authority, were exposed to continual threats from without, and lacerated within their walls by the attacks of would-be tyrants. On the other hand, the Guelph cities lived in continual terror of the king's ambitious designs; but Charles's position was not sufficiently assured for him to be able to use his temporary and limited office as a pretext for asserting sovereign power over

Tuscany, although such was his secret aim. For the moment it was enough to play the part of high protector of all civic rights and privileges, so that the Guelph cities might be tricked into counting on his help both against Ghibelline attacks from without and internal treason in favour of tyranny.

The Florentines, however, were not easily hoodwinked regarding either future or present events. They had asked Charles to accord them his protection, but only within certain limits, which, at any cost, they were determined should not be overstepped. They too nourished a secret aim— namely, to use the king's forces, not for the increase of his power, but towards the establishment of their own supremacy in Tuscany. The authority of the Empire was much diminished in Italy; the temporal strength of the Papacy was also on the wane, and the Communes, realising their greater independence, hastened to enlarge their respective territories. All Italian cities now had this end in view. But if one city waxed powerful, all its neighbours had either to pursue the same course or become its prey. Thus there was continual war between this and that city, less from party strife or jealousy than in necessary defence of their own interests. Besides, with the new custom of hiring foreign soldiers and captains of adventure, any one with gold at his command could quickly collect a powerful force and attack some of his neighbours. Hence every city or state had to be always on the alert and continually enlarging its strength and power. It was for this purpose that the Florentines now resolved to turn to account the authority, prestige, and forces of King Charles.

Accordingly when (1267) his mandatories, the Podestà Emilio di Corbano,[300] and Marshal Philip de Montfort,[301] with eight hundred French knights, arrived in Florence, a Florentine army, composed of recruits from two *sestieri* of the city, in junction with the French cavalry under Montfort, immediately marched to the siege of St. Ilario, or St. Ellero, in which castle a number of Ghibellines had sought refuge with their leader, Filippo da Volognano. The castle was taken, and its eight hundred Ghibelline defenders were all either killed or captured.[302] They comprised many members of the highest Florentine nobility, Uberti, Fifanti, Scolari, &c., and party hatred was then so fierce that a youthful scion of the Uberti, finding surrender inevitable, threw himself from the top of a tower to avoid falling into the hands of the Buondelmonti.[303] In the course of this campaign the castles of Campi and Gressa were captured; and many cities, including Lucca, Pistoia, Volterra, Prato, San Gimignano, and Colle, being won over to the Guelph cause by the expulsion of their Ghibellines, joined the Florentines in the League, or *Taglia*, commanded by the French marshal.

Pisa and Sienna still remained Ghibelline; the former had always been and still continued to be the strongest bulwark of the party in Tuscany; the latter had, as usual, given refuge to the banished Ghibellines of Florence, and also to some of Manfred's Germans who had escaped the massacre of Benevento. The Florentines had not yet succeeded in revenging the rout of Montaperti, and were burning to pluck this thorn from their side; while King Charles, equally eager for the destruction of all surviving friends and supporters of the Suabian line, was preparing to come to Tuscany to lead the war against Sienna in person. Pending his arrival, the Florentines, after an abortive attack on the city, laid waste the surrounding territory, and finding that the exiles, the Germans and other Ghibellines, were entrenched at Poggibonsi, marched against that town with the French contingent and the Guelphs of the *Taglia*, and began preparations for a regular siege. At the same time King Charles entered Florence, and was naturally welcomed with great joy. All the chief citizens went forth to meet him, with the *Carroccio*, as a sign of the highest honour, and after spending a festal week in the city and raising several persons to the knighthood, the king repaired to the camp before Poggibonsi. The siege lasted four months, and then, towards the middle of December, 1267, the stronghold was driven to surrender by famine. Charles left a Podestà there to govern in his name, and began to build a fortress, providing for that expense, in his accustomed way, by levying heavy taxes from the cities of the League. Florence had to contribute 1,992 *lire*. After this, the army was immediately marched against Pisa. The reduction of this powerful and warlike republic proved no easy task; the king had to be satisfied for the time with humiliating it, by seizing Porto Pisano and levelling the towers there. In February, 1268, he repaired to Lucca, and marching thence to the siege of Mutrone, captured that castle and gave it to the Lucchese. Thus, by a series of small victories, which, although of slight importance, were achieved with dazzling rapidity, he greatly raised the authority and prestige of the Guelph party, which had not only contributed troops to the war, but borne its entire expense, granting all the large sums of money continually demanded by their imperious protector. In fact, by the end of February, 1268, Florence alone had disbursed no less than seventy-two thousand *lire*, twenty thousand of which were devoted to the reduction of Poggibonsi, although Charles had not fulfilled his promise of erecting a fortress there. But at this moment a war-cry was raised, stirring all Italy to alarm, and the monarch was suddenly threatened by so imminent a peril, that after some hesitation he was compelled to decide on flying to the defence of the Neapolitan kingdom.

II.

Prince Conradin, son of Conrad, and grandson of Frederic II., was the last representative of the Suabian line in Germany, and the last hope of the Ghibellines in Italy. He was rightful heir to the crown of Naples that Charles of Anjou had forcibly usurped; and in many quarters he was regarded as the future emperor of Germany. On attaining the age of fifteen years, numerous exiles, from Naples, Sicily and other parts of Italy, sought his presence, imploring him to reconquer his kingdom and restore the Imperial party in Italy. Conradin was a youth of precocious intelligence, full of ardour and ambition; so, fired by this flash of hope, he instantly resolved to cross the Alps. Selling what little property remained to him, and collecting the most devoted of his adherents, he gathered a small army and entered Verona on the 20th of October, with three thousand horse and a considerable number of infantry. From this city he despatched letters to all the Christian powers, recounting his misfortunes: the injuries inflicted on him by the usurpation of King Charles and the hatred of Pope Urban IV., who, not content with summoning a French pretender to trample on the Imperial rights, had gone to the length of excommunicating the legitimate heirs of the Empire itself. By way of reply, Pope Clement now renewed the sentence of excommunication on Conradin, tried to stir all the powers against him by means of violent and venomous epistles; and wrote pressingly to Charles, now waiting to give battle in Tuscany, bidding him hasten to defend his kingdom from the threatened and imminent danger. In fact, the Ghibelline movement was now spreading throughout Italy. Pisa and Sienna were roused to great hopes, for the cities of Romagna, Naples, and especially of Sicily, had all risen against the French. By April, 1268, Conradin was already in Pisa with his army, and numerous adherents flocked to his standard, although the emptiness of his purse had caused some of the Germans to desert. By this time Charles had reached Naples, was making preparations for defence, and laying siege to Lucera, where Manfred's Saracens had hoisted the Suabian flag. Conradin was ready to fly thither, without even halting in Tuscany to encourage the cities revolted in his favour. Pisa and Sienna openly sided with him; Poggibonsi had promptly thrown off the Florentine yoke; and other places were preparing to do the same. Meanwhile, the German troops at once directed their march on Rome, where the Senator Errico of Castile was awaiting them. The French in Florence sallied forth to intercept their passage, but were driven back with heavy loss, to the great encouragement of Conradin and his followers.

But the prince's fate was to be decided by the battle of Tagliacozzo, fought near the banks of the Salto on August 23, 1268. At the beginning of the engagement Charles's inferior forces seemed almost routed, so that the German horse rode forward on all sides in pursuit. But while all were scattered, riding down and pillaging their retreating foes, Charles suddenly fell on them with the reserve of eight hundred horse he had kept in ambush, and quickly turned the fortunes of the day. The same evening, in a frenzy of delight, he announced his victory to the Pope, who was equally exultant. The prisoners were treated with unparalleled cruelty, being mutilated, beheaded, or even burnt alive. Conradin escaped with about five hundred men, and escorted by Henry of Austria, Galvano Lancia, Count Gherardo Donatico of Pisa, and other devoted friends, made for Rome. But being then deserted by most of his followers, he had to fly to the Maremma and seek shelter in the Castle of Astura. But here, by the sea, when on the point of embarking for Sicily with a handful of friends, he was seized by Giovanni Frangipani, lord of Astura, who handed him over to Charles, and was rewarded by grants of land.

The French monarch hastened to manifest his joy by renewed acts of cruelty. It is said that one of the towers of Corneto was garlanded with the corpses of some of the most distinguished and valiant Ghibellines. In all the Neapolitan cities he excited the populace to the fiercest excesses against the nobles of Conradin's party. And his ministers in Sicily outrivalled one another in ferocity, for it is said that, among other barbarities, so many unhappy Sicilians were put to death in one day at Augusta, that the executioner became exhausted with fatigue, and wine was poured down his throat to give him strength to continue the slaughter. But the king's ferocious mind was chiefly devoted to considering what should be Conradin's fate. To murder thousands of fellow Christians, and let them die amid the worst torments, was a matter of very slight consequence to him; but where a victim of royal and Imperial blood was in question, he felt obliged to hesitate a little. In fact, it is said that he sought counsel from the Pope; but then, without waiting the reply, he sought to give an honest colour to his revenge by investing it with a false air of legality. He presumed to treat the rival whose throne he had usurped as one who had rebelled against a legitimate sovereign, and to treat a prisoner of war as a criminal guilty of high treason, and justly responsible for all the excesses of the German soldiery during the campaign. Yet, although the tribunal consisted of foes of the Hohenstauffen selected by the king, some of its members spoke nobly in Conradin's defence. It was affirmed that Guido du Suzzara, a juris-consult of Emilia, renowned in his day, pleaded the youthfulness of the accused, his belief in his own right to the Neapolitan crown, the motives of the campaign. It was also reported that many of the judges remained silent, and that one alone openly declared against the prisoner. But all was in vain. Charles, who had already put some of the barons to death, and forced one of them, Count Galvano Lancia, to witness the strangling of his own son before being executed, never intended the trial to be more than a sham, so, choosing to interpret the judges' silence as a sign of consent to the prince's death, gave sentence accordingly. The verdict was communicated to Conradin in prison while he was playing chess with his cousin Frederic of Austria. On October 29, 1268, both were led to the scaffold on the Market Place at Naples. The protonotary Roberto di Bari, counsel for the prosecution, read the sentence aloud, in the presence of the exultant King Charles. It is asserted that even many of the French were stirred to rage and humiliation by this cruel scene. An immense throng filled the Piazza, and many fell on their knees touched with pity. Conradin removed his cloak, glanced at the silent people, threw his glove to them, as an augury of vengeance in time to come, and then submitted his neck to the axe. Thus died the Emperor Frederic's heir, the last of the Suabian line. Frederic of Austria tried to kiss his cousin's head, but was instantly seized by the executioner and put to the same death. Many details, either historical or legendary, are added by the chroniclers in describing this dismal tragedy. Although a Guelph, Villani believed the false rumour (vii. 29) to the effect that Count Robert of Flanders, son-in-law to Charles, on hearing the sentence read by di Bari, was moved to such fury that he drew his sword and slew the protonotary forthwith before the king's eyes. At least, this tale serves to show what was the general impression produced by the deed. Opinions vary as to the Pope's share in the tragedy. It is certain that he beheld it in silence.[304]

III.

Although these events excited general and very severe condemnation in Italy, they wrought immediate benefit to Charles and the Guelphs. The Florentines profited by the opportunity to launch new sentences against the Ghibellines, and shortly afterwards prepared to make fresh attacks on their neighbours, and particularly on Sienna. For they still yearned to avenge the defeat at Montaperti, and were now additionally irritated by seeing their exiles again flocking to Sienna, and heartily welcomed there. They also held that city responsible for the recent revolt of Poggibonsi, and their action in devastating the latter's territory sufficed to start hostilities afresh. The hopes of the Siennese had been greatly inflamed by Conradin's passage, and even now they were not disposed to be easily worsted. The chief ruler of the city was still Provenzano Salvani, one of those who had advised the battle of Montaperti and given notable proofs of valour in the fight. Since then his fame had been increased by many noble deeds. It was said that when a friend of his was seized by King Charles and condemned to pay a fine of ten thousand crowns in exchange for his life, Provenzano came to the rescue, and as neither he nor the prisoner's kindred could contrive to pay the ransom, he stretched a carpet on the Piazza and stood there, asking public alms for his friend until the required sum was collected. Consequently he had great influence with the people, was a Ghibelline and the declared enemy of Florence. Sienna likewise contained a considerable number of Spaniards and Germans, old soldiers of the Ghibelline wars, and there was also Count Guido Novello, who, although of little worth, continually agitated in favour of hostilities. Thus an army was recruited, consisting, Villani says, of fourteen hundred horse and eight thousand foot, and this force besieged the Castle of Colle in Val d'Elsa, as a reprisal for the devastation of Poggibonsi. Thereupon the Florentines took the field with a small body of infantry, led by the vicar of King Charles, and eight hundred horse, and notwithstanding their inferiority of numbers advanced against the Siennese, gave them battle (June 17, 1269), and achieved their defeat. Count Guido Novello secured his safety, as usual, by flight; but Provenzano Salvani justified his fame by dying sword in hand. His head was carried round the field on the point of a spear. This was the fulfilment of a prophecy made to him before the battle: "Thy head shall be the highest in the field," although he had interpreted the saying as an omen of success. The Siennese received no quarter from their foes, who returned home in triumph, and thinking they had now avenged the rout of Montaperti, began negotiations for peace. The first condition exacted was that Sienna should no longer harbour Ghibelline refugees, who, in fact, were soon compelled to depart and wander from place to place, everywhere exposed to persecution and cruelty. Among others were the Pazzi, who, having excited the Castle of Ostina to revolt, were seized and hacked to pieces.

After a devastating raid on Pisan territory, executed by the Florentines and Lucchese, Pisa signed a treaty of peace with Charles in April, 1270. Florence herself concluded an alliance with that republic on the 2nd of May, stipulating almost the identical terms and the same politico-commercial agreements previously arranged by the peace of 1256.[305] Just at that time Azzolino, Neracozzo, and Conticino degli Uberti, together with a knight named Bindo dei Grifoni, left Sienna to take refuge in the Casentino, and were captured by the Florentines on the way. The latter asked Charles what should be done with these prisoners, and he replied, that they were to be punished as traitors, save Conticino the youngest, who was to be sent to him. The others were speedily beheaded, by order of the Podestà Berardino d'Ariano (May 8, 1270). It is related that on nearing the scaffold Neracozzo said to Azzolino: "Whither are we going?" To which his kinsman quietly replied: "To pay a debt bequeathed us by our fathers." Conticino perished in a

Capuan dungeon. This instance clearly proves the great supremacy exercised by Charles over the Commonwealth. But the Florentines were willing to tolerate anything from him in order to assure their predominance in Tuscany by his help, and restore the prestige of the Guelph party. The latter aim was already practically achieved, for all Tuscany now adhered to the Guelphs, and both old and recent injuries had been avenged. At this time Florence also demolished the Castle of Pian di Mezzo in the Val d'Arno and razed the walls of Poggibonsi.

Meanwhile, however, the power of the Angevins had swelled to a formidable extent. Charles was firmly established on the Neapolitan throne; and during the interregnum had been nominated by the Popes senator of Rome and vicar-imperial of Romagna as well as Tuscany. Accordingly, while restoring the strength of the Guelph party, he had notably aggrandised his own authority. His lurking ambition to be master of all Italy was now clearly discernible, and accordingly the Florentines began to kick against his perpetual interference, and to object to every commune being subject to a Podestà of his choice exercising absolute judicial power in his name and under his authority. And as though this were not enough, there was also a royal marshal or vicar in Tuscany who jointly with the rest perpetually harassed the city by threatening demands for fresh subsidies. But even greater than elsewhere was the jealousy excited in Rome. The Popes had summoned the Angevins to the overthrow of the Suabians, less on account of these being Ghibellines, those Guelphs, than because the Suabians had entertained the identical ambition that Charles was now beginning to conceive. Accordingly, there was now the same motive for combating him.

Niccolò Machiavelli has often repeated that the Popes "always feared every one who rose to great power in Italy, albeit his power was exercised by favour of the Church. And inasmuch as they [the Popes] sought to lower that power, frequent tumults would arise and frequent changes of power, since fear of a tyrant led to the exaltation of some feebler personage, and then, as his power became increased, he in turn was feared, and, being feared, his overthrow was desired. Thus, the government taken from Manfred was conceded to Charles; thus, later, when he excited fear, his ruin likewise was planned."[306] In fact, Urban IV. had invited Charles to seize the kingdom of Naples; Clement IV. had named him his vicar; Gregory X. was now beginning to oppose him, and succeeding pontiffs followed his example. Thus three different political games were now being played in Central Italy: the Angevins already yearning for the dominion of Italy; the Florentines scheming to use the French monarch's power to assure their own predominance in Tuscany; and the Popes seeking to check the king's ambition

173

and resume their former supremacy over that state.

IV.

The first sign of this alteration in the Papal policy was quickly detected by Florence, although Rome used every device to conceal the real cause and object of the change; and, indeed, to prevent its change of purpose from appearing on the surface. Gregory X. began by expressing regret that a city so rich and powerful as Florence should still be divided by the party strife of the Guelphs and Ghibellines. He desired to see them at peace. No wish should have seemed more natural on the part of the Head of the Church; but it roused the king's suspicions to find the Pope suddenly inflamed by such unusual compassion towards the Ghibellines. His distrust was heightened on seeing how cheerfully the Florentines accepted the proposals of the Pope. They had already shown signs of wishing to shake off the royal yoke by requesting the king to give them an Italian Podestà, as their statutes required, and already in January, 1270,[307] he had felt obliged to make this concession in a graciously worded decree. Instantly divining the real intention of Rome, the Florentines now understood that the moment had come to second it for their own advantage. They were all the more willing to do so not only to impose a check on the growing tyranny of the king, but in order to remedy another evil wrought by his supremacy in Florence. Charles was always surrounded by his own barons and captains, whose foreign presence was unwelcome, and by Guelph nobles and knights not only of Tuscany, but from other parts of Italy as well. In Florence he constantly favoured the old Guelph nobility, and on every visit to the city created new knights. Thus, ennobled Guelph merchants were joined to the other aristocrats, and assuming the rank of *grandi*, soon became opposed to the people, and revived the old antipathy of the Florentine democrats, who, just as they had rebelled in past times against the feudal pride of the Ghibellines, now refused to tolerate that of the old and new Guelph patriciate. Therefore it was necessary to curb the *grandi* at any cost, and it seemed the wisest plan to recall the Ghibellines, who were equally opposed to them and the king. Thus the people would be strengthened by the division of the nobles, and the latter, by quarrelling among themselves, would lessen the number of those most subservient to Charles. The king, however, could not be blind to the hidden purpose of these intrigues, and was quite awake to the Pope's real intentions. He knew that the latter was now urging the Germans to elect Rudolf of Hapsburg as King of the Romans, in order to put an end to the Imperial interregnum, and consequently to his own tenure of the vicariate. Why should the Pope desire the election of an emperor save for the purpose of weakening the Angevin power? Meanwhile both pontiff and king preserved a feint of amity, and seemed to be on the best possible terms, although their mutual distrust continually flashed forth.

Gregory X. had decreed the convocation of a Council at Lyons in 1274 in order to promote a crusade against the infidels; and reaching Florence on June 18, 1273, suspended his journey for awhile for the purpose, as he said, of re-establishing the general peace. He arrived with his whole train of cardinals and prelates, accompanied by the Emperor of Byzantium, Baldwin II., who came to ask Christian aid against the Infidel, and escorted by Charles of Anjou, whose sense of the honour due to the pontiff, so he said, forbade leaving him alone in Florence. And as the Pope found the city to his liking, he decided to spend the whole summer there. The 2nd of July was the day fixed for the solemn reconciliation of the Guelphs and Ghibellines, and the syndics, or leaders, of either party were gathered in the town. On the waste of dry sand in the bed of the Arno by the Ponte alle Grazie wooden platforms had been erected, and here the Pope, the Emperor Baldwin, and Charles of Anjou were seated in state. The oath of peace was sworn in the presence of a great throng of spectators; the syndics exchanged kisses, and the Pope gave his benediction, threatening excommunication on all who should dare to break the peace. Both sides gave hostages and yielded castles as pledges of faith, and everything seemed to be arranged in accordance with the benevolent intentions of the Pope. The Holy Father was lodged in the palace of his bankers, the Mozzi, Baldwin in that of the bishop, while Charles occupied several houses in the Frescobaldi gardens. There was now time to enjoy life in Florence before the return of the banished Ghibellines and the festivals to be given in their honour. But suddenly it was learnt that the Ghibelline syndics, instead of carrying out the concluding terms of the peace, had hastily fled from Florence. And the reason alleged for this was, that the king's vicar had sent them an intimation that unless they left the city without delay, he would have them all cut to pieces at the request of the Guelph nobles. Thereupon the Pope instantly set out for the Mugello, much enraged not only with the king, but even more with the Florentines for their indifference to the whole farce, and he punished their violation of the oath by pronouncing an interdict on the city.

Meanwhile Charles continued his aggressive policy with regard to the Ghibellines, and was seconded by the Florentines, who marched out under the banner of the Commune, sometimes alone, but oftener in junction with the French cavalry, to impose peace and assure the triumph of their party in all the neighbouring towns. But their arrogant daring was sometimes pushed too far. When the Ghibellines were expelled from Bölogna, the Florentines immediately set out to proffer their unrequested aid to that city. But, much to their amazement, on reaching the banks of the Reno, they found the Bölognese waiting to drive them back. The latter had achieved their purpose of banishing the Ghibellines, but had no intention of allowing the haughty Florentines to come to disseminate their own party rancours under pretence of assisting the city. The Podestà of the Florentines was killed in trying to push through the opposing force, and the humiliated expedition had to retrace its steps (1274).

They were more fortunate with regard to Pisa. That city, being torn by party strife, had banished Giovanni Visconti, judge of Gallura, and Count Ugolino della Gherardesca di Donoratico, two ambitious Ghibelline nobles, who, deserting their own for the Guelph cause, applied to the Florentines for help. They immediately granted it, and joining forces with their new friends and the French, invaded the territories of their old rival, capturing the Castle of Asciano in September, 1275. The following June, at the instigation of the same exiled nobles, they resumed hostilities with a larger army, aided by the Lucchese and other Guelphs, and accompanied by the king's marshal. Again victorious, they compelled Pisa to make peace on June 13, 1276, and recall her exiles, especially the Count Ugolino, whose ambition was destined to bring fatal consequences on himself and his native town.

Meanwhile Pope Gregory had returned from Lyons and reached Tuscany in December, 1275. Still highly irritated against Florence, he refused to enter its gates; but as the Arno was too swollen to be fordable, he was obliged to cross one of its bridges, and therefore raised the interdict from the city, although only during the time required for his passage. His death took place shortly afterwards, January 10, 1276, and in a single year three new Popes rapidly succeeded him: Innocent V., Adrian V., and John XXI. Then, on November 25, 1277, Nicholas III. was elected to the pontifical Chair, and during his three years' reign followed the same policy pursued by Gregory X., and with even greater zeal. Full of haughtiness and ambition, Nicholas sought to aggrandise his own family as well as the Papal power. He renewed the scandalous practice of nepotism and simony by making some of his kinsmen cardinals and appointing others to high offices of the State. But on trying to negotiate the marriage of one of his nieces with a nephew of King Charles, the latter mortally wounded his pride by the reply, that although the Pope had crimson hose, his blood had not been sufficiently ennobled to be mixed with that of French royalty.[308] Nicholas III., already disgusted with the king, and suspicious of his motives, could not easily pardon this affront. Hence he seized the first opportunity to let Charles know that although Rudolf of Hapsburg had not yet been crowned emperor in Rome, he had been already elected king of the Romans in Germany, and that accordingly it was no longer needful for Charles to fill the post of vicar-imperial, only granted him during the interregnum. Thus the French monarch was finally compelled to resign the vicariate of Tuscany, the title of Roman Senator, and even his jurisdiction over Romagna and the Marches, that had been partly accorded to, partly usurped by him. Perceiving that there was no possibility of evading this blow, the king instantly yielded the point without showing the slightest resentment, so that the Pope was driven to declare: "This prince may have inherited his fortune from the House of France, his cunning from Spain, but his shrewdness of address could only have been acquired by frequenting the Court of Rome."[309] Nevertheless, he was not in the least deceived by the king's apparent calmness, and neglected no chance of diminishing his power and aggrandising that of the Holy See. Thus, when Giovanni da Procida was going through Italy seeking help for the Sicilian revolution that was soon to burst forth, he received encouragement from the Pope. Then, after showing much favour to Rudolph of Hapsburg, Nicholas profited by the occasion to obtain his sanction for extending the states of the Church as far as the Neapolitan frontier on one side, and for including the March of Ancona, Romagna and the Pentapolis on the other. And down to our own day the states of the Church preserved these boundaries almost unaltered. Although at the time, the domination of the Popes was chiefly nominal over part of this territory, yet by dint of insistence they gradually achieved practical supremacy over the whole of it.

V.

As a first step in this direction, Nicholas III. sent his nephew, Cardinal Latino de' Frangipani, to establish peace in Romagna. As a Dominican monk, Frangipani had shown great powers of oratory, and was therefore fitted to enforce the new authority of the Church. Count Bertoldo Orsini was also sent with him. After a short stay in Romagna, the cardinal was transferred to Florence to renew with better success the reconciliation of hostile parties Gregory X. had failed to conclude. Now, however, the Florentines themselves seemed really desirous of peace. Although freed from the too oppressive protection of King Charles, they still suffered from the evil results of his policy. The *grandi*, turbulent as ever, and with increased numbers and strength, were threatening division even among the Guelphs. Villani says of them that, "Resting from victories and honours won in wars abroad, and fattening on the lands of exiled Ghibellines and other fruits of enterprise, they began from pride and envy to fall out with one another; so that many quarrels and feuds arose among the citizens of Florence, and much killing and wounding."[310] First the Adimari began to stir riots from hatred against the Tosinghi, next the Pazzi and Donati came to blows; and this was seen to be a prelude to greater evils. Accordingly the Guelphs sent messengers to the Pope, praying him to send some one to pacify the city, unless he wished to see the party divided against itself. The Ghibellines seemed equally anxious for peace. They were weary of prolonged exile and continual confiscation of their property, and cherished hopes that the popular hatred, being now inflamed against the Guelph nobles, would be softened towards themselves.[311]

Accordingly Cardinal Latino entered Florence on October 8, 1279, with three hundred knights and prelates in his train, and was received with every token of honour. The Florentine clergy went to meet him in procession, and the Republic sent forth the *Carroccio* with a great number of standard- bearers. Being a Dominican, he was lodged in the monastery of Santa Maria Novella, and laid the first stone of the celebrated church of that name. He immediately began the negotiations for the arrangement of peace.

On the 19th of November platforms were raised in the Piazza of Santa Maria Novella Vecchia, and the parliament being assembled there in the presence of the magistrates and councils, the cardinal asked and obtained the power of concluding peace with the same authority possessed by the people— that is to say, the right of imposing fines, decreeing confiscations, and occupying castles, to guarantee the due performance of the terms about to be sworn. He next essayed to reconcile the bitterest foes: Guelphs who had come to a rupture, quarrelsome Ghibellines, and hostile Guelphs and Ghibellines. All went well until he came to the Buondelmonti and Uberti, whose ancient hatred was too deeply rooted. It was impossible to persuade them to be reconciled, for some of them indignantly rejected the proposal. Hence the Cardinal had to decree their excommunication, and banish the more obstinate from the Commune. Finally, January 18, 1280, was fixed for the conclusion of the general peace. Great preparations for the ceremony were made in the Piazza of Santa Maria Novella Vecchia; the platforms were hung with tapestries, and the whole square carpeted with cloth. Hither came the Twelve, the Podestà, the Captain of the people (then styled Captain of the mass of the Guelph party), and their councils, together with all the rest of the magistrates, and a great concourse of spectators. Lastly came the cardinal with his attendant prelates, and the general excitement was heightened by the expectation of his speech, since he was known to be one of the most eloquent orators of his time. He gave an address on the merit and necessity of making peace, and finally the treaty was read aloud. It was to put an end to all the old hatreds; it stipulated the restitution of confiscated property to the Ghibellines, with some interest on the capital; all sentences, oaths, leagues, and associations made by the one party to the hurt of the other were declared null and void, and every clause of the statutes tending to the perpetuation of strife was to be cancelled. Either party was to furnish fifty sureties, and bound to forfeit the sum of fifty thousand silver marks, in case of any violation of the peace. As an additional guarantee certain castles were to be given up, and the right was reserved of demanding more hostages should occasion require. Then came a long string of minute stipulations, all directed to the same end. Many of the chief families were to be confined to fixed places until they made peace with their foes and gave money and hostages in pledge of good faith. The delegates of both parties kissed one another on the mouth, the documents of the treaty were solemnly registered, and party decrees of banishment and other sentences cancelled or burnt. The exiles were authorised to return; and, without prejudice to the functions of the Podestà, the captains, and guild- masters, were charged with the strict maintenance of the terms of peace. For this reason the Captain was no longer to be entitled Captain of the Guelph party, but Captain of the city and conservator of peace. Also, the office of vicar-imperial granted to Charles having now lapsed, it was decreed that henceforward the Podestà and Captain were to be nominated for two years by the Pope, and have each the command of fifty horse and fifty foot soldiers. After two years the right of election would be resumed by the people, provided their nominees were not opposed to, but actually approved by, the Head of the Church. Each Captain would then have the command of one hundred horse and one hundred foot, but, for the better preservation of peace, the said troops must neither be citizens nor natives of the territory. The guilds were likewise sworn to assist in maintaining peace. It was farther decreed that the statutes should be revised, the government of the city reformed, and an estimate made of the property of all persons who had been condemned to pay fines or damages.[312]

This would seem to show that the cardinal was almost in the position of a provisional dictator, with arbitrary power of decision. But he first consulted the magistrates as to many clauses proposed by him, while regarding other conditions of the agreement the Florentines obeyed them or not as they chose. The people desired peace for the reasons we have already described and the cardinal was therefore given full powers to conclude it on his own authority and that of the Church. But his success was far more apparent than real. In fact, the constitution of the Guelph party remained in force, and as soon as he had gone, the city was again torn by faction strife. He left Florence on April 24, 1280, after receiving a recompense of "mille floreni auri in pecunia numerata, et alie zoie empte pro Comuni Florentie."

Nevertheless, during February and the beginning of March, he was so satisfied with his imagined success as to attempt the reconciliation of many adversaries confined to fixed domiciles. He likewise tried to give effect to the constitutional reforms prescribed by the peace; above all, that of replacing the twelve worthies by fourteen "good men," composed of eight Guelphs and six Ghibellines. These functionaries, in co-operation with the Captains and the councils, formed the government of the city, and were changed every second month. Nevertheless, the Podestà and Captain remained in office for one year more. The authority of the Podestà, as the nominee of King Charles, had been much diminished under the latter's rule; accordingly increased powers were now conferred on the Captain and Twelve, and the latter being augmented to fourteen,[313] constituted the supreme power or Signory of Florence.

This custom of changing the Signory every second month—a custom maintained to the close of the Republic—has given rise to much discussion. Certainly, this rapid mutation of the highest power in the State could not be favourable to peace; but, as we have had frequent occasion to note, the new constitution of the guilds had reduced the attributes of the central government to a minimum. Besides, the manifest tendency of all Italian republics to degenerate into despotism made the Florentines distrustful of any Signory of longer duration. Now, too, the Ghibellines having returned, there was special cause to fear that the government might be induced to conspire in favour of some ambitious personage disposed to play the tyrant at a moment's notice. For these reasons, it was decided on the one hand to lessen the authority of the Podestà, and on the other to frequently change not only the heads of the government but even, as will be seen, other political functionaries as well. Later on, election by ballot was adopted as another means of preventing the carrying out of any prearranged design against freedom.[314]

VI.

Meanwhile the King of the Romans was sending his vicar to Italy, with an escort of three hundred men only, to ascertain the temper of the land, and whether the cities still acknowledged the suzerainty of the Empire. On arriving in Tuscany, the vicar made halt at San Miniato al Tedesco, and found the Pisans still Ghibellines, and eager to swear fealty. But when the other Tuscan cities refused to recognise the rights of the Empire the Florentines corrupted the vicar with bribes, and, showing him the futility of his mission, persuaded him to depart acknowledging the force of the privileges granted them by the Pope.

Thus they dexterously contrived to make the altered policy of Rome a means of advancing their own interests and damaging those of King Charles, whose power over Central Italy was entirely lost. By once more calling the Empire to the front, and encouraging Rudolph of Hapsburg to assert himself against Charles, Nicholas III. succeeded in weakening both, while giving new strength to the Papacy. So, too, with equal sagacity, the Florentines had made use of the king to dominate Tuscany; of the Pope to enfeeble the king; and, finally, of both to avoid yielding submission to Rudolph.

Nicholas III. died in 1280. He had compelled Charles to leave Tuscany, and be satisfied with receiving from Rudolph the investiture of Provence and the kingdom of Naples. To render this agreement more binding, by means of a family alliance, Rudolph gave his daughter in marriage to a grandson of King Charles. But naturally the latter accepted the arrangement most reluctantly, and took every opportunity of secretly exciting the Tuscan Guelphs against the Ghibellines, who were again coming to the front. Also, having learnt by his own experience the serious difference between having the Popes as friends or as foes, he hastened to Orvieto, where the new conclave was sitting, determined to use every means to procure the election of some candidate favouring his views. As usual, he pursued this purpose unhesitatingly and without scruple. Perceiving that the cardinals were temporising, and dreading the consequences of delay, he excited a revolt, during which the populace captured two cardinals of the Orsini house, relations of the deceased Pope, and decidedly opposed to the Angevin interests. After this event the election took place, and on February 22, 1281, Martin IV. was proclaimed. The new pontiff was French, and being very friendly to Charles, immediately undertook to forward his policy and support the Guelphs.

But the general conditions of Italy were much changed, and therefore the king's triumph at Orvieto failed to prevent the consequences entailed by his cruelty in Naples, and by the policy of Nicholas III. from producing their natural effect. The latter's agreement with Rudolph was ratified by the new Pope, who counselled the cities of Italy to accord a hearty welcome to the emperor's daughter, when she came as the bride of the king's nephew. Even Florence was obliged to give the princess an honourable reception, although she was accompanied by an Imperial vicar, who, as usual, abode at San Miniato, in order to attempt to resuscitate the rights of the Empire in Tuscany. But a far graver change occurred in March, 1282, when the Sicilians, wearied of misgovernment, at last snatched up the gauntlet thrown by Conradin to the people, and with the sanguinary revolt of the Vespers began the long and glorious war that was to free Sicily for ever from the Angevin yoke. In order to keep faith with the Guelph party and avoid unnecessarily irritating the Pope or the king, the Florentines sent five hundred horse to the latter's aid; and this contingent, commanded by Count Guido di Battifolle of the Guidi house, and bearing the banner of Florence, took part in the siege of Messina. But the revolution was everywhere triumphant; the Florentines shared in the general defeat, and had to return, leaving their flag in the enemy's hands. The island was inevitably lost to the French.

Even before the outbreak of the Sicilian Vespers the Florentines had naturally begun to be on the alert and watchful of their own interests. Noting that the vicar was only attended by a small force, and gained few adherents, they soon tried to win him with gold, and succeeded in persuading him to leave the country after confirming the concessions previously granted to them. At the same time, profiting by the emperor's weakness in consequence of troubles at home, and by the fact of Charles being at a distance in Naples and already gravely preoccupied concerning the approaching crisis in Sicily, they seized the opportunity to make some constitutional reforms. First of all, now that the Podestà and Captain were no longer elected by the king, but named instead by the Pope, they decided to grant them ampler powers, in order to keep the city quiet by checking the arrogance of the Ghibellines and tyranny of the *grandi*. Both factions were daily becoming more threatening; and particularly the latter, which cancelled magisterial decrees by absolute force, prevented the laws from being executed, committed murder either directly or indirectly for the sake of party revenge, and kept the city in a perpetual turmoil. It was therefore decreed to allow the Podestà greater freedom of action in the general repression of crime, and give the Captain a larger force with which to maintain order and punish criminals to whom the Podestà might have been too lenient. The *grandi* were not only bound to swear obedience to the laws, but to give hostages for their good faith; so that even should they succeed in escaping from the city after committing any crime, those who had given surety, or stood hostage for them, would have to suffer in their stead all punishments or fines to which the contumacious were condemned. To ensure the execution of all these decrees a thousand armed men were chosen among the citizens. Of this number two hundred were contributed by the Sesto of St. Piero Scheraggio, as many by that of the Borgo, the four other Sesti each giving 150 men, and then the whole thousand being divided in companies with the banners of the different quarters, or rather *sestieri* of the city, 450 men were placed at the orders of the Podestà, and 550 under the Captain's command. They bore colours given them by either magistrate in the presence of the public parliament, and whenever the bell rang the signal for their assembly no gatherings of the people were allowed in the city.[315]

This reform seemed the more indispensable, seeing that under Charles's rule the employment of citizen soldiers commanded by the gonfaloniers of the guilds had fallen into disuse, and order was maintained by means of foreign troops. Thus the Captain had forfeited much of the authority that it was now sought to restore to him. Now, too, we find the Fourteen empowered to conduct the government without summoning the Council of One Hundred, of which the documents cease to make mention. Owing to this, and also to the lack of concord between the eight Guelph and six Ghibelline members, the authority of the Fourteen, instead of being strengthened, suffered decline. Accordingly, another reform was in course of arrangement, when the outbreak of the Sicilian Vespers gave the Florentines more freedom of action. They had three special objects in view. Firstly, to make the Republic independent of Pope, emperor and king; secondly, to close accounts with the Ghibellines, because they were nobles, and as constant adherents to the Empire supported its pretensions in Tuscany; thirdly, to lower the pride of the *grandi*, whether Guelphs or Ghibellines, because their tyrannous deeds kept the city in continual disturbance. This, indeed, was one reason why the terms of Cardinal Latino's peace were no longer observed; and why, above all, the promised indemnities to injured Ghibellines had never been paid. Also, on February 8, 1282, a Guelphic League was concluded with Lucca, Pistoia, Prato, Volterra, and Sienna, whose adherence was compulsory; and San Gimignano, Colle, and Poggibonsi were also given permission to join. The members of the League swore to remain united ten years for the common defence, and were each pledged to hire five hundred horse with the customary number of squires. Also, as usual, the allies joined in a species of convention touching the exchange and passage of merchandise.

But the most important point for Florence was the internal reform of the city. All the guilds, and especially some of greater, were becoming more strongly organised, and acquiring increased political influence. In fact, the *capitudini*, or guild-masters, figure more frequently in the public records, side by side with the Fourteen, the Captain, and Podestà. It is at this period(1282–3) that we even find mentioned a *Defensor Artificum et Artium*, together with two councils, an indubitable sign of the growing power of the guilds.[316] For, although the *Defensor* disappears later on, and his office is deputed to the Captain, this change only occurred when the government of the Republic was actually carried on by the guilds. Meanwhile they already shared in the election of the Fourteen, and aided them with their advice. The chroniclers tell us that by a reform enacted in June, 1282, the priors of the guilds were finally raised to office in place of the Fourteen; but in fact the change happened less suddenly than might be inferred from their account of the matter. For we find that—as was always the case with Florentine reforms— the Fourteen continued to govern in co-operation with the new priors, until, overshadowed by the growing importance of the latter, they gradually disappeared altogether. It is certain that on June 15, 1282, three *Priors of the Arts* were made chiefs of the Republic—namely, the priors of the Calimala, Money Changers, and Woollen Guilds. They were attended by six guards (*berrovieri*), and had six heralds to summon the citizens to council; they dwelt in the Badia, without leaving it during their whole term of office, and generally deliberated in junction with the captain. The Fourteen remained in office with them for some time longer, but chiefly *pro forma.*[317] After the first two months it was deemed necessary to increase the number of the priors, not only because three were found to be insufficient; but also being necessarily chosen from one or the other half of the six *sestieri*, they invariably seemed to represent one division only of the citizens. Accordingly, to avoid delay, in the August of the same year, the three guilds of Doctors and Druggists, Silkweavers and Mercers, Skinners and Furriers, were added to the original number. Other guilds also were subsequently added, but the number of the priors remained restricted to six, one for each *sestiere*. Compagni says that "their laws [or functions] consisted in guarding the property of the Commune, and in seeing that the signories did justice to every one, and that petty and feeble folk were not oppressed by the great and powerful."[318] At the end of their two months' term the priors, assisted by the guild-masters and a few additional citizens, designated as *arroti*, elected their own successors to office.

Villani affirms that the title of prior was derived from a verse of the Gospel, where Christ says to His disciples, "Vos estis priores." What is certain is that by means of this reform the guilds, or rather commerce and trade, had the whole government of the Republic in their hands; and it should also be noted that although the above-mentioned guilds, together with that of the jurists and notaries, constituted the seven greater arts, yet the legal guild— perhaps because it represented neither industry nor commerce—is left unnoticed by the chroniclers at this point. Henceforward the Commonwealth is a true republic of traders, and only to be governed by members of the guilds. Every title of nobility, whether old or new, becomes an impediment rather than a privilege.

Consequently many of the principal families began to change their names in order to disguise their former rank. The Tornaquinci divided into Popoleschi, Tornabuoni, Giachinotti, &c.; the Cavalcanti became Malatesti and Ciampoli; and others assumed fresh names.[319] Nevertheless, many proudly clung to their ancient appellations and titles; and when King Charles' son, the Prince of Salerno, was summoned to Naples from Provence, he halted in Florence by the way on purpose to imitate his father by creating new knights. By these artificial devices it was hoped to give new strength to an aristocracy that was doomed to decline by the natural course of events; but the means employed were too utterly opposed to the political and social temper of Florence to have the slightest success there. No longer fettered by Pope and emperor, and emancipated from the oppressive patronage of King Charles, who was now absorbed in Sicilian matters, the Florentines had organised the constitution in the manner that suited them best, and by entrusting the greater guilds with the management of the State gained a real predominance in Tuscany that they turned most skilfully to account for the extension of their trade. The politico-commercial league, concluded in March, 1282, to which we have already alluded, proved most beneficial to their interests, and the subjection of neighbouring towns and territories was another means to the same end.

Nevertheless, the two Ghibelline cities of Arezzo and Pisa still remained hostile to Florence. The former was a threatening presence in the upper Val d'Arno, while the latter, with its wealth, power, and command of the sea, was a danger to the lower valley, and, standing on the road to Leghorn and Porto Pisano, was an obstruction to the maritime trade of Florence. Hence it was obvious that sooner or later the Republic would be forced to combine with friendly neighbours and new allies against both these foes, and especially against Pisa. Free access to the sea-board was more indispensable than ever to the Florentine trade, and should Pisa continue to block the way, the Republic would reap nothing from the successes it had already achieved.

Meanwhile the Florentines enjoyed the benefits of peace for two quiet years. During this time Charles' son, the Prince of Salerno, and other members of the royal house were received in the city with all due pomp and parade. In March, 1283, the king came in person to Florence on his way to Bordeaux, where he was to engage in single combat with Peter of Aragon, who had been proclaimed Lord of Sicily by the people of the island. By this much-talked-of duel, that never took place, the war desolating Southern Italy was to be brought to an end. Even on this occasion the king, although noisily welcomed in Florence, and probably oppressed by grave anxiety, insisted on creating more knights, regardless of the trouble he caused to the people. Nevertheless, after he had gone, the merrymakings were continued with greater zest than before. On St. John's Day, always a great festival in Florence, a company was formed of a thousand young men, who, clothed in white robes and led by one of their number representing the "Lord of Love,"[320] inaugurated games and diversions of every kind, giving dances in the streets and within doors to persons of all ranks—ladies, knights, and common folk. This Court of Love was in imitation of certain French customs first introduced into Florence by the Angevins. It now numbered three hundred knights, so-called *di corredo*, chiefly created by King Charles, according to the French mode. They gave banquets and had a train of pages, courtiers, and buffoons imported from various parts of Italy and France. But all this was a fruitless attempt to introduce customs opposed to the city's traditions, a childish means of asserting the existence of a new patrician order. The populace was enchanted with these gay doings; but the thriftier citizens at the head of the government, and constituting the real strength of the Republic, highly disapproved of them, and were disgusted to find that after struggling so long to repress the nobility fresh efforts were needed to stamp out its remains. Throughout Tuscany, indeed, fresh warfare was impending, for the Sicilian Vespers seemed to have roused the Imperialists to new vigour. For this reason Corso Donati had declared, at a *consulta* held on February 26, 1285, that all districts appertaining to the Empire (*de Imperio*) and bordering the Florentine territory were to be subject *ad iurisdictionem Comunis Florentiae*.[321] New agreements were made to this effect with the other Guelph cities.[322] But the most urgent consideration of all was how to overcome the pride and power of Pisa, that obstinately Ghibelline city with whom Florence had always been compelled to struggle, and must now struggle anew. But how was success to be assured? Florence was neither willing nor able to depend on the help of the French king, and even with the combined aid of all its allies could not muster sufficient strength for the enterprise. Therefore much sagacity and diplomatic skill were required in order to multiply the resources of the Republic, and the

Florentines proved equal to the occasion.

VII.

Although the city of Pisa derived all its strength and influence from its maritime trade, nevertheless—either from being always on the Imperial side, or because such was the predestined fate of all Italian sea-board republics—it was dominated by a powerful aristocracy to the same extent as were Genoa and Venice. With their usual astuteness, the Florentines had long sought to bring their influence to bear on the Pisan nobles, in order to create discord among them. Giovanni Visconti, entitled Judge of Gallura, from the high and remunerative post once held by him in Sardinia, as governor of several provinces, for the Pisan Republic, had been subsequently (1274) exiled on account of his Guelph proclivities, and had then joined the vicar of King Charles and the Guelph League against his native state. He died in 1275; and just at that time Count Ugolino della Gherardesca, one of the most powerful and ambitious nobles of Pisa, who aspired to establish a despotism there, was driven into banishment with other formidable Guelphs (1275). These exiles not only made alliance with the Florentines, but, in conjunction with the League, or *Taglia*, made war on Pisa and captured several castles, Vico Pisano included. In the September of the same year they returned to the attack in co- operation with the Angevin vicar-royal, Florentines, and Lucchese, and, defeating their fellow-citizens at three miles' distance from Pisa, seized the Castle of Asciano, which was handed over to the Lucchese. In 1276 the war was resumed by Florence and Lucca, and again at the instigation of Count Ugolino and his friends. This was the occasion alluded to at an earlier page, when both sides brought powerful armies into the field and came to a pitched battle between Pisa and Pontedera, on the banks of the so-called Fosso Arnonico, a canal into which the Pisans had formerly diverted the waters of the Arno for the better defence of their territory. Again the Pisans were worsted, and the bitterness of defeat enhanced by having to accept peace on the terms proposed by Florence, of which the first and hardest condition was the readmittance in their city of all the banished Guelphs, and particularly of the ambitious Count Ugolino, whom they hated so deeply.

Pope Gregory X. was highly displeased by this war, and by the ardour and pertinacity with which it was pursued, for he considered the Ghibelline spirit of Pisa a barrier to the growing power of the Florentines, who, in spite of being Guelphs, used every effort to become wholly independent of the Papacy. Wherefore, after vainly enjoining them to put an end to the war, he excommunicated their city. But the Florentines offered slight excuses, and until 1276 paid no attention to his thunders. Then at last peace was declared, but during its very brief duration plans were arranged for new expeditions.

After this the Republic of Pisa enjoyed a few tranquil years, and owing to the vastness of its trade and the extension of its colonies, its finances were rapidly restored to their former prosperity. Unfortunately, certain Pisan families had become so powerful by means of their wealth that, no longer satisfied with republican equality, they sought to dominate the internal affairs of the State and direct its foreign policy in favour of their personal ambition rather than of the interests of the State. The Judges of Gallura and Arborea, Counts Ugolino, Fazio, Neri, and Anselmo della Gherardesca, all had their own little courts and men-at-arms after the fashion of princes. Absorbed in covetous rivalries, they distracted the attention of the magistrates from the dangers threatening their republic, and daily becoming graver and more imminent. For, in fact, the strength of the Republic was not only almost exhausted by the continuous attacks of the Guelph League, but for some time past the rivalry of Genoa had been threatening to culminate in a still deadlier strife. As both these maritime cities were Ghibelline, they had every reason to be at peace with each other and combine in defending their interests against the far greater sea power of Venice. But, on the contrary, this only seemed to exasperate their reciprocal jealousy. Their fleets were constantly in collision in Levantine waters. They had a desperate encounter in 1277 near Constantinople and on the Black Sea. It ended in disaster for the Pisans, who had been the assailants, and from that moment they panted for revenge. Nor were opportunities lacking. While the Venetians were asserting absolute dominion over the Adriatic, the Genoese and Pisans, hard by on the Mediterranean, were always crossing each other's tracks, inasmuch as both were engaged in the same trading ventures, and both possessed colonies in the same islands of Corsica and Sardinia. Thus, they were involved in continual conflict. Then, too, as the Guelph League was specially hostile to Pisa, it supplied Genoa with perpetual pretexts for beginning the hostilities which the Florentines were seeking to incite by every political manœuvre. At last their reciprocal hatred reached so high a pitch that the Pisans themselves were the first to provoke the war. Their burning desire for reprisals was continually kept aflame by the greed of the nobles, who hoped to convert the conflict into a ladder to power, and whose own ambitions were spurred by the crafty encouragement of Florence.

Corsica was ruled by a certain Sinucello, bearing the title of Judge of Cinarca. He had been educated in Pisa, and the Republic had assisted him to regain and increase his hereditary possessions in the island. Governing there as a vassal of Pisa, he nevertheless transferred his allegiance to the Genoese, who occupied another part of the island. Later on, after perpetrating every species of cruel and tyrannous deeds, he turned against the Genoese and devastated their Corsican towns. Taking refuge at Pisa, that republic granted him protection as a former vassal, equally regardless of the subsequent treaties, by which he had sworn fealty to Genoa, and of all the barbarities he had committed. Pisa tried to reinstate Sinucello in Corsica by force, but as the Genoese were determined to keep him at a distance, this served to provoke hostilities. In fact, being sent back to the island with 120 horse and 200 foot, he was able to recapture his possessions; but from that moment (1282) the Genoese and Pisan ships were always chasing one another over the Mediterranean in order to engage. Accordingly, from the end of 1282 to the August of 1283, a continual series of sanguinary conflicts took place, sometimes attaining the proportions of real naval battles; and although the Pisans were generally defeated, they always rallied their forces, and prepared to resume the struggle. On one occasion half their fleet perished in a storm; nevertheless, shortly after this (1284) they sent twenty-four galleys to escort Count Fazio to Sardinia, where collisions with the Genoese were of constant occurrence. In fact, on the 1st of May, they encountered the latter's fleet, gave battle, and carried on an obstinate fight that lasted the whole day. Finally, however, the Pisans were beaten off, leaving thirteen galleys and a great number of prisoners in the enemy's hands. Notwithstanding this reverse, the same year witnessed another naval battle between the two republics, that proved one of the most memorable fights on record in the Middle Ages.

Genoa, whose victories had cost her dear, caused vessels to be built and equipped in every port of the Riviera; while Pisa, although exhausted by so many conflicts on sea and land, made prodigious efforts of all kinds. By appealing to the patriotism of her noblest families, she elicited a worthy response. The Lanfranchi, a numerous Pisan clan, equipped no less than eleven galleys at their own expense; the Gualandi, Lei, and Gaetani, furnished six; the Sismondi three; the Orlandi four; the Upezzinghi five; the Visconti three; the Moschi two; and other families joined in equipping one. Andrea Morosini, the Venetian, one of the highest naval celebrities of the time, was chosen Podestà, with full powers to make all requisite preparations for the war, and to then assume the chief command of the fleet at sea. Thus both sides sent forth the most formidable armaments to be seen in those times. Genoese writers reckon their vessels to have been ninety-six in number, and those of Pisa seventy-two; whereas Pisan historians reckon their fleet at 103 sail against 130 of the Genoese. At any rate, both are agreed that the Genoese fleet outnumbered the Pisan, and that its superiority was enhanced by the greater skill of its commanders. The two armadas cruised in search of each other for some time, and then tacked about before giving battle, each trying to gain the better position. It is averred that the Pisans sailed to the entrance of the port of Genoa, discharging silver arrows and balls covered with purple cloth, in order to make a display of wealth, after the usage of the time. Anyhow, it is known that some of their galleys were anchored off Porto Pisano, and others lying in the Arno, between the two bridges of the city, when the news came that the Genoese fleet had been sighted. All Pisa was in a turmoil; scattered crews hastened on board, and the archbishop, attended by his clergy, and bearing the banner of the Republic, appeared on the Ponte Vecchio, and blessed the fleet. Thereupon, amid joyful shouts, the galleys weighed anchor, and swept down the river to the sea. It is related that at the moment the benediction was pronounced the crucifix on the standard fell down, which was judged a bad omen.

The 6th of August, 1284, was a memorable day. The two fleets met off Meloria, at a short distance from Porto Pisano. Here in past times the Genoese had been severely defeated by the Pisans, and here they now sought revenge in the famous battle so fully recorded by our historians. The remoteness of the event, and the discrepancies between Tuscan and Genoese accounts, make it very difficult to obtain absolute knowledge of all the details of this fight. Accordingly it will be safer to fix our attention on the best ascertained and more remarkable points.

The Pisan fleet consisted of three squadrons. Of these, Admiral Andrea Morosini commanded the first; while the second was under Count Ugolino, who, in spite of his courage, was no trustworthy leader, on account of the devouring personal ambition urging him to subordinate the interests of the State to his own greed for power. The third was commanded by Andreotto Saracini. Oberto Doria, an officer of great courage and experience, was high admiral of the Genoese fleet. As it first hove in sight, this armada seemed no greater than that of the Pisans, but only because a reserve of thirty galleys, commanded by Benedetto Zaccaria, lay hidden behind Meloria—or, according to other accounts, behind Montenero—ready to join in the fight when required. Soon after midday the battle began, and raged for some hours without any decisive result. But when the two flag-ships met, both fleets closed in a general engagement. On either side vast numbers of combatants, killed, wounded, or stunned, were hurled into the sea. The waves were crimsoned with blood; drowning men clutched at oars to save their lives, but were relentlessly thrust under by the rowers' next strokes, owing to the impossibility of checking the manœuvres in the thick of the fight, and at the most critical moment. Just then Benedetto Zaccaria, having been signalled for, hove in sight, full sail, and with sweeping oars, in time to decide the fate of the day. Seeing him draw near, the Pisans knew they were outnumbered, and their courage began to fail, although they continued the fight with undiminished ardour. As Zaccaria dashed in, he contrived to bring his galley alongside Doria's, so as to wedge Morosini, whose flag-ship was making a gallant defence. At the same time the galley bearing the Pisan standard was also surrounded by the foe. On all sides the sudden arrival of the reserve squadron had given fresh courage to the Genoese and diminished the hopes of Pisa. The struggle was now too unequal; nevertheless, both sides were unwilling to end it, for each bitter enemy was seeking to destroy not only the other's fleet, but the very life of the rival Republic.

But the conflict could not go on for ever. The Pisan banner, on its tall iron shaft, was suddenly seen to bend, and the next instant it fell with a horrible crash beneath a storm of blows, while at the same moment the admiral's flag-ship began to give way, and Morosini, who had been shockingly wounded in the face, was forced to surrender. At this juncture Count Ugolino, for his own treasonable purposes, gave the signal for flight, and thus completed the catastrophe. Seven Pisan galleys were sunk, twenty-eight captured by the foe, while, according to the inscription on the Church of St. Matteo at Genoa, no less than 9,272 prisoners were taken. Certain Pisan writers raise the number to eleven, and some even to fifteen thousand; but this may have included many of the slain, who may undoubtedly be reckoned at five thousand. At all events, after the battle of Meloria, it became a common saying in Tuscany that one must now go to Genoa in order to see Pisa.

When those who had escaped returned to Pisa, all the town flocked into the streets to ask news of their kindred, and nearly all had to mourn the loss of some killed or captured relations. A host of old men, women, and children wandered about the city maddened with despair, so that at last the magistrates were forced to ordain that all should keep to their own homes. Soon all the inhabitants were clad in black, and only women were seen in the streets. Genoa, on the contrary, rejoiced and made glad; but victory had no wise softened its hatred against Pisa. This was proved when the fate of the prisoners came to be discussed. Some citizens proposed putting them to a heavy ransom; others to exchange them for the Castel di Castro in Sardinia, the key of the Pisan possessions there; but neither suggestion was approved. Orators raised their voices, crying that it were best to retain the prisoners until the war should be really at an end. Thus the women, being practically widowed, but unable to re-marry, population would be checked, and the Pisan army prevented from repairing its losses. In fact, the war continued sixteen years longer; and by the time the prisoners were released, their number was reduced to one thousand and odd, all the rest having succumbed to disease, old age, injuries, or hardships.

VIII.

It is difficult to decide which rose to greater proportions during these years—the heroic endurance of calamity on the part of the Pisans, or the insatiable hatred of their victors. Soon after the catastrophe of Meloria, Florence and Lucca proposed an alliance with Genoa, in order to join that power in completing the extermination of the rival republic. This alliance was to be maintained for twenty-five years from the conclusion of the war. Hostilities were to commence within fifteen days, Genoa being pledged to provide fifty galleys, and Florence and Lucca to furnish an army. Thus the allies could make combined attacks by sea and by land, and were bound to carry on the campaign for at least forty days every year. Pisa understood that her total overthrow was decreed, and her detestation of Lucca, and still more of Florence, was so keen that, to avoid yielding to those states, she professed her readiness to accept instead the terms of submission Genoa had sought to impose. But it was now too late. On the 13th of October the treaty of alliance was subscribed, in the Badia at Florence, by delegates from Lucca and Genoa, together with the representatives of Florence, of whom Brunetto Latini was one. An arrangement was also made allowing the other Tuscan cities to join the League, and, what was far more remarkable, another clause provided for the admission of Pisan prisoners of influential position who should have sworn to make war on their own state. Even Count Ugolino, his sons, and the Judge of Gallura, were to be admitted on the same terms, provided they became Genoese citizens and acknowledged the suzerainty of Genoa over their estates. Nevertheless, no prisoners were to be admitted without the general consent of the allies, and were not to exceed twenty in number. This clause clearly proves that many Pisans were traitorous, or disposed to treason. Nor was Florence forgetful of the aim she had constantly in view; for even on this occasion she took care to insert profitable commercial agreements in the treaty of political alliance.[323]

Several other cities of Tuscany speedily adhered to the League, and preparations for war began. Pisa was soon surrounded on all sides. The Florentines marched into Val d'Era, the Lucchese captured several castles, while Spinola's Genoese squadron attacked Porto Pisano and wrought much damage there. Suddenly, however, the Florentines showed so much slackness in lending their aid, as to excite the grave discontent of Lucca and Genoa. Their chief object was to promote their own commerce; hence, while anxious to break Pisa's pride, and reduce the city to submission on the plan pursued with other Tuscan towns, it did not suit their views to let the Genoese usurp the chief share of the work, much less the lion's share of the profit. Yet, as things stood, the latter's naval superiority rendered this result only too certain.

For, were Genoa once mistress of Pisa, the Mediterranean would be practically hers, and, with so much increased power, would be truly formidable to Florence.

Accordingly, after raising such a host of enemies against Pisa, the Florentines now tried to turn things to their own exclusive advantage, and, with the usual double dealing of the period, paid little respect to the treaties they had sworn to observe. The Pisans instantly saw their opportunity and sought to profit by it; but in so bungling a fashion as to hasten their ruin. As we have already related, they had vainly attempted to come to terms with Genoa, and, their grievous calamities rendering them unable to cope with assailants equally formidable by land and by sea, they now made endeavours to conciliate Florence. For this purpose they nominated Count Ugolino to the office of Podestà, and even entrusted him subsequently with the direction of the war, in spite of the general belief that he had played the traitor at Meloria. For, knowing him to be Guelph, and secretly favourable to the Florentines, they considered him fitted to fulfil their purpose of detaching the latter from the Genoese interests. They knew, also, that the count was absorbed in the single idea of establishing his own domination in Pisa; therefore he would be ready to come to terms, if required, with the enemies of his country, and be capable of the worst crimes in order to gratify his enormous ambition. But, this ambition once sated, the Pisans believed that, possessing many friends among the Guelphs, his courage and astuteness would enable him to arrange satisfactory terms. This proved to be the case, but his intervention led to very unexpected results.

The chroniclers relate that Ugolino sent the rectors of Florence a present of Vernaccia wine, with gold florins at the bottom of every flask as a bribe.[324] This legend merely signifies that he was considered capable of employing any means to attain his own ends. At all events, he was obliged to impose very cruel sacrifices on Pisa before the Florentines could be induced to suspend hostilities. It was necessary to cede important domains, castles such as Sta Maria a Monte, Fucecchio, Sta Croce, and Monte Calvoli, and to restore the city to the Guelphs by banishing all the Ghibellines—the direst humiliation to a republic that had always been steadfastly Ghibelline. But, with her very existence at stake, Pisa was bound to submit even to this.

When, however, the Genoese and Lucchese discovered that the Florentines had deserted them and were siding with Pisa against Lucca, they complained so bitterly of this breach of faith, that Count Ugolino deemed it well to at least silence Lucca by the cession of Bientina, Ripafratta, and Viareggio. In this manner the haughty Pisan Republic was stripped of nearly all its territories outside the city gates, and deprived of all power of defending the coast, at a time when its ships were being chased and plundered by the Genoese on every sea. Amid the general ruin and desolation, however, Ugolino triumphed; for now, being absolute lord of Pisa, his dearest desire was fulfilled. Nevertheless, his power was much less secure than he supposed, for the fiery Pisan spirit was not entirely extinguished, and already the majority of the citizens were growing intolerant of a tyranny at home failing to spare them humiliations abroad. The smallest occasion served to show that public feeling was on the verge of an outbreak.

Much discontent was also provoked in the course of negotiations with Genoa for the restitution of the prisoners, comprising many of Pisa's best sons. Their release was desired at any cost; but the count, knowing them to be Ghibellines, and consequently opposed to himself, daily invented fresh obstacles to prevent their return, and by proposing terms the Pisans could not accept, always caused fresh delays. Thus, as he intended, no conclusion could be arrived at. But his arrogance finally produced discord even among his own party. His nephew, Nino Visconti, judge of Gallura, and the natural head of the Guelph faction, began to make overtures to the Ghibellines for the purpose of combating his uncle. Thereupon Ugolino promptly sent many other Ghibellines into exile, and demolished ten of their grandest palaces. This produced an outburst of indignation. Nino made close alliance with the Gualandi and Sismondi, and all tried to hasten the prisoners' release, while the count found fresh pretexts for delay by reviving causes of dispute with Genoa.

After vain attempts to rouse the people against him, Nino and his friends resorted to legal measures, hoping in this way to curb his tyrannous excesses. He had been nominated Captain-general of the people, but had illegally usurped the office of Podestà in addition, and fixed his residence in the palace of the Signory, where he had no right to dwell. His nephew and the others sued him for this before the *Anziani*, and obliged him to leave the palace in conformity with the law. He obeyed for a short time, but soon resumed his former supremacy by force. Meanwhile, party hatred grew stronger, the count fomenting discord with Genoa, while his enemies, as another means to his overthrow, were doing their utmost to conclude peace and deliver the prisoners.

At last the count discerned his peril, and tried to find some way of escape. Seeing that certain Guelphs were no less hostile than the Ghibellines and had joined with them against him, he decided on conciliating the latter, in order to detach them from the Guelphs who had forsaken his cause. Thus he might at once defeat these deserters, and, having isolated the Ghibellines, find it easy to destroy them later on.

But, in spite of these ingenious devices, both parties finally combined against him, under the command of Archbishop Ruggiero, one of the most powerful of the Ghibellines. Civil war raged in the city; the public palace was alternately seized by the archbishop, and re-captured by the count; while the latter, blinded by his fury for revenge, rejected the warnings and advice of even his closest adherents. One day, when the popular discontent had come to a climax, in consequence of the high price of provisions, and no one ventured to inform him of it, one of his nephews demanded audience, explained the state of things, and advised him to suspend the levying of customs, so as to lower the price of food. But this enraged the count to such a point that, drawing his dagger, he stabbed the speaker in the arm. A nephew of the archbishop chanced to be present, and being a friend of the wounded man, rushed forward to shield him from further attack. Thereupon the count, maddened with fury, caught up an axe that lay near, and with one blow stretched the intruder dead at his feet.

The Archbishop Ruggieri dissimulated for a while, waiting his chance to take revenge. It came at last. On July 1, 1288, the council of the Republic was assembled in the Church of St. Sebastian to discuss the arrangement of peace with Genoa. Both the Ghibellines and people yearned for peace at any cost; but the count raised fresh obstacles, still relying on the support of his friends. As the meeting dispersed, the archbishop perceived that the favourable moment had arrived, and that no time must be lost. The Gualandi, Sismondi, Lanfranchi and other houses joined with him, and all proceeded to attack Ugolino. The latter made a valiant resistance, aided by two of his sons, two nephews, and a few devoted followers. After the first encounter, in which Ugolino's natural son was slain before his eyes, he took refuge in the palace of the people, and defended it from midday to dusk, when the besiegers decided to set it on fire. Then, forcing their way through the flames, they captured the count, with his two younger sons, Gaddo and Uguccione, and his nephews Nino, surnamed Brigata, and Anselmuccio. The prisoners were thrown into the Gualandi tower on the Piazza degli Anziani, and Ruggieri kept them most closely confined there for several months. [325] Finally the key of the tower was cast into the Arno, and all left to die of starvation, amid the torments immortalised by Dante's pen. [326]

IX.

These events, while still further reducing the strength of the unfortunate city, likewise caused the overthrow of the Pisan Guelphs, by once more driving them into exile, and promoted the hopes of the Ghibellines, who now seemed to have gained new life in Tuscany. Accordingly Florence was again compelled to recur to arms. Charles I of Anjou was no more, and Pope Honorius, being favourable to the Ghibellines, had instigated his kinsman, Prenzivalle del Fiesco, to assume the post of vicar-imperial in Tuscany, But as the cities of the League gave him a very rough reception, he retired to Arezzo, and vainly promulgated edicts against the Guelphs. By this time no one heeded the words of Imperial vicars. On realising this he went back to Germany, leaving Arezzo a prey to conflicts, in which the Ghibellines won the victory, with the help of numerous Florentine exiles. The Guelphs sought refuge in neighbouring castles, whither reinforcements reached them from the Florentine Signory. Thus the war spread even to the Upper Val d'Arno; for as the Ghibellines had returned to power, both in Arezzo and Pisa, led by the spiritual lord of either town, they had now to be encountered on two sides. In Pisa their chief was the Archbishop Ubaldini, in Arezzo, Guglielmo degli Ubertini, an equally Ghibelline prelate. The latter was also a better warrior than priest, the lord of many strongholds, and being of a very slippery nature, first attempted to betray the city to the Florentines, in return for an agreement guaranteeing him his possessions. The men of Arezzo contrived, however, to compel him to keep faith with his own party. On June 1, 1288, the army of the League took the field. It comprised nobles and *popolani* from every part of Tuscany, and together with the mercenary troops reached a total of 2,600 horse and 12,000 foot. They carried on the campaign for twenty-two days, capturing and razing about forty castles, great and small, on the Aretine territory; but then a great storm wrought so much damage to their encampments, that they were forced to beat a retreat. As a mark of insult to the enemy, they had held races under the walls of Arezzo, naming twelve knights *di corredo*;[327] but then, raising the siege, they went back to Florence, leaving their foes unconquered and undismayed. In fact, when the Siennese separated from the main body on the way to their own city, they were surprised by a band of Aretines in ambush, and thoroughly routed.

During the month of August the Florentines joined with the Pisan Guelph exile, Nino di Gallura, made raids on Pisan lands, and occupied the Castle of Asciano; then, in September, they marched against the Aretines, who had now gathered an army of seven hundred horse and eight thousand foot. No pitched battle, however, took place, for the enemy retreated before the Florentines, leaving them to devastate the country at their will, but afterwards made reprisal in the beginning of 1289, by laying waste the Florentine territory, and penetrating almost as far as San Donato. These variously important skirmishes paved the way for more serious hostilities.

All Tuscany was now preparing for war. The captain elected by Pisa was

Count Guido da Montefeltro, who had risen to the highest distinction by his victory over the French troops of Charles of Anjou at the battle of Forlì. He was undoubtedly one of the bravest warriors of the time, and on his arrival in Pisa quickly reorganised the militia, and created a new body of light infantry of three thousand crossbowmen, able to do good service against the heavy cavalry then considered the chief strength of an army. On the other hand, the Aretines increased their forces so much, that when Charles II. of Anjou passed through Florence on the way to his coronation in Naples, the Florentines were obliged to grant him an escort of their best horse and foot soldiers, to protect him from the attack threatened by the men of Arezzo. On this occasion they asked the king for a good leader, to enable them to pursue the campaign energetically, and Amerigo de Narbonne being appointed to the post, he joined them, accompanied by William de Durfort and one hundred men-at-arms.

On June 2, 1289, the new captain, Narbonne, took the field with an army of one thousand horse and ten thousand foot soldiers of the League. It comprised the flower of the Florentine nobles and commons, including six hundred of the best-equipped knights ever furnished by the city. Prato, Pistoia, Sienna, and all the allies, including the Guelphs of Romagna, had sent their due contingents. Meanwhile the Aretines had collected all the Ghibellines from neighbouring cities, and were encamped at Bibbiena with eight hundred horse and eight thousand foot, under the command of their captains, the greatest of whom was the daring Bishop Guglielmo degli Ubertini. On finding that he could not make terms with Florence to secure his own strongholds, without being exposed to the vengeance of the Aretines, he had plunged into the war with youthful ardour. His conduct was arrogant and full of assurance; for he relied on his own courage and that of his men, and despised the Florentines, because, so he said, they were as sleek as womenfolk.

On the 11th of June the two armies met in the plain of Poppi, near Campaldino, where the engagement began. The battle is known by that name, and rendered all the more celebrated by the fact of Dante Alighieri—then young and unknown—having fought in it. The Florentines had placed a mixed host of infantry, crossbowmen, and bucklermen in the van, and their wings were formed of 150 skirmishing light horse, who were all picked men. Vieri de' Cerchi was among the latter; for, having been entrusted with the choice of those of his *sestiere*, he insisted, in spite of illness, on accompanying his son and nephews to the battlefield. In the rear of the first division a stronger force of heavy cavalry and infantry was drawn up, with the baggage-train behind. Corso Donati led a band of about 250 foot and horse from Lucca, Pistoia, and foreign parts. He was Podestà of Pistoia at the time, and was directed to hold his reserve back until the commander-in-chief gave the signal to advance. On either side there was a fever of emulation between the Guelphs and the Ghibellines, and to gratify the ambition of their respective leaders, some were awarded the honour of knighthood that day, in order to spur them to greater feats. The Florentines were under orders to await the enemy's charge, and Messer Simone dei Mangiadori of San Miniato shouted to his men, "Signori! our Tuscan battles used to be won by vigorous assault, but are now to be won by standing still." The Aretines, on the contrary, trusting to their own courage and their leader's skill, made so impetuous a charge to the cry of *"Viva San Donato!"* that the Florentine army wavered, and gave way before the shock. Nearly all the light horse were hurled from their saddles, and the main body fell back. But the foot soldiers flanking the second corps moved forward to the cry of *"Narbona cavaliere!"* and by threatening to surround the enemy, checked its advance, and thus gave their comrades time to re-form. Count Guido Novello, in command of 150 Aretine mounted skirmishers, lost his presence of mind, and by failing to attack the foe at the moment when their ranks were in confusion, caused much harm by the delay. But this was his usual behaviour, and presently, as the fight grew hotter, he took to flight—also as usual. On the other hand, Corso Donati, although instructed to keep his men steady, and not to advance until expressly summoned, could not remain inert on beholding the Florentines waver at the first shock of encounter, and cried aloud, "If we lose, I will perish with my fellow-citizens; if we win, let who likes come to Pistoia to punish our disobedience;" and so saying, gave the command to take the enemy in flank. Thus the attacking Aretines were now charged in their turn. They made an admirable resistance, and their cavalry being insufficient, the infantry crawled on all fours among the advancing troops, and disembowelled their steeds. But no prodigies of personal courage could avail to decide the battle. There was a fierce and prolonged mêlée; the Florentines fought stubbornly, and nearly all the leaders of the Aretines were killed. Archbishop Ubertini fell, sword in hand; so, too, his nephew, Guglielmino dei Pazzi, held to be one of the bravest captains in Italy, and Buonconte, the Count of Montefeltro's son. Many Florentines perished, including three of the Uberti and one of the Abbati. Count Guido Novello alone saved his skin by flight. The Aretines were thoroughly routed, and, according to Villani, left seventeen hundred dead on the field, and two thousand prisoners in the enemy's hands. But of these only 740 reached Florence, the rest having escaped or been ransomed. This is not very surprising, when we remember that in these Guelph and Ghibelline wars fellow-citizens, and old friends or relations, often had to meet in combat; and that consequently leniency was more natural than hatred, although there are only too many instances of the ferocity to which the latter feeling was carried. The Florentine losses were slight and unimportant.

Corso Donati, whose daring charge greatly contributed to decide the struggle, and Vieri de' Cerchi were both covered with glory. Many men previously deemed of little account won high reputation that day, while many others forfeited their fame. At any rate, all the best citizens and captains returned safely to Florence, and there was general rejoicing in the city.[328]

The Florentines had felt assured of victory from the outset. In fact we are told that the priors, having fallen asleep on the day of the battle, worn out by their previous vigils, they were suddenly awakened by the sound of a voice seeming to cry: "Arise, for the Aretines are beaten." At that moment all the citizens were in the streets, waiting impatiently the arrival of news. At last the desired messenger appeared, and there was an outburst of joy and festivity. Later on discontent was excited by hearing that the army had failed to follow up the victory by giving pursuit to the foe. For had the latter been driven back into Arezzo, that town might have been easily seized. Instead of this, the forces captured Bibbiena, belonging to the bishop, plundered several castles, and devastated the country for twenty days. They ran races round the walls of Arezzo, and used their rams to drop asses crowned with mitres into the town, in order to insult its inhabitants. But they suspended all serious hostilities for the time, although, when the new priors had been chosen, the government at once despatched two of them to the camp, in order to push forward the war in person, and hasten the capture of the city. But the favourable moment had passed, for the Aretines made some successful sallies, and set fire to all the besiegers' engines of assault. Accordingly, leaving a sufficient force to guard the captured castles and unfinished siege-works, the Florentines returned home on the 23rd of July, much to the displeasure of the citizens, who murmured that the enemy's gold must have been poured into the camp. Nevertheless, a great victory had been won, and the soldiers were received with vast demonstrations of delight. All the people, with the banners and insignia of every guild, and the whole of the clergy, went forth in procession to welcome the conquerors. The Captain, Amerigo de Narbonne, and Ugolino de' Rossi, the Podestà, entered the town in state, beneath sumptuous canopies of cloth of gold, borne by the noblest of Florentine knights. The entire cost of the campaign was paid by levying a property tax of six *lire*, six *soldi* per cent. in the city and its territory. This tax soon yielded a product of thirty-six thousand gold florins, owing, as Villani remarks (vii. 132), to the admirable administration and organisation of the financial affairs of the Commune at that time.

After humiliating the two hostile cities of Arezzo and Pisa, the Florentine Republic had overthrown the Ghibellines and assured the triumph of the Guelphs throughout Tuscany, and thus gained almost unlimited influence, both political and commercial. Hence there was a vast and rapid increase of prosperity. Great festivities and banquets were held in all the wealthiest houses, and palace courtyards, covered with silken canopies and draped with gorgeous stuffs, served as places of entertainment for the citizens. In token of rejoicing the womenfolk paraded the streets wearing garlands of flowers. Nevertheless, there was a general wish to continue the war, in the hope of completing the overthrow of the two most powerful Ghibelline cities. This, however, was no easy task.

In 1289 there were fresh skirmishes between the Guelphs and Ghibellines, although none of any importance. The Florentines made several attempts to capture Arezzo by force and by fraud, but always in vain. In November they had contrived a secret arrangement by means of which it was hoped to surprise the city. A decree was suddenly issued summoning all able- bodied men to assemble outside the walls before a candle lighted at one of the gates should have time to burn down. The army thus hastily gathered made a forced march on Arezzo; but the treason plotted there had been already discovered: a dying man, rumour said, having revealed it to his confessor. At any rate, the army was obliged to withdraw from a bootless errand.

In the June of the ensuing year, 1290, the Florentines resumed the campaign with an army of 1,500 horse and 6,000 foot, furnished by the League. Surrounding Arezzo, they devastated the territory within a circuit of six miles, for the space of twenty-nine days, but without achieving any farther result. At that period all cities were fortified, and before the invention of gunpowder siege operations had no chance of success, save by treason, against a resolute defence. Now, too, the Florentines were trying to carry on a double campaign, against Arezzo on the one hand and Pisa on the other. In fact, presently leaving three hundred horse and a considerable number of foot soldiers to garrison the neighbouring strongholds, they transferred the rest of the army from the Upper to the Lower Val d'Arno, to act against Pisa.

In the preceding year, aided by Florence and the League, Lucca had taken the field with four hundred horse and two thousand foot, in order to carry on the war with Pisa, while the Florentines were busied with Arezzo. This force encamped before Pisa, and, according to usage, held races there; harried the territory for twenty-five days, captured the Castle of Caprona, and made several assaults on Vico Pisano, but achieved no farther result. Now, in 1290, the Florentines resumed the attack in combination with all the great forces of the League. And while this army was making a general attack by land, the Genoese fleet swooped down on the coast with deadly effect. Leghorn and Porto Pisano were taken, the four towers guarding the harbour were thrown into the sea, and the Meloria lighthouse destroyed in the same way, together with its keepers. Before setting sail the Genoese blocked the mouth of the harbour by sinking four ships laden with ballast, and demolished all warehouses and palaces. But the havoc wrought by land was confined to the destruction of crops and the demolition of petty strongholds. Meanwhile the Pisans made a brave resistance on all sides. Guido di Montefeltro, their captain, used his newly invented troop of light horse to excellent effect against the Tuscan infantry of the League and the heavy cavalry in its pay. By his successful sallies he repeatedly achieved a bloody revenge for past losses. In December, 1291, the Pisans marched on the Castle of Pontedera, and finding it slackly defended, accomplished its capture, and shortly afterwards stirred the Castle of Vignale to revolt against San Miniato. Thereupon the Florentines decided on sending an army to provoke a fresh engagement; but the expedition was too long delayed, and the troops had hardly started before torrents of rain inundated the country and compelled them to retreat.

Military operations now slackened more and more, for mischief was brewing in the city, and all men foresaw that worse troubles were at hand. Therefore, although urged to resume hostilities by their valiant and energetic leader, the Judge of Gallura, the Florentines so sorely needed tranquillity that they finally concluded a treaty of peace at Fucecchio on June 12, 1293. According to its stipulations, all prisoners of war were to be released; no duties were to be levied on inhabitants of the communes of the League in passing through Pisa, nor on Pisans passing through the said communes. The office of Podestà or Captain of Pisa was only to be held by a member of the League, and it was expressly forbidden to confer that post on any rebel or adversary of the said League, or any scion of the Montefeltro house. Further, Count Guido, the brave chief who had shown so much energy and daring in defence of the Pisan Republic, was to be dismissed, together with all the foreign Ghibellines; and twenty-five citizens of the best Pisan blood were to be given in hostage to secure the due observance of the terms. Such was the reward of the veteran leader's fidelity and heroism! On being paid off, he entered the council chamber, and after reproving the ingratitude of the Pisans in dignified words, took his leave without expressing any wish for revenge. Yet, being still in command of an experienced army devoted to himself, vengeance lay in his power, had he chosen to follow the fashion of the times. Another clause of the treaty provided that the descendants of Count Ugolino and the Judge of Gallura should be freed from outlawry and reinstated in all
329
their possessions.

X.

From this moment the Florentines devoted their chief attention to the affairs of the city, although these had not been altogether neglected, even during the last wars. Continual improvements had been made in the administration of the Republic, and in many respects it was a model administration, while there was also a notable increase of commerce, trade, and wealth. At the same time many public works had been completed under the direction of the famous architect Arnolfo di Cambio, the creator of some of the grandest public buildings in Florence. He planned the alterations for the enlargement of the city, first undertaken in 1285, and afterwards built the third circuit of walls, the which work was also superintended by the celebrated chronicler Giovanni Villani. It was likewise by Arnolfo's care that the Loggia of Or' San Michele, then used as a corn market, was built in and paved, the Piazza dei Signori supplied with a pavement, and the Badia embellished and restored. Folco Portinari, the father of Dante's Beatrice, founded, at his own expense, the church and hospital of Santa Maria Nuova. The Piazza of Santa Maria Novella was laid out, and many other public works of a similar kind were begun. [330]

Meanwhile political reforms were uninterruptedly carried on, and among them the notable measure passed in 1289, reducing the Podestà's term of office from twelve to six months. [331] The post was then conferred on Rosso Gabrielli of Gubbio, a city supplying many Podestàs and Captains of the people not only to Florence, but to all parts of Italy. At that period Romagna, Umbria, and the Marches seemed to be a nursery of these dignitaries, the inhabitants of those provinces being not only well trained to arms, as is proved by the horde of captains and soldiers of adventure they sent forth, but also well versed in the legal lore of the neighbouring university of Bologna. This reduction to six months of the Podestà's tenure of office was not long maintained, but had been decreed for the same motives as the change of Signory every two months. The power of a magistrate authorised to administer justice, in command of the army and invariably escorted by a body of armed followers in his private pay, might be easily transformed into a formidable despotism, as several Italian republics had already found to their cost. Hence it was endeavoured to avert this danger from Florence by changing the magistrates so frequently as to allow no time for hatching plots against the Commonwealth, or forming a party whose adherence could be counted on for any length of time.

But political and social changes of a very different and far graver kind were now brewing among the citizens of Florence. Signs of a new and radical transformation were becoming daily more pronounced; hence the greater need of assuring peace in order to withstand the inevitable and imminent shock of coming revolutions. The presence of the Angevins in Florence, the example set by their nobles, and their continual creation of new knights, had swelled the arrogance of the leading Guelphs to a boundless extent. These patricians were now known by the name of *grandi*, and in imitation of the French nobility assumed manners ill-suited to a republican state, trying to rule everything and all men according to their will. A serious riot took place in 1287, because one of these chieftains, named Totto Mazzinghi, being condemned to death by the Podestà for murder and other crimes, Messer Corco Donati, one of the leading nobles of Florence, attempted to rescue him by force on the way to the scaffold. Thereupon the Podestà, resenting such open violation of the law, caused the alarm bell to be rung. The people flocked to the place of execution sword in hand, some mounted, some on foot, to the cry of "*Giustizia, Giustizia!*" and the sentence was then carried out with the uttermost rigour of the law. The condemned Mazzinghi was dragged through the streets before being hung; the promoters of the revolt against the magistrates were heavily fined, and order was re-established in the city. But these disturbances were indicative of deeper evils to come, and Florentine statesmen were full of anxiety. In order to check the arrogance of the *grandi*, and prevent them from combining with the populace, the middle-class Guelphs began to grant political rights on a continuously wider scale, while restricting the power of the nobles. As we have already seen, the latter had been obliged to provide sureties personally responsible for their actions, to swear to abstain from deeds of vengeance, from oppressing the people and so forth. The very remarkable law passed on August 6, 1289, served to overthrow the might of the nobles, both within and without the city walls, and to enhance that of the people by destroying the last lingering remains of the feudal system. Thanks to this decree, serfdom was entirely abolished throughout the territory; for in terms resembling a proclamation of the rights of man, it declared liberty to be an imprescriptible, natural right, a right never to be dependent on another's will; and that the Republic was determined not only to maintain liberty intact throughout its dominions, but likewise increase the same.[332] Thus every species of bondage, whether for a term or for life, was abolished, together with all contracts or agreements infringing on the liberty of the individual.

It has been thought by some writers that the Commune of Bölogna had already achieved this most important reform in 1256, and that Florence only followed its example thirty-three years later. But this was an error induced by supposing that in the Italian communes the abolition of serfdom was completed at one stroke, whereas, on the contrary, it was carried out very slowly and in different degrees. In the territory there were not only *nobles* and their *serfs*, but also *fideles*, whose personality was already recognised by law, but who still remained dependents of the *nobiles* and bound to yield them service and tribute. At a later date the condition of the *fideles* was further ameliorated; they could hold land in fee from their lords, or by payment of a yearly rent (a *livello*), but remained bound to them on terms of villeinage, and therefore bound to the soil. For this reason the lords believed, or feigned to believe themselves entitled to sell the soil, together with the *fideles* attached to it, even when this was no longer in accordance with the spirit of the law. The Bölognese abolished serfdom in 1256, but the peasantry remained in their master's dependence, that is, more or less as *fideles*, and although these conditions were ameliorated in 1283 they were not altogether abrogated. But even earlier than 1289 serfs had ceased to exist in the Florentine territory, and, judicially, the *fideles* had been long considered almost independent of their masters, although the latter, by the abuse of purely personal contracts, often compelled them to remain attached to the soil and claimed the right of disposing of them, as well as of the land. These were the abuses condemned and suppressed by the Florentines in 1289, as being adverse to liberty, "the which is a natural and therefore inalienable right." The new law likewise decreed that in consequence of this natural right all the above-mentioned sales became null and void; and cancelling every illegal contract, it finally guaranteed complete freedom to the peasantry. And by another clause every peasant was thenceforth enabled (irrespective of any sale of the land) to purchase his emancipation from any personal contract binding him to the proprietor of the soil. Thus the law of 1289 did not abolish serfdom, inasmuch as that institution had been already suppressed by the Florentines some time before, but it assured, for the first time, complete liberty to the cultivators of the soil. Economically, the new law was very advantageous to the Commune, by converting the peasantry into direct contributors, and no less advantageous to the democracy, inasmuch as it broke the last links of the feudal system, and weakened the power of the nobles throughout the *contado*.[333]

Many other measures were also passed in 1289 and 1290 for the purpose of strengthening the position of the people in the city, and serving to show that Florence steadily pursued the work of political and social transformation. First of all, the number of legally constituted guilds was increased by adding five more to the seven greater guilds, and all having their special insignia, organisation, arms, and political attributes.[334] We now find records of twelve greater guilds in the archives of the Republic, whereas, previously to this date, seven only were mentioned. It is true that the number was very soon reduced again to seven; but then the five omitted were joined to nine others, these fourteen designated as the lesser guilds, and the total number of the guilds was finally fixed at twenty-one. In 1290 another law was passed, called *the law of prohibition*, decreeing that no prior could be re-elected to office until three years had elapsed. Later on this prohibition was partially extended even to the kinsmen of a prior.[335] The scope of these measures was always to prevent the rise of any future tyranny and to keep the growing arrogance of the nobles in check.

Other laws were also framed for the same purpose. As, for instance, the two decrees carried almost unanimously on June 30, and July 3, 1290.[336] By these all guild-masters were prohibited, under severe penalties, from forming monopolies, agreements, compacts, fictitious sales, or other arrangements tending to the imposition of arbitrary prices, regardless of the rules prescribed by statute. And not only the individuals guilty of such infringement were subject to punishment and to be mulcted in the sum of 100 *lire*, but the guild to which they belonged was also subject to a fine of 500 *lire* for neglecting to enforce obedience to the laws, and its rectors and consuls were to be mulcted in 200 *lire*.

On January 2, 1291, another law was passed of a far weightier import, with the clearly expressed aim of curbing by force the wolfish rapacity of the nobles (volentes lupinas carnes salsamentis caninis involvi).[337] This decree rigorously prohibited recourse to any tribunal or magistrate save to the legally constituted authorities, such as the priors, the Captain, Podestà, or the judges in ordinary of the Commune. All persons having obtained from the Pope, Emperor, King Charles, or their respective vicars exemptions of any kind, or right of appeal to other magistrates, and pretending to exercise such right, and all persons who, with the same intent, should assert the power of exercising old feudal privileges, were warned to refrain from attempting to use such rights under penalty of the severest punishment. The new law minutely described different forms of similar fictitious exemptions, and determined the penalties incurred by their use. What seems strangest of all is, that this law decreed the punishment not only of persons asserting and trying to exercise the above-mentioned rights, of the notaries transcribing the acts, and the lawyers declaring them valid; but in cases where the real criminals should escape punishment, it likewise held responsible the relations and distant connections of the guilty, and even their labourers and tenants. At that period the populace, the well-to-do burghers and the nobles (*grandi*) formed as it were three classes of citizens, or, indeed, three distinct social bodies, who both for offence and defence, in all questions of party rancour, revenge or political privilege, acted as though every one was willingly and of necessity bound to be responsible for the deeds of his colleagues. Hence, recognising this state of things, certain extreme measures were decreed, which, although opportune and even imperative at the moment—in order to forward the democratic cause by assisting the weak to struggle against the powerful class —were none the less arbitrary. However, the necessity of employing the most stringent remedies was becoming daily more obvious. The nobles had been too much uplifted by the favours heaped on them by the Pope and the Angevins. And the brilliant success recently achieved at Campaldino, where victory had been decided by the prowess of Corso Donati and Vieri de' Cerchi, had so swelled their pride that they openly vaunted their contempt for the law, and constantly violated its prescriptions. This state of things finally produced the revolution of 1293, resulting in the constitution of the second popular government (*il secondo popolo*) and the total overthrow of the nobles.

NOTE A.

"In Dei nomine amen. Anno sue salutifere incarnationis millesimo ducetesimo octuagesimo nono, indictione secunda, die sexto intrante mense augusti. Cum libertas, qua cuiusque voluntas, non ex alieno, sed ex proprio dependet arbitrio, iure naturali multipliciter decoretur, qua etiam civitates et populi ab oppressionibus defenduntur, et ipsorum iura tuentur et augentur in melius, volentes ipsam et eius species non solum manutenere, sed etiam augmentare, per dominos Priores Artium civitatis Florentie, et alios Sapientes et bonos viros ad hoc habitos, et in domo Ghani Foresii et Consortum, in qua ipsi Priores pro Comuni morantur, occasione providendi super infrascriptis unanimiter congregatos, ex licentia, bailia et auctoritate in eos collata, et eisdem eshibita et concessa in Consiliis et per Consilia domini Defensoris et Capitanei et etiam Comunis Florentie, provisum, ordinatum extitit salubriter et firmatum: Quod nullus, undecumque sit et cuiuscumque conditioni dignitatis vel status existat, possit audeat vel presumat per se vel per alium tacite vel espresse emere, vel alio aliquo titulo, iure, modo vel causa adquirere in perpetuum vel ad tempus aliquos Fideles. Colonos perpetuos vel conditionales, Adscriptitios vel Censitos vel aliquos alios cuiuscumque conditionis existant, vel aliqua alia iura scilicet angharia vel perangharia, vel quevis alia contra libertatem et condictionem persone alicuius, in civitate vel comitatu vel districtu Florentie; et quod nullus, undecumque sit, et cuiusque condictionis, dignitatis vel status existat, possit, audeat vel presumat predicta vel aliquid predictorum vendere, vel quovis alio titulo alienare, iure modo vel causa concedere in perpetuum vel ad tempus alicui persone, undecumque sit, vel cuiusque condictionis dignitatis vel status, in Civitate vel comitatu vel districtu Florentie, decernentes irritum et inane et ipso iure non tenere, si quid in contrarium fieret in aliquo casu predictorum. Et tales contractus et alienationes quatenus procederent, de facto cassantes, ita quod nec emptoribus vel acquisitoribus ius aliquod acquiratur, nec etiam ad alienantes vel concedentes ins redeat, vel quomodolibet penes eos remaneat: sed sint tales Fideles, vel alterius conditionis astricti, et eorum bona, et filii et descendentes libere condictionis et status. Et nihilominus tales alienantes, vel quomodolibet in alios transferentes, in perpetuum vel ad tempus, per se vel per alium et quilibet eorum, et ipsorum et cuiusque eorum sindici, procuratores et nuntii, et tales emptores, vel alio quovis titulo, modo, causa vel iure acquirentes, per se vel per alium in perpetuum modo vel ad tempus, et eorum procuratores, sindici et nuntii et iudices et notarii et testes, qui predictis interfuerint vel ea scripserint, et quilibet eorum, condempnentur in libris mille f. p., que effectualiter exigantur, non obstantibus aliquibus pactis vel conventionibus, etiam iuramento vel pena vallatis, iam factis vel in posterum ineundis, super predictis vel aliquo predictorum vendendis, permutandis vel alio quovis modo vel titulo transferendis. Quos contractus supradicti domini Priores et Sapientes nullius valoris et roboris fore decreverunt, et quatenus de facto processissent vel procederent, totaliter cassaverunt et cassant. Decernentes etiam quod si aliquis non subiectus iurisdictioni Comunis Florentie, et qui non respondeat in civilibus et criminalibus regimini florentino, vel non solvat libras et factiones Comunis Florentie, undecunque sit, per se vel per alium, predictos contractus vel aliquem predictorum iniret aliquo modo iure vel causa, quod pater et fratres et alii propinquiores ipsius, si patrem vel fratrem non haberet, et quilibet eorum condempnentur in libris mille f. p., que pena effectualiter exigatur; reservantes etiam sibi et populo florentino potestatem super predictis et quolibet predictorum acrius providendi contra tales concedentes vel concessiones recipientes per se vel per alium in aliquibus casibus de predictis. Et quod in predictis omnibus et singulis et circa predicta domini Potestas et Defensor et Capitaneus presentes et futuri et quilibet eorum plenum, merum et liberum arbitrium habeant et exercere debeant contra illos, qui in predictis vel circa predicta committerent in personis et rebus, ita et taliter quod predicta omnia et singula effectualiter observentur et executioni mandentur. Salvo tamen quod Comuni Florentie quilibet possit licite vendere et in ipsum Comune predicta iura transferre; et etiam ipsi Fideles et alii supradicti se ipsos et eorum filios et descendentes et bona licite possint redimere sine pena; et illi tales qui talia iura haberent, possint ipsa iura ipsis fidelibus volentibus se redimere vendere et eos liberare a tali iure licite et impune. Et hec omnia et singula locum habeant ad futura et etiam ad preterita, a kallendis ianuarii proxime presentis citra, currentibus annis Domini millesimo CC°

LXXXVIII° indictione secunda."

This law was read and approved of in the general and special council of the captain and of the *capitudini*, as was the custom, but not in that of the Podestà. It has been published many times, but not without mistakes and omissions: by the lawyer Migliorotto Maccioni in a work of his in favour of the Counts of Gherardesca (vol. ii. p. 74); by C. F. Von Rumohr, "Ursprung der Besitzlosigkeit des Colonen in neuren Toscana" (Hamburg, 1830), pp. 100–103; and in the "Osservatore Fiorentino" (vol. iv. p. 179). Florence: Ricci, 1821. We give it as it is in the original text in the State Archives of Florence, *Provvisioni* Registro 2, a. c. 24–25.

NOTE B.

The defender of the artisans and of the guilds, Captain and *Conservatore* of the city and commune of Florence, brought forward the proposal in the special and general council on June 30, 1290, "presentibus et volentibus Dominis Prioribus Artium," and the proposal, carried almost unanimously (*placuit quasi omnibus*), ran as follows:
—"Quia per quamplures homines civitatis Florentie fide dignos, relatum est coram officio dominorum Priorum Artium, quod multi sunt artifices et comunitates seu universitates Artium et earum Rectores, qui certum modum et formam indecentem, et certum precium incongruum imponunt in eorum mercantiis et rebus eorum Artium vendendis contra iustitiam et Rempublicam." It ended by strictly forbidding every sort of monopoly and every contract of sale arranged in a manner contrary to custom or to the laws, "et quod dogana aliqua vel compositio non fiat contra honorem et iurisdictionem Comunis Florentie, per quam vel quas prohibitum sit a Rectoribus vel Consulibus ipsorum Artis, quod aliqui vel aliquis ad certum modum et certam formam et certum precium vendant, vel vendere debeant mercantias," ec. To which Guidotto Canigiani added, that the signory should henceforward formulate other articles, not so as to weaken the said provision, but only to strengthen it more and more in the interest of the guilds. And his amendment was approved together with the provision itself (State Archives, Florence, *Provvisioni*, Registro iv. c. 29). And on the 3rd of July, by reason of the former amendment, the *priori* of the guilds, together with the other wise men consulted by them, decreed: "Quod nulli Consules vel Rectores alicuius Artis, aut aliquis alius, vice et nomine alicuius Artis, vel aliqua singularis persona alicuius Artis, utatur aliquo ordinamento scripto vel non scripto, extra

Constitutum Artis approbatum per Comune Florentie, vel aliter vel ultra quam contineatur in statuto talis Artis, ec.... Et siqua facta essent in contarium vel fierent in futuro tacite vel expresse, non valeant nec teneant ullo modo vel iure, sed sint cassa et irrita ipso iure ec. Et quod nullus notarius vel alius scriptor scribere debeat aliquid de predictis vel contra predicta, et nullus nuntius vel alius precipiat aliquid aliquibus artificibus contra predicta: sub pena Rectori et Consuli contrafacienti auferenda librarum cc. pro quolibet et qualibet vice; et Arti, librarum quingentarum; et sub pena librarum centum pro quolibet, qui observaret talia ordinamenta vel precepta prohibita; et sub pena libr. centum cuilibet qui de predictis ordinamentis prohibitis faceret precepta Arti seu artificibus alicuius Artis." This provision was to be read in the captain's council every month and cried about the city. (*Provvisioni*, Registro, iv. a. c. 30–31.)

NOTE C.

On the 31st of January (new style, 1291) a provision was made, beginning with this singular proemium:—"Ad honorem, ec. Ut cives et comitatini Florentie non opprimantur sicut hactenus oppressi sunt, et ut hominum fraudibus et malitiis que circa infrascripta committi solent, debitis remediis obvietur et resistatur, quod quidem videtur nullomodo fieri posse, nisi iuxta sapientis doctrinam, dicentis quod contraria suis purgantur contrariis; ideoquo volentes lupinas carnes salsamentis caninis involvi et castigari debere, ita quod lupi rapacitas et agni mansuetudo pari passu ambulent, et in eodem ovili vivant pacifice et quiete," ec.

It goes on to severely forbid that any one should dare to: "aliquas litteras impetrare vel impetrari facere, aut privilegium vel rescriptum, per quas vel quod aliquis vel aliqui de civitate vel districtu Florentie citentur vel trahantur ad causam, questionem vel litigium aut examen alicuius indicis, nisi coram domino Potestate, Capitaneo et aliis officialibus Comunis Florentie;" and that he who, having falsified, did not cease from falsifying, when reprimanded, and failed to pay damages and interest within three days, was to be fined one hundred small *fiorini*, or more, according to the judgment of the *Podestà* or of the captain, or of any other magistrate who had undertaken the prosecution. And if any one sought to disobey or escape from the jurisdiction of the magistrates, "teneantur Potestas et Capitaneus, qui de predictis requisitus esset, condemnare patrem vel filium vel fratrem carnalem vel cuginum ex parte patris vel patruum et nepotes eius, ec., in dicta pena, et dictam condemnationem exigere cum effectu, et etiam in maiori pena, ad arbitrium eorum et cuiuscunque eorum, si eis vel alteri eorum videbitur expedire. Et nichilominus compellat eos et quemlibet eorum dare et facere tali contra quem dicerentur tales littere vel privilegium vel rescriptum impetrata, omnes expensas quas faceret vel fecissit, occasione predicta, credendo de predictis expensis iuramento huiusmodi contra quem dicerentur predicta vel aliquod predictorum impetrata."

Moreover, as we have said before, any one, who in the city, Commune, or district of Florence, directly or indirectly published such acts, together with the notary who wrote them out, and the lawyer who defended them, was subject to severe penalties. The Podestà and the captain could proceed as they pleased against any one who, "audeat vel presumat facere precipi eis vel alicui eorum, quod faciant aliquid vel ab aliquo desistant, vel citari Potestatem vel Capitaneum vel Priores vel Consiliarios vel aliquem officialem Comunis Florentie, vel eorum offitia impedire vel retardare coram aliquo vel aliquibus, ex autoritate aliquarum licterarum, privilegii vel rescripti, vel ex auctoritate alicuius indicii ordinarii, delegati vel subdelegati, vel vicarii." And as usual the penalties could be applied to relations.

As it happened that many requested the support of civil justice (*brachium seculare*) "in deffectum iuris et in lesionem et in preiuditium personarum et locorum subdittorum Comuni Florentie," ec., it was decreed that this support should be given only when the suit was over, before competent magistrates, and after it had been examined. If in this case the magistrates refused, then action could be taken against them. But otherwise, those who should demand an unjust sentence were subject to penalties, together with their relations, according to the first paragraph of this law. "Verum si consanguineos, ut dictum est, non haberet, procedatur contra bona talis pretentis brachium seculare, et contra inquilinos, laboratores, pensionarios et fictaiuolos eiusdem potentis, et illorum cuius occasione petitur, et ad alia procedatur, prout ipsis dominis Potestati vel Capitaneo et Prioribus videbitur expedire." Two other paragraphs follow, of which there are ten in all, but at this point a gap occurs in the manuscript, (*Provvisioni*, Registro ii. a. c. 175–177).

CHAPTER VI.

THE COMMERCIAL INTERESTS AND POLICY OF THE GREATER GUILDS IN FLORENCE.[338]

I.

THE end of the thirteenth century marks the opening of a new era in the history of Italy and of Europe. During the period of political disorder prevailing throughout Northern Europe ever since the days of Charlemagne, a literary culture was nevertheless developed, which, although little heeded in past times, has been most clearly elucidated by recent learned research. The literature of Provence, the romance of chivalry, the poems arranged in the cycles of Charlemagne, the Round Table, the Nibelungen Lied, the innumerable ballads, the splendid cathedrals reared on both banks of the Rhine and constituting an art never to be surpassed by its countless imitators, were one and all the offspring of the mighty, primitive culture of the Middle Ages, in which, for a long time, Italy had no share. In Northern Europe, where conquerors and conquered amalgamated with less difficulty, national art and literature were sooner able to spring into being. In Italy, on the contrary, the conquered were oppressed, but never entirely fused with their conquerors; gradually, rather, they began to assert their individuality and their rights. The original rise of the communes was the result of this struggle. Accordingly, at the time when France was composing love-songs and poems of chivalry, Italy was absorbed in founding political institutions and preparing to win freedom.

At the beginning of the fourteenth century the scene was completely changed. Every branch of mediæval literature seemed smitten with an instantaneous decay, northern imagination and fancy to be suddenly withered. Even there, in the north, men begin to strive, slowly and painfully, at the task of political organisation. Meanwhile, the Italian communes being already constituted, our country had already given birth to a national literature, of so dazzling a splendour as to banish all others from view, and relegate to centuries of oblivion the fruits of earlier culture elsewhere. It was precisely at this moment that Florence, then the chief seat and centre of the new Italian culture, was subject to the rule of the greater guilds. The Empire seemed to have abandoned its pretensions with regard to Italy; the Papacy, weakened and menaced, no longer dared to impose its commands on the secular world in its former imperious fashion; the struggle between conquerors and conquered had come to an end, all distinction between the German and Latin races having utterly disappeared, and Italy being peopled by Italians alone.

Now, too, the prolonged conflict waged by the democracy of Florence against the feudal aristocracy was about to terminate in the former's victory, and the Commonwealth could be justly entitled a Republic of merchants, whose trade was soon to enrich them to an apparently fabulous extent. All seemed to herald a new era of peace, prosperity, and concord. But in the light of after events we perceive that the Republic continued to be sorely harassed by internecine strife; also that, in spite of the splendid results achieved in art and commerce, political institutions were on the wane, and the loss of liberty becoming almost a foregone conclusion. How was it that a Commune, enabled to assert its existence at the beginning of the twelfth century and steadily progress in the face of tremendous obstacles, should now show symptoms of decline in the heyday of its triumph? How was it that civil war should still be carried on when all motive for discord seemed extinguished by the victory of the popular party now at the head of the State? We shall discover the answer to this problem by investigating more closely the new conditions of Florentine society, and more particularly the conditions of the trade guilds constituting its chief strength and nucleus.

The number of the Florentine guilds welded in associations had been, after various changes, finally fixed at twenty-one: seven greater and fourteen lesser guilds, although often found otherwise divided into twelve greater and twelve lesser. At any rate, the guilds of first rank and decidedly highest importance were the following:—

1. The Guild of Judges and Notaries.

2. The Guild of Calimala, or Dressers of Foreign Cloth.

3. The Guild of Wool.

4. The Guild of Silk, or of Porta Santa Maria.

5. The Guild of Money-changers.

6. The Guild of Doctors and Druggists.

7. The Guild of Skinners and Furriers.

As every one can see, the first on the list is altogether outside the limits of trade and commerce, and seems rather to belong to the learned professions. But it may be remarked that in those days judges and notaries contributed very largely to the advancement of the guilds, and were continually employed in their service. Together with the consuls, they constituted the court or tribunal of every guild, and gave judgment in all commercial suits tried there; they arranged all disputes, pronounced or suggested penal sentences. Then, too, it was the peculiar function of the notaries to draw up new statutes, continually reform them, and provide for their due enforcement. They were likewise engaged to prepare contracts, and were frequently the mouthpieces of the consuls at the meetings of the greater and lesser guilds. Good judges and notaries were in great demand throughout Italy, and, as necessary instruments of prosperity, richly remunerated for their services. Accordingly, their guild became one of the most influential in Florence, and its notaries were reputed the best-skilled in the world. Goro Dati speaks of this guild in his "Storia di Firenze," saying that "it has a proconsul at the head of its consuls, wields great authority, and may be considered the parent stem of the whole notarial profession throughout Christendom, inasmuch as the great masters of that profession have been leaders and members of this Guild. Bologna is the fountain of doctors of the law, Florence of doctors of the notariate."[339] At public functions the proconsul took precedence over all the consuls, and came directly after the chief magistrate of the Republic. As head of the judges and notaries he held judicial authority, as it were, over all the guilds.

The four next in order—*i.e.*, the Calimala, Wool, Silk, and Exchange—commanded the largest share of Florentine commerce and industry. They were of very ancient origin. Ammirato remarks that the consuls of the guilds are mentioned in a Patent of 1204, but there is documentary record of them at a much earlier date. But, although boasting so old an existence, the guilds passed through a long period of gradual formation, only developing their strength much later, and each at a different time. The oldest and also the first to make progress were the Calimala and Wool Guilds, virtually exercising almost the same industry, inasmuch as both dressed woollen stuffs, and carried on an extensive business with them. Nevertheless, seeing that each pursued its trade in a way peculiar to itself, and achieved thereby a special individual importance, the two guilds always remained separate and distinct from each other.

From the earliest mediæval times the manners and customs of the Italians had been more refined and civilised than those of barbarian peoples, and their handicraft far more advanced. We learn from a chronicler, quoted in Muratori, that when Charlemagne was in Italy he wished to go out hunting one day, and suddenly summoned his courtiers from Pavia. Precious Eastern stuffs having been already brought to that town by the Venetians, the courtiers were able to appear before the emperor clad in the richest attire. But during the hunt their precious stuffs and feathers were totally spoiled by rain and thorns, whereas the emperor's plain tunic of goatskin was as good as before. Thereupon Charlemagne turned to his followers and said, rather jeeringly: "Why do you throw away your money so fruitlessly, when you might wear skins, the most convenient, lasting, and least expensive of garments?"[340] We may certainly doubt the historic truth of this incident; but the chronicler's tale proves two things at all events, *i.e.*, that the custom of wearing the skins of goats or lambs was so general in the ninth century, that even an emperor might not disdain their use; and that, although Italian industry was then very undeveloped, beautiful stuffs were procured from the Levant through the Venetian traders.

II.

The art of weaving coarse woollen stuffs is, however, so easy that it must have been soon revived in Italy, and was probably never completely abandoned. It would seem to have first begun to progress by imitating the simpler fabrics of the Eastern Empire, where cultivation and industry had survived to a much later date. In fact, all the earlier Italian stuffs bear names indicative of their Byzantine derivation, such, for instance, as *Velum holosericum, Fundathum alithinum, Vela tiria, bizantina, Crysoclava, &c.*[341] Nevertheless, although the craft of woollen manufacture is of very early origin, and was even practised by pastoral tribes, there were many obstacles to its development in Italy. Improvement in the breeding of sheep, and consequently in pasturing and agriculture, was required for its progress. But, whereas the Italian communes showed great solicitude for the promotion of trade, they not only despised but often crushed agriculture. The Republic was constituted and governed by artisans, who, after overthrowing the feudal lords, rose to supremacy; but the agricultural class, although far better treated in Tuscany than elsewhere, remained long bound to the soil, and never enjoyed rights of citizenship. This fact alone serves to indicate the rest. All laws and decrees relating to trade are full of good sense and foresight; while all concerning agriculture seem dictated by prejudice or jealousy.

Then, too, regarding pasturage and consequently the woollen industry, it should be added that Tuscany, being a mountainous country, is adapted to the culture of vines and olives and excellent cereals, but deficient in meadowland, whether natural or artificial. Accordingly, it was an exceedingly difficult task to improve the quality and quantity of the wool produced there. Although the Florentines soon succeeded in manufacturing the woollen stuffs called *pignolati, schiavini*, and *villaneschi*, these very coarse fabrics, the names of which sufficiently indicate their quality, only served for a limited trade in the territory or just beyond the borders of the Republic. And when it was attempted to improve the manufacture serious difficulties arose. To weave fine cloth from coarse wool was a fruitless labour; while to procure foreign wool from distant countries was no easy task in times when industry and commerce had scarcely any existence, and the cost of transport would have devoured the profits. Nevertheless, it was by conquering all these obstacles that the Florentines gave the first proofs of their genius for trade.

In Flanders, Holland, and Brabant far better wool was obtainable, and the art of weaving it so long established there that, as in the case of the linen webs of North Germany, the origin of the craft is lost in the obscurity of almost pre-historic times. But, notwithstanding the good quality of the yarn, the woollen stuffs manufactured in those countries were decidedly coarse, sent to market undressed, badly-finished, and dyed in very ugly and evanescent colours. Accordingly the Florentine merchants conceived the idea of importing these foreign stuffs in order to dress and dye them in their own workshops. Hence the origin of the Calimala or Calimara craft.[342] Bales of cloth began to arrive from Flanders, Holland, and Brabant, and these so-called *Frankish* or *ultramontane* stuffs were carded, shaved, dressed, and cut in Florence. This treatment removed all the knots coarsening the surface, and as the material was much finer than Italian wool it could be easily dyed in very delicate tints, and the Florentines soon surpassed all competitors in this particular art. Then, after being carefully ironed, faced, and folded, the cloth was re-sold in a very different condition and at a much higher price. From the first there was a great demand for these goods in Italy, and they were afterwards sent to the East, and bartered for drugs, dyes, and other Asiatic products. Finally, as their quality went on improving, they found their way to France, England, and the same markets whence they had originally come, and where they were sold in exchange for undressed fabrics. Thus the lack of original material was not only supplied, but foreign manufactures served to swell Florentine gains. A very extensive trade was carried on with comparatively little trouble, and as the process of wool-dressing gave employment to many hands, the Calimala Guild attained a position of great influence that was naturally shared by the Guild of Wool.[343]

In fact, the latter being stirred by emulation and greed for profit, used the utmost care to improve its manufactures. And the development of the craft was equally assisted by the labours of private individuals and the wise measures decreed by the State. At that time there was a monastic order in Italy known as the Humble Friars, originally founded by a few Lombard exiles, who, on being banished to North Germany in 1014 by Henry I., had learnt the very ancient craft of wool-weaving practised there. Later on, having formed a pious association, the exiles laboured at the trade for their bread, and after five years' absence returned home a united band of workers. Down to the year 1140 they remained laymen, but then decided to form a religious order, afterwards sanctioned by Pope Innocent III. Once admitted to the priesthood, they no longer worked with their own hands, but retained the management of the business, had it carried on by laymen under the direction of a *mercatore*, and continually introduced new improvements. It was natural that cultivated men, with members of their order scattered over various provinces, should be able to forward the progress of the trade they had founded. In fact, they acquired so much celebrity for their administrative talents that we find them engaged at Florence and elsewhere as treasurers of the public revenue (*camarlinghi*) and as army contractors in time of war. Wherever a house of their order was established the wool-weaving craft immediately made advance. Hence, with its usual sharpsighted wisdom touching all questions of trade and commerce, the Florentine Republic, considering the houses of the *Umiliati* to be great industrial schools, invited the friars to establish a branch in the neighbourhood of Florence.

Accordingly in 1239 the Humble Brethren arrived and settled near the city in the Church of San Donato a Torri, granted to them by the State. Their presence led to the expected result. Before long their house became one of the principal centres of Florentine industry, so that the guild-masters complained of the friars' distance from the town, and urged them to move their establishment nearer to the walls. In 1250 they obtained buildings and land in the suburb of Sta Lucia sul Prato, and exemption from all taxes on their property, the which privilege was usually accorded by the Florentines to any one introducing a new branch of trade in the city. Then, in 1256, the Umiliati founded the church and monastery of Sta Caterina, in Borgo Ognissanti, and carved their arms over the entrance, *i.e.*, a wool-pack fastened crosswise by ropes. From that moment the wool craft made enormous advance in Florence, and in every European market Florentine cloths began to rank above all others. Efforts were made to improve the rough material and to use additional care in dressing it, finer wools being imported from Tunis, Barbary, Spain, Portugal, Flanders, and lastly even from England. Thus so vast a trade was established, such great wealth accumulated, that the wool craft rivalled and surpassed the Calimala itself. Both guilds became great commercial powers in Europe, while in Florence the government dared not oppose their decisions.[344]

Giovanni Villani informs us, in his valuable account of Florentine statistics during the year 1338, that there were more than two hundred wool factories, turning out from seventy thousand to eighty thousand pieces of cloth, of the total value of one million two hundred thousand florins, "of the which sum a good third was kept at home for the works, without counting the earnings of the wool dressers in the said works, the which supplied a living to over thirty thousand persons." The chief profits of the trade were obtained by perfection of manufacture, rather than by any increase of produce. Even Villani remarked that thirty years earlier, that is, in 1308, the factories were more numerous, actually as many as three hundred, and producing one hundred thousand pieces of cloth: "but these stuffs were coarser, and of only half the value, having no intermixture of English wool, the which indeed they had not yet learnt to dress with the skill since acquired."[345] This clearly shows that the craft owed its first improvement in the thirteenth century to the Humble Friars, and was carried to perfection in the fifteenth century by the introduction of English woollens.

In the same year of 1338 the Calimala Guild owned twenty warehouses in Florence, "yearly receiving more than ten thousand pieces of cloth, to the value of three hundred thousand florins, all sold in Florence, and without including those sent out of the city."[346] The Calimala craftsmen were exceedingly skilled as refiners and dyers, and particularly successful in preparing the crimson cloth for which there was a great demand in Florence, as it was used for the *lucco*, a hooded robe worn by all citizens entitled to enter the Public Palace and sit in the tribunals or councils of the Republic. The two guilds afterwards made a division of labour in order to avoid infringing each others rights. The statutes absolutely prohibited the Calimala from dying anything save foreign stuffs, and the Woollen Guild had dyers of its own, forming, as it were, a subordinate association. These dyers were bound to deposit three hundred florins with the guild as a warranty, and fines were deducted from this sum whenever the goods delivered were soiled or dyed a bad colour. The officers of the guilds were exceedingly severe on these points. Every inch of cloth underwent the minutest examination, and the least defect in colour, quality, or measure exposed the workman to heavy penalties. Some of these great Florentine guilds were not composed solely of one trade, but were often agglomerations of various crafts, particularly in the case of the Wool Guild, which included many kinds of workmen, ranging from carders of the rough material to dyers and finers of the most costly fabrics. Thus, the guild being able to carry on the manufacture in all its details, and the different craftsmen required for the common end being all bonded together, there was no fear that any one branch of the trade would raise its prices to the detriment of the rest. The emblem of the Wool Guild was a lamb bearing a flag (*Agnus*

Dei), while the Calimala showed a red eagle on a white bale corded with many twists.

During the whole of the fourteenth and a considerable part of the fifteenth century these two guilds continued to progress, and maintained their supremacy in the markets of Europe. Nevertheless, they were always in a difficult position, since Italy could not supply them with sufficient raw material, nor could they obtain the number of hands required to carry on all the work connected with their business. To establish branches of the trade in neighbouring states and subject cities was an idea that found no place in the economic and political theories of the Middle Ages. In those days trade formed the chief strength and social power of the communes: hence every commune wished to have the monopoly of its advantages, and the statutes bristled with decrees inspired by this blindly jealous exclusiveness. For this reason, while pursuing the system of keeping the finer and more profitable processes of the manufacture in their own hands, the Florentines had opened factories for the first and coarser stages of the work in every place where the best wool could be found, that is in Holland, Brabant, England, and France. And even in these factories they took care that the more difficult and profitable share of the process should be done only by Florentine hands. Their chronicles prove that they then spoke of foreigners in the same terms now used by the latter with regard to ourselves: jeering at the indolence and stupidity of the northerners, who even on their own soil allowed strangers to snatch the bread from their mouths. But this state of things could not last long. From very early times the Flemings had always been a strong, hard- working race, and were very soon equalled by the French and English. So gradually the eyes of the northerners were opened, and the Florentines saw new factories rising abroad, side by side with and soon rivalling their own, and were obliged to admit that, to their own despite, they had taught foreigners the very trade of which they had meant to preserve the monopoly. Nor was this the end of the matter. Being now on the alert, the northerners tried to check the exportation of their wools and of their uncut, or rather undressed, cloths; and from the end of the fifteenth century Henry VII. of England began to take measures to that effect. Thenceforth the Guilds of Wool and Calimala were doomed to decline in Florence. Fortunately, however, before this came about, the silk trade had assumed the same importance in Florentine commerce that was gradually slipping away from the other two crafts.

As every one is aware, the art of silk-weaving, though of very early origin in the East, was only introduced much later to the Western world. The Romans obtained a few silk stuffs from Persia, India, and China at an enormous expense; they also had certain insects from which material for highly esteemed fabrics was procured; but until the closing years of the Middle Ages the real silkworm was unknown in Italy, and the details of its first introduction in the West have not yet been fully ascertained. It is related that during the sixth century B.C. two Persian monks concealed some silkworm seed inside their staffs, and thus succeeded in bearing it to Constantinople, where they taught the art of rearing the insects. In this wise the silk trade is supposed to have been originated in the dominions of the Byzantine Empire, and carried thence by Arabs and Mahomedans to Sicily and Greece. When Roger II., Count of Sicily, conquered the Ionian islands, he returned to Palermo with numerous prisoners (1147–48), who greatly assisted the progress of the silk trade there. Thence it easily penetrated to Lombardy and Tuscany; but was first established and perfected in Lucca, all the Florentines being still devoted to the profitable wool trade.

The consuls of the Silk Guild—or of Por' Santa Maria, as it was designated in Florence, from the name of its street—are mentioned among other guild-masters in public treaties; but although this craft too may be of ancient date, it certainly began to flourish much later than the rest. Noting the fact that Giovanni Villani makes no allusion to the Silk Guild in his very minute account of Florentine trade and commerce in 1338, we are inclined to believe that it had made very little advance at that period.[347]

We know that when Uguccioni della Faggiola besieged and took Lucca (1314), fugitives from that city brought their improved method of silk-weaving to Lombardy, Venice, and Tuscany, and the art being particularly undeveloped in Florence, many chroniclers gave the Lucchese the credit of having first introduced it there. Nevertheless, for many years afterwards the silk trade was carried on by importing the raw material from the East. But as the wool craft began to decline, Florence gave its whole attention to silk, and the trade speedily began to prosper. In the early years of the fifteenth century, Gino Capponi—he who was commissary to the camp at the siege of Pisa—taught the Florentines the art of spinning the gold thread they had hitherto imported from Cologne or from Cyprus to interweave with their silk. This was the beginning of that delicate manufacture of gold and silver brocades, in which by the combination of technical skill with artistic sense, the Florentines soon surpassed all rival manufacturers. The markets from which their woollen stuffs had been ousted, were speedily reconquered by their silken cloths and brocades. During the latter half of the fifteenth century, in fact, we find Benedetto Dei, a merchant of the Bardi Company, writing a letter to Venice praising the glory and greatness of Florentine commerce and saying: "We have two crafts worthier and greater than any four contained in your city of Venice." And the gist of his subsequent remarks was to this effect: "Our woollen stuffs go to Rome, Naples, Sicily, the Morea, Constantinople, Broussa, Pera, Gallipoli, Schio, Rhodes, and Salonica. Then, as to the silk and gold brocades, we produce more than Venice, Genoa, and Lucca combined, and you see that we have houses, banks, and warehouses at Lyons, Bruges, London, Antwerp, Avignon, Geneva, Marseilles, and in Provence." [348] This long list of cities plainly shows that in Dei's time Florentine woollens, though still prized in the East, had been driven from the principal markets of the West, and replaced by silk stuffs; and thus the two guilds shared commerce between them, one in the East, the other in the West. Also, according to Dei, Florence then possessed eighty-three factories, where various tissues of silk, gold, and silver were produced known by the names of damasks, velvets, satins, taffetas, and *maremmati*, and most of the raw silk used in their fabrication was still imported from the East by Florentine galleys. [349]

This is one of the trades longest preserved in Florence and other parts of Italy, and to this day silk is among the most important of our products. With this difference, however, that whereas in past times the weaving of the silk was our chief source of profit, at present we frequently export the raw material, repurchasing at an enormously increased price the fabrics returned to us from foreign looms. In old times we imported woollen and silk yarn, and exported Italian cloth and brocade; in these days, on the contrary, we send no small portion of our raw silk to Lyons, and receive it back in a manufactured state. In the same way other raw materials, which we might easily work up ourselves, are despatched to foreign factories.

III.

There was one branch of industry, however, almost solely the product of human talent and energy, in which the Florentines stood positively first. From the opening of the thirteenth to the end of the fifteenth century the money-changers' craft was an essentially Florentine business. For as soon as the merchants had established commercial relations with all the markets of the East and the West, they naturally put into circulation a large quantity of specie. Therefore it naturally ensued that if any trader of Antwerp or Bruges wished to forward money to Italy or Constantinople, the easiest and safest plan was to apply to some of the Florentine merchants in his own town. The latter bought up the wool and rough cloths, which, after being dressed in Florence, either returned to Northern Europe, or found their way to Constantinople, Caffa, or Tana (Azov), in exchange for silks, dyes, and spices. Accordingly the transmittal of any sum to any part of the then known world cost them little more trouble than the despatch of an ordinary letter, and was always a source of gain. For they received *agio* on their money, and by sending it in the form of merchandise, reaped a second profit. When, on the contrary, any Florentine wished to send a hundred florins to London, he had only to walk a few steps to find some merchant of the Calimala or Por' Santa Maria, who, by a line to his correspondent in Lombard Street, caused the payment to be made. These so-called letters of exchange (*lettere di cambio*) proved one of the most useful of inventions for the advancement of modern trade. There has been much discussion as to whom this discovery was originally owed. Some attribute it to the fugitive, persecuted Jews in France and England; while others ascribe it, at a much later date, to the Guelphs banished from Florence in the thirteenth century. But it is very difficult to ascertain who was the first author of what cannot be justly styled a discovery, seeing that it is an arrangement so readily occurring to the mind, that examples of it are even to be found in very remote antiquity. Besides, the real importance of the letter of exchange consists not in its invention, but in its legally authorised value, its extensive use, and the thousand different ways in which it may be turned to account for the speedy transmission and increase of capital. On these points the Florentines of the period were altogether unforestalled and unsurpassed, being superior masters of the art of finance.

When the exiled Guelphs went wandering about the world in the thirteenth century they strengthened the widespreading commercial ties established by Florence, and founding banks in all parts, gave a tremendous impulse to the money-changers' trade. Accordingly they were credited with the invention of the "letters of exchange," which now being widely circulated, gained added importance. In fact, all subtle and ingenious devices for multiplying gold, by despatching it to every market where, being scarce, it consequently commanded the highest price and interest, and almost all the complicated and difficult operations practised by our modern bankers, were already familiar to the Florentines. Whenever the Republic was obliged to borrow money it obtained loans from the bankers of Florence on precisely the same system and method in use at this day, no source of profit being unknown to those financiers. Also, when the total of these loans was formed into the so- called *Monte Comune*, paying interest on the consolidated capital, the *luoghi del Monte*, which would nowadays go by the name of "shares of the public debt," were negotiated precisely as at present. We find the Florentine merchants under the Arcades of the New Market, speculating on the rise and fall of stock, like modern men on "'Change" in great capitals.[350] And the profits of similar ventures were far greater at a time when lawful interest varied between 10 and 20 per cent., and few felt any scruples against carrying it up to 40 per cent. by means of fictitious contracts. For instance, the lenders would fix an impossibly early date for the receipt of the lawful interest, and after that date took 40 per cent. with the pretext that the extra amount was the fine agreed upon in case of non-payment.

It should be kept in mind that the Florentines reaped great advantages in all these banking operations from the excellent quality of their coinage, for the Republican Mint always kept the best interests of commerce in view. To this end, in the year 1252, the gold florin of twenty carats was struck, with the figure of St. John on one side and the lily of Florence on the reverse; and, owing to the goodness of the metal and its alloy, soon obtained currency in every Eastern as well as European market. Eight of these florins weighed one ounce, and a single florin was valued at about twelve Italian *lire*. The Florentines, however, usually made their calculations in *lire*, *soldi*, and *denari*. The silver *lira*, then the conventional standard, consisted of twenty *soldi*, and the *soldo* of twelve *denari*. The florin seldom altered in value, but the *lira*, either from the greater variability in the price of silver, or from other causes, was constantly altering its rate with regard to the florin. In 1252 the latter was equivalent to the *lira*, and therefore similarly divided into twenty *soldi*; in 1282 it already consisted of thirty-two *soldi*; in 1331, of sixty *soldi*, or three *lire*, and always changing in value, rose to four *lire*, eight *soldi* by the year 1464.

The Florentines had discerned how greatly their commerce was benefited by the use of a coin universally prized in all markets supplied with their goods. But in the beginning of the fifteenth century, when their trade penetrated farther into the East, they found themselves forestalled by the Venetians, whose gold ducat, somewhat larger and heavier than the florin, was already current there. Accordingly, in 1422, they decreed the issue of another florin, equivalent to the Venetian ducat in weight, size, and value, and therefore easily exchanged for it. And as this new and larger florin was to be carried to the Levant on board-ship, they named it the "broad florin," or the "galley florin," to distinguish it from the older "sealed florin" (*fiorino di suggello*). In 1471 the older coin only was re-issued, and kept in circulation down to 1530, when it was held equivalent to seven *lire*, and was then withdrawn for a time.[351] Thus we see that for a considerable period two different florins were in use, that the *lira* altered in value from one year to another; and if we likewise remember that economists are still unagreed as to the exact difference between the present value of gold and silver and their value in the days of the Republic, we shall recognise the difficulty of making any calculation sufficiently exact to afford any precise idea of the relative prices of things. It is asserted by some writers that a given quantity of gold was only worth in those days double its present value; while others exaggerated its value to fortyfold. Sismondi believes that in the fourteenth and fifteenth centuries gold must have been worth four times as much as at present. Certainly the florin, or *zechin*, as it was called later, is worth about twelve Italian *lire*. But the difference in the value of gold remains involved in uncertainty. Besides, when old writers reckon by *lire*, it is needful to remember that these coins varied in value; that it is impossible to make even an approximative calculation without knowing the exact date referred to.

Returning to the Guild of Changers, we must again insist on the point that, in addition to the extended commercial relations, the wise measures enforced by the Republic and the singular activity of the citizens, the rapid prosperity of the Florentine bankers was also greatly enhanced by their nearness to Rome. The revenues of the Holy See and of its prelates in all parts of Christendom were all poured into the Eternal City. There gathered the spiritual lords, bishops, and cardinals, holding rich benefices in the East or the West; thither from all the remotest ends of the known world believers sent sums of "St. Peter's pence," together with the costly offerings suited to a period of religious faith and fanaticism. The keen-witted Florentines quickly recognised the advantage of becoming bankers to the Pope; for thus the largest floating capital in the world would have to pass through their hands. So, from the first, they used the most persistent efforts to obtain that position. If we find them clinging to the Guelph cause through all changes of time and circumstance, and preserving the name of Guelphs, even when the term had lost all meaning, we must attribute no little weight to commercial as well as to political motives. Placed in the centre of Italy, and not far from Rome, they had to struggle chiefly against the Siennese, who were still nearer to the Eternal City. For this reason we soon find them engaged in warfare and jealous strife with Sienna, the which republic was subsequently worsted, not only in fight, but also by the wider-stretching enterprise of Florentine commerce. It is proved by the correspondence of Gregory IX. that even in 1233 the Tuscans were forwarding remittances to the Pope from various parts of the world; and gradually the monopoly of this business became more exclusively concentrated in Florentine hands. When the Pontifical Seat was transferred from Rome to Avignon (1305), and on its restoration later to Rome again, there occurred, twice at least, an enormous displacement of interest, a great movement of capital, and a necessity for large remittances in cash; and, according to the best authorities, this was the favourable moment when the Florentine contractors of the Papal revenues were enabled to become the principal bankers of Rome. From that time their fortune was assured, the greatest banking business in Europe passed through their hands, and they rose to so high a repute, that all sought their help and advice on matters of finance.

We see the Florentines invited to manage the mints, and fix the weights and measures of various European states. In 1278 a convention between the King of France and the Lombard and Tuscan *Universitates* invites both to find money for the former's government. In 1306 the Modenese people issued a decree, appealing for the same purpose, to the notaries and bankers of Florence. Then in 1302, when the King of France, lacking funds wherewith to make war, decided on repeated debasement of the coinage, this fatal step was attributed to the advice of two Florentines, Bicci and Musciatto Franzesi. These men were severely censured by their fellow-citizens, many of whom had been ruined by the bad French currency. On all occasions when the French sovereigns were on the eve of a great war, they were practically compelled to first secure the aid of some known Florentine banker in bearing the expense. Some of these bankers held the same position in Europe as the Rothschilds of the present day, and accumulated fortunes of apparently fabulous amounts. In 1260 the Salimbeni house lent twenty thousand florins to the Siennese. In 1338 we find the Bardi and Peruzzi creditors of King Edward III. of England for one million three hundred and sixty-five florins, the which, without reckoning the difference in the value of gold, would amount to about sixteen millions of Italian *lire*; and allowing for that difference, would amount, as Sismondi has calculated, to no less than sixty- four millions. Pagnini adds a list of many other loans, amounting to a positively enormous total. In 1321 the Peruzzi had a credit of 191,000 florins on the Order of Jerusalem alone, and the Bardi another of 133,000 florins. In 1348 the house of Tommaso di Carroccio degli Alberti and his kinsmen had banks at Avignon, Brussells, Paris, Sienna, Perugia, Rome, Naples, Barletta, Constantinople, and Venice.[352] And at the close of the fifteenth century Philippe de Commines declared that Edward IV. of England owed his crown to the help of Florentine bankers.

The Money-changers' Guild was one of the oldest in Florence, its consuls being named on the same footing as the rest in all public records; and a copy of its statutes, dated 1299 (1300 new style), makes reference to an earlier code of 1280, that was not the earliest of all. This craft prospered and waned with the commerce of Florence. It was carried on in the New Market, where it had shops with counters or *tavoletti*, money-bags, and ledgers. All business had to be performed in the shop, and registered in the account book, and heavy penalties were exacted for any infringement of the rule; nor was any one allowed to exercise the craft without being inscribed on the matriculation list, a privilege only to be obtained by having given proofs of capacity and honesty during matriculation, and sworn to obey the statutes of the guild. In 1338 there were about eighty of these money-changers' stalls, and Florence coined from 350,000 to 400,000 gold florins.[353] In 1422 these stalls numbered seventy-two, while it was calculated that Florence had a capital of two million florins in circulation, without including the value of the merchandise in the city.[354] In 1472, partly because the first signs of the decline of trade were appearing, and partly because trade was becoming restricted to a more and more limited number of firms, the banks were already reduced to thirty-three,[355] although the chronicler Benedetto Dei still remarked with pride that these bankers did business in the East and the West, "as is well known to the Venetians and Genoese, and likewise to the Court of Rome."[356] They were everywhere known by the names of changers, lenders, usurers, Tuscans, and Lombards, and, together with other Italian houses, had a street of their own both in London and Paris.

IV.

In order to complete the list of the greater guilds, we must say a few words concerning the Doctors and Druggists, and Skinners and Furriers, and particularly the former. Although of less importance commercially than the guilds already described, they had a great share in promoting Florentine trade in the Levant, whence nearly all drugs and spices were received in exchange, and no less than twenty-two different qualities of fur, many of which, being the skins of rare animals, formed some of the dearest articles of luxury. Therefore these two guilds likewise rose to great influence, inasmuch as the Eastern trade has invariably proved the main source of wealth for all nations, and most of all for Italy. It served to sustain the high fortunes of Venice; it had enriched Amalfi, Genoa, and Pisa; and accordingly was constantly coveted by the Florentines, whose highest prosperity indeed was only attained when the Black Sea being opened to their galleys, they could enjoy the same rights as the Venetians in Egypt, Constantinople, and the Crimea. This, so long their principal aim, was not, however, quickly attained: they continued to wrestle for it throughout almost the whole of the fourteenth century.

The struggles maintained by the Florentines for the extension of their trade play a very important part in the history of the Republic, not only demonstrating the progress of their wealth, but likewise the ruling motives of their policy. In fact, the moment they had won their first successes against the nobles of the *contado* surrounding them on all sides, they immediately tried to monopolise the whole trade with Lombardy. One of the first treaties signed by them was with the Ubaldini, lords of the Mugello, for the purpose of opening that highway for their products; and shortly afterwards they made a treaty with the Bölognese (1203). But in course of time the latter, profiting by their position, exacted heavier tolls on the merchandise now continually passing through their territory; whereupon the Florentines promptly came to terms with Modena, opening a fresh road for their commerce, and thus compelling Bölogna to respect the original agreement. In 1282, at the time of the war against Pisa, they arranged treaties guaranteeing free passage to their merchandise through Lucca, Prato, Pistoia, and Volterra, and thus began their domination over the commerce of Tuscany. Nearly all their wars were undertaken for purposes of trade, and ended with trading agreements. In 1390 they entered into conventions with Faenza and Ravenna, and then step by step with the majority of the Italian cities.

The continual increase of Florentine commerce by land made the necessity of free access to the sea ever more pressing and indispensable. But to reach either Porto Pisano or Leghorn, the only ports convenient for their trade, they must necessarily traverse the republic of Pisa, their powerful neighbour and rival. For if the Florentines were masters of nearly the whole Tuscan trade by land, the Pisans were lords of the sea, and had no intention of allowing their realm to be snatched from them by so industrious and energetic a race as their competing neighbours. Accordingly the Pisans had only to demand heavy tolls for the passage of those neighbours' goods, and the Florentines were left with no remedy save recourse to arms. Hence the continual warfare and perpetual rivalry of the two republics. After the capture of Volterra by the Florentines in 1254, the threatening attitude of their victorious troops drove the Pisans to grant free passage to their merchandise, and in 1273, 1293, 1327, and 1329 similarly compelled them to adhere to the same terms. Pisa, however, never yielded the point with a good grace, but merely to avoid war, or in consequence of defeat.

Meanwhile the Florentines were continually extending their trade to remoter parts of the East, and concluding fresh treaties there. This, while increasing their desire to command the sea, fanned the jealousy of Pisa to a fiercer flame. In Pagnini's work on "La Decima" we find an essay on the "Practise of Trade" ("Pratica della Mercatura"), written early in the fourteenth century by an agent of the Bardi firm, one Balducci Pegolotti. Next to Marco Polo's "Milione," this work is one of our most important sources of information regarding Italian travels and trading enterprises in the Levant, and furnishes specially minute details of Florentine traffic. From what Pegolotti tells us of his own doings, we may judge what was done by his fellow-citizens in general. In 1315 he succeeded in securing for them in Antwerp and Brabant similar franchises to those already enjoyed by the Genoese, Germans, and English. He afterwards went to the Levant, and found at Cyprus that the Bardi and Peruzzi alone shared the privilege granted to the Pisans of only paying 2 per cent. import and export duty; whereas all other Florentines had either to pay 4 per cent., or feign to be Pisans, a device exposing them to many spiteful reprisals from the latter, who treated them *worse than slaves or Jews*. These proceedings aroused Pegolotti's wrath, so that, although he was one of the Bardi firm, he made great and successful efforts to have the same privilege of franchise extended to the rest of the Florentines (1324). Thus, their common interests being promoted no less by the energy of individuals than by that of their government, these merchants continued to make advance in the East, and stir the Pisans to greater envy. In fact, the latter decided in 1343 to reduce the exemptions allowed on Florentine merchandise, decreeing that goods only to the value of 200,000 florins might pass untaxed through their city; all the rest being charged two *soldi* the *lira*—*i.e.*, at the rate of 10 per cent. This left the Florentines no choice save to make war, or find some mode of avoiding the Pisan highway. To prove that their trade was not altogether at the mercy of Pisa, they preferred the second alternative. By making treaty with the Siennese, they obtained the concession of Porto Talamone, and at great expense, and in the teeth of many difficulties, finally succeeded in making it a vast emporium for their wares. The road to Talamone was long and inconvenient; but the Pisans, soon perceiving that they had done greater damage to themselves than to Florence, and that although they might inflict annoyance on the latter, there was no hope of destroying its trade, were therefore presently reduced to permit the free passage of merchandise. Accordingly the Florentines felt braced to more extensive enterprise in the Levant.[357]

The Egyptian route was the easiest and most direct for trading purposes; but sultan and califs barred the road to Christians. The Venetians alone, from having concluded treaties, it was said, "in the holy name of God and Mahomet," had made some way in that country to the jealous exclusion of all other Italians, who therefore usually travelled by Constantinople and the Black Sea, where they, and more especially the Genoese, had founded some populous and flourishing cities. Farther on, by the Sea of Azoff, a mile or so from the mouth of the Don, stood the town of Tana (Azov), a great business centre for traders from Russia, Arabia, Persia, Armenia, Mogul, and Southern China; and the chief place of exchange for Eastern and Western products. The Italians brought silk or woollen fabrics, oil, wine, pitch, tar, and common metals, and bartered them for precious stones, pearls, gold, spices, sweetmeats, sugar, Eastern tissues of silk, wool, or cotton, raw silk, goatskins, dye-woods, and likewise for Eastern slaves of either sex, who were to be seen in Italy down to the end of the fifteenth century.[358] All this varied commerce, originally started by Amalfi and other southern states, was afterwards carried on by the Venetians, Genoese, and Pisans. The argosies of those republics traversed all parts of the Archipelago, the Bosphorus, and the Black Sea. Italian was spoken in all the harbours of the East, where, besides Italian banks, workshops, and factories, there were cities founded and inhabited solely by Italians, with buildings in the Genoese or Venetian style, but where Italian, and especially Venetian, architecture became modified by Oriental influences. A great number of Genoese were settled in those parts. To give some idea of the naval strength of Venice, it will be enough to say that during the Crusade of 1202 that Republic equipped a fleet able to convey 4,500 horsemen, 9,000 squires, 30,000 infantry, and stores for nine months. Their galleys, never less than 80 feet in length, sometimes measured 110 by 70 in width, and in the fifteenth century were forty-five in number, with a total of 11,000 seamen. At the same time they also possessed 3,000 other vessels of from ten to one hundred tons, with 17,000 men, and 300 big ships with 8,000 men. In all, therefore, 3,345 vessels, with 36,000 seamen,[359] a strength that seems positively incredible, when we remember that the 'Serenissima' Republic of Venice was a city built on the sandbanks of the lagoons; that the entire management of its policy and trade was in the hands of men born within the narrow bounds of those lagoons. Accordingly we may imagine how great was the united strength of all the maritime republics, and how signal the courage of the Florentines in competing with them so obstinately for the Levantine trade.

Before launching a single galley, the Florentines had already established many houses and banks in every place, and contrived to introduce their merchandise in all the principal Eastern ports. We not only find them doing a vast business at Tana with great energy and enterprise, but also pushing on thence to far remoter regions. Pegolotti minutely describes the route followed by them, their manner of travelling, and the time employed in it. They journeyed, he tells us, through Astracan (Gittarchan), to Saracanco (Sarai) on the Volga, thence by Organci in Zagataio,[360] not far from the Caspian Sea, and crossing Asia by many places of which the names cannot be identified with any known at this day, they penetrated as far as Gambaluc, or Gamulecco, the chief city of China, that is to say, the city of Pekin. They employed eight or ten months to go from Tana to Pekin. Thus a period of almost two years was required for the journey there and back and time of sojourn, and when we also calculate the voyage from Porto Pisano or Leghorn to Tana and back, it is plain that a Florentine bound for Pekin could rarely count on returning home within three years.[361]

During the growth of this Eastern trade, carried on with such indomitable energy, amid difficulties of all kinds, the Florentines were always aiming at the command of the seaboard, and never losing sight of the necessity of having a port of their own. And when, by the capture of Pisa in 1406, that long-desired object was finally attained, a new era began for their commerce. All their business concerns became most rapidly extended, and the first half of the fifteenth century was the time in which their greatest wealth was accumulated. In 1421 they appointed "consuls of the sea," who were ordered to immediately build two wide-beamed merchant galleons (*galee di mercato*) and six narrow galleys, and to continue to launch one of either kind every six months, for the which purpose a monthly sum of one hundred florins was assigned from the revenues of the Pisan university. Accordingly Florence soon possessed a merchant fleet of eleven stout galleons and fifteen narrow galleys continually employed in the Eastern traffic by command of the Republic. All these vessels had strict sailing orders as to the course to be taken, the ports to be touched at, and the freight to be carried. Announcements of their departure and arrival were hung in the arcades of the New Market; and the vessels being chartered by private individuals, the government was enabled to keep the Eastern routes open to all, without any outlay. In 1422, when, as already related, the "galley florin" was coined, the Florentines, at the instance of one Taddeo Cenni, a merchant long established in Venice, despatched two envoys to Egypt to obtain the right of having a church, warehouses, dockmen, and porters of their own at Alexandria. The negotiation proving successful, in 1423 they instructed the "consuls of the sea" to appoint extra consuls at every port where their presence might be useful to Florentine trade. Some had been established for more or less time at Constantinople, Pera (1339), and London (1402); but from this moment we find them at Alexandria, Majorca, Naples, and other ports in all directions. These consuls had offices and clerks of their own, interpreters, men-at-arms, and places of worship; and all their expenses, salary included, were deducted from the freight dues received by them.[362]

To fully understand to what extent and in what way the Florentines profited by the new conditions resulting from their conquest of Pisa, it is necessary to point out that this event not only marks the time of their highest commercial prosperity, and the beginning of their navy and merchant fleet, but also indicates the date of their first attention to nautical and astronomical studies. We gain another proof of their great intelligence and untiring activity when we see that their first efforts in a branch of learning of which they had no previous knowledge enabled them to initiate the era of scientific triumphs, opening with Paolo Toscanelli, the first inspirer of Christopher Columbus, continued by Amerigo Vespucci, and closing with Galileo Galilei and his imperishable school.

V.

The seven guilds, already described by us, were styled the greater guilds, as being those of most importance and having the chief trade and wealth of the State in their hands. Several of these guilds consisted, as we have seen, rather of different crafts banded together, than of a single branch of industry; they gave employment to many workers, gathered and made use of enormous funds. But Florence also possessed the so-called lesser guilds numbering fourteen in all, namely: Linenmakers and Mercers, Shoemakers, Smiths, Salters, Butchers and Slaughterers, Wine-dealers, Innkeepers, Harnessmakers, Leatherdressers, Armourers, Ironmongers, Masons, Carpenters, Bakers.[363]

Certain smaller Florentine crafts had also obtained great repute in Italy: for instance, that of the wood and stone carvers, who were esteemed as some of the best in the world. In all work demanding any share of artistic ability the Tuscans stood unrivalled. Thus the Florentine moulders of waxen images were considered to have incomparable skill, and we even find this remarked by the chronicler Dei. But neither the carvers nor the wax moulders formed an association, and were artists rather than artizans. But, leaving this question aside, the lesser guilds, although numerous and energetic, failed to achieve any noteworthy influence. Their difference from the greater guilds mainly lay in the fact that, being solely concerned with the local trade of the Republic, they were confined to a very limited field of business and enterprise, while the others engaged in the trade with the East and the West, were enabled to attain a high position even in politics, and to finally become masters of the State.

Looking back on the period in which the greater guilds rose to power, we shall see that they simultaneously held in their grasp the commerce, wealth, and government of the Florentine Republic. We shall also readily understand the enormous energy they must have displayed in order to use politics as a means for increasing the opulence that, in the existing conditions of Italy, had become the chief strength of our communes. The Florentine merchants, having long divined that the future would belong to them, were always the firmest supporters of the Guelph party against the Imperial Ghibellinism of the nobles and had vowed eternal hatred to the latter. We may now imagine Florence as a huge house of business, situated in the centre of Tuscany, and surrounded by others all competing with it in the race for success. International law and equity were unknown to the Middle Ages: hence when any State felt envious of its neighbour, the obvious course to adopt was to prohibit that neighbour from traversing its territory, and exact unbearably heavy dues from the rival it feared. Accordingly, the Republic of Florence, being the object of still fiercer jealousy on account of the continual increase of its commerce, and lacking room to breathe, as it were, without access to the sea, would have been speedily reduced to impotence had it not resisted its neighbours by force of arms. Hence, the necessity of defending its existence involved the State in an uninterrupted series of wars, invariably terminated by treaties of commerce, in which the unfailing subtlety of the Florentines always won the advantage.

We have seen from the beginning how Florence combated the neighbouring barons in order to secure the progress of its dawning trade, and subsequently obtained a passage through the Mugello for its increased traffic with Romagna and Lombardy. Later on, we have seen it engaged in fiercer struggles, and, after many vicissitudes, subduing almost all the Ghibelline cities of Tuscany, as, for instance, Volterra, Sienna, and Arezzo. And when inquiring why Florence should have remained so obstinately Guelph, even in the face of Papal threats, and repeating the same question Farinata put to Dante—

"Dimmi, perchè quel popolo è si empio

Incontro a' miei in ciascuna sua legge?"[364]

the invariable reply has been that in addition to political motives of a more general nature, it must be kept in mind that the plutocracy now risen to power had first attained wealth by doing its chief business with Rome. Sienna, Arezzo, and Volterra being on the road and closer to Rome, were doomed to defeat in any competition with Florence.

Then, as soon as the Republic had secured its hold on Roman affairs and the Lombard trade, we saw its irresistible need of access to the sea, and that a war of extermination with Pisa had become altogether inevitable. To suppose that this prolonged, constantly renewed and sanguinary conflict was solely caused by a blind instinctive hatred of Pisa, when other and more serious reasons were so plainly existent, would be to deny the evidence of facts. From beginning to end it was simply the clash of violently opposed interests. The Pisans were perfectly aware that to yield a free passage to the power already commanding the chief trade in the interior of Italy—the power that, without having as yet a single galley afloat, had already made its way to all the harbours of the East—the power so persistently struggling for absolute supremacy in Tuscany—could only lead to their own lasting subjection. Therefore they resisted to the utmost of their strength. Their resources were undoubtedly great, and as many other Italians were equally hostile to the supremacy of Florence, the latter could never have succeeded in reducing the Pisans, had it not constantly employed the shrewdest devices in addition to its efforts in the field. In fact there is no better proof of the political ability of the Florentines than their mode of conducting this war and the means they employed to attain the object that, throughout the whole course of their history, had been their chief and invariable aim. We find them steadfast in their friendship to Lucca, and always prompt to succour that city at all costs, because Lucca was never well disposed to the Pisans, and might prove a most useful ally in any campaign against them. So, too, we always find Florence on good terms with Genoa, and avoiding every risk of giving offence to a power that was Pisa's natural rival on the seas. Indeed, the Florentines always did their best to foster that rivalry, inasmuch as without an ally strong enough to assist them by crushing Pisa's power by sea, they could never hope to overthrow it by land. And at last the Pisans were defeated by the Genoese in the naval battle of Meloria (August 6, 1284). From that day the conquest of Pisa by the Florentines, although still to be long contested, was a foregone conclusion, and from that moment also their friendship for the Genoese began to lose warmth. While desiring assistance in overcoming Pisa, they wished to avoid aggrandising the power of a Ghibelline republic, already very mighty on the sea. Accordingly, after having so furiously attacked and enfeebled Pisa, we find them aiding that state to withstand the Genoese, until the moment came when the latter having abandoned the idea of conquering Pisa, they could successfully undertake its conquest on their own account.

With equal sagacity they pursued the same course in the years during which they were menaced by the powerful Dukes of Milan who sought to become masters of all Italy, and also when threatened from the south by the enmity of King Ladislaus of Naples. The art of stirring division among their foes, of supporting the weaker party against overbearing neighbours, of constantly contriving to rouse half Italy against every potentate risen to sufficient strength to be a terror to their own Republic, was the invariable means by which Florence maintained her independence in the midst of States who were losing their liberty, and in the midst of the numerous and formidable foes pressing about her on all sides. And this successful policy was the work of the greater guilds, or rather of the prosperous trading class (*popolani grassi*).

These mercantile aristocrats ruled the Republic with so much energy and zeal, precisely because the aggrandisement of Florence conduced at the same time to the increase of their own wealth and commerce. Thus a city whose population was seldom more than 100,000, and often shrank far below that number, and whose narrow territory was surrounded by so many enemies, was enabled to become a State feared by the rest of Italy, and respected throughout Europe. These Florentine merchants were so jealous of their liberty as to deem no sacrifice too vast for its preservation, and were neither bewildered nor daunted by any danger, even when their trade was at stake. In fact, although so obstinately Guelph, and connected with Rome by so many commercial interests and ties, we find them ready to combat the Pope himself, when he made attacks on their liberty, and see them giving the name of the *Eight Saints* to the magistrates charged to conduct the campaign against Gregory XI. (1376). In the like manner we find them carrying on a war with the Visconti of Milan at a yearly cost of millions of florins, without the resources of the Republic being exhausted, or the courage of its rulers worn out.

VI.

Nevertheless, it would be an error to suppose that the domination of the greater guilds was assured and uncontested in the interior, at least, of the city. On the day when the scheme was first mooted, in the Calimala court, of placing these guilds at the head of the government, they speedily recognised that the possibility of success was solely owed to the fact of their having fought and conquered the nobles with the help of the lesser arts. Hence, on the one hand, they had to face their natural and inveterate foes, the survivors of the feudal order, and on the other the lesser guilds coveting a share in the government which they had helped to establish. Thus the Republic comprised three classes of citizens and three separate parties. It is true that the greater guilds constituted by far the stronger of the three factions, but the others might become, if united, a very formidable opposition. And their union was no impossible contingency.

The difference, in fact, between the greater and lesser guilds was not merely one of degree as regarded their respective wealth and power; what divided them was the diversity of interests urging them to pursue an opposite policy. The wool-dresser or silk merchant was always ready to sacrifice his last florin, provided the Republic could gain possession of Leghorn or Porto Pisano. Accordingly he invariably kept a strict watch on the policy of Lucca and Genoa, to prevent them from making friendly advances to the Pisans. The Florentine banker was anxious that his Republic should always possess skilful ambassadors and consuls, able to supply full details of all that occurred in Rome, Antwerp, or Caffa, and impede the Siennese, Genoese, Venetians, and Lombards from gaining too much influence in those cities. Where any question of this kind was concerned the members of the greater guilds were always disposed to promote hostilities, no matter how prolonged, expensive, or dangerous, and to subject both themselves and the State to unlimited sacrifices. But financial and political interests weighed little with the blacksmiths, masons, carpenters, and other members of the fourteen lesser guilds, which nevertheless formed so considerable a part of the Florentine population. It mattered far more to them that Florence should be inhabited by rich and splendid gentry; that sumptuous palaces, villas, and monumental churches should have to be built; that there should be a continual increase of luxury and good living among the citizens of rank and wealth, by whom they earned their subsistence. Warfare, on the contrary, put a check upon luxury, and the greater guilds were always issuing decrees against it, precisely on account of the exigences of the wars they so constantly had on hand. Hence the poorer classes detested the opulent burghers, whom they had helped to raise to power, who had subsequently excluded them, as well as the nobles, from the government, and who, while accumulating untold millions, often lived in the city on a footing of Spartan frugality; the men daily promulgating new edicts against female luxury in dress; forbidding the use of gold and silver ornaments, prohibiting all lavish expenditure for entertainments or wedding banquets, even going so far as to limit the number and choice of viands, and exclude gold and silver plate from festive tables; but who, nevertheless, were always very ready to squander millions in attacks on the Pisans, the King of Naples, the Visconti of Milan, or even for a church, or an additional consul at Caffa or Pera. This difference of temper generated party hatred. Nor should it be omitted that some of the bitterest outcries against the greater guilds came from the women of Florence, who, being naturally opposed to warfare, and addicted to extravagance, objected to the vexatious restrictions imposed by law, while yet contriving to evade them with indescribable ingenuity.[365]

It is very easy to realise how good an opportunity this afforded the nobles of gaining the favour of the populace by stirring these germs of discord. They exercised no trade, lived on their revenues, but spent freely and lavishly in Florence. Accordingly, whenever engaged in fresh attempts to seize the government, or preserve their remaining share in it, they always allied themselves with the mob that lived—or at least believed itself to live—solely at their expense, and roused its resentment against the *popolani grassi*—or well-to-do burghers—by dwelling on the fact that whereas all the guilds were equally engaged in trade and commerce, a considerable number of them had no share in the power exclusively monopolised by the rest. The democratic spirit was far too lively in Florence for these devices to assure the safety of the nobles, much less their return to power; but they had the effect of stirring the masses to a burning and irresistible thirst for power, and of awakening revolutionary passions in the mob. Thus, at the moment of finally losing their old supremacy in the city, the nobles achieved the revenge of bequeathing to Florence a prolonged inheritance of strife that kept the Republic divided, and hastened its fall.

In fact, when at last the lesser guilds obtained a share in the government, they were never at one with the greater trades. Their hostility was continually shown in all councils, tribunals, and public gatherings; and they sometimes resorted to the perilous means of inflaming the worst passions of the mob which, as usual, served as a ready tool for ambitious aims. In this way a spirit of anarchy was unloosed, leading first to the revolt of the Ciompi, then to the necessity of seeking a protector for the Republic, and finally to the rule of the Medici. But before arriving at these extremities, there were two centuries of struggle, during which Florentine affairs were almost invariably in the hands of the burghers. On several occasions the reins of power seemed to have slipped from their grasp, but they always managed to retain enough influence to secure the election of magistrates of their own choice. In this way victory was restored to them, and they again took possession of the government. When, on the other hand, the triumph of anarchy made it requisite to seek a protector, and this protector, summoned to the defence of the Republic, sided with the malcontents and tried to establish a tyranny, the burghers then contrived to unite every faction in the interest of their common freedom and reinstate the Republican government, thus giving it a fresh lease of life. By dint of incredible sagacity, daring, and steadfastness, they managed to struggle on amid a thousand dangers, both within and without the walls. Although plunged in perpetual conflict with those who desired peace and claimed ever wider rights; although surrounded by most powerful external foes now attempting to destroy their trade, now their Republic, their energy and patriotism never wearied, never failed to be on the alert. It was a feverish time of unceasing stress and strain, and freedom, though always on the verge of annihilation, was kept alive for two centuries in the midst of communities where it was perishing. And even as the burghers had managed to create all sorts of financial combinations for the increase of trade and multiplication of wealth, so they showed inexhaustible ingenuity in devising new schemes and institutions to prolong the life of their Republic.

In matters of foreign policy Florentine diplomats became so renowned for sagacity and quick-wittedness, that on certain points they enjoyed even higher repute than the famed ambassadors of Venice. The latter, in fact, with their old traditions of statecraft, pursued the invariable policy of a strong, calm and self-reliant government. Their strength was the outcome of the strength and wisdom of a republic commanding both fear and respect, and whose voice seemed to be heard in the speech of its envoys. Every Florentine ambassador exercised, on the contrary, a direct personal influence, due to his own sharpness of intellect, extraordinary knowledge of mankind, and marvellous aptitude for comprehending everything and making everything clearly understood. Undoubtedly the State acted in him and by him; but less because he served as its mouthpiece than because it had succeeded in evoking and training all his mental powers and rendering him an intelligent and independent personality. Florentine merchants, notaries, administrators, and diplomats were universally prized, and seemed at home in every corner of the globe. Hence it is said that one day Pope Boniface VIII., seeing that the ambassadors sent to him from different parts of the world were one and all Florentines, quietly remarked, "You Florentines are the fifth element in creation."

It was in the midst of these political conflicts, of this ferment of the human mind, that art and literature rose to such splendour, that the whole world was, as it were, illuminated by the radiance shed by Italian cities, and shining most brightly from Florence. The far-reaching energy of this city of commerce and trade was felt almost everywhere; but even at points where this had failed to penetrate, the genius of Florentine literature and art seems to have asserted its power and initiated modern culture in Europe.

VII.

All this, however, was carried on in the face of continual and new dangers, threatening the very life of the Republic, and sometimes only to be averted by super-human efforts. Memory instinctively carries us back to the Florence of old with its council and its Consuls, yearly taking the field united and agreed, for the purpose of abasing the nobles and clearing the highways for the march of its trade; and then, having reduced the hostile barons one by one, compelling them to live within the walls, subject to the equal pressure of republican laws;—to the times when the State could only overcome its more powerful neighbours by emancipating the slaves of the soil and granting political privileges to traders hitherto unpossessed of any such rights. On recalling those times, we easily recognise that they contained the germs of future greatness for the Commune that by dint of continual warfare succeeded in augmenting its resources in every direction. Later, however, things were radically changed, owing to many causes, and above all in consequence of the new method of warfare to which we have already alluded and which must now be more fully described.

Down to the fourteenth century republican armies were composed of foot soldiers, lightly equipped with sword, shield, and helmet, and some slight defensive armour for leg or breast. The horse were few in number and never decided the fate of a battle. All barbarian armies had been composed much on the same plan, excepting those of the Huns and Moors, who were almost always mounted, and of the Byzantines, whose cavalry had frequently defeated the Goths. Frederic Barbarossa's Italian campaigns had been chiefly carried on by infantry and withstood by the infantry of our communes, who could then turn all able-bodied citizens into soldiers at a moment's notice. But in the campaigns of Frederic II., Manfred and Charles of Anjou, a new method of war had been imported into Italy from Germany and France. The Florentines had learnt this to their cost at the battle of Montaperti, when their numerous army was routed by the charge of a few German horse. From that moment the issue of all Italian battles began to be decided by heavy cavalry or by men-at-arms. The mounted soldier was clad in steel from head to foot, although not yet, as at the close of the fifteenth century, encased, together with his steed, in such ponderous armour, that, once fallen, neither could rise from the ground without help. Armed with a very long lance, the horseman could overthrow the foot soldier before the latter could approach him with his short sword. Besides, this weapon never served to pierce the armour either of

239

man or horse; and the arrows of the bowmen were equally useless. Accordingly, a few hundred men-at-arms pushed forward like a movable and impregnable fortress into the midst of a host of infantry sufficed to rout it in a very short time. This state of things lasted until the invention of powder and firearms produced a radical change in the condition of the Italian communes. For mounted troops required much training and great expenditure. It was not enough to maintain great arsenals, to create and train a new breed of horses, but every trooper had also to be kept in steady practice, devote his whole time to warfare, and keep two or three squires continuously drilled and employed. These squires carried all the armour and weapons and led the knight's charger, which was only used in battle. Only then, too, were knight and steed in full harness, otherwise both would have been exhausted in the hour of danger. Hence it was impossible for our republics to raise cavalry, seeing that citizens, earning their living by trade and commerce, could not forsake their daily work to acquire the art of war. Therefore, soldiering became a regular trade, and all choosing it for their career speedily began to put a price on their swords. Thus from the closing years of the thirteenth century we begin to find *soldiers* of various nationalities—Catalans, Burgundians, Germans, and other foreign horse—in the ranks of republican armies, and the number of these mercenaries was continually on the increase.

Gradually, also, tradesmen were obliged to recognise that they had become personally useless in the field. Accordingly, whenever the republics were threatened with attack, they no longer ventured to give battle without hiring some captain with a band of foreign horse. Italian valour rapidly lost its prestige, and "Companies of Adventure"—soon to be the cause of our direst calamities—began to be formed. Later on, it is true that when Alberico da Barbiano, Attendolo Sforza, Braccio da Montone, and others adopted the same career, they rivalled and even surpassed the foreign adventurers, who had now often to yield the palm to Italian courage. Soon, in fact, many came from afar to learn the new art of war under these Italian captains whose skill first reduced it to a science. Nevertheless, few citizens of free states were able to devote their whole life to war. It was the nobles, the exiles, the unemployed —knowing no other trade—and the subjects of petty tyrants who joined the "Companies of Adventure." And whether small bands or large, Italian or foreign, they invariably hastened the ruin of all our communes, and more especially of Florence. The continual wars in which this State was now engaged no longer served to foster the military spirit and energy of its people. Always compelled to rely on the help of foreign mercenaries, it soon lost all confidence in its own resources, the which therefore rapidly declined. A campaign simply implied some financial operation, or the levying of fresh taxes to furnish sufficient capital for the hire of one of the captains of adventure, who always closed with the highest bid. The money found, it was often enough to send it to the State's surest and most powerful ally, who undertook to complete the affair by engaging the captain best able to hire the largest number of men. So the chief thing was to know how to gain friends and excite enemies against the foe, and in this the Florentines always showed masterly skill. But these devices were no proof of military capacity. The most important personages despatched by them to the seat of war were commissioners charged to superintend the general proceedings, the administration of the army, and the political object of the campaign, and although we sometimes find these commissioners suddenly transformed into captains, taking command of the forces and deciding the fate of a battle with singular daring, their functions were always civil and diplomatic rather than military.

It is easy to foresee the final results of this method with regard to the future of the Republic, and the morals of its inhabitants. The stout burghers at the head of the government were engaged in the continual practice of cunning and craft. It was requisite to show adroitness in the council chamber; to thwart the nobles; to remain constantly on the alert to prevent the populace from growing unruly, while persuading it to furnish funds to carry on wars which were indispensable to secure the safety and prosperity of the foreign trade. Hence, still greater subtlety was needed in diplomatic negotiations to avoid being isolated, and to continually maintain the equilibrium of Italian States in the way most advantageous for the Republic. Even actual warfare being now reduced, as we have seen, to a financial operation, had come to be a fresh proof of ingenuity. There were no longer any of those vast sacrifices of citizens' blood and citizens' lives which serve towards the continued regeneration of a people, no longer any deeds of open and generous violence. And at times when the rich burghers were not absorbed in politics, they and all the rest of the citizens were devoted heart and soul to commerce, employing their leisure moments in the study of Tacitus, Virgil, or Homer, kept ready to hand under their counters. But, invariably, it was only the intelligence that was kept always in training, while the nobler faculties remained strangled and atrophied by the constant use of cunning and trickery. This was destined to lead, sooner or later, to the inevitable decay of the Republic's moral and political life, and to the decline of the highest mental culture. If the manner in which wars were planned and conducted caused fatal results, no less fatal were the ulterior consequences of victorious campaigns. For the hired troops once paid off, changed from friends into foes, and instantly sought to sell their services to some other employer. Failing to find one, and therefore receiving no pay, they dispersed in armed bands, ravaging town and country, by a species of military brigandage. Generally, it was found requisite to come to terms with them, and bribe them to keep the peace.

But the most important point to be noted at this juncture is that the conquest of fresh territory, although become an absolute necessity to the Republic, now began to be a serious danger and the source of future calamities. During the Middle Ages the Italian Commune had been a fertile cause of progress; but as its possessions outside the walls began to increase, it proved wholly powerless to convert the free city into what we call a State without working radical changes in its constitution. In fact, even in Florence, the most democratic of our communes, citizens were only to be found within the circuit of the walls. Laws were framed to ameliorate the condition of the territory outside and to abolish serfdom there, but no one contemplated endowing inhabitants of the *contado* with political rights. The title of citizens always remained, as it were, a privilege only granted to a minority, even of dwellers within the walls, and was never extended to the people at large. Whenever a new city was conquered and subjected to the Republic, it was governed more or less harshly; allowed to retain more or fewer local privileges; sometimes even permitted to retain a republican form of government, subject to the authority of a Podestà, captain, or commissary, and paying the taxes imposed by them; but its inhabitants never enjoyed the freedom of the City, nor were their representatives by any chance admitted to the councils or political offices of Florence. Accordingly, as the State became enlarged by fresh conquests, the cluster of citizens monopolising the government, and already very limited in number, sank to a still smaller minority compared with the ever-increasing population subject to their rule. Similarly to all other republicans of the Middle Ages, the Florentines were altogether unable to conceive the idea of a State governed with a view to the general welfare. On the contrary, the prosperity and grandeur of Florence formed the one object and aim to which every other consideration had to be subservient. Nor had the lower classes and populace, who were always clamouring for increased freedom, any different or wider views on the subject. Their ideas, indeed, being restricted in a narrower circle, were even more prejudiced, as their passions were blinder. Consequently it was considered at that time a greater calamity to be subjugated by a fellow republic than by a monarchy; inasmuch as princes brought their tyranny to bear equally on all alike, and thus, at any rate as regarded politics, the chief majority of the conquered suffered less injury. When Florence, however, by achieving the long-desired conquest of Pisa, at last became mistress of the sea, and witnessed the rapid increase of her commerce, she discovered that the annexation of a great and powerful republic, full of life and strength and possessed of so large a trade, brought her none of the advantages which might have ensued from a union of a freer kind with an equal distribution of political rights. The chief citizens of Pisa and all the wealthier families left the country, preferring to live in Lombardy, France, or even in Sicily under the Aragonese, where at least they enjoyed civil equality, rather than remain in their own city subject to the harsh and tyrannous rule of Florentine shopkeepers. The commerce and industry of Pisa, her navy, her merchant-fleet, all vanished when freedom fell; while her *Studio*, or university, one of the old glories of Italy, and afterwards reconstituted by the Medici, was done away with, and the city soon reduced to a state of squalid desolation. All conquered cities suffered this fate; those once of the richest and most powerful in the days of their freedom being treated with still greater harshness than the rest.[366] This makes it easy to understand why, when Florence was in danger, all conquered cities in which life was not altogether extinguished invariably seized the opportunity to try to regain their independence, and always preferred a native or foreign tyrant to cowering beneath the yoke of a republic that refused to learn from experience the wisdom of changing its policy. Nor could it have effected such change without radically altering its whole constitution and manner of existence.

Thus, in accumulating riches and power, Florence was only multiplying the causes of her approaching and unavoidable decline. The Commune seemed increasingly incapable of giving birth to the modern State, and accordingly, when its chief support, commerce, began to decay, the strength of the burghers was sapped, and the oppressed multitude, now a formidable majority, speedily looked to monarchical rule for their relief. Thus the Medici were enabled to attain supremacy in the name of freedom, and with the support of people and populace. Thus, likewise, by violence, or fraud, or by both combined, the communes of Italy were all reduced to principalities; and wherever, from exceptional causes, the republican order still lingered on for a while, it was only as a shadow of its former self, and no longer rendering any of the advantages for which it had been originally designed. Populations which had failed to establish equality by means of free institutions, were now forced to learn the lesson of equality beneath the undiscriminating oppression of a despotic prince. Signories formed the necessary link of transition between the mediæval commune and the modern state. For these Signories traced a way towards the just administration and method pursued by the vast kingdoms then in course of formation on the continent of Europe, and which also remained absolute and despotic monarchies until the French revolution effected in town, country, and throughout every class that work of social emancipation which the Italian communes had so admirably initiated, but had never learnt to extend beyond the circuit of their walls.

Florence maintained a prolonged resistance, but finally shared the fate of her fellow republics.

CHAPTER VII.[367]

THE FAMILY AND THE STATE IN ITALIAN COMMUNES.[368]

I.[369]

IT is certain that no real national history of Italy can be written until the statutes and laws of our communes have been published, studied, and thoroughly investigated by the light not merely of historical but of legal research. The necessity for such investigation was first proclaimed by the learned Savigny, subsequently recognised by many Italian scholars, but has never yet been entirely satisfied. An accurate study of those old laws and statutes would make us acquainted with the public law of the communes, and place before our eyes a clear and exact picture of their political institutions which have been hitherto very imperfectly understood. Moreover, what is certainly of no less importance—it would enlarge our knowledge of our ancient private law, to which many learned authorities, among others Francesco Forti, attribute the origin of modern jurisprudence, and the germs of many jural provisions, afterwards accepted by us as novelties derived from the French Code.

Public and private law have far more affinity than is generally supposed, and each conduces to the plainer and more exact comprehension of the other. Society and the State have both their birth in the family, reacting upon and modifying it in turn. No student therefore who seeks to discover the true key to political institutions developing themselves in a country spontaneously, should neglect the constitution of the family wherein are to be found the earliest beginnings of civil law, with which political law also is more or less connected. Cases, it is true, frequently occur of one people adopting the civil law of another, without altering its own political institutions; while in other instances both are imposed simultaneously by a superior foreign force. This has led many to question the reality of the connection which in fact subsists between them. But these cases have nothing to do with that natural and spontaneous development of law of which we are now speaking. In this development, politics and jurisprudence, the State and the family, are found to be closely interconnected.

In the course of Florentine history we often see political revolutions break out suddenly and apparently without warning; but on closer examination we perceive them to be the result of deep social changes which have been maturing for a long time, and although imperceptible at first, afterwards assuming such proportions as to become suddenly visible to all eyes and productive of political reforms. Thus it happens that private law, which always accompanies social movements and changes with them, not unfrequently enables us to trace the sources and unfold the true tendency and inexorable necessity of revolutions, even before they come to pass. Accordingly, the habitual neglect of this particular study in connection with the history of Italy has proved a serious defect. No one at the present day would venture to write the political history of Rome without giving attention to the Roman jurisprudence. Nevertheless, we have written the history of our republics over and over again, without bestowing a thought on their civil and penal legislation.

It is true that the investigation required presents very great difficulties, inasmuch as our history was subject, during the Middle Ages, to a series of changes, always rapid and always different. The number of our republics is infinite. Every province of Italy, every fragment of Italian territory is divided and subdivided into communes, every one of which has a distinct history, and political institutions which are constantly changing. This perpetual mutation is faithfully reflected in the statutes of the Commune. On the margins of these statutes we find alterations and corrections registered from year to year, and formulated, not unfrequently, after the streets of the city had begun to run with blood. When annotations and corrections reach a certain number, the statutes are drafted anew, and of these re-drafts also many copies are still extant. It was the duty of the officials in charge of the statutes (*statutari*) to enter from time to time such farther modifications as were afterwards approved of in the Councils of the People. Hence it sometimes happens that on referring to the statutes of a given year, we may find the duties of some chief magistrate of the Republic set forth in their text with the most minute detail, whereas if we look to the notes it will appear that these duties have already been changed. If we next consult the remodelled statute it will be found that the magistracy itself no longer exists. How is it possible, therefore, to give any idea of the political form of a municipality fashioned in such wise? This can only be done by gleaning from the mass of the statutes the history of the constitution through all its successive changes of form. In a word, we must recognise that, instead of being confronted by a system crystallised, fixed and immutable, we are watching a living organism develop under our eyes in obedience to a settled law. This law alone is uniform, and it is this we must endeavour to trace, since it alone can solve the mystery and supply exact ideas. Turning from public law to private legislation, our difficulties rather increase than diminish. For, in perusing this, by no means less important portion of the statutes, we come upon a confused medley of legal systems differing from and often opposed to one another. When we meet with such terms as *meta* and *mundium*, *wergild* and *morgengab*, *dos* and *tutela*, testamentary succession and succession by agreement, we recognise that Longobard law, Roman law, feudal law, and canon law are all present, and perceive that they are blended in constantly varying proportions. These diverse legal systems act and react one upon the other, producing reciprocal changes. Into the Roman law, provisions are constantly filtering which indubitably belong to the Longobard law, while the latter in its turn is profoundly modified ("mutilated and castrated," as Gans expresses it) by the Roman law. How are we to explain this congeries of different laws? Is there any new and original principle that assimilates the heterogeneous elements and constitutes a new law? If so, what is it? This is the knotty problem which Savigny encouraged us to attack, but which we have hitherto failed to unravel. But although the question remains unsolved, its importance is now universally acknowledged; it has been carefully studied, and many treatises, including some of the highest value, have been published on the subject. Accordingly certain observations may at last be offered to the public.

The constitution of the family and its relation with the State are, as it were, the chief centre round which all fresh researches must revolve, and these form the subject of this short and summary essay. As a preliminary step towards the solution of the problem, an accurate investigation is required of the various forms that the family assumed under the various systems of law which succeeded one another in Italy, in order to ascertain how it was that from the combination of those various forms, another and widely different one should have resulted. The first question therefore that presents itself has reference to the condition of the Roman law and the Roman family at the time of the barbarian invasion. As regards the Italian communes, it is only natural that the Roman jurisprudence should strike the deepest and strongest root in their social system, and that the history of our laws should originally find in it their first beginning. Here, however, we are forced to enter on a digression which, although seemingly apart from the point, will presently help us to a clearer understanding of the new society in course of development. With regard to this digression it should also be said that so much learning and research have been directed to the study of Roman law, that we are able to arrive at certain trustworthy conclusions which, by affording evidence of the close connection between the Roman family, and the political society derived from it, will show us what path to take in pursuit of the same connection in the history of Italy.

II.

Every student of the Pandects knows that the words "Roman law" denote the outcome of long preliminary labours, and the ultimate form of a jurisprudence which cannot be rightly understood without analysing all the historical elements employed in preparing and building it up. Treated in this way, the history of Roman law becomes, as it were, instantly transformed into a history of many different legislations following one another at intervals. From the Twelve Tables down to Justinian, this law never halts for an hour in its constant course of development. Even during the Middle Ages, when the compilations made at Constantinople were studied with religious zeal by expounders and commentators whose sole object was to faithfully reproduce and diffuse this law, even thus, in the hands of those interpreters, influenced by the altered spirit of the times and by new social developments, it underwent changes of which they were not themselves conscious. It is not until the fifteenth century that this historic development can be said to have ceased among us, and Roman law become mainly a subject of learned research. It is at this time that a new and modern system of jurisprudence first reveals itself to history, endowed with a separate life, and with a form of its own, though borrowing much from the Roman law, which in consequence continues to be of the utmost value to us, and still deserves our most assiduous attention, although for a very different purpose from that with which it was studied during the Middle Ages. Our object is now to familiarise ourselves with an immortal monument of ancient wisdom, to shape our legal education by it, to be helped by it to a clearer understanding of our own codes, and to contemplate it in its successive manifestations, while we search for its regulating law. It is in fact the discovery of this law that has at once thrown a new light upon the whole history of Roman jurisprudence, which we perceive to have been always and unceasingly governed by it, and thus forced to assume a character so constant and continuous through all its various transformations, that what had before seemed to be a series of distinct legislations takes an entirely new aspect, making us spectators, as it were, of the evolution of a single idea, the progressive development of a work of Nature.

All this continuous progress or evolution was the result of two forces, of two different elements. The true, primitive law of Rome was the special law of the Quirites, of which we find the remains in the Twelve Tables: a severe and restricted law abounding in formulas which had to be sacredly observed, and its administration was entrusted to a small number of citizens who alone were acquainted with its rules, whose authority was sanctioned by religion. The smallest mistake of form made void the most just decree, and where the law omitted to define the formula to be observed, no valid action could be brought. When the due formula, making the contract binding, had once been pronounced, no proof of mistake or fraud could annul it. "Uti lingua nuncupassit ita ius esto." A slave to forms, the judge could not listen to the voice of morality or rectitude; the most just complaint failed to move him, unless supported by a text of law. The defendant dared not stir a step without the continual guidance of the legislator, inasmuch as every juridical formula was sacred and inviolable; and as the science of law was monopolised by the College of Pontiffs, the most aristocratic and conservative body in Rome, it became a kind of occult science. It was this very character, however, apparently so restricted and pedantic, that gave its great force to the law in Rome. For law, being now freed for the first time from every extraneous element belonging to morals and good faith, became firm and inexorable. Any one who had the law in his favour was safe to see it promptly carried out. History affords no example elsewhere of legal sanction and redress being applied so swiftly and surely as in Rome. In Athens, indeed, where the laws were more philosophical, and the popular conscience gave judgment, investigating motives, despising formulas, and looking only to substantial justice, caprice often prevailed, and law never attained the iron strength and tenacity of the Roman jurisprudence.

But with changing times, all things changed in Rome. This jurisprudence revered as sacred, but described by Vico as *made up of formulas and phrases*, was well adapted to a rude and primitive people. Ideas had greatly altered in the days of Cicero, who in his speech *pro Murena* severely satirises a science which, in his eyes, had become ridiculous: "res enim sunt parvæ, prope in singulis literis atque interpunctionibus occupatæ." He looked upon the whole thing as a fraud designed by the priests to secure themselves a monopoly. Was he in the right or the wrong? Vico, in examining a similar question, showed that Cicero was mistaken on this score. Cicero and his contemporaries, he said, lived in too cultivated an age to comprehend rude and primitive jurisprudence; they could not grasp its true significance, but formed their judgment of the ancient laws according to the ideas and principles of their own times. This view, which was first broached in the *Scienza Nuova*, was afterwards accepted by many other writers; and it is now placed beyond a doubt that the primitive Roman law was not the artifice of a learned few, but was a spontaneous and necessary growth among the people with whom it had its origin. At first, custom, clearly distinguished from the law formulated and written, tempered its rigid severity. Good faith and equity, disregarded and rejected by the law, found their sanction in custom, were administered by a separate tribunal, and were always respected, inasmuch as the sentence pronounced by the officiating magistrate was morally, though not legally, binding, and was therefore of great efficacy as the genuine expression of public opinion. The sentence of condemnation could not be carried out by force; but it made the condemned man infamous, and, as a last resort, the magistrate could cite the accused before the people, as the supreme legislator and judge.

But at a later date customs grew corrupt, and no longer sufficed to protect public good faith and morality, which were driven to seek asylum and sanction in the law, and so began gradually to modify its primitive character. Substance now prevailed over form, equity over the ancient text of the law, the intention of the contracting parties over words uttered by mistake; the law became more moral as customs grew more degraded. This transformation, though very gradual at the beginning, was afterward, accelerated by the new conditions of the Republics in which a change took place not unlike that occurring in the history of jurisprudence, towards the beginning of the seventeenth century. At that time the various European States, with their various systems of law, having contracted new relations with one another, came to recognise the necessity of establishing some fixed rules by which all should be bound, and thus, under the auspices of Hugh Grotius, the so-called School of Natural Law was built up. The same occurred in Rome, if not in the science, at any rate in the practice of law. As the dominion of the Republic became extended in Italy, its relations increased with neighbouring nations, among whom the more philosophical and less severe laws and principles of the Greek jurisprudence prevailed. It was impossible to impose upon all these nations, without modification, the rigid law of the Roman patriciate. Accordingly a new system of law, of a simpler character and wider reach, took shape and rapidly grew. This was named the *jus gentium*, to distinguish it from the other, the *jus civile*. "Jus gentium est quod naturalis ratio inter omnes homines constituit." This system, however, was not deduced from philosophic theories concerning human nature, as was the, appropriately styled, natural law of the eighteenth century; it originated in the practical needs of the Romans and their new relations with other Italian peoples: it was fostered by the principles of Greek jurisprudence that had been transplanted into Southern Italy; it met the new requirements of the Romans themselves; and taking the place that custom had previously filled in the Roman courts, grew side by side with the law of the Patricians with which it long maintained its union.

There were thus two systems of law in force in Rome; and we accordingly find on the one hand judges and courts faithful to the ancient formalism, on the other, judges and courts taking cognizance of equity and good faith, and almost discharging the duties of the Censor. The continuous onward progress of the *jus gentium*, the reciprocal action of the two legal systems ultimately fusing them into one, wherein the old Roman formation gradually lost its rigidity, and equity, becoming incorporated with the civil law, began to assume a more definite and regular form, were all consequences of the principle which dominates the life and history of the Roman law, and may even be said to constitute it. For it has been moulded and diffused through the world, inheriting from the old Quirites its frame of iron; from contact with other races and from such germs as it could assimilate of Greek civilisation, its more comprehensive and human spirit. Assuming thus a character at once exact and philosophical, it seemed as though destined to become, from its superiority, the universal jurisprudence, the indispensable foundation, as it were, of all future legislation. This union of legal systems was effected by the Prætor. He it was who represented both the modern spirit and the ancient, enlarging the old law with the defences of equity which he strengthened by submitting it to the trammels of a formal procedure. This in substance was what took place with regard to customs, letters, and everything else. The fusion of Greek civilisation with the Roman constitutes the history of the ancient world.

III.

As is natural, we also meet with the same phenomena in the history of the family, from which the civil law is to a great extent derived. In fact, whoever contemplates the primitive Roman family, at once recognises it as the basis upon which the future juridical and political greatness of Rome was erected. The family is sacred; the father is absolute master of the goods, the liberty and the life both of his wife and of his children. He is priest, judge, supreme arbiter: wife, children, and grandchildren form with him a single joint society, one legal entity of which he is the representative. The woman may be bartered away, killed, or sold in execution; freed by marriage from the despotic control of her father, she at once falls under that of her husband; her legal incapacity lasts through her whole life. But primitive customs so temper this harsh law that we find no other people of antiquity so observant of the sanctity of family, or showing so much respect to woman. Matrimony is styled "consortium omnis vitæ, divini et humani iuris communicatio." Divorce on the part of the husband (*repudium*) is not forbidden by law, but any man who repudiates his wife is dishonoured by the Censor, excommunicated by the priest, and for a period of five centuries few cases of repudiation are recorded. In ancient Greece some traces of oriental polygamy are still discernible, but in Italy monogamy is coeval with Rome itself. Natural children, as such, never rank as members of the family, but they may be legitimated. Adoption is a solemn act, the moral propriety of which is referred to the decision of the pontifex, as the guardian of the sanctity of the family, and is thus submitted to the popular sanction. The woman is never seen in places of public resort, nor does she attend popular gathering; but within doors she is *domina*, and the husband addresses her by that title. The *Atrium* is the centre and sanctuary of the house. Here relations, friends, and strangers meet together; here stand the domestic hearth, the altar dedicated to the *Lares*, and all those objects which the family holds sacred: the nuptial coach, the ancestral likenesses moulded in wax from the faces of the dead, the matron's rock and spindle, the chest containing the household records and monies. All these possessions are entrusted to the care and superintendence of the mother of the family, who, together with her husband, sacrifices to the gods and assists him in the management of the common patrimony: she directs all domestic work, and watches over the education of her children. In the annals and legends of Rome the name of some heroine, such as Virginia or Lucretia, is indissolubly linked with the chief glories of the Eternal City. It is not so in Greece. In instituting and sanctifying the family, the Romans laid the foundation-stone of the Capitol. But to maintain this primitive nucleus of Roman society firm and compact, the law must always watch with vigilance and multiply its ordinances. The property of the family must be kept together as strictly as possible and for the longest possible time. The father is its sole master and arbiter; but on his death the patrimony is equally divided between sons and daughters. The *unity* of the family must also be guarded and defended by the law, since there is serious danger that a woman marrying may carry away from the family an interest in the family property. She is accordingly subjected by the law to a perpetual tutelage which prevents her from disposing at will of her own property. On the death of her father the woman comes under the tutelage of the agnati. In Cicero's day, when as Vico has noted, the true significance of primitive Roman law had been lost, lawyers believed that this tutelage of women had been established on account of the weakness of the sex, *propter sexus infirmitatem.* But Gaius refers to this opinion as a plausible and prevalent error, and maintains that the restriction was instituted in the interest of the agnati, so that the woman, whose presumptive heirs they were, should have no power to alienate, diminish, or otherwise defraud them of their inheritance.[370]

So long as the woman remained under the tutelage of her father, inasmuch as she had not yet inherited, the law allowed her to incur legal obligations. The danger for the family began when, on her father's death, she became an heir. It was from that precise moment, accordingly, that she came under the tutelage of her own heirs the agnati, and could no longer bind herself without their consent. This tutelage, therefore, became not merely a duty on the part of the agnati, but was also a right and privilege. Where the agnate was a minor, of weak mind, or otherwise incapacitated, he did not forfeit this right, but it had to be exercised by a third party. The tutor fixed the dowry to be given with the woman on her marriage; but the remainder of her patrimony had to be preserved intact, that it might return afterwards to the agnati. No woman could make a will, that she might not have it in her power to defraud the family. On passing *in manus viri*, the woman underwent a *capitis diminutio*. She entered another family, as it were, *loco filiæ*, and her new relations became her lawful heirs. Under these circumstances the law permitted her to make a testamentary disposition, whereby, notwithstanding her new relationships, she might restore her patrimony to her own original family.

When the woman was under the *manus* of her husband, she was emancipated from the paternal authority and from the tutelage of her agnates. The displeasure thereby caused to her own family was so great that, before long, marriage by simple consent was resorted to, according to which the woman became personally subject to her husband's authority, but he had no right of *manus* over her, and consequently no power over her property. In this way the woman remained under the power of her father or of the agnates, and at the same time came under the authority of her husband, an arrangement that inevitably led to many collisions, and hastened the advent of the most radical change in the Roman family—the complete independence of woman. But, before reaching this point, disputes were for a long time kept in check and efficaciously remedied by the mediating influence of a most important institution—the domestic tribunal. This family council, regulated by usage, not law, was composed of agnates, cognates, relations, and sometimes also of friends. It presided at espousals and at the assumption of the *toga virilis*; it protected orphans; it aided the head of the family in adjudicating and in awarding punishment, and acted as a restraint on his authority. By law, the father could act even without the co-operation of the Council; but by doing so, he exposed himself to being publicly blamed and noted with ignominy by the Censor, who, if necessary, might accuse him before the people. The marriageable maiden was subject to and protected by this Council.

Becoming a wife by that form of marriage which brought her *in manus viri*, she left her own family to become member of another; but if not married under that form, she still remained subject to the family Council, in which her husband was now included.

IV.

In the age of Cæsar, the Roman family is no longer what it was at first. Laws, usages, ideas, all are changed; and everything is moving onward to a still more radical transformation. The *jus gentium* seems to have become identical with the more rigorous *jus civile*. The *fideicommissum* has almost the force of a testament in solemn form, and has become part, as it were, of the *jus civile*; *verbal contract*, the ancient *stipulatio*, once so hampered by formulas, is grown so flexible as to resemble a contract under the *jus gentium*. But the greatest change of all has taken place in the family. The domestic hearth is no longer the household sanctuary. The *Atrium* is transformed into an open courtyard, enlivened with flowers and limpid fountains, ornamented with gilded busts and statues, often of an obscene character. Sacrifices are no longer offered there to the gods amid the stillness and purity of domestic and religious affection; it now serves the enriched and corrupt patrician as a place of reception for his numerous friends and clients. The family of former days, once almost a State within the State, is now dissolved, and, as it were, swallowed up by the political power. The agnates no longer cleave together, the domestic tribunal has either lost its strength or has entirely disappeared. Paternal authority, though less absolute, is more oppressive, being no longer in harmony with the changed customs. If a father disinherits his son, the judge cancels the will. Should he refuse consent to his son's marriage, the State compels him to grant it; should he punish his son with death, the emperor sends him into exile; he cannot ill-use even his slaves without being punished by the law, for the law has grown moral as manners become more corrupt. By gradual degrees woman escapes from tutelage, and from *manus*, and ultimately attains her independence. But the more she is emancipated from her family and relations, the greater becomes her subjection to the State. In her new independence she incurs new disabilities, no longer resulting from her position as daughter or wife, but from the fact of her sex, disabilities no longer imposed in the interest of the family, but created as a protection for her infirmity. This explains how it was that the lawyers of later days were mistaken as to the significance of the old law touching the *tutela* of woman. The wife's dowry is guaranteed to her more and more strictly, until it finally becomes her almost inseparable property. It must neither be alienated nor diminished. On her becoming a widow, being divorced, or returning to the paternal roof, she remains absolute mistress of it. A husband who surprises his wife in adultery can no longer—hiding his dishonour within his own walls— judge and put her to death with the consent of the domestic tribunal. He must now leave the State to avenge his wrongs, and must resort to the courts, even though seeking only minor penalties. Divorce has become a public act of not unfrequent occurrence. The woman, in short, is no longer under her husband's *manus*, no longer subject to the *patria potestas*, no longer under the tutelage of the *agnati*: she is protected by the State. When the law still requires her to have a *tutor* or Procurator, she can choose a stranger who becomes her servant rather than her master. Eventually even this last shadow of subjection disappears. Absolutely her own mistress, the woman may now hold property, increase her fortune, make her will, lose her virtue; but her dowry, guaranteed and kept intact by law, remains hers to the end of her life.

Nevertheless, as regards succession, the woman's rights are not yet the same as the man's. It is true, that should her father die intestate, she takes an equal share with her brothers of the inheritance; but in all other cases of intestacy the nearest female agnate stands after the most distant male. The woman cannot now do any legal act for others, though this had not been forbidden previously; she cannot be a witness; she cannot stand security for the debts of others. The *Senatus-consultum Velleianum* lays it down as a fixed rule, which, to a certain extent, has remained in force to our own days—that the woman must not undertake any obligation on behalf of others. She may alienate her possessions in others' favour, may incur a direct obligation, contract a debt, and transfer the money to others; but she cannot bind herself to pay another's debt, nor guarantee its payment. In the legislator's opinion, the infirmity of her sex leaves her enough intelligence to escape danger in assuming direct obligations, or by alienating her property, but not enough to guard her from lightly undertaking remote and indirect liabilities which are often no less serious.

But the progressive changes in the Roman family are not yet at an end. To the numberless causes for change already in existence another is added, when Christianity finds its way into the Empire, into literature and law, and subverts all things. According to the law of Christ, man and woman are equal; father and mother have equal rights and duties in respect of their children, for whose advantage all things must be ordered; whereas, by the old law, the rights of the children were subordinated to the interests of the family. A new element is now introduced into Roman law which further changes its character, already much modified by Greek philosophy and by Byzantine despotism. The Canon law accepts the principles of the Roman, recognises the wife's absolute interest in her marriage portion, and rejects the pretensions of the husband. Woman remains excluded from every office which the ancients deemed proper to man; she cannot enter into obligations for others, nor arbitrate, nor lay an accusation, nor bear witness in court; her evidence has no legal effect. On the other hand, Roman law tends inexorably to democratic equality, natural equity, and to the absolute predominance of the State. The public authority deprives domestic authority of its last remnant of power; it may almost be said that the family, as a body-politic, disappears, to be reconstituted on the footing of reciprocal affection. The final seal to these alterations was imposed by the famous law of succession (Nov. 118 and 127) enacted by Justinian in the years 543 and 547, which, suppressing every privilege of sex and agnation, fixes rights according to the degree of relationship, and makes them reciprocal. It moreover enlarges the amount of the legitim, and ordains that the dowry of the wife should be met by a *donatio propter nuptias* of equal value from the husband, and that, in the interest of the children, both should be inalienable. Even with the consent of his wife, the husband cannot sell the dowry; he may only administer it, and there must be complete reciprocity. The wife is not only the owner of the dowry, she has besides a general charge over her husband's property for its restitution, with a right of action to enforce it as against all his other creditors. In inheriting from their children the mother has equal right with the father, and she is now qualified to be their guardian. Even the *Senatus-consultum Velleianum*, which forbade women to incur obligations on behalf of others, is modified with the same scope. Justinian, indeed, from his desire to protect the property of the woman against all danger, is strenuously opposed to her incurring obligations on behalf of her husband; but he is much more indulgent in respect to obligations undertaken on behalf of a stranger. These, if incurred for manifestly good cause, are valid if renewed after two years. Thus modified, the *Senatus-consultum Velleianum* is treated with respect throughout the Middle Ages. Reciprocal equality is now achieved, but the ancient unity of the family is dissolved; the compact and iron nucleus of Roman society is broken to fragments by the continual and increasing action of the State. In all her institutions, Rome has succeeded in arriving at democracy and equality, but at the cost of complete individual liberty, and by sacrificing the development of special associations and of local life to the unity of the State. How to conciliate these two elements without destroying the one in the interest of the other will be the problem of a new era and a new civilisation.

However highly we may rate the amazing and indisputable greatness of the labours of Imperial legislators and juris-consults collected in the *Corpus iuris* in the time of Justinian, it is nevertheless certain that the ancient and primitive character of Roman law has been profoundly changed by it, and that the despotism of the State, always prevalent in Rome, has been enormously increased. It is for this reason that Tocqueville, and others with him, go so far as to maintain that the great diffusion of the Justinian law among the Latin races has more than once proved hurtful to political freedom. To many, such an assertion may seem absurd; but granting that there is a close bond of connection between private and public law, and that the final changes in Roman law were introduced by the action of the growing despotism of the State, the opinion advanced by the French writer is not without its value.

V.

However that may be, it is undeniable that the family, as we now find it constituted, or, more correctly speaking, weakened, by the Justinian law has not the qualities which would enable it, in the ages of barbarism now at hand, to withstand the violent onset of the advancing Germanic peoples, much less to be the nucleus and germ from which the new society of the Italian Commune may take birth. In fact, in the statutes we find the family constituted on a very different footing. Agnation has recovered its ascendancy. The woman is under a new species of guardianship; and although the dotal system is rigorously observed, there are innumerable regulations designed to keep family property together, or make it revert to the family, so as to preserve the domestic patrimony intact. Here an important question arises, namely, whether this new constitution of the family, which stands in close relation with the public law of the communes, is a return to the pre- Justinian law, or derived from Germanic institutions and the Longobard law, in which we find, in fact, precedence accorded to agnate kin and a more stable family organisation? Italian writers, the earlier writers more especially, adhered for the most part to the former theory, while the majority of German authors, who have recently found disciples even among ourselves, adopt the second view. Thus, on either side we find theories propounded as to the constitution of the Italian family in the Middle Ages, analogous to those concerning the origin of the communes.[371]

The persistence of Roman law in the Middle Ages, even when the condition of the Italians was most wretched, and when all things seemed to be subject to the law of the Longobard, was maintained with marvellous learning and acumen in the immortal work of Savigny. But, in truth, though public law and penal law might readily be altered under the rule of the conqueror, there was little likelihood that the civil law which, for so many centuries, had filtered into the usages and into the very blood of the Romans, which had regulated the manifold relations of a civilised people and satisfied its countless requirements, should perish utterly beneath the sword of barbarians unconscious of those requirements and not always able to comprehend those relations. Matters of which they were to a great extent ignorant, or as to which they were indifferent, must often have been passed over without notice in the laws framed by the barbarians, or have evaded their action. Various provisions, therefore, of the Roman law—those, for instance, relating to marriage, to succession, and to contract—must often have continued to be applied by the Italians in conformity with ancient usage. This will be more readily understood if we reflect that while the Roman law had become the law of *all* in those countries in which the Roman conquest had taken deep root, the laws of the barbarians, on the contrary, according to Teutonic usage, always presented a personal character—that is to say, extended only to the people with whom they originated, and were not easily communicated to others. In fact, when, as a consequence of successive invasions, different Germanic tribes, whether independent of each other or in subjection one to another, came together in the same country, each of them continued to be governed by its own peculiar laws. The Romans, on the contrary, regarding their law as universal in character, communicated it to, and imposed it upon all. It was almost the first germ of the greatness and the civilisation of Rome, and for that reason its diffusion was considered the most sacred of duties by this sovereign people. Thus it was that, even under the harshest barbaric oppression, the Roman law continued to be the private law of the Italians in all those cases, and they were not few, in which the German laws failed to notice it, and neither abrogated it directly nor substituted another in its place.

But the presence of two diverse legislations, the one imposed by force, the other preserved by custom, the radical change of conditions occasioned by the destruction of the old Roman State and the formation of a new society, could not fail to originate a new life, a new history for the Italian law. In the statute books of our communes we find Roman and Longobard law confronted and almost contending, each modified in turn by the action of the other. But under which of the many forms through which it has passed is the Roman law found among us at the moment when it seemed on the point of being overcome by the Germanic law? Was it in the literary and philosophic form given to it by Justinian, or was it in the *pre*-Justinian form, which, while less systematic, was also less altered by Byzantine ideas, and more in accordance with usage? Savigny roundly asserts that the Pandects on their completion were at once sent into Italy, and that immediately after the power of the Goths had been shattered by the Greeks Justinian hastened to issue the Constitution (534), whereby legal effect was given to them in the land. In consequence of this, he continues, the Pandects were then to be met with in every corner of Italy, where they were at once received with favour, inasmuch as the Justinian law was specially adapted to the requirements of the land. This, he goes on to say, likewise explains why it was that all the earliest Italian commentators or glossators devoted themselves exclusively to the study of the *Corpus iuris*. The reader, however, may easily discover that, on this head, Savigny has pushed his inferences too far. More than once, indeed, he is compelled to put a false interpretation on documents that they may not contradict his theories; and more than once the documents themselves seem to warn him that, even in the Middle Ages, vestiges of a *pre*-Justinian law are to be traced; but he persists still more resolutely in considering all this to be only a survival of antiquated forms. Many new documents have recently been published, and the question again presents itself, always with the same urgency.

As a German writer, well versed in the subject, has recently observed, everything tends to show that the history of Roman law in the Middle Ages should be divided into two entirely distinct periods.[372] During the first it endured by force of custom, and accordingly many pre-Justinian formulas survived with it; in the second and much later period the Justinian law prevailed, promoted still further by the literary study of the Pandects undertaken by the Bolognese professors; it was only then that the most ancient formulas wholly disappeared. This view is supported by documentary evidence and harmonises with the character of the times and with the requirements of society, and is confirmed by our old writers and our literary traditions.

SUPPOSED PALACE OF THEODORIC, IN RAVENNA.

[*To face page 383*

In fact, Savigny himself examines and recognises the full importance of the various sources of *pre*-Justinian law diffused in the Middle Ages. The code of Theodosius (438) which then possessed great authority, and the edict drawn up by order of Theodoric the Ostrogoth (500), were direct compilations of the old Roman Jurisprudence.

If in these compilations we turn our attention to the constitution of the family, more particularly as regards succession, we find it exactly as it was before the law was interwoven with the Imperial edicts.[373] The Breviary of Alaric ("Lex Romana Visigothorum") and the so-called *Papian* code ("Lex Romana Burgundioram"), both posterior to the year 500, are likewise compilations of *pre*-Justinian law, and are found to be diffused in several provinces of the Empire. The often-mentioned "Lex Romana Utiniensis, seu Curiensis," which seems to be ninth century *rimpasto* of Alaric's Breviary for the use of Italians in lands previously under Longobard rule, also shows the same characteristics. It is true that, according to the hypothesis of Savigny, the

Breviary of Alaric must have been in use among the Franks and brought by them to Italy after the expulsion of the Longobards. In this case we should find the old law to have been in force among us only before and after the period of the Longobards; while during their oppressive rule we should discover no certain trace of it. But it is very difficult to suppose that the ancient law, based as it was upon custom, should have died out precisely when custom might have preserved it, or that Roman law should at that time have assumed the literary Justinian form and afterwards have returned to a form more primitive. Had the legislation of Justinian in its genuine form been once accepted, it must have continued to gain ground with the advance of civilisation and under the less severe rule of the Franks, whose mode of life approached much nearer to that of the Latins. The fact is, that throughout the Middle Ages we meet with pre-Justinian legal forms, more or less modified, even among the laws of the Longobards.[374] As to the remark that the earliest Italian commentators, the *glossators*, directed their studies to the Pandects and the whole of the *Corpus iuris*—this only shows that on the revival of the communes and of letters they turned, as was natural, to the most authoritative and literary source of jurisprudence. From that time, in fact, no other is looked for.[375]

THE TOMB OF THEODORIC, RAVENNA.

[To face page 384

It should also be remembered that, when the Greeks came into Italy to combat the Goths, they found the ancient Roman customary laws in force and sanctioned by the edict of Theodoric; that the Goths were definitely vanquished in 553; that in 568 the Greek domination was followed by that of the Longobards; that the latter confined their rivals to Southern Italy, whence they were afterwards expelled by the Normans. There, in the south, the corrupt Byzantine despotism proved no less fatal than the oppression of the barbarians, and was perhaps the prime cause of the many disasters and prolonged neglect into which those provinces afterwards fell. But was it possible for a dominion so brief and troubled to diffuse the law of Justinian in Italy with such effect as not only to make it universally accepted, but also so thoroughly incorporated with customary law, that it could survive even when its binding legal effect was no longer recognised by the barbarians?

Such an hypothesis will seem even less tenable as regards everything relating to the family and to succession, if we reflect that the reforms introduced into this branch of the law by Justinian at Constantinople in no way corresponded to the conditions in which Italy then stood. Notwithstanding the diffusion of Greek philosophy among us, the spirit of Byzantium was by no means identical with that of Rome, and there was still less identity in their social conditions. In Constantinople Oriental despotism corrupted, nay, suffocated society by excess of luxury and over-refinement of culture; the State assuming everything to itself, imparted a new character to the laws. In Italy, on the other hand, society, no less corrupt, had become disintegrated, and was already falling to pieces; the ancient unity and strength of the State were continually diminishing and losing strength, and less and less resistance was opposed to the assaults of the barbarians. At Constantinople the State was omnipotent, while in Italy its vigour was on the wane. Among us, accordingly women and all who were weak were naturally driven to seek refuge in private associations, and above all in the bosom of the family. And if the natural force of events had power to urge in any direction, and determine any new tendency, it certainly could not have aimed at enfeebling the family bond by subjecting it to the authority of a tottering State, but must rather have sought to strengthen it as the only possible safeguard amid the dangers that were threatening on every side. This, in fact, is the course always followed in barbaric societies, where, the State being powerless, the care of the weak and the punishment of injuries are entrusted to the kinsmen. In short, both the disordered condition of Latin society and the example of the barbarians themselves combined to offer grave obstacles to the diffusion of Justinian's laws, more especially when the old Roman customs were seen to be better suited to the new and increasing needs of society, and useful for the reconstruction, on a firmer basis, of the old family system, now become more essential than before to the common welfare. No other way was left for beginning anew the social task and advancing afterwards to new methods and institutions. Nor need we attach much importance to the constitution of the year 534, knowing how wide is the difference between the promulgation of a law (especially when it is passed by a short-lived and feeble Government in a society that is lapsing into disorder) and its actual enforcement and incorporation with custom. Even under the Roman Republic, or under the Empire, old laws did not at once disappear when new ones were proclaimed. Even in modern societies we may note how tenaciously ancient customs continue to be observed when they are more in harmony with the character and requirements of the people.

The principles of the Napoleonic code were proclaimed in our Southern provinces during the French domination and afterwards confirmed by subsequent legislation; and according to that code, every patrimony was bound to be divided equally among the children. Nevertheless, in the two Calabrias and many other Southern provinces, property is still kept undivided in the family, since, by common consent, only one of the sons marries, the others remaining single. For the same reason, the smallest possible sum is assigned to the daughters; nor do all of them marry, some being persuaded or forced to take the veil. Social progress alone will slowly give real effect to the principles of equality sanctioned by the codes.

Everything therefore points to the conclusion that Roman law survived among us to the downfall of the Western Empire, preserving by usage many of the forms that had belonged to it before the compilation of the *Corpus iuris*. While in this state it came into contact with the Germanic code, and thereupon began the series of mutual alterations, from which the Italian family emerged, reconstituted in a totally new way, and together with it the Commune. It was a slow transformation, during which Latin ideas and traditions steadily gained ground, and gradually fused or destroyed the barbarian laws and institutions. When communal liberties were finally proclaimed, a new culture was inaugurated, and with it a new epoch in the history of Roman law. The university of Bologna became the centre for the diffusion and study of the Pandects, and the *Corpus iuris* became speedily regarded as the primary and perennial source of common law in our country. The tradition, according to which the Pandects of Amalfi, carried off by the Pisans, were by them discovered and made known for the first time to the Western world, dates this event about the year 1135, that is to say in the same age that witnessed the rise of the communes, and in which, as related by another tradition, Guarnerius founded the Bolognese school at the request of

Countess Matilda. [376] Thus our conclusions are supported alike by history, legend, and logic.

VI.

In Italy, therefore, at the beginning of the Middle Ages, the family accorded a preference to the agnates, and, in consequence of the continuous weakening of the State, was obliged to seek in itself for increased strength. The inroads of the barbarians brought with them a different constitution of the family, but this could effect no great change in our own family system until the Longobards had firmly established their dominion over us. There then began a great change in the social condition of Italy, which was forcibly compelled to assume a form more or less barbaric. Hence it concerns us to study the Longobard family system, that we may see how far and in what way it could thus alter ours.

ANCIENT SHRINE, RAVENNA.

[*To face page 388*

Like every other barbaric society, that of the Longobards was founded upon force; in time of war it was compactly united under a king; during peace it split into groups, from want of vigour in the central authority, and from the excessive independence of subordinate chiefs. Hardly had barbarian kingdoms begun to be erected in the West with a certain degree of stability, than we find them subdividing into marquisates, dukedoms, separate groups, and at a later period into feudal holdings. If we look to the primitive conditions of these barbarians before they come among us, we find them scattered over the country, without any city properly so-called, and with no true conception of the State, which for them seems to consist in a confederation of secondary groups. The social unity of the barbarians is to be found in the villages or even in the tribes, which are societies originally derived perhaps from a single family. Everywhere the State assumes family forms. The social strength of the Germans is more manifest in the lesser groups, and consequently in the family. We ought not to be surprised, therefore, at finding the family constituted more solidly with them than among the Latins, who now, for many centuries, had been altering and modifying it under the growing pressure of State control.

Originally the barbarian family had been, like the Roman, an association consecrated by religion. A tutelary goddess presided over the domestic hearth; the father was priest and protector of the family. In Rome the control was in the hand of a single person, who ruled with an iron authority, but in Germany this authority was shared by all male members of the family fit to bear arms. At Rome the family was an absolute monarchy, its senior members being always regarded as the most powerful; but in Germany it more resembled a Republic, consisting of all the adult male members, except such as were disqualified by bodily infirmity. The family council aided the Roman father and tempered his rigid despotism; whereas in Germany the council predominated and assumed to itself the chief share of the family power. The Roman father could rupture every domestic tie at his will; he could remove his son from the family, sell him, or put him to death. The German son, on the contrary, when able to bear arms and fight by his father's side, might, if he chose, separate himself from his original family and join another tribe. Among the Germans bodily strength, property held in common, and natural ties of blood constituted the family; in Rome it was the conception of the family in itself that dominated over everything and made it authoritative and sacred. In Rome the individual was merged in the State, the son in the father; whereas, among the Germanic tribes, individual liberty was much greater, and if to us the State has the appearance of a confederation, the family seems a society of more independent members united by mutual agreement. Punishments, transgressions, property, all were in common; if any member of the family suffered wrong, it was the kinsmen's part to avenge him and obtain retribution. For sales and donations, as well as for acts of revenge, the consent of every member was required, inasmuch as the property belonged to the whole family, and ought to stay with it: whence the inutility of testamentary dispositions, which were in fact unknown to the barbarians. Property was sacred; it constituted the family, conferred social rights and obligations, and rested chiefly in the hands of the males. In this family, and in this society founded wholly on force, the woman, being incapable of bearing arms, was committed, like all other weaklings, to the defence and protection of her armed kinsmen, and so came under their perpetual guardianship (*mundium, munt, manus*). This tutelage being established on account of the weakness and infirmity of the sex, could never come to an end, as it might in Rome, where it had been constituted wholly in the interest of the family. But the Germanic woman, although oppressed, liable to be deprived of her property, to be sold, or made a slave, was under a power which, being divided among many, was feebler and less despotic than the Roman domestic rule. She was a dependent member of the family, but the authority of her father, brothers, or sons was shared by all her other kinsmen. Hence it was easy for the woman to find a protector. Her incapacity by reason of her infirmity did not entail incapacity in the eye of the law. She could appear in court, choose some one to represent her there; she could own property; she could inherit, although taking a less share than would have come to her had she been a man. The man listened to her advice, and treated her with religious respect; but it was the respect due to her weaker sex, not as in Rome, where respect was offered to the mother, to the wife, to the sacred character which was the foundation at once of the Roman family and of Roman greatness.

Longobard law, essentially Germanic, prevailed long in Italy, where plain traces of its survival are to be recognised as late as the fourteenth century. Under the stronger influence of the Roman jurisprudence it very soon lost its native rudeness and originality. As to this change, Gans, in his "History of the Law of Succession," has observed: "The fact that after the historical redaction of this law, another and systematic compilation of it was made, should prove to us how it was that the more confused, but at the same time more natural, spontaneous, and vigorous character of the Germanic law must necessarily have been altered, and as it were crystallised into a form that rather belongs to the Roman." It was precisely this form that so greatly promoted its diffusion among us.

VII.

With the Longobards, as with all the Germanic nations, woman was never released from tutelage (*mundium*), never became her own mistress (*selbmundia*). The man who desired to make her his wife must first of all pay the price of the *mundium* or guardianship which the marriage would give him over her; next he must bind himself to make good the *meta*, a species of dowry noticed by Tacitus when he remarks that, among the Germans, the husband brought the dower to the wife, instead of the wife bringing it to the husband. To the *meta*, also known afterwards under the name of *dotalitium*, *dos*, *sponsalicium*, &c., there was added the *faderfium*, which the father might, if he chose, give to his daughter. On the morning of the day after the wedding the husband presented his bride with a gift (*morgengab*), attended, according to a very questionable interpretation, as the price of her virginity. When Longobard customs came to be affected by the growing influence of the Roman law, the amount of the *meta* and of the *morgengab* was restricted. In the age of the communes, the *faderfium*, now transformed into a dower, was also limited by law. The *meta*, *faderfium*, and *morgengab* belonged to the wife, who could require them to be given up to her on her husband's death.

But by a peculiarity of the Germanic law, retained in its entirety even by the Longobards, the Roman regulation, which made the dower the separate and independent property of the wife [even during her husband's lifetime], was never accepted. The only property owned absolutely and exclusively by the woman was what was given her by the husband. The Germanic law favoured the principle of common ownership. As to this, Gans observes:—"It is not necessary with us, as with the Romans, that a woman should have separate property of her own in order to assert her juridical personality, and prove her equality with her husband. She possesses what her husband possesses, and her equality rests on the mutual affection which makes all differences disappear." In the ordeal by combat the husband represented the wife, since she was under the protection of his sword; if she were taken in adultery he might put her to death. All her possessions, movable or immovable, including even nuptial gifts made to her by friends, became the property of her husband, who had only to provide against the contingency of the marriage being dissolved by death: whence the necessity of the *meta* and the *donatium*.

If the wife died without issue, everything went to the husband; on the husband's death, the wife was entitled to receive the *meta* and *morgengab* (donation). For anything more she was entirely dependent on the generosity of her husband, who, at a later period, was permitted to leave her the half, and, eventually, the whole usufruct of his possessions.

While the marriage laws of the Longobards and the Romans differed thus widely, their laws relating to guardianship were also different. The *mundium* of the Longobards, as we have seen, is not to be confounded with the *tutela* to which the Roman woman was subjected. Originating in the incapacity to bear arms, it was of limited duration in the case of males, and ceased with their incapacity. At first the limit was fixed at the age of twelve, at a later period of eighteen years. But for the woman, who could never become capable of bearing arms, it was perpetual. From the *mundium* of her father, she passed, on marriage, under that of her husband; and on the death of her father, if then a widow, under the *mundium* of her own son, or of the agnates, who were also her heirs.

In default of other guardians she was protected by the *Curtis Regia*. But in every case, whether under father, husband, son, agnates, or *Curtis Regia*, the *mundium* was identical in character, having for its object the protection of the weak. This could not be said of the Roman *tutela*, which had its origin in the Roman conception of the family. The *tutela* of the Roman father over his children lasted all his life; but he could divest himself of it. The *mundium* of the Longobard father lasted while his children were incapable of bearing arms, and, as a logical consequence, ceased when the incapacity terminated.

While it cannot be positively asserted that emancipation was unknown to the Longobards, it may be believed, from the tendency of their law, to have been of rare occurrence. When the Roman woman was subjected to the *potestas* of her father, the *manus* of her husband, the *tutela* of the agnates, there were three kinds of guardianship very different from each other, corresponding with the difference in the domestic relations of those who exercised the right. No one of them had anything in common with the *mundium*.

The Longobard father had the right to sell his sons; he represented them in courts of law; whatever they acquired was his. But, as we have already shown, his authority was tempered by the family council, in which the brothers of the mother—the children's natural protectress—had much to say.

The Longobard family law has marked peculiarities in regard to succession as well as to marriage. And first, it should be noted that the disposal of property by will was recognised by the Longobards. This seems contrary to the usage of the Germanic tribes, among whom wills were unknown, but may be referred to the modifying action of the Roman on the Longobard law.

The fact, however, that with the Longobards donations and wills were irrevocable, indicates a Germanic character, or rather the trace of it, for the main feature of the Roman will consisted in its revocability. Of the essential principles of the Roman *Testamenti factio* the Longobards were ignorant. Legitimate children came first in the order of inheritance, and with them came natural children also, the latter—though not in strictness forming part of the family—being admitted to succeed along with the former, though taking a less share. They might, however, be put on an equal footing by being legitimated. At a later period this essentially Germanic peculiarity of the laws of succession was done away with by the action of the Roman and Canon laws, which exclude natural children. Originally, by the Longobard law, a legitimate child took two-thirds of the inheritance, leaving one-third only to the natural children. If there were two legitimate children, the natural children took only a fifth; if three, a seventh.

It was forbidden to leave more than the prescribed share to natural children, and no child could be disinherited without just and manifest cause. The reasons for disinheriting a child were borrowed from the Roman code. It was allowable, however, to favour one son more than the rest.

The preference accorded to males over females is a point of much importance, and is another of the special characteristics of the Longobard law. When the testator had one son and one or more unmarried daughters he was obliged to leave a fourth of the inheritance to the latter, but when there were several sons the daughters only received a seventh part. Married daughters had no right to any share in the inheritance, but had to be content with what they had received on the day of their marriage, and could claim nothing more. Failing male issue, daughters were next heirs, and whether married or single inherited as though they were males. Another peculiarity of Longobard law was the great favour shown to daughters or sisters of the testator domiciled in his house—*in capillo*. A brother is excluded in favour of a daughter or niece —a remarkable instance of this strange and singular preference accorded to females. We likewise find that unmarried daughters and sisters inherit on equal terms when living under the parental or fraternal roof.

We have already noticed that the statutes of the Italian communes accord, as does also the Longobard law, a decided preference to *agnates* over *cognates*, and that this circumstance has given rise to keen discussion. Many persons, indeed, insist on detecting in this preference an absolutely Germanic characteristic transfused into the statutes from the Longobard law. But we have seen that through the greater part of its history the Roman law also gave a preference to the agnates, and that it was only at a very late period that it lost this feature, which was still to some extent retained in Italy at the time of the barbarian invasions. That the preference of the agnates was not borrowed by the statutes from the Longobard law will be even more conclusively shown if we consider the manifest differences which prevail on this very point between the Germanic and the Italian laws; and bear in mind the important fact that the preference continued to increase in strength, at the very time when the action and influence of the Roman law are increasingly apparent in the statutes. In truth, the more closely we examine the matter, the more we are compelled to recognise that it was political reasons altogether peculiar to the Italian communes and to Italian society in the Middle Ages that led to this preference of the agnates. But even here the reciprocal action of the one law upon the other is clearly traceable, for we can perceive that the succession of the agnates, under the Longobard law, has itself been modified by the Roman, which has made it careless of the nature of the property of which the inheritance consists; whereas it is the peculiar and constant characteristic of the Germanic law that such succession should be ruled according both to the degree of kinship and the nature of the inheritance.

In conclusion, it may be said generally that with the Longobards the ties of blood predominate; that in their family there is greater individual freedom, and the family itself is much less affected by the action of the State. With the Romans, on the contrary, the conception of the family is stronger than the ties of blood; the unity of the family depends at first on an absolute paternal despotism, afterwards destroyed by the authority of the State, which to a great extent assumes its place.

From this time the State is predominant in all things; it reduces the family to fragments, and aims at the complete equality of all without having the strength to consolidate a society in which neither individual liberty, local activity, nor free associations were allowed sufficient scope for their development. Yet all these were absolutely necessary for the preservation of a huge social structure made up of distinct races, and consequently destitute of the national character and unity which the Republic and the Empire had imposed. It was precisely these new elements that were introduced among us by the barbarians. And thus it was that two peoples, two forms of family and society, I might almost say two ideas, two wholly different types of society were brought together, of which the one had become the necessary complement of the other. From their forests the Germans brought individual freedom, personal independence, the force of small associations; the Latins had already discovered the unity of the State, the wider and more organic conception of society, and the political idea of the family which we shall see hereafter triumphing in the Commune.

From the fusion of these two different societies that modern society is to arise in which the action of the one is seldom dissociated from that of the other, and it becomes impossible to ascribe the result exclusively to either.

VIII.

But while the co-existing and contending laws of the Romans and Longobards are the two juridical elements most plainly to be recognised in the Italian statutes, there are others also claiming remembrance, and among these the feudal and the Canon law must be noticed. Feudalism is one of the most important institutions in the history of the Middle Ages; it is the first form that society assumes on emerging from the chaos of barbarism, and it is stamped with a character essentially Germanic. With it, property and the family take a new and peculiar shape. We may pronounce it to be the first and chief political and social manifestation of Germanic individualism. The barbarian tribe had a natural tendency to split into small groups, into families solely united by the bond of common danger. During invasions the tribe transformed itself into an armed band, left behind all weak or incapable members, accepted recruits even from neighbouring tribes, and being under the command of one chief, was forced by the exigencies of war to be firmly and compactly united. The attacks previously made on them by the Romans had, for like reasons, the effect of creating among the barbarians certain strong and powerful kingdoms by the union of different tribes; but these never lasted long, since as soon as peace was restored they began anew to fall apart and dissolve. Scarcely had the barbarians begun to settle themselves in the West, than their incapacity to establish the unity of a State was made clearly manifest. The moment peace was declared the leaders of the various armed bands proceeded to divide the conquered territory. They then separated, and their king, or supreme chief, remained, as it were, isolated, and with very scant authority. Every leader tried to possess himself of some stronghold where he might rule as an absolute lord, barely acknowledging his dependence on the king. In the fief thus created, ownership and sovereignty became confused, but were both considered to be held (*per beneficium*) as of favour from a more powerful lord, subject to certain burthens and obligations. Originally a temporary grant, the *benefice* or *fief* only became hereditary at a later time. At first it could be resumed by the donor; it reverted to him on the death of the feudatory, that it might be transmitted by a new grant to the feudatory's heirs; it then gradually, by use, abuse, or special act of concession, became an hereditary estate. Eventually all property, possession, or ownership came to be held, during the Middle Ages, on feudal tenure. The want of vigour in the supreme political power obliged the weak to seek protection elsewhere. Many independent landowners voluntarily accepted the position of vassals; while, on the other hand, the obstacles encountered by the great lords in enforcing their authority over wide territories compelled them to cede part of their land in *benefice* to lesser vassals. In this way the State, the Church, all things assumed a feudal form. This system was completely established in the eleventh century, when the communes arose in Italy to combat and overthrow it.

In a fortified castle it was natural that the ties of the family should become continually stronger: a fortress must suffice for itself. It was, as it were, the independent world of the lord who dwelt in it, and divided his time between perilous adventures and domestic life. All historians have noted that feudalism produced increased respect, affection, and chivalrous regard for woman, and made man more resolute and energetic. Save in times of war, the baron was almost absolute and independent lord of his small realm, wherein all were his subjects. From him his vassals received the posts of seneschal, count of the palace, equerry, and the like, which offices, being granted in a form more or less feudal to persons of noble birth, had a tendency to become hereditary. A numerous retinue somewhat relieved the loneliness of the castle. The sons of subordinate nobles frequented the court of their liege lord, to be trained to polite manners and the arts of chivalry, and finally to receive the sword from his hands and be proclaimed knights. All this gave prestige to the castle, and secured the fidelity of the vassals to their lord, while at the same time it flattered the pride of the inferior nobility.

The Longobard feudal law is found to have points of connection with the laws of Rome which, though very different in spirit, are often called to its aid. Often, however, they are found to be in opposition. There can be no doubt that the Roman law manifests in Italy its persistent action on the feudal law. The fief, as is well known, not being absolute independent property, but only a limited and conditional grant, cannot, from its nature, be subject to the hereditary principle. On the contrary, the right of the heir must be recognised anew in his person, since, as we have seen, he does not derive it from any right in his predecessor. And this continued to be the practice even after custom had begun to make the tenure hereditary. According to feudal law, the successor was not then considered to represent the person whose heir he was; the original grant was renewed in his behalf. Moreover, when a fief has once become hereditary, the whole family has a right to it, not derived from the will of the last holder at his death, but already existent during his life. It is therefore necessary to establish an order of succession to determine which member of the family shall be preferred, and this order of succession begins to be borrowed from the Roman code. Although differing from the true and correct order of succession, it is gradually confounded with it, and finally alters and dissolves the fief. Thus the Roman law penetrates and modifies the feudal.

CHURCH OF SAN VITALE, RAVENNA.

[To face page 401

From the very nature of a fief, female descendants cannot inherit, and the male descendants of deceased sons succeed equally with surviving sons. Nevertheless there are certain fiefs which, having been originally bestowed upon females, must, in default of heirs male, naturally pass to females; but as soon as the male line is established, male heirs have the preference. Ascendants cannot succeed, because succession is determined, not by relationship, but by the original grant; accordingly the reversion falls, not to the ascendant, but to the original granter of the fief. Collaterals of the last holder, unless descendants of the first, are not entitled to succeed; nor can brothers, as such, succeed, unless their father has held the fief. Nor can husband and wife succeed to each other. But under the growing influence of common law all these primitive characteristics likewise disappear. Feudal law has little importance in the Italian statutes; but the political and social importance of feudalism in the history of our communes is immense. It represents a society distinguished by laws and usages of its own, and that appeals to the Emperor, whose judgments and judges it always prefers to the laws and magistrates of the Republic which it despises, and would fain ignore. The Republic in consequence looks on the nobility as a foe to be destroyed, but this it can only effect after sanguinary struggles in the course of which it will be itself profoundly changed.

Canon law undoubtedly plays a part in the history and formation of the communes that should not be overlooked, though by no means corresponding with the greatness of the political, social, and religious influence of the Church. Made up of fragments from the writings of the Fathers, ordinances of ecclesiastical councils, papal decretals, and with a large admixture of Roman law, it appeals also to the authority of reason and of Holy Writ. It thus declared itself favourable to natural equity, as opposed to legal sophistry, tempered the harshness of barbaric laws, protected the weak, upheld the sanctity of the family, and aided the triumph of the Roman law over that of the Longobards. But it also sought to subordinate the civil power to the ecclesiastical; it added to the number of exceptional tribunals; it favoured inquisitorial jurisdiction, torture, and trial by ordeal. Moreover, its constant tendency to encroach on the field of civil law found an open door in the oath which every magistrate, the Podestà included, had to take, with the prescribed formula: "saving conscience" (*salva la coscienza*) expressed or understood. As it rested with the clergy to determine cases of conscience, so also it was for them to decide on the validity of oaths. This naturally fostered the diffusion of canon law. The exclusion of natural children from succession and the suppression of divorce are not a little due to the operation of this law. Its action is to be seen plainly enough in the statutes, but still more clearly in the struggle between the civil authority and the ecclesiastical, wherein the latter endeavours to maintain its inviolable privileges, its exceptional tribunals, its supremacy even in causes civil and political.

IX.

In the statutes therefore, we find four different legislations, contending, as it were, with one another: the Longobard, the Roman, the Feudal and the Canon law. These, however, may almost be reduced to two, seeing that feudal law is Germanic, and canon law, in so far as it affects the statutes, is mainly Roman. So that here again we are met by the old hostility between Germans and Latins. The two races are opposed, as also their institutions, laws, and ideas; their minds seem to challenge one another wherever they meet, whether in the field of letters, politics, or art. Yet each has need of the other, and both must disappear to make way for a new social system and a more comprehensive spirit which, resulting from the fusion of two warring elements, will remain sole victor in this prolonged contest. In Italy, however, the Latin strain always predominates, as we see even in the statutes, wherein Roman law forms the keystone of the whole juridical structure.

EMPEROR JUSTINIAN.

(*From a Mosaic, Ravenna.*)

[*To face page 403*

The earliest compilation of the statutes dates from the very time when a knowledge of the *Corpus iuris* begins to be diffused throughout Italy from the University of Bologna. From that time forth the legislation of Justinian was regarded as an epitome of juridical philosophy, as the law *par excellence*, and is recognised by all our Republics as the common law, the law to be applied whenever the statutes are silent. For this reason that part of the statutes which relates to the civil law is very much less developed than the political part; and for this reason those teachers whose studies have been directed chiefly to civil jurisprudence occupy themselves much more with Roman, canon, feudal, and Longobard law than with the law of the statutes. These they examined, especially at first, rather as a result of the study of the Roman law, than as deserving careful attention on their own account; they regarded them as the written expression of popular custom to which no great scientific value could be attached, as something outside the one legal system which alone merited universal admiration.

A long period elapsed before writers on law began to apply their minds to the consideration of the statutes, the great importance of which has been only completely recognised in our day. Venice is perhaps the only Commune in which it was customary, in the absence of statutory provisions, to appeal to natural reason: whence Bartolo's remark that the Venetian magistrate gave judgment *manu regia et arbitrio suo.*[377] But even in Venice such decisions must always have been inspired or guided by a knowledge and admiration of the Roman law.

EMPRESS THEODORA AND COURT, RAVENNA.

[To face page 404

What has been said will put in a clear light the extraordinary importance accorded to the University and the professors of Bologna in connection with their labours in annotating and interpreting the *Corpus iuris* so as to make it intelligible to all, and an instrument for instructing and training all those who sought to follow the legal profession, whether as notaries, judges, Podestàs, or captains of the people. That these teachers possessed a very slender knowledge of history is seen from their writings. Their merit lay in the intelligent exposition of a system of law which had never become extinct. It was a precept of theirs that "as the unskilled rider must hold on by the pommel, so the judge should stick to the gloss." In this way the school of Bologna became, as it were, the depository of an universal law which was looked upon as almost sacred. Thither popes sent their decretals, emperors their edicts for registry or revision. The Emperor was, however, regarded as the living source of legislation, as alone entitled to add new laws to the Roman. Any one speaking evil of the Emperor met with condign punishment. Any one who questioned his universal authority was declared heretical by the jurists themselves. This authority belonged to him as lord of all nations, and was transmitted to him from the Roman Empire as its rightful heir. It was natural, therefore, that to determine the extent and limits of this authority, recourse should again be had to the professors of Bologna, the veritable depositaries of the Roman law, who accordingly acquired a constantly increasing importance. The *ratio scripta* was what was always called for; and the communes, even while avowing their determination to preserve their ancient liberties undiminished, never forgot to profess their willingness to leave the Emperor all the *veteres justitias* which belonged to him, and which they declared themselves desirous to respect. The only question was to ascertain what these were, and hence fresh occasion to consult the professors of Bologna.

Before the great contest between the Lombards and Frederic Barbarossa, a genuine judicial trial was held, ending with the condemnation of the Milanese, who were declared rebels, *adstipulantibus judicibus et primis de Italia*. At Roncaglia, Frederic exercised judicial and legislative authority, with the assistance of four professors from Bologna, who maintained the Emperor's rights, not from any hostility to their own country, but because, as professors of Roman law, they were the natural champions of the Holy Roman Empire. Nor did the communes themselves raise any objection to these claims. After Frederic's defeat they continued to draw up their statutes, laws, and public instruments in his name. Even as late as the fifteenth century, we find that notaries still gave validity to public documents by making them run in the name of the Empire. At the peace of Constance the power to appoint magistrates, civil and criminal, consuls, Podestà, and notaries, was expressly reserved to the Emperor, whose prerogative in such matters, as well as of deciding causes of serious importance on final appeal, was fully recognised. If, in fact, the Milanese paid little regard to the Emperor's authority, his right was not questioned. The Lombards acknowledged themselves his lawful subjects, though they afterwards chose to act as if free and independent.

When Henry VII. came to Italy, in Dante's time, he too, brought the Italian cities to trial, pronounced sentence on them, exacted fines on men and money, and cited King Robert of Naples to appear before him. At that time many must have deemed these proceedings farcical; but they were echoes of a bygone age, of a past which even Alighieri's immortal genius thought to recall to life, as his letters and his book, "De Monarchia," serve to show. The Church, it is true, constantly withstood the Empire, but during the whole of the Middle Ages the Emperor's political and juridical authority was never called in question, was invariably recognised.

While the continual struggle between Church and Empire, communes and feudal lords, Guelphs and Ghibellines, was being waged, the statutes were framed. In these were recorded, not only new customs written down as they were formed, but also all the old customs that had been modified by the new. Although the jurists of Bologna thought it no concern of theirs to study a system of law, which being in common use was then well known, and which had its source in that Roman jurisprudence which engaged their attention through their whole lives, for us it is certainly a study of grave importance, as a means of accurately estimating the value and character of this communal life in the Middle Ages. We may have very long to wait before we can completely solve the problem. Nevertheless we may make a beginning by examining the various statutes, comparing them with one another, and also comparing the different forms which each of them received at different stages of drafting, in order to discern the evolution of the new law, to ascertain and understand the principle which governs it.

X.

The whole life of the Commune is embraced in the statutes: the election and functions of political magistrates; public, civil, criminal, administrative, and commercial law. Public law is the subject most fully dealt with; while, for reasons already explained, civil law is left very incomplete. Nevertheless the statutes handle, with more or less detail, such matters as personal *status*, dowers, contracts, judicial procedure, succession, wills, rights arising in respect of contiguous lands or houses, and, above all, the family. They aim at a simple and summary procedure, free from chicanery, whereby causes may be settled fairly and promptly; but from defective drafting, from admitting a running commentary, altogether out of place in legal enactments, and from leaving too much to the discretion of the judge, they generally lead to a contrary result. It is indeed astonishing to observe how, during those centuries in which a splendid literature was growing up, when the most unpretentious writings offer us an example of good style, and when judges, notaries, and professors of law had the imperishable model of the *Corpus iuris* constantly before their eyes, the statutes should have been written in a form so illiterate that we may often pronounce it barbarous, and always involved and confused. The statutes constitute a legislation based upon custom, mutable, popular, still uncertain of itself, which, taking its birth in the midst of civil wars, always retained their likeness, and never arrived at classical elegances, which in any case would have been made impossible by the scholastic jargon that still prevailed in our Universities and among our jurists. Petrarch's animadversions, directed chiefly against the obscure phraseology of the professors of law in his time, were fully justified. The classical revival which sought to introduce a purer and more elegant latinity had to make a beginning outside, and often in opposition to the Universities. It spread far and wide during the fifteenth century, but always retained a literary and philosophical rather than a juridical character.

Notwithstanding the greatness of its merits and aims, the Italian Commune has in it something of the transitory and mediæval; it constantly indicates a period of change. It is the germ from which, at a later time, modern society is to issue, but the birth cannot be accomplished until the germ itself is destroyed; consequently it always remained in a state of incessant transformation. Sprung from the conjunction of two different societies, the Roman and Germanic, it derived from the former the general idea of the State, from the latter individual liberty, local activity, and the force of special associations. The problem it had to solve, and that constitutes its essential life and history, lies precisely in its ceaseless efforts to harmonise those two elements which long remained not only separate but often opposed. Until complete fusion was effected by the destruction of the Commune itself, the contest continued to be waged, and was accompanied by inevitable disorder. In the Commune, government and public policy have an importance unknown to barbaric society, but the Commune still wears the character of a powerful assemblage of small associations rather than of a single society, or of a State in the true and strict sense of the word. Life indeed courses more swiftly through these numberless groups, and is quickened by their activity. Social vigour is chiefly to be looked for in family cliques, and in the Companies of the Arts and Trades, of the Nobles and of the Burghers, all of whom have laws, statutes, magistrates, and tribunals of their own. Hence arises an extraordinary interlacing of ordinances, of conflicting passions, of diverging or clashing interests. True individual liberty, true equality before the law is not yet understood; but the individual is trained and protected by the association to which he belongs, which lends him a certain degree of strength, and secures him an increasing share of freedom. These subsidiary groups, however, unlike those which we have already met with in the Germanic societies, cannot be separated, but must live together in the State, outside of which there is no reason for their existence. The infinite multiplication of these groups, their jealousies and continual jarrings and collisions, made the Republic all the more indispensable to them, all the more the object of their hopes and love. Every one of these merchant-citizens was ready to give his life for this Republic, on which, both in peace and in war, his own welfare and that of the various associations depended. The heads and leading members of these associations were privileged to sit in the Councils of the State, governed it as masters, and found it their only sure defence against the countless rivals with whom each of them had to contend. Individual and general interests thus worked in concert, and the fragmentary power divided among so many hands, was nevertheless able to guard the liberty of all, at a time when no true conception of the State or of general equality had yet arisen. Still, it is easy to imagine how ill-arranged and inconclusive must have been the legislation of republics thus divided and subdivided, in which at every step some new special statute or tribunal was encountered. And this at a time when judicial and political power were so strangely intermixed, that whoever had a share in the one necessarily shared in the other.

The dominant feature in all the civil enactments of the statutes seems to be a jealousy of neighbouring communes, and a fear lest, as a result of marriage, property should be withdrawn from the city, the society, or the family. To guard against this, both law and custom provided so efficaciously, that even in a Republic as democratic as that of Florence, wherein every vestige of aristocracy was destroyed, and the Ciompi obtained the upper hand, we find landed property so strictly tied up that there are families who, to this day, own the same estates which were held by their ancestors in the fourteenth century. The necessity for keeping families, associations, and party-circles intimately united, and making each member of them bound for the rest, is so strikingly apparent, that it is these political and social considerations which determine the tendency of the civil law, and often impede its natural development. So that even here, notwithstanding the weakness of the State, we again recognise the old Latin tradition, which always accords an excessive importance to political considerations, and consequently a preponderating influence to public over private law. The Italian statutes, therefore, can only be explained and understood in connection with the history of the communes, which they illustrate in their turn. And this is another reason why the professors of Bologna, accustomed to the philosophical character of Justinian's legislation, and unfamiliar with the methods of historical exposition, so long neglected the statutes.

Also, as might be expected, the predominating action of political considerations is most clearly shown in the constitution of the family. Here the rights which flow from the Commune's conception of the family prevail over the ties of blood which by the Germanic law are much more respected.

The regulations of the Roman law as to dower are fully accepted, but the dower itself is restricted to a small amount. Males have a marked precedence over females, and over descendants in the female line. But in all circumstances the woman is entitled to alimony. It is not meant that she should be rich, or should divide the domestic patrimony, and transfer it to another family, much less to another Commune; but in any event she must be assured of a suitable maintenance, according to her rank of life. She remains under the perpetual protection of the *mondualdo* (legal guardian), but the *mundium* assumes in the statutes the character of the later Roman *tutela*, with which it almost seems to be confounded. The woman may call upon the judge to assign her a *mondualdo*, and may choose him herself when she requires him for any special business. Everywhere, indeed, we see this tendency to transform Longobard institutions into Roman, so that often nothing is left to the former save the name.

Immovable property was so strictly settled that a very small part of it could be disposed of by the father at his death. No one, therefore, born of a family in easy circumstances was exposed to any anxiety as to his future. It is to be noted, however, that in our communes, all of which resembled great commercial houses, the proportion of immovable to movable property was extremely small; and that if, as regards the former, there was much security and stability, for the latter there were rapid gains, unforeseen fortunes, and sudden fluctuations of capital.

The father's authority was held in veneration, and the utmost confidence reposed in guardians of his choice; but we do not find in the statutes any great development of the *patria potestas*. On the contrary, as in other cities, the marked characteristic of the family is their doing everything in common. All affairs of moment are settled by the family council, by an assembly of relations. Both law and custom continue to follow this course. In the family, the party-circle, or *clique*, and the association, the community of interests is sometimes carried to extraordinary lengths. Not only may a father or brother be summoned to pay the debts of a son or brother, but every creditor of a consociation can sue its individual members, and one associate may be made liable even for the crimes of another. Within the circle of the family or association, disputes were settled by arbiters, whose awards had the validity of legal sentences. The trade associations, as we have already stated, had regularly constituted, special tribunals of their own. These incidents and characteristics of statutory law certainly cannot be referred to the Roman legislation, but find their explanation in the very beginnings of Italian history to which Germanic races and institutions undoubtedly contributed in no small degree. The distinctive character of the Commune remains always the same. On the one hand particular associations attain great development; on the other the action of the political power is sometimes too feeble, but at times exercises a pressure such as would seem excessive even at this day. In a society in which the State is so feeble that its very existence seems continually threatened, it is certainly strange to find it interfering so directly and extensively in the private affairs of the citizens. The emancipation of sons is to be effected with due solemnity at a full meeting of the Council of the People, in the presence of the heads of the Republic. Should a noble citizen desire to change his abode and move to another quarter of the city, the matter must be brought before the same Councils of the People and the Commune, and decided by a special Act.[378] We find the chief magistrates of the Florentine commonwealth continually altering the boundaries and extent of the Quartieri or Sestieri of the city, enlarging or contracting now one and now another in order to preserve the balance which is always being threatened by parties and sects, and prevent any one quarter from winning undue predominance. A change of abode from one district of the town to another might drag a citizen into a different sect or party, and so become of political importance. All this shows more and more clearly that society had not yet found its natural and permanent basis. The manifold new and varied elements entering into its composition were being developed on all sides; but the synthetic power which unites and assimilates could never be attained by the Italian Commune.

XI.

Coming now to a particular examination of the statutory provisions which most nearly concern the subject in hand, we shall direct our attention more especially to the Florentine statutes which, for us, have a twofold importance. We have undertaken this study as an aid to the clearer comprehension of certain political reforms in Florence, which are only to be explained by the social conditions of the Republic. In this study of the Florentine Commune it is necessary to bear in mind that in no other Commune was aristocracy so radically destroyed and democracy so thoroughly triumphant. Every trace of feudalism, every foreign element disappears from its statute book, which consequently, in spite of perennial alterations, preserves a uniform and consistent character, and tends always towards the scope that it finally attains. Other statute books, on the contrary, are no less copiously altered; but the alterations are due to less permanent causes, to elements most extraneous to the life of the Commune, and which therefore make it still more difficult to understand what are the true principles moulding the laws and determining their historical character.

If we begin by examining the paternal authority as set forth in the statutes, we at once perceive the uncertainty that prevails in this legislation. At first we find the Longobard *mundium*, but this gradually takes the shape of the Roman *patria potestas*, as regulated by Justinian's legislation, which finally prevails, although never absolutely. In the various provisions of the statutes, which, even on this point, are always defective, we sometimes find the son placed under a stricter subjection than by Roman law, while at other times, the Longobard law predominating, he enjoys the greatest independence. Generally there are special political or commercial reasons at the root of this illogical inconsistency. By the Roman statutes the son is entitled to appear in criminal cases, without permission from his father, who is not held liable for crimes committed by his son. The son, however, may be punished by his parents at their discretion. The natural children of magnates are in an inferior position, both civilly and politically, to sons born in wedlock, inasmuch as they are never eligible to any public office.[379] According to the Pesaro statutes, a son may dispose by will of all his earnings, provided he leaves the obligatory usufruct to his father; but sons marrying without their father's consent may be disinherited.[380] When a son is condemned to pay a fine, the father must give him his share of the inheritance wherewith to pay it. Should a father beat his sons or grandsons or their wives, *in nihilo puniatur, nisi pro enormi delicto.*[381] In Lucca, a son who is eighteen years of age, may contract a loan, even without his father's leave. But a father may send his son, whether emancipated or under tutelage, to prison if he has dissipated his private means or led an evil life. The magistrates must execute the father's decision without calling for proofs.[382] A son may thus be arbitrarily confined to the house, fettered and imprisoned by his father, who is only bound to supply him with the necessaries of life. The same rule obtains with regard to other descendants. If in all this great variety of laws we try to discover any one characteristic peculiar to the statutes, we must seek it in the *unitas personæ* between father and son, which is often carried to a great length. This, too, is a result of the general conception of the family recognised by the statutes. In Urbino and elsewhere the father may be punished for the son, the master for the servant.[383] As to the liabilities of commerce, these are shared, not only by father and son, but by the whole body of the relations, as we find was the case in Genoa, Florence, and many of the principal trading cities. In Florence, the father, grandfather, and great-grandfather incur the same liability for a descendant (even if under guardianship) who engages in trade, as though they stood surety for him. To escape this responsibility they must make a public and formal disclaimer of liability.[384] Thus, if an unemancipated son is agent or factor of a company or house of business, the father is responsible for him, unless he has given the parties legal notice to the contrary. For the same reason the emancipation of the son must be publicly performed and communicated to the Society of Merchants.[385] When a daughter marries, she ceases to be subject to the paternal authority, and can no longer be held in any way responsible for her father, either as regards civil obligations or criminal, should the father have evaded punishment by flight.

In Florence, the woman is under the perpetual protection of the *Mondualdo*. The term was still retained in the eighteenth century, but under the statutes the *mundio* soon becomes almost identical with the Roman tutelage; as time goes on it gradually falls into disuse, but the rights of women are never made equal with those of men. In respect of marriage the intermixture of different legal systems is most marked. Professor Gans has noted how the Pisans, finding that the Roman law forbade a woman to re- marry within a year from her husband's death, that the Canon law (interpreting the apostle's words as an unqualified permission) contained no such prohibition, and that the Longobard law forbade re-marriage only for thirty days, fixed by their statutes the prohibited period at six months. But this rough compromise neither met the object intended by the Roman law, namely, that a second marriage should not take place during the pregnancy which might possibly result from the first, nor conceded the liberty allowed by the Canon law and the Longobard. More commonly, however, the union of different laws is brought about by the gradual transformation of one into another. The Pisan statutes, for instance, regulate marriage almost entirely according to the Roman Code. To the dower (*dos*) brought by the wife, and the donation (*donatio propter nuptias*, called also *antefactum*) given by the husband, they join other gifts, to which they give the name "*corredo*," which, on the dissolution of the marriage, belong to the wife: should they then be found to have been consumed or made away with, she would be entitled to two-thirds of their value. As a rule Pisan husbands and wives hold their property entirely separate, so that marriage seems sometimes to involve a hostile relation, rather than a community of interests.[386]

Certain statutes admit the *dos* and *donatio propter nuptias* together with the *meta* and the Longobard donation. The Florentine statute speaks of a dowry, of a donation that must be equal to one half of the dowry—provided this does not exceed the sum of fifty *lire*—and of an augmentation. Failing sons, grandsons, or grandsons of sons, the wife, at her husband's death, recovered possession of her dowry, with the donation and augmentation; otherwise she had her dowry alone, and whatever her husband might leave her by will. If the husband died before receiving the dowry, the wife took the promised donation, limited however to one-eighth of her husband's estate, over which, to the extent of her dower, she had a preferential mortgage. Nor had the wife's consent to the sale or alienation of her husband's property the effect of releasing her right to the subjects so sold or alienated. This regulation, however, only comes into force from the year 1388.[387] This date, which is given in the printed Florentine statute of 1415, shows that the dotal system and the separation of property had by this time made great progress, a fact farther confirmed by the statutes.

The wife could not maintain her right to her husband's property (*defendere bona viri*) against her husband's creditors at large, but only against those who were liable for the restitution of the dower. Dotal property, of which no valuation had been made, might be claimed by her as against any creditor, and if her husband fell into difficulties, she could always demand restitution of her dower.[388] Property acquired or inherited by the wife during the husband's life, belonged to her; but she could not alienate it without the consent of the husband, who was also entitled to the usufruct. On the decease of the husband, whatever remained of the usufruct might be claimed by the wife, or, if she too were dead, by the children.

XII.

The dotal system and separation of conjugal property are not only recognised in all the statutes,[389] but are often enacted in an exaggerated form, as seems to be the case in the statutes of Pisa. Thus gifts between husband and wife are forbidden, sometimes even gifts from them to strangers, where there is ground to suspect that these are meant to disguise a gift between the spouses. Zealous precautions to hinder property being withdrawn from the family, still more from the city, are universal. In Urbino, for instance, no alien could inherit *ab intestato*, without first pledging his word to reside within the city or territory.[390] At Pesaro a similar pledge was exacted from any alien who sought a bride in that city; he had also to obtain the consent of the Podestà.

In Verona,[391] women might, under a will, share equally with their brothers; but *ab intestato*, they had only their dower. In Pisa, testate succession was regulated in accordance with the Roman law: *de ultimis voluntatibus pen legem romanum iudicetur*. The lawful share, however, was fixed on almost the same scale as by Longobard law; and, as provided by that law, one child might be favoured more than the rest. As regards intestate succession, male heirs had, as always, marked preference. Failing descendants in the male line, females inherited, but even in the succession to maternal estate, male descendants had priority when there were no surviving daughters.[392] This rule prevails in all statute books, not excluding the "Consuetudini" of Naples, of Amalfi, and of Sorrento, although in these cities the influence of the Longobard law was much less felt.[393] The real object of these regulations is clearly expressed in the statutes themselves. In the statutes of Mantua it is thus set forth: "Ut familiarum dignitas, nomen et ordo serventur, et bona morientium in eorum agnatos et posteros transmittantur, per quos nomina generis conservantur, statuimus et ordinamus,"[394] &c.

It would seem that in Ravenna the prolonged continuance of the Byzantine rule had the effect of suppressing this preference of the agnates, and that there the Novel of Justinian was in force. The same was the case at Osimo. Adoption was of rare occurrence; legitimated children were postponed to legitimate; natural children who, under the influence of the Longobard law, had been favoured in earlier statutes, were afterwards neglected, in consequence of the growing ascendancy of Canon and Roman law. The whole statutory law of succession is so dominated by the political conception which, so far from losing, is constantly gaining ground, that the disposing power of the testator—always extremely restricted—can only arrive at a result slightly more equitable and natural, but never attains to absolute freedom of decision in the Roman sense of the word. In this, as in every branch of civil law, the Florentine Statute Book, like all the others, does not present us with a complete treatise, but only with fragments, the statutes making constant reference to the Roman law.

No woman succeeds *ab intestato* to her sons or daughters, when there are direct descendants or ascendants even in the third degree; and uncle, brother, sister, son, or grandson of a brother are preferred to her. Though excluded from succession, she can nevertheless claim alimony from those who by law exclude her. If there be no such relatives, she inherits *ab intestato* one-fourth of her son's estate, provided it does not amount to more than five hundred *lire*. In any case, she only receives money, not real property. If there is no money, she will be entitled to the price of the lands forming her inheritance. The same provisions apply when a grandmother, great-grandmother, or descendants in the maternal line succeed *ab intestato*.

A woman could not succeed *ab intestato* to a brother leaving children, grandchildren, or brothers; but when thus excluded from the succession, she was still entitled to alimony. She could not succeed even to her father; but was entitled to receive her dowry from the agnates, and could meanwhile, even if a widow, claim alimony from them.[395]

It is plain from all these provisions that the woman's rights of succession were very limited; but she was always insured of the wherewithal to live. We find, indeed, from the Florentine statutes, that while the preference given to the agnates increases as time goes on, so too the woman's rights to alimony increase. The statute of 1355 concedes to her the usufruct of the paternal inheritance, on failure of male issue, while under the same circumstances, later statutes deny her this right, allowing her alimony instead.[396] Speaking of aliment, and of those bound to supply it, the statute of 1324 says: "Si filius, nepos vel pronepos facultatis abundarent,"[397] so that they can *commode subvenire*, &c.; and the statute of 1355 imposes the same obligation, with the same conditions.[398] But the printed statute of 1415 is far more explicit; the father, mother, grandfather, grandmother, great-grandfather, and great-grandmother are all entitled to alimony, and the Podestà is bound to enforce the law. The female inherits *ab intestato* from her mother or other female ascendants, but only on failure of male issue. Uterine brothers, being of the female line, cannot succeed one another should there be relations of the deceased in the male line as far as the fourth degree,[399] these being preferred to the mother and relations in the female line. The Florentine statute goes on to declare that the wife is to be preferred to the public treasury, *uxor mariti defuncti præferatur fisco*; showing how little the woman's rights were considered, when an express enactment was needed to prevent the revenue authorities from depriving her of her husband's estate. Natural children were also preferred to the treasury, which only succeeded on failure of relations as far as the fourth degree. Relations, however, could succeed to bastards, as though these had been legitimate.[400] It should be added that Florentine custom did not allow natural children to be left without some means of support, or without provision for their education, as is shown by many still existing wills. In the case of males, the father generally tried to obtain employment for them; in the case of females, to find them husbands, and he recommended them to the care of his legitimate heirs.

The husband succeeded to his wife's dowry, failing children or other near descendants. Of her extra-dotal property he was entitled to one-third, and the wife could not dispose of her dowry either by will or donation, so as to exclude her husband or children.[401]

XIII.

Besides the law of succession, there is another branch of the Italian statutes in which the action of the political idea upon civil law is equally apparent, namely, that which treats of rights between neighbours, and of the obligations *in solidum* attaching not only to the members of families, but likewise to the members of sects and associations. We have already observed that these are carried so far as to make one member responsible for another's debts, and even for his delicts: this is a law to which we shall have more than once to return and give our attention. When real property is sold, we find that the agnates and cognates have always a preferential right of purchase. In the March of Ancona, the blood-relations of a prisoner condemned to death may be compelled to purchase his estate.[402] At Bologna, relations are often made legally responsible for one another, and, by the rules of the corporations of merchants in that city, the brothers of any bankrupt, who have lived in community with him within a month before his failure, are held responsible for his debts—even if they have separated from him since that time.[403]

According to the Florentine statute, the creditor of any Commune or of any *Universitas* (corporation) might proceed against it, *sicut procedi potest contra alias singulares personas debitrices, in persona*. This was carried so far, that it was permissible to proceed against every individual member of the association, and even to have him arrested, *liceat ipsi creditori capi et detinere omnes et singulares personas dicti Communis vel Universitatis, quousque fuerit integre satisfactum.*[404] If landed property had been laid waste or houses burnt, the proprietor was entitled to compensation from the author of the deed; from his associates (*consorti*), were he a noble, or from his relations, even to the fourth degree, if a commoner. Nay more, the injured person might also proceed against the Commune, University, or district (*plebatum*) in which the crime had been committed; he was at liberty to follow any of these modes of redress, and if unsuccessful in one to try another.[405] The statute prescribed the form of procedure and the terms of the sentence.[406] The Commune, University, or district was thus compelled to be always ready to raise the alarm, when similar acts were perpetrated, and to pursue and arrest the criminal, since, in case of failure, they were held responsible.[407]

In all matters, even such as purchases or sales, great importance was assigned to the condition of the persons concerned. In some cases, where land was to be sold, the law required that it should be sold to a neighbour; commoners, however, were not compelled to sell to magnates.[408] Similarly no one might buy, sell, or acquire the usufruct of lands held in common, or any piece of land or house touching another man's wall, without according the joint-owner, associate, or neighbour the right of pre-emption.[409]

In case of a dispute between relations or associates, *qui consortes sint de eadem stirpe, per lineam masculinam usque ad infinitum,*[410] the judge was bound, at the request of one of the parties concerned, to leave the matter to the decision of arbiters chosen by the parties themselves; but no plebeian could act as arbiter between nobles.[411] In reviving a law of much earlier date, the statute of 1355 informs us that arbiters were therein mentioned, as blood-relations.[412] Whence it may be inferred that similar compromises began to be customary, at a very remote period, between relations and associates who voluntarily selected arbiters from their own group. Down to the year 1324, the custom had been sanctioned by law; at a later time it lost its primitive character of a voluntary and domestic agreement, and assumed the shape of a regular legal trial.

XIV.

If we now compare the Florentine Statute Book with those of other Italian cities, we shall find it marked by various distinguishing characteristics, chiefly resulting from the fact that in it democratic freedom was carried to the farthest point obtainable during the Middle Ages. Not only had every feudal privilege gradually disappeared from it, but the great nobles had ended by finding themselves in a position inferior to that of the commonalty. Florence, as we have already seen, was one of the first Italian cities to abolish serfdom in her outlying territory by the law of 1289.[413] And although her rural population was always treated much worse than the inhabitants of the city, it nevertheless enjoyed far better conditions than prevailed in a great number of communes. We have proof of this in the contract of *Mezzeria*, which makes the cultivator of the soil an actual partner with the proprietor, and which still remains a great monument of civilisation and the cynosure of modern economists who have never been able to devise any better system.[414]

The freedom and strength of associations, the extraordinary ease with which any one might participate in the government of the Commune, all contributed to the triumph of democracy on the widest basis. Another general characteristic to be noted, not only in the Florentine, but in almost all the Italian statutes, is the constant endeavour to shake off the intervention of the ecclesiastical authority, which labours with incredible obstinacy to maintain its privileges undiminished, and even seeks to increase them; but which, nevertheless, finds them gradually reduced almost to zero. The statute of 1415 ordains that "no person, university, or church, no religious or clerical house shall presume to question the jurisdiction of the Commune under pretence of 'benefice' or privilege, and that any one who opposes this enactment shall be imprisoned until he renounce such privilege.[415] No excommunication nor interdict shall hinder or diminish the action of the magistrates or the effect of their decrees.[416] Every man may freely exercise his rights over all Church property derived from secular sources."[417]

XV.

Turning now to a general view of the Italian statutes, we must remark that although the history of statutory law presents many difficulties, owing to the infinite number of different provisions to be found in it, the diversity of these provisions is chiefly due to accidental and temporary causes, extraneous to the natural and spontaneous development of the law itself, which, examined apart and with reference to its essential characteristics, presents a striking uniformity. It may, however, be noted that in the republics of Northern Italy the Longobard law is far more predominant; while in those of Central and Southern Italy Roman law obtains an early and rapid ascendancy, and, subject to the changes which have been indicated, ends by dominating at all points. This progress becomes more apparent from year to year, so that even in examining the statutes, the very same conflict of antagonistic elements which we have already noted, throughout the entire history of the communes and of Italian civilisation, is brought before our eyes in civil wars, in sanguinary struggles between Guelphs and Ghibellines, in art, in literature, in all things. It is true that the statutes only treat of juridical ideas and enactments; but these seem to strive with the same ardour, and to aim at the same ends, as the men whom they control.

Towards the close of the fourteenth century Italian commerce began to make enormous advance, and this gave a new impetus to Italian legislation. In fact, we find a series of enactments enabling all mercantile affairs to be transacted with much greater celerity, avoiding legal quibbles, releasing merchant's credits from mortgage or sequestration, and severely punishing all frauds and fraudulent bankruptcies. In a word, we clearly discern the inchoation of the modern commercial code with which these enactments are frequently in unison.

But in all these laws we always recognise the consequences of commerce being divided and split into a multitude of separate associations with statutes of their own, judges of their own, and an exuberance of vitality. At the same time, we recognise that the central authority, though aware that its natural rights are threatened and usurped on all sides, continues to exert its influence, without method, indeed, or uniformity, but not without vigour, and occasionally even with violence. At one moment it seems to be vanquished; at another it comes forth victorious. The entire history of the Commune demonstrates a constant tendency to harmonise all these distinct and often jarring elements—political, social, and legislative—but this problem it never succeeds in solving, and ends by relapsing into despotism. A true conception of social unity was wanting; the idea of a due distribution of authority was still unknown, either in real life or in theory; accordingly whoever happened to have a share in the executive authority, also assumed, as necessarily connected with it, a share not only in judicial, but likewise in administrative and legislative functions. Wherefore it seemed that the only way to preserve liberty was to parcel out the government among an infinity of hands, and so to contrive that parties, associations, *cliques* (*consorterie*), families, and quarters of the town should each and severally serve as checks upon all the others. In this process of division and subdivision all the elements afterwards constituting modern society were prepared, but the State, in its true sense, was never discovered. Without ballast to steady her, the ship of the Commune, driven hither and thither in a ceaseless storm and buffeted by winds from all quarters, could neither find anchorage nor keep a settled course. No clear and certain conception was ever reached of that law which, by limiting and defining the amount of liberty guaranteed to each individual, secures freedom to all.

The political life of communes, moreover, was always confined within the walls of the dominant cities, since not only the outlying territory was excluded from it, but likewise all towns that had been annexed or conquered. Every form of representative government was as yet unknown. All who enjoyed political rights entered, each in his turn, the Councils of the Republic, and sooner or later nearly all rose to power. This made it necessary that the States should have very circumscribed borders, as otherwise it would have been impossible to govern them at all. The French Revolution, by achieving for the first time, in behalf of the nation at large, what the Italian communes had effected for the cities, was able to proclaim the civil and political equality of all who formed part of the nation, and who were in consequence to be recognised as citizens. From that time democracy became the predominant characteristic of modern societies which, by means of representative institutions, have found it possible to secure freedom, even in large states, reconciling the unity and vigorous action of the central government with personal independence and with local liberty and activity. But the Commune always wavered between the opposing elements of which it was made up and which it never succeeded in fusing into a true political organism.

The history of our republics may, in fact, be summed up in an account of the varying predominance of one or other of the great associations of which they were composed. In Florence, we have, first of all, the conflict of nobles and commons which is maintained with changing fortunes. When the fraternities (*consorterie*) of the leading magnates obtained such ascendancy as to menace popular liberties and destroy the social balance, notable reforms were made in the statutes; the Commune was completely transformed, and by means of the Ordinances of Justice (of which we shall soon have to speak), the nobles were overthrown and their associations broken up. But as these associations were an integral part of the State, their downfall was followed by a phase of rapid corruption and decay. To the passions and interests of caste succeeded personal ambitions, hatreds and passions of a still more dangerous character. Families began to be at strife; men who were at once powerful and ambitious, came to the front; and Corso Donati, or some other like him, would have soon become master and tyrant of the Republic, save for the fact that a mighty people, enriched by the speedy gains of an extended commerce, devoted to freedom and opposed to the nobility, had first to be disarmed. Thus to the supremacy of the leagues of the magnates succeeded the predominance of the Greater Guilds, between whom and the Lesser Guilds a struggle was entered upon in the course of which the latter obtained, in their turn, a share of power. At a later period, the populace, represented by the plebeian Ciompi, comes to the front, and threatens the utter dissolution of the old social form of the Republic. Then new personal ambitions, more fatal to freedom because more fortunate, occupy the scene. The struggle between the Albizzi, Pitti, and Medici terminates in the triumph of the last-named family in the person of Cosimo the Elder, who slew the Republic. Yet nothing of all this should cause us much surprise. For if we bear in mind the beginnings of the Commune and the elements out of which it was constituted, we may readily see that all that happened was, in the main, unavoidably bound to occur.

CHAPTER VIII.

THE ENACTMENTS OF JUSTICE.[418]

I.

THERE are many reasons why the history of Florence in the closing years of the thirteenth century should demand our fullest attention. It was the period of the very important political revolution resulting in the establishment of those Enactments of Justice of which the authorship is attributed to Giano della Bella, and which Bonaini has entitled the Magna Charta of the Florentine Republic. Even should this comparison seem strained, it is certain that those enactments, sometimes strengthened, sometimes modified, and occasionally suspended, remained in vigour nevertheless for more than a century—a fact of no small weight in so mutable a commonwealth as that of Florence. Sooner or later many neighbouring cities imitated these enactments, and in 1338 the Romans sent to request a copy of them, in order to re-organise their city by the same means. On this subject Villani wrote as follows: "It is known how times and conditions change, for the Romans, who of old built the city of Florence and gave it their own laws, now, in our days, have sent to ask laws from the Florentines."[419] It is likewise during this period that we behold arts and letters suddenly blossoming to the greatest splendour in the bosom of the Republic. Language, poetry, painting, architecture, sculpture had already put forth their first shoots in various Italian cities; but all are now permanently rooted in Florence, and initiating a new era in the history of the national intellect, suddenly flash forth into a glory of light, irradiating all Europe as well as Italy. Hence it behoves us to investigate most minutely the nature of the favourable conditions, both political and social, which rendered Florence the centre of such marvellous activity and the focus of all those far-spreading beams.

The remark might certainly occur, that although this period has such undoubted claims upon our attention, its history is already very familiar to us; it has been recounted by contemporary writers such as Compagni and Villani, who were not only eye-witnesses, but often active participants in the events they described; it has been corroborated by many original documents, and recently expounded afresh by some most illustrious modern writers. Nevertheless, the attentive student is compelled to recognise that those times are less well known than might be supposed; for even in perusing the works of the newest historians we are perplexed by numerous difficulties and doubts. In point of fact, what is it we learn from Machiavelli, Ammirato, Sismondi, and Napier, and even from Vannucci, Giudici, and Trollope, who wrote subsequently to the publication of many newly discovered original documents? That, after the battle of Campaldino the arrogance of the nobles in Florence exceeded all bounds; that they insulted, oppressed, and trampled on the people; that there arose a daring and generous man named Giano della Bella, a noble devoted to the popular party, who when holding the office of Prior proposed a new law as a permanent remedy for these evils; that this law was passed and sanctioned under the name of Enactments of Justice, and that it excluded the nobles—or, rather, the magnates—from every political post; that it only permitted those really engaged in some trade or craft to share in the government of the Republic; that it punished every grave offence against the people, on the part of the nobles, with exceptionally severe sentences and penalties, such as chopping off hands, death at the block, and, more frequently, by confiscation of property; that slighter offences were only punished by fines; that the magistrates were empowered to chastise any man of the people (*popolano*) showing hostility to the Republic or breaking its laws, by proclaiming him a noble, and that this sentence immediately excluded him from the government and placed him under the same restrictions to which aristocrats were subject. Furthermore, that if any magnate convicted of offence should escape justice, one of his relations or associates would have to expiate the crime in his stead.[420]

"A fact without parallel in the world's history!" Giudici exclaims. For truly, although a fundamental law of the Republic, this decree seems rather a freak of revenge solely inspired by the blindest party spirit. Accordingly almost every word of the decree excites our suspicion. How can it be explained that Dante was one of the Priors in office at the time, together with others who undoubtedly were not artisans, or only so in name, if it were true that the enactments excluded all who were not *practically exercising* some trade? And apart from a thousand lesser doubts, the fact that innocent men were then condemned to death merely because they were relations or fellow associates of criminals who had escaped justice, is a point that we cannot possibly understand. In a period of the densest barbarism, it would be barely comprehensible; in Dante's age, it is a mystery and a contradiction, confusing all our ideas concerning those times. Therefore renewed investigation of the subject cannot be altogether futile. It is requisite to penetrate the true nature of the revolution that had then been accomplished, and of the law that resulted from it, and to bring both into harmony with the times and with the history of Florence.

II.

Towards the end of the thirteenth century the Republic had acquired very high importance throughout Italy as well as Tuscany. The fall of the Hohenstauffens, the coming of the Angevins, the vacancy of the Imperial throne had given an enormous ascendancy to the Guelph party which in Florence was that of the democracy. Its three great Ghibelline rivals, Pisa, Sienna, and Arezzo, had been humiliated and conquered by the subtle diplomacy of Florence and Florentine arms; and these victories had not only re-established the Republic's political authority in Tuscany, but opened and secured to it all the chief highways of commerce. Through Pisa it had access to the sea; through Sienna and Arezzo, to Rome, Umbria, and Southern Italy; it could pass to the north through distant Bologna, peopled with friendly Guelphs. Accordingly the commerce of Florence was then rapidly increased, and this republic of merchants, surrounded by other republics equally devoted to trade and industry, stood at the head of all Tuscany. On the other hand, however, the augmented power of the Angevins was beginning to excite the jealousy of the Popes who had first called them to Italy, and who now turned their eyes towards Germany in order to revive the Imperial pretensions, and thus check the growing ambition of the French king. For Charles of Anjou, whom they had named Senator of Rome and Vicar-Imperial of Tuscany, now seemed determined to follow the daring policy of the Swabian line by aspiring to supremacy over Italy.

During this state of things, the Florentines managed to keep their balance with marvellous *finesse*, and by leaning this way, or that, frequently turned the scales on the side they preferred. They utilised the king's soldiery to crush Ghibelline cities and Ghibelline nobles; they leaned on the Pope, to check Charles's arrogance; and they showed readiness to favour the Empire, when the Pope tried to assert temporal supremacy, as though, in the present *interregnum*, he were the natural inheritor of the imperial rights. By this means, the Republic not only preserved its independence, but became a State commanding the fear and respect of all Italy.[421] This was all the result of the shrewdness, energy, and intelligence of its burghers, who governed with so much thriftiness and wisdom as to achieve an unparalleled prosperity. "It is a known thing," says Villani, "that down to this time and for long past, such was the tranquillity of Florence, that the City gates stood unlocked by night,[422] no duties were exacted in Florence;[423] and rather than impose burdens, when money was needed, old walls and bits of land within and without the City were sold to the owners of conterminous portions of the soil."[424] With few taxes and no debts, the administration was excellently

299

conducted; it left the citizens unhampered, and increased the general well-being.

III.

Nevertheless, beneath this tranquil surface the seeds of deep-rooted discord lurked in the bosom of the State, and occasionally broke forth in sanguinary conflicts, of which the discontent of the nobles was the principal cause. It would be a serious mistake to believe that they were first excluded from the government in virtue of the Enactments of Justice. The measure had been prepared long before, and although not then rigorously carried out, may be said to have been already sanctioned in 1282, by the decree placing the Priors of the Guild at the head of the Republic. But it should not be thought on this account, that the nobles had lost all actual power in the city at the time. First of all, the new system of warfare, in which municipal armies, composed of artisans, unprovided with cavalry or men-at-arms, proved very incompetent, had made the assistance of the nobles indispensable, and also began to render it necessary to employ foreigners: soldiers of adventure from Germany, France, and Spain, who earned their living by war alone. At Montaperti (1260) the terrible defeat of the Republic's Guelph host had been achieved by Manfred's Germans, and the Ghibelline nobles banished from Florence. At Campaldino (1289) it was Corso Donati, Vieri de' Cerchi, and other Florentine nobles or potentates who had decided the fate of the day. The nobles knew this, and constantly boasted of it, in their contempt for the artisans and people. Being trained to arms, and undisturbed by commercial cares, they sorely chafed against being excluded from the government by rougher folk far less fitted for war than themselves. Accordingly, political animosities became more and more heated; the nobles could neither be still nor leave others in peace.

It should also be remarked that the nobles of the period were no longer the feudal lords of former times, who, isolated in their well-guarded strongholds, like so many sovereigns, depended solely from the Empire and were foes to the Republic. Having been ousted from the territory, and obliged for some time back to reside in the city, they now clung to the latter, but desired to hold rule over it. Being surrounded on all sides by a powerful population banded in trade guilds and masters of the Government; being forcibly made subject to Republican laws refusing all recognition of feudal rights, the nobles had been obliged, in self-defence, to form Associations or Societies of the Towers, which being ruled by custom rather than law, were all the more firmly knit together. Originally, the nobles had been chiefly united by family ties which were still more closely respected on the disintegration of the feudal order, when, in order to maintain their strength, kinsmen banded together in separate castes or associations and gave admittance to a widening circle of members. They clustered together in neighbouring palaces, often lining one or more of the city streets; they lived in the midst of their adherents, squires, domestics, and grooms, and in moments of danger even summoned to their aid the peasantry of their rural estates. Their possessions were always handed down to their families or the Society to which they belonged, and their disputes were settled by chosen arbiters.[425] Besides all this, their deeds of vengeance were decided upon in common, and the individuals charged to execute them were always placed in safety by their comrades, the whole association assuming the responsibility of every deed of this kind. Often, between one house and another, or in one of their palace yards, there was an archway under which they administered torture to any one they chose. In fact, speaking of the Bostichi family, Compagni tells us that: "They committed many evil deeds, and continued to do them for long. In their own palaces, situated in the New Market, in the centre of the city, they would string men up, and put them to the torture at mid-day. And it was a common saying in the land that there were too many tribunals; and in counting the places where torture was applied, people said: 'In the Bostichi house, by the Market.'"[426] All this continued to be done, notwithstanding the very severe laws already promulgated against the nobles. A man of the people could be flogged, stabbed, or tortured, without the author of the misdeed being brought within the grasp of the law. Out in the country these same nobles used all sorts of devices to perpetuate serfdom, although for many years it had been legally abolished, and by threats or open violence induced their peasants, by means of fictitious contracts, to acknowledge obligations from which they were lawfully exempt.[427]

Thus citizens, already powerful in virtue of their social position, contrived to retain much strength and great political influence in the Republic, notwithstanding the laws designed to keep them in check. Being excluded from the Signory they could neither enter the Council of One Hundred nor the Councils of the Captain, in which the more important questions were discussed. But they were admitted to those of the Podestà, and this official, being of necessity a knight, often gave judgment in favour of the nobles. Also, they were continually employed as ambassadors, and given the first posts in war; but they enjoyed most prominence in the institution entitled the Guelph Society (*Parte Guelfa*), and were specially appointed to all its chief offices. This Society, founded, as we have previously shown, in 1267, after the expulsion of Count Guido Novello, was charged with the administration of all confiscated Ghibelline property which had been formed into a *monte* or *mobile*, or, as would now be said, capitalised. This property was to be employed for the subjection of the Ghibellines and the support of the Guelphs, of whom Florence was the Tuscan headquarters. It was on this account that Cardinal Ottavio degli Ubandini had exclaimed: "Now that the Guelphs have formed a fund in Florence, the Ghibellines will never return there;" and his prophecy was fulfilled.[428] In fact, the Ghibelline party was gradually swept away by the steady persecution to which it was subjected on the complete overthrow of the Suabian line; and Florence, having become exclusively Guelph, was divided between the parties of burghers and populace, and that of the nobles and magnates or *grandi*. The latter, although excluded from the government, or from *honours*, to use the phraseology of the time, could never be ousted from the Guelph Society, and continued to administer its large revenues. This Society was ordered in the fashion of a miniature republic, and notwithstanding numerous attempts to introduce an increasing burgher element within its pale, these efforts proved so fruitless and were so invariably thwarted, that the statutes compiled in 1335, and now extant in print, record the fact that money premiums were offered to promote the nomination of new knights. To each of the six knights elected during the year the sum of fifty gold florins were awarded, "so that a city of such great magnificence may be duly glorified by the number of its knights." Thus while, on the one hand, every means was taken to abase the great nobles, almost to the extent of securing their extermination, on the other, this threatened class continually gained reinforcement and support.[429]

IV.

With all these advantages, had the nobles been united, they might have regained their position even after the defeats of '66 and '82 and succeeded in dominating the people. But they were divided, and hotly at strife even among themselves. "There was much warfare" (Villani says) "between the Adimari and Tosinghi, between the Rossi and Tornaquinci, between the Bardi and Mozzi, between the Gherardini and Manieri, between the Cavalcanti and Buondelmonti, and likewise between certain of the Buondelmonti and Giandonati; between the Visdomini and Falconieri, between the Bostichi and Foraboschi, between the Foraboschi and Malespini, and among the Frescobaldi themselves, and between the members of the Donati family, and also among those of many other houses."[430] Nor is it surprising that such strong and powerful cliques should have felt jealous of one another. Added to this, the Guelph nobles included the remains of the Ghibelline party, which cherished Imperial tendencies; thus another germ of discord was sown that encouraged and excited the people to prosecute the war of extermination it had already set on foot. The popular party was far better organised and united; it was banded in various guilds forming part of the general constitution of the State, and on every occasion showed an energy and singleness of purpose never possessed by nobles. It is true, that even at this juncture, some seeds of jealousy were beginning to be discernible between the greater and lesser guilds and the populace; but open discord was long delayed. For the moment there was no hint of it. Certain special conventions, drawn up in regular documentary form, had been arranged between the members of one or more of the guilds, and these agreements were designated at the time *Legbe, Posture*, or *Convegni*. But their object was chiefly commercial, being designed to keep the price of certain commodities up to a forced standard, and create illegal monopolies, and was seldom the result of political interests or animosities. They were not sanctioned by law, they certainly did not promote concord, but their importance was slight.

Thus the city became increasingly divided and subdivided into groups, and was apparently in danger of falling to pieces. The lower classes were still undoubted rulers of the government, but the nobles were also powerful, if in a different way; hence unity and concord were continually and seriously imperilled. Necessarily, therefore, the chief aim to be pursued, in order to avert a catastrophe, was the attainment of greater equality among the citizens, of greater union and strength in the various societies as well as in the government itself. In fact, for a long time past, Florentine legislation and successive revolutions had alike kept this object in view. The law of August 6, 1289, abolishing serfdom in order to emancipate the peasantry, was also another step towards equality. Those of June 30, and July 3, 1290, prohibited all agreements in any way opposed to the lawful constitution of the guilds. The law of January 31, 1291, imposed a fresh check on the nobles, by obliging all citizens, without any exception, to submit to the jurisdiction of the regular courts, and decreeing the severest penalties on any one asserting, or trying to obtain, the privilege of trial by special tribunals.[431]

But a more notable point is the fact that every fine decreed in such cases fell upon the fellow-associate or relation of the criminal, should the latter contrive to evade justice. However strange this rule may appear to the modern mind, its explanation is to be found in the account we have already given of the mode in which property was held at the time, and of the constitution of families and associations. When almost the whole of the patrimony was shared by the family in common, it would have been very difficult, and even dangerous, to inflict a fine on any one member of the house while exempting the rest, and for this reason the invariable tendency of the law was to insist on their solidarity. This principle seemed still more logical when it was a question of inflicting fines on nobles banded in closely united associations, and who, keeping all their interests in common, decided on acts of vengeance, and proved their intention of holding all things in common and dividing one another's responsibilities. Where property belonged to the whole family, it was only just that the whole family should be liable for the fine; where an act of vengeance was done in common, and the gravest offences committed in the name, and with the sanction, of the whole kindred, there could be nothing extraordinary in the law compelling one associate or kinsman to be mulcted in lieu of another, beginning with his nearest relations. Precisely for these reasons, it had long been customary in drawing out the list of the nobles, for the law to compel the said nobles to *sodare*, that is, to compel every one of them to stand surety not merely for himself alone, but also for his relations, by depositing the sum of two thousand *lire*. In this way, since money- penalties seldom exceeded the said amount, whenever a noble was fined he could use the money he had already deposited, or it could be employed for the same end by the kinsman bound surety for him, in case he should have

escaped or contrived to evade the law by some unauthorised device.[432] These were exclusively and precisely the principles upon which the Enactments of Justice were also founded. Accordingly it is impossible to consider them the personal invention of Giano della Bella, seeing that they were merely a logical consequence and natural result, inevitably evolved from preceding revolutions, institutions, and laws. Indeed, for the most part they only sum up and arrange older laws, so as to accentuate more plainly their primary and enduring intent.

V.

Giano della Bella was neither a legislator nor a politician, but a man of action. A noble by birth, he had fought at Campaldino, where his horse was killed under him; he afterwards joined the popular side, by reason, it was averred, of a quarrel at San Piero Scheraggio with Piero Frescobaldi, who had dared to strike him in the face, and threaten to cut off his nose.[433] Whether this tale were true or not, it is certain that Giano was a man of violent disposition, great daring, small prudence, and disinterested love of freedom; but he was by no means devoid of the passion for revenge that even his admirers laid to his charge. "A forcible and very spirited man" (says

Compagni), "he was so daring, that he defended matters forsaken by others, said things others left unspoken, did his utmost to bring justice to bear on the guilty, and was so much feared by the Rectors that they dared not conceal evil deeds."[434] According to Villani "he was a most loyal and upright *popolano*, and more devoted to the public good than any man in Florence, one that gave help to the Commune without seeking his own profit. He was overbearing and obstinate in wreaking revenge, and also achieved some deeds of vengeance on his neighbours, the Abati, by using the authority of the Commune,"[435] for which the worthy chronicler severely blames him.

When appointed Podestà of Pistoia, he immediately plunged into party strife, persecuting one side and favouring the other, with so much ardour that, instead of fulfilling his duty of pacifying the different factions, he inflamed their hatred to such a pitch that it was impossible for him to remain there to the end of his official term.[436] The whole course of his conduct in Florence proves, as we shall see, that he must have been a man of scant prudence and great impulsiveness. It was precisely these characteristics which made him a leader of the people instead of a legislator, and likewise an implacable enemy of the nobles.

After the battle of Campaldino the latter showed more audacity and growing insolence. "It was we who won the victory at Campaldino," they continually repeated, "and yet you seek our ruin." Bent on forcing their way to the front and gaining command, they daily insulted or injured some man of the people. The law was powerless against them, inasmuch as the offenders could never be unearthed; the latter were carefully sheltered, and no one desired or dared to testify against them. A *popolano* could be surrounded, attacked, even stabbed, yet nobody had seen the doer of the crime. Or some one would be dragged into the houses of an association, maltreated, beaten or tortured on the cord, yet all that occurred in those places remained unrevealed. If some noble was condemned to a fine, he made haste to declare that he possessed no separate estate, and by his own negligence, or that of the magistrates, had failed to give surety, while his relations repeated the same story.[437] Hence it was necessary to recall the old laws into vigour, make them still stricter, and decide on new and sterner measures. So at last the priors in office from the 15th of December, 1292, to the 15th of February, 1293, urged on by the public voice, under Giano's guidance, commissioned three citizens, Donato Ristori, Ubertino della Strozza, and Baldo Aguglioni, to frame a new law fitted, not only to meet present dangers, but to assure greater stability to the Republic in the future. On the 10th of January, the Bill being then drawn up, the Captain of the People assembled the Council of One Hundred, and

proposed that the required Councils should be asked to grant them full powers
(balìa)[438] to proclaim it, if it were approved by the magistrates and by certain citizen worthies. Some proposed, in amendment, that it should be first read and discussed by the councils; but this would have entailed a risk of the whole thing coming to nothing. Accordingly the more practical course was chosen, and by seventy-two votes, against two negatives only, the requested balìa was granted. On the 18th of January the new law, entitled "Ordinamenti," or "Ordini di Giustizia," was proclaimed in the names of the Podestà, captain, and priors, and with the concurrence of the Heads of the Twenty-one Guilds
and certain citizen worthies.[439] There is every reason to believe that Giano della Bella was one of the worthies in question; but although historians suppose him to have been the creator and initiator of the law, since, as leader of public opinion, he compelled the Signory to pass it, yet he was not in the
government at the time, nor does his name appear in any official decree.[440] Therefore he was by no means the sole author or compiler of the new law.

VI.

What, then, are these enactments? In replying to this question it is requisite to leave the historians aside and turn to the law itself. But there are several old compilations of it, differing so much from each other, that one form only comprises twenty-two rubrics, whereas some have more than a hundred. Accordingly, the first thing to be done is to ascertain which is the genuine and primary law passed on the 18th of January, 1293, since on this alone can an accurate judgment be based, and no other starting-point is possible. There are six of these very different compilations—four in print, and two still inedited. Two of the number may be summarily dealt with as unnecessary to our purpose. One is included in the general collection of Florentine statistics, formed in 1415 by Bartolommeo Volpi and Paolo de Castro, and printed with the false date of Friburg, towards the close of the eighteenth century (1778–1783). This consists of laws of entirely different periods arranged haphazard, without regard to chronology, and including the enactments, but these are given with all the modifications and changes introduced at a later date, and are also confusedly jumbled. No historian engaged on the times of Giano della Bella can make any use of a collection of this kind, since it shows no proof of authenticity. For the same reason we may also reject the Miscellany preserved in the Florence Archives, and that Bonaini calls "a *huge medley*," containing unconnected laws of different periods, and different tendencies, some enforcing and others modifying the

Enactments of Justice. Hence, while possibly of some importance with regard to the history of the "Ordinamenti," this Miscellany cannot help us to discover their primary form.

Four other compilations remain, one of which only is inedited. Examination quickly shows that the one brought out by Bonaini comprises no more than twenty-one rubrics, and that the last of these, forming a general summary, is mutilated; the other compilations contain a greater number of rubrics, but, in all three, the general special enactments of January, 1293, are invariably given under the first twenty-eight rubrics.[441] In fact, from the twenty-ninth forward, appendices and posterior laws begin to occur, often separately dated, and seemingly tacked on to the enactments, in order sometimes to modify, sometimes to strengthen them, or again to diminish their effect, or because of their relation to cognate matters. All the laws and statutes of the Republic suffered more or less the same fate. Thus the notable divergences found in the various compilations are reduced to very narrow limits as regards the original body of enactments. Certain doubts still assail us, however, seeing that we not only find twenty-two rubrics on the one hand against twenty-eight on the other, but because these rubrics clash on various points. First of all, then, let us remark that the oldest compilation is undoubtedly the one published by Bonaini in 1855, from the original MS. in the State Archives. The editor felt assured of having discovered the original document of the enactments, but conscientiously preferred to entitle it the original draft,[442] seeing that, as Hegel has since ascertained, it is not the actual law that was approved and proclaimed by the magistrates. The codex is of great antiquity, and may be ascribed to Giano della Bella's day. In fact, in one heading, first inscribed and then cancelled, we find the date of 1292 *de mense ianuarii* (1293, new style).[443] The usual formula heading all decrees of the Republic is missing, and the said formula not only gave the date and title, but occasionally added the names of the magistrates promulgating the law. The codex is of small size, full of erasures, alterations, and additions written by different hands: often, too, there are empty spaces left between one rubric and another to allow room for future additions or corrections. Everything plainly shows that this old codex is only a rough copy of the law, standing exactly as it was drawn up, at the request of the magistrates, by the three previously mentioned citizens, and before it had been cast in its final form, or legally sanctioned by those charged to discuss and approve it, prior to its promulgation. Accordingly it is impossible to decide with any certainty whether it was modified at all, or in what degree. But although this rough draft is somewhat anterior to the actual law itself, the existing compilations are all posterior to it, and may consequently include later appendices and modifications. Thus, on examining the Latin compilation edited by Fineschi in 1790, and the Italian one brought out by Giudici in 1853, both derived from old and authentic manuscripts, we find each to have all the characteristics of a regularly proclaimed law. Both begin with the official formula, and are dated the 18th of January, 1292 (1293, new style). On reading the rubrics appended to the second (the Italian copy), which is much longer than the other, we find various dates given, including that of 1324; whereas the first (the Latin version) contains none later than the 6th of July, 1295. Therefore the latter is the older of the two, and the occasional divergences existing even among its first twenty-eight rubrics are undoubtedly caused by amendments introduced at a subsequent time. Nevertheless, even the first rubrics of the Latin compilation evidently contain modifications of an earlier date than the 6th of July, 1295. For instance, in rubric vi. we find the number of witnesses—a point left undecided in the rough draft (rubric v.)—fixed at three in the two posterior compilations, and this point (as we shall see) can be proved on documentary evidence to have been settled by law in July, 1295. Therefore we are justified in concluding that it is the Latin and older compilation that gives the enactments as they stood in July, 1295; while the Italian copy, although proved, by examination of the codex, to be an official translation, occasionally includes alterations of even a later date than 1295. If, however, we only keep in view their first twenty-eight rubrics, and collate these with Bonaini's draft, it will be seen that, saving for the non-appearance in the latter of six rubrics, chiefly of a very insignificant kind, all other divergences are rather formal than substantial. In any case, wherever the three versions are found to agree, we may be sure of possessing the law passed on the 18th of January, 1293, in the precise shape it wore at the time; but wherever, on the contrary, divergences exist, we must seek the aid of the chroniclers and of any new documents, should such be found, before arriving at a definite conclusion.

Following these rules, we may therefore proceed to examine the law.[444]

VII.

What, then, were these Enactments of Justice, as originally framed, and what is to be learnt from them? They work a political and social change in the Republic, for the evident purpose of promoting civil equality, giving greater unity to the government and increased strength to the guilds; also of assuring the harmony and concord of the people, and curbing the arrogance of the nobles. The more strictly political reform is confined to establishing safe rules for the election of Priors, and creating a new and more powerful magistrate, the Gonfalonier of Justice, to sit in junction with the Priors.

By request of the Captain of the People, the Priors authorised him to call a meeting of the Heads, or Consuls of the Twelve Guilds, in order to deliberate as to the safest and most fitting mode of choosing their own successors. All candidates to the priorate had to be enrolled in some guild, and to exercise its trade, as the surest means of proving that they were not of the aristocracy— always the chief point to be ascertained. In fact no one remaining a noble could be eligible to the Signory, even if engaged in trade.[445] By means of subtle and often quibbling interpretations of the law, it was possible to compromise as to the actual practice of a craft, but never as to being absolutely free from all taint of aristocracy.[446] Thus Giano della Bella, in spite of merely having, as Villani relates, some slight commercial interests in France, was qualified, on discarding his rank and becoming one of the people, to enter the Signory in February, 1293. In July, 1295, as we shall see, the enactments were modified, and it was sufficient for candidates to be enrolled in some guild without practically exercising its trade, always providing they did not belong to the nobility. Many regulations were added to assure an equal division of public posts among all the Sestieri of the city and all the guilds, while prohibiting the nomination of several Priors belonging to the same Sestiere, family, or guild. None leaving office could be re-elected to it within two years, and this prohibition was extended to his relations as well. The office of Prior was held for two months; no one was allowed to ask or intrigue for it, but neither might one refuse to accept it. The Priors had to dwell altogether in one house, where they lived and ate in common, without accepting invitations elsewhere or giving private audiences.[447]

The next subject considered was the election of the new magistrate, namely, the Gonfalonier of Justice. He was chosen every two months from a different Sestiere of the city, and his electors were the incoming Priors, captains, and guild-masters, with the addition of two worthies of each Sestiere. He was elected on precisely the same terms as the Priors, saving that he might return to office after one year instead of two; he lived with the Priors as *primus inter pares*; he received the same honorarium of ten *soldi* per day, expenses included, so that he was practically unremunerated. But having higher attributes in the eyes of the law, he became speedily and of necessity the chief of the Signory.[448] At the public parliament the Gonfalon of the People was solemnly consigned to him, and one hundred *pavesi*, or shields, and twenty-five cross-bows with bolts were placed at his disposal, for the better equipment of part of the thousand *popolani* yearly selected to serve under him, the Podestà and Captain to preserve order and enforce the execution of the new laws.[449] No relation of the Priors in office could be elected to the Gonfaloniership. The creation of this new post certainly serves to prove that the necessity of giving increased unity and supremacy to the Government was already acknowledged. But at that period Republican jealousy was too strong to sanction anything more than a mere show of supremacy. Accordingly, the Gonfalonier was only the most influential of the Priors, and liable to be changed on the same terms, albeit the fact of having the free disposal, at given moments, of the citizen army undoubtedly endued him with higher authority.

In treating of the branch of the enactments bearing on social rather than political cases, we should remark first of all that to these enactments was owed the settled constitution of the Florentine guilds, which now hastened to reframe or renew their own special statutes. The normal number of the guilds was likewise established by the enactments, and from that moment remained fixed at twenty-one.[450] In fact, the first rubric decreed that the guilds should take a solemn oath to maintain union and concord among the people. The second rubric annulled and forbade, under heavy penalties, all *companies, leagues, promises, conventions, obligations,* and *sworn pacts,* that is, all agreements among the people unprovided or unsanctioned by the laws, and opposed or alien to the constitution of the guilds. Both procurators and stipulators of similar agreements were liable even to capital punishment; and any guild known to be concerned in such agreement would be mulcted in one thousand *lire*; the consuls of the said guild, and the notary who had drawn the deed, in five hundred *lire.*[451] All this plainly proves that the law was not devised, as once believed and asserted, for the sole purpose of wreaking vengeance on the nobles, but was also framed with the intent of reforming the city and government by solidly organising the guilds and granting them higher political importance. Nevertheless, the humiliation of the leading nobles was certainly one of the principal objects of the law. Therefore we may now proceed to examine the clauses directed to that end.

VIII.

First of all, to punish the nobles for their continual attacks on the people it was requisite to make them guarantee their collective responsibility, since, in defiance of preceding laws, they frequently contrived to shirk that obligation. Most offences being punishable by fines, persons bound by no guarantees could easily evade the prescribed penalty on some pretext or another: therefore the enactments were framed to prevent such evasion of justice.[452] They likewise gave fresh force to old laws which had been too often violated. "Further, to prevent the numerous frauds daily committed by certain leading nobles of the city and territory of Florence with regard to the guarantees pledged, or rather, bound to be pledged by the said nobles according to the terms of the statute of the Florentine Commune, as decreed under the rubric: 'De la securtadi che si debbono fare da' grandi de la città di Firenze,' and beginning with the words: 'Acciò che la isfrenata spezialmente de' grandi,' &c.—it is provided and ordained," &c.[453]

Consequently, all the nobles already enumerated in the above-mentioned statute, and of whom a new list was then made, were ordered to give guaranty, from the age of fifteen years to seventy, without exception, by the payment of two thousand *lire*, a sum generally sufficient to cover the highest fines exacted, apart from confiscation, which penalty was not only commonly, but abusively employed. The fact of being enrolled in a guild did not suffice to exempt any of these nobles from the duty of giving guarantees; the privilege of exemption being solely granted to him whose entire family, for this or that reason, even by special indulgence, had been spared the duty of giving guarantees for five years at least, or declared absolutely free (*francata*). In either case the family was considered to be thoroughly of the people, and entitled to all the advantages deriving therefrom. The Signory was empowered to reduce the sum guaranteed (*il sodamento*) in the case of the poorer nobles, but it was precisely this clause that opened the door to partiality and fraud.[454] The law proceeded to state that the fixed time for giving guarantees was the month of January or February at the latest: any one refusing or delaying obedience, no matter in what way, would be banished, and his nearest kin in the male line compelled to give surety in his stead. The penalty of any crime committed by an unguaranteed person was to fall on that person's relations. But when the penalty was death, and the criminal had fled, his relations must pay three thousand *lire* instead of the guaranteed two thousand. But in case of mortal feud between the members of a family their obligation of giving surety for one another was cancelled. This plainly shows that when community of interests and passions had ceased to exist the law no longer insisted on the collective responsibility of kinsmen or associates. This assists our better comprehension of the real scope of the enactment.[455]

When, however, the members of associations acted in common, as one entity, the law framed for the purpose of dissolving those associations made the members reciprocally responsible, obliging them to guarantee and pay for one another. But no penalties save fines, and these only within certain limits, were exacted from relations and fellow associates, since an association was only fined as a collective body. This will explain what Compagni and Villani meant by saying that according to the enactments, "one associate was bound for the other."[456] We may see how Machiavelli blundered, or at least exaggerated, in his interpretation of their words when he stated in general terms that "the associates of a criminal were made to suffer the same penalty to which the latter was condemned;"[457] and we can also note the mistake committed by modern writers in clinging to an interpretation, that is totally contradicted by the terms of the enactments, which would be otherwise in opposition to the culture of the period and the most fundamental principles of law. The measures specially directed against the nobles may be reduced to two leading clauses, namely the revival in a more rigorous shape of the old laws excluding the nobles from office and obliging them to guarantee and pay one another's fines; and the increased severity of the punishments inflicted on them by—to use Villani's words—"a different mode of doubling ordinary penalties."[458] Let us now see what these penalties were in their aggravated form.

According to the enactments, should a noble murder or procure the murder of one of the people, both the noble and the doer of the deed are to be condemned to death by the Podestà, and their property destroyed and made confiscate.[459] Should they escape by flight, they are to be sentenced in contumacy, and their property confiscated. Nevertheless their guarantor will have to pay the sum for which he stood surety, but with right of reimbursement from the confiscated and demolished property of the fugitive criminal. All other nobles who, without being direct accomplices in the crime, have had any share in it, are sentenced to a fine of two thousand *lire*; if failing to pay this, their property is confiscated, and their kinsmen or guarantors bound to pay it in their stead. But when the crime in question was that of inflicting serious bodily hurt, the doer of the deed and its instigators were sentenced to a fine of two thousand *lire*. If refusing to pay the penalty, their hands were chopped off; if escaping the reach of justice, their possessions were sacked, their funds confiscated, and their guarantors bound to pay the fine, but with the usual right of reimbursement from the sums confiscated by the State. For slighter offences, slighter penalties were adjudged. In every case the guilty were forbidden to hold any public office until five years had elapsed. For murderous attempts, the sworn testimony of the injured person or his nearest relation, together with that of two witnesses to the public voice on the matter (*testimoni di pubblica fama*), was considered sufficient proof of the crime; nor was it necessary for the two witnesses to have seen the crime actually committed. This was the clause most obnoxious to the nobles. In general they were little disturbed by threatened punishment, even of the severest kind, since they always hoped to escape it. But they were roused to fury as well as alarm, when measures were taken for the rigorous enforcement of the penalties prescribed. And this was precisely the chief intent and soul of the enactments. The whole course of procedure enjoined by them was almost as summary as that of martial law, and allowed much weight to public opinion, which, in the midst of party strife, was no trustworthy guide. The close union prevailing in associations had made ordinary legal procedure very difficult, if not impossible. Hence it was ordained that whenever a crime was perpetrated, the Podestà was bound to discover its author within five, or at most eight days, according to the gravity of the deed, under pain, in case of neglect of loss of office and a fine of five hundred *lire* for minor offences. In such case, however, the Captain was charged to take the matter in hand, and subject to the same penalties. All shops were then to be closed, the artisans called to arms, and the Gonfalonier to be on the alert to punish all recusants. But when the Podestà discovered the criminal, and it was a case of homicide, he and the Gonfalonier together were to ring the tocsin without waiting for the sentence of the court, and assembling the thousand select men, proceed to demolish the houses belonging to the criminal. The guild-masters were prompt to obey the Captain's summons. When slighter offences were in question the criminal's houses were not destroyed until sentence had been passed.[460] It should be remarked that this pulling down of houses was never carried to the point of total demolition, and, particularly in cases of petty crimes, the Gonfalonier and Podestà always settled beforehand what damage should be wrought.[461]

Very severe penalties were imposed both on injured persons failing to denounce crime,[462] and on the makers of false accusations.[463] When one of the people received hurt through joining in some quarrel of the nobles, or in cases of conflict between master and man, the enactments were not applied, and the common law was again enforced.[464] Other clauses followed touching unjust appropriation of the people's property on the part of the nobles, and obstacles interposed by them to bar the former from due receipt of income, for which offences, fines varying between one thousand and five hundred *lire* were prescribed in the customary way.[465] A noble sentenced to any fine was forbidden to beg or collect the amount from others, since this would have made it easier to commit deeds of vengeance in common and pay the penalty by means of a general subscription. Therefore any noble begging contributions from others was condemned to a special fine of five hundred *lire*; while all trying to collect money for him, as well as those supplying it, were mulcted in one hundred *lire*.[466]

No appeal of any sort was permitted against sentences pronounced according to the enactments,[467] since these overruled all ordinary statutes, and it was forbidden either to prorogue, suspend, or alter them, under penalty of incurring the severe punishment prescribed in the *General Conclusion*.[468]

IX.

Thus the Enactments of Justice were framed. As already stated, their object was to fortify the guilds, give greater unity to the Government and the people, humble the nobles, and promote the dispersal of associations. Only it was to be doubted whether a law of this kind could be fully carried out, or would not rather be violated by the nobles, thus sharing the fate of many earlier laws promulgated for the same purpose. Giano della Bella used his best efforts to avert this danger. He had not compiled the enactments, nor was he in office when they were discussed and passed; but he undoubtedly assisted in promoting them. On the 15th of February, 1293, shortly after they were proclaimed, he was elected to the "Priors," and on the 10th of April— namely, ten days before his term of office expired—we find that a new law, devised for the purpose of "fortifying" the enactments among which it was subsequently incorporated, was presented, discussed, and passed by all the State Councils.

This additional law, one decidedly accordant with the spirit of action rather than of debate, possessed by Giano della Bella, was of a very simple kind. It ordained that another thousand men, together with one hundred and fifty *magistri de lapide et lignamine* and fifty *piconarii fortes et robusti, cum bonis picconibus*,[469] should be added to the force of one thousand *popolani* at the disposition of the Gonfalonier of Justice, of the Captain and Podestà. The object of this new measure was self-evident: it was intended to inflict real punishment; to thoroughly confiscate the property and demolish the abodes of all nobles doing injury to the people. Accordingly the aristocrats were provoked to fury, and their hatred of Giano could no longer be restrained. But he was nowise alarmed; on the contrary, it spurred him to new efforts, and he planned another measure, that, if carried into effect, would have proved a deathblow to the nobles.

As we have seen, the latter's position as magistrates of the Guelph Society still kept their power intact; so, in order to humble them, Giano proposed to deprive their captains "of the Seal of the Society, and of its property, which was considerable, and hand these over to the Commune. Although a Guelph, and of Guelph nationality, he hoped, by this measure, to humble the power of the magnates."[470] In fact, once deprived of the seal, that was the symbol, as it were, of their separate entity; once their movable property, or funds, transferred to the Commune, their caste would have been notably enfeebled, if not destroyed, and the last stronghold of nobility lost. Giano's proposal was likewise justified by a law established by the Guelph Society, decreeing the latter to be only entitled to one-third of the property confiscated from the Ghibellines, while as matter of fact it had appropriated the whole. Hence there was some reason for compelling the Society to disgorge at least the two-thirds it had unduly usurped. To what extent Giano's plan was fulfilled, the absence of documents leaves us in ignorance. Although the incident is recorded by historians,[471] the Guelph Society long continued to exercise tyrannous rule. At any rate the mere fact of proposing this law suffices to explain the increasing hatred developed against Giano, and the speedily visible signs of approaching disaster in the city.

X.

Thereupon the people rose to the emergency, and in order to be prepared for events, hastened to avert all risk of foreign war by concluding peace with the Pisans, in spite of the latter being already reduced to such extremities, that the continuation of the war would have certainly led to their still deeper humiliation and abasement. But the Florentines decided for peace in order to "fortify the position of the people, and lower the power of nobles and potentates, who often acquire renewed strength and vitality by war."[472]

Negotiations were set on foot during the Gonfaloniership of Migliore Guadagni (April 15 to June 15, 1293), and concluded soon afterwards during that of Dino Compagni. The terms arranged were: the restitution of prisoners; free passage through Pisa for the merchandise of all communes included in the Tuscan League, and the same right of passage, free of duty, for Pisan merchandise through the States of the League. For the term of four years the Pisans were to contrive the election of their Podestà and Captain, in such wise that one of the pair should always belong to one of the communes of the League, the other to some house not rebelled against the same, and no member of the family of the Counts of Montefeltro was ever to be chosen. Now the Pisan leader who had defended the city so valiantly, and filled the offices of Podestà, Captain of the people and of war, was precisely Count Guido Montefeltro. Hence, by the terms of the treaty, he was now forced to leave Pisa, together with all the foreign Ghibellines; and twenty-five leading citizens were also to be given in hostage. Thus the Pisans were compelled to behave with the harshest ingratitude. The count, indeed, might have made them pay dearly for it, being still in command of a numerous and most devoted army; but he preferred to bear the insult with dignity. Appearing before the Council, he recounted his services to Pisa, the ill return made for them, and then, having received the monies due to him, instantly went away. The Pisans were likewise pledged to dismantle the walls of the fortress of Pontedera, and to fill up the trenches; farther, to recall to the city all the leading Guelph exiles. On the other hand, Florence was to give back their castle of Monte-Cuccoli, and all their other possessions in Vald'Era.[473]

Having thus put an end to what seemed for the moment their wealthiest concern, the Florentines devoted more energy to the less important undertakings on hand. Various districts or castles, such as Poggibonsi, Certaldo, Gambassi, and Cutignano were reduced to submission. The Counts Guidi were deprived of jurisdiction over numerous domains in the upper valley of the Arno. Also possession was resumed of many others in the Mugello, which had been illegally usurped by the said Counts Guidi, the Ubaldini, and other powerful lords. A commission of three burghers of the lower class was then appointed to estimate all possessions appertaining to the city and its territory. These commissioners likewise cleared the lands of the St. Eustachio Hospital, near Florence, of many unlawful occupants, and put the estate under the direct protection of the Consuls of the Calimala Guild.[474] Another fact should also be noted, if only to prove what universal energy was displayed at this juncture by the Florentine people who, as Villani phrases it, "were heated with presumption and consciousness of power." A certain man fled to Prato after committing some crime, and was given refuge there. The Republic immediately demanded his extradition, and on Prato's refusal, sentenced the Commune to a fine of ten thousand *lire* and the surrender of the criminal, despatching a single messenger with a letter to this effect. As the authorities of Prato were still recalcitrant, war was promptly declared, horse and foot called to arms, and the town was finally compelled to yield the point.

"And this is how the hot-blooded Florentines managed their affairs."[475]

XI.

Just when all was safe and tranquil outside the walls, the worst of dangers began in the city. The nobles were determined to prevent the Enactments of Justice from taking effect, and accordingly contrived that after all attacks upon the people, the offenders should be cited before judges belonging to their own party. These conducted the trial to their advantage, and thus the Podestà, without being aware of it, punished the innocent instead of the guilty. For the nobles sheltered evildoers, protected their fellow associates, and on every attempt to enforce the law, did their best to raise riots. All these proceedings were fiercely combated by the people, under the guidance of Giano della Bella, who was always reiterating the cry, "Perish the city rather than justice!" Accordingly public feeling became so inflamed that the most sanguinary measures were threatened in retaliation on the nobles. The first family to incur the worst penalties decreed by the enactments were the Galli. One of that line having mortally wounded a Florentine merchant in France, their dwellings in Florence were demolished.[476] This instance easily prepared the way for sterner measures. The people clamoured for new and more vigorous sentences; therefore it was feared, says Compagni, "that were the accused left unpunished, the rector would be left to bear the brunt, and thus no accused person was granted impunity." The fury of the nobles reached its climax, and they complained, with some show of reason, that "if a horse at full gallop chanced to whisk its tail in the face of a *popolano*, or some one in a crowd pushed against another man's breast, or small children came to blows, there was no reason why their property should be ruined on such slender pretext."[477]

Accordingly they conceived the idea of conspiring to the bodily hurt of Giano, the ringleader and head of the people, and thus getting rid of him for ever. To compass his assassination seemed easy, by reason of his straightforward impetuosity and incautiousness. He had great influence over the populace, but even this was a point open to attack. As we have seen, the Lesser Guilds and the populace lived by petty industry and small trades carried on within the city; and their chief profits being derived from noble customers, the latter had much ascendancy over them and no few adherents in their ranks. Besides this, a certain amount of jealousy had already sprung up between the lowest class and the well-to-do burghers, who, being mainly

317

concerned in the export and import trade,[478] were independent of the nobles, hated them, and sought their destruction. Nevertheless these burghers could not approve of Giano's attempts to rouse the ambition and increase the strength of the lowest class, which was disgusted at being excluded from the Government and yearning to have a share in it.

Another element of strife was soon to be introduced by the election of Pope Boniface VIII. (December, 1294). This Pontiff had an immoderate appetite for temporal power, and believed that owing to the interregnum of the Empire, its rights could now be assumed by the Papacy throughout Italy and Europe. He was particularly anxious to increase his power in Florence, the leading city of Tuscany, where his own predecessors had appointed Charles of Anjou to the post of imperial vicar. Therefore he quickly began to open negotiations with the nobles, whose present weakness increased their readiness to come to terms with him, and who would have willingly resumed the government of the city in his name, just as their Ghibelline ancestors had often held it in the name of the emperor. But this was naturally opposed by the burghers, who being determined, on the contrary, to maintain the liberty and independence of the Republic, could not, albeit staunch Guelphs, side with the Pope at that moment.

Secret intrigues between Boniface and the nobles were now carried on through the Spini, rich Florentine merchants, who, as bankers to the Curia, had agents in Rome. The first step hazarded was to call to Tuscany a certain Giovanni di Celona,[479] who was already on the march towards Italy with several hundred men, in response to a summons from the Pope and the nobles. The latter, intending to use his force for their own ends, had made him many promises, and with the concurrence, it would seem, of certain of the burghers. But the affair dragged, and men's passions were now outstripping the political manœuvres employed to feed the flame. Accordingly, without further delay, it was decided to hatch a scheme for the murder of Giano della Bella. "The shepherd struck down, his flock will be scattered," so said the nobles.

Only, as it fell out, the party in favour of craft prevailed over the side preferring violence. At this moment frequent excesses, perpetrated by the people, remained unpunished through the pusillanimity of the judges. The butchers in particular, led by one Pecora, an audacious ruffian, who had publicly threatened the Signory, committed worse outrages from day to day. Hence, at the popular meetings frequently held by Giano, the nobles, knowing his love of justice, would whet his indignation by saying, "Dost not see the violence of the butchers? Dost not see the insolence of the judges, who, by threatening to punish the rectors when the time of investigation arrives,[480] wrest unjust favours from them? Suits are suspended for three or four years, and sentences never pronounced." Thereupon the loyal Giano would promptly reply, "May the city perish, rather than this state of things be continued! Let laws be framed to repress all this wickedness." And then the nobles would maliciously hasten to inform judges and butchers that Giano meant to crush them with new laws.[481] In pursuance of this cunning scheme, they suggested a law against exiles, in the hope of soon being able to apply it to Giano himself. It seems that he was on the point of falling into the trap, but received timely warning. So then, refusing to hear another word, either from friends or foes, he forbade that any law whatever should be proposed, and threatened his enemies with death. Accordingly the meeting only served to increase the general heat and ferment.[482]

The nobles were not to be checked so easily. Seeing that Giano still retained many friends, and that there was no hope of conquering by craft, they held a private sitting in the church of San Jacopo Oltrarno, to discuss what should be done; and violent measures were once more suggested. Giano's personal enemy, Betto Frescobaldi, the same who had once struck him in the face at San Piero Scheraggio, spoke to this effect: "Let us cast off this slavery; let us arm and rush to the Piazza; let us kill both friends and enemies of the popular class, as many as we find of them, so that neither ourselves nor our sons may ever be crushed by them." But the promoters of intrigue were again in opposition, and Baldo della Tosa replied very quietly, "The wise knight's counsel is good, but too risky, since, should the scheme fail, we should all perish. First let us conquer (our enemies) by cunning, and excommunicate them with soft words…. And when thus excommunicated, let us harry them in such sort that they can never lift their heads again."[483]

But quite suddenly a fitting opportunity for violence spontaneously arose. Corso Donati, one of the most powerful and arrogant of Florentines, induced some of his followers to assault Messer Simone Galastroni, and a riot ensued in which one man was killed and two wounded. Both sides laid complaints; but when the affair was brought before the judges charged to try the case, one of them, influenced by the usual party spirit, arranged that the notary should reverse the depositions of the witnesses. When the case, thus garbled, was brought before the Podestà, Giano di Lucino, he acquitted Donati, and condemned Galastroni. Thereupon the people who had witnessed the riot, and knew all the circumstances, rose to arms, shouting through the streets: "Perish the Podestà; he shall perish by fire!" They made for the palace, faggots in hand, to burn down the door, and expecting to be actively assisted by Giano della Bella. But, on the contrary, he sided with the magistrates, whose authority he invariably held in respect. Nevertheless, the door of the Podestà's palace was consumed, his horses and chattels were stolen, his men captured, and his papers scattered and torn. And as many persons knew him to possess indictments against them, they took care to destroy his official documents. He and his wife contrived to escape to an adjoining house, and obtained refuge there. Corso Donati, who was in the palace at the time, saved his life by flying from roof to roof.

The Councils assembled the next day, and for the honour of the Republic decided to restore all the Podestà's stolen property to pay him his salary and send him away. Thus order was re-established at once, but public feeling was still very inflamed, and the nobles saw that the moment for wreaking vengeance on Giano had finally arrived. In fact, some of the people were his foes, owing to the numerous calumnies purposely launched against him, and among others the charge of having promoted decrees to the hurt of the judges and butchers; some, again, were furious because he had sided with the Podestà, while others denounced him as the author of the riot. Accordingly, profiting by the general confusion and uncertainty, his enemies succeeded in obtaining the premature election of a Signory opposed to his views; and he was speedily cited before the new magistrates on the charge of having caused the disturbance. At this the whole city rose in tumult. Some desired his condemnation; but the populace hastened to assume his defence. Thereupon he decided to go away, and left Florence on the 5th of March, 1295, for he shrank from being the cause of civil strife, hoped that his departure would open the eyes of the wiser citizens, and that the latter would speedily procure his recall. However, in this his calculations were at fault, for he had many more enemies than he imagined. Accordingly he was sentenced in contumacy in the name of the enactments he had urged, and of which he was held to be the author. The Pope hastened to congratulate the Florentines, and Giano realised that his star had set. So, acting with his usual impetuosity, he unhesitatingly removed to France, where he possessed some share in the Pazzi bank, and died there in exile. His Florentine houses were demolished, his friends and relations condemned to punishment, but the Enactments of Justice long remained in force.[484] With regard to Giano, Villani remarks that "every one who became a leader of the people or the masses in Florence was invariably deserted." He adds that "on account of this novelty, there was great perturbation and change in the people and city of Florence, and that henceforth the artisans and populace had little power over the Commune; and that the government remained in the grasp of rich and powerful burghers."[485]

SCENE IN CORN MARKET, FLORENCE.

(From early XIV. Century MS. in the Laurentian Library.)

[*To face page 475*

XII.

These concluding words from the chronicle of a skilled observer such as Villani enable us to understand more completely the general character of the revolution described; for as this was the natural outcome of many preceding disturbances, its study throws a new light on earlier events.

When the Florentines succeeded in destroying the castles of feudal and Ghibelline nobles scattered over their territory, and in forcing the conquered to inhabit the city, the Republic became split, as we have seen, in two parties, constantly at strife: the one composed of Ghibelline lords, the other of Guelph *popolani*. When the Hohenstauffens of Naples and Palermo called all the Ghibellines of Italy to arms, the magnates of the party took the lead in Tuscany, with Frederic and Manfred to back them, again dominated Florence and drove out the Guelphs. But when the Swabians fell and were replaced by the House of Anjou, the Empire became weakened, and Italian policy took a new turn. The Guelphs once more triumphed in Florence, and the democratic element, already constituting the real strength of the State, wreaked vengeance on the Ghibellines, who seemed to be almost annihilated. Only as it chanced, at this moment, the Guelphs were split into two factions, the nobles on one side, the people on the other; and this division led to another and equally bitter struggle, undertaken for the purpose of crushing the magnates outright. Thus the latter were driven to crave admission to the guilds, to assume democratic habits, and even to discard their old family names, unless resigned to exclusion from the government. After a prolonged series of different legal measures and revolutions, the Enactments of Justice finally achieved the aim that the Florentine Republic had so long—and, indeed, from its birth—kept in view, namely, the triumph of democracy.

RIOT IN CORN MARKET, FLORENCE.

(From an old MS. in the Laurentian Library.)

[*To face page 476*

But the Republic comprised the populace as well as the people; and although both orders were united in fighting the nobles, they split apart as soon as their common victory was assured. Thus the party of the rich burghers, or Greater Guilds, gradually sprang into being. At first there were twelve of these guilds, and they seemed to be at one with the nine Lesser Trades, afterwards increased to fourteen; but, as time went on, these fell more widely apart from the remaining seven, and strictly Greater, Guilds, and began to struggle against them, thus constituting the party of the rich burghers or *popolo grasso*. The formation and successful career of this party, so long at the head of the Government, dates, as Villani tells us, from the defeat of Giano della Bella, whose downfall was caused by the temporary alliance of the nobles and the more powerful section of the people. The latter soon divided both from the nobles and lower class, was equally victorious over either party, and constituted one of the most energetic, sharp-witted, and intelligent democracies of which history has record. It comprised the richest and most vigorous section of the people, known for that reason as the *popolo grasso*, and gradually became master of the city. And albeit this state of things was a natural result of past revolutions, it was undoubtedly precipitated by the Enactments of Justice. These had been promoted by Giano, with the aid of the people, to be used as a weapon against the nobles. He fell a victim to the latter, when they hoodwinked the people by feigning to unite with them for the nonce. It was certainly altogether against his own will that Giano helped to promote the formation of a party, that, issuing from the wreck of the nobles and populace, finally excluded both alike from all participation in the government of Florence.

For a long time, at any rate, this party raised the power of the Republic to a very lofty height, and directed its policy for more than a century. The moment of its consolidation coincided with that in which Florence became the seat of Italian culture, and hence of the general culture of Europe. Nor is there any cause to be surprised by the vast intellectual, political, and moral success of the commercial democracy of Florence. In the days of the Hohenstauffen, the Italian aristocracy undoubtedly constituted the most cultivated and civilised part of the nation; all great political questions, and the great struggles between the Papacy and the Empire, in which the whole of Europe took so lively a share, were alike carried on by that class. The Court of Frederic II. had been the headquarters of those contests, and the most dazzling centre of mental light in the world at the time. The language spoken there was the language of courtiers; the Court was sceptical, and the first poets were princes or barons. The Emperor Frederic, his son Enzo, and his secretary, Pier della Vigna, gave voice to the first notes of the Italian muse. It was a privileged and limited order, in which literature and science still retained the characteristics of chivalry and scholasticism. In imitation of their French and Provençal masters, these poets lauded some imaginary woman or some fantastic and unreal love in obstinately artificial verse. They were never able to cast off mediæval and conventional forms. At the same time, however, the merchants and working men of our republics, more especially of Florence, were scouring the world, founding banks and business firms throughout the East and the West; they were studying jurisprudence, always and everywhere demonstrating a special aptitude for framing laws, creating new institutions, and directing vast concerns. By this means they acquired that practical knowledge of mankind and the universe, that sense of truth and reality, so entirely absent from pre-existent literatures, and precisely required to originate the first literature of the modern world.

Naturally, however, those merchants, solely versed in commerce and petty local politics, lacked the breadth and loftiness of thought, the mental culture and refinement needed to solve the hard problem without help. At the same moment, Florence, the most active and intelligent of Italian republics, was enduring the series of great and radical changes, already described, which after much sanguinary strife and a new rearrangement of social conditions, suddenly raised her to a truly fortunate position. Owing to her successes in war, Florence now commanded every highway of commerce, and, by the amazingly rapid extension of her trade, was enabled to acquire mighty and no longer contested preponderance in Tuscany and become its chief as well as its central city. The actual antagonism between the Pope and the Angevins, together with the altered conditions of the Empire, enabled her to steer cautiously between those rival powers and assume for the first time great and genuine political importance in Italy. Thus the extent of her concerns and the circle of her ideas were simultaneously enlarged. The two most intelligent and most hostile classes of her citizens, namely, the now powerful traders and the nobles now reduced to equality with them, became transformed and definitely fused in one class during the course of their fierce conflict, excluding, on the one hand, the lowest order of the people, and on the other, those of the nobles who, whether aspiring to absolute rule or obstinately clinging to feudal customs and the authority of the Empire, remained blindly opposed to municipal institutions which were nevertheless predestined to triumph. Need we then feel surprised if at this moment art and literature put forth their fairest blossoms, and in the life-giving air of freedom were seen to expand their leaves and shed their fragrance through the world? It is enough to read the records and glance at the laws of the Republic in order to discern that in the closing years of the fourteenth century a new spirit was stirring the people and a new sun, as it were, rising in the sky.

Every page of the chronicles records the undertaking of very important public works, the erection of city squares, canals, bridges, and walls. And simultaneously with these, the most enduring monuments of modern art were springing up from the ground. During the same period Arnolfo di Cambio worked on the Baptistery, began the church of Santa Croce, and, according to the chroniclers, received from the Signory a solemnly worded order to reconstruct the old cathedral from the foundations by erecting a new one "of the most magnificent design the mind of man could conceive, rendering it worthy of a heart expanded to much greatness by the union of many spirits in one."[486] Undoubtedly it was then that Arnolfo laid the first stone of the fane considered by many the finest church in the world. At the same time a great number of monumental buildings and public works were being also carried on: Santo Spirito, for instance, Orsammichele, and Santa Maria Novella. In 1299 Arnolfo likewise began the Palace of the Signoria, another marvel of modern architecture, that seems to be so thoroughly in character with the Republic and expressive of the youthful vigour then animating the Florentine people. In the same year the construction of new walls, suspended since 1285, was also resumed. And while churches, public buildings, and private palaces were rising on all sides, Giotto's brush was employed to cover their walls with a lavish profusion of lofty and immortal compositions; sculpture rivalled painting in decorating temples with imperishable works, and gave birth to the Tuscan school that was afterwards to culminate in Donatello, Ghiberti, the Della Robbia, and Michelangelo. What, too, are the names most frequently occurring in the records of those times, and amid the struggles promoting or following the Enactments of Justice? At every turn, among the Priors, the Gonfaloniers, and ambassadors, or at hot debates in council, we meet with Dante Alighieri, Brunetto Latini, Giovanni Villani, Dino Compagni, and Guido Cavalcanti, the creators of Italian poetry and prose. The Divine Comedy bristles with continual allusions to the events, amid which it was conceived, and which all seem to be informed by the same spirit, since, even in a thousand varying garbs, it always asserts its identity. Therefore the Enactments of Justice are neither the work of a single individual, nor suddenly improvised by Giano della Bella, but rather the outcome of many revolutions: a body of statutes proving and explaining the definite form and character of the Florentine Republic. The same character, albeit less splendidly displayed, appertained in varying degree to the other Italian communes. But of them all Florence was ever the most original and brilliant example.

NOTE TO CHAPTER VIII.

At this point it is necessary to allude to a question that has recently arisen concerning the Enactments of Justice. Signor Salvioli and Prof. Pertile, when describing certain Bolognese statutes of 1271 for keeping the nobles in check, took it for granted that the Florentine enactments of 1293 had been copied from those. But the Bolognese statutes of 1271 having never been unearthed, the hypothesis met with little favour. When Prof. Gaudenzi edited the "Ordinamenta sacrata et sacratissima" of Bologna in 1282–84 (Bologna, the Merlani Press, 1888), he noted their marked resemblance to the Enactments of Justice of 1293, and considered it to be beyond a doubt that the latter had been derived from the former. Indeed, he went to the point of asserting as a fact "Che in genere i rivolgimenti e gli ordini di Firenze non furono che l'imitazione di quelli di Bologna" (Preface, p. v.).

The decided injustice of this last assertion has been already pointed out by Dr. Hartwig, in his recent precious work on Florentine history ("Ein Menschenalter Florentinische Geschichte, 1250–1293" (Freiburg, 1889–91), extracted from vols. i., ii., and v. of the "Deutsche Zeitschrift für Geschichtwissenschaft"). For in truth Florentine laws and institutions issue very directly from the history of Florentine society and Florentine revolutions, which are very different from those of Bologna.

As to the other question, that is, whether the Florentine enactments, of 1293 were really derived from the Bologna statutes of 1282, I feel considerable doubt, and believe that no definite solution can be reached until fresh researches in the Florence Archives have corroborated the result of Prof. Gaudenzi's studies of Bolognese documents. Meanwhile I need merely remark—That the people's struggles with the magnates, and the harsh and often cruel laws promulgated against them, were not exclusively confined to Florence, but incidents of very common occurrence in the history of our communes. Notwithstanding many points of general resemblance, these conflicts and laws varied very much in different communes. Hence, in order to prove to what extent the Bolognese enactments served as models for those of Florence, it is not enough to compare the two codes and note their respective dates. As plainly proved by the events we have related, and additionally confirmed by all the later researches of Hartwig, Del Lungo, and Perrens, the Florentine ordinances are found to be a synthesis of other and much earlier laws against the nobles, and sometimes literal reproductions of them. The enactments themselves quote a law of 1286 frequently mentioned by historians, and, as we have seen, even the "Consulte" of 1282 refer to an earlier law against the nobles. These anterior laws are the veritable source of the Florentine enactments, which, however, are not solely designed, like the Bolognese ordinances, for the repression of the nobles, but to promote the transfer of the government to the Greater Guilds, a change already inaugurated in Florence as far back as 1250. It is this double purpose that constitutes their specific character. It behoves us to unearth more of these laws in the Florence Archives and collate them with those of Bologna before deciding that the Enactments of Justice, so peculiarly connected with the whole course of Florentine history, were mere copies of the Bolognese ordinances. Professor Gaudenzi's publications do honour to his historical research. But I venture to repeat that, in my opinion, the question cannot be really settled without fresh investigation of the Florentine rolls. This task is now being carried on by Signor Salvemini, and I hope that he may make some new and profitable discovery. The problem is interesting enough to claim solution.

DOCUMENTO.[487]

V.

In nomine domini amen. Liber defensionum et excusationum Magnatum Civitatis et comitatus Florentie, qui se excusare volunt a satisdationibus Magnatum non prestandis, receptarum per me Bax. de Amgnetello notarium nobilis Militis domini Amtonii de Fuxiraga de Laude, potestatis Florentie.

In anno currente Millesimo ducentesimo ottuagesimo septimo.

Ad defensionem

Absoluti $\left\{\begin{array}{l}\text{Dardoccii quondam domini Uguicionis}\\\text{Manni fratris sui}\end{array}\right.$ $\left.\begin{array}{l}\text{de Sachettis}\\\text{producta fuit}\end{array}\right\}$

intentio singnata per Credo (*sic*), et ad ipsam probandam producti fuerunt infradicti testes.

Baldus Brode populi sancti Stephani de Abatia, iuratus die suprascripta de veritate dicenda, et lecta sibi intentione per me Bax., dixit quod bene vidit dictum Dardocium et Mannum eius fratrem facere artem cambii in Civitate Florentie, iam sunt xx anni, et ab eo tempore citra, et credit eos fecisse. Set propter guerram et brigam quam nunc habent, predicti fratres Dardocci non tenent tabulam in mercato, set stat in doma sua, et ibi facet (*sic*) artem canbii. Interrogatus si ipsi palam tenent banchum et tapetum ante dischum domus sue sicut faciunt alii campsores, respondit non, quia est consuetudo prestatorum et non campsorum tenere tapetum. Interrogatus, dixit quod predictus senper cotidie exercuit.

Lapus Benvenuti qui vocatur Borrectus populi sancti Petri Maioris iuratus die suprascripto (?) ut supra, lecta sibi intentione per Be., dixit quod ipse testis est consocius predictorum Dardoccii et fratris in arte canbii; et vidit dictum Dardoccium et fratrem dictam artem in civitate Florentie continue [exercere], et predictum Mannum vidit in Borgongna facere dictam artem per decem annos et plus, quibus stetit in Borgongna; set dixit quod predictus Dardocius[488] propter guerram quam ad presens habet, non audet uti ipsa arte in mercato sive in pubblico, set ea continue utitur in domo sua, et vidit ipse testis; et vox et fama est in populo dictorum fratrum et in civitate Florentie, quod ipsi fratres fuerunt et sunt campsores.

L. S. Ego Ruffus Guidi notarius predicta ex actibus Communis Florentie exemplando transcripsi, pubblicavi rogatus.

CHAPTER IX.[489]

THE FLORENTINE REPUBLIC IN DANTE'S TIME.

I.

AFTER the enforcement of the Enactments of Justice (1293) and the expulsion of Giano della Bella, the Florentine Republic passed through a phase of extraordinary and almost delirious confusion. Its incidents are very familiar to us, owing to the splendid series of chroniclers and historians who, from that moment, began to record the minutest particulars of all that occurred under their eyes. Modern writers have also studied that period and ransacked its archives; more especially Professor Del Lungo, who has recently given proofs of an industry and learning which cannot be sufficiently praised. Nevertheless, I believe that some useful work may be done by trying to bring all those facts together and scrutinising their organic unity, in order to ascertain whence they proceeded, whither they tended, and thus explain, if possible, the primary cause of so much disorder and the real significance of the new revolutions undertaken. I may also add that such investigation might prove to have much historical importance, since it concerns the time in which not only a new art, new literature, and new civilisation first sprang into being, but when the old mediæval social order was decaying and fading away, and the society of the Renaissance beginning to take shape.

In the midst of these events the figure of Dante Alighieri stands forth in giant mould, instantaneously arousing the most earnest attention, and enhancing the value of all his surroundings.

As we have frequently observed and repeated, the history of Florence runs a very plain course down to the year 1293, through the series of wars and revolutions, during which the Guelph inhabitants of the city first attacked the Ghibelline feudal lords, who, castled on every surrounding hill, impeded all trade; and then, having conquered them, demolished their strongholds, and forced them to dwell inside the city walls, subject to the laws of the Commune. Next, the people were compelled to combat and break down the surviving feudal element that sought to assert itself in the city. Before the year 1293 this too had been destroyed, and only the *Grandi* were left, namely, nobles stripped of their titles and of the old feudal privileges of their class. The Enactments of Justice, which dissolved their associations and excluded them from all share in the government, had increased, on the other hand, the strength of the guilds and the people. These accordingly were the masters of Florence, and the new law supplied them with a most efficacious means of continuing the persecution and routing the nobles in the tribunals of the State. The terms Guelph and Ghibelline were still retained, but had lost their original meaning. The old aristocracy, constituting the real nucleus of the Ghibelline party, having now disappeared, the city was wholly Guelph. The general condition of Italy also fostered this state of things. In fact, owing to the fall of the Hohenstauffens and the success of the Angevins, summoned to Italy by the Pope, the Guelph party had triumphed throughout the Peninsula. The murder of Conradin (1298) had proved the death knell of the Ghibellines.

The triumph of France was more and more assured, and during the interregnum of the Empire Philip the Beautiful played almost the part of an emperor. At the same time Boniface VIII. loudly declared that the Pope stood above all kings and princes of the earth, and that all were bound to yield him submission.

But division still reigned in Florence. First of all, germs of future discord were lurking in the bosom of the people itself, owing to its subdivision into rich people (*popolo grasso*), or the Greater Guilds, and small people (*popolo minuto*), or Lesser Guilds, having the populace at their back. The Greater Guilds, at the head of the principal manufacturing business and the vast export and import trade, were always ready to undertake fresh wars, which, by burdening the city with taxes, greatly diminished the internal luxury upon which the Lesser Guilds, engaged in small crafts, depended for their daily support. It needed little to convert this clash of material interests into a political conflict, especially when we remember that the Greater Guilds had taken possession of the government without allowing the Smaller Crafts any share in it. For the moment, however, the lower class, although so turbulent and numerically strong, lacked cohesion and experience, and had no leading men at its head. But although without real elements of political strength, and still incapable of forming a party, it was excellently suited to swell the ranks of already constituted parties having the wit to use its aid in their progress to power.

The nobles, on the other hand, although defeated, persecuted, and oppressed, were by no means stamped out, and still retained some measure of influence and skill. The expulsion of Giano della Bella was an instance in point; for, by contriving to make the people believe him its foe, they induced it to desert him and then provoked the mob to attack him. Although deprived of legal authority, the nobles were still practically strong. Always boasting of their victory of Campaldino, they had undoubtedly played a prominent part in all the greater wars of the Republic in past times, and even now made far better soldiers than the popular class. As the wealthy proprietors of town and country mansions, castles, and farms, they were undistracted by commercial cares, and had more leisure for military pursuits; while the material independence they enjoyed made them all the more sensitive to the sting of political ambition. It was natural that they should seek and obtain the co-operation of the populace in their contest with the burghers. Thus, in junction with the former, they constituted a vast and dangerous body of agitators, but without organic cohesion, and all equally ineligible to office, inasmuch as the nobles had been excluded from power in 1293, and the populace had never been allowed any share of it.

II.

At this time the world began to perceive what results the subtle craft of the Florentines was capable of achieving. The art of secretly becoming masters of the State, that, at a later period, gave Cosimo and Lorenzo dei Medici such triumphant supremacy in the Republic, enabling them to hold sovereign rule while remaining private citizens in the eyes of the law, this art was now discovered by the nobles. It consisted in leaving republican institutions untouched, and showing no desire to be concerned in them, yet contriving that none save personal adherents should be admitted to power. The offices of the Guelph Society afforded an efficacious means to this end, for, as we know, the nobles were eligible to those offices, and when holding them could declare any citizen a Ghibelline, confiscate his property, and exclude him from the government at their own pleasure. Thus, without being members of the Signory, they had found a more or less legal method of preventing their worst enemies from entering it. Giano della Bella was fully awake to this danger, and had tried to avert it; but the nobles had frustrated his purpose by compassing his expulsion from the city.

As another useful means of regaining their forfeited power, the nobles managed to obtain the right of choosing the magistrates, in order to exercise a personal influence over them. Many of the magistrates were foreigners who came provided with foreign notaries, chancellors, and subordinate judges, while certain others, as, for instance, the Podestà and the Captain of the People, were necessarily bound to be knights—that is to say, nobles. They gave judgment in political as well as civil and criminal cases. In fact, it was the function of the Podestà and Captain, in junction with the Gonfalonier, to enforce the enactments; and besides this, political and common law were so intermixed at the time, that it was impossible to separate the one from the other. Originally, as we have already seen, the Podestà was the virtual head of the Commune. He commanded the army, signed treaties of peace; and even as ancient historians recorded Roman events in the name of the Consuls in office, so the Florentine chroniclers registered the events of their city under the name of its Podestà and even occasionally of its Consuls. But towards the close of the thirteenth century things were changed. With the destroyal of feudalism, the development of civil equality and increased recognition of Roman law, the political importance of those offices was lessened. The Podestà and Captains of the People were gradually lowered to the status of ordinary high judges. Hence both they and their subordinates steadily declined in authority and strength; and being worse paid and less feared, became more open to bribery, and more easily subjected to the influence of the nobles. Many of these officers came from Romagna, and the Marches, and the greater number from Gubbio. Reared under tyrannical governments and trained to Roman law in the school of Bologna, they had no previous knowledge of the real significance of party conflicts in Florence, and seldom succeeded in acquiring it; hence they also failed to discern the true meaning of laws such as the Enactments of Justice, which were mainly political laws. All this contributed to render them easily and blindly subservient to those desiring to use them as tools. In fact, the whole literature of the period teems with fierce invectives against "the wicked, accursed, and perverted judges bringing ruin upon cities."[490]

Thus by favour of the lower class and the mob, by the unjust verdicts of the Captains of the Guelph Society and the corruption of alien judges, the nobles endeavoured to regain their lost ground and again seize possession of the government. Nor was it an altogether impossible plan, seeing that at this moment (as will be presently shown) they received powerful foreign aid. But unity was indispensably required, and no unity was to be secured among a party composed of not only different, but heterogeneous elements. Accordingly it was already easy to foresee that, sooner or later, the fiercest discord must inevitably break out in their midst.

Dino Compagni remarks in his Chronicle, that "the powerful citizens were not all nobles by birth, but were sometimes styled *Grandi* for other reasons."[491] The *Grandi*, in fact, were composed of ancient aristocratic families, despoiled of feudal privileges and titles; of old-established burghers raised to a higher position on the score of their wealth and of those proclaimed *Grandi* by the people for the sole purpose of subjecting them to the penalty of exclusion from power. Naturally the old aristocracy were full of distrust and contempt for new-comers, who often continued (if not personally, by means of their kinsmen) to carry on trades and manufactures, and thus maintain their relations with the rich burghers opposed to the lower classes, whereas the latter were more in sympathy with the really influential and aristocratic section of the *Grandi*. Nor was this all. The latter party likewise comprised country nobles, such as the Ubertini, the Pazzi of Valdarno, and more particularly the Ubaldini owning nearly the whole of the Mugello and dominating it with their fortified castles. The fortress of Montaccenico, one of their main strongholds, guarded by a triple circuit of walls, had been founded by the Cardinal Ottavio degli Ubaldini, who has a place in Dante's "Inferno," and who once said, "If I ever had a soul, I have lost it, for the sake of the Ghibelline cause." All these territorial lords clung to their feudal traditions with far greater tenacity than the rest, and being very hostile to the people, were equally opposed to the Republic, which was always at strife with them. When residing in the city they were undoubtedly compelled, like the others, to obey the common laws; but in their own castles they and their kindred still asserted the rights of feudal barons.

In order to sap the strength of the Pazzi and Ubertini, the Florentines, in 1296, established the two colonies of San Giovanni and Castelfranco between Figline and Montevarchi in the Upper Valdarno. All adherents of the nobles willing to settle on these domains were freed from vassalage and exempted from taxation for ten years.[492] But measures of this kind would have been useless against the Ubaldini, and prolonged and sanguinary hostilities had to be engaged with them. By logical rule these territorial lords should have been Ghibellines and imperialists; but the Empire was now distant and feeble, France and the Pope were menacing close at hand. Accordingly they rather tended to combine with the Guelph nobles of Florence, and more particularly with those of ancient descent, thus forming a new element in that curious agglomeration of diverse forces. Also, seeing that private jealousies and hates are always readier to burst into flame when unrestrained by the organic unity and common interest of a well-organised party, it will be easy to understand what confusion and disorder prevailed.

III.

Notwithstanding the powerful support of one kind or another furnished to the nobles from abroad, and in spite of their really menacing attitude, there remained one inexorable truth that must be always kept in view, since it affords the best explanation of the phase of Florentine history. It consisted in the fact that the aristocratic faction, doomed to decay and dissolution, was confronted by the young and vigorous party united in the Greater Guilds, bound by common interests, and constituting the real motive power and future of the Commune. The history of those times is nothing more, in short, than the history of the process by which the Greater Guilds succeeded in becoming the very core of the Republic, in spite of the numerous obstacles in their path, and likewise succeeded in eliminating all hostile or alien elements. For some time past these guilds, and especially the first five, on which all the others were more or less dependent,[493] had been prospering to an extraordinary degree. And when their position was farther strengthened by the Enactments of Justice, their statutes, with the amendments then introduced, very clearly showed that in augmenting their own wealth they purposed not only to enrich the Republic, but also to heighten its power. Before long the five leading guilds jointly constituted an *Universitas Mercatorum* that rose to the authority of a regular commercial tribunal in 1308, and issued a definite set of statutes in 1312. Indeed all this may be considered the main part of the reforms promoted by Giano della Bella,[494] and the point on which, favoured by the conditions of the period, he was most successful. We have the best proof of this in the fact that incessant party strife notwithstanding, the prosperity of Florence increased, at that time, to a positively prodigious extent. Villani repeatedly alludes to this state of prosperity and general well-being, adding that continual festivities were then held in Florence, and that the Republic could call to arms as many as 30,000 men in the city, and 70,000 in the territory.[495] What was of still greater moment, its bankers manipulated the chief trade of the world, and flooded all markets with Florentine goods. They conducted the affairs of the Roman Curia; they managed nearly the whole commerce of France and Southern Italy; all the sovereigns of Europe came to these bankers for aid, and frequently employed keen-witted, enterprising Florentines in their mints, their treasuries, and their embassies. Thus money flowed into the city from all sides; and it was at this moment, so it is said, that Boniface VIII., giving audience to the ambassadors of various powers, and finding to his surprise that all of them were Florentines, cried out, "You Florentines must be the fifth element!" As a natural result of this state of things the petty Republic became a first-class power, wielding everywhere, and over Italy in particular, a preponderating influence. All neighbouring cities, great and small, tried to copy the laws and institutions they deemed the source of its amazing prosperity. Even Rome herself seemed desirous to organise her magistracies, councils, and Commune on the Florentine pattern.[496]

It was this that most irritated the Popes in their perpetual struggle with the Roman municipality, and now specially irritated Boniface VIII., who seemed determined to crush the Commune. But he was strenuously opposed by the nobility and people, who gave him no truce, and drove him to wander, almost a fugitive, from town to town. Of haughty temper and boundless ambition, his conception of the papal authority rose to the height of craving universal rule. Hence he could not be resigned to the stubbornness of the Romans, and still less to the example and encouragement afforded them by Florence. He therefore conceived the plan of subduing the latter city and reducing it almost to the condition of a fief of the Church, under a governor of his own choice. Having once formed this scheme, he began to prosecute it with his customary ardour. There was certainly a good chance of success, save for one insurmountable obstacle that he omitted to take into account. The chance in his favour was the fact that Florence, being now a republic of traders, had small means of offering armed resistance. The army of 100,000 men, so proudly enumerated by Villani, consisted of a species of national guard of artisans and peasants having the barest smattering of military training, with no officers and no generals fitted to take command. It comprised no mounted troops, since nobles alone could find time for the requisite cavalry training. The Commune naturally feared to place any trust in the nobles of the town, while those of the territory were avowedly hostile. The Companies of Adventure, afterwards open to hire, had not yet begun to be established. Nevertheless, an army was needed, and, moreover, one commanded by competent leaders, if the Republic wished to preserve its authority in Italy, and protect its trade from the growing jealousy of its neighbours. This was the reason formerly inducing its rash acceptance of Vicars nominated by the Popes, and that had also induced it to confer supremacy for ten years on Charles of Anjou, who had accordingly supplied the State with captains and soldiery. Why should not Boniface be able to clench a similar bargain on even more effective and permanent terms? The Republic's need of a military leader was as urgent, nay, more urgent than before; while the consent and support of the nobles might be considered assured. But the insurmountable obstacle, unforeseen by the Pope, was that the Florentines had always wanted and still wanted defenders, but refused to have rulers; nor would it be easy to induce them to yield this point, either by craft or persuasion. The subject on which they were most tenacious, and would never give way, was the popular government of the guilds, and this government would have to be destroyed or reduced to submission before the Pope's scheme could be carried into effect.

The task certainly had its difficulties. In fact, the problem could only be solved by force, and Boniface was not the man to shrink from employing it; hence collision was unavoidable. As an additional complication, the Republic, about to bear the brunt of the Pope's fury, was thoroughly and determinately Guelph, not only Guelph from sentiment or by force of old traditions, but even more from motives of interest. In fact, it had risen to existence by centuries of struggle with powerful Ghibellines and aristocrats, and had finally built up the government of the guilds on the ruins of those adversaries' strength, and greatly assisted therein by the success of the Angevins summoned to Italy by the Popes. The chief trade of the Republic, and main source of its vitality and power, was that carried on with France, with Southern Italy—now held by the Angevins—and with Rome. Hence it could not entertain the idea of rousing the enmity of the French king, Pope, and Angevins, who were all allied at the time. Besides, the Ghibelline party in Tuscany was then represented by all the cities hostile to Florence. Sienna, Arezzo, and Pistoia inclined more or less openly to the Ghibelline side. The Pisan Republic, which had so zealously assisted Conradin's cause, still flaunted the Ghibelline flag. This State was in perpetual rivalry with Florence, and sought to bar her from access to the sea, the command of which was now more pressingly needed than before. The strife between these republics could only end in the annihilation of the one or the other. Therefore the Florentines were compelled to keep on good terms with the Pope, yet at the same time forced into opposition against him. In this condition of affairs all will understand why Florentine history should be so complicated and obscure.

IV.

After the expulsion of Giano della Bella, the nobles seemed again masters of the city for a time; and their spirits were immoderately raised by their success in procuring the election of a Signory (June 15, 1295) exclusively composed of their own friends. By the beginning of July they had concerted their plans, and repaired to the Piazza armed for the fray. But the people were already gathered there and in superior force, so that civil war would have instantly broken out had not certain friars and citizens intervened, and fortunately contrived to pacify the public excitement. Nevertheless, the Signory being favourable to the nobles, determined to turn the opportunity to account, and on July 6, 1295, managed to get the Bill passed that, as we have previously related, was incorporated in the enactments for the purpose of modifying them and considerably attenuating their severity.[497]

Some of these modifications were of a purely formal kind, but others encroached on the substance of the law. As the enactments now stood, accomplices in the offences decreed punishable were no longer classed with the direct authors of crimes, a single *Capitanus homicidii* now being recognised. Nor was the testimony of two witnesses of good repute any longer considered sufficient proof of the crime, the testimony of three witnessesnow being required. Finally it was no longer indispensable that candidates to the Signory should be practically engaged in some trade, *continue artem exercentes*; their enrolment in the guild of the trade being decreed sufficient proof of their eligibility, *qui scripti sint in libro seu matricola alicuius artis*. This last concession was, in fact, slighter than it appeared, seeing that even before then the *practical* exercise of trade had been more often apparent than real. But the principle for which men had fought was now cast aside, and putting together the various concessions granted in 1295, we plainly see that the amendment of the law was a genuine victory for the nobles. In fact, the popular discontent ran high at the passing of this Bill, and Villani tells us that the Signory who had proposed and carried it were treated with much contumely and scorn on leaving office, and even greeted with volleys of stones in the public streets.[498] Accordingly a popular reaction ensued that proved to be the germ of new and serious discord among the citizens. The first step taken was to deprive the nobles of certain of their weapons; the next to proclaim some of the less factious aristocrats members of the popular class, in order to weaken their party.[499] Besides this, fresh laws were soon decreed to restore the pristine force of the enactments, followed by other measures of the same kind, culminating in the creation of a new magistrate for the express purpose, as will be seen, of ensuring the strict fulfilment of the law. But it was impossible for these changes to be effected without fresh discord and bloodshed in the city.

For there was not only fiercer strife just then between the nobles and the people, but the former now split into two divisions, formed respectively of those bent on doing away with the enactments, and those who had renounced that idea. These new factions were designated by the names of the two families acting as leaders, namely, the Donati and the Cerchi. The latter were of humble origin, but had made their way up and were now counted among the richest merchants in the world. They boasted a wide-spreading kindred, numerous friends, owned vast estates both in town and country, and lived in grand style. They had recently purchased many palaces of the Counts Guidi, members of the oldest Florentine nobility; and by lending their houses at St. Procolo to the Signory, to whom no palace had yet been assigned, were more easily enabled to keep in favour with the heads of the State. Villani, being of the opposite party, says that the Cerchi were "easy-going, innocent, and savage." They were, in fact, business folk, unpractised in warfare, and with small aptitude for political intrigue. The term "savage" was applied to them on account of their humble descent, and Dante himself, though an adherent of their party, speaks of it as "savage" (*selvaggia*). In virtue of their origin and continued practice of trade, they were liked and esteemed by the people, and their avowed opposition to the Donati[500] won them still higher favour. Besides the advantages of wealth and of wide-spreading family ties, their courtesy of manner helped to advance their popularity.

On the contrary, the "gentle-born and warlike" Donati, as Villani calls them, were of old feudal descent. Messer Corso, the head of the family, was a daring, shrewd, hard-hitting man, of moderate means, but so immoderately haughty and ambitious as to tolerate no equals, and least of all among the enriched merchants. He was known as the baron, and Compagni, who was on the Cerchi side, says that whenever Corso rode through the streets, "he seemed the lord of the earth" (*"che la terra fosse sua"*). Many magnates of the city, many nobles of the territory, and particularly the Pazzi of the Upper Valdarno, considered him their leader. Some of the merchants also adhered to him, and among others the Spini, who owned a bank in Rome, and as business agents for the Pope and the Curia, drove a very profitable trade. This Donati faction was detested by the burghers, but in favour with the populace, who greeted the baron with shouts of applause as he passed through the streets. But although Corso's courage and subtlety stood him in good stead during the struggle now impending, his arrogance alienated many followers and disposed them to join the Cerchi. The Cavalcanti were among his opponents, and that graceful poet and valorous knight, young Guido Cavalcanti, had conceived so special and deadly a hatred for him that the two never met in the streets without drawing their swords. The Donati's influence in the city was chiefly owed to the favour of the captains of the party, while that of the Cerchi was maintained by the support of the Signory. Thus the palace of the Guelph Society and of the Priors became the headquarters, as it were, of the two opposing camps. The two families likewise owned neighbouring estates in the country and dwelt near each other in town. Their respective houses were situated in the St. Piero quarter or *sesto* of the city, which, on account of the continual disturbances occurring there at the time, was known by the name of "The Scandalous Sesto" (*Sesto dello Scandalo*). Everything served as fuel to the flame. Words uttered by either party were reported and exaggerated to the other. How Corso Donati always spoke of Guido Cavalcanti as Guido Cavicchia; how, when alluding to the head of the family and party chief, Vieri de' Cerchi, he would ask, "Has the ass of Porta brayed to-day?" On the other hand, the Donati were styled by their adversaries "The Ill-famed," as being men of bad repute and doers of evil.

It is not easy to exactly ascertain how and when these parties first became known as *Bianchi* and *Neri*, for the chroniclers are rather vague and not altogether agreed upon the point. Both names were of old usage in Florence as distinctive family appellations; in fact, there had already been White Cerchi and Black Cerchi, but the latter afterwards became the chiefs of the White party.[501] The same names had then been employed to designate two opposite factions of the Cancellieri house waging fierce strife in Pistoia. The Florentines, who exercised great authority in that town, mediated between the two sides to bring them to make peace; and to achieve this intent sent some members of the Pistoian, Bianchi, and Neri to Florence. The Whites were quartered in the Frescobaldi palace, the Blacks in the house of certain Cerchi, to whom they were related. But this measure had a very unexpected result, for, as Villani[502] remarks, even as one sick sheep infects another with disease, so the Pistoians communicated their party hatred to the Florentines, who thus became increasingly divided. At all events, from that time the Donati were Blacks, the Cerchi Whites.

Hence it may be clearly seen that this division of parties no longer corresponds with that of the Guelphs and Ghibellines. Principles are set aside and personal passions and hatreds more and more dominant. But, in the nature of things, no Florentine family at the time could have a better claim to be entitled Ghibellines than the Donati, a line boasting feudal descent, and connected with the oldest nobility of the city and its territory. The head of the house was Messer Corso, who, after the death of his first wife, contracted a second marriage with one of the Ubertini, an old Ghibelline family that had been always opposed to the popular government, and seemed to have the very blood of the tyrants of Romagna and Lombardy in its veins. Yet it was principally through Corso Donati that events again took another unexpected turn. Spurred by his devouring ambition, he started a secret intrigue with Boniface VIII. through his Roman agents, the Spini, and the Pope believed that at last he had found a man after his own heart.[503] And before very long these secret practices produced visible results.

V.

The Pope's purpose of exercising undue interference in Florentine affairs was plainly seen when the question was discussed as to revoking the banishment of Giano della Bella. Though without any lawful voice in the matter, he not only made violent opposition to the proposal, but also, on January 23, 1296, addressed a letter to the Florentines, threatening them with interdict, unless they abandoned the idea.[504] No one, however, was yet aware that he had already formed a scheme, and was secretly plotting to carry it into effect; nor did any one imagine that *Papa Bonifacius volebat sibi dari totam Tusciam,*[505] although this was afterwards ascertained to be the case, and written proof of it is extant in an old document that serves to explain his real aims.[506] These were also formulated clearly enough by the chronicler Ferreto, when he wrote that Boniface meditated "faesulanum popolum iugo supprimere, et sic Thusciam ipsam, servire desuetam, tyrannico more comprehendere."[507] In fact, in May, 1300, the Pope had already sent word to the Duke of Saxony that the Tuscan factions having infected his own States, it was impossible for him to achieve any result without first reducing Tuscany to subjection. And he continued that although able to do this on his own authority, he nevertheless preferred to gain the consent of the electoral princes, and likewise that of Albert of Austria, king of the Romans, to whom he forwarded a minute of the act of renunciation.[508] Donati, being privy to the scheme, had hastened to assume the attitude of the most Guelph of all Guelphs, and denounce the Cerchi as Ghibellines. Consequently all who distrusted the Pope were increasingly willing to join the Cerchi side.

Suddenly Florence was startled by receiving well certified news of the clandestine intrigues Donati was carrying on in Rome through the agency of the Spini. Messer Lapo Salterelli, an advocate of much skill but doubtful integrity, and always ready to go with the tide, came before the magistrates accompanied by two personal friends,[509] and publicly accused of treasonable attempts against the State three Florentines domiciled in Rome at Spini's bank, three "mercatores Romanam Curiam sequentes."[510] Corso Donati was not in Florence at the time, but at Massa Trabaria, a city in the States of the Church and close to the Tuscan frontier, where he had just been appointed rector by the Pope, a circumstance that heightened suspicion, and made the danger appear all the more serious and imminent. Determined to be on the alert, without giving undue provocation to the Pope, the magistrates immediately sentenced the three citizens in question to pay heavy fines, but awaited fresh intelligence before proceeding against all the other persons undoubtedly concerned in the plot. To allay the suspicions roused against him, the Pope should have now maintained a prudent silence, but his impetuous nature brooked no restraint. Therefore, giving vent to his fury, he wrote on April 24, 1300, threatening excommunication on the city for daring to sentence *his own familiars*, and summoned the three accusers to come to Rome without delay.[511] He gained nothing by this move—on the contrary,

342

Lapo Salterelli, having just been elected a prior, raised the question of jurisdiction by denying his right of interference with the internal affairs of the Republic. Meanwhile Boniface had called Vieri de' Cerchi to Rome, for the purpose of inducing him to make peace with Donati, who had already arrived there. But Cerchi, without betraying any knowledge of the trial, merely declared that he bore no hatred to any man, and alleging other vague excuses, declined the proposed reconciliation, thus stirring the Pope's wrath to the highest degree.[512] It was naturally very important for him to pacify the nobles, since this was the only means of compassing the subjection of the people. But precisely on that account the people preferred to keep them divided, and therefore throwing its weight on the side of the Cerchi, vehemently urged the latter to oppose the Donati.

VI.

Such was the state of public feeling on the day known to some as the fatal May Kalend. According to an old custom, the maidens of Florence greeted the coming of spring in the year 1300 by performing a dance in the Sta Trinità Square. Crowds flocked to the spot, struggling for a better sight of the festivity. Certain youths on horseback, both of the Bianchi and Neri factions, came into collision while pressing to the front. Hot words were exchanged followed by blows, swords flashed out, and many wounds were inflicted. Ricoverino de' Cerchi had his nose slashed off, an injury naturally demanding mortal revenge. So, in the same way that the Buondelmonti tragedy was declared by the chroniclers to have given birth to the Guelph and Ghibelline factions, this May-day festival was now considered by others to be the origin of the White and Black factions.[513] Yet this, too, was only the sudden outburst of long repressed passions, now raised to boiling point by the plots of the Pope. In consequence of these disturbances, the councils immediately passed a decree (4th of May), granting the Signory full powers to reduce the city to order; to enforce the Enactments of Justice; to guard "the ancient, customary, and continued independence of the Florentine Commune and people, in present danger of being changed to servitude by many perilous innovations *tam introrsum, quam etiam de foris venientes.*"[514] The concluding words clearly referred to Boniface, and accordingly on the 15th of May the Pope despatched from Anagni a most violent letter to the bishop and the inquisitor of Florence. He made complaint against those "children of iniquity who, in order to turn the people from their submission to the Keys of St. Peter, were spreading the rumour that he sought to deprive the city of its power of jurisdiction, and diminish its independence, whereas, on the contrary, he wished to enlarge its freedom." But he then proceeded to cry: "Is not the Pontiff supreme lord over all, and particularly over Florence, which for special reasons is bound to be subject to him? Do not emperors and kings of the Romans yield submission to us, yet are they not superior to Florence? During the vacancy of the Imperial throne, did not the Holy See appoint King Charles of Anjou Vicar-general of Tuscany? Was he not recognised as such by themselves? The Empire is now vacant, inasmuch as the Holy See has not yet confirmed the election of the noble Albert of Austria." And thus, in a rising *crescendo*, he threatened the Florentines that, failing obedience, "he would not only launch his interdict and excommunication against them, but inflict the utmost injury on their citizens and merchants, cause their property to be pillaged and confiscated in all parts of the world and release all their debtors from the duty of payment." He again inveighed against the three audacious informers, vowing to have them treated and punished as heretics, and wrote with special acrimony of Lapo Salterelli for having dared to declare that the Pope had no right to meddle with the tribunals of the Commune. And he wound up by insisting that the sentence on his three familiars should be annulled.[515]

The Florentines refused to heed his words, and the Neri then began to feel anxious, dreading lest the White, or, as they already called it, the Ghibelline party, "should be exalted in Florence, which, under pretence of good government, already wore a Ghibelline aspect."[516] They accordingly induced the Pope to send the Cardinal of Acquasparta to arrange the pacification of the nobles. The Cardinal arrived at the beginning of June, at once requested full powers to conclude the agreement, and likewise proposed that the Signory should be chosen by lot, in order to avert the disturbances always accompanying their election.[517] The Florentines lavished verbal promises on him, but refused to invest him with the desired Balia. Previous experience had warned them that peace between the nobles meant "ruin to the people," and a fresh proof to this effect was afforded at the moment. In fact, the Cardinal had barely begun to dispose the nobles towards reconciliation, than they rose to arms, and on St. John's Eve (23rd of June), almost under the Cardinal's eyes, made a violent assault on the Consuls of the Guilds, who were bearing offerings to the shrine of the saint, and shouted while raining blows on them: "We are the men that routed the foe at Campaldino, yet you have driven us from office and power in our own city."[518] So enormous an outrage demanded heavy punishment, and as the Signory was then composed of burghers of the White party, including Dante Alighieri, it exiled several nobles of either side within twenty-four hours.[519]

The Bianchi promptly obeyed the decree and withdrew to Sarzana; but the Neri rebelled against it, and only when threatened with worse chastisement, removed to Castel della Pieve in the Perugian territory. It was said that they had ventured to resist because they had the Cardinal's permission to await help from Lucca, which after all was never sent. And it was added that this succour was withheld because the Florentines, gaining some inkling of the scheme, had prepared for defence, and advised Lucca to that effect. Whether this were true or false, it is an ascertained fact that the public wrath was so hot against the Cardinal, that the people aimed their crossbows at the windows of the bishop's palace where he was lodged. One of the bolts actually struck the beam of his ceiling, and so greatly alarmed him, that after first removing to another house he took his departure, leaving the city under interdict and excommunication.[520] Nevertheless, animosity and riot continued to prevail; and before long the exiled Bianchi were permitted to return. This indulgence was accorded them, partly because the climate of Sarzana was so unhealthy that Guido Cavalcanti contracted an illness there, of which he subsequently died, but partly too because the Bianchi nobles were on far better terms with the people. The Neri, on the contrary, joined more actively than before in the Pope's plots, and seconded by the Captains of the Party, conspired for the purpose of trying conclusions by force.

Meanwhile Boniface was pressingly urging Charles of Valois, the king's brother, to march into Tuscany from France, and Charles II. of Anjou had already implored that prince to come to aid him in his struggle with the Sicilians. The Valois was an enterprising and cruel leader. During the Gascon campaign of 1294 he had hung sixty citizens, and slaughtered the inhabitants of Rèole after they had laid down their arms. He had fought in Flanders at the beginning of the year 1300, and after capturing various cities, had compelled the reigning Court to open to him the gates of Ghent. Then, after swearing in the name of the king to restore his States, he nevertheless sent him to Paris, and in violation of the oath he had taken, annexed the county to France.[521] This was the man now summoned to Florence by the Pope. To induce him to come promptly and with good will, the Pope even dazzled him with hopes of the imperial crown. In any case, by right of the authority he asserted during the interregnum, he would appoint him vicar-general and peacemaker in Tuscany, "to enforce the execution of his purpose there."[522] In what that purpose consisted, even Villani, who was on his side, admits that Boniface intended "to crush the people and the Whites."[523] Accordingly the Blacks own displayed great activity, with the aid of their adherents in town and country. They held various meetings, of which the most notorious and turbulent was that assembled in June at Santa Trinità, for the purpose of urging the Pope to send Charles of Valois to straighten their affairs, and declaring that, for their own part, they were ready to join him at any cost.[524] Naturally all this could not be kept secret, and in fact the Signory immediately sentenced the conspirators to various penalties. Messer Corso, being absent, was condemned in contumacy to confiscation as well as personal punishment; some of the Blacks were relegated to a fixed domicile; others mulcted in 2,000 lire each, and even their friends at Pistoia expelled from that city, for the greater enfeeblement of the party.

Meanwhile Charles of Valois marched across the Alps, and the same summer was already in occupation of Parma, "cum magno arnese equorum et somariorum."[525] Reaching Bologna on the 1st of August he found convoys from the Bianchi and the Neri awaiting him there. The latter party had already handed over to the "curia domini Papæ" the large sum of 70,000 florins to assist the expedition which was now absolutely decided.[526] As a preliminary step, Valois went to Anagni with 500 knights, saw King Charles of Naples, and made arrangements with him concerning the Sicilian campaign. The Pope hastened to create Valois Count of Romagna, and afterwards, in the name of the vacant Empire, Mediator (*Paciaro*) in Tuscany.[527] So, without farther delay, the Court started for Florence, joined on the road by the exiles who flocked to his ranks. His mission was to crush the Bianchi and the people and to uplift the Neri. He had deliberately undertaken the task, but rather for the purpose of satisfying the Pope, of whose support in Sicily the Angevins had now pressing need, than from any personal motive. In fact, knowing that he could never hope to be lord of Florence, he felt very little interest in the matter. Nevertheless he counted on being able to extort a considerable sum of money from the city, and to this end brought Messer Musciatto Franzesi with him to serve, Villani tells us, as his *pedotto*, *i.e.*, as guide and factotum. This man was a well-known merchant of the Florentine territory, who had made his fortune in France by illegal as well as lawful means and had been knighted by the French king in reward for many services, among others for having suggested a device for replenishing the treasury during the war in Flanders by debasing the coinage.[528] Charles of Valois hoped to gain much by this man's assistance; whereas the Florentines regarded the said *pedotto* with great distrust.

On the 13th of September all the councils assembled in the palace of the Podestà—Dante Alighieri sitting among them that day—to decide "quid sit providendum et faciendum super conservatione Ordinamentorum Iustitiæ et

Statutorum Populi." [529] This, and not the struggle between the Bianchi and Neri, was always the main point with the Florentines. Hence it was resolved that, for the present, everything should remain in the hands of the magistrates of the Republic, and that it would be advisable to dispatch an embassy to the Pope. Whether Dante Alighieri was one of the ambassadors sent, as asserted by the historians, has been no less disputed than all other incidents of the poet's life. At that time he was ardently devoted to politics, and although belonging to the old nobility, was not only enrolled in the guilds and a partisan of the Bianchi, but thoroughly at one with the people, a supporter of the Enactments of Justice, and opposed to the Pope's designs. From the 15th of June to the 15th of August, 1300, he had been one of the Priors who had exiled the leaders of the Bianchi and the Neri. In the "Consulte" of 1296 we find him combating the proposal of furnishing a subsidy to Charles of Anjou, to assist his Sicilian campaign. In 1301 he took an even more prominent share in the debates of the councils, and always manifested unchanged opinions. In fact, during the debates of the 14th of April, when it was proposed to supply a hundred soldiers at the expense of the Commune, for the Pope's service, Dante twice, at least, made reply, "Quod de servitio faciendo domino Papæ

nihil fiat." [530] He had been also frequently employed in other public posts: accordingly it is quite possible that he may have been sent to Rome at this time, as many of his biographers have stated. What could be said to the Pope? It was now hopeless to expect him to refrain from sending Charles of Valois; but in addition to soothing him with fair words, it might be neither inopportune nor useless to endeavour to make him understand that it could not serve his purpose to expel the Bianchi and aggrandise the Neri, seeing that the government of the city would still remain in the hands of the guilds. It would, therefore, be wiser for him to come to terms with the people, which was steadfastly Guelph, and, once pacified, might consent, as in past times, to accept from him, in the future, a provisional Vicar, always provided that the freedom of its popular government, its statutes and enactments, were left intact. But this popular government was precisely what the Pope was determined not to tolerate any longer. Therefore, without many words, and almost without giving any heed to the ambassadors, he only replied to their arguments by saying, so Compagni relates: "Make humiliation to us." According to the same chronicler, two of the ambassadors returned to Florence without delay, but Dante, who was the third, lingered in Rome for a while. [531]

VIII.

Meanwhile Valois, with his usual deceit, and to hoodwink every one more completely, wrote to the Commune of San Gimignano on the 20th of September in the following terms: "Be assured that neither the Pope nor I have the slightest intention 'de juribus iurisdictionibus seu libertatibus, quæ per comunitatis Tusciæ tenentur et possidentur, in aliquo nos intromictere, sed potius … favorare.'"[532] The Florentines, however, were not to be tricked by these false promises, and on the 7th of October elected a new Signory, in advance of the usual time, trying to assign either faction an equal share in it, in the hope of effecting some mitigation of party rancour. But, as justly observed by Compagni, this was rather the time "for the sharpening of swords." Valois, being at Sienna on the 14th, dispatched ambassadors thence to announce his arrival, and these envoys were received by the councils in full assembly, including that of the Guelph Society. Accordingly many Neri and Grandi being present, and joining with those who at every time and everywhere invariably go with the winning side, they all vied warmly with one another in proposing to welcome the stranger with open arms.[533] In point of fact, no one was inclined to oppose what had now become an unavoidable necessity, particularly as Charles had again given the Florentine envoys at Sienna written as well as verbal assurances of his intention to respect the city's laws and rights of jurisdiction.[534] So, on All Souls' Day, 1st of November, welcomed with great pomp and display of force, Valois entered Florence as "Peacemaker," and, as Villani says, "with his men disarmed." But in the "Divina Commedia" Dante describes his entry thus:—

"Per far conoscere meglio sè e i suoi,
Senz 'armi n'esce solo con la lancia
Con la qual giostrò Giuda, e quella ponta
Si che a Fiorenza fa scoppiar la pancia."[535]

His troops had gained so many recruits by the way as to now amount to about 800 foreign and 1,400 Italian horse. They were certainly too few to besiege or enslave Florence; but Valois had the influence of Rome and France at his back, and the Neri were ready to fly to arms. Hence, assured of safety, he established his quarters across the river (Oltrarno) in the house of the Frescobaldi, once friends, but now foes of the Cerchi. After resting there quietly for a few days, in order to mature his plans, he demanded the lordship and custody of the city, with a view to its pacification. Accordingly a solemn meeting was held in Santa Maria Novella on the 5th of November, attended by all the leading citizens and magistrates of Florence. Valois's request was granted when he pledged his princely word to preserve the city in good order, peace, and independence. Villani, who was present at the ceremony, and favourable to Charles, relates, nevertheless, that "he" (Valois) "and his troops immediately began to do the contrary." In fact, by the advice of Musciatto Franzesi, who had connived with the Neri to that effect, violence was resorted to without delay, and all Florence rose in a tumult, perceiving that the moment for assault and treachery had now arrived.

The Signory being attacked by the Neri, betrayed by Charles and forsaken by the Bianchi on the charge of having allowed itself to be surprised unprepared for defence, was utterly powerless, and the Republic was left without a government. The new Podestà, Messer Cante dei Gabrielli of Gubbio, had entered the city with Charles de Valois, and for what purpose may be easily divined. At this juncture Corso Donati appeared, sword in hand, with his followers at the Pinti gate. Finding it closed, he managed to break through the postern door, with the help of friends within, and, entering the city, was hailed by the mob with the usual cries of "Viva Messer Corso, viva il Barone!" Hastening first to throw open the prisons, he then went to the Public Palace, and driving out the Signory, compelled them to return to their homes. Villani relates that "during all this laceration of the city, Charles, violating the terms he had just sworn to observe, never attempted to check the fray, but only looked on."[536] The Bianchi were speedily overpowered, many wounded and killed, and their houses sacked. This "pestilence lasted for five days in Florence, and for eight in the territory, armed bands scouring the country, maltreating the inhabitants, and plundering and burning their dwellings. Some of the worst and most ferocious excesses were committed by the Medici family.[537] By the 7th of November the Signory were so overwhelmed with terror as to suggest a decree authorising them to withdraw before the legal expiration of their term. Therefore on the following day a new Signory was appointed to hold office until the 14th of December, when, according to the law, another one would have to be elected in regular course. The existing Signory hastened to announce to all the fortunate triumph of the Church party under the auspices of the Pope and Valois, by whose means "Populus roboratus, Status et Ordinamenta Iustitiæ, iurisdictiones, honores et possessiones Populi et Comunis Florentiæ suorumque civium observata."[538] In spite of these very hypocritical words, we know that even then no one dared attempt to annul the enactments, or to remove the government from the grasp of the people; while it was equally true that with a Signory composed of Neri, a Podestà such as Cante dei Gabrielli and Valois, with Musciatto Franzesi and Corso Donati at his elbow, the Bianchi were doomed to destruction. In fact, the work of pillage never ceased; exiled friends were recalled, the banishment of adversaries was rigidly maintained, and Charles began to extort money from the citizens by threat.[539] His first victims were the members of the late Signory, who were given the choice of opening their purses or being sent as prisoners to Puglia, an alternative of which the meaning was clear.[540]

Meanwhile, the Pope having little confidence in Valois, or in the latter's scanty knowledge of Florence, and still adhering to his plan of reconciling the magnates in order to crush the people, again sent the Cardinal of Acquasparta, for the purpose—as stated in his letter dated 2nd of December, 1301—"of seconding Charles's efforts, by checking dissension among the citizens and converting them to peace and charity."[541] These were vain hopes, however. The Cardinal did his utmost, and arranged a few reconciliations and even some marriages between Bianchi and Neri; but when he proposed that either party should have an equal share in the government, the Neri, backed by Charles, made the most vehement opposition. And as the Cardinal persisted in his fruitless endeavours, Messer Niccolò de' Cerchi, when riding out to the country for a day's pleasuring with his friends, was attacked in Piazza Santa Croce, pursued by Corso Donati's son Simone, and murdered by him on the Africo bridge. But in the course of the struggle the victim dealt his assailant a mortal wound that soon brought him also to the grave.

As Simone was Corso's favourite son, it may be imagined how this effected the peace that the Pope had hoped to establish through the Cardinal's mediation. Messer Cante dei Gabrielli had already begun to pronounce sentences on the Bianchi, which were subsequently transcribed on the first pages of the still extant "Libro del Chiodo." Four of the Bianchi faction were exiled on the 18th of January, 1302; five more, including Dante Alighieri, on the 27th. In February four other verdicts were issued for the banishment of over one hundred nobles and burghers of the city and territory.[542] Enraged by these proceedings, the Cardinal hurried off, again leaving Florence under interdict, but not before he had received the 1,100 florins assigned to him on the 27th of February, 1302, in remuneration of his abortive efforts.

In the meantime Charles of Valois had gone to Rome, though for what purpose is scarcely ascertained. Compagni says that he went to seek money from the Pope, who replied to him: "I have sent thee to the source of gold; now profit by it as best thou canst." It is, therefore, highly probable that he went to convince the Pope of the impossibility of the pacification His Holiness had dreamt of arranging, and that the only thing to be done was to exalt the Neri and crush the Bianchi, together with the people abetting them. Knowing little of the Italian communes in general or of Florence in particular, he failed to discern, that though the Bianchi might be crushed, not so the people. To quell the latter, nothing short of wholesale slaughter could suffice, and even this would have failed in the long run.

At any rate, on returning to Florence on the 19th of March, Valois feigned to have discovered that the Bianchi had formed a plot against him with the connivance of one of his barons, Pietro Ferrando of Provence; and an agreement signed and sealed by the conspirators was actually produced.[543] The chroniclers, Villani included, declare that the plot was entirely fictitious; nevertheless, the agreement in question, dated 26th of March, is still extant in the Florentine Archives.[544] Either it was forged at the time to furnish an excuse for fresh arrangements, or was drafted by Pietro Ferrando for the purpose of entrapping the Bianchi and giving Charles another weapon against them. In fact, he immediately subjected them to fresh persecutions. The heads of the party were cited to appear; but disregarding the summons, they hastily fled to Pistoia, Arezzo, and Pisa, there reinforcing, the Ghibellines and all other enemies of Florence. Eleven of their number were outlawed as rebels; their houses and property confiscated or destroyed.

Having dealt the Bianchi this fresh blow, and secured the triumph of the Neri, Valois took his departure, but not without obtaining a promise of further subsidies from his friends. In fact 20,000 florins were awarded him in December, and 5,000 more sent in October, 1303.[545] Meanwhile the Podestà, Messer Cante, continued to rain penalties on the town. By May no fewer than 250 condemnations had been pronounced, and as his successor pursued the same course, more than 600 sentences of confiscation, exile, and death were issued during the year 1302.[546] Villani says in conclusion: "Thus by the agency of Charles and the orders of Boniface VIII., the hated Bianchi faction was defeated and expelled, wherefrom great trouble ensued later on."[547] Up to this point the succession of events may be traced with sufficient ease. But from the moment the exiles sought friends abroad, and waged war on their native city, it became increasingly difficult to disentangle the chaos of parties, and comprehend the real meaning of all that took place. Therefore this is the moment to test whether our previous remarks have served to cast any new light upon a period of history that is still somewhat obscure, in spite of the close study and deep learning devoted by so many writers to its investigation.

CHAPTER X.[548]

DANTE, FLORENTINE EXILES AND HENRY VII.

I.

AFTER Valois's departure and the events by which it was followed, the history of Florence enters on a new phase. The exiles united with the nobles of the territory and the Ghibelline cities in raising a rebellion against the Republic, in order to pave the way for their own recall. This naturally brought about a temporary reconciliation and agreement between the magnates of the Black party, who made greater boast than ever of being the only genuine Guelphs, and stigmatised all the exiles as Ghibellines. Pistoia and the fortress of Piantravigne were the first to revolt, but were speedily reduced to submission. Then, on the 8th of June, 1302, the leading exiles, of whom Dante Alighieri was one, assembled in the church of St. Godenzio among the Apennines, and arranged explicit terms of alliance with the Ubaldini, undertaking to compensate them at their own expense for the injuries caused by the war to that family's possessions in the Mugello, where the stronghold of Montaccenico was to serve as headquarters for the adversaries of Florence. Thereupon the Florentines at once proceeded to ravage all the lands of the Ubaldini on either side of the Apennines.[549] By tremendous exertions, and with the support of Pisa and Bologna, the exiles managed to collect an army of 800 horse and 6,000 foot, and in the spring of 1303 beleaguered the Castle of Pulicciano, appertaining to the Florentines. But even there they had little success. The "people and knights" of Florence took arms and hastily marched against them. The Pisans failed to send the promised succour, the Ubaldini remained inert, and as the Bolognese withdrew declaring themselves betrayed, the Bianchi, being left unassisted, ignominiously dispersed. So the Neri returned to the city in triumph, after taking many prisoners, some of whom were killed on the way and others beheaded by the Podestà. They afterwards surprised the Castle of Montale near Pistoia, and ravaged the surrounding territory. Thus the war seemed at an end, and the hopes of the exiles fallen.

But at this juncture discord again broke out in Florence. Preliminary manifestations of turbulence and rebellion had already led to some fresh sentences of exile and a few executions. But matters now grew more serious.

Corso Donati's arrogance once more produced its usual results. By disgusting his friends he drove them to side with the rich burghers they despised. Being alienated from the nobles of the territory who had made common cause with the exiles, he tried again to become the leader of the more intolerant section of the magnates, and curried favour with the populace, declaring it to be unjustly overtaxed, merely to fill the pockets of certain fat burghers. "Let the people see where that great sum has gone, for no such amount can have been expended on the war." And he demanded an inquiry, thus beginning, as Villani remarks, "to sow discord by a feint of justice and compassion."[550] Much discussion, great turmoil ensued, but nothing was done, although a law was actually passed (24th of July, 1303) granting the Podestà and captain full powers of inquiry and decision. Meanwhile much irritation was felt by the "fat burghers" against whom the accusation had been launched, and in order to strike a fresh blow at the magnates, they obtained the recall of certain exiles belonging to the popular party, who had not broken bounds. They likewise recalled a few of the Cerchi family, thereby gaining the approbation of the Pope, who was much troubled by the disturbances the Bianchi were exciting on all sides and even in cities belonging to the Church.[551] Thus, as Del Lungo happily expresses it, "by dint of fishing magnates out of the crucible,"[552] Corso Donati was enabled to gather about him more than thirty families, including some of the burgher class and a few returned exiles. Several members of the Tosinghi house were adherents of the Bianchi, and amongst them the valiant Baschiera della Tosa was one of the exiles. There were also Donati's former foes, the Cavalcanti, a very wealthy and numerous clan, comprising members of all parties, although more Bianchi than Neri, and who, as the owners of a mass of houses, shops, and magazines in the centre of the city and tenanted by merchants, were naturally on good terms with the trading class. Accordingly the Donati no longer commanded a party, but rather an ill-assorted crowd, only united by the common bond of hatred against the people. In fact, Messer Corso was wont to say that they were all "captive and enslaved to a herd of fat burghers, or rather dogs, who tyrannised over them and robbed them of power."[553] Nevertheless, the real magnates, namely, noblemen by birth and temper, mostly leaned to his side, while those unable to tolerate his insolence preferred to play the part of spectators. Another of Corso's allies was Messer Lottieri della Tosa, Archbishop of Florence, who was making warlike preparations within the walls of his palace. In opposition to these confederates, several families, such as the Spini, Pazzi, Gherardini, and certain of the Frescobaldi had banded together under the lead of Messer Rosso della Tosa, another man of soaring ambition, who, in pursuance of the policy formerly employed by Vieri dei Cerchi, inclined to the burghers' side. And by means of some of his bravest followers, more particularly certain democrats of the Neri party, named Bordoni, "serving him," Compagni says, "as pincers to seize hot iron,"[554] he daily harassed the Donati in the councils of the State.

II.

Thus matters seemed again at the same point as before the arrival of Valois. In fact, we see Rosso della Tosa and his following combining with the people in defence of the Signory; while, on the other hand, Donati, backed by the captains of the party, was continually threatening and attacking it. Again, the citizens daily drew swords and came to blows; again, robbery, bloodshed, murder, and arson were rife in the town and throughout the territory. Even from the tower of the bishop's palace a mangonel hurled stones on Corso Donati's foes. Both the Signory and Podestà were reduced to impotence. Things reached at last such a pitch that recourse was had to the very strange plan of transferring the government to the Lucchese for sixteen days to see whether they could succeed in quieting the city. They re-established order, but without punishing the guilty; consequently, as soon as they were gone everything went on as before. It was even endeavoured to choose a Signory (solely of the people, however) approved by both parties, but the attempt came to nothing.[555] What brought the confusion to a climax, and rendered it permanent, was the fact that whereas the split between the magnates and the people had caused two genuine parties to be formed, the division among the magnates now convulsing the city, solely proceeded from the ambition of Corso Donati and a few others, had no political motive, and no basis of general principle or general interest. As we have seen, in fact, Donati's following comprised magnates of every shade, returned exiles owning friends and relations still in banishment, together with a sprinkling of the lower class. Nor could there be much cohesion in the ranks of the adverse party supporting the Signory, since this was also made up of aristocrats and men of the people, conflicting elements whose union could never be permanently assured. If the foes of the Signory were held together by Corso's energy and ambition, its supporters were chiefly united by their common hatred for him. Therefore, owing to this predominance of the personal element, both the parties were exposed to perpetual division, subdivision, and change, to a perpetual shifting of the pieces, and restless passing and repassing from one group to another.

Confusion was now to be heightened by the death of Boniface VIII. (October 11, 1303) and the election of Pope Benedict XI., a man of gentler fibre and uncertain will. The new pontiff yearned to re-establish peace in Florence at all costs, and procure the recall of its exiles; for the latter were keeping his own states in a turmoil, and even in Rome itself he had already encountered so much opposition from the nobles and people, that shortly after his election he had been compelled to seek refuge at Perugia, namely, on the borders of disturbed, restless Tuscany. Nor was it now possible, amid all these calamities, to count on any help from France, inasmuch as he had brought a suit against the authors of the criminal attempt at Anagni causing the death of Pope Boniface, that had been actually devised by the king of the French. For these reasons, and at the earnest solicitation of the Bianchi in Florence and elsewhere, Pope Benedict dispatched a peacemaker to the city on the 31st of January, 1304, in the person of Cardinal da Prato, a supposed Ghibelline. The Cardinal arrived on the 10th of March, and tried to conciliate all alike; magnates, people, exiles, Bianchi, the Neri led by Corso Donati and the Neri under Rosso della Tosa. But what chiefly disturbed public feeling and brought confusion to a climax was his scheme of recalling banished men and reconciling them with the city. Nevertheless the popular class was less opposed than others to the plan, discerning in it a possible means of enfeebling the magnates by promoting fresh discord in their ranks. Rosso della Tosa, on the contrary, was decidedly hostile to the exiles' return, considering that this would strengthen the opposite party, which was already favourable to many of the banished men. These views were shared by some of his faction. On the excuse of suffering from an attack of gout, Corso Donati remained a passive spectator for the nonce. But the Cavalcanti warmly approved of the suggested treaty, and were seemingly the first to promote it.

Having received full powers from the people, the Cardinal at once began to arrange reconciliations, and with success as regarded the Bishop and his former comrade, Messer Rosso della Tosa. He next appointed Corso Donati Captain of the Guelph Society, and reorganised the old popular militia, on the original plan, under nineteen Gonfaloniers of Companies. But in spite of bestowing commands on some of the magnates, the latter murmured bitterly against his reforms, saying that they tended to increase the people's strength, that the Cardinal was a Ghibelline, would end by leaving the city in the hands of the Bianchi, and that the latter would forthwith claim restitution of all property and estates made confiscate for the benefit of the Guelph Society. Regardless of these complaints, the Cardinal persisted in holding meetings to ratify the agreement. In fact, on the 26th of April, several Neri of the Donati and Tosa factions exchanged pledges of amity in the Square of Santa Maria Novella. Great festivities were given in honour of the occasion, among others a grand performance arranged by the Company of Borgo San Frediano, who announced throughout Florence that all persons desiring news of the other world might obtain it by assembling on the banks of the Arno on the evening of the 1st of May. Blazing fireworks represented the infernal regions, while boatloads of masks figured as condemned souls undergoing various torments. The people flocked in vast numbers to the river and on to the Carraia Bridge, which being only a wooden structure at the time, gave way beneath their weight. Many were seriously injured, and many others really went to the next world. The catastrophe was regarded by all as a bad omen, and was truly the prelude of fresh calamity.

III.

Meanwhile, those most opposed to the recall of the exiles craftily advised the Cardinal to begin by undertaking a mission of peace to Pistoia, declaring that so long as that city remained in the power of the Bianchi, Florence could never be really pacified. But the Pistoians resisted his efforts so vigorously, that not only was he compelled to leave the town without concluding any arrangement, but on seeking to enter Prato, found the gates of his native city closed in his face. The Pope, being highly enraged by all this, addressed an indignant letter to the Florentines on the 29th of May.[556] But they were in so disorderly and riotous a state, that after imploring the Pontiff to find them a Podestà, they refused to accept either of the four individuals proposed by him. Yet the Cardinal obstinately clung to his idea of re-establishing peace. At his instance, safe conducts were given to twelve delegates from the exiles, six Ghibellines and six Bianchi, in order that they might come to Florence to settle terms with as many representatives appointed by the City, each Sesto contributing one of the Donati and one of the adverse faction.[557] These twenty-four citizens were all magnates, and felt so much reciprocal distrust that the twelve exiles, although well received by the people and quartered under State protection in the Cardinal's own residence at the Mozzi Palace, were most anxious to depart, fearing to be cut to pieces at any moment. But they were advised by their friends to take arms and seek refuge in the houses of the Cavalcanti, seeing that with the latter's help they would be enabled, if necessary, to repulse and overcome their enemies by force. The Cavalcanti seemed well disposed to the plan, and began to arrange preliminaries. But after thus rousing the suspicion and increasing the animosity of their foes, they suddenly drew back, thereby disgusting even their friends. Accordingly on the 8th of June, 1304, the exiles hurried away from Florence as though flying for their lives.[558] Thereupon there was a loud outcry against the Cardinal; he was charged with having betrayed the city by his stealthy manœuvres, and it was even added that he had encouraged the exiles to appear before the walls in warlike array. Letters bearing his seal were shown, and it was affirmed that the exiles had marched from the Mugello as far as Trespiano, and only beaten a retreat on learning the failure of the meditated scheme. Villani declares that these reports were mere slanders;[559] but even the epistles attributed to Dante Alighieri lead us to infer that the Cardinal really desired the exiles' return and had negotiated with them to that effect.[560] But his patience being now exhausted, he departed on the 10th of June, again leaving the city under interdict, and exclaiming: "Since ye prefer to be at war and accursed, will neither hear nor obey the messenger of God's Vicar, nor be at rest and at peace among yourselves, remain under the curse of Heaven, under the curse of Holy Church."[561]

At this moment the Cavalcanti and their friends were at a truly terrible pass. Their present junction with the Donati was insufficient to blot out old animosities, which had been only laid aside for a while in order to second the return of the Bianchi, at the expense of the Tosinghi faction. The latter remained practically isolated, forsaken even by the rich trading class, who, wearied of perpetual civil war, had been persuaded by the Cardinal to promote a reconciliation between the Cavalcanti and Donati. But the former's unexpected withdrawal at the last moment, and when all seemed arranged, had stirred the old hatred to new fury, and the Cavalcanti were now between two fires. Messer Corso, being unwilling to join hands with the Tosinghi, kept his rage in check for the nonce, and feigning to be ill with gout, still remained passive, leaving his followers to do as they chose. But Rosso della Tosa was a ferocious enemy of the Cavalcanti, by whom he had been brought to the verge of ruin, and his hatred was not to be restrained. So the Cardinal had scarcely disappeared before a catastrophe became imminent in Florence. The Cavalcanti recognised their peril; but they were numerous, courageous, and powerful. They could count on the Gherardini, Pulci, and Cerchi del Garbo; they owned many friends even outside the walls and among the exiled Bianchi; they had also adherents of the burgher class, no few of whom tenanted their houses in the centre of Florence. The foes now arming against the Cavalcanti were aristocrats, not *popolani*. The Cerchi del Garbo began to scuffle day and night with the Giugni. The Cavalcanti and their friends hastened to the former's assistance, and so effectively as to be able to press on from Or San Michele to Piazza San Giovanni almost unopposed. But while at this distance from their own quarter a serious fire broke out there. Their enemies had set the Cavalcanti houses ablaze with combustibles kept in readiness for some days past. The first man to start the fire, beginning with the dwellings of fellow associates, was Neri degli Abati, prior of San Piero

Scheraggio; and his incendiary example was followed by many accomplices, including Simone della Tosa and Sinibaldo Donati, Messer Corso's son.[562] It was the 10th of June, 1304, and a strong north wind was blowing. Accordingly, the fire spread with great rapidity to the Calimala street, the Old Market, and Or San Michele, thus destroying the whole centre of Florence as well as the Cavalcanti houses—in fact, as Villani expresses it, "all the marrow, the yolk, and dearest spots of our city of Florence."[563] He adds, that the palaces, houses and towers consumed amounted to more than seventeen hundred, with enormous loss of property and merchandise, seeing that everything saved from the fire was stolen when carried away, and that fighting and pillage went on even in the midst of the flames.[564] Paolino Pieri relates in his chronicle, that one-tenth of the city was burnt, and one-sixth of its whole property. Many families and associations were ruined, but the worst sufferers were the Cavalcanti, who seemed paralysed with terror on beholding all their possessions devoured by the flames. Yet so ferocious was the hatred cherished against them, that even after these cruel calamities they were driven from Florence as rebels.

IV.

Let us see what were the political consequences of these events. The Donati and Della Tosa factions having combined for the undoing of the Cavalcanti and their friends, it was decided at first that the magnates, emboldened by union and victory, should next attempt to annul the Enactments of Justice, and take the government in their hands. And, in the midst of the General dismay, the project might have succeeded, Villani says, had the nobles been really in unison. Instead, "they were all at strife, and split into sects, wherefore either side courted the people so as not to lose ground."[565] The division of parties remained substantially the same. That is, on the one hand, there were the quarrelsome magnates seeking support from the people against their personal foes, and, on the other, the people trying to profit by the magnates' dissensions. Of course the merchants had also suffered heavily by the fire; but their wealth was of a kind to be rapidly replaced, whereas the nobles had no means of repairing their still greater losses. For the prosperity of the Florentine people was so prodigious at the time that, even after this wholesale destruction, their riches seemed nowise diminished. But there was a notable decline in the power of the magnates, who disappeared almost entirely from the first circuit, or centre of the city, where the old families had their dwellings. Therefore Capponi has some reason to say in his history: "From that moment the supremacy of the nobles seems to have been uprooted, and new social orders established."[566] Thus, as always happened in Florence, even this great calamity proved advantageous to the people.

In consequence of these lamentable events, added to the reports sent by Cardinal da Prato to the Pope in Perugia, the Holy Father cited twelve leading magnates of Florence to appear before him there. Among the persons thus summoned were Corso Donati and Rosso della Tosa, once bitter enemies but now friends for the moment. They set out towards Perugia with a great train of followers, forming a mounted company of five hundred men in all. So the exiles considered this a most favourable opportunity for making a fresh attempt to re-enter their native city. As usual, it was rumoured that the Cardinal had encouraged them to expect a good reception; and it was further announced that he had instigated Pisa, Bologna, Arezzo, Pistoia, and the whole of Romagna to come to their aid. But although some of the exiles' direst foes were absent from Florence at the time, on the other hand, the position of their adversaries must have been considerably strengthened by the slaughter of the Cavalcanti and Gherardini. Likewise, although the Greater Guilds had once been induced to favour the return of banished men, and particularly those of the popular class, it was not to be expected that they would now be disposed to welcome exiles advancing on Florence under the wing of the Pisans, and joined with the Ghibellines of Tuscany and Romagna. This league with the enemies of the State naturally roused all Florence against them.

Nevertheless the exiles seemed very hopeful. Thanks to their new allies, they had contrived to collect an army of 9,000 foot and 1,600 horse, and on the 19th of July marched into Lastra, to await other reinforcements from Pistoia. These were to be commanded by Tolosato degli Uberti, a valiant Ghibelline leader, of an ancient Florentine house, persistently hated by the Guelphs, in memory of the rout at Montaperti. As Uberti failed to appear, the exiles resolved to move on without him; but the twenty-four hours' delay had sufficed to destroy their chance of taking Florence by surprise. In fact, only twelve hundred horse rode to the city in peaceful array, bearing olive boughs in their hands; and passing the unfinished girdle of new walls, halted beneath the old bastions, in the Cafaggio fields, between St. Mark's and the Church of the Servi. There, on the 20th of July, panting from fatigue, without water, and exposed to the burning sun, they vainly waited for the gates to be opened to them. Meanwhile a small band of their men had managed to enter the city by forcing the Spadai gate, and advanced as far as Piazza San Giovanni. But instead of finding friends there, they were met by 200 horse and 500 foot, who drove them back, capturing some of their number, and leaving a good many wounded and slain. This gave the signal for a retreat, soon converted into a general flight. The force waiting at Cafaggio, exhausted from hunger and heat combined, had already thrown down their weapons and dispersed with "bands of volunteers" in pursuit. Many were killed or died of fatigue, others were stripped, seized and strung up on trees. News of the defeat reached Lastra before the fugitives returned; accordingly those encamped there took to flight, and although Tolosato degli Uberti met them on the way, he found it impossible to rally them to the attack. Among other narratives of the affair we have that of Villani, who witnessed all that occurred in Florence.[567] Dante Alighieri was not with the army at Lastra, having separated from his companions in exile shortly before, and almost in anger. He was probably disgusted by their hybrid alliance with all the enemies of Florence, by the secret agreements set on foot between Donati and the Cavalcanti, and saddened by the internecine slaughter so blindly provoked in the vain expectation of compassing the recall of a few banished men.[568]

The victory at Lastra must have undoubtedly augmented the daring and power of the magnates. It may have been on this account that certain of their number now insisted on their names being erased from the rolls of the guilds.[569] Additional proof to this effect is furnished by another important event occurring on the 5th of August, 1304. One of the Adimari having perpetrated a crime, was brought before the Podestà to be judged. But his associates made a violent assault on that magistrate as he was leaving the Priors' palace, and after wounding or killing several of his escort, broke into the prison and rescued the criminal. Thereupon the Captain of the People, Messer Gigliolo da Prato, temporarily acting as Podestà (since the continual disturbances in the city had deterred every one from assuming that office), departed from Florence in high indignation. Accordingly, to provide for the due administration of justice, the Florentines were obliged to elect a committee of twelve citizens, one noble and one *popolano*, from every Sesto, to fulfil the duties of a Podestà.[570] Presently, however, the resumption of hostilities outside the walls reduced the city to quiet for a time.

V.

The exiles had again begun to scour the land, stirring neighbouring strongholds to revolt; and the Florentines instantly marched against them. The first place to be attacked was the castle of Stinche, which had been incited to rebel by the Cavalcanti. Its reduction was easily effected (August, 1304), and all the captives were lodged in the new prisons, henceforth entitled the "Stinche." A more serious expedition had to be undertaken in 1305 against Pistoia, when it rose to arms in the Bianchi cause, aided by Arezzo and Pisa, and under the command of Tolosato degli Uberti. A long and vigorous siege was the result. The beleaguering force of Florentines and Lucchese was led by Duke Robert of Calabria, who, as Captain of the League, had furnished a large contingent of foot and 300 Catalan horse.[571] The town held out during the whole winter, but in April, 1306, the Pistoiese were compelled to surrender from famine. Their walls and towers were demolished, their territory divided between the Florentines and Lucchese. Pope Clement V. had vainly endeavoured to put an end to this war which dealt another cruel blow to the Tuscan Ghibellines. He was a native of France, had transferred the papal see to Avignon, and had no knowledge of Italy. Nor could Italy feel any love for an alien Pope who had deserted Rome. In fact, the Florentines declined to listen to the messengers of peace he despatched to their camp, and paid no heed to the interdict he launched against them. For although the Duke of Calabria withdrew, this was only a feint, seeing that he left them all his men under the command of Captain Pietro de la Rat. So the campaign was carried on to the end.

Nor did the other envoy of peace, Cardinal Napoleon Orsini, meet with any better fortune, for he was not only ill received in Tuscany and Romagna, but robbed of his goods and even in danger of his life. As for his excommunications, interdicts, and counsels of peace, every one laughed at them. The Florentines were determined to do the work thoroughly, and even before the conclusion of the war with Pistoia, started another expedition against the formidable castle of Montaccenico, chief stronghold of the Ubaldini, dominating the whole of the Mugello and serving as the exiles' headquarters. By dint of scattering bribes among the Ubaldini themselves, the Florentines finally won the castle by treason, and, after reducing it to ruin, immediately resolved to plant the towns of Scarperia and Firenzuola in its vicinity, "to serve as scarecrows to the Ubaldini, and harbours of refuge to faithful subjects." All willing to inhabit the little town founded for that purpose, were to be exempt from every form of vassalage. The first stone of Scarperia was laid, without delay, on the 7th of September, 1307; but the construction of Firenzuola was postponed to a much later date (1332).

We must now consider what was the object the Republic had in view, and what it achieved by means of these continual campaigns, in which even the magnates took a part; what too by the reduction of Ghibelline cities, and the destruction of castles throughout the whole territory? On the one hand, its political predominance in Tuscany was rapidly increased, and new outlets of commerce acquired; while, on the other, the power of the magnates outside Florence was overthrown by the aid of those within the walls, who, in their blind fury against the exiles, did not realise what they were doing. The Florentines of old had demolished the castles, which at one time reached nearly to their gates; they had forced the barons to dwell in the city, had subjected them to republican laws, and lowered their pride by excluding them from the government. Profiting by their disputes, the citizens had next spurred them to destroy one another; and, in conclusion, were now making them turn their weapons against more distant nobles, and overthrow the latter's strongholds in the Casentino, Mugello, and valley of the Arno. All this was invariably advantageous to the guilds and the people. Therefore, in 1306, while the Pistoian campaign was still going on, the Florentines reorganised citizen-armed bands under nineteen Gonfalonieri. This was the constitution of "the good Guelph people," a reform made, according to Villani, "in order to prevent the 'Grandi' and other powerful folk from presuming to show arrogance on the strength of having gained many victories over the Bianchi and Ghibellines."[572]

But this was not all, for the real gist of the new reform consisted in the law of the 23rd of December, 1306, by which the enactments were strengthened and an Executor of Justice was appointed to enforce their more rigorous application. The object of the law was clearly expressed by the introductory words explaining that it was intended "to preserve the liberties of the Florentine people, and break the pride of iniquitous men, which has swollen to such extent that our eyes fail to discern its limits."

In point of fact, the guilds showed no mercy to the magnates, even when fighting side by side with them against common foes. The "Executor" was required to be a Guelph, a man of the people, and a foreigner, *i.e.*, of non-Tuscan birth, from some city or place, subject to no lord, and not less than eighty miles from Florence. He was neither to be a knight nor a *law judge*, a prohibition caused by the growing hatred against *perverse judges* and fatal experience of recent Podestàs. The "Executor" was to remain in office for six months, and he was to bring with him one judge, two notaries, twenty *masnadieri*, or guards—all of whom were to be Guelphs and aliens—and two war-horses. His office was to protect the people and all the weak against powerful personages, and to call the companies to arms whenever any crime should be committed, for the prompt enforcement of the penalties prescribed. It was to be his special duty to ensure the due execution of the Enactments of Justice, and whenever the Podestà or Captain failed to do their part, he was instantly to assume their functions according to the rules minutely laid down in the new law, that was henceforth an integral portion of the enactments. He was likewise to deal punishment on all frauds and dishonest tricks practised in the offices of the Commune. Should the Podestà fail to demolish buildings (churches always excepted) in which conventicles or meetings had been illegally held, he was to enforce the said demolition, and impose a fine of 500 *lire* on the Podestà. Capital punishment was to be inflicted on all who held meetings, to plot treason against liberty or the popular government. In such case, if nobles were concerned the penalty was to be adjudged by the Podestà, and should the Podestà hesitate to act, the Executor was to mulct him as usual, and assume his functions. When the guilty were *popolani* the Executor alone was to condemn them to death and degrade their descendants to the rank of nobles. Likewise all *popolani* accessory to crimes perpetrated by nobles were to be condemned by the Executor to double the penalty prescribed by the common law. It was also the Executor's task to examine the actions of the outgoing Podestà and Captain, and he, in due turn, was subjected to investigation by persons appointed by the Priors and

Gonfaloniers of the Companies.

VI.

Meanwhile the Pope's anxiety being stirred by the increasing agitation provoked by the Florentine exiles, throughout Romagna and the Marches, as well as in Tuscany, again began to insist upon peace. But the person charged to open negotiations to this effect was Cardinal Orsini, a man of strong party feeling and doubtful integrity. For when at Arezzo in 1307, he had called there, in addition to the Florentine exiles, many adherents of his own from the adjoining States of the Church, thus assembling a force of 1,700 cavalry and a great number of foot soldiers. It appears that he had come to terms with Corso Donati and received money from him for the undertaking in view. Messer Corso, whose ambition was still unassuaged, had married a third time, and was now related, through his wife, with the Ghibelline lord, Uguccione della Faggiuola. This circumstance naturally exposed him to much suspicion on the part of the Guelphs, and accordingly, being even more angered and discontented than before, he was again bitterly hostile to Messer Rosso della Tosa and his followers, who in their turn, and as an inevitable consequence, had again combined with the wealthier burghers. Hence, the latter, on noting the Cardinal's preparations, and Donati's new manœuvres, speedily collected an army of 3,000 horse and 15,000 foot, and without further hesitation marched towards Arezzo, ravaging the enemies' lands by the way. Thereupon, by way of displaying his military tactics, the Cardinal directed his march on Florence through the Casentino. But as the Florentines outwitted him, by doubling back and reaching the city before him, he was obliged to retreat to Arezzo in a very crestfallen mood. He then opened negotiations with the Florentines, who, feigning willingness to entertain his proposals, despatched two ambassadors to gull him with fair words. Compagni remarks that "no woman was ever more flattered and then abused by betrayers than he (the Cardinal) by those two knights."[575] So that all he could do was to go off with his tail between his legs, once more leaving the city under sentence of excommunication.[576] In revenge for this, the Florentines imposed fresh taxes on the clergy, punishing those who refused to pay.[577]

The worst sufferer was Corso Donati, for the Cardinal, after extracting money from him by promising to come to Florence to crush Della Tosa and his Black faction, had not even dared to approach the walls. But without acknowledging his defeat, Donati immediately plunged into fresh and more daring schemes. After a short absence from Florence, probably to gain funds and allies, he returned there in 1308. Increasingly blinded by party passion, counting on assistance from his father-in-law, Uguccione della Faggiuola, now lord of Arezzo, as well as from Prato and Pistoia, he called a meeting of his adherents in Florence. After explaining his hopes and vowing to do away with the Enactments of Justice, he urged them to draw their swords and make an end of those Neri, who, after receiving so much help from him and gaining victory by his means, now treated him so iniquitously. But the rumour being already abroad that he expected aid from that bitterest foe of Florence—the formidable Uguccione—the popular feeling against him was excited to the highest pitch.[578] After being repressed for some time the general fury burst out all at once, and took Donati unawares. Suddenly, on the 6th of October, 1308, the Signory sounded the alarm-bell, and the people, rising to arms, united with the Della Tosa faction, other friendly magnates, and De la Rat's Catalan troops. Donati was denounced to the Podestà, Piero della Branca of Gubbio, as a traitor to his country, and in less than an hour he was accused, tried, and condemned. Immediately afterwards, the Signory, Podestà, Captain, and Executor, with their respective familiars, the Catalan troops, knights, and citizen-trained bands, marched to St. Piero Maggiore to attack the Donati houses. But Messer Corso and his friends resisted so valiantly, that had Uguccione and the others fulfilled their promise of coming to the rescue in time, the affair might have taken an ugly turn. It is supposed that the Aretines were already on the march, when, hearing that all Florence had risen against Donati, they decided to turn back. At all events, no succour arrived, and Messer Corso soon found that even many of his Florentine friends had ceased to defend the chain barricades, and relinquished the struggle. Thereupon the people broke through, and soon demolished the houses he had been forced to abandon. Accompanied by a few devoted adherents, he fled from the town by the Croce gate, with the citizens and Catalans in hot pursuit. The first man captured on the banks of the Africo was Gherardo dei Bordoni, who was instantly slain. Next, the crowd cut off his hand and nailed it on the door of the Adimari house, because Tedici degli Adimari had first instigated the dead man to join with Donati. A few moments later the Catalans overtook Donati himself at San Salvi, and in obedience to orders killed him on the spot. According to another version of the tale, he first tried to bribe them to spare his life, but without success; so, to avoid falling into the hands of his Florentine foes, he cast himself on the ground and was dispatched by a spear- thrust in the throat. The monks of San Salvi bore away his dead body, and the following day buried him in the Badia without any pomp for fear of provoking the public wrath.[579]

The cause of this sudden and irresistible burst of popular fury is clearly explained by the letters which the Commune shortly addressed to the Lucchese, in whose territory the Bordoni had found refuge. "It is known to all Tuscany that the Donati had planned a war to the death, in order to give the city of Florence and the Guelph party into the hands of the Ghibellines, and subject to their yoke, to the utter extermination and destruction of the Guelph Government. Those rebels intended to break all bounds, and subdue the city to their rule, although Messer Corso and his followers shamelessly styled the Signory Ghibelline instead."[580] These words were written by the Signory in March, 1309. In fact, the Neri being split into Donati and Tosinghi factions, and the latter having united with the wealthier burghers, from whom could the Donati hope assistance, save from the Ghibellines? The lower class of the people was weak, and the distant Pope increasingly urged the return of the exiles. The latter had now combined with Donati's whilom allies, the nobles of the *contado*, standing aloof from many of the burgher Bianchi, who had been expelled at the same moment, but were gradually permitted to return; and they had also separated from all independent men, such as Dante Alighieri. The poet, in fact, being opposed to Donati, and a promoter of the Enactments of Justice, had been finally driven to adopt an individual attitude. Thus the Bianchi, though exiled for having sided with the people, were now on the side of the magnates, the Ghibellines, Uguccione, and even of Corso Donati, the only person likely to profit by so hybrid an alliance. Accordingly his death had the immediate result of giving another terrible shock to the magnates' power, both within and without the city. Speedy proof was afforded of this when, at the beginning of 1309, the proud Ubaldini came to make submission to the Florentine Commune, promising to guard the passes of the Apennines, and supporting their offer by fitting guarantees of good faith. In consequence of this they were accepted as friends, with the condition, "that in every act and deed they should behave as good subjects and citizens."[581]

Throughout the whole of its history the Florentine Commune invariably adopted this plan when admitting nobles to its midst. But it had also the effect of enabling conquered and subject magnates to gain increased strength in the city itself. Therefore, first without and then within the walls, they unceasingly combated the people and the Republic, down to the distant time when they were finally crushed by the State. If Florentine prosperity as yet showed no signs of diminution during the sanguinary struggle now described, it was for two reasons which should be duly kept in mind. The successive conflicts we have narrated, all proceeded from the constant necessity of preserving the merchant-republic from the impact of the extraneous feudal body threatening to check its natural growth. These civil wars, however, were carried by a comparatively small number of citizens, eager to gain possession of a government that had far less influence on society than is generally supposed. The true motive-power of the Republic proceeded less from the Signory, which was changed every two months, than from the commercial and political constitution of the guilds, which were firmly organised and, so far, thoroughly in unison. The conditions of an all-absorbing modern State, wherein every shock affects society at large, had not yet sprung to life in the Middle Ages. The Italian republics were miniature confederacies of separate associations, under a central government of so feeble a kind, that even when totally suppressed for a time, no great harm seemed to result from its loss.

VII.

Corso Donati's death put an end to the tragedy of which the expulsion of the Bianchi had formed the first act; and now the condition of all Italy, as well as Florence, was changed by a new event. This was the murder of Albert of Hapsburg by his nephew, on the 1st of May, 1308. Therefore the election of a new king of the Romans and future emperor was now imminent. Philip the Beautiful aspired to win the Imperial crown, if not for himself, at least for his brother, Charles of Valois, through the help of Clement V. As the Pope was residing in France, he could not directly oppose the design, but had certainly no intention of favouring it. With the Angevins at Naples, the Holy See transferred to Avignon, and Rome in revolt against him, the choice of a French emperor would have placed him entirely at Philip's mercy.

Accordingly he gave secret support to Henry of Luxembourg, who was elected to the throne as Henry VII. on the 27th of November, 1308. This emperor, born on the French frontier, and educated in France, presented a combination of Germanic and Latin characteristics. As lord of a petty State, he had no real strength or power of his own; but having great nobility of mind and an imagination disposed to mysticism, he had formed a lofty idea of the dignity and might of the universal Empire that he hoped to restore to Rome. He seemed totally unable to comprehend that the feudal union of Germany and Italy, which had missed success even at the beginning of the Middle Ages, had become totally impossible now that feudalism itself, the principal basis of the Holy Roman Empire, was almost annihilated in Italy. Nevertheless, when Henry first raised the Imperial flag, enormous hopes were conceived by the Ghibellines, and rapidly spread throughout the peninsula. All men seemed to be suddenly stirred to genuine enthusiasm.

The Ghibellines of that day were no longer the Ghibellines of old, and in Italy the conception of the Empire had undergone a total change. The hostile attitude of the Popes towards republican freedom and independence; their persistent struggle against the Roman Commune; the fact of Clement V. being at a distance, in France, and weakly dependent on the French monarch; the necessity, now beginning to be generally recognised, of building up, from the ruins of old municipalities, new forms of government, such as were now arising in France and elsewhere; the revival of classical studies, enabling men to glean from the Republic and Empire of ancient Rome some literary conception of the unity and strength of the secular State required to meet present needs;—had all combined to transform the mediæval idea of the Empire. For now that France and other countries were detached from it, the Empire was no longer universal, but simply Germanico-Roman; while to Italian eyes it was beginning, though still very vaguely, to seem a revival of the old Rome that had always been the spiritual head of the civilised world, and the possible centre of an Italian confederated State. This idea was clearly expressed for the first time in Dante's "Monarchia," which then served as the manifesto of the Ghibelline party. The same idea was afterwards more widely developed in the "Defensor Pacis" of Marsilio da Padova, and at a subsequent date inspired the fantastic enthusiasm of Cola di Rienzo. The latter's attempt —so lauded by Petrarch—to create a new Roman, Italian, Imperial Republic was a confused dream of scholastic, classico-humanistic, feudal, and mediæval ideas, but nevertheless a dream containing in embryo some vague conception of the future Italian State as it was already dimly foreseen, although with no comprehension of its real nature. Such as it was, however, this incoherent jumble of ideas became the standard of the Italian Ghibellines.

The Guelphs had no philosophical programme of their own to flaunt in return. The force of events, and the pressing need of maintaining the independence of Italian cities against Pope and emperor, was then the war-cry of the Florentine Guelphs. To Florence, the coming of the emperor signified the revival of the old Ghibelline party, consequently the revival of Arezzo, Pistoia, Pisa, and other hostile cities, all ready to compress her within a circle of steel, and strangle her commerce. For this reason she called on the Guelph cities, and all seeking to preserve freedom and escape foreign tyranny, to join in an Italian confederation, with herself at its head. It was, therefore, at this moment that the small merchant-republic initiated a true national policy, and became a great power in Italy. So, in the mediæval shape of a feudal and universal Empire, on the one hand, and in that of a municipal confederation on the other, a gleam of the national idea first began to appear, though still in the far distance and veiled in clouds. Both sides fought eagerly for the interests of the moment, and both were inspired with the presentiment of a new future; but neither discerned that this future was only to be attained by the destruction of both parties alike.

At this juncture the Pope seemed favourable to Henry VII., for he encouraged his project of going to Rome to assume the Imperial crown, and urged the Italians to accord him a good reception. Nevertheless—as the Florentines had known from the first—he could not wish to see Italy subject to the Empire, having too keen a remembrance of all that the Church had endured at the hands of Frederic II. Following, therefore, the traditional policy of the Roman Court, he simultaneously encouraged Robert of Naples, formerly Duke of Calabria, who, having succeeded to the throne at the death of King Charles II. (May 3, 1309), was naturally prepared to resist Henry's pretensions to the utmost. At first the Florentines appeared disposed to be passive lookers on, but were not deceived by the Pope's pretence of encouraging Emperor Henry. They desired a closer alliance with Clement, but he too was very resentful with regard to their past conduct, and with some reason, secretly echoed the words of Benedict XI.: "Who could imagine that those men" (the Florentines) "should presume to be sons of the Church, while fighting against her?" But nowise dismayed by this, they treated with King Robert, who still allowed them to retain the services of Captain De la Rat and his Catalan horse, and now sent them his flag in addition. With the help of this contingent the Florentines made repeated attacks on Arezzo, refusing to desist even when Henry warned them to respect that city as a fief of the Empire. Their attacks were invariably successful, and they even forced their way into the town, but were prevented from holding it by the treachery of the magnates, as it was rumoured at the time.[582] All acts and decrees of the Commune bore the heading: "In honour of Holy Church and His Majesty

King Robert, and to the defeat of the German king."[583]

VIII.

In 1310 Henry set out for Italy, leaving the affairs of Germany to his son's care. Louis of Savoy, the newly elected Senator of Rome, was sent on in advance, and reached Florence on the 3rd of July, accompanied by two German prelates. The latter were admitted to the council; but in answer to their request that Florence should prepare to receive the emperor with due honour, Betto Brunelleschi replied: "That the Florentines had never lowered their horns before any lord whatsoever;" and this somewhat indecorous response was sufficiently indicative of the public feeling. In fact, the Imperial envoys, though everywhere well received, obtained nothing from Florence, and even failed to put a stop to the war with Arezzo. And when ambassadors from nearly every city of Italy sought audience of Henry at Lausanne, no Florentine envoys appeared. On the contrary, Florence was energetically preparing for defence; the new walls were raised about sixteen feet higher, and surrounded by moats from the Prato gate to that of San Gallo, and thence to the Arno.[584] On the 30th of September Robert arrived in Florence from Avignon, where the Pope had crowned him King of Naples, and likewise appointed him Vicar of Romagna, to prevent Henry from seizing that province which had recently seceded from the Empire. King Robert soon came to an understanding with the Florentines, and arranged measures with them for their common defence. Notwithstanding this, Henry continued to advance, heading all his decrees with the phrase, *in nomine regis pacifici*, and assuming the part of a just and impartial judge. He summoned both Guelphs and Ghibellines to his side, promising equal welcome to all. He reached Susa by the 24th of October, and on the Feast of the Epiphany (January 6, 1311) assumed the Iron Crown in the Church of St. Ambrogio at Milan.

But in this city his dream of peace was disturbed by a sudden outburst of civil war. The Guelph Torriani were expelled by the Visconti before his eyes; and from that moment, being forcibly dragged into the vortex of party strife, Henry renounced his mission as peacemaker, and was again a German, foreign, and *barbarian* emperor. It was averred that the Florentines had bribed Guido della Torre to raise a rebellion, and that this was the cause of his expulsion. We have no certainty that this was the case, but it is an ascertained fact that they sent money, despatches, and envoys to Cremona, Lodi, Brescia, Pavia, and other Lombard cities, and succeeded in stirring them to rise against

Henry.[585] They also sent ambassadors to Naples, France, and more particularly to Avignon, where they lavished heavy bribes on the officials of the Curia, for the purpose of learning when the Pope spoke truly or falsely. On all sides they displayed such feverish activity that one day the Cardinal da Prato exclaimed in the presence of the French king: "How great is the insolence of these Florentines in daring to tempt every lord with their lousy small coin!"[586]

Even in crises such as these the magnates of Florence could not lay aside their animosities, but continued to disturb the city by fresh riots now and then. In February, 1311, the Donati murdered Betto Brunelleschi, whom they considered responsible for Messer Corso's death, and immediately afterwards disinterred the latter's corpse at San Salvi, and reburied him with due pomp now that he had been avenged.[587]

Nevertheless, order was quickly restored, since there was little leisure for private feuds, and men's minds were absorbed in graver concerns. At the beginning of June, 1311, Florence, Pisa, Lucca, Sienna, and Volterra gave their formal adherence to the Guelph League, and swore to combine in armed defence against Henry. On the 26th of June, the Florentines despatched De la Rat to Bologna with 400 Catalan horse, while the Siennese and Lucchese forwarded another contingent to King Robert in Romagna, where that monarch was harrying and incarcerating all the Ghibellines and exiled Florentine Bianchi who were then trying to stir the Papal cities to revolt.[588] And when it was rumoured that the king was seeking to make terms with Henry, the Florentines wrote to him, insisting on his entering Rome at once, according to his promise, and likewise warning him that they would stand no half-measures, and that if he delayed, or attempted any pact with the emperor, they would instantly withdraw their forces from the League. "Inasmuch as your Royal Majesty has repeatedly promised us to make no terms with the German king, but to supply us with an armed force and go in person to Rome to exterminate our common foe."[589] This missive had some effect, for Robert speedily despatched 400 horse to Rome under his brother John, who, with the help of the Orsini, soon won the chief vantage-points of the city. The king still feigned to act in the interests of the Empire; but no one was deceived by this pretence, and the Florentines were satisfied.

Meanwhile Henry, still faithful to his original plan, and quite unconscious of the extraordinary change that was going on, had reduced Cremona to submission, and was now besieging Brescia, which opposed a more stubborn resistance. The "peaceful" monarch vented his rage on his prisoners and put one of the Guelph leaders to a most atrociously cruel death. But the Brescians still refused to surrender; the flower of the German army was perishing from sickness and wounds, and Henry's brother died of his hurts. During these days of slaughter, Florence wrote to the Brescians, saying, "Remember that the safety of all Italy and all Guelphs depends on your resistance. The Latins must always hold the Germans in enmity, seeing that they are opposed in act and deed, in manners and soul; not only is it impossible to serve, but even to hold any intercourse with that race."[590] At the same time they wrote to encourage other cities to make a stand and rise to arms. They summoned the Perugians "to shake off their bonds of vassalage, and proclaim the sweets of liberty"; repeating to all that, for their own part, they would unceasingly devote their arms, men, and gold to the task of resistance.[591] Also, for the greater reinforcement of the citizens and the Guelph party, they removed the ban from all exiles, probably well disposed to the Guelphs, only maintaining it against several hundred supposed Ghibellines, Dante Alighieri among the number. This modification of the Law of Banishment was known as the Amendment of Baldo d'Aguglione, one of the Priors by whom it was passed on September 2, 1311.[592]

Meanwhile, after an heroic defence, Brescia was forced to accept terms of surrender, whereupon Henry immediately set out towards Genoa, entering that city on October 21, 1311. Here, though deeply grieved by the death of his wife, he allowed no delay in the necessary preparations for continuing his journey to Rome by the Pisan route. And, being informed of this, the Florentines redoubled their efforts. They strengthened the garrison of San Miniato al Tedesco, recalled from Bologna De la Rat and his troops, despatched reinforcements to Lucca, Sarzana, Pietrasanta, and the fortresses in Lunigiana, and the western Valdarno.[593] But remarkable as it may seem, they never neglected the interests of their trade, even at this critical time. In fact, they chose this moment to address the King of France, explaining the serious difficulties in which Henry's descent had involved them, and lamenting that the present war should have led His Majesty to take measures hurtful to the interests of their merchants, upon whom the prosperity of Florence so largely depended, "*cum Civitas nostra ex predictis Florentinis ex maiori parte consistat.* You have always hitherto protected them," they said in conclusion, "and our chief hopes are placed, after God, in your Majesty, especially now that Henry threatens to go to Pisa and march against us, *qui firmavimus et parati sumus nostram quam a vobis et a vestris recognovimus, defendere libertatem.*" They likewise besought the king to order matters in such wise, that their trade with France might be pursued without interruption, even during the war.[594]

Meanwhile the emperor had despatched another embassy to Florence, composed of Bishop Niccolò of Botrintò, and Pandolfo Savelli; but when these envoys finally reached Lastra, after encountering many mishaps by the way, they were not only robbed, but placed in mortal danger. The bells rang the alarm at their approach, armed men poured into their lodging, and the Podestà and Captain of Florence arrived barely in time to save their lives. Accordingly, by the advice of those functionaries, the strangers quitted the town in the utmost haste.[595] Thereupon (20th of November, 1311) the emperor cited the Florentines to appear before him in Genoa to tender apology and submission. Then, finding that—as was to be expected—they disregarded his summons, he placed their city under the ban of the Empire.[596] Even this was received with the same indifference as the interdicts of the Pope. But recalling their merchants from Genoa, they hastened their preparations for war.

The magnates now gave another proof of their irrepressible turbulence. Precisely at this moment, and heedless of the grave danger menacing the Republic, they plunged the city in disorder with their private feuds. On the

11th of January, 1312, Pazzino de' Pazzi, one of the leading men, and much beloved by the people, was set upon and killed, as he rode to the chase, by Paffiera dei Cavalcanti, to avenge the loss of Masino de' Cavalcanti and Betto Brunelleschi, whose murder was attributed to Pazzi. The victim's body was carried to the Priors' Palace, and the indignant people rising to arms, marched under their own banner to the Cavalcanti houses, and burnt them to the ground. As the speediest way of checking these tumults, the Signory exiled the Cavalcanti at once, conferred knighthood on four of the Pazzi family, and presented them with certain lands and property in the gift of the Commune.[597] Thus, even at this juncture, order was soon re-established.

IX.

During this time Henry was preparing to go to Rome. In the Imperial camp minstrels were chanting the piteous tale of Conradin's death, and the popular muse of the Ghibellines continued to shower laudatory greetings on the just judge, the celestial peacemaker. Men of letters, poets, jurisconsults, and philosophers persisted in regarding Henry as the new redeemer who was to restore the Imperial crown to Rome, give Italy freedom and peace. Cino da Pistoia cried, "Nunc dimittis servum tuum, Domine, quia viderunt oculi mei salutare tuum."[598] But Dante Alighieri was the most exultant of all, for at this moment he was virtually the chief representative of the Imperial party in Italy. On Henry's first approach to the Alps he had addressed an epistle to the princes and governments of Italy, exclaiming, "Hosanna to thee, suffering Italy, now wilt thou be envied of all, for 'Sponsus tuus et mundi solatium et gloria plebis tuæ, clementissimus Henricus, Divus et Augustus et Cæsar, ad nuptias properat.' Let the oppressed rejoice, for their redemption draweth near. Let all who have endured injuries like unto mine forgive and grant pardon, for now the Shepherd that cometh from God will lead us all back to the fold."[599]

Afterwards, however, when Henry was about to march on Cremona, and the Florentines had already declared openly against him, Alighieri's joy turned to wrath, and from the source of the Arno in the Casentino hills, he wrote another epistle, dated 31st of March, 1311, and addressed, "*Scelestissimis Florentinis.* Know ye not, God hath ordained that the human race be under the rule of one emperor, for the defence of justice, peace, and civilisation, inasmuch as Italy was always a prey to civil war whenever the Empire lapsed? Do ye dare, ye alone, to cast off the yoke of freedom and seek for new kingdoms, even as though *alia sit florentina civitas, alia sit romana*? Most foolish and insensate men, ye shall succumb perforce to the Imperial eagle. Know ye not that true liberty consisteth in voluntary obedience to Divine and human laws? Yet while presuming to claim liberty, ye conspire against all laws!"[600]

Then, when instead of marching forward, Henry tarried in Lombardy, to attack the cities stirred to revolt against him by Florence, Dante's indignation rose to its highest pitch, and on the 16th of April of the same year he addressed another epistle to the emperor, saying, "Men declare that thou dost waver in thy purpose, and wouldst turn back from it, disheartened. Art not, then, the man expected by us all? When my hands touched thy feet, I exultantly cried, 'Ecce Agnus Dei, ecce qui abstulit peccata mundi.' Why tarriest thou? If thine own glory move thee not, let thy son's, at least, stir thee.

"Ascanium surgentem, et spes hæredis Tuli
Respice, cui *regnum Italiæ*, romanaque tellus
Debetur.... (Æn. iv. 272.)

What may it profit thee to subdue Cremona? Brescia, Bergamo, Pavia, and other cities will continue to revolt until thou hast extirpated the root of the evil. Art ignorant mayhap where the rank fox lurketh in hiding? The beast drinketh from the Arno, polluting the waters with its jaws. Knowest thou not that Florence is its name? Florence is the viper that stings its mother's breast, the black sheep that corrupts the whole flock, the Myrrha guilty of incest with her father. In fact it is Florence who rends the bosom of the mother—Rome, that created her in the likeness of herself, and violates the commands of the Father of the Faithful, who is agreed with thee. And Florence, while contemning her own sovereign, sides with an alien monarch and others' rights. Delay no more, but haste to slay the new Goliath with the sling of thy wisdom and the stone of thy might."[601]

This semi-scholastic, semi-Biblico-classical, and often inflated language, admirably represents the ideas of the period, and proves the excited state of Dante's mind. He was undoubtedly the first to put clearly into words the new Ghibelline theory that had been gradually developing and maturing in his mind ever since he had indignantly parted from his fellow-exiles, and turned to solitary study. Although, as we have already remarked, this new conception —more amply developed in Dante's "Monarchia"—was certainly theoretical and literary rather than practical, it was deeply rooted nevertheless in the thought of the period, and the work devoted to its disclosure already shows, by unmistakable signs, that the spirit of the age was about to be transformed. In reading the "Monarchia" we are often plunged back in the Middle Ages, but the pale gleaming of a new dawn often shimmers before our eyes. "The Empire represents the law upon which human society is firmly based; it is derived accordingly from God, the source of the Imperial, as of the Papal power." In this we may already discern the conception of an independent secular society emancipated from the Church, and thus the idea of a State founded upon law—an idea inspired by ancient Rome, and suggested by new practical needs—is first put into words at the close of the Middle Ages which had denied its possibility. But even Dante failed to see that the new State must be intrinsically national, neither could he perceive that the universal Empire he invoked, and now represented by Henry VII., was precisely what made it impossible for that State to be formed. Thus the novel and almost prophetic portion of his book is neutralised by its theoretic and scholastic elements. The independent secular State, foreseen by his lofty intellect, was indeed bound to triumph; but its victory implied the destruction of the mediæval Empire of which his book was intended to be the apotheosis. On the contrary, the "Monarchia" became its epitaph, as some one has justly remarked. Nevertheless, some vaguely distant conception of the State, and even of the national State, occasionally flashes forth in Dante's book, though still battling with the mists of revived classic lore. The Empire is not, in fact, to be separated from the Eternal City that gave it birth, and of which it is the heir. Rome, the natural and permanent seat of empire, was to be restored to her ancient grandeur by the coming of the emperor. Also, were not Rome and Italy one and the same thing? Henry VII. was the representative, not only of law but of peace, freedom, and civilisation, therefore by him Italy's woes would be brought to an end, and Italy's freedom guaranteed. Was not Henry the master of the world? Hence he could desire nothing more, and could not fail to be the just lord and father of all, respecting every legally acquired right and jurisdiction. But it was precisely the emperor's yearning to be lord of all men and all things that was so opposed to the national spirit that was already beginning to stir many minds, and that—if almost unawares—Alighieri was so earnestly lauding, while practically denying it by imploring the resurrection of the Empire.

This contradiction gave a truly tragic hue to Dante's mental state at the time. He was profoundly sincere, profoundly persuaded of the truth of his ideas. Inflamed with holy wrath against all supporters of the Pope and the Angevins, mindful of the deeds he had seen committed in Florence by Boniface VIII. and Charles of Valois, he had a premonition, amounting almost to second sight, of the numerous calamities to be wrought upon all Italy by the obstinacy of his opponents. But he failed to see that his own political theory would have thrust Italy back into the feudal Middle Ages, neutralising the work of the communes and the result of the prolonged struggles, in which he himself had been recently involved. The conflicting emotions stirring within him found vent in the "Divine Comedy" depicting two different and often contrasting worlds, and wherein the past is touched and transformed by a new spirit, made the source of a new future, new art, new literature and new civilisation. In this great poem the reality of human passion and human life breaks through the mystic clouds of the Middle Ages, and finally disperses them for ever. Therefore philosophers and historians may find in the poem all the constituents of an age in which one form of society was dying out, and another springing, almost visibly, to life. But although the conflict of thought in Dante's mind might produce immortal verse, it could not possibly create any efficient political system.

On the latter point the advantage lay with the Florentines, inasmuch as they always clung to actualities and the needs of the moment. They weighed and counted their bales of silks and woollens, and calculated the probable damage to their import and export trade from the triumph of the Empire in Italy. They saw that it would inevitably ruin their commerce; and by assuring victory to their foes, *i.e.*, to the magnates, Pisans, and many petty Italian tyrants, would overthrow their own freedom and the government of the guilds. Was not this belief justified by the fate of Milan, Cremona, and Brescia? This was why the Florentines called the Guelph cities to their side, and in the name of Italy, freedom, and their common independence, united them all in a defensive alliance against the foreign foe. Nevertheless they had also leagued with King Robert and espoused the cause of France and the Pope, whose triumph was destined to prove fatal to Italian liberty and independence. As we have previously shown, the nation could only be built up on the ruins and by the destruction of both parties. The long and difficult course of historic evolution requisite to prepare the way for a distant future was then unknown to all. The Florentines only thought of securing present safety, and in this they were well advised and fortunate.

X.

Meanwhile that "crowned victim of his own fate," as Del Lungo calls Henry VII., continued his advance with untroubled self-confidence. The royal peacemaker felt no remorse at having drenched Italian cities in blood and disseminated discord. Not even the loss of wife and brother, the slaughter of his best soldiers, the desertion of numerous adherents, nor the scathing contempt of his foes availed to shake his self-assurance and certainty of success. Calm and composed as ever, he entered Pisa on the 6th of March, 1312, was welcomed with great pomp, and remained amid this truly friendly population until the 23rd of April. While at Lausanne he had already received sixty thousand florins from the Pisans, and they now showed the sincerity of their submission to him by accepting new magistrates at his hands and promising a second gift of money equal to the first.[602] Neither did he feel the slightest alarm on hearing that the army of Robert's brother, Prince John, had gained reinforcements in Rome.

That prince had brought with him a force of over six hundred Catalan and Apulian horse, and had now been joined by two hundred of the best Florentine cavalry, led by De la Rat, who, in addition to his Catalan troops, had also collected one thousand foot. Fresh contingents had poured in from Lucca, Sienna, and other towns. The Capitol, the Castle of St. Angelo, and Trastevere, and all the fortresses were therefore held by the prince. And as a final stroke, the Neapolitan king, after first stating that he occupied Rome for the Empire, now declared openly against Henry. Nevertheless the latter continued his march with only one thousand horse and a body of infantry, and on the 7th of May, 1312, entered the Eternal City. He quickly attacked and won the Capitol; but in seeking to force his way to St. Peter's to grasp the Imperial crown, a real battle took place in the streets; and a *sortie* from Castle St. Angelo repulsed him with heavy loss. Nor would his coronation have been accomplished at all, had not the Roman people declared in his favour and by threats of violence compelled the prelates to disregard custom and perform the solemn rite in the Lateran Church on the 29th of June. But Henry was now obliged to recognise that even the Pope was adverse, when the latter commanded him to refrain from attacking Naples, to make a twelvemonth's truce with the king, to leave Rome on the day of his coronation, to renounce all rights over the Eternal City, and never re-enter it without permission. At last the Pope had dropped his mask, and the Florentines were proved good prophets. But at the very moment in which their Guelph policy triumphed, and the breach between Pope and emperor was so plainly revealed, the people proclaimed Rome an Imperial city and their Capitol the permanent seat of the emperor, whose authority was to be acknowledged as emanating from the Roman people alone. "Dum sola tribunitia, exterminatis Patribus, potestas adolevisset illo sub magistratu … omnia hæc parari Cæsari, ipsum evocandum in Urbem, vehendumque triumphaliter in Capitolium, principatum ab sola plebe recogniturum."[603]

Dante's own idea was now uttered by the voice of Rome.

At last, and after much hesitation, Henry decided to adopt the advice proffered by the great poet some time before, and went to lay siege to Florence. Crossing the Roman Campagna in August, his army was decimated by fever, and after the capture of Montevarchi and San Giovanni, he halted at

Figline.[604] The Florentines, without good commanders and with most disorderly haste, marched a large force of infantry and 1,800 horse to the Castle of Incisa. But they then declined to accept battle, and the emperor continued his journey by another route, vigorously repulsing every *sortie* made from Incisa for the purpose of arresting his passage. On the 19th of September he invested Florence on all sides, establishing his headquarters at San Salvi. The citizens, having received no news from the army, were almost taken by surprise, but, snatching their weapons, hurried to the walls under the banners of the people, and accompanied by their bishop, sword in hand, together with all his clergy. Two days later the troops sent to take the field against the emperor made their way back to Florence across country; reinforcements arrived from Lucca, Sienna, Pistoia, Bologna, Romagna, and in short from all the cities of the League. Thus, Villani tells us, an army was collected of 4,000 horse and innumerable infantry. The emperor having only a force of 800 German knights, 1,000 Italian horse, and a considerable body of foot, was merely able to ravage the land. Fortunately for him, the year's harvest had been so abundant that there was no difficulty in provisioning his troops. Even now, in spite of their great numerical superiority, the Florentines still shrank from attempting a pitched battle; but inside the town they felt so completely secure that they only closed the gates facing the emperor's camp, leaving the others open to traffic as in times of peace. This state of things lasted to the month of November, but then Henry's patience being altogether exhausted, he raised the siege and set out for Poggibonsi and Pisa. The Florentines started in pursuit, and attacked him several times on the road, with varying results. The emperor tarried at Poggibonsi to the 6th of March, 1313, without provisions, or funds, and his army was so reduced that his cavalry had dwindled to 1,000 horse. Nevertheless he continued his march, and although, according to Villani, his assailants were four to one, he contrived to fight his way to Pisa, and arrived there on the 9th of March.

At this time, although his health was ruined by mental worry and bodily hardship, his purse emptied, and his army melted away, the emperor was still calm and hopeful. In Pisa he made many attempts to pursue the war by legal devices: depriving the Florentines of their judicial rights, dismissing their judges and notaries, imposing heavy fines, and condemning many of their citizens to confiscation and punishment. And regardless of the fact that these sentences had no effect, he continued to launch them as before. He prohibited the Florentines from coining money, while permitting Ubizzo Spinola of Genoa and the Marquis of Monferrato to fabricate within their own territories false florins marked with the Florentine stamp. Naturally an act so damaging to the public credit provoked severe blame.[605] He condemned King Robert as a traitor to the Empire, and made alliance with Frederic of Sicily and the Genoese. He also determined to march against Naples, although the Pope had threatened excommunication on any one attacking that kingdom, which was considered a fief of the Church. Burning with zeal for this new enterprise, he demanded money and men from Lombardy and Germany. He was thus enabled to collect 2,500 foreign and 1,500 Italian horse, besides an army of foot soldiers. Seventy galleys were equipped by the Genoese; fifty by King Frederic. The Pisans, who had already sacrificed everything to his cause, managed to furnish twenty galleys. He also obtained a certain amount of money, and set off on the 8th of August, 1313, with some reasonable hope of success. But his sudden death at Buonconvento, on the 24th of May, brought everything to an end.

On the 27th of the same month the Florentines exultantly announced to their allies that "Jesus Christ had procured the death of that most haughty tyrant, Henry, entitled King of the Romans and Emperor, by the rebel persecutors of Holy Church, to wit, your Ghibellines and our foes."[606] During Henry's life they had conferred the lordship of Florence on Robert for five years, and now stretched the term to three more, on the well-understood condition that their free, Guelph, and popular government should be left intact. All they asked from him was a military leader bearing the king's flag, acting in his name, contributing a few sturdy men at arms, and competent to take command of the citizen army in order to protect the Republic from possible attacks on the part of Pisa or Genoa, and against Ghibelline captains such as Uguccione della Fagguiola and others. Pisa and Uguccione were their most dreaded foes. The latter, indeed, had already hired one thousand of Henry's soldiers, composing the first of those Free Companies destined to speedily become the real scourge of Italy.[607]

The Pope, now reduced to be the slave of France, threw himself into the arms of King Robert, and named him Senator of Rome, thus causing the return thither of Angevin vicars. As the Pontiff hoped to be able to assume the authority of the Empire during the interregnum, he annulled Henry's decree against Robert, and appointed him Imperial Vicar in Italy for a term extending to two months after the election of the next emperor.

Notwithstanding Robert's augmented power and his lordship over their city, the Florentines were now vastly improved in strength, both morally and materially, since they had foreseen future events far more accurately than others, had been the chief authors of all that had occurred, and were the friends and allies of those who had triumphed with them. The people were substantially supreme; the magnates were overthrown; and trade which had gone on uninterruptedly during the war, attained more vigorous development now that peace was restored. But what had become of the Guelph Federation, and of the name of Italy invoked to call it into being? All had vanished in a flash. The very fact of the Florentines now feeling compelled to crave protection from a king, clearly proves that their vast prosperity, notwithstanding the Republic, had neither sufficient self-reliance nor strength to preserve its independence unaided. This state of things necessarily involved new complications and new dangers which could be in no case long averted. The Italian Commune was doomed to decay; the modern State destined to be born; but the moment of its birth lay beyond a period of oppression. The same fate was already distantly impending over Florence.

After Henry VII. was dead, both the nature of the Empire and its relations with Italy were changed. So, too, the Pope's alliance with France radically transformed the attitude of the Papal power towards the Italian communes, for it became increasingly hostile to their freedom and independence. The Middle Ages had come to an end, and an entirely new epoch was now opening in the history of Florence and of Italy in general.

THE END.

FOOTNOTES

[1] Originally published in the Milan *Politecnico*, March, 1866.

[2] "Lettres sur l'hist. de France." close of Letter xxv.

[3] See, for example, Goro Dati's "Storia di Firenze."

[4] Since this paper first appeared many important researches have been made on the origin of Florence and its Commune, particularly by Professor D. O. Hartwig, of whose estimable work we shall speak later on. Several general histories of Florence have also been published, of which the more noteworthy are the "Storia della Repubblica di Firenze," by the Marquis Gino Capponi (Florence, Barbera, 1875, 2 vols.), and "L'Histoire de Florence," by Mons. Perrens (Paris, 1877–90, 9 vols.), both to be mentioned farther on.

[5] At the time when this sentence was written Malespini was held to be anterior to Villani, and the latter his plagiarist. Later, the contrary was proved by Scheffer-Boichorst, many of whose arguments admit of no reply. But Marchese G. Capponi refused to be convinced, on the strength of certain indications establishing, as he thought, that Malespini had written at an earlier date than Villani. Later again the diligent researches begun by Professor Lami confirmed the fact that Malespini's work is a compilation, chiefly, from Villani, and perhaps, though only here and there, from some other chronicler of possibly earlier date. The latter hypothesis would explain the deductions of Gino Capponi.

[6] Published in Florence, 1838, 2 vols., at "The Sign of Dante" printing office. See also Gervinus, "Geschichte der florentinischen Historiographie." Frankfurt, 1833.

[7] Capellæ, "Commentarii," of which eleven editions appeared between 1531 and 1542. Ranke, "Zur Kritik neurer Geschichtschreiber." I may now add that in my opinion Ranke

was exaggeratedly hostile to Guicciardini, whose historic merits are proved by documentary evidence. *Vide* my work on Machiavelli, end of vol. iii.

[8] Here allusion is made to Capponi's "History," which was still unpublished at the time.

[9] *Vide* "Discorso Storico," chap. i.

[10] Gino Capponi, "Lettere sui Longobardi."

[11] Everything connected with the division of the land has been the theme of much dispute, both in Italy and abroad. It was learnedly treated by Troya, in his work on the "Condizione dei Romani vinti dai Longobardi"; Capponi and Capei discussed it with much subtlety in their "Lettere sui Longobardi" (appendix of the "Archivio Storico Italiano," vols. i. and ii.); so too Manzoni, Balbo, &c. The question turns on the interpretation of two passages in "Paulus Diaconus." The passage alluding to the first division made, when the Longobards seized one-third of the revenues of the land, is clear enough: "His diebus multi nobilium Romanorum ob cupiditatem interfecti sunt. Reliqui vero per hospites divisi, ut terciam partem suarum frugum Langobardis persolverent, tributarii efficiuntur." But the other is much less clear, and has been variously interpreted. This is the reading most generally adopted: "Hujus in diebus" (*i.e.*, in Autari's reign) "ob restaurationem Regni, duces qui tunc erunt, omnem substantiarum suarum mediatatem regalibus usibus tribuunt; populi tamen agravati per langobardos hospites, partiuntur." But a tenth-century version, in the Ambrosian Codex, runs as follows: "Aggravati pro Longobardis, hospitia partiuntur." The division of the land (*hospitia*), and not of the fruits of the land, would seem more clearly indicated in this second reading, accepted by Balbo. Prof. Capei, on the other hand, while accepting the first reading, asserts that the word *partiuntur* should be interpreted in an active sense. The conquered *divided* their lands with their conquerors, and therefore were oppressed (*aggravati*), being compelled to yield one-half of their estates, but they had at least the advantage of retaining the other half in their own possession.

[12] Among other authorities, *vide* Gino Capponi, note to doc. 3, vol. i. of the "Archivio Storico Italiano."

[13] Codex 772 of the Vatican Palatine Library, containing the so-called Lombard collection of Longobard laws. The discovery of the Florentine annals on the back of sheet 71 is owed to the librarian Foggini. He communicated his find to Professor Lami, who published part of the fragment, with notes. The whole was afterwards edited by Professors Pertz and Hartwig, and finally Professor C. Paoli issued an exact photo- type of the fragment in No. 1 of the "Archivio paleografico Italiano," edited by Prof. Monaci, of Rome.

[14] This is a codex from Santa Maria Novella, now No. 776, E. A. (Suppressed Monasteries section), of the Magliabecchian Library. It consists of forty-six records, part of which (the first twenty-five, down to the year 1217) were published by Fineschi in his "Memorie Storiche degli uomini illustri di S. M. Novella," vol. i. pp. 330–332.

[15] D. O. Hartwig, "Quellen und Forschungen zur Altesten Geschichte der Stadt Florenz." Part i. of this work was published in Marburg, 1875; part ii., containing both series of annals, at Halle, 1880.

[16] First published by Fineschi (op. cit., vol. i. p. 257) and afterwards by Hartwig (ii. 185 and fol.), with many notes and additions. Some new names of Consuls are contained in the so-called "Chronicle" of Brunetto Latini, to be mentioned later on.

[17] One was discovered by Pro. C. Paoli in the Laurentian Library, Codex xxviii. 8, *vide* his paper "Di un libro del Dr. O. Hartwig," in the "Archivio Storico It.," tom. ix., anno 1882. Other copies were discovered by the late Prof. Lami, who intended to mention them in an essay on Malespini.

[18] Discovered, but not published, by Follini, the editor of Malespini, in a codex of the Magliabecchian Library at Florence, shelf ii. No. 67.

[19] In the Archives of Lucca, in a codex of the Orsucci Collection, O. 40.

[20] This date (Hartwig i. 64) is not found in the Latin version, which is consequently held to be of earlier date.

[21] "Appendice alle Letture di famiglia," vol. i. Florence: Cellini, 1854.

[22] Hartwig, "Quellen und Forschungen," etc.

[23] *Vide* Professor Santini, in pt. i. doc. 18 of his forthcoming work, gives a document dated June 14, 1188, with the signature, "Ego Sanzanome index et notarius." In the Acts of the Tuscan League of 1197 (Santini, vol. i. 21, p. 37) we find the name of "Sanzanome de Sancto Miniato" among the signatures following that of the Consul of San Miniato.

[24] Professor Paoli makes the same statement in his before-mentioned work. The Codex in question is the Magliab.- Strozz., Cl. xxv. 571. The "Gesta" were published about the same time by Hartwig (op. cit.) and by the Tuscan "Deputazione di Storia patria" (Cellini, 1876).

[25] Just at this point there are several gaps in the Codex.

[26] *Vide* Weiland's edition in the Mon[ta.]-Germ[a.] xxii. 377–475, and the same editor's remarks in the "Archiv. der Gesellschaft für ältere deutsche Geschichte," vol. xii. p. 1 and fol.

[27] Ciampi, the editor of one part of it, and Scheffer Boichorst in his "Florentiner Studien."

[28] Prof. Santini, who gave much attention to the subject, discovered in Florence twelve copies of Martin Polono, and three of its translations, all of the fourteenth century. Other copies have been found since by Prof. Lami.

[29] "Impressum Florentiæ apud Sanctum Jacobum de Ripoli, Anno Domini mcccclxxviii." Other editions were produced in the sixteenth century. Prof. Santini has discovered three fourteenth-century MSS. of this work in Florence.

[30] The Naples Codex is marked xiii.-F. 16. A similar codex of the fifteenth century, carried down to the death of Henry of

Luxemburg, is in the Laurentian-Gaddiano Collection, cxix.

[31] In pt. ii. of his "Quellen," &c., where these extracts are given under the title of "Gesta Florentinorum und deren Ableitungen und Fortsetzungen."

[32] In mentioning certain Saracen nobles, sent as prisoners that year *alla Chiesa di Roma*, he adds: "*et io gli viddi*" ("and I beheld them").

[33] It comes down to 1303, but the concluding paragraph seems to be written by a later hand. But the preceding paragraph narrates events of 1297, and Brunetto Latini certainly died before then (1294).

[34] Florence National Library, cl. xxv. Cod. 566.

[35] This has also been clearly proved by Prof. Santini's numerous verifications.

[36] Two very short records, or rather notes, were added by another hand where the gap occurs, namely: "Pope Adrian V., born of the Fiesco family of Genoa, 1276, reigned as Pope thirty days; the Chair vacant twenty-eight days. Pope Innocent VI. elected, who came from Portugal." The second note is certainly erroneous. Innocent VI. (Etienne d'Albert) was a Frenchman of Limousin birth, and was raised to the Papacy in 1352. But Adrian's successor was John XXI., a Portuguese. The author mistook *Johannes* (probably written in an abbreviated form) for *Innocentius*, XXI. for VI. Even in other chronicles the two records stand together, and almost in the same words, but without the same blunder.

[37] Codex Laur. Gadd. 77. On the back are these words: "Cronica romanorum Pontificum et Imperatorum." This title explains the connection of the Chronicle with Martin Polono, and why the MS. so long escaped the researches of students of Florentine history. The work of Professor Santini from which we have quoted being an essay sent in for his B.A. examination, was discussed at the Istituto Superiore, and an account given of it in the "Arch. Stor. It.," Series iv. vol. xii. No. iv. p. 483 and fol., 1883. The paper itself has remained unpublished, as Alvisi's discovery made its demonstrations

superfluous. Santini regarded the Chronicle as one of great importance, since it records the names of certain consuls, omitted in all the others, but contained in newly discovered documents, now in type, and forming part of the work that will soon, we hope, be published by Signor Santini.

[38] Baluzio Manzi, "Miscellanea," tom. iv. This Orsucci Codex, in the Lucca Archives, has been very minutely described by Hartwig (vol. i. xxx. and fol.), who, as before mentioned, brought out the Italian version of the legend he had extracted from it.

[39] VIII. 36.

[40] I. 1.

[41] VIII. 36.

[42] In the Acta Sanctorum.

[43] "L'estoire de Eracles empereur, et la conqueste de la terre d'outremer (Receuil des historiens des Croisades)," translated into Latin, Greek, German, Spanish, Italian. For the sources consulted by Villani, *vide* Busson, "Die florentinische Geschichte der Malespini" (Innsbrück, 1869), and Scheffer-Boichorst, "Die Geschichte Malespini, eine Fälschung," in his "Florentiner Studien."

[44] *Vide* Paoli's article on Hartwig's work.

[45] "Il y en eut (des consuls) tout au moins en 1101." And after quoting the document he adds this note:—"Devant de fait si positif, il serait oiseux de S'arrêter aux conjectures des auteurs même presque contemporains," p. 209.

[46] Perrens, pp. 152–4.

[47] Borghini, "Discorsi," vol. ii. pp. 27 and 93. Florence, 1755.

[48] The ninth and last volume is now published, and extends to the fall of the Republic (1530–32).

[49] Concerning the numerous errors contained in this first volume, Dr. Hartwig has written at some length in Sybil's "Historiche Zeitschrift," vol. iii. No. 3, anno 1868. Of the other volumes nothing need be said at this point.

[50] Servius writes, in his Commentary on the Ænead (bk. iii. v. 104): "Dardanus Iovis filius et Electrae, profectus de Corytho [Cortona], civitate Tusciae, primus venit ad Troyam." And farther on (Com., bk. iii. v. 187), he says that "Dardanus et Iasius fratres … cum ex Etruria proposuissent sedes exteras petere ecc." In tracing the genealogy of Æneas, he begins thus: "Ex Electra Atalantis filia et Iove Dardanus nascitur." This must have partly inspired the legend, although, according to the latter, Electra is the wife of Atlas and the daughter of Jove. *Vide* Hartwig, vol. i. xxi.

[51] Even Brunetto Latini, in bk. i. of his "Tesoro," makes the Catiline legend relate to the origin of Florence, records the great slaughter occurring at the battle wherein Catiline was routed, and also the subsequent pestilence. "E per quella grande peste di quella grande uccisione, fu appellata la città di Pistoia" (bk. i. chap. 37, in the vulgate of Bono Giamboni). The principal authorities for the historical information in the "Tesoro" are Dictys of Crete, and the "De excidio Troie," attributed to Dares the Phrygian. Undoubtedly the latter is also one of the sources of our legend. *Vide* Thor Sundy, "Della vita e delle opere di Brunetto Latini," translated, with many additions, by Prof. R. Renier. Florence: Le Monnier, 1884.

[52] The "Libro fiesolano" styles them Africans instead of Franks, *una compagnia venuta d'Africa*, as elsewhere, instead of *Ottone* or *Otto*, it says *Ceto*, a blunder also found in the MS. that was printed. The blunders probably originated from some ignorant copyist of the legend, and were frequently repeated by later scribes. John of Salisbury ("Polikratikus," vi. 17, edit. Giles), in mentioning the cities built by Brennus, according to history, repeats the same story of Siena contained in the legend. He remarks that all this is not real history, *sed celebris traditio est*, adding, however, that tradition is confirmed by the fact that in their constitution, beauty and customs, the Siennese resemble "ad gallos et Britones a quibus originem contraxerunt." John of Salisbury's words are also recorded by Benvenuto da Imola in

his Commentary on the "Divina Commedia," where he mentions that Dante intended to allude to this resemblance ("Inferno," xxix. 121) in the lines:

"Or fu giammai
Gente si vana come la senese?
Certo non la francesca si d'assai."

Boccaccio's "Commento" gives the same explanation of these lines.

[53] The Latin compilation says: *quingentos annos et plus*; the Italian, and more modern versions, merely say, "five hundred years."

[54] Even history tells us that Totila was in Tuscany towards the middle of the sixth century.

[55] "Libro fiesolano", chap. xv.

[56] This is also mentioned by Hartwig, i., xxiv., and fol.

[57] The first to note this was Hegel: "Ueber die Anfange der florentinischen Geschichtschreibung," in Sybel's Historical Journal, No. 1, anno 1876.

[58] Chaps. xvi. and xvii. of Follini's edition.

[59] Villani, i. 41.

[60] Villani, iii. 3.

[61] *Vide* G. Rosa, "Delle Origini di Firenze," in the "Archivio Storico Ital.," Series iii., vol. ii. p. 62 and fol. Hartwig, op. cit., and Milani, "Scavi di Mercato Vecchio," in the "Notizie degli scavi nel mese d' Aprile, 1887, Atti dell' Accademia dei Lincei."

[62] In digging a sewer in the street called Borgo dei Greci, in 1886, the discovery was made in Professor Milani's presence, "at the depth of about three metres beneath the street level, and exactly beneath the pavement of the first circuit of the Amphitheatre, ... of a half *asse onciale*, weighing 12 grammes 25, undoubtedly coeval with the construction of the

Florentine Amphitheatre. This kind of coin assuredly dates from 89 B.C., and was issued after the Plautian-Papirian decree reducing the weight of the aes from 1 oz. to ½ oz. The aes cut with a chisel were only in currency for a short time, and were withdrawn when the new coins were issued. Accordingly they must have ceased by the date of the second triumvirate (43 B.C.), when the aes was further reduced to the third of an ounce. We may therefore accept the conclusion that the Florence Amphitheatre was of the Sullian period. Opposed to this conclusion is the fact that, according to the report of Dione (li. 23), the first stone amphitheatre built in Rome was that of Taurus, dating from anno 30 B.C. But recalling how Cicero accused Sulla of having wasted treasures on magnificent buildings, exactly when he was under Fiesole, one is justified in assigning the construction of the Florence amphitheatre, and also of that of Pompei, to Sulla's day. Likewise the basements of the *Tuscanic* columns, found *in situ* near the Amphitheatre, and some architectural fragments discovered in 1887 on the south side of Santa Maria del Fiore, confirmed the opinion that some of the chief public buildings of Florence were connected with the times of Sulla and also with the last days of the Republic." (From a letter by Prof. Milani addressed to myself.)

[63] The inscription (now lost) beginning thus: "Col[*onia*] Iul[*ia*] Aug[*usta*], Flor[*entia*]", should be differently interpreted, according to Mommsen, as referring to Vienne in Dauphiny. *Vide* "Hermes," 1883, p. 176 and p. 180, note 1. Prof. Milani takes the same view regarding the new and important inscription recently found in the excavation of the Mercato Vecchio, containing the following words:

"... Genio Coloniae
... Florentiae."

Vide "Scoperte epigrafiche nel Centro di Firenze," in the "Nazione," April 15, 1890.

[64] Milani, "Relazione degli scavi," &c.

[65] Villani, ii. 1 and 2, and also the "Chronica de Origine Civitatis."

[66] Ibid., ii. 1, 2, 3.

[67] *Vide* Hodgkin, "Italy and her Invaders," vol. iv. p. 446 and fol.

[68] Lami, "Lezioni," pt. i. p. 293. From a document also quoted by Maratori and Tiraboschi, it would seem that Florence was included, as it were, in the *city of Fiesole*; and therefore some of the Florentine churches were described as being in Fiesole. *Vide* also pt. ii. p. 429 of the same work.

[69] This is described in detail by Lami, Borghini, and Hartwig.

[70] Villani, iii. 3.

[71] Ibid., iv. 1.

[72] Lami, "Lezioni," at preface to pts. cvi.-viii; Hartwig, i. 85, 86.

[73] Villani, iv. 6.

[74] Villani, iv. 7.

[75] It is related by St. Pier Damiano in the letter quoted farther on.

[76] Petri Damiani, "Epistolarum libri viii." Parisiis ex-officina nivelliana, 1610, *vide* p. 727. The epistle (p. 721 and fol.) is addressed: "Dilectis in Christo civibus florentinis, Petrus peccator, monachus, fraternae charitatis obsequium."

[77] Tocco, "L'Eresia nel Medio Evo," bk. i. chap. iii. pp. 207–228.

[78] Passerini, "Arch. Storico Italiano," New Series, vol. iii. pp. 43, 44; Perrens, i. 85 and fol.; Hartwig, i. 88, 89; Capecelatro, "Vita di S. Pier Damiano," bk. vii. two vols. Florence: Barbera, 1862.

[79] "Ad hec ille se inquit, neutrum jubere, neutrum velle, neutrum recipere. Quin etiam edictum a Preside per legatos suos impetravit, ut quicumque laicorum, quicumque clericorum se ut episcopum non coleret suique imperio non obediret, ad

Presidem victus non duceretur, sed traeretur: si quis autem his minis territus, de civitate fugeret, ad dominium Potestatis assumeretur quicquid possedisset." Thus runs the letter dated *Millesimo lxviii idus februari*, and beginning, "Alexandro prime sedis reverentissimo, ac universali episcopo, clerus et populus Florentinus sincere devotionis obsequium." It was repeatedly, but incorrectly printed (*vide* Brocchi, "Vite di Santi e Beati," p. 145. Florence, 1742; "Acta Sanctorum," iii. luglio, pp. 359, 379), in the two lives of St. G. Gualberto; included in the Laurentian Cod. xx. 22, in sec. xi. The letter placed at the end of the Codex itself is written in a different and somewhat later hand; but, according to the opinion of Prof. Paoli, who examined it at my request, the writing has every characteristic of the eleventh century, "and could not possibly be of later date than the first half, or rather first quarter of the twelfth century." It more resembles a narrative in an epistolary form than a genuine letter. The title given it in the Codex also supports this view: "Incipit textus miraculi quod Dominus," &c. We shall have to recur to the subject later on.

At any rate, it is plain that the *Potestas* above-mentioned has no relation with the Podestà of a later period. Here the term signifies *superior authority—i.e.,* that of the Duke Goffredo. The *Preside* I consider to mean Goffredo's representative in Florence. Both are old-fashioned, rhetorical terms, similar to those afterwards employed by Sanzanome.

[80] The same letter, after narrating how certain persons, having taken refuge in an oratory, were threatened with expulsion, "extra Civitatem pellerentur," unless they made submission, also adds that those persons refused to obey. "Hincque factum est ut ... municipal. presid ... illos extra emunitatem oratori ... eiceret." The two abbreviated words in the Codex were printed in many different ways, changing the verb and often altering the whole phrase, to the reader's great confusion. Several colleagues I have consulted agree with my view, that the words should be rendered *municipale praesidium*.

[81] This description is also taken from the same document.

[82] The *Nuova Antologia* of Rome, June 1, 1890.

[83] In the Laurentian Codex previously referred to.

[84] *Rhetor* was then synonymous with *causidicus*.

[85] Ficker's work pays great attention to this point, and is also treated by Fitting. *Vide* "Die Anfänge der Rechtsschule zu Bologna." Berlin and Leipzig, 1888.

[86] "Lege Digestorum libris inserta, considerata." So styled in a *placito* of 1076, pronounced by an envoy of Beatrice at Marturi, near Poggibonsi ("prope plebem Sancte Marie, territurio fiorentino"), where the presence is also noted of Pepone, the precursor of Irnerius (Werner). A Florentine, who was contesting certain lands with the monastery, adduced the *temperis praescripto*, on the authority of the Digest, that, according to the legal custom of the time, he produced in court. *Vide* Fitting, op. cit., p. 88. Zdekauer, "Sull' Origine del manoscritto Pisano delle Pandette Giustiniane." Sienna: Torrini, 1890. In a document of 1061, treating of a dispute between two Florentine Churches (*vide* Della Rena e Camici, vols. ii. 2, p. 99), we find "Indices secundum romanae legis tenorem, utramque ceperunt inquirere partem." According to Ficker, the judges in question were Florentines: "und zwar schienen das die gewöhnlichen städtischen Iudices von Florenz zu sein." Ficker, iii. par. 469, at p. 90. Goro Dati, a chronicler who died at the beginning of the fifteenth century, stated in his Chronicle that the Florence notaries were the best reputed of all, although the most celebrated doctors of law were those of Bologna. *Vide* Dati, "Storia di Firenze," Florentine edition of 1735, at p. 133.

[87] Petrus Damiani, "De parentelae gradibus," in his "Opera, Opusc, viii," chaps. i. and vii. He combats here the opinion expressed by the *sapientes* of Ravenna, in contradiction to the canonical law, as to the degrees of relationship prohibiting marriage. Touching a wise man he asserts to be a Florentine, he adds: "promptulus cerebrosus ac dicax, scilicet acer ingenio, mordax eloquio vehemens argumento."

[88] Ficker says, in mentioning the before-quoted document of 1061: "Diese Romagnolen scheinen nun weiter kaum nur zufällig zu Florenz gewesen zu sein."

[89] As regards the ever-increasing action of Roman law in Tuscany there is a very remarkable passage in the Pisan

Statutes of 1161, in which it is said of that city, "a multis retro temporibus, vivendo lege romana, retentis quibusdam de lege longobarda." In a Siennese document of 1176, edited by Ficker (vol. iv. doc. 148), the Consuls declare: "Item nos professi sumus lege romana cum tota Civitate vivere." The mixture of Roman with Longobard or other legal systems is very frequent throughout the whole of the eleventh century, and even later on. Often, women who professed to live according to the Roman law, declared themselves at the same time as being under the *mundium* of their sons or of others.

[90] Lami, "Lezioni," preface, p. cxv and fol. *Vide* also the documents published in Fiorentini's "Memorie delle gran Contessa Matilde" (Lucca, 1756); Della Rena e Camici, "Serie cronologica-diplomatica degli antichi duchi e marchesi di Toscana," pt. ii. These documents clearly show in what manner Matilda's tribunal was composed.

[91] *Vide* Fiorentini, doc. at p. 168; Della Rena e Camici, pt. ii. vol. ii. docs. xv. and xvi. pp. 106 and 108; vol. iii. p. 9; vol. iv. doc. xiv. p. 61.

[92] *"Unthätiger Vorsitzende,"* says Ficker, when clearly proving this fact. Vol. iii. par. 573, p. 294 and fol.

[93] On this head Ficker remarks: "Dass schon früher die Gerichtsbarheit in der Stadt nicht durch die Feudalgewalt, sondern durch Bürger der Stadt als rechtskundige Königsboten geübt wurde." Vol. iii. par. 584, pp. 315–16.

[94] "Consuetudines etiam perversas a tempore Bonifactii Marchionis duriter eisdem impositas, omnino interdicimus." Ficker, vol. i. par. 136, pp. 255–6, and the text of the document in vol. iv. pp. 124–5; Pawinski, "Zur Entstehungsgeschichte des Consulats in den Comunen Nord und Mittel-Italiens." Berlin, 1867, p. 29.

[95] "Nec Marchionem aliquem in Tusciam mittemus sine laudatione hominum duodecim electorum in Colloquio facto sonantibus campaniis." Murat., "Antiq." iv. 20. Also *vide* Ficker and Giesebrecht, before cited, and Pawinski at p. 31.

It has been suggested that some interpolations have been made in these patents (of which only an ancient copy survives, not the original), and especially in the second, but Ficker and Pawinski oppose this view. At any rate, the substance of both documents is now accepted by all the most competent writers. *Vide* Ficker, vol. iii. p. 408; Giesebrecht (4th ed.), vol. iii. pp. 537–8.

[96] Amari, "Storia dei Musulmani in Sicilia," vol. iii. p. 1 and fol.

[97] We use the word *grandi* here for the sake of clearness, although in this particular sense it only came into general use in Florence at a later date, and more particularly in 1293 in the days of Giano della Bella.

[98] Pawinski, p. 31, note 3.

[99] "Nec domum in predictis terminis relevari, neque ad triginta sex brachia interdici, permittemus" (Pawinski, p. 34).

[100] Bonaini, "Statuti inediti della città di Pisa," vol. i. p. 16.

[101] Frequent mention is made of counts and viscounts of whom, so far, there was no record in Florence. Later on, from causes that will be related, some few were found there.

[102] But I cannot agree with Pawinski when, in noting this characteristic of Pisa and other similar communes, he neglects the popular, commercial element, that even in Pisa, as elsewhere, was very influential, and considers that the birth of the Italian Commune should be solely attributed to the nobles.

[103] "Nisi fortitan communi Consilio Civitatis, vel maioris partis Bonorum vel Sapientum ... ad commune Colloquium Civitatis ... supra-dictorum hominum consensu et omnibus Pisae habitantibus" (Bonaini, op. cit., vol. i. p. 16).

[104] Murat., "Antiq.," iii., 1099. A poem attributed to Guido da Pisa narrates the campaign of 1087 carried on by the Pisans, in alliance with Genoa, Amalfi, and Rome, against the Saracens in Africa, and cites the names of four Pisans:—

"Vocat ad se Petrum et Sismundum
    Principales Consules,
Lambertum et Glandulfum
    Cives cari [clari?] nobiles."

This, however, is a poetical work, and in order to accept it as a proof that these Consuls existed in 1087 it would be necessary to carry back to that year, at least, the first *concordia* of Bishop Daiberto. This might not be impossible, seeing that he held the bishopric from 1085 to 1092, when he was named archbishop. *Vide* Pawinski, p. 31, note 3. Leonardo Vernese recounts the expedition to the Balearic Isles (1113–15) in his "Carmen," and says:—

"Inde duo et denos de culmine nobilitatis
Constituere viros, quibus est permissa potestas
Consulis atque ducis."

But the existence of Consuls at that time has been already proved by other documents. *Vide* Pawinski, pp. 38–9.

[105] The chronicler designates the chief families as *anteriores*, possibly because they were the first to settle in Venice; he represents them as a supreme and governing class,

and in the list he gives of them mentions what trades they carried on. "Cerbani de Cerbia venerunt, anteriores fuerunt de omni artificio ingeniosi. Signati (variant: Cugnati) Tribuni Ianni appellati sunt, anteriores fuerunt, mirabilia artificia facere sciebant caliditate ingenii. Aberorlini … anteriores fuerunt; non aliud operabantur nisi negocia, sed advari et increduli." And so on regarding other families exercising from generation to generation the same trade, commerce, or liberal profession. As to the guilds or *ministeria*, we find many expressions affording hints of their embryo organisation. "Hetolus autem appellatus est, quia ipse erat princeps de his qui ministerii erant retinendis." They were sadlers, cattle-herds, &c. Many more of these families are named in the list given in the Chronicle, and all seems to denote the continuation of a state of things that had existed during the lower Empire.

[106] This document is in the Vatican (Urb. 440), and has also been examined by Gfrörer. The ironsmith, Giovanni Sagornino, "insimul cum cunctis meisparentibus," appeals first to the Doge Pietro Barbolano (1026–31), and then to the Doge Domenico Flabiabico (1032–43), against the *gastaldo* of the guild, who sought to compel him to labour at iron-work for the prisons in the palace yard, whereas Sagornino asserted his right, according to custom, of making the iron-work at his own house, when fulfilling his gratuitous task for the State. A regular suit was carried on; and being decided in favour of the appellant, the latter was permitted to do the work in his own shop. All this proves that well-defined traditional customs prevailed before the guild possessed written statutes (sec. xiii.), since these would have been mentioned had they existed at the time.

The document we have quoted speaks at one point of the *gastaldo of the doge*, and at another alludes to him as the *gastaldo of the smiths*, because the director of the guild heldhis nomination from the doge. This is clearly evidenced in the thirteenth century by a decree (*pro-missione*) of the Doge Jacopo Tiepolo, dated March 6, 1229, and by another of the Doge Marco Morosini (June 13, 1249). Thus we see, on the one hand, how much the organisation of the Venetian guilds differed from that of the Florentine, while, on the other, we note how ancient and persistent in all Italian communes was the character of their institutions in general and of the trade guilds in particular. For the details given in this and the preceding note we are indebted to Prof. Monticolo, a man of great learning, and now engaged in important researches on Venetian history, of which the results will soon be published. Meanwhile we seize this occasion to express our thanks in print.

P.S.—We may now add that Prof. Monticolo has already begun to publish his discoveries in "Le Fonti della Storia d'Italia," issued by the Istituto Storico Italiano.

[107] Repetti, article on Gangalandi and Monte Orlando.

[108] "Dum in Dei nomine, Domina inclita Comitissa Matilda, Ducatrix, stante ea in obsedione Prati," &c. Anno 1107. *Vide* "Fiorentini," op. cit., bk. ii. p. 299. Villani, vol. iv. pp. 25 and 26; Hartwig, vol. ii. pp. 45 and 47; Repetti, art. "Prato"; "Arch. Stor. It.," Storie v. vol. v. disp. i., p. 108 and fol. Villani's narrative, however, is crammed with fantastic details concerning Prato. The destruction of Monte Orlando is not mentioned in vol. i. of the "Annales," which only begin with the year 1110; but is recorded in the Codex Neap. and in Tolomeo da Lucca.

[109] The "Annales florentini," ii., followed by Villani, merely relate the destruction of the castle in 1113, without any comments, for the next event they mention relates to the year 1135. The "Annales florentini," i., say nothing about it in 1113, and place the "secunda et ultima destruccio murorum" in 1114. In 1119 they record two other attacks on the castle, "quem marchio Rempoctus defendebat": by the second of which the Florentines "Monte Cascioli ignem (*sic*) consumpserunt." It seems clear that three attacks were made in succession, and farther dispute on the point would be superfluous.

[110] The "Annales," i. and ii., omit this event. The Neap. Codex assigns it, as does Villani, to the year 1117, but only says that the Pisans went to the Balearic Isles, and that "the Florentines guarded the city of Pisa" (Hartwig, ii. 272). The same account is given by Tolomeo da Lucca, but he dates the event in 1118; so, too, the pseudo Brunetto Latini, who records the gift of two porphyry columns, "by reason that the Florentines guarded their lands, while they were at the war,"

but adds nothing more to this statement. As to the error of date, we will merely remark that Capmany, in his "Memorias historicas sobra la marina ... de Barcelona," vol. i. p. 10, after narrating the expedition of 1113–15, goes on to say that Raimondo Berengario III. came to Pisa and Genoa in 1118, in order to promote another campaign. Perhaps the remembrance of this visit contributed to the mistake, the which, once made, was repeated by many subsequent writers.

[111] Dr. Hartwig quotes particulars received from Dr. Wüstenfeld of a patent dated 1114, which would seem to show that the Florentines also took part in the expedition, in which case, he observes, the columns might have been the gift of the Pisans, and nevertheless part of the spoil taken in common. I caused a search to be made for the diploma in the Pisan Archives, and obtained it through the courtesy of Prof. Lupi. It is inserted in another patent, dated *vi. idus Augusti, 1233*, whereby King James of Aragon confirms the Pisans in the privileges conferred on them by the preceding diploma that "Berengarius Barchinione gloriosissimus Comes Pisanis fecit." This older patent is reproduced in the document, and bears this date: "M.C. quarto decimo ... septimo idus septembris, indictione sexta." Although several other words stand between those of decimo and septimo, this mode of writing the date may have been another cause of the blunder committed by the chroniclers who dated the event in 1117.

Whatever may be thought of these very disputable theories, it is certain, on the other hand, that the privileges were conferred on the *populo pisano*, and that three of their Consuls were invested with them, and received "vice aliorum Consulum tociusque pisani populi," and that this concession was made "coram marchionibus, comitibus, principibus romanis, lucensibus, florentinis, senensibus, volterranis, pistoriensibus, longobardis, sardis et corsis, aliisque innumerabilis gentibus, que in predicto exercitu aderant." Therefore it was no mere alliance between one or two cities: it was the Pisan people in conjunction with many potentates from different parts of Italy. The chancellor of the Pisan Consuls drew up the diploma, in the presence of the Archbishop of Pisa, "qui Dompni apostolici in predicto exercitu vicem gerebat," of two *vice comites* and nine Consuls, the names of the latter being given. This diploma had never been published in Italy; therefore Amari, who was much interested in the subject, wished to print, just before his decease, the copy I had sent him, although he had ascertained that it was already published in Spain by Moragues y Bover in the notes to a "Historia de Mallorca," by Don Vincente Mut, printed at Palma in 1841.

[112] *Vide* "Documenti che illustrano la memoria di una monaca del secolo xiii." ("Arch. Stor. It.," Series iii. vol. xxiii.). These documents are among the earliest of the thirteenth century, and contain the depositions of witnesses, alluding almost always to events of the twelfth century, and continually mentioning the monastery of Rosano, and of one who "defendit ipsum monasterium a Teutonicis" (*vide* pages 206, 391–2, and other parts also).

[113] The "Annales," i., record two fires (1115 and 1117), which destroyed the whole place; the Neap. Codex only mentions the second. Thomas Tuscus, writing in Florence about 1279, speaks of both the fires in his "Gesta Imperatorum et Pontificum," attributing to that cause the destruction of many chronicles which he supposes to have existed, but which probably never existed at all. Villani adopted the same theory, being equally unable to understand that the Commune might have had no historians of earlier date.

[114] Petrus f. Mingardole, who, "*ad defendendum se de crucifixo*," passed through the fire unhurt. Certain historians, unwilling to credit the existence of heresy in Florence at that time, have disputed as to the words *de crucifixo*, and proposed this reading instead: *cum crucifixo* or *de crimine infixo*. But the facsimile of the Codex, published by Prof. Paoli, leaves no doubt on the point.

[115] In fact, Simone della Tosa, a later chronicler, who may have copied from Villani at this point, after relating the second burning of the city in 1117, goes on to say that "the heresy of the *Paterini* was then abroad in Florence." Pope Innocent III. (1198–1216), in discoursing on heretics, wrote: "Impii Manichaei qui se Catharos vel Paterenos appellant" (Ep. lib. x. ep. 54, in Migne's ed. vol. ii. p. 1147). Also, in the "Annales Camaldulenses" (vol. iii. app. p. 396) there is a sentence

pronounced at Sutri, in 1141, running as follows: "Igitur universi qui vulgo Paterenses vocantur, eo quia, sub iugo peccati, retinebant omnia que de predicta ecclesia sancte Fortunate accipiebant." Therefore it is plain that the name of *Paterini* (although strictly speaking that of a special sect, quite separate from others) was here applied to all those occupying Church lands, or opposed in any way to the Church. Hartwig, vol. ii. pp. 17 and 21.

[116] *Vide* the Chronicle, *ad annum*. As we have already observed, all information regarding this period is derived from the Gaddi Codex, discovered in the Laurentian Library a few years ago. The part beginning from 1181 is also contained in the autograph Chronicle that has been longer known to us; but being very difficult to decipher has not been much studied.

[117] "Would to God that Ghibellines were declared to be *Paterini*!" So says the pseudo Brunetto Latini in the year 1215.

[118] The MS. of the "Annales," i., writes, *Rempoctus*, not *Remperoctus*, as it was printed elsewhere.

[119] Ficker, vol. ii. pp. 223, 224, par. 310; Murat., "Antiq.," iii. 1125.

[120] Murat., "Antiq.," i. 315.

[121] The "Annales," i., say that, "deo auctore, Florentini Monte Cascioli igne consumpserunt." The MS. really seems to run, *de auctore*, but this would be nonsense. Lami proposed the reading, *des auctoritate*, but this too would lack sense. The interpretation preferred and adopted by ourselves was suggested by Prof. Paoli. In combating the Empire and fighting for the Church, the Florentines believed themselves to be under Divine protection, and considering their adversaries as enemies of God, accordingly named them heretics and *Paterini*.

[122] "Teneanla certi gentiluomini Cattani, stati della città di Fiesole, e dentro vi si riducevano masnadieri e sbanditi e mala gente, che alcuna volta faceano danno alle strade e al contado di Firenze" (iv. 32).

[123] According to the "Annales," i., the war lasted less than

three months, while Sanzanome stretches it to three years. Possibly the latter included all the attacks and skirmishes by which the war may have been prefaced.

[124] Soldani, "Historia Monasterii S. Michaelis de Passiniano," p. 109, quoted by Lami, "Lezioni," i. 288.

[125] In Passerini's collection of documents, quoted above, one finds, at p. 211, the following words: "Domina Sofia dixit et dicit quod est lxxx. annorum et plus, et recordatur de destructione Fesularum." Others give testimony to the same effect.

[126] In a sentence given on December 30, 1172, we find seven Consuls named, a judge in ordinary, and three proveditors. The Consuls instal the judge, "huic missioni in possessum auctoritatem prestans." This document and many similar ones are in the Florence Archives, Curia di S. Michele. Some have been printed separately by Prof. Santini, in pt. ii. of a volume soon, we hope, to be given to the world. We call the reader's attention to the fact that we quote from his work not only with regard to documents which are still inedited, but also touching those already edited by other writers, because we know that he has carefully collated all with their originals. In his forthcoming work he will probably indicate which documents were discovered by himself, which simply reproduced. *Vide* Santini, pt. ii. doc. i. In October, 1181, three Consuls preside "super facto iustitiae, nominatim in mense octobris." The judge *Restauransdampnum* confirms the sentence (ibid., doc. ii.). There are other documents to the same effect, though we also sometimes find two Consuls for one month. On January 27, 1197, there are two Consuls of justice for January and February (Santini, pt. ii. doc. ix.), and so on for some time, two Consuls for two months. On February 28, 1198, the two Consuls are judges by profession; but, nevertheless, the assistance of a judge in ordinary—one *Spinello Spada*—is still required (ibid., doc. x.). This is an additional proof that the Consuls of justice did not exactly fulfil the function of real judges. From 1201 downwards we find one Consul of justice *per totum annum* (ibid., docs. xiii., xv.).

[127] On April 18, 1201—there being then a *Potestà*—we

only find "Gerardus ordinarium iudex cognitor controversiae … hanc sententiam tuli ideoque subscripsi," without a Consul of justice, who reappears soon afterwards (Santini, pt. ii. doc. xi.). It would seem that at Pisa it was the rule to nominate special judges, *electi*, or *dati a Consulibus et universo populo*, who pronounced judgment on their own account, sometimes in the presence of the Consuls. Elsewhere we find *Consules de placitis*, or *Assessores Consulum* (as at Parma, for instance), who pronounced judgment without the intervention of the Consuls of the Commune (Ficker, iii. pars. 584 and 585).

[128] Originally, Florence was divided in quarters (*quartieri*). The old city did not then comprise the part beyond the Arno, Oltrarno, which was only inhabited by a few "low folk of small account" (Villani, iv. 14). Afterwards, but from the earliest days of the Commune, the city was arranged in *sestieri*, of which the Oltrarno formed one. In the year 1343 (Villani, xii. 18) the division in four quarters was resumed.

[129] It is dated January, 1165, and is to be found in the Florentine Archives (S. Appendix ii. doc. i. p. 517). It is an act of donation, giving part of a house to the members of the *Società della Torre* of Capo di Ponte: "Tam qui modo sunt, aut in antea fuerunt ex Societate vestre turris de CapitePontis."

[130] On two scraps of parchment dated 1179 and 1180, together with a document, part of which dates from May 16, 1209, and part from an older period, in the Florence Archives. The Statute of the Podestà (in 1324) also mentions the Societies of the Towers. The whole question has been minutely studied by Prof. Santini in his learned work on the "Società delle Torri in Firenze," first published in the "Arch. Stor. It.," Series iv. t. xx. 1887, and subsequently in a separate form. In Appendix ii. of his previously quoted work the author includes several documents relating to these societies. They are respectively dated 1165, 1179, 1180, 1181, 1183, 1201, 1209, &c.

[131] In the above-quoted, separate, work, at p. 55, and fol. Prof. Santini names many of these families, and supports his statements by documentary evidence.

[132] On this point I differ from Santini. The rural societies

he has been able to discover are few in number, of a different nature from the others, and of less ancient date. Out in the country the principal basis of the society was lacking—*i.e.*, the tower surrounded by houses belonging to different members.

[133] Villani (v. 32) also tells us that Florence was under "the rule of Consuls chosen from the greatest and best of the city, with a council of the senate", that is of one hundred worthies, and that, as in Rome, all these Consuls "guided and governed the city, holding office for one year." He arbitrarily fixes their number at four or six, according to the division of the city in quarters or sixths, and adds that, whenever mentioned, only the chief Consul was named. January seems to have been the time fixed for the election. In 1202 we find the same Consuls in the first and second half of the year (March 1 and October 1). This would likewise prove that the year was not then begun on the 25th of March, according to Florentine style (Santini, doc. v.). In Sienna, January was the time of the election, and on the evidence of the chroniclers one may infer that it was the same in Florence.

[134] The first document recording the names of consuls is dated March 19, 1138 (quoted by Hartwig, ii. 185, from the "Memorie di Lucca," vol. iv. p. 173, doc. 122), and states that *"Broccardus et Selvorus"* promise *"pro se et pro sociis suis."* The second is dated June 4, 1138 (Santini, pt. i. doc. ii.), and in this a Count Ugicio (or Egicio) receives "launechild et meritum a Burello et Florenzito Consulibus, vice totius populi." These two documents of the same year do not contain identical names, perhaps because they only give those of the *Consules priores*, who sat in turn, as we have before remarked. Even in Sienna the *Consules priores* seem to have been continually changed. *Vide* Caleffo Vecchio for June, August, October, 1202; Caleffo dell' Assunta, 1202. And when Consuls were replaced by Governors, each of these was *Prior* for one week.

In two Florentine documents, among the Capitoli, dated April 7, 1174, and April 4, 1176 (Santini, pt. i. docs. vi. and ix.), all the Consuls—ten in number—are named, possibly the Consuls of justice being omitted. But, on the other hand, in an oath sworn by the men of Mangona to Florence (October 28, 1184, in Santini, pt. i. doc. xv.) we read: "Annualiter dabimus unam albergariam xij. Consulibus Florentie." Even in 1204 we find twelve; but more than twelve are recorded in the documents of the League (1197–8), and likewise in the year 1203. We have already given the probable explanation of this fact. The *Consules priores*, also existing in other communes, are seldom mentioned in Florence by the name of *Priores*, especially in early days. But there is one doc. dated October 24, and November 7, 1204 (S. pt. i. doc. liii.) saying: "Potestas Florentie vel Consules eiusdem civitatis, omnes vel maior pars vel Priores aut Prior eorum." So, too, another document dated October 15, 1200.

[135] Santini, pt. i. doc. xii.

[136] Ibid., pt. i. doc. xv.

[137] There were, in fact, Consuls of the Commune, of the guilds, of the Arno, of the city gates, of the Societies of the Towers, and the latter were more specially styled Rectors. Yet even "Rectors" was a generic term, indicating all who governed, and there were Rectors of the Towers, of the city, and of the guilds. *Potestas* then indicated the supreme authority in general, and was only converted later on into a special and separate office.

[138] There are so many examples of this, that quotation is unneeded. It was the usual formula in other cities as well as in Florence. In the treaty drawn up between Lucca and Florence (July 24, 1184), from which we have already quoted, there was a proviso in case there might be no Consuls at Lucca, no *Lucana Potestas*, and this addition was accordingly made "aut bonos viros lucensis civitatis, si Consules vel Rector aut Potestas tunc ibi non fuerit."

[139] "Forte Belicocci Senator eiusdem [Florentiae] Civitatis" (in a document dated April 15, 1204, Santini pt. i. doc. li). Another document of November 13 and 14, 1197, in the Acts of the Tuscan League, we find the name *Bilicozus* among the *consiliarii* present. In the "Breve Consulum Pisane Civitatis," of 1162, edited by Bonaini, the councillors are styled *senatores*.

[140] This document (Santini, pt. i. doc. xxii.) is that of November 13 and 14, 1197, and also one of those of the Tuscan

League. It should be remarked, however, that even at this grave juncture there were more than twelve Consuls; so, too, for similar reasons, either the number of the councillors was augmented, or else (being towards the end of the year) some of the newly elected members sat together with those about to retire.

[141] The term *arengo, arrengo, aringo,* or *arringo,* was derived from the verb *arringare,* to harangue, in the same way as parliament from the verb *parlare,* to speak.

[142] In Italian communes *habitatores,* and even *assidui habitatores,* are clearly distinguished both from *cives* and foreigners. Florentine documents often mention *cives salvatichi,* a term that indicates, I believe, the quasi citizenship of persons living in the country, but bound to dwell in the city during part of the year. These greatly increased in number later on, and in course of time became real and entire citizens, in accordance with certain rules not yet fully known to us.

[143] Many examples of this have been found by us among *provvisioni* (or decrees) of later date.

[144] *Nuova Antologia.* Rome, July 1, 1890.

[145] Ficker, vol. ii. par. 310, p. 223. Here the names of many of these envoys are given, and what scanty details are known concerning them. To Rabodo (died 1119) succeeded a Corrado (1120–27), afterwards a Rampret (1131), then an Englebert (1134), then Errico of Bavaria (1137), immediately followed by Ulrico d'Attems, then the Duke Guelfo (1160–62), uncle to the Emperor Frederic I., by whom he was sent.

[146] "Annales," i.

[147] "Annales," i.; Sanzanome, Florentine ed., p. 128; Villani, iv. 36.

[148] "Annales," i.; 16 kal. Iulii. Ingelbertus Florentiam est ingressus."

[149] "Annales," i.; Otho of Friesland, *vide* Pertz, xx. 264, and the Annali Senesi.

[150] Sanzanome, Florentine ed., p. 129.

[151] This is related by an eye witness in the Passerini collection of documents (often quoted to us) at p. 389. The "Annales," i., manifestly err in assigning precisely this date of 1147 to the capture of Monte Orlando, which really happened in 1107. The erasures in the Codex just where the date and places of the event narrated are written—*i.e.*, before the entry in Florence of Henry IV., 1111—also serve to prove that a blunder had been made.

[152] The above-quoted Passerini Documents make repeated mention of the reconstruction of the walls, both at p. 394 and p. 217. It records at the same point the subsequent destruction of Monte di Croce: "Et dixit quod sunt lx. annos quod fuit destructus Mons Crucis." Both Villani (iv. 37) and the pseudo Brunetto Latini give the date of 1154; the "Annales," ii., the Neapolitan Codex, and Paolino Pieri, that of 1153. Sanzanome, according to his frequent practice, gives no precise date even here (at p. 130). He merely says that the first attack on the castle took place in 1146.

[153] Santini, i. doc. iii. dated April 4, 1156.

[154] "Constituit etiam Teutonicos principes ac dominatores super Lombardos et Tuscos, ut de caetero eius voluntati nullus Ytalicus resistendi locum habere ullatenus posset. Vita Alexandri," in the year 1164. In the "Cronica Urspergense," of the year 1186, we read that: "Cœpit Imperator in partibus Tusciae et terrae romanae castra ad se spectantia, suae potestati vendicare, et quaedam nova construere, in quorum presidiis Teutonicos praecipue collocavit." *Vide* Ficker, vol. ii. par. 311, p. 227.

[155] "Nullus enim Marchio et nullus nuntius Imperii fuit, qui tam honorifice civitates Italiae tributaret, et romano subiceret Imperio." *Vide* the Annali Pisani, in Pertz's Mon^ta. Ger^ma. xx. 249. Ficker, vol. i. par. 137, p. 259.

[156] Ficker, vol. i. par. 122–4.

[157] *Vide* the Passerini Documents, pp. 208, 394–400.

[158] Some of these depositions have been printed before, but the whole collection is now given in Santini, i. doc. xlv. They are dated May, 1203, but naturally refer to a much earlier period. *Vide* Santini, pp. 115, 117–19.

[159] *Vide* the treaty given in Santini, i. doc. iv.

[160] Count Macharius was the Imperial representative at San Miniato. Ficker gives a list of other German counts in that castle (vol. ii. par. 311, p. 227 and fol.).

[161] "Castrum autem intelligimus recuperatum etiam sine superiori incastellatura."

[162] At this moment many former partisans of the Empire were fighting against it. Pisa is one example.

[163] Nevertheless it was not kept among the *Capitoli* comprising real official documents, but among papers of an almost private nature. Hartwig was the first to bring it to light (ii. 61); and it was afterwards reprinted verbatim in Santini, pt. iii. doc. i.

[164] Tommasi, "Storia di Lucca," in the "Arch. Stor. It.," vol. x. *ad annum*; Roncioni, "Istorie Pisane," in the "Arch. Stor. It.," vol. vi. *ad annum*; Marangoni, i. 285; Ottoboni, "Annales," i. 95; Hartwig, ii. 58–63.

[165] *Vide* Santini, i. docs, v., vi., vii., viii. The first of these is dated Feb. 23, 1173; the others are of April 7, 1174.

[166] "Annales," ii., year 1170; Villani, v. 5.

[167] "Annales," ii.; Sanzanome; Villani, v. 6; Neapolitan Codex (here, however, the event is ascribed to the year 1175); Repetti, art. "Asciano"; Hartwig, ii. 64–5.

[168] This treaty (in which not only the emperor, but also Christian of Mayence, and Count Macharius, who was then at San Miniato, are expressly named) is in the Siennese Archives, Caleffo Vecchio, at c. 9, and Caleffo dell' Assunta, at c. 53. Dr. Hartwig published a large summary of it, made by Wüstenfeld. Thanks to the kindness of Cavaliere Lisini, Director of the Sienna Archives, we were enabled to obtain a copy of the treaty, and of other documents connected with the peace. Some belonging to Florence are comprised in Santini's work, i. docs. ix., x., xi. (April 4 and 8, and December 11, 1176).

[169] "Et quod Comunis Senensis acquisierit extra eorum episcopatus et comitatus, dabo medietatem Florentinis." In the above-quoted treaty among the Siennese Archives.

[170] Nevertheless, in the year 1174, we find a Guido Uberti on the list of Consuls. Santini, i. doc. vi.

[171] Villani, v. 8. The "Annales," ii., of 1177, say that "Orta est guerra inter Consules et filios Uberti; eodem anno combusta est civitas florentina." The Neapolitan Codex dates the first fire the 4th of August, as Villani also does, and gives the commencement of the civil war immediately afterwards, the which "filled two years." Paolino Pieri dates the first fire August 4, 1174, and the fall of the bridge and the second fire in 1178. Tolomeo da Lucca merely states that a revolution broke out in 1177 and lasted for two years.

[172] Chronicle of the pseudo Brunetto Latini, *ad annum*.

[173] We subjoin an extract from the pseudo Brunetto Latini, as it stands in the Gaddi Codex, with all its blunders. After giving an account of the revolution, the chronicler goes on to say: "Then in the year 1180 the Uberti gained the victory, and Messer Uberto degli Uberti and Messer Lamberto Lamberti were consul and rector of the city of Florence, together with their companions, and these formed the first consulate of the city, the which was brought about by violence, only afterwards they began to rule the city according to reason and justice, every one preserving his own position, so that it was decided by the citizen Consuls to summon powerful nobles of foreign birth to fill the post of Podestà, as will be shown to you in writing farther on." It is strange that the chronicler should ascribe the origin of the Consuls to so late a date. But, seeing that his list of these magistrates only begins at this point, it would seem that he really believed them to have no earlier origin. Nevertheless, shortly before, in writing of 1177, he had stated that the Uberti began to make war on the Consuls; hence it is clear that even in his opinion they had existed before the year 1180. Still, blunders and incongruities of this sort are frequently found even in Villani and other chroniclers of the same period.

[174] Santini, i. doc. xii. This is the document stating that the tribute of fifty pounds of "good money" was to be paid to the Consuls of the city, or, failing these, to the Consuls of the merchants, authorised to receive it for the Commune.

[175] This had been granted them in an Imperial patent, given at Pavia *iv. Idus Augusti*, 1164, the which has been published several times, and is also included in the "Storia della guerra di Semifonte," by Messer Pace da Certaldo (p. 5). As all know, this is a counterfeit "Storia" dating from the beginning of the seventeenth century.

[176] Santini, i. doc. xiii. This is the document with the erroneous date, 1101, rectified by Marquis Capponi to 1181 (modern style, 1182).

[177] Villani, Paolino Pieri, the Neapolitan Codex, and the pseudo Brunetto Latini. The "Annales," ii., wrongly assign the

event to 1172.

[178] Santini, i. doc. xiv. The terms were not to be altered without the consent of the Consuls of either city, together with that of at least twenty-five councillors on either side; and the Consuls of the soldiery and of the merchants were to be included in the number. We note that in naming the Consuls a hint is already given of the possible election of a Podestà, although none had as yet been chosen in Florence. This subject will be resumed later on. Meanwhile, the words of the document run as follows: "Inquisitis florentinis Consulibus, vel florentina Potestate, sive Rectori vel Dominatore a comuni populo electo." On Lucca's side mention is also made of the "bonos viros lucensis civitatis, si Consules vel Rector aut Potestas ibi non fuerint."

[179] The "Annales," ii., the pseudo Brunetto Latini, and the Neap. Cod. date the event in 1185; Villani (v. ii.) dates it instead 1184, and says that Pogna was occupied by nobles, who were *cattani* and hostile to Florence. We follow Villani, for otherwise it would be impossible to explain the captivity of Count Alberto in 1184, an event confirmed by documentary evidence.

[180] Santini, i. doc. xvi. and xvii.; the first dated November, 1184, and the second, November 29, 1184.

[181] Hartwig, ii. 79.

[182] Villani, v. 12.

[183] The "Annales," ii., and Paolino Pieri except Pisa alone; Villani, the Neap. Cod., and the pseudo Brunetto Latini except both Pisa and Pistoia.

[184] The chroniclers only say, with obvious inexactitude, for ten miles round.

[185] This diploma is given in Ficker, iv. doc. 170, p. 213. Henry (then Henry VI., King of the Romans, afterwards, as emperor, also called Henry V.), after granting the concession, adds: "Excepto ac salvo iure nobilium et militum, a quibus etiam volumus ut Florentini nihil exigant." The diploma only

refers in general terms to the services rendered by the Florentines to Henry and to his father, Frederic I. Villani considers the grant a reward for their prowess in the Crusade; but the Crusade took place in 1189, and the grant was made in 1187; for although he wrongly dates the latter in 1188, this blunder does not suffice to remove the anachronism. Besides, he also states that the concession was granted through the intervention of Pope Gregory VIII., who was elected in 1187, and died the same year.

[186] In 1186 Perugia was granted judicial rights over the *contado* beyond the walls: "Exceptis domibus et possessionibus, quas habent marchiones et monasterium S. Salvatoris," and, excepting several nobles, specified by name, "in quibus nihil iuris Perusinis relinquitur." Ficker, i. par. 128, p. 242. Sienna, after being deprived of the *contado* in June, 1186, received it back in October, under the same conditions, and so, too, Lucca in the same year. Ficker, i. par. 125. p. 239, and par. 128, p. 2 2.

[187] Ficker often gives the names of these Imperial Podestà, as gleaned from the depositions of witnesses. *Vide* Ficker, vol. iii. p. 440. Hartwig (ii. 192) cites one *Henricus comes florentinus*, also mentioned by Stumpf and who seems to have been a Podestà of the *contado* in September, 1186. After all this, it is not surprising that the Imperial authority should be often referred to in documents of the latter half of the twelfth century. We may cite some instances from the rolls of the Florence Archives: October 14, 1175 (Passignano), "Sub obligo Consulum Florentinorum vel Nuntio Regis"; October 9, 1185 (Passignano), "Sub duplice pena Imperatoris et eius Missi aut quicumque habuerint dominium pro tempore." (Reference is here made to the *contado*, and is another proof of the uncertain rule previously described by us.)

[188] "Liberalitate benefica ipsos respicere volentes, concedimus," &c. ... "huius munifice nostre concessionis."

[189] In 1184, *vide* in addition to the chroniclers, Santini, i. docs. xiv., xv., xvii. and Hartwig, ii. 191. For the years 1185, 1186, and 1187, besides the names recorded by the pseudo Brunetto Latini, the documents furnish frequent allusions of the

following kind: April 30, 1185 (Passignano), "Sub obligo Consulum Florentie resarcire promitto"; December 13, 1185 (Santa Felicità), "Sub obligo Consulum Florentie"; April 26, 1186 (Passignano), "Penam ad Consules Florentie"; September 21, 1187 (Arch. Capitolare, 629), "Consulum vel Rectorum pro tempore Florentie existentium (Actum Florentie)." The rolls of the Arch. Capitolare were examined by Santini, to whom we are indebted for the information; those of the Florence Archives we have personally examined, but some of these were first brought under our notice by Santini.

In 1189 there were undoubtedly Consuls. Not only are the names of three of them recorded by the pseudo Brunetto Latini, but documents give the names of the Consuls of justice. Santini, ii. docs. v. and vi.

[190] Ficker (ii. par. 313, p. 234) cites the words of Pillius, a jurist of the period: "Ut quando faciunt castellanos vel comites in Tuscia"; and, further on: "Sicut fit hodie illis, qui pracficiuntur in singulis provinciis, vel in parte alicuius provinciae, ut in comitatu senensi, florentino vel aretino."

[191] They are both named in the Passerini documents, from which we have frequently quoted.

[192] According to the results of Hartwig's inquiries, between 1150 and 1180.

[193] We find in the Passerini documents (p. 206) that one of the witnesses states that Count Guidi "defendit ipsum monasterium [of Rosano] a Teutonicis et a Renuccio de Stagia, quando erat Potestas Florentinorum, et a Consulibus Florentinis."

[194] October 14, 1175 (Passignano), "Sub potestate consulum Florentinorum vel Nuntio Regis"; July 5, 1191 (Arch. Capitolare, 347), "Sub pena Consulum Florentie vel Potestatis"; April 15, 1192 (Arch. Capitolare, 449), "Sub obligo Potestatis vel Rectorum pro tempore Florentie existentibus"; November 7, 1192 (Passignano, in the Church of St. Biagio), "Sub obligo Potestatis in hac terra existentis" (here allusion is possibly made to some Podestà of the *contado*); May 9, 1193 (Passerini documents in the Florence Archives), "Sub obligo

Potestatis vel Consulum Florentinorum … Actum Florentie."
According to these and other rolls examined by me in the
Florence Archives, the change is seen to have been carried out
in a regular and steady manner. The ancient formulas reappear
from time to time.

[195] "Inquisitis florentinis Consulibus, vel florentina
Potestate, sive Rectore vel Dominatore … florentini Consules
vel florentina Potestate sive Rector vel Dominator" (Santini, i.
doc. xiv).

[196] Santini, i. doc. xx.

[197] Santini, ii. doc. viii. His name is *Corsus*, and at one
point he is styled a councillor *super facto iustitie*, at another,
consul iustitie.

[198] In the years 1193 and 1195 he still mentions the
Consuls, and even by name. These may have been the *consiliarii*
of the two Podestà known to have existed in those years. It is
well to observe here that all this would have been impossible in
the case of Imperial Podestà, had there ever been any in
Florence. They could never have appeared in the light of chief
Consuls.

[199] Florence Archives, "Bullettone," c. 131. July 10, 1196:
"Dominus Petrus episcopus habuit tenutam a consulibus curie
Communis Florentie." In the years 1197–99, *vide* the documents
of the Tuscan League, quoted later on, and Hartwig,
ii. 194.

[200] In the year 1197, Paolino Pieri tells us: "San Miniato al
Tedesco, or rather its fortress, was destroyed." In 1198, he tells
how "San Genesio was pulled down by the inhabitants"
(*terrazzani*), who then returned to the hill-top, and rebuilt San
Miniato. Villani (v. 21) says that San Miniato was destroyed, and
its inhabitants came down to St. Genesio in the plain. *Vide* also
the "Annales," ii., and the Neap. Cod., *ad annum*. Hartwig (ii.
93) has examined the question minutely, and swept away all
inaccuracies and exaggerations.

[201] "Annales," ii., Neap. Cod., *ad annum*, Villani (v. 22).
From the reports of eye witnesses, published by Passerini, one

sees that Montegrossoli was troublesome to its neighbours, and even Villani says that it was held by *cattani*, who made continual attacks on the Florentines.

[202] *Vide* the "Acts of the League" (November 11 and December 14, 1197; February 5 and 7, 1198), in Santini, i. doc. xxi., and in Ficker, vol. iv. p. 242, doc. 196. Ficker uses some of the documents preserved in Florence, and also some of those at Sienna which are more complete and correct at certain points.

[203] Sed Podiumbonizi possit recipi per capud.

[204] *Vide* the "Acts of the League" in Ficker, vol. iv. p. 246.

[205] "Atti della Lega." The Florentines swore to the League on November 13 and 14, 1197. The document in Santini, i. doc. xxiii. gives the names of sixteen Consuls and 133 councillors who took the oath. In a preceding document, also relating to February 5 and 17, 1198, there are the names of ten Consuls, but three of them are not the same on both days, so that there must have been more than twelve Consuls in February, 1198. Some, too, were already in office even in November, 1197, and this confirms our previous hypothesis that, on the great occasion of the League, all or part of the withdrawing Consuls remained in office with those just elected. Nor is this a solitary instance. On April 2, 1212, the Commune of Prato, in arranging a treaty with Florence, sent three *Consules veteri*, and three *Consules novi eiusdem terre* to conclude it. Santini, i. doc. lx.

[206] Innocentii III., "Epistolae," i. 15, 27, 34, 35; Ficker, vol. ii. par. 363, p. 384.

[207] Instead of mentioning the *Ducatus Tusciae*, he now spoke of the *magna pars Tusciae, quae in nostris privilegiis continetur*. To the Pisans he wrote, "Post correctionem adhibitam, nihil invenimus quod in ecclesiastici iuris vel cuiusquam maioris vel minoris personae praeiudicium redundaret." And in February, 1199, he urged them to join the League. Innocentii, "Ep.," bk. i. 401 and 555; "Gesta Innocentii," c. ii.; Ficker, vol. ii. par. 363, pp. 385–6.

[208] Santini, i. docs. xxiii., xxiv., xxv. The first is dated the

10th; the second, April 15, 1198; and the third, giving the names of the men of Figline swearing fealty to the League, is also dated the 15th of April. The second alludes to the chief Consuls: "Comandamenta Consulum florentine civitatis omnium vel maioris partis aut priorum ex eis." The third informs us (pp. 43 and 44) that the oath was sworn: "In Florentia, in ecclesia S. Reparate et Parlamento, coram florentino populo iuraverunt." Also further on: "In ecclesia S. Reparate, in Aringo." This is another instance of the parliament being convened in a church.

[209] Santini, i. doc. xxvi. Obedience was sworn to the Consuls or Rectors *vel segnoratico aliquo extante*. This, too, is an expression having very little savour of the more democratic temper of former times.

[210] In Villani (v. 26) he is wrongly styled Count Arrigo della Tosa. The Della Tosa family were not counts. The pseudo Brunetto Latini speaks of him in an undated paragraph, anterior to his record of 1200, as "Messer Arrigo, count of Capraia."

[211] As we have stated, it seems to be for this reason that the pseudo Brunetto Latini dates the office of Podestà from this moment: "A novel thing was done, and for the first time a Potestade was elected in Florence, from jealousy of the Consuls, the which Potestade was Paganello Porcaro of Lucca."

[212] Santini, i. doc. xxvii. (February 12 and 23, 1200); doc. xxviii. (February 12 and 19); doc. xxix. (February 12 and 23, and March 25). In these papers the Podestà is always mentioned with the councillors, and the office of the Consuls is also invariably recorded: "Sive parabola Potestatis et Consiliariorum vel Consulum sive Rectorum Florentie" (p. 49). "A Potestate vel Consiliariis eius, sive a Consulibus Florentie vel Rectoribus" (p. 48). In a posterior document (Santini, i. doc. xxxvii., dated August 14, 1201), we find the councillors representing the Podestà: "Sitio filio condam Butrighelli, Melio filio Catalani Consiliarii domini Potestatis Florentie, recipienti (*sic*) vice et nomine dicte Potestatis et totius Comunis Florentie" (p. 72). These councillors did not yet form a special council, but were on the way to it, since the council or senate of the city being already called the general council, the existence

of a special one is implied: "In Florentia, in ecclesia S. Reparate, coram generali consilio civitatis, iuraverunt." Santini, i. doc. xxviii. p. 53.

[213] Santini, i. doc. xxx.

[214] It may be roughly rendered:

"Florence, get out of the way,
Semifonte's a city to-day."

[215] Santini, i. doc. xxxiv.

[216] This treaty was concluded April 27, 1201; about five hundred inhabitants of Colle swearing adhesion to it on the 28th, 29th, and 30th of April. Santini, i. docs. xxxv. and xxxvi.

[217] "Per quinquennium guerra durante et eidem omnibus de Tuscia prestantibus patrocinium.... Tacere tamen nolo magnalia quae inter caetera vidi, guerra durante." Sanzanome, Florentine ed., pp. 134–5.

[218] The document is given in the "Delizie," of Ildefonso di San Luigi, vii. 178. Perpetual exemption from all taxes was decreed to Gonella and his comrades, "qui mortui fuere in turre de Bagunolo et in muris apud Summumfontem, in servitio Communis Florentie." *Vide* also in Hartwig, ii. 100.

[219] Santini, i. xxxviii., xxxix. The treaty of peace was concluded between Alberto da Montauto, lord of San Gimignano, for the people of Semifonte, and Claritus Pillii, Consul of the merchants for Florence.

[220] This letter, published by Winkelmann (Philipp von Schwaben, i. 556), is taken from a MS. of the Florentine Boncompagni, in the Archives of Berne, No. 322, fol. 18, and part of it is referred to by Hartwig, ii. 102.

[221] About eight hundred men of Montepulciano swore to these terms on the hand of the Florentine Consul. Santini, i. doc. xl. October 19, 24, 1202.

[222] Santini, i. docs. xlii., xliii., xliv., and xlv. These papers, dated April and May, 1203, give the names of all the Siennese

citizens and country people sanctioning the arbitration in the name of their city. The last document contains the depositions of the witnesses examined by Ogerio. Doc. xlvii., June 4, 1203, is the verdict pronounced by him.

[223] On the days 4th, 7th, and 8th of June, the Bishop and Commune of Sienna gave up all that was due to Florence, in accordance with the verdict. Santini, i. doc. xlviii. On the 6th of the same month one hundred and fifty Siennese councillors swore observance to the terms. Santini, i. doc. xlix.

[224] Santini, i. doc. lii.

[225] Ibid., i. doc. xlvi.

[226] Murat., "Antiq. It.," iv. 576–83. *Vide* also Ficker (vol. ii. par. 312, p. 229 and fol.), who gleaned from this important document the list of the Podestà established as Imperial envoys in the Siennese territory. These Podestà are mentioned by the witnesses as "Comites teutonici, Comites comitatus senensis pro imperatore Federigo," and occasionally even as "Comites contadini."

[227] "Per distruggere questa capra, non ci vuol altro che un lupo." *Vide* Repetti, art. "Capraia e Montelupo"; Hartwig (ii. 106–9) rectifies some chronological and other blunders made by Villani.

[228] The treaty is probably extant in the Archives of Pistoia. Repetti, in citing it from the "Aneddoti" of Zaccaria, dates it the 3rd of June; other writers date it July.

[229] Dated October 29, November 17, 1204, in Santini, i. doc. liii. The oath sworn before the Consul Guido Uberto was of obedience to the commands "que ... fecerint Potestas Florentie vel Consules Civitatis vel maior pars vel priores aut prior eorum." Thus the Podestà's name came first, even at a time when there were Consuls in office, before whom the oath was sworn, in presence of "Angiolerii Beati, Doratini et Burniti Paganiti sexcalcorum Comunis Florentie." Even the office of *sexcalcus* is new (it is also mentioned in another document of the 30–31st of May, in Santini, i. xlvi.), and seems to us a sign of the change tending to a more aristocratic form of

government in Florence. The communal oath sworn on October 29, 1204 (Santini, i. doc. liv.) began thus, "Hec sunt sacramenta, quae Potestas et Consules Comunis et Consules militum, mercatorum et Priores Artium et generale Consilium, ad sonum campane coadunatum, fecerunt Guidoni Borgognoni comiti et filiis et Caprolensibus." The Consuls took the oath, not the Podestà, for there was none, although nominally heading the formula.

[230] Recorded in the "Acta Sanctorum," the 1st of May, at p. 14, and also in the list (known as that of Sta. Maria Novella) of the Consuls and Podestà. *Vide* Hartwig, ii. 197. But the documents of this year only refer in general to the Consuls and Podestà without giving any names.

[231] Sizio Butrigelli, or Butticelli, is mentioned in the Sta. Maria Novella Catalogue. Hartwig, ii. 197.

[232] Sanzanome, pp. 139–40; Hartwig, ii. 111–12.

[233] Santini, i. doc. lviii. and lix. A great number of Siennese swore to the treaty in the presence of the Podestà Gualfredotto Grasselli, *vice et nomine Comunis Florentie recipienti*, without the *consiliarii*. But the ceremony being very lengthy, he delegated Ildebrandino Cavalcanti to represent him, *procuratoris nomine*. Some of the documents of this peace are in Florence, the others in Sienna. The former were discovered by Santini, and all are mentioned by Hartwig, ii. 113–14.

[234] This chapter was originally published in the *Politecnico* of Milan, numbers for July and September, 1866.

[235] The details of this event are differently told by Villani (v. 38), by the pseudo Brunetto Latini (*ad annum*), and by Dino Compagni at the beginning of his Chronicle. But the gist is the same in all three, and we have mainly adhered to the first and second authorities, whose accounts are longer and more detailed than that of Compagni.

[236] Villani, v. 38.

[237] Villani, vi. 5.

[238] Villani (vi. 33) says: "Albeit the said parties existed among the nobles of Florence, and they oftentimes came to blows from private enmities, and were split into factions by the said parties," nevertheless the people "remained united, for the good and honour and dignity of the Republic" (vol. i. p. 253). The "Annales," ii., of the year 1236 relate that the palaces of the Commune and of the Galigai were destroyed, which would certainly seem to be a proof of a genuine revolution.

[239] Ammirato, "Storie," lib. xi. (with additions made by Ammirato the younger). Anno 1240.

[240] In this year we find the first official mention of the Florentine Guelphs. Frederic II. complains of their conduct, saying: "Pars Guelforum Florentiae, cui dudum nostra Maiestas pepercerat." The "Annales," ii., first name the Guelphs in 1239, and in 1242 mention the Guelphs and the Ghibellines. *Vide* Hartwig, "Quellen," &c., vol. ii. pp. 159–60 and 164. This author believes that the names of the two Florentine parties first came into use in the year 1239.

[241] Lami, "Antichità Toscane," lesson xv.; Passerini, "Istituti di Beneficenza—Il Bigallo." Florence: Le Monnier, 1853.

[242] *Vide* "Statuta Populi et Communis Florentiae," published in Florence, but with the mark of the Friburg press, vol. i.; Cantini, "Saggi," vol. iii. chap. xvi.; "Delizie degli Eruditi Toscani," vol. ix. p. 256 and fol.

[243] Villani says: "They stripped all power from the Podestà then in Florence, and dismissed all the officers" (vi. 39). As usual, Malespini copies from Villani (chap. cxxxvii.). But reading farther we see clearly that the Podestà was elected as before, and that a palace was built for his use. The chronicler's real meaning was that the form of government was changed, and the actual governors dismissed from office. The term Podestà was used in its general sense of magistrate-in-chief.

[244] Villani, vol. vi. pp. 39 and 40. *Vide* also Coppo Stefani.

[245] It is thought to be the work of Lapo or Jacopo, the

supposed master of Arnolfo Brunelleschi.
[246]

[247] Villani, vi. 39.

Vide Marchionne di Coppo Stefani, "Storia Fiorentina," bk. ii. rubric 63. In relating the first rupture of the Guelphs and Ghibellines, the author says: "Almost all the families on the Ghibelline, or Imperial side, were nobles of the *contado*, because these held lands or castles in fief from the Empire." Also Ammirato, who was well versed in contemporary chronicles and documents, in relating what was said by men of the people as to the reforms of 1250, makes them continue their statement that the Uberti, as leaders of the nobles, were the authors of all the misfortunes of Florence, with the following words: "Who but the Uberti waste our substance and our strength by exorbitant taxes and imposts? These haughty men deemed it an honourable thing, among their other grand and noble usages, to be our foes; inasmuch as, exulting in their descent from the princes of Germany, they consider us to be churls and peasants, and despise us, as though we were of a different clay from their own." Ammirato, "Storie," bk. ii. *ad annum.*
[248]

In fact, Villani only mentions them at a much later date. But there is documentary evidence of their previous existence. *Vide*, for instance, the "Arch. Stor. Ital.," Series iii. vol. xxiii. p. 222. Doc. dated April 30, 1251. *Vide* M. di Coppo Stefani, rub. 90.

[249] Giannotti, "Opere," ed. Le Monnier, vol. i. p. 82.

[250] Machiavelli, "Storie," bk. ii. On this point it may be well to repeat our former remarks, to the effect that Machiavelli is often as inaccurate in his definition of facts as profound in his intuition of their character and tendency. After the first book of his "Storie," giving a general introduction to the Middle Ages, he begins to narrate the history of Florence in the second book. He was the first writer, after L. Aretino, to put aside nearly all the fabulous tales of the chroniclers touching the origins of Florence, and start from well-authenticated facts. For although he, too, believes that Florence was destroyed by Totila and rebuilt by Charlemagne, and even credits the destruction of

Fiesole by the Florentines in 1010, it is easy to condone these blunders, remembering how many other legendary tales were rejected by him, and how much time elapsed before some germ of historic truth could be gleaned from the less incredible traditions to which he adhered. But why did Machiavelli pass over almost at one bound the interval between 1010 and 1215 without saying anything of the first and second Florentine constitutions, or alluding to the numerous deeds of war and political revolutions occurring during that period? Regarding these events, he might have derived information from the chroniclers. But he clings to the theory that the Buondelmonti tragedy was the primary cause and origin of all internecine strife in Florence, although the evidence of contemporary chroniclers and his own historical acumen might have saved him from this error. Continuing with the same strangely unaccountable negligence, he skips another period—from 1215 to 1250— saying that then at last Guelphs and Ghibellines came to an agreement, and "deemed the moment come to establish free institutions," almost as though this were the first time that the Florentines had contemplated organising a free government. Yet we have seen that Florentine liberties were assured, and the first constitution founded in 1115; that the constitution of 1250 was the third, not the first, and established by the Guelph *popolani*, to the hurt of the Ghibelline nobles, instead of being formed, as Machiavelli states, by the united efforts of the Guelphs and the Ghibellines. Nor is this the last of his blunders, for Machiavelli goes on to say: "Likewise to remove causes of enmity arising from judgments delivered, they [the Florentines] decreed the establishment of two foreign judges, with the respective titles of Captain and Podestà, authorised to administer justice to the citizens in all cases, whether civil or criminal." In this manner he converts the two chief political authorities into ordinary judges, places both on the same level, and fails to remark that, although the Captain was a newly created functionary, the Podestà had been in existence for more than half a century. He also states that the *carroccio* was instituted in 1250, to give prestige, or *maestà*, to the army, although the Florentines had adopted the use of the *carroccio* long before this date. He shows equal negligence in his account of the organisation of the army, and without drawing any distinction between the forces of the Commune and those of the people, although this point is fully elucidated by the chroniclers. Villani, for instance, tells us: "Inasmuch as we have treated of the gonfalons and banners of the people," it is fitting to make mention of those "of the knights and the army proper" (*guerra*). Nevertheless, whenever Machiavelli pauses to consider the general character of Florentine revolutions, and particularly of those subsequent to 1250, his definitions excel those of any other writer.

[251] November, 1252.

[252] "Arch. Stor. It." Series iii. vol. xxiii. p. 220.

[253] Villani and Ammirato, *ad annum*.

[254] Villani, vi. 51. Ammirato, *ad annum*.

[255] Ammirato, *ad annum*, contains a summary of the treaty of peace.

[256] Villani and Ammirato, *ad annum*.

[257] VI. 70.

[258] *Scaggiale*—a leathern belt with a buckle.

[259] *Tassello*—a square of cloth attached to the cloak so as to be used as a hood.

[260] Villani, vi. 70.

[261] *Vide* "I Capitoli del Comune di Firenze, inventario e regesto," vol. i., edited by C. Guasti. Florence: Cellini, 1866.

[262] Ammirato, *ad annum*, gives a summary of the treaty.

[263] Villani, vi. 62. This incident, highly praised by Villani as a magnanimous example, has been quoted by others as a proof that the Florentine people must have been corrupt at a time when so exceptional a monument could be decreed to one of the citizens simply because he had refused to betray his country. But it should be noted, first of all, that he was not honoured with a monument merely because he had rejected a bribe, but, as Villani goes on to say, because "Aldobrandino died in such excellent repute for his virtuous deeds for the good of the Commune." Even should Villani's praises of the deed in itself seem too marked and consequently indicative of general corruption, this corruption might be more fitly attributed to Villani's own days than to the earlier period of Aldobrandino and the *Primo Popolo*, when genuine virtue and true patriotism were undoubtedly predominant.

[264] "Storie," lib. ii.

[265] Villani, vi. 65.

[266] C. Paoli, "La battagali di Montaperti" (extract from vol. ii. of the "Bollettino della Società Senese di Storia patria"). Sienna, 1869. In 1889 Prof. Paolo added another very important publication to this work, *i.e.*, "Il libro di Montaperti," in the "Documenti di Storia Italiana," brought out by the Royal Commission for Tuscany, Umbria, and the Marches, vol. ix.

[267] Marchionni di Coppo Stefani, "Stor. fior.," rubric 120.

[268] Villani and other Florentine chroniclers.

[269] The figures given by Florentine chroniclers are never exact, and must be therefore regarded as approximate ones only.

[270] Here is an instance extracted from a law of 1284: "Item quod nullus presumat consulere, vel arengare super aliquo quod non sit principaliter propositum per dominum Potestatem, vel aliquem loco sui. Et qui contrafacerit, in soldos sexaginta florenorum parvorum vice qualibet puniatur, et plus et minus ad voluntatem domini Potestatis. Et quicquid dictum vel consultum contra propositionem, non valeat, nec teneat." "Consigli Maggiori, Provvisioni e Registri," i., sheets 12 *retro*. Archivio di Stato, Florence.

[271] Too coarse to be translated.—*Translator's note.*

[272] Villani, vi. 78.

[273] Aldobrandini, "Chroniche," p. 9; Paoli, "La battaglia di Montaperti," p. 46.

[274] In the cathedral of Sienna certain poles are shown traditionally believed to have belonged to the Florentine *Carroccio*. But Siennese scholars now justly maintain that these poles formed part of their own *Carroccio* instead.

[275] Paoli, op. cit., p. 58.

[276] Sismondi, after comparison of the chroniclers' accounts, raises the number of killed to 10,000 and the wounded to the same figure.

[277] VI. 19.

[278] Lord of the Castle of Poppi in the Casentino. He had separated from the other Counts Guidi, who were Guelphs.

[279] All this is narrated by Villani and other chroniclers, and is likewise recorded by Dante in the "Divina Commedia." A few writers have tried to throw doubt on the incident, but, as Dr. Hartwig justly observes, it is difficult to suppose that Guelph chroniclers would have invented a legend so entirely favourable to the Ghibelline chief.

[280] Prof. Del Lungo gives a full account of these demolitions in his paper, "Una vendetta in Firenze," in the "Arch. Stor. It.," Series iv. vol. 18, p. 355 and fol.

[281] P. Ildefonso, "Delizie," &c., vol. ix. p. 19 and fol.

[282] Machiavelli, "Storie," lib. i. p. 37.

[283] It is said that Manfred, on witnessing their attack, showed his admiration for their courage by exclaiming, "Whoever may win the victory, these Guelphs will not lose it."

[284] Dante (Purgatorio, iii. 121–32). The poet places Manfred in purgatory, although at the period he was classed as a heretic together with the Emperor Frederic, Farinata, and many other Ghibellines:

"Orribili furon li peccati miei,
  Ma la bontà infinita ha si gran braccia
  Che prende ciò che si rivolve a lei.
  Se il pastor di Cosenza, che alla caccia
  Di me fu messo per Clemente, allora
  Avesse in Dio ben letta questa faccia,
  L'ossa del corpo mio sarieno ancora
  In co' del ponte presso a Benevento,
  Sotto la guardia della grave mora.
  Or le bagna la pioggia e move il vento,

Di fuor del Regno, quasi lungo il Verde,
Ove le trasmutò a lume spento."

[285] Machiavelli, "Storie," lib. ii. p. 73.

[286] This result had come to pass at a much earlier period, was of frequent occurrence in Florentine history, and was now more assured than at any previous time. Malespini's Chronicle, chap. 104, even before the coronation of Frederic II., refers to certain families who "were beginning to be prominent, although too obscure to be mentioned a short while ago.... The Mozzi, Bardi, Jacopi detti Rossi, Frescobaldi, all these were of recent creation, inasmuch as they were still merchants and of petty origin: likewise the Tornaquinci and Cavalcanti, also traders, were of petty origin, and the same may be said of the Cerchi, who shortly began to rise higher than the aforesaid."

[287] Most of these letters are given in Martène, others are published by Del Giudice in his "Codice diplomatico di Carlo I. and Carlo II d'Angiò."

[288] Machiavelli, "Storie," lib. ii. p. 75.

[289] "Il Codice diplomatico di Carlo I. e II. d'Angiò," published by Del Giudice, in Naples, serves to rectify many blunders made by the chroniclers on this point.

[290] "The citizens of ancient times being either entirely extinguished, or, at least decayed by age, another race began to spring up, as it were, in a new city." Ammirato, "Storie."

[291] There are so many discrepancies among Florentine authorities regarding this question that, after careful study and comparison of the different accounts given by the chroniclers, we have chosen Villani as our guide. He is the most celebrated of the old writers and the nearest to the times described. On close consideration of his words (*vide* Villani, lib. vii. chap. xvi.) we see that the councils are to be specified as those of the Twelve, of the Captain and of the Podestà. But reference to the State Archives, the *Consulte*, or first volume of *Provvisioni*— dated a few years after the reform of which we speak—will serve to prove that sometimes the Council of One Hundred was assembled; at others both the special council of the Captain and

his council-general and special were summoned; sometimes again the Podestà's special council—likewise styled the Council of Ninety—with his council-general and special, amounting in all to 390 members (300 + 90). We also find that admittance to these four last-mentioned councils was usually granted to the seven masters (*capitudini*) of the greater guilds, and that in course of time the number of the masters increased, and that they were sometimes summoned to meet as a separate council. By studying the number of votes given at the councils, we find sufficient proof of the accuracy of Villani's statements. In special councils the voting was done with black and white balls, a record being kept of their respective numbers. But at that period general councils only signified their verdict by standing up or remaining seated, and the votes were not recorded in writing. But regarding these points the rules changed as circumstances required, for the magistrates were frequently authorised to consult *whichever councils they preferred.*

In affairs of the highest importance, and in discussions carried on in a strictly legal way, every measure proposed had to be first approved by the twelve worthies, who were likewise allowed to ask the advice of confidential private persons, afterwards denominated *advisers* (*richiesti*). The proposal was next submitted to the One Hundred, then to the Captain's two councils, and finally to those of the Podestà. All these details are confirmed by the documents in the Archives; and as a more easily verified instance, although of later date than the period now described, we may quote the opening sentence of the "Statuto dell' Esecutore di Giustizia," given in the Appendix to Signor Giudici's "Storia de' Municipi Italiani," p. 402 (1st edition). "In the name of God, *Amen.* In the year of His Holy Incarnation, 1306, &c., firstly, in the Council of One Hundred, and subsequently in the council and through the special council of *Messere lo Capitano* and the masters of the twelve greater guilds (these having already increased in number) … and farthermore, at once, without delay, in the council and through the general and special council of *Messere lo Capitano* and of the people of Florence, and of the masters of the guilds … done, confirmed, and carried the vote by sitting and rising, as prescribed by the same Statutes…. Likewise after these proceedings, in the same year, same '*indiction*' and day, in the council and by the general council of three hundred and special council of ninety men of the Florentine Commune, with the aforesaid guild-masters, by order of the noble gentleman, Messere Count Gabrielli d'Agobbio of the same city and Commune of Florence, Podestà, &c." Here it should also be noted that although in this case the councils of the Podestà assembled on the same day as those of the captain, yet according to law and usage the former should not have been convoked until one or two days had elapsed.

[292] *Vide* "Delizie degli eruditi Toscani," by P. Ildefonso, vol. vii. pp. 203–286.

[293] Del Lungo "Una Vendetta," in "Firenze Arch. Stor. It.," Series iv. vol. xviii. p. 354 and fol.

[294] The *Giornale Storico degli Archivi Toscani*, anno i., No. 1, contains "Lo Statuto di Parte Guelfa," of 1335, edited by Bonaini, whose learned commentary on the same appeared in subsequent numbers. Villani tells us (vii. 17) that, "by mandate from the Pope and the king, the said Guelphs *nominated three* knights as rectors of the party." But this must be a blunder, since, according to the statutes of the party, three knights and three men of the people were named to the office. A document dated December 12, 1268, appended to Del Lungo's "Una Vendetta in Firenze," mentions, *"Unus de sex Capitaneis Partis Guelforum."* Villani, in the same chap. xvii., confuses Pope Clement with Pope Urban, deceased in 1264. The statute of 1335 adds a third council, of one hundred, to the others, and this probably served the same purpose with regard to the councils as that fulfilled by the parliament to the Republic.

[295] The English word "milliner" is derived from *Milan*.

[296] The term *calimala* seems to have been taken from the name of the street in which the guild was situated. The street led to a house of ill-fame, hence the name *Calis malus*, in the sense of *Via mala*—evil road or lane.

[297] A statute of the Calimala Guild, dated 1332, is given in the appendix of Giudici's "Storia dei Municipi Italiani." Another, dated 1301–2, has been published, with a commentary by Dr. Filippi, "Il più antico Statuto dell' Arte di Calimala."

Turin: Bocca, 1889. The statutes formulated regulations already long in vigour by means of special laws.

[298] All these details of the Calimala Guild are to be found in the statutes cited above. We have quoted from the earliest statutes.

[299] Originally published in the Milan *Politecnico*, Nos. for November and December, 1867.

[300] Ammirato (ed. of 1846; Florence, Batelli), i. 248.

[301] The chroniclers say Guy de Montfort, but the latter only came in 1269. *Vide* Del Giudice, Cod. Dipl. ii. 23.

[302] Villani, vii. 19. The frequent mention of eight hundred knights by the chroniclers of this period excites doubts as to their accuracy. It is never safe to accept their statements regarding the number of this or that army. Probably eight hundred horse was a species of regulation number, signifying a squadron of French men-at-arms.

[303] Villani, vii. 19; Marchionne Stefani, rubric 138; Ammirato, lib. iii.

[304] Gregorovius, vol. v. chap. 8: Cherrier, "Storia della lotta dei Papi e degli Imperatori di Casa Sveva," lib. x.

[305] Ammirato, i. 262; "Delizie degli Eruditi," vol. ix. p. 41.

[306] Machiavelli, "Storie," vol. i. p. 77. Italy, 1813.

[307] "Ipsas petitiones benigne accessimus et audivimus cum effectu, primo de conservando iure et honore Comunis Florentie; contra Pisanos et Senenses invasores et Gibellinos et exiticios terre vestra et infideles Podiibonizi proditores nostros proponimus, cum Dei auxilio atque vestro, facere vivam guerram, donec peniteant de commissis, et vos de factis vestris habeatis comodum et honorem.... Vicarium Ytalicum virum providum discretum et fidelem, cuius devotionem, fidem et probitatem in magnis factis nostris cognovimus, firmiter et ab experto vobis concessimus secundum quod vestra postulatio continebat, et volumus quod sit contentus salario et expensis et

emendis, prout in ipsius Civitatis statutis continetur, nec ultra aliquid exigat." Del Giudice, "Codice Diplomatico," ii. 116–17.

We find that several Italian Podestà were afterwards appointed in Florence by Charles.

[308] Villani, vii. 54.

[309] Raynaldi, anno 1278; Sismondi, vol. ii. chap. vii.

[310] Villani, vii. 56.

[311] Ammirato, vol. i. p. 274.

[312] Ammirato the younger was the first writer to give an exact report of this agreement, with minute details derived from State papers, in his additions to the elder Ammirato's "History" (Anno 1279 and 1280). Several documents are given in the "Delizie degli Eruditi Toscani," by Padre Ildefonso, vol. ix. p. 63 and fol. Still ampler details are given by Bonaini ("Della Parte Guelfa in Firenze") in the *Giornale Storico degli Archivi Toscani*, vol. iii. p. 167 and fol. *Vide* also A. Gherardi's recent and very important work, "Le Consulte della Repubblica Fiorentina" (Firenze, Sansoni). The original document of the Peace is to be found (mutilated) in the State Archives of Florence.

[313] The Fourteen are mentioned together with the Twelve in the cardinal's treaty of peace, and for some time later both bodies are simultaneously mentioned in the "Consulte," according to the usual Florentine custom of enumerating the old as well as the new magistrates. Subsequently the Fourteen alone are recorded, and the Twelve disappear entirely.

[314] Villani, vii. 56; Ammirato (Florentine edition of 1846), lib. iii. p. 275, &c.

[315] The old chronicles contain indications of these particulars, but for the minute description of them, corroborated by documentary evidence, *vide* Ammirato the younger, in his appendices to the "Storie" of Ammirato the elder.

[316] Dr. Hartwig, who first called attention to this point, also

remarked that the office of *Defensor* is first recorded in the "Consulte," in November, 1282, and that the first Defender mentioned by name is Bernardino della Porta. "Consulte," pp. 116, 132, 133, 140, from November 6, 1282 to February 6, 1283.[317]

Dr. Hartwig also ascertained that in the "Consulte" the first mention of the priors occurs on June 26, 1282. Their names are recorded after those of the Fourteen; on April 24, 1283, they are given precedence over the latter; and from December forwards they are mentioned alone, without the Fourteen.[318]

[319] Bk. i. p. 25 and fol. (the Del Lungo edition).

[320] Villani, vii, 79; Ammirato, iii. pp. 288–90.

Villani says (vii. 89) that this "was the most noble and renowned *court* ever held in the city of Florence."[321]

[322] "Consulte," vol. i. pp. 169–70.

Hartwig, "Ein menschenalter florentinische Geschichte" (1250–93). Freiburgi B., 1889–91, p. 111.

[323] Ammirato gives full details of this treaty. A summary of the original document was afterwards included by Canale, in his "Nuova Istoria della Repubblica di Genova" (the Le Monnier edition), vol. iii. p. 34.

[324] Villani, vii. 98; Malespini, ccxliii.

[325] Some of the chroniclers assert that the archbishop hoped to extract large sums of money from his captives before making an end of them.

[326] For details of the Pisan war with Genoa and Florence, *vide* "Storie e Cronache Pisane," edited by Bonaini and others in vol. vi. (pts. i. and ii.) of the "Archivio Storico Italiano"; Canale, "Nuova Istoria della Repubblica di Genova"; Villani; Flaminio dal Borgo; Muratori Script., vol. xv.; Sismondi; "Hist. des Rep. It.," T. ii. chap. 8.

[327] An order of knighthood limited to the nobility.

[328] G. Villani, Dino Compagni, and the other Florentine chroniclers.

[329] Villani, Compagni, Ammirato, and the Pisan historians previously quoted.

[330] Villani, vii. 99; Vasari, "Vita di Arnolfo"; Ammirato (Florence: Batelli and Co., 1846), vol. i. pp. 310–11.

[331] Ammirato, vol. i. p. 337.

[332] *Vide* Note A at the end of this chapter.

[333] Prof. P. Santini has treated of this question in his article entitled "Condizione personale degli abitanti del contado nel secolo xiii.," "Arch. Stor. It." (Series iv. vol. xvii. p. 178 and fol.). He justly remarks that there is no basis of comparison between the Bolognese law of 1256 and the Florentine law of 1289, seeing that they relate to persons of a different class and to two different periods of the movement set on foot in every commune for ameliorating the conditions of the inhabitants of the *contado* (p. 188 and fol.).

[334] Villani, vii. 132.

[335] Ammirato, bk. iii. *ad annum.*

[336] *Vide* Note B at the end of this chapter.

[337] *Vide* Note C at the end of this chapter.

[338] Originally published in the *Politecnico* of Milan; Nos. for June and July, 1867.

[339] *Vide* the Florentine edition of 1755, p. 133.

[340] This anecdote is related by the Friar of St. Gall, "De rebus bellicis Caroli Magni." *Vide* Muratori, Dissertazione xxv.

[341] Muratori, Dissertazione xxv. *Vide* likewise Pignotti, "Storia della Toscana," vol. iv. Saggio iii. Florence, 1824.

[342] We have already mentioned the probable derivation of this term.

[343] *Vide* Pagnini, "Della Decima," vol. ii. sec. 4 and 5.

[344] Pagnini, "Della Decima," ibid.

[345] Villani, lib. xi. chap. 94.

[346] Villani, lib. xi. chap. 94.

[347] It would seem that the Guild of Por' Santa Maria originally traded in Florentine woollen stuffs, and that the silk merchants formed a secondary and separate branch. Gradually, however, they became amalgamated with the guild (early in the thirteenth century), and then became its principal components, until at last the Silk Guild and Por' Santa Maria were entirely fused in one.

[348] *Vide* the "Cronaca" of Benedetto Dei (1470–92), preserved among the MSS. of the Magliabecchian Library. Many interesting portions of this "Cronaca" have been published in the appendix to vol. ii. of Pagnini's "Decima."

[349] *Vide* the same "Cronaca" of Dei.

[350] "Again, a law was passed in 1371, inasmuch as many men traded the shares of the Monte in this wise: One said to another: 'the shares of the Monte are at thirty; I wish to do some business with you to-day. This time next year I'll sell to you, or you to me, at what price shall we say?' At thirty-one the share [of one hundred]? 'What premium do you ask for this?' So they bargained, and the terms were fixed. When shares fell, the merchant bought, if they rose, he sold out, and the stock changed hands twenty times in the year. Accordingly a tax was charged of two florins in the hundred for every transfer." Marchionne di Coppo Stefani, vol. viii. p. 97, in the "Delizie degli Eruditi Toscani," vol. xiv.

[351] Vettori, "Il Fiorino d'oro"; Orsini, "Storia delle Monete." Florence, 1760.

[352] Pagnini, "Della Decima," vol. ii. sec. iii. chaps. i.-iv.

Other details are supplied by Ammirato, Dei, and more especially by Villani (xi. 88, and xii. 55).

[353] G. Villani, xl. 54.

[354] Ammirato, lib. 18, *ad annum*.

[355] "Cronaca" of Benedetto Dei, given in Pagnini.

[356] Ibid., vol. ii. p. 275.

[357] Ammirato, *ad annum*; Pagnini, loc. cit.

[358] This led some writers to believe that slavery still existed in Italy many centuries after it had disappeared. A praiseworthy article on this theme, by Signor Salvatore Bongi, was published in the *Nuova Antologia*, anno I. No. 6.

[359] *Vide* the Speech of Tommaso Mocenigo, so often reproduced by chroniclers and historians; Pagnini, "Della Decima," vol. ii. p. 7 and fol.; Romanin, "Storia documentata di Venezia," vol. ii. pp. 156–7.

[360] Urghanj, the chief city of Khwarezm, the country now called Khiva. New Urghanj, the present commercial capital of Khiva, is sixty miles from the ancient city.

[361] Balducci Pegolotti, in Pagnini's book. Colonel H. Yule's "Cathay, and the Way Thither, being a Collection of Mediæval Notices of China" (London, printed for the Hakluyt Society, 1866), is a very important work, includes a series of documents translated by the author, and is prefaced by a learned dissertation from his pen.

[362] Pagnini, vol. ii. sec. i. K. Sieveking, "Geschichte von Florenz." This very brief but excellent work was published anonymously at Hamburg in 1844. It has furnished many of the details given in this chapter.

[363] The first five were frequently joined to the greater guilds, which were then increased to twelve.

[364] "Inferno," Canto x.

[365] Franco Sacchetti tells us that while he was a member of the government the magistrates of the Republic never succeeded in enforcing the laws against luxury. One of them, having been severely reprimanded on this score and threatened with dismissal from office, gives the following account of the devices by which Florentine women evaded the regulations established by law:

"*Signori miei*,—All my life I have sought to acquire reason; and now, when methought I knew something, I find I know nothing; inasmuch as when searching for forbidden ornaments, according to your orders, the women bring forward arguments of a kind never found by me in any law; and among others I will quote these: There comes a woman with an embroidered trimming turned down over her hood, and the notary says, 'Give me your name, since you wear an embroidered trimming.' The good woman takes off this trimming, which is fastened to the hood by a pin, and, holding it in her hand, declares it is a garland. He goes to another woman and says, 'I find you have too many buttons on the front of your gown; you must not wear those buttons.' But she replies, 'Yes, Messere, I can, for these are not buttons, but bosses; and if you do not believe me, see, they have no shanks, and neither are there button-holes.' The notary passes on to another woman wearing ermine fur, saying to himself, 'What excuse can she allege for that? You wear ermine,' and he begins to write her name. The woman says, 'Do not write me down, for this is not ermine, but *lattizzi* fur.' Says the notary, 'What are these *lattizzi*?' 'They are animals....' One of the magistrates says, 'We are trying to fight against a wall.' And another remarks, 'It were better to attend to affairs of more importance!'" (Novella, 137.)

[366] Guicciardini, "Considerazioni sui Discorsi del Machiavelli" (Opere inedite, vol. i., Barbéra, Florence). Full confirmation of the above statements are to be found in this work. In treating of chap. xii. bk. i., where Machiavelli charges the Popes with having prevented the unity of Italy, the author qualifies his approval of the remark by adding: "But I feel uncertain whether it were a good or an ill chance for this province to escape being absorbed in a kingdom; for although to be subject to a republic might prove a glory to the name of Italy and a happiness to the dominant city, it could only bring calamity to all other cities, seeing that, oppressed by the latter's shadow, they were unable to rise to any greatness, it being the wont of republics 'to give no share of the fruits of their independence and power to any save their own citizens.... This reason does not hold good in a monarchy wherein all subjects enjoy more equality, and therefore we behold France and many other provinces living contentedly under a king.'"

[367] Originally published in the Milan Politecnico, July and August, 1868.

[368] To avoid the addition of too many notes to a chapter treating of the general course of events, and only purposing to throw some light on the political conditions of our communes, more especially of Florence, I may say once for all, that besides

the statutes, quoted in due place, the authorities most frequently referred to are: Savigny, "Storia del Diritto Romano nel Medio Evo"; Francesco Forti, "Istituzioni Civili e Trattati inediti di giurisprudenza"; Gans, "Il Diritto di Successione nella Storia Italiana," translated by A. Torchiarulo: Naples (Pedone, Lauriel, 1853); Gide, "Etude sur la condition privée de la femme": Paris, 1868; Schupfer, "La Famiglia Longobarda," in the Law Archives of Bologna, Nos. 1, 2. At this date it is scarcely necessary to remark that since 1868 these studies have made enormous progress in Italy, and that many works of signal importance have been produced which were naturally unknown to me while engaged on these pages, only intended— at the moment—to assist my pupils to a clearer comprehension of the Florentine revolution of 1293, and the "Ordinamenti di Giustizia," which were its inevitable and long needed results.

[369] *Translator's note to Chapter VII.*—With regard to this chapter, I am greatly indebted to the kindness of my learned friend Mr. Ninian Thompson, late judge at Calcutta, since without his skilled collaboration and revision it would have been impossible to cope with the legal technicalities of the text. My thanks are also due to Signor Del Vecchio, Professor of Jurisprudence, for his valuable explanation of ancient terminology.—LINDA VILLARI.

[370] Gaius, i. pp. 890–2.

[371] Comitis Gabriellis Verri, "De ortu et progressu iuris mediolanensis," &c. In Book I. of this work we find, among others, the following words: "Quæ omnia manifeste demonstrant, maiores nostros maximum atque perpetuum studium, contulisse ad agnationem conservandam pro veteri xii. tabularum iure, a Justiniano postea immutato, quo certe nihil ad servandum augendumque familiarum splendorem … utilius, commodius, aptius, commendabilius potuit afferri."

Another of those old writers on law who steadfastly maintain this view is Cardinal De Luca, who, in his "Theatrum veritatis et iustitiæ," makes a singularly angry attack upon Justinian and all agreeing with his views on the subject of agnation. According to De Luca, the Italians never accepted the reforms, or, rather, as he calls them, the *destructions and corruptions*, favoured by Justinian.

Even Giannone, in his "Storia Civile del Regno di Napoli" (bk. iii. paragraph v.), says that Justinian's works met with no favour among us. "They found no acceptance either in Italy or in our provinces, nor could they be planted and strike deep roots here, as on foreign soil; on the contrary, the ancient books of the juris-consults were retained, and the code of Theodosius lost neither its reputation nor its authority."

Here it may be well to remark that the persistence of the Roman law in Italy during the Middle Ages, maintained by Savigny, but combated by others, is now admitted on all hands.

[372] Dr. J. Ficker, "Forschungen zur Reichs und Rechtgeschicte Italiens," 4 vols. Innsbruck, 1868–74.

[373] Gans, while accepting the ideas of Savigny as to the diffusion of the Justinian law in Italy, also takes this view, which is in accordance with his own theory that the new forms of the Italian law were derived from the laws of the Longobards.

[374] Baudi de Vesme, in his notes on the Longobard laws, repeatedly remarks: "Theodosiani juris vestigia hic agnoscere mihi vedetur." Del Giudice has recently proved that certain passages are taken from the Justinian law and others from the Theodosian code.

[375] This discussion may now be considered superfluous, it being generally acknowledged at the present day, that even subsequently to Justinian's constitution, the Theodosian code continued in force. In this way the Justinian and pre-Justinian forms had a contemporaneous existence, only the Pandects were longer neglected.

[376] According to Savigny, the school of Guarnerius was already flourishing in 1113–18. It is now well ascertained that this school was preceded by others adhering far less closely to Justinian forms.

[377] The ancient statute of Giacomo Tiepolo, of which the MS. is extant in the Archives of the Frari, in Venice, and which has been frequently printed, concludes its first prologue with these words: "Et se alguna fiada occorresse cosse che per quelli

statuti non fossero ordinade, perchè l'è de plui i facti che li statuti, s'el occorresse question stranie, et in quele alcuna cossa simela se trovasse, de simel cosse a simele è da proceder. Aver, secondo la consuetudine approvada, oltremente, se al tuto sia diverso, over si facta consuetudine non se trovase, despona i nostri iudexi come zusto et raxionevole a la so providentia apparèrà, habiendo Dio avanti i ochi de la soa mente, si fatamente che, al di del zudixio, de la streta examination davanti el tremante (*tremendo*) Iudexe render possa degna raxione." [378]

Many examples to this effect will be found in the volumes of "Provvisioni" in the Florence Archives. [379]

[380] "Statuta Romæ," Romæ, 1519, ii. 110, 111, and iii. 17.

"Statuta Pisauri, noviter impressa," 1531, ii. 79, 84, 106, 107. [381]

"Statuta Pisauri, noviter impressa," 1531, ii. 79, 84, 106, 107. [382]

"Etiam nullis probationibus, *quia volumus quod* nuda patris assertio plenam probationem faciat." *Vide* "Statuta Civitatis Lucensis," 1539, ii. 66, 67, 68. [383]

"Statuta Civitatis Urbini, impressa, Pisauri," 1519, vi. 30. *Quod pater pro filis, dominus pro famulo teneatur in damnis datis.* [384]

[385] "Statuta Florentiæ" (edition dated from Friburg), ii. 110.

[385] "Statuta Florentiæ" (edition dated from Friburg), ii. 110.

[386] *Vide* "Statuti Pisani," edited by Bonaini.

[387] "Statuta Florentiæ," ii. 61, 62, 63.

[388] "Statuta Florentiæ," ii. 64.

[389] Ibid. ii. 65. *Vide* also the statutes of 1324 (ii. 36 and 74)

and of 1355 (ii. 39) in the State Archives.

[390] "Nisi promiserit de continuo habitando in dicta civitate, vel comitatu Urbini" ("Statuta Urbini," Pisauri, 1519, ii. 54).

[391] "Liber juris civilis urbis Veronæ," chap. xliv. Verona, 1728.

[392] See Gans, *op. cit.* This author made a very careful examination of the Pisan law in the statutes (then unpublished) contained in a MS. Codex at Berlin.

[393] *Vide* the "Consuetudini della città d'Amalfi," edited and annotated by Scipione Volpicella, p. 22; and the "Consuetudini della città di Napoli," under the heading, "De successionibus ab intestato." The same provisions are found also in the "Consuetudini Sorrentine." See also Dr. Otto Hartwig's work, "Codex iuris municipalis Siciliæ." Heft 1, "Das Stadtrecht von Messina." Cassel und Göttingen, 1867.

[394] "Statuta Comunis Mantuæ," Rubric li., "De successionibus ab intestato." *Cod.* MS. F. T., 1, fourteenth century, Mantua Archives. Similar terms are used in the Veronese statutes ("Statuta Veronæ." Veronæ, 1588, bk. ii. chap. 82). "*Ut bona parentum in filios masculos et cæteros per lineam masculinam descendentes conserventur*, pro conservandis domibus et oneribus Communis Veronæ sustinendis, *statuimus*," &c.

[395] "Statuta Florentiæ," ii. 130.

[396] Statutes 4 (of 1324), ii. 70, and 9 (of 1355), ii. 73, in the State Archives, declare in fact that when there are no surviving sons, but only brothers or their sons, the woman is entitled to have the usufruct of her father's, grandfather's, or great-grandfather's estate: "Tunc ipsa mulier habeat usufructum omnium bonorum talis patris, avi, vel proavi defuncti." This is the usufruct for which alimony is afterwards substituted.

[397] State Archives, "Statuti," 4, bk. ii. 50, and 9, bk. ii. 51.

[398] "Statuta Florentiæ," ii. 32.

[399] Ibid. ii. 130.

[400] "Statuta Florentiæ," ii. 126.

[401] Ibid. ii. 129.

[402] "Constitutiones Marchiæ Anconitanæ." Forolivii, 1507.

[403] "Statuti della honoranda Universitate deli Mercanti de la Citade di Bologna," 1530, file 98 and following.

[404] "Statuta Florentiæ," ii. 51.

[405] Ibid. ii. 76.

[406] "Statuta Florentiæ," ii. 75.

[407] Ibid. ii. 77.

[408] Ibid. ii. 108.

[409] Ibid. ii. 109.

[410] The frequent repetition of this phrase is worthy of note, since it enables us to understand the manner in which associations were usually constituted.

[411] "Statuta Florentiæ," ii. 66.

[412] State Archives, "Statuti" 9, ii. 30. The same provision is found in the statutes of 1324 (ii. 87), and was already comprised in those of Pistoia dated 1296 (ii. 6), having been copied from another Florentine statute of earlier date.

[413] The *Mezzeria* system obtains not only throughout Tuscany and Lucca, but over a considerable part of Romagna. But the terms and contracts most favourable to the peasantry are to be found near Florence and in the Pistoian district. Contracts implying a system of *Mezzeria* more or less rudimentary, and dating from about the close of the twelfth century, are still extant.

[414] Two of 1250 and 1251, in the Florentine territory, have

been edited by Ruhmor (*vide* also Capei in the "Atti dei Georgofili," vol. xiv. p. 228); other hardly less ancient examples have been found at Cortona by the Notary L. Ticciati, and published by him in the "Archivio Storico Italiano," Series v., vol. x., No. 4, 1892. Nevertheless, contracts on the true *Mezzeria* system cannot have been in general use earlier than the commencement of the fourteenth century. A common contract drawn up in 1331 on Siennese territory was communicated by Prof. C. Paoli to Baron S. Sonnino, and published by the latter in 1875 Florence, in his work "Sulla Mezzeria in Toscana." In a review, entitled "L'Agricoltura Italiana," nineteenth year (1893), Nos. 274–5, Marquis L. Ridolfi justly remarks that the difficulty in finding old *Mezzeria* contracts in the Florentine territory proceeds from the custom prevailing there of seldom referring to a public notary for the purpose. As a rule, the parties concerned merely exchange written copies of the agreement.

[415] "Statuta Florentiæ," ii. 18.

[416] Ibid. ii. 21.

[417] Ibid. ii. 23. *Vide*, on this subject, Salvetti, "Antiquitates Florentinæ."

[418] "Nuova Antologia," Florence, July, 1869.

[419] G. Villani, "Cronica," xi. 96.

[420] P. E. Giudici, "Storia dei Comuni Italiani," bk. vi., paragraphs 53 and 54. Florence, Le Monnier, 1866. Vannucci, "I primi tempi della libertà fiorentina," chap. iv. p. 161 and fol. Florence, Le Monnier, 1861. Napier's "Florentine History," vol. i. chap. xiii. p. 342. London, 1846. T. A. Trollope, "A History of the Commonwealth of Florence," bk. ii. chap. iii. p. 212. London, 1865. It should be noted that although Mr. Trollope failed to overcome every difficulty, he was enabled to avoid various blunders on this head by merely translating certain parts of the enactments without explaining the more obscure items. Mons. Perrens, in a recent work, written after the first publication of this chapter, has generally accepted its conclusions and corroborated them by fresh researches of his own.

[421] *Vide* chaps. v. and vi. of the present work.

[422] It is impossible to believe that there were no duties of any kind. Villani himself (bk. xi. chap. xcii.) enumerates a great many imposed between 1336 and 1338, and certain of these were unquestionably of earlier origin. Perhaps he meant to express that the duties were few and slight.

[423] "Per non mettere gravezza." Whenever taxes were imposed on the property of citizens, an estimate was made of it, as the tax in question was paid in *lire* or *libbre*, the term *far libbra, allibbrare*, was often used to signify making valuations of property as well as the imposition of taxes.

[424] G. Villani, viii. 2.

[425] *Vide* the preceding chapter.

[426] Dino Compagni, bk. ii. p. 201, the Del Lungo edition. I quote from this edition, as being far more correct than the others, although it was only published in 1879, ten years after the first appearance of this chapter in the form of a separate essay.

[427] *Vide* in Padre Ildefonso's "Delizie degli Eruditi Toscani," the document appended to vol. viii. It consists of a petition presented by certain inhabitants of Castelnuovo after having been attacked by the Pazzi and others, *armata manu, cum militibus et peditibus*, who had burnt their houses, killed several persons, and compelled others to sign a contract, under false pretence of a law suit, that had never occurred, *et scribi faciendo litem contra eos esse super renovationem servitiorum*.

[428] G. Villani, vii. 16.

[429] *Vide* the "Statuto della Parte Guelfa," chap. xxxix. It may be found in vol. i. (1857) of the "Giornale storico degli Archivi Toscani," that was published for some years jointly with the "Arch. Stor. It." This statute of 1355 (edited by Bonaini) is the earliest known statute of the *Parte Guelfa*, but does not appear to be the first that was compiled. In the above- mentioned "Giornale," vol. iii. (1859), Bonaini began a

monograph, entitled, "Della Parte Guelfa in Firenze," which was continued in several numbers, but then left incomplete. *Vide* also G. Villani, vii. 17, describing the original formation of the Society. Its precise condition in 1293 is as yet imperfectly known, but this may be inferred from what it was shortly before and after that period.

[430] G. Villani, viii. 1.

[431] The first of these laws, already known to the public, and the others which were then inedited, have been fully examined in chap. v. of this work and are printed in the appendix to the same.

[432] In fact the "Ordinamenti" (rubric xviii. of the Bonaini edition) refer to this law, dated October 2, 1286 ("Provvisioni," i. 27), and comprised in the statute. Both the rubric and title are quoted in the "Ordinamenti." A *Consulta* (or decree) of March 20, 1280 (81), given in Gherardi's collection, p. 33, had also cited a similar and still older law: "De securitatibus prestandis a magnatibus," which was afterwards amended by that of 1286.

[433] Ammirato, at commencement of bk. iv.; also in "Provvisioni," ii. 72, Florentine Archives.

[434] Dino Compagni, bk. i. p. 56.

[435] G. Villani, viii. 8.

[436] Ammirato, bk. iv. p. 348.

[437] In fact, many neglected to give surety (*sodare*), and several laws were framed to compel the contumacious to obey.

[438] This is known from the terms of the debate, which has been published by Bonaini in the "Arch. Stor. It.," New Series, vol. i. p. 78, document B.

[439] At the period there were twelve Greater and nine Lesser Guilds.

[440] Many historians assert that he was among the priors when the "Ordinamenti" were compiled. But these are officially

dated the 18th of January, and Compagni states that Giano entered the Signory on the 15th of February. This statement is supported by the list of priors given by Coppo Stefani, in his "Delizie degli Eruditi Toscani," and likewise by documentary evidence.[441]

Another inedited compilation also exists in the Florence Archives. Certain new rubrics were inserted in this at a later date, and even, as we shall show further on, among the first twenty-eight.[442]

Dr. K. Hegel, "Die Ordnungen der Gerechtigheit," Erlangen, 1867. This is a *Prolusion*, in which the learned author of the "Storia della Costituzione dei Municipi Italiani," very carefully examines the code edited by Bonaini, and compares it with others. But he does not investigate the value or intrinsic importance of the enactments, and merely gives a brief summary of them.[443]

"Arch. Stor. It.," New Series, vol. i. (1855) p. 38, note 1. [444]

Until this draft was published, we could only refer to posterior compilations, and had no means of ascertaining to what extent they differed from the law in its original form. Although Bonaini had failed to discover the original document of the law as approved, his publication of the first draft brings us very near to the real thing. And this is a point of no small importance, seeing that the laws of the Florentine Republic underwent such radical changes from one day to another, that a compilation, dated only two or three years after the original law, might be very different from it. For instance, Document A, published by Bonaini ("Arch. Stor. It.," New Series, vol. i. p. 72), contains a rider or addendum to the Ordinamenti passed on the 9th and 10th of April, 1293. This was inserted as part of the original law in the compilations edited by Fineschi and Giudici.

In the following bibliographical notices I shall be obliged, for the sake of greater clearness, to occasionally repeat or sum up previously related facts.

1. Of the various compilations of the enactments, that included among the printed statutes was the first to be

published.

2. P. F. Vincenzo Fineschi published a second compilation in his "Memorie storiche, che possono servire alle vite degli uomini illustri di Santa Maria Novella," &c., Florence, 1790.

3. The third published compilation was given by Prof. P. E. Giudici in the appendix to his "Storia dei Municipi Italiani," Florence, Poligrafia italiana, 1853; reprinted in 3 vols., Florence, Le Monnier, 1864–66. The Italian compilation, divided in 118 rubrics, the last of which is mutilated, was published from a codex in the State Archives of Florence ("Statuti," No. 8). By some oversight the author chanced to omit the three concluding rubrics.

4. The last published compilation is that brought out by Bonaini in the "Arch. Stor. It.," New Series, vol. i, No. 1, 1855, of which we have already spoken, and shall have to mention again farther on.

5. Another compilation, to which previous allusion has been made (p. 89, note 92), is also deserving of notice. It is among the MSS. of the Florence Archives (ch. ii., dist. i., No. 1), and is still inedited. Padre Ildefonso published certain fragments of it, however, in vol. ix. of the "Delizie degli Eruditi Toscani," and Bonaini published an index of its rubrics, 134 in number.

6. In conclusion, we may mention the Miscellany or "Zibaldone," likewise referred to before, which in addition to many decrees issued between 1274 and 1465, some of which augment the force of the enactments, also includes a petition presented by the people of Florence in June, 1378—namely, the year in which the Revolt of the Ciompi occurred, imploring that the Enactments of Justice should be again enforced, the which request was granted. This codex is also a useful contribution to the history of the enactments.

Recently both Prof. Del Lungo (*vide* "Bullettino della Società Dantesca," Nos. 10, 11, of July, 1892) and Sig. G. Salvemini, undergraduate of the Instituto Superior, Florence (*vide* "Arch. Stor. It.," Series v., vol. x. 1892), have published the provision of July 6, 1295, introducing several modifications and mitigations in the enactments. Although this provision was already known to the world, by Prof. Del Lungo's previous careful examination of it in his work on "Dino Compagni" (vol i., 1078–80), Salvemini's clever commentary has gleaned fresh information from it. This provision includes all the modifications made in the enactments in 1295, and often gives fragments of the law as it previously stood, together with the changes then introduced. Hegel, having examined all the documents edited in his day, was the first to prove, on assured evidence, that the rough draft edited by Bonaini, although, as he thinks, omitting certain rubrics and comprising some disparities, mostly of form, contained the real gist of the original enactments. This in itself was an important result. Regarding the disparities noted by Hegel, and the missing rubrics, Salvemini was enabled, by studying the document of July 6, 1295, to make some novel remarks, to which we shall refer later on.

[445] Rubric iii. of the draft states that "De prudentioribus, melioribus et legalioribus artificibus civitatis Florentiæ, continue artem exercentibus, dummodo non sint milites." Also farther on: "Aliquis qui continue artem non exerceat, vel aliquis miles non possit nec debeat modo aliqui eligi, vel esse in dicto officio Prioratus." "Arch. Stor. It.," New Series, vol. i. pp. 44, 45. Rubric xviii., p. 66, enumerates the persons bound to give guaranty as nobles, although exercising a trade, "non obstante quod ipsi vel aliquis eorum de dictis domibus et casatis … sint artifices vel artem seu mercantiam exerceant."

[446] *Vide* on this point a document of 1287 appended to this chapter. It proves that the practical exercise of a trade or craft was held indispensable before 1293, and shows what precautions were required to prevent the law from being easily evaded.

[447] Rubric iii., G. We generally quote from Giudici's Italian compilation as being more widely known than the others. But we are careful to collate it with the versions of Fineschi and Bonaini, taking note of significant divergences. The letters B. G. F. are used to indicate the respective editions of Bonaini, Giudici, and Fineschi.

[448] Mons. Perrens (vol. ii. p. 385, note 2) doubts this fact, and states that it only occurred in 1305. It is certain that the Gonfalonier's function was to enforce the enactments, and that when released from this duty by the creation of an "Executor" in 1306, he then began to be more specially considered as the chief of the Signory; but it is none the less certain, that among seven magistrates, all of the same legal standing, the one possessed from the first of loftier attributes and more direct command of the army, was virtually, if not nominally, their president and chief.

[449] Rubric iv., G. and F. We should note that the Latin draft reduces the Gonfalonier's interval of ineligibility to one year only, while the other compilations extend it to two years, as in the case of the Priors and as subsequently enforced. We have followed the Latin draft, for the additional reason that, in the law of 1293, edited by Bonaini (Doc. A. at p. 74), we find it ordained that Priors and Gonfalonier should share the same benefits and privileges, "salvo et excepto quod quæ in Ordinamento iustitie, loquente de electione Vexilliferi, continentur circa devetum et tempus deveti ipsius Vexilliferi, et circa alia omnia in ipso ordinamento descripta, in sua permaneant firmitate." This is repeated even under rubric xxxi.,
G. and F., whence we are forced to conclude that the prescribed interval before re-election to the Gonfaloniership was originally different from that established with regard to the Priorate, and only equalised with the latter at a subsequent time. Besides, in Compilations F. and G. no thought was given to correcting the rule laid down in rubric xxxi., where it is taken for granted that the original diversity was still in force. Florentine laws were always made and amended bit by bit. All doubts, however, are solved by the document from which we have quoted, dated July 6, 1295, extending the term of prohibition, as regarded the Gonfalonier, from one to two years. Salvemini has found proofs in the "Provvisioni" and "Consulte" that this rule had been already applied in December, 1294.

[450] As we shall see farther on, Dr. Lastig was the first writer to point this out.

[451] Rubrics i. and ii. in Compilations B., F., and G.

[452] Rubrics lxiii.-lxv., which, as we have noted, were added by another hand in 1297, to the codex edited by Fineschi, and correspond with rubrics lxxxii.-lxxxiv. of the codex edited by Giudici, there is renewed reference to the tricks employed in order to avoid giving guarantees or nullifying their effect. When a noble committed a crime and refused to pay the prescribed fine, his nearest relation was legally bound to pay it in his stead. But in this case the said relation frequently made declaration, "that the guilty person who had either failed to give guarantees or offered pledges unsuited to the case, possessed one or more legitimate or natural children, aged one year, or more or less; and that for this reason the next of kin, or those supposed to be responsible in virtue of the said enactment, are exempt from the penalty prescribed by the same." (Rubric lxxxii., G., lxv., F.)

[453] Rubric xvii., G. The law quoted here is of October 2, 1286 ("Provvisioni," i. 27).

[454] Rubric xvii., B., F., G. The two later compilations have an addition tacked on at the end, that is not included in Compilation B. In the Italian codex (G.) this addition is undated, but in the Fineschi compilation is dated July 6, 1295. Its purpose is that of attenuating the law by declaring that all omitted from the list of nobles in the statute, or who have changed their name, and are known by another, are not to be considered nobles. This addition was contemporaneous with the extension of the legal number of witnesses from two to three.

[455] Rubrics xviii. and xix., F., G. These and rubric xx. also are not in the Latin draft, as we shall have again to remark farther on.

[456] Compagni, i. 11; Villani, viii. 1.

[457] "Storie," bk. ii. p. 80, Italy, 1813.

[458] viii. 1.

[459] The nobles frequently employed friends or dependents to execute their deeds of vengeance or assault—hence the enactments nearly always refer to authors of crime in the plural

as those chiefly charged with the deed. The law of the 6th of July, 1295, was attenuated on this point, as we shall see, by its recognition of a single leader or "captain" of the crime, the others being only punished as accessories.

[460] Rubric vi., F. G. and V. B.

[461] This is derived both from the terms of the enactments and from the chroniclers. According to the latter, criminals occasionally obtained partial compensation because the destruction of their property had been carried too far.

[462] Rubric xii., F. G., vii., B.

[463] Rubric xiii., F. G. This being a codicil added in 1295, it is not comprised in Compilation B.

[464] Rubrics vi., vii., F. and G. Not comprised in B, having been added in 1295. It should be remarked that in the legal phraseology of the time "common law" signified Roman law; the law as prescribed by the statutes being held almost in the light of a special or exceptional code. But as the enactments constituted in themselves an exception, with regard to the statutes, the latter are referred to wherever *common law* is mentioned. When the question was of two municipalities, one of which was subject to the other, the subject municipality was always allowed (excepting in political concerns) to retain its own statutes; but in cases where these proved insufficient, it had recourse to those of the dominant city, as though these constituted the common law.

[465] Rubric ix., F. G., and vi., B. In this case two witnesses were always needed to prove the offence, and on this point all the compilations, including the rough draft, are agreed. Regarding the other cases, Compilation B (rubric v.) only says *per testes*, meaning more than one, that is, two or three. On the 6th of July, 1295, *per testes* was changed to *per tres testes*, and so it stands also in rubric vi., F. and G.

It should be remarked that in the Italian compilation this rubric ix. has a codicil that is neither comprised in the draft nor even in Fineschi's compilation, and this is an additional proof that the Italian compilation was of later date than the Latin text, of which it is generally the faithful translation. The codicil decrees that the fine is to be paid to the Commune either by the offending party himself or his nearest relation.

Rubric xi., F. and G., answering to rubric xvi., B., treats of the rights acquired by nobles over real property appertaining to the people, and alludes in this connection to the *associates* or *relatives of the popolani*. This proves that the custom of joining in associations was very general at the time, and likewise shows how nearly the ties of association resembled ties of relationship.

[466] Rubric xvi., F. and G., rubric ix., B.

[467] Rubric xxvi., G., xxi., B.

[468] This "Conclusion" is mutilated in the xxii. and final rubric of Compilation B. It exists in full in rubric xxvii., F., and rubric xxv., G.

It should be noted at this point that, leaving aside other partial disparities, those rubrics, included in Compilations G. and F., and entirely omitted from Compilation B. (whether as the results of later decrees, or actually passed at the time when the draft was engrossed in its definite official shape, we have no means of really ascertaining), were those indicated in Compilations G. and F. by the numbers xviii., xix., and xx.

[469] This law, drawn up in full official form, is contained in Document A. of the Bonaini Compilation, but still as a separate law. On the other hand, in Compilations F. and G. we find it incorporated with the enactments it was designed to strengthen. In Compilation G. it is dated April 10, 1293, so also in the Latin Codex, but is undated in Compilation G. We should remark in this connection that the law edited by Bonaini is not only incorporated with the enactments in Compilations F. and G., but in both comprises codicils of a later date—such, for instance, as giving power to call nearly the whole of the city and territory to arms, up to the number of 12,200 men. Had this clause been passed in Giano's time, the chroniclers could not have failed to record it. Villani states that at first one thousand men only were enrolled—that is, the same number authorised by the earlier enactments; the number was afterwards raised to

two thousand, as enjoined by the new law, and later still to four thousand (viii. 1). Therefore, even according to Villani, the number was progressively enlarged.

[470] Villani, viii. 8.

[471] After Villani, Ammirato wrote: "For in addition to the measures ordained, Giano had deprived the Captains of the Society of their seal; and had provided that the funds of the said Society, which amounted to a large sum, should be consigned to the Commune" (vol i. bk. iv. p. 346, Batelli edition, Florence, 1846–49).

[472] Villani, viii. 2.

[473] Villani, viii. 2; Ammirato, *ad annum*, vol. i. pp. 339.

[474] Ibid. viii. 2; Ammirato, vol. i. pp. 340, 341.

[475] Villani, viii. 2; and "Cronica" of the pseudo B. Latini, *ad annum*.

[476] Ibid. viii. 1. Compagni gives a different version in vol. i. 12. He relates that the offenders were of the Galigai family, and that he, being Gonfalonier at the time, had to demolish their dwellings. We have adhered to Villani, who states the fact to have occurred under the first Gonfalonier, Baldo Ruffoli (in office from February 15th to April 15th), whereas Compagni held the Gonfaloniership from June 15th to August 15, 1293, and it is scarcely probable this could have been the first occasion on which the enactments were enforced. It is known that Compagni's Chronicle is only extant in copies dated after his time, and therefore probably containing blunders, alterations, and additions made by its transcribers. Compagni's chronology is often extremely vague. While Gonfalonier he may have undoubtedly seen some sentences executed; but the first sentence on the nobles seems to have been carried out as related by Villani, and also corroborated by Coppo Stefani, bk. iii., rubric 198, Ammirato, vol. i. p. 338, and other historians of weight. Some years after the first publication of this essay, Professor Scheffer Boichorst produced the famous work (*vide* "Historische Zeitschrift," xxiv. p. 313, 1870) that raised the very heated controversy as to the authenticity of Dino

Compagni's Chronicle. At a later period Professor Del Lungo's learned volumes induced the German scholar to cede many of the points in dispute. Accordingly we may still continue to refer to Dino Compagni, although not without careful sifting and discrimination.

[477] Compagni, i. 12, p. 55.

[478] *Vide* chap. vi. of this work.

[479] Jean of Châlons in Burgundy.

[480] It is known that the Podestà, Captain, and many other magistrates were subjected to an investigation or *sindacato*, on retiring from office.

[481] Dino Compagni, i. 13; Villani, viii. 10.

[482] Dino Compagni, i. 13. The author does not explain the nature of these meetings in which nobles and people were brought together. They may have been private or preliminary assemblies. But even at the Councils of the Guelph Society, as also at those of the Podestà, nobles and people sat together, and therefore had continual opportunities for talking over affairs of the State and discussing proposed bills.

[483] Dino Compagni, i. 15.

[484] We have gleaned this narrative from Villani and Compagni, endeavouring to make their accounts agree, although this is no easy task, seeing that the two are at odds on many points. Accordingly we have tried to collect all the details given by both which are not in contradiction. Compagni, i. 16, 17; Villani, viii. 8.

[485] Villani, *loc. cit.*

[486] This famed decree, quoted in Del Migliore's "Firenze Illustrata" (Florence, Ricci, 1821), vol. i. p. 6, and repeated by numerous writers, is certainly a very beautiful one; but the original document of it has never been discovered, and the form in which it has come down to us leads to the belief that some changes at least must have been made in it by a modern hand.

[487] Florence Archives, the Strozzi-Uguccioni Collection, 127. This document was discovered by Signor Salvemini, who has kindly placed it at our disposal.

[488] This Daddoccio was admitted into the Money-Changers' Guild on the 14th of December, 1283, and on the 1st of December, 1287, paid his rate as member of the same (Strozzi-Uguccioni Collection, 1283, 14th of December).

[489] Originally published in the "Nuova Antologia" of Rome, December 1, 1888.

[490] Many just observations and important notes on this subject are to be found in L. Chiapelli's work, "L'Amministrazione della Giustizia in Firenze" ("Arch. Stor. It.," Series iv., vol. xv. p. 35 and fol.); and Francesco Novati's "La Giovinezza di Coluccio Salutati" (Turin, Loescher, 1888, chap. iii. p. 66 and fol.). But in my opinion both writers have devoted all their acuteness and learning to proving the corrupt state of justice at the time, without dwelling on the origin of that corruption and its notable increase during the fourteenth century. Its origin should, I think, be sought in the changed conditions of the Podestà, Captains of the People, chancellors, notaries, judges, &c. What was said of judges in the fourteenth century, certainly could not have applied to those of the times of Piero della Vigna, Rolandino dei Passeggieri, or of the numerous mediæval Podestà wielding so much power, that they tried, and often with success, to become absolute tyrants of the communes. These were not men to act as blind tools of others' party passions; on the contrary, they strove for their own ends alone. It may have been owing to the political decline of the Podestà's office, and to his consequent inclination to serve party strife, that, dating from 1290, his term of power was reduced from one year to six months (*vide* Ammirato, *ad annum*). Naturally the Captain's term also had to be similarly shortened.

[491] "Cronica," i. 13, p. 57.

[492] G. Villani, viii. 17.

[493] The Calimala, or Guild of Dressers, Finers and Dyers of

foreign woollen stuffs; the Changers or Bankers, the Guild of Wool; the Porta Sta Maria, or Silk Guild; lastly, the Guild of Physicians, Druggists, and Mercers, with whom the Painters were also joined. Dante Alighieri was a member of this guild.

[494] Lastig, "Entwicklungswege und Quellen des Handelsrechts," Stuttgart, Enke, 1877, p. 251 and fol. Among many other just observations, the author notes that the enactments fixed the number of the guilds at twenty-one, that this number remained unchanged from that time, and that in the statutes of the guilds, the year 1293 is continually referred to as their "normal year," "wiederholt geradezu als Normaljahr" (p. 244). *Vide* also p. 267 and fol.

[495] Villani, bk. viii. chaps. 2 and 39.

[496] *Vide* "Il Comune di Roma nel Medio Evo," in my "Saggi Storici e Critici," Bologna, Zanichelli, 1890.

[497] Villani, viii. 12. *Vide* also the Provision of July 6, 1295, that has been previously quoted.

[498] Villani, viii. 12.

[499] Del Lungo, "Dino Compagni e la sua Cronica," i. p. 162. The author believes that Dante Alighieri may have been one of the nobles proclaimed men of the people.

[500] The chroniclers have much to relate on this subject. Compagni says (pp. 86–7) that the Cerchi "made friends with the people and the rulers;" farther on he remarks that "all holding the views of Giano della Bella gathered round them" (the Cerchi) (p. 106). Stefani (iv. p. 220) states that the people "adhered to the Cerchi from party spirit, and chiefly because they were merchants."

[501] Professor Del Lungo supplies special information on this subject in several passages of his work.

[502] Villani, viii. 38.

[503] The aims of Pope Boniface and his plots with the Blacks have been placed in a new light by the careful

researches of Signor Guido Levi and the documents discovered by him. *Vide* his excellent work, "Bonifazio VIII. e la sue Relazioni col Comune di Firenze," first published in vol. iv. of the "Archivio Storico della Società Romana di Storia Patria," and subsequently in separate form. Rome, Forzani, 1882. My quotations are taken from the latter.

[504]

[505] Levi, Doc. i.

Vide Ficker, "Forschungen," iv. n. 499, p. 506; Levi, p. 49.

[506] The words quoted above form the heading of a copy of the document mentioned by Signor Levi (p. 49, note 2), and were taken as a motto for his work.

[507] Levi gives the whole passage at p. 51, note 2.

[508] Levi, pp. 48, 49, and Doc. iii.

[509] Bondone Gherardi and Lippo, son of Ranuccio del Becca.

[510] Levi, pp. 39, 40. According to a letter of the Pope, published by Signor Levi, in Doc. iv., the three persons accused were: "Simonem Gherardi familiarem nostrum, nostræque Cameræ mercatorem; Cambium de Sexto procuratorem in audientia nostra; Noffum de Quintavallis, qui tunc ad Curiam nostram accesserat."

[511] Levi, Doc. ii.

[512] Ibid. p. 66.

[513] Villani, too, compares it with the Buondelmonti affair (viii. 39).

[514] Levi, p. 42; Dino Compagni, "Cronica," i., xxii. note 9.

[515] G. Levi, Doc. iv.

[516] Villani, viii. 40.

[517] Ibid. viii. 40.

[518] Dino Compagni, i. pp. 96–7.

[519] Prof. Del Lungo, with his usual careful research, notes that all the exiled were Grandi. Levi, in repeating the remark (at p. 59), considers this a singular fact, "seeing that the evil germs of discord had then spread through the mass of the citizens." Yet the fact seems easily accounted for by the circumstances related above.

[520] Villani, viii. 40; Compagni, i. 21.

[521] Perrens, "Histoire de Florence," vol. iii. p. 31.

[522] Villani, viii. 43.

[523] Villani, viii. 42.

[524] Signor Levi gives a very clear explanation of the case by distinguishing between various facts confused together by the chroniclers.

[525] "Chronicon Parmense," in Muratori, r. i., ix. 843.

[526] Del Lungo, vol. i. p. 230; Dino Compagni, bk. ii. 8, note 3.

[527] Villani, viii. 43 and 49; Del Lungo, vol. i. p. 206.

[528] Villani, viii. 56. Boccaccio also alludes to Franzesi as "a trader turned knight."

[529] Fraticelli's "Storia della Vita di Dante" (Florence, Barbèra, 1861) includes at p. 135 and fol. fragments of the debates in which Dante took a part, and the same were republished more correctly and completely in Imbriani's work, "Sulla Rubrica Dantesca del Villani," first published in the "Propugnatore" of Bologna for 1879 and 1880, and afterwards in a separate volume. Bologna, 1880; Del Lungo, p. 209.

[530] Fraticelli and Imbriani, *op. cit.*

[531] One of the first writers refusing belief in this embassy was Professor V. Imbriani in his already mentioned essay,

"Sulla Rubrica Dantesca del Villani." Subsequently, my colleague and friend, the late Professor Bartoli, applied his learning to a re-examination of Dante's entire career, in vol. v. of his "Storia della Letteratura Italiana," and without explicitly denying that the embassy in question had been sent, expounded the doubts which might be raised about it. He included in the volume an essay by Professor Papa, who, with youthful daring, decidedly disbelieves in the embassy. But that learned scholar, Professor Del Lungo, asserts that it really took place. This is a very important question with reference to Dante's career, but very unimportant as regards the general history of Florence, since even if the embassy were really sent, it produced no practical result. Nevertheless, without presuming to decide the lengthy dispute, I will show my reasons for crediting the fact of the embassy.

Although Villani says nothing on the subject, it is mentioned by Dino Compagni (ii. 25), the authenticity of whose chronicle is maintained by Bartoli, Papa, and Del Lungo. Hence, if any of these writers intends to deny the fact of the embassy, without denying Compagni's authenticity, he must suppose this special passage to be an interpolation. Yet it is impossible that such interpolation could have been made at a later date in the fifteenth century manuscript containing the passage. Besides, the testimony of nearly all Dante's biographers has still to be dealt with. Leonardo Bruno (born 1369) makes very explicit mention of the embassy; Filippo Villani, Giovanni Villani's grandson, who expounded the Divine Comedy in 1401, by order of the government, speaks of a mission undertaken by Dante "ad summum Pontificem, urgentibus Reipublicæ necessitatibus." Boccaccio also alludes to it, but far more indirectly and vaguely. Certainly the latter is no trustworthy historian, nor were the other two contemporaries of Dante. But after acknowledging all this, and even granting that some one of those writers may have borrowed from the others, and likewise admitting the theory of an interpolation inserted during the fifteenth century, in Compagni's chronicle, we are still met by the undisputed fact, that those who studied Dante's works, and wrote Dante's life at a period little removed from his own day, and therefore enjoying better opportunities than we possess for learning its details, all believed in the fact of his mission to Rome.

Until fresh documents are found, what reasons can be alleged to justify us in denying it at this distant date? In no case, says Professor Papa, could such an adversary as the author of the "Monarchia" have gone as ambassador to Boniface VIII. First of all, however, the period in which the "Monarchia" was written is still disputable and disputed. Professor Del Lungo and many others ascribe the work to a much later period. As far as we know, Dante was still a Guelph then, but certainly no favourer of the Papal pretensions against which the Florentine Government sent him to protest. Hence, so far there is nothing to make us think his mission incredible.

But Professor Papa winds up with an argument that, as he thinks, should finally dispose of the question. If, as asserted by Compagni and Aretino, Dante was really sent ambassador to Rome, and departed thence, after a time, without returning to Florence, how is it that the decree sentencing him to banishment should set forth, as it does, that he had been cited by the Nuncio to appear in Rome? According to the statute, *forenses*, or absent persons, had to be cited by letter. Therefore, if the citation was made through the Nuncio, it proves that Dante was undoubtedly in Florence, and had not gone to Rome. But *forensis* does not signify an absent person, *i.e.*, one who *extra civitatem manet*, but, on the contrary, signifies— according to the statute—one having no domicile either in the city, *contado*, or district.

Accordingly Dante, having a domicile in Florence, was not *forensis*, and if he went to Rome was only *absent*; his embassy, decreed in September, must have been speedily ended, since a new and adverse government came into office the 8th of November; and Dante's banishment was only proclaimed on the 27th of January of the following year. Together with three other persons he was cited to appear and be heard in his own defence and exculpation. As neither he nor the others appeared, and none of them would have consented to appear, even if in Florence, they were condemned, as they would have been in any case. Thus, strictly speaking, it cannot be said that even in this instance there was any violation of legal procedure, although in those days legality, justice, and humanity were trampled under foot without the slightest scruple.

Therefore, as Professor Bartoli admits, there is no absolute proof of the impossibility of the embassy in question. Even if Villani's silence may seem strange, Compagni's statement to be considered an interpolation, the fact remains that the embassy was credited at a time little removed from Dante's day, and credited by men better acquainted than we can be with the circumstances of his career. For these reasons, while admitting the weight of often reiterated doubts, pending absolute proof to the contrary, I shall retain my belief in the embassy.

[532] *Vide* Del Lungo, vol. i., Letter in appendix vi. pp. xlv. and xlvi.

[533] Compagni, ii. 8.

[534] Villani, viii. 49. Compagni says that he saw the sealed (*bollate*) letters.

[535] "Purgatorio," xx. 72–5.

[536] Villani, viii. 49, p. 53.

[537] Ibid. viii. 49. Many other details are given in the Chronicles of Compagni, Paolino Pieri, Neri degli Strinati, &c., &c.

[538] *Vide* Del Lungo (vol. i., Appendix, Doc. vi. p. xlv.) in the Letter dated 12th of November, sent to the Commune of San Gimignano.

[539] *Vide* the "Provvisione" in Del Lungo, vol. i. p. 290.

[540] Compagni, "Cronica," ii. 20 and 21.

[541] Potthast, Boniface's Letter in the Regesta Pont. Rom., p. 2006.

[542] *Vide* the notices and documents collected in Professor Del Lungo's monograph, "Sull' Esilio di Dante," Florence, Le Monnier, 1881. Some fragmentary information on this subject had been already published in the "Delizie degli Eruditi Toscani."

[543] Bk. viii. chap. 49, p. 53.

[544] Dino Compagni, ii. 25; Prof. Del Lungo, pp. 212–13, note 3.

[545] Del Lungo, i. p. 305.

[546] *Vide* the "Libro del Chiodo."

[547] G. Villani, bk. viii. chap. 49, p. 54.

[548] First published in the "Nuova Antologia" of Rome, in issue of 16th of December, 1888, and 16th of January, 1889.

[549] Villani, viii. 52, 53; Del Lungo, Appendix xii. to Compagni's "Cronica," p. 562, and fol.; "Le guerre Mugellane e i primi anni dell' esilio di Dante."

[550] Villani, viii. 58. Dino Compagni, "Cronica," ii., xxxiv., and notes 13 and 14.

[551] Dino Compagni, "Cronica," ii., xxxiv., note 20 (document).

[552] Del Lungo, p. 546.

[553] Compagni, iii. 11.

[554] Ibid. iii. 11.

[555] Villani, viii. 68.

[556] *Vide* the letter given by Del Lungo at pp. 556–7.

[557] Dino Compagni, iii., vii.

[558] Villani, viii. 69; Compagni iii., vii.

[559] Villani, viii. chap. 69, p. 87.

[560] An anonymous and undated epistle addressed to Cardinal Da Prato by the Captain Alessandro (supposed to be Alessandro da Romena) and the council and university of the

Bianchi party, was published among Dante's Letters as one composed by him for the use of his fellow-exiles, and was long attributed to him by his biographers. But the Captain's name is not given in the old manuscript from which the letter was printed, but merely indicated thus: *A. ca.* (Epistle I. of the Fraticelli edition, Florence, Barbèra, 1863).

This epistle says in reply to letters and advice from the Cardinal that the Bianchi are grateful to him and disposed to peace. "Ad quid aliud in civile bellum corruimus? Quid aliud candida nostra signa petebant? Et ad quid aliud enses et tela nostra rubebant, nisi ut qui civilia iura, temeraria voluptate truncaverunt, et iugo piæ legis colla submitterent, et ad pacem patriæ cogerentur?" Therefore the gist of Dante's words would have been: The desire to have our laws and liberties respected was the sole cause of our rebellion; all that we now wish is to see justice and peace again triumphant. This language is worthy of the poet, we think.

But doubts have lately arisen as to his authorship. Professor Bartoli, after examining the subject from all points, and ingeniously discussing all different theories respecting it, concludes his prolonged and careful inquiry by stating that there is no historical evidence to prove whether the letter were really by Dante or not ("Storia della Letteratura Italiana," vol. v. chaps. 8–10). Professor Del Lungo says that the style of the letter is Dantesque, in its merits as well as in certain defects; but that this fact does not justify him in decidedly attributing it to the poet's pen, since it may have proceeded from some contemporary in similar circumstances. Indeed, after examining the contents of the letter, he considers that it cannot have been written by Dante, and, among other reasons, chiefly because the words *candida nostra signa*, and *enses et tela nostra rubebant*, &c., are almost identical with those used by Compagni in describing the fight that occurred at Lastra on the 20th of July, 1304. Hence, he is of opinion that the letter undoubtedly refers to that event, and was therefore only written after that date. And seeing that Dante had separated from the exiles before that time, Del Lungo considers that the letter cannot be by him.

For my own part, I doubt whether the letter really referred to the Lastra affair. Surely the words in question: "Our white ensigns were displayed, and our weapons flashed," may have been used either in reference to Lastra or any other battle fought by the exiles, in spite of their resemblance to, and apparent translation from the passage in Compagni relative to the fight at Lastra. This being the case, without altogether rejecting Del Lungo's view, I will merely remark that his argument is insufficient to disprove Dante's authorship, since the poet may have written the letter in the name of the exiles, when they were carrying on those negotiations with the Cardinal on the subject of peace, afterwards leading, as we have seen, to the despatch of twelve delegates to Florence. The failure of those negotiations, the cruel slaughter of the Cavalcanti and their friends, the wholesale destruction by fire and pillage, the partial junction of the Bianchi with Corso Donati, and the union of the exiles with the Bolognese, Pistoiese, Pisans, and all foes of Florence, immediately followed up by the foolish attempt at Lastra, may well suffice to explain, not only Dante's indignant withdrawal from the exiled Bianchi, but likewise the withdrawal of many other citizens. In fact, the latter's non-appearance at Lastra may be perhaps assigned to the same motive, as we shall have occasion to show later on.

[561] Villani, viii. 69. This chronicler dates the Cardinal's departure the 4th of June; Dino Compagni, the 9th; Paolino Pieri and the "Cronica," designated by Del Lungo as the "Cronica Marciana-Magliabecchiana," give the date of the 10th. This is also adopted by Del Lungo, p. 563. *Vide* Dino Compagni, "Cronica," iii. 7, note 26.

[562] Compagni, iii. 8.

[563] Villani, viii. 71.

[564] Ibid.

[565] Villani, viii. 71.

[566] "Storia della Repubblica Fiorentina," vol. i. chap. 6, p. 116 (edition of 1875).

[567] Villani, viii. 72.

[568] *Vide* the well-known words pronounced by Cacciaguida

in Canto xvii. of the "Paradiso":

"E quel che più ti graverà le spalle
Sarà la compagnia malvagia escempia,
Con la qual tu cadrai in questa valle;
Che tutta ingrata, tutta matta ed empia,
Si farà contra te; ma poco appresso
Ella, non tu, n'avrà rotta la tempia.
Di sua bestialitade il suo processo
Farà la pruova, si che a te fia bello
L'averti fatta parte per te stesso."
("Paradiso," xvii. 61–69.)

[569] Del Lungo notes this fact (vol. i. p. 577), and observes that it was frequently repeated between 1301 and 1304.

[570] Villani, viii. 74; Del Lungo, pp. 578–9.

[571] These Catalans, after fighting the Moors in Spain, scattered to different parts of the world, and refused to return to their own country.

[572] Villani, viii. 87.

[573] This law is placed under rubric lxxxiii. of the enactments. *Vide* Giudici, "Storia dei Comuni Italiani," vol. iii. p. 119 and fol. Florence, Le Monnier, 1864–66.

[574] Other clauses tending to increase the rigour of this law were added on to it in 1307, 1309, and 1324, as may be seen in Bonaini's edition, published in the "Archivio Storico Italiano," new series, vol. i., 1885.

[575] Dino Compagni, iii. 18, p. 326.

[576] Villani, viii. 89.

[577] Ibid.

[578] Ibid. viii. 96.

[579] Villani, viii. 96; Dino Compagni, iii. 20, 21.

[580] Dino Compagni, iii. 20, note 29; Del Lungo,

Introduction, p. 607. Prof. Del Lungo, the editor of these documents, does not believe that Corso was favourable at that time to the exiles and Ghibellines. Besides, the latter were no longer the genuine Ghibellines of older days. Therefore the Signory could have no motive for deceiving their friends, the Lucchese, and their letters are likewise corroborated by the previous events we have described.

[581] Villani, viii. 100.

[582] Villani, iii. 118, 119.

[583] Compagni, "Cronica," iii. 35, note. 26.

[584] Villani, ix. 10.

[585] Villani, ix. 11.

[586] Compagni, iii. 32.

[587] Villani, ix. 12.

[588] Ibid. ix. 18.

[589] *Vide* the letter sent by Florence, June 17, 1311, in Gregorovius (3rd edition), vol. vi. p. 39, note 2.

[590] Bonaini, "Acta Enrici VII.," ii., lv., lxxxvi., Florence, Cellini, 1877.

[591] Ibid. ii., xcviii., xcix.

[592] Published in the "Delizie degli Eruditi Toscani," and given more completely in Prof. Del Lungo's "Dell' Esilio di Dante," &c., p. 107 and fol.

[593] Villani, ix. 21, 24, 26, 29.

[594] "Ita quod ipsi Florentini possint uti, pro eorum faciendis negotiis et mercationibus, regno vestro, non obstantibus novitatibus antedictis." This letter is dated 1311, and though the month is not indicated, it alludes to Henry's arrival in Genoa as a recent event. *Vide* Desjardins, "Négociations diplomatiques de la France avec la Toscane,"

vol. i. p. 12. and fol.

[595] The Bishop of Botrintò gives an account of his strange and perilous journey in his work, "De Henrici VII. imperatoris itinere italico." This is to be found in Muratori, R. I., and has been recently republished by Doctor Heyck (Innsbrück, 1888).

[596] Villani, ix. 26–29; Del Lungo, p. 632.

[597] Villani, ix. 33. The fact of making the Pazzi knights by way of compensation, serves to prove that the title of *cavaliere* was already losing its former significance. For, at the close of the thirteenth century, when used as a sign of nobility, possession of this title helped to exclude a man from the Government.

[598] Perrens, vol. iii. p. 145.

[599] This letter was written about the end of 1310 and beginning of 1311. It is No. v. of the Fraticelli edition.

[600] Epistola vi. of the Fraticelli edition.

[601] Epistle vii.

[602] Gregorovius, vol. vi. p. 40; Perrens, iii. 172; "Cronaca di Pisa," R. T. S., xv. 985; Malavolti, par. ii. bk. iv. f. 66; Mussato, bk. i. rub. 10.

[603] Mussato, in Gregorovius, vi. 73, note 1.

[604] Villani, ix. 45, p. 170.

[605] Villani, ix. 49.

[606] Bonaini, *op. cit.*, ii., ccclxv.

[607] Gregorovius, vi. 89.

INDEX

Abati, 210, 445

Acquasparta, Cardinal of, 506, 517

Adimari, 208, 441, 543

Adrian V., Pope, 46, 257

Agnati, 372, 373, 375, 376, 388, 393, 394, 396, 419, 421, 423

Aguglioni, Baldo, 446

Albert of Austria, 503, 506

Albert of Hapsburg, 546

Alberti, House of, 101, 145, 146, 155, 160, 163, 331

Albizzi, 430

Aldobrandeschi, House of, 196

Aldobrandino, Count, 210

Alexander II., Pope, 75

Alfonso of Castile, 205

Alighieri, Dante, 406, 480, 485, 507, 510, 511, 521, 529, 535, 544, 556, 557, 563

Altino Chronicle, 98

Amalfi, 387

Ammirato, 11, 53, 262, 267, 283, 432

Amphitheatre, Florentine, 66

Angevins, 434, 435, 478, 495, 496, 510, 546, 560

Anglona, Giordano d', 205, 206

Arnolfo di Cambio, 479

Arras, Count of, 210

Art and Literature, 238, 239

Artisans, 91

Arts, Association of, 232

Bonaini, 431, 448, 449, 450, 451

Boniface VIII., Pope, 350, 470, 486, 493, 494, 501, 502, 504, 508, 519, 525, 526, 560

Bonifazio III., 82, 83, 90, 91

Bordoni, Gherardo dei, 543, 544

Bostichi, 438, 441

Bouillon, Godfrey de, 55

Breviary of Alaric, The, 383

Brunelleschi, Betto, 550, 551, 555

Buondelmonti, The, 132, 173, 213, 260, 441, 505

Byzantine, 382, 385

Cadolingi, Castle of, 114

Cadolingi, The, 102, 103

Calabria, Duke of, 537

Calimala, Court of, 232, 345

Calimala Guild, 124, 233 *et seq.*, 269, 319

Cambio, Arnolfo di, 297

Campaldino, 432, 437, 444, 445, 487

Caponsacchi, Gherardo, 154, 155

Capponi, Marquis Gino, 11, 15, 18, 36, 54

Capraia, Siege of, 184

Caprona, Castle of, 295

"Captain of the People," 13, 189, 226, 262, 268

Carroccio, The, 177

Cascioli, Monte, 102, 103

Castelfranco, 491

Castro, Paolo de, 447

474

UNWIN BROTHERS, LIMITED, PRINTERS, WOKING AND LONDON.